BOOKS BY

ANTHONY POWELL

THE MUSIC OF TIME

A Question of Upbringing

A Buyer's Market

The Acceptance World

A Dance to the Music of Time
(A COLLECTION OF THE ABOVE THREE NOVELS)

At Lady Molly's

Casanova's Chinese Restaurant

The Kindly Ones

A Dance to the Music of Time: Second Movement
(A COLLECTION OF THE ABOVE THREE NOVELS)

The Valley of Bones

The Soldier's Art

The Military Philosophers

A Dance to the Music of Time: Third Movement
(A COLLECTION OF THE ABOVE THREE NOVELS)

OTHER NOVELS

Afternoon Men

Venusberg

From a View to a Death

Agents and Patients

What's Become of Waring

Books Do Furnish a Room

GENERAL

John Aubrey and His Friends

*Brief Lives: and Other
Selected Writings of John Aubrey*

A Dance to the Music of Time

Third Movement

A Dance to the Music of Time

Third Movement

THE VALLEY OF BONES
THE SOLDIER'S ART
THE MILITARY PHILOSOPHERS

BY

Anthony Powell

★ ★ ★

LITTLE, BROWN AND COMPANY
Boston   *Toronto*

LIBRARY OF CONGRESS CATALOG CARD NO. 70-161417

T09-71

PRINTED IN THE UNITED STATES OF AMERICA

A Dance to the Music of Time

Third Movement

THE VALLEY OF BONES
THE SOLDIER'S ART
THE MILITARY PHILOSOPHERS

The Valley of Bones

for
Arthur and Rosemary

1

SNOW FROM YESTERDAY'S FALL STILL LAY in patches and the morning air was glacial. No one was about the streets at this hour. On either side of me in the half-light Kedward and the Company Sergeant-Major stepped out briskly as if on parade. Some time in the past – long, long ago in another existence, an earlier, less demanding incarnation – I had stayed a night in this town, idly come here to cast an eye over a countryside where my own family had lived a century or more before. One of them (rather a hard case by the look of it, from whom Uncle Giles's failings perhaps stemmed) had come west from the Marches to marry the heiress of a small property overlooking a bay on this lost, lonely shore. The cliffs below the site of the house, where all but foundations had been obliterated by the seasons, enclosed untidy banks of piled-up rock against which spent Atlantic waters ceaselessly dissolved, ceaselessly renewed steaming greenish spray: *la mer, la mer, toujours recommençée*, as Moreland was fond of quoting, an everyday landscape of heaving billows too consciously dramatic for my own taste. Afterwards, in the same country, they moved to a grassy peninsula of the estuary, where the narrowing sea penetrated deep inland. There moss and ivy spread over ruined, roofless walls on which broad sheets of rain were descending. In the church nearby, a white marble tablet had been raised *in memoriam*. Those were the visible remains. I did not remember much of the town itself. The streets, built at constantly changing levels, were not without a bleak charm, an illusion of tramping through Greco's Toledo in winter, or one of those castellated upland townships of Tuscany, represented without great regard for perspective in the background of *quattrocento* portraits. For some reason one was always aware, without knowing why the fact should be so inescapable, that the sea was not far away. The poem's emphasis on ocean's aqueous reiterations provoked in the mind a thousand fleeting images, scraps of verse, fragments of painting, forgotten tunes, disordered souvenirs of every kind: anything, in fact, but the practical matters required of one. When I tried to pull myself together, fresh daydreams overwhelmed me.

Although they had remained in these parts only a couple of generations, there was an aptness, something fairly inexorable, in reporting under the badges of second-lieutenant to a spot from which quite a handful of forerunners of the same blood had set out to become unnoticed officers of Marines or the East India Company; as often as not to lay twenty-year-old bones in the cemeteries of Bombay and Mysore. I was not exactly surprised to find myself committed to the same condition of service, in a sense always knowing that part of a required pattern, the fulfilment of which was in some ways a relief. Nevertheless, whatever military associations were to be claimed with these regions, Bonaparte's expressed conviction was irrefutable – French phrases seemed to offer support at that moment – *A partir de trente ans on commençe à être moins propre à faire la guerre.* That was exactly how I felt myself; no more, no less. Perhaps others of the stock, too, had embarked with reservations on a career by the sword. Certainly there had been no name of the least distinction for four or five hundred years. In mediaeval times they had been of more account in war; once, a long way back – in the disconcerting, free-for-all manner of Celtic lineage – even reigning, improb-

2

able as that might now appear, in this southern kingdom of a much disputed land. One wondered what on earth such predecessors had been like personally; certainly not above blinding and castrating when in the mood. A pale, mysterious sun opaquely glittered on the circlet of gold round their helmets, as armed men, ever fainter in outline and less substantial, receded into the vaporous, shining mists towards intermediate, timeless beings, at once measurably historical, yet at the same time mythically heroic: Llywarch the Old, a discontented guest at the Arthurian Table: Cunedda – though only in the female line – whose horse men had mounted guard on the Wall. For some reason the Brython, Cunedda, imposed himself on the imagination. Had his expulsion of the Goidels with great slaughter been at the express order of Stilicho, that Vandal captain who all but won the Empire for himself? I reviewed the possibility as we ascended, without breaking step, a short, very steep, very slippery incline of pavement. At the summit of this little hill stood a building of grey stone surrounded by rows of spiked railings, a chapel or meeting house, reposing in icy gloom. Under the heavy portico a carved scroll was inscribed:

SARDIS
1874

Kedward came smartly to a halt at the entrance of this tabernacle. The Sergeant-Major and I drew up beside him. A gale began to blow noisily up the street. Muffled yet disturbing, the war horns of Cunedda moaned in the frozen wind, as far away he rode upon the cloud.

'This is the Company's billet,' said Kedward, 'Rowland is meeting us here.'

'Was he in the Mess last night?'

3

'Not when you were there. He was on his rounds as Captain of the Week.'

I followed Kedward through the forbidding portals of Sardis – one of the Seven Churches of Asia, I recollected – immediately entering a kind of cave, darker than the streets, though a shade warmer. The Sergeant-Major formally called the room to attention, although no visible presence stirred in an ominous twilight heavy with the smell of men recently departed, a scent on which the odour of escaping gas had been superimposed. Kedward bade the same unrevealed beings 'carry on'. He had explained earlier that 'as bloody usual' the Company was 'on fatigues' that week. At first it was not easy to discern what lay about us in a Daumier world of threatening, fiercely slanted shadows, in the midst of which two feeble jets of bluish gas, from which the pungent smell came, gave irregular, ever-changing contours to an amorphous mass of foggy cubes and pyramids. Gradually the adjacent shapes contracted into asymmetrical rows of double-decker bunks upon which piles of grey-brown blankets were folded in a regulated manner. Then suddenly at the far end of the cave, like the anthem of the soloist bursting gloriously from a hidden choir, a man's voice, deep throated and penetrating, sounded, rose, swelled, in a lament of heartbreaking melancholy:

> 'That's where I fell in love,
> While stars above
> Came out to play;
> For it was *mañana*,
> And we were so gay,
> South of the border,
> Down Mexico way . . .'

Another barrack-room orderly, for that was whom I rightly judged the unseen singer to be, now loomed up from

4

the darkness at my elbow, joining in powerfully with the last two lines. At the same time, he swung his broom with considerable violence backwards and forwards through the air, like a conductor's baton, finally banging it with all his force against the wooden legs of one of the bunks.

'All right, all right, there,' shouted the Sergeant-Major, who had at first not disallowed the mere singing. 'Not so much noise am I telling you.'

As one's eyes grew used to the gloom, gothic letters of enormous size appeared on the walls of the edifice, picked out in red and black and gold above the flickering gas-jets, a text whose message read straight across the open pages of a huge volume miraculously confronting us high above the paved floor, like the mural warning at Belshazzar's feast:

> 'Thou hast a few names even in Sardis
> which have not defiled their garments:
> and they shall walk with me in white:
> for they are worthy.'
> Rev. III. 4.

'Some of these blankets aren't laid out right yet, Sergeant-Major,' said Kedward. 'It won't do, you know.'

He spoke gravely, as if emphasising the Apocalyptic verdict of the walls. Although he had assured me he was nearly twenty-two, Kedward's air was that of a small boy who had dressed up for a lark in officer's uniform, completing the rag by rubbing his upper lip with burnt cork. He looked young enough to be the Sergeant-Major's son, his grandson almost. At the same time, he had a kind of childish dignity, an urchin swagger, in its way quite impressive, which lent him a right to be obeyed.

'Some of the new intake was taught different to fold them blankets,' said the Sergeant-Major cautiously.

5

'Look at that – and those.'

'I thought the lads was getting the idea better now, it was.'

'Never saw anything like it.'

'A Persian market, you might think,' agreed the Sergeant-Major.

Cleanshaven, with the severely puritanical countenance of an Ironside in a Victorian illustration to a Cavalier-and-Roundhead romance, CSM Cadwallader was not as old as he looked, nor for that matter – as I discovered in due course – nearly so puritanical. His resounding surname conjoined him with those half-historical, half-mythical times through which my mind had been straying a minute or two before, the stern nobility of his features suggesting a warrior from an heroic epoch, returned with dragon banners to sustain an army in time of war. Like the rest of the 'other ranks' of the Battalion, he was a miner. His smooth skull, entirely hairless, was streaked with an intricate pattern of blue veins, where coal dust of accumulated years beneath the ground had found its way under the skin, spreading into a design that resembled an astrological nativity – his own perhaps – cast in tattoo over the ochre-coloured surface of the cranium. He wore a Coronation medal ribbon and the yellow-and-green one for Territorial long service. The three of us strolled round the bunks.

'Carry on with the cleaning,' said Kedward sharply.

He addressed the barrack-room orderlies, who, taking CSM Cadwallader's rebuke as an injunction to cease from all work until our party was gone, now stood fidgetting and whispering by the wall. They were familiar later as Jones, D., small and fair, with almost white hair, a rarity in the Battalion, and Williams, W. H., tall and dark, his face covered with spots. Jones, D., had led the singing. Now they

began to sweep again energetically, at the same time accepting this bidding as also granting permission to sing once
more, for, as we moved to the further end of the room,
Jones, D., returned to the chant, though more restrainedly
than before, perhaps on account of the song's change of
mood:

> 'There in a gown of white,
> By candlelight,
> She stooped to pray . . .'

The mournful, long-drawn-out notes died for a moment.
Glancing round, I thought the singer, too, was praying;
then saw his crouched position had been adopted the better
to sweep under one of the bunks. This cramped attitude no
doubt impeded the rendering, or perhaps he had paused for
a second or two, desire provoked by the charming thought
of a young girl lightly clothed in shimmering white – like
the worthy ones of Sardis – a picture of peace and innocence
and promise of a good time, very different from the stale,
cheerless atmosphere of the barrack-room. Rising, he burst
out again with renewed, agonised persistence:

> '. . . The Mission bell told me
> That I mustn't stay
> South of the border,
> Down Mexico way . . .'

The message of the bell, the singer's tragic tone
announcing it, underlined life's inflexible call to order,
reaffirming the illusory nature of love and pleasure. Even
as the words trailed away, heavy steps sounded from the
other end of the chapel, as if forces of authority were already
on the move to effect the unhappy lover's expulsion from
the Mission premises and delights of Mexico. Two persons

7

had just come through the door. Kedward and the Sergeant-Major were still leaning critically over one of the bunks, discussing the many enormities of its incorrectly folded bed-clothes. I turned from them and saw an officer approaching, accompanied by a sergeant. The officer was a captain, smallish, with a black moustache like Kedward's, though much better grown; the sergeant, a tall, broad shouldered, beefy young man, with fair hair and very blue eyes – another Brythonic type, no doubt – that reminded me of Peter Templer's. The singing had died down again, but the little captain stared angrily at the bunks, as if they greatly offended him.

'Don't you call the room to attention when your Company Commander comes in, Sergeant-Major?' he asked harshly.

Kedward and CSM Cadwalladar hastily straightened themselves and saluted. I did the same. The captain returned a stiff salute, keeping his hand up at the peak of the cap longer than any of the rest of us.

'Indeed, I'm sorry, sir,' said the Sergeant-Major, beginning to shout again, though apparently not much put out by this asperity of manner. 'See you at first, I did not, sir.'

Kedward stepped forward, as if to put an end to further fault finding, if that were possible.

'This is Mr Jenkins,' he said. 'He joined yesterday and has been posted to your company, Captain Gwatkin.'

Gwatkin fixed me with his angry little black eyes. In appearance, he was in several respects an older version of Kedward. I judged him to be about my own age, perhaps a year or two younger. Almost every officer in the unit looked alike to me at that very early stage; Maelgwyn-Jones, the Adjutant, and Parry, his assistant sitting beside him at the table, indistinguishable as Tweedledum and Tweedledee, when I first reported to the Orderly Room the evening before. Later, it was incredible persons so dissimilar could ever for one moment have appeared to resemble one another in any but the most superficial aspects. Gwatkin, although he may have had something of Kedward's look, was at the same time very different. Even this first sight of him revealed a novelty of character, at once apparent, though hard to define. There was, in the first place, some style about him. However much he might physically resemble the rest, something in his air and movements also showed a divergence from the humdrum routine of men; if, indeed, there is a humdrum routine.

'It's no more normal to be a bank-manager or a bus-conductor, than to be Baudelaire or Genghis Khan,' Moreland had once remarked. 'It just happens there are more of the former types.'

Satisfied at last that he had taken in sufficient of my appearance through the dim light of the barrack-room, Gwatkin held out his hand.

'Your name was in Part II Orders, Mr Jenkins,' he said without smiling. 'The Adjutant spoke to me about you, too. I welcome you to the Company. We are going to make it the best company in the Battalion. That has not been brought about yet. I know I can rely on your support in trying to achieve it.'

He spoke this very formal speech in a rough tone, with the barest suggestion of sing-song, his voice authoritative, at the same time not altogether assured.

'Mr Kedward,' he went on, 'have the new intake laid out their blankets properly this morning?'

'Not all of them,' said Kedward.

'Why not, Sergeant-Major?'

'It takes some learning, sir. Some of them is not used to our ways yet. They are good boys.'

9

'Never mind whether they are good boys, Sergeant-Major, those blankets must be correct.'

'Indeed, they should, sir.'

'See to it, Sergeant-Major.'

'That I will, sir.'

'When was the last rifle inspection?'

'At the pay parade, sir.'

'Were the Company's rifles correct?'

'Except for Williams, T., sir, that is gone on the MT course and taken his rifle with him, and Jones, A., that is sick with the ring-worm, and Williams, H,. that is on leave, and those two rifles the Sergeant-Armourer did want to look at that I told you of, sir, and the one with the faulty bolt in the Company Store for the time being, you said, and I will see about. Oh, yes, and Williams, G. E., that has been lent to Brigade for a week and has his rifle with him. That is the lot I do believe, sir.'

Gwatkin seemed satisfied with this reckoning.

'Have you rendered your report?' he asked.

'Not yet, sir.'

'See I have the nominal roll this evening, Sergeant-Major, by sixteen-hundred hours.'

'That I will, sir.'

'Mr Kedward.'

'Sir?'

'Your cap badge is not level with the top seam of the cap-band.'

'I'll see to it as soon as I get back to the Mess.'

Gwatkin turned to me.

'Officers of our Battalion wear bronze pips, Mr Jenkins.'

'The Quartermaster told me in the Mess last night he could get me correct pips by this evening.'

'See the QM does so, Mr Jenkins. Officers incorrectly dressed are a bad example. Now it happens that Sergeant

Pendry here, who is Battalion Orderly Sergeant this week, will be your own Platoon Sergeant.'

Sergeant Pendry grinned with great friendliness, his blue eyes flashing in high-lights caught by the gas-jets, making them more than ever like Peter Templer's in the old days. He held out his hand. I took it, not sure whether this familiarity would conform with Gwatkin's ideas about discipline. However, Gwatkin seemed to regard a handshake as normal in the circumstances. His tone had been austere until that moment; intentionally, though perhaps rather unconvincingly austere. Now he spoke in a more friendly manner.

'What is your Christian name, Mr Jenkins?'

'Nicholas.'

'Mine is Rowland. The Commanding Officer says we should not be formal with each other off parade. We are brother officers – like a family, you see. So, when off duty, Rowland is what you should call me. I shall say Nicholas. Mr Kedward told you his name is Idwal.'

'He has. I'm calling him that. In practice, it's Nick for me.'

Gwatkin gazed at me fixedly, as if not altogether sure what I meant by 'in practice', or whether it was a term properly to be used by a subaltern to his Company Commander, but he did not comment.

'Come along, Sergeant Pendry,' he said, 'I want to look at those urine buckets.'

We saluted. Gwatkin set off on his further duties as Captain of the Week – like the Book of the Month, I frivolously thought to myself.

'That went off all right,' said Kedward, as if presentation to Gwatkin might have proved disastrous. 'I don't think he took against you. What must I show you now? I know, the ablutions.'

11

That was my first sight of Rowland Gwatkin. It could hardly have been more characteristic, in so much as he appeared on that occasion almost to perfection in the part for which he had cast himself: in command, something of a martinet, a trifle unapproachable to his subordinates, at the same time not without his human side, above all a man dedicated to duty. It was a clear-cut, hard-edged picture, into which Gwatkin himself, for some reason, never quite managed to fit. Even his name seemed to split him into two halves, poetic and prosaic, 'Rowland' at once suggesting high deeds:

> . . . When Rowland brave, and Olivier,
> And every paladin and peer,
> On Roncesvalles died!

'Gwatkin', on the other hand, insinuated nothing more impressive than 'little Walter', which was not altogether inappropriate.

'Rowland can be a bloody nuisance sometimes,' said Kedward, when we knew each other better. 'He thinks such a mighty lot of himself, do you know. Lyn Craddock's dad is manager of Rowland's branch, and he told Lyn, Rowland's not all that bloody marvellous at banking. Not the sort that will join the Inspectorate, or anything like that, not by a long chalk. Rowland doesn't care much about that, I expect. He just fancies himself as a great soldier. You should keep the right side of Rowland. He can be a tricky customer.'

That was precisely the impression of Gwatkin I had myself formed; that he took himself very seriously, was eminently capable of becoming disagreeable if he conceived a dislike for someone. At the same time, I felt an odd kind of interest in him, even attraction towards him. There was about him something melancholy, perhaps even tragic, that was hard to define. His excessively 'regimental' manner was certainly over and above anything as yet encountered among other officers of the Battalion. We were still, of course, existing in the comparatively halcyon days at the beginning of the war, when there was plenty to eat and drink, tempers better than they subsequently became. If you were over thirty, you thought yourself adroit to have managed to get into uniform at all, everyone behaving almost as if they were attending a peacetime practice camp (this was a Territorial unit), to be home again after a few weeks' change of routine. Gwatkin's manner was different from that. He gave the impression of being something more than a civilian keen on his new military role, anxious to make a success of an unaccustomed job. There was an air of resolve about him, the consciousness of playing a part to which a high destiny had summoned him. I suspected he saw himself in much the same terms as those heroes of Stendhal – not a Stendhalian lover, like Barnby, far from that – an aspiring, restless spirit, who, released at last by war from the cramping bonds of life in a provincial town, was about to cut a dashing military figure against a backcloth of Meissonier-like imagery of plume and breastplate: dragoons walking their horses through the wheat, grenadiers at ease in a tavern with girls bearing flagons of wine. Esteem for the army – never in this country regarded, in the continental manner, as a popular expression of the national will – implies a kind of innocence. This was something quite different from Kedward's hope to succeed. Kedward, so I found, did not deal in dreams, military or otherwise. By that time he and I were on our way back to the Mess. Kedward gratifyingly treated me as if we had known each other all our lives, not entirely disregarding our difference in age, it is true, but at least accepting that as a reason for benevolence.

13

'I expect you're with one of the Big Five, Nick,' he said.

'Big five what?'

'Why, banks, of course.'

'I'm not in a bank.'

'Oh, aren't you. You'll be the exception in our Battalion.'

'Is that what most of the officers do?'

'All but about three or four. Where do you work?'

'London.'

Banks expunged from Kedward's mind as a presumptive vocation, he showed little further curiosity as to how otherwise I might keep going.

'What's London like?'

'Not bad.'

'Don't you ever get sick of living in such a big place?'

'You do sometimes.'

'I've been in London twice,' Kedward said. 'I've got an aunt who lives there – Croydon – and I stayed with her. I went up to the West End several times. The shops are bloody marvellous. I wouldn't like to work there though.'

'You get used to it.'

'I don't believe I would.'

'Different people like different places.'

'That's true. I like it where I was born. That's quite a long way from where we are now, but it's not all that different. I believe you'd like it where my home is. Most of our officers come from round there. By the by, we were going to get another officer reinforcement yesterday, as well as yourself, but he never turned up.'

'Emergency commission?'

'No, Territorial Army Reserve.'

'What's he called?'

'Bithel – brother of the VC. Wouldn't it be great to win a VC.'

'He must be years younger than his elder brother then. Bithel got his VC commanding one of the regular battalions in 1915 or 1916. I've heard my father speak of him. That Bithel must be in his sixties at least.'

'Why shouldn't he be much younger than his brother? This one played rugger for Wales once, I was told. That must be great too. But I think you're right. This Bithel is not all that young. The CO was complaining about the age of the officers they are sending him. He said it was dreadful, you are much too old. Bithel will probably be even older than you.'

'Not possible.'

'You never know. Somebody said they thought he was thirty-seven. He couldn't be as old as that, could he. If so, they'll have to find him an administrative job after the Division moves.'

'Are we moving?'

'Quite soon, they say.'

'Where?'

'No one knows. It's a secret, of course. Some say Scotland, some Northern Ireland. Rowland thinks it will be Egypt or India. Rowland always has these big ideas. It might be, of course. I hope we do go abroad. My dad was in this battalion in the last war and got sent to the Holy Land. He brought me back a prayer-book bound in wood from the Cedars of Lebanon. I wasn't born then, of course, but he got the prayer-book for his son, if he had one. Of course that was if he didn't get killed. He hadn't even asked my mum to marry him then.'

'Do you use it every Sunday?'

'Not in the army. Not bloody likely. Somebody would pinch it. I want to hand it on to my own son, you see, when I have one. Are you engaged?'

'I was once. I'm married as a consequence.'

'Are you really. Well, I suppose you would be at your age. Yanto Breeze – that's Rowland's other Platoon Commander – is married now. The wedding was a month ago. Yanto's nearly twenty-five, of course. What's your wife's name?'

'Isobel.'

'Is she in London?'

'She's living in the country with her sister. She's waiting to have a baby.'

'Oh, you are lucky,' said Kedward, 'I wonder whether it will be a daughter. I'd love a little daughter. I'm engaged. Would you like me to show you a photograph of my fiancée?'

'Very much.'

Kedward unbuttoned the breast-pocket of his tunic. He took out a wallet from one of the compartments of which he extracted a snapshot. This he handed over. Much worn by constant affectionate reference, the features of the subject, recognisably the likeness of a girl, were otherwise all but effaced. I expressed appreciation.

'Bloody marvellous, isn't she,' said Kedward.

He kissed the faded outlines before returning the portrait to the notecase.

'We're going to get married if I become a captain,' he said.

'When will that be, do you think?'

Kedward laughed.

'Not for ages, I suppose,' he said. 'But I don't see why I shouldn't be promoted one of these days, if the war goes on for a while and I work hard. Perhaps you will too, Nick. You never know. There's this bloody eighteen months to get through as second-lieutenant before you get your second pip. I think the war is going on, don't you? The French will hold them in the Maginot Line until this country builds up her air strength. Then, when the Germans try to advance, chaps like you and me will come in, do you see. Of course we might be sent to the help of Finland before that, fight the Russkis instead of the Germans. In any case, the decisive arm is infantry. Everybody agrees about that – except Yanto Breeze who says it's the tank.'

'We shall see.'

'Yanto says he's sure he will remain with two pips all the war. He doesn't care. Yanto has no ambition.'

I had met Evan Breeze – usually known by the diminutive 'Yanto' – in the Mess the previous night, a tall, shambling, unmoustached figure, not at all military, who, as an accountant, stood like myself a little apart from the norm of working in a bank. Gwatkin, so I found in due course, did not much like Breeze. In fact it would be true to say he hated him, a sentiment Breeze quietly returned. Mutual antipathy was in general attributed to Gwatkin's disapproval of Breeze's unsmart appearance, and unwillingness to adapt himself to army methods and phraseology. That attitude certainly brought him some persecution at the hands of Gwatkin and others in authority. Besides, Breeze always managed to give the impression that he was laughing at Gwatkin, while at the same time allowing no word or act of his to give reasonable cause for offence. However, there was apparently another matter. When we knew each other better, Kedward revealed that Gwatkin, before his marriage, had been in love with Breeze's sister; had been fairly roughly treated by her.

'Rowland falls like a ton of bricks when he does, believe me,' Kedward said, 'when he takes a fancy to a girl. He was so stuck on Gwenllian Breeze, you would have thought he had the measles.'

'What happened?'

17

'She wouldn't look at him. Married a college professor. One of those Swansea people.'

'And Rowland married someone else?'

'Oh, yes, of course. He married Blodwen Davies that had lived next door all their lives.'

'How did that work out?'

Kedward looked at me uncomprehendingly.

'Why, what do you mean?' he said. 'All right. Why should it not? They've been married a long time now, though they haven't any kids. All that about Gwen Breeze was years ago. Yanto must have forgotten by now that Rowland could ever have been his brother-in-law. What a couple they would have been in one family. They would have been at each other like a dog-fight. Rowland always knows best. He likes bossing it. Yanto likes his own way too, but different. Yanto should clean himself up. He looks like an old hen in uniform.'

All the same, although Breeze might not possess Kedward's liveliness, ambition, capacity for doing everything with concentrated energy, I found later that he was not, in his own way, a bad officer, however unkempt his turnout. The men liked him; he was worth consulting about the men.

'Keep an eye on Sergeant Pendry, Nick,' he said, when he heard Pendry was my Platoon Sergeant. 'He is making a great show-off now, but I am not sure he is going on that way. He has only just been promoted and at present is very keen. But he was in my platoon for a time as a corporal and I am not certain about him, that he can last. He may be one of those NCOs who put everything into it for two or three weeks, then go to pieces. You'll find a lot like that. They have to be stripped. There is nothing else to do.'

It was Breeze, on the evening of the day I had been shown round the lines by Kedward, who took me to the bar of the

18

hotel where the officers of the unit were billeted. After dinner, subalterns were inclined to leave the ante-room of the Mess to the majors and captains, retiring to where talk was less restricted and rounds of drinks could be 'stood'. This saloon bar was smoky and very crowded. In addition to a large civilian clientele and a sprinkling of our own Regiment, were several officers from the Divisional signals unit located in the town, also two or three from the RAF. Pumphrey, one of our subalterns, was leaning against the bar talking to a couple of army chaplains, and a lieutenant I had not seen before, wearing the Regiment's badges. This officer had a large, round, pasty face and a ragged moustache, the tangled hairs of which glistened with beer. His thick lips were closed on the stub of a cigar. In spite of the moustache and the fact that he was rather bald, he shared some of Kedward's look of a small boy dressed up in uniform for fun, though giving that impression for quite different reasons. In strong contrast with Kedward's demeanour, this man had an extraordinary air of guilt which somehow suggested juvenility; a schoolboy wearing a false moustache (something more than burnt cork this time), who only a few minutes before had done something perfectly disgusting, and was pretty sure that act was about to be detected by the headmaster with whom he had often been in trouble before. Before I could diagnose more, Kedward himself came into the bar. He joined us.

'I will buy you a bitter, Idwal,' said Breeze.

Kedward accepted the offer.

'Finland is still knocking the Red Army about on the news,' he said. 'We may go there yet.'

Pumphrey, another of our non-banking officers (he sold second-hand cars), beckoned us to join the group with the chaplains. Red-haired, noisy, rather aggressive, Pumphrey was always talking of exchanging from the army into the RAF.

'This is our new reinforcement, Yanto,' he shouted, 'Lieutenant Bithel. He's just reported his arrival at the Orderly Room and has been shown his quarters. Now he's wetting his whistle with me and the padres.'

We pushed through the crowd towards them.

'Here is Iltyd Popkiss, the C. of E.,' said Breeze, 'and Ambrose Dooley that saves the souls of the RCs, and is a man to tell you some stories to make you sit up.'

Popkiss was small and pale. It was at once evident that he had a hard time of it keeping up with his Roman Catholic colleague in heartiness and avoidance of seeming strait-laced. Dooley, a large dark man with an oily complexion and appearance of not having shaved too well that morning, accepted with complaisance this reputation as a retailer of hair-raising anecdote. The two chaplains seemed on the best of terms. Bithel himself smiled timidly, revealing under his straggling moustache a double row of astonishingly badly fitting false teeth. He hesitantly proffered a flabby hand. His furtiveness was quite disturbing.

'I've just been telling them what an awful journey I had coming here from where I live,' he said. 'The Adjutant was very decent about the muddle that had been made. It was the fault of the War Office as usual. Anyway, I'm here now, glad to be back with the Regiment and having a drink, after all I've been through.'

I thought at first he might be a commercial traveller by profession, as he spoke as if accustomed to making social contacts by way of a kind of patter, though he seemed scarcely sure enough of himself for that profession. The way he talked might be caused by mere embarrassment. The cloth of his tunic was stained on the lapels with what seemed egg, the trousers ancient and baggy. He looked as if he had consumed quite a few drinks already. There could be no doubt, I saw with relief, that he was older than myself. If he had ever played rugby for Wales, he had certainly allowed himself to run disastrously to seed. There could be no doubt about that either. He seemed almost painfully aware of his own dilapidation, also of the impaired state of his uniform, at which he now looked down apologetically, holding out the flap of one of the pockets from its tarnished button for our inspection.

'When I'm allotted a batman, I'll have to get this tunic pressed,' he said. 'Haven't worn it since I was in Territorial camp fifteen or more years ago. Managed to spill a glass of gin-and-italian over the trousers on the way here, I don't know how.'

'You won't get any bloody marvellous valeting from your batman here, I'm telling you,' said Pumphrey. 'He'll be more used to hewing coal than pressing suits, and you'll be lucky if he even gets a decent polish on those buttons of yours, which are needing a rub up.'

'I suppose we mustn't expect too much now there's a war on,' said Bithel, unhappy that he might have committed a social blunder by speaking of pressing tunics. 'But what about another round. It's my turn, padre.'

He addressed himself to the Anglican chaplain, but Father Dooley broke in vigorously.

'If I go on drinking so much of this beer, it will have a strong effect on my bowels,' he said, 'but all the same I will oblige you, my friend.'

Bithel smiled doubtfully, evidently not much at ease with such plain speaking in the mouth of the clergy.

'I don't think one more will do us any harm,' he said. 'I drink a fair amount of ale myself in civilian life without bad results.'

'You want to keep your bowels open anyway,' said

21

Dooley, pursuing the subject. 'That's what I believe in. Have a good sluicing every day. Nothing like it.'

He held up his glass to the light, as if assessing the aperient potentialities of the contents.

'Army food gives me squitters anyway,' he went on, roaring with delight at the thought. 'I've hardly had a moment's peace since we mobilized.'

'It makes me as constipated as an owl,' said Pumphrey. 'I should just about say so.'

Dooley finished his beer at a gulp, again giving his jolly monk's laugh at the thought of man's digestive vicissitudes.

'Even if I'm all bound up, I always carry plenty of toilet paper round with me,' he said. 'Never be without it. That's my rule. You can't know when you're not going to be taken short in the army.'

'That's a good notion,' said Pumphrey. 'We must follow His Reverence's advice, mustn't we. Take proper precautions in case we have to spend a penny. Perhaps you do already, Iltyd. The Church seems to teach these things.'

'Oh, why, yes, I do indeed,' said Popkiss.

'What do you take Iltyd for?' said Dooley. 'He's an old campaigner, aren't you, Iltyd?'

'Why, yes, indeed,' said Popkiss, evidently pleased to be given this opening, 'and what do you think? In my last unit, when I took off my tunic to play billiards one night, they did such a trick on me. You'd never guess. They wrapped a french letter, do you know, between those sheets of toilet paper in my pocket.'

There was a good deal of laughter at this, in which the RC chaplain amicably joined, although it was clear from his expression that he recognised Popkiss to have played a card he himself might find hard to trump.

'And did it fall out in the middle of Church Parade?' asked Pumphrey, after he had finished guffawing.

'No, indeed, thank to goodness. I just found it next day on my dressing table by my dog-collar. I threw it down the lavatory and pulled the chain. Very thankful I was when it went away, which was not for a long time. I pulled the chain half a dozen times, I do believe.'

'Now listen to what happened to me when I was with the 2nd/14th—' began Father Dooley.

I never heard the climax of this anecdote, no doubt calculated totally to eclipse in rough simplicity of language and narrative force anything further Popkiss might attempt to offer, in short to blow the Anglican totally out of the water. I was sorry to miss this consummation, because Dooley obviously felt his own reputation as a raconteur at stake, a position he was determined to retrieve. However, before the story was properly begun, Bithel drew me to one side.

'I'm not sure I like all this sort of talk,' he muttered in an undertone. 'Not used to it yet, I suppose. You must feel the same. You're not the rough type. You were at the University, weren't you?'

I admitted to that.

'Which one?'

I told him. Bithel had certainly had plenty to drink that day. He smelt strongly of alcohol even in the thick atmosphere of the saloon bar. Now, he sighed deeply.

'I was going to the 'varsity myself,' he said. 'Then my father decided he couldn't afford it. Business was a bit rocky at that moment. He was an auctioneer, you know, and had run into a spot of trouble as it happened. Nothing serious, though people in the neighbourhood said a lot of untrue and nasty things at the time. Nothing people won't say. He passed away soon after that. I suppose I could have sent myself up to college, so to speak. The money would just about have run to it in those days. Somehow, it seemed too late by then. I've always regretted it. Makes a difference to a man, you know. You've only got to look round this bar.'

He swayed a little, adjusting his balance by clinging to the counter.

'Had a tiring day,' he said. 'Think I'll smoke just one more cigar and go to bed. Soothing to the nerves, a cigar. Will you have one? They're cheap, but not bad.'

'No, thanks very much.'

'Come on. I've got a whole box with me.'

'Don't really like them, thanks all the same.'

'A 'varsity man and don't smoke cigars,' said Bithel, speaking with disappointment. 'I shouldn't have expected that. What about sleeping pills? I've got some splendid ones, if you'd like to try them. Must use them if you've had just the wrong amount to drink. Fatal to wake up in the night when that's happened.'

By this time I had begun to feel pretty tired myself, in no need of sleeping pills. The bar was closing. There was a general move towards bed. Bithel, after gulping down a final drink by himself, went off unsteadily to search for a greatcoat he had mislaid. The rest of us, including the chaplains, made our way upstairs. I was sleeping in the same bedroom as Kedward, Breeze and Pumphrey.

'Old Bithel's been allotted that attic on the top floor to himself,' said Pumphrey. 'He'll feel pretty lonely up there. We ought to make a surprise for him when he comes to bed. Let's give him a good laugh.'

'Oh, he'll just want to go quietly to bed,' said Breeze, 'not wish for any tomfoolery tonight.'

Kedward took the opposite view.

'Why, yes,' he said, 'Bithel seems a good chap. He would like some sort of a rag. Make him feel at home. Show him that we like him.'

I was glad no such welcome had been thought necessary

24

for myself the previous night, when there had been no sign of horseplay, merely a glass or two of beer before bed. There was perhaps something about Bithel that brought into being such schemes. What shape the joke should best take was further discussed. The end of it was we all climbed the stairs to the top floor of the hotel, where Bithel was housed in one of the attics. The chaplains came too, Dooley particularly entering into the idea of a rag. At first I had envied Bithel the luxury of a room to himself, but, when we arrived there, it became clear that such privacy, whatever its advantages, was paid for by a severe absence of other comfort. The room was fairly big, with a low ceiling under the eaves. Deep shelves had been built along one side, so that in normal times the attic was probably used as a large linen cupboard. The walls were unpapered. There was a strong smell of mice.

'What shall we do?' asked Kedward.

'Put his bed upside down,' suggested Pumphrey.

'No,' said Breeze, 'that's plain silly.'

'Make it apple-pie.'

'That's stale.'

The padres wanted to see the fun, but without too deeply involving themselves. The idea that we should all lie on the shelves, then, when Bithel was already in bed, appear as a horde of ghosts, was abandoned as impracticable. Then someone put forward the project of making an effigy. This was accepted as a suitable solution to the problem. Pumphrey and Kedward therefore set about creating a figure to rest in Bithel's camp-bed, the theory being that such a dummy would make Bithel suppose that he had come into the wrong room. The shape of a man that was now put together was chiefly contrived by rolling up the canvas cover of Bithel's valise, which, under the blankets, gave the fair semblance of a body. Two of Bithel's boots were placed so that they stuck out at the foot of the bed, a head on the pillow represented by his sponge-bag, surmounted by Bithel's 'fore-and-aft' khaki cap. No doubt there were other properties too, which I have forgotten. The thing was quite well done in the time available, a mild enough joke, perfectly good natured, as the whole affair would not take more than a couple of minutes to dismantle when Bithel himself wanted to go to bed. The effigy was just completed when the sound came of Bithel plodding heavily up the stairs.

'Here he is,' said Kedward.

We all went out on to the landing.

'Oh, Mr Bithel,' shouted Pumphrey. 'There is something you should look at here. Something very worrying.'

Bithel came slowly on up the stairs. He was still puffing at his cigar as he held the rail of the banisters to help him on his way. He seemed not to hear Pumphrey's voice. We stood aside for him to enter the room.

'Such a fat officer has got into your bed, Bithel,' shouted Pumphrey, hardly able to control himself with laughter.

Bithel lurched through the door of the attic. He stood for several seconds looking hard at the bed, as if he could not believe his eyes; not believe his luck either, for a broad smile spread over his face, as if he were delighted beyond words. He took the cigar from his mouth and placed it with great care in the crevice of a large glass ashtray marked with a coloured advertisement for some brand of beer, the sole ornament in the room. This ashtray stood on a small table, which, with a broken chair and Bithel's camp-bed, were its only furniture. Then, clasping his hands together above his head, Bithel began to dance.

'Oh, my,' said Breeze. 'Oh, my.'

Bithel, now gesticulating whimsically with his hands, tripped slowly round the bed, regularly changing from one foot to the other, as if following the known steps of a ritual dance.

'A song of love...' he intoned gently. 'A song of love...' From time to time he darted his head forward and down, like one longing to embrace the figure on the bed, always stopping short at the moment, overcome by coyness at being seen to offer this mark of affection – perhaps passion – in the presence of onlookers. At first everyone, including myself, was in fits of laughter. It was, indeed, an extraordinary spectacle, unlike anything before seen, utterly unexpected, fascinating in its strangeness. Pumphrey was quite scarlet in the face, as if about to have an apoplectic fit, Breeze and Kedward equally amused. The chaplains, too, seemed to be greatly enjoying themselves. However, as Bithel's dance continued, its contortions became increasingly grotesque. He circled round the bed quicker and quicker, writhing his body, undulating his arms in oriental fashion. I became gradually aware that, so far as I was myself concerned, I had had sufficient. A certain embarrassment was making itself felt. The joke had gone on long enough, perhaps too long. Bithel's comic turn should be brought to a close. It was time for him, and everyone else, to get some sleep. That was how I felt. At the same time, I had nothing but admiration for the manner in which Bithel had shown himself equal to being ragged; indeed, the way in which he had come out completely on top of those who had tried to make him look silly. In similar circumstances I should myself have fallen far short of any such mastery of the situation. Nevertheless, an end should now be made. We had seen enough. You could have too much of a good thing. It must, in any case, stop soon. These were idle hopes. Bithel showed no sign whatever of wanting to terminate his dance. Now he placed the palms of his hands together as if in the semblance of prayer, now violently rocked his body from side to side in religious ecstasy, now whirled past kicking out his feet before him in a country measure. All the time he danced, he chanted endearments to the dummy on the bed. I think Popkiss was the first, after myself, to begin to tire of the scene. He took Dooley by the arm.

'Come along, Ambrose,' he said, 'Sunday tomorrow. Busy day. It's our bedtime.'

At that moment, Bithel, no doubt by this time dizzy with beer and dervish-like dancing, collapsed on top of the dummy. The camp-bed creaked ominously on its trestles, but did not buckle under him. Throwing his arms round the outline of the valise, he squeezed it with abandon, at the same time covering the sponge-bag with kisses.

'Love 'o mine . . .' he mumbled, 'Love 'o mine . . .'

I was wondering what would happen next, when I realized that he and I were alone in the room. Quite suddenly the others must have decided to leave, drifting off to bed, bored, embarrassed, or merely tired. The last seemed the most probable. Their instincts told them the rag was at an end; that time had come for sleep. Bithel still lay face-downwards on the bed, fondling and crooning.

'Will you be all right, Bithel? We are all going to bed now.'

'What's that?'

'We're all going to bed.'

'You lucky people, all going to bed . . .'

'I'll say good night, Bithel.'

'Night-night,' he said, 'Night-night. Wish I'd decided to be a 'varsity man.'

He rolled over on his side, reaching across the dummy for the remains of his cigar. It had gone out. He managed to extract a lighter from his trouser pocket and began to strike wildly at its mechanism. Hoping he would not set fire to the hotel during the night, I shut the door and went down the stairs. The others in the room were at various stages of turning in for the night.

'He's a funny one is old Bithel,' said Breeze, who was already in bed.

'A regular caution,' said Kedward. 'Never saw anything like that dance.'

'Went on a bit long, didn't it,' said Pumphrey, removing a toothbrush from his mouth to speak. 'Thought he'd be at it all night till he fell down.'

However, although there was general agreement that Bithel had unnecessarily prolonged the dance, he did not, so far as his own personality was concerned, seem to have made a bad impression. On the contrary, he had established a certain undoubted prestige. I did not have much time to think over the incident, because I was very tired. In spite of unfamiliar surroundings, I went to sleep immediately and slept soundly. The following morning, although there was much talk while we dressed, nothing further was said of Bithel. He was forgotten in conversation about Church Parade and the day's routine. Breeze and Pumphrey had already finished their dressing and gone downstairs, when Pumphrey's soldier-servant (later to be identified as Williams, I.G.) came up to Kedward in the passage as we were on the way to breakfast. He was grinning.

'Excuse me, sir.'

'What is it, Williams?'

'I was ordered to look after the new officer till he had a batman for hisself.'

'Mr Bithel?'

'The officer don't seem well.'

'What's wrong with him?'

'Better see, sir.'

Williams, I.G., enjoyed giving this information.

'We'll have a look,' said Kedward.

We went upstairs again to the attic. Kedward opened the door. I followed him, entering a stratosphere of stale, sickly beer-and-cigar fumes. I half expected to find Bithel, still wearing his clothes, sleeping on the floor; the cap-surmounted sponge-bag still resting on the pillow. However, in the manner of persons long used to turning in for the night the worse for drink, he had managed to undress and get to bed, even to make himself reasonably comfortable there. His clothes were carefully folded on the floor beside him, one of the habits of the confirmed alcoholic, who knows himself incapable of arranging garments on a chair. The dummy had been ejected from the bed, which Bithel himself now occupied. He lay under the grey-brown blankets in a suit of yellow pyjamas, filthy and faded, knees raised to his chin. His body in this position looked like a corpse exhumed intact from some primitive burial ground for display in the showcase of a museum. Except that he was snoring savagely, cheeks puffing in and out, the colour of his face, too, suggested death. Watch, cigar-case, sleeping pills, stood on the broken chair beside the bed. In addition to these objects was another exhibit, something of peculiar horror. At first I could not imagine what this might be. It seemed either an ornament or a mechanical contrivance of complicated design. I looked closer. Was it apparatus or artefact? Then the truth was suddenly made plain. Before going to sleep, Bithel had placed his false teeth in the ashtray. He had removed the set from his mouth bodily, the jaws still clenched on the stub of the cigar. The effect created by this synthesis was extraordinary, macabre, surrealist. Again one thought of an excavated tomb, the fascination aroused in archaeologists of a thousand years hence at finding these fossilized vestiges beside Bithel's hunched skeleton; the speculations aroused as to the cultural significance of such related objects. Kedward shook Bithel. This had no effect

30

whatever. He did not even open his eyes, though for a moment he ceased to snore. The sleeping pills must have been every bit as effective as Bithel himself had proclaimed them. Apart from gasping, snorting, animal sounds, which issued again so soon as his head touched the pillow, he gave no sign of life. Kedward turned to Williams, I.G., who had followed us up the stairs and was now standing in the doorway, still grinning.

'Tell the Orderly Corporal Mr Bithel is reporting sick this morning, Williams,' he said.

'Right you are, sir.'

Williams went off down the stairs two at a time.

'I'll come and have a look at old Bithel later,' said Kedward. 'Tell him he's been reported sick. Nothing much will be expected of him this morning, Sunday and newly joined.'

This was prudent handling of the situation. Kedward clearly knew how to act in an emergency. I suspected that Gwatkin, confronted with the same situation, might have made a fuss about Bithel's state. This show of good sense on Kedward's part impressed me. I indicated to him the false teeth gripping the cigar, but their horror left him cold. We moved on to breakfast. It had to be admitted Bithel had not made an ideal start to his renewed army career.

'I expect old Bithel had a glass too much last night,' said Kedward, as we breakfasted. 'I once drank more than I ought. You feel terrible. Ever done that, Nick?'

'Yes.'

'Awful, isn't it?'

'Awful, Idwal.'

'We'll go along early together, and you can take over your platoon for Church Parade.'

He told me where to meet him. However, very unexpectedly, Bithel himself appeared downstairs before it was time for church. He smiled uncomfortably when he saw me.

'Never feel much like breakfast on Sundays for some reason,' he said.

I warned him that he had been reported sick.

'I found that out from the boy, Williams, who is acting as my batman,' said Bithel. 'Got it cancelled. While I was talking to him, I discovered there was another boy called Daniels from my home town who might take on being my regular servant. Williams got hold of him for me. I liked the look of him.'

We set off up the street together. Bithel was wearing the khaki side-cap that had been set on the sponge-bag the night before. A size too small for him, it was placed correctly according to Standing Orders – in this respect generally disregarded in wartime – squarely on the centre of his head. The cap was also cut higher than normal (like Saint-Loup's, I thought), which gave Bithel the look of a sprite in pantomime; perhaps rather – taking into consideration his age, bulk, moustache – some comic puppet halfway between the Walrus and the Carpenter. His face was pitted and blotched like the surface of a Gruyère cheese, otherwise he seemed none the worse from the night before, except for some shortness of breath. He must have seen me glance at his cap, because he smiled ingratiatingly.

'Regulations allow these caps,' he said. 'They're more comfortable than those peaked SD affairs. Cheaper, too. Got this one for seventeen bob, two shillings off because slightly shop-soiled. You don't notice the small stain on top, do you?'

'Not at all.'

He looked behind us and lowered his voice.

'None of the rest of them were at the 'varsity,' he said.

'I've been making inquiries. What do you do in Civvy Street – that's the correct army phrase, I believe.'

I indicated that I wrote for the papers, not mentioning books because, if not specifically in your line, authorship is an embarrassing subject for all concerned. Besides, it never sounds like a serious occupation. Up to that moment, no one had pressed inquiries further than that, satisfied that journalism was a known form of keeping body and soul together, even if an esoteric one.

'I thought you might do something of the sort,' said Bithel, speaking with respect. 'I was trained for professional life too – intended for an auctioneer, like my pa. Never cared for the work somehow. Didn't even finish my training, as a matter of fact. Always been more or less interested in the theatre. Had walk-on parts once or twice but I'm no actor. I'm quite aware of that. I like doing odd jobs in any case. Can't bear being tied down. Worked for a time in our local cinema, for instance. Didn't have to do much except turn up in the evening wearing a dinner jacket.'

'Does that sort of thing bring in enough?'

'Not much cash in it, of course. You'll never make a fortune that way, but I rub along all right with the few pennies I have already. Helps not being married. I expect you're married?'

'I am, as a matter of fact.'

He made marriage sound as if it required some excuse.

'I thought you would be,' he said. 'As I mentioned, I'm not. Never found the right girl somehow.'

Bithel looked infinitely uncomfortable when he admitted that. There was a pause in our conversation. I could not think of anything to suggest. Girls certainly did not appear much in his line, though you never could tell. I asked how he came to be in the Territorial Army Reserve, which seemed to require explanation.

33

'Joined the Terriers years ago,' he said. 'Seemed the thing to do. Never thought I'd wear uniform again when I gave them up. Rather glad to get back now and have some regular money rolling in. I've been out of a job, as a matter of fact, and what I've got doesn't support me. We draw Field Allowance here, so I heard last night. I expect you know that already. Makes a nice addition to the pay. Funds were running rather low, to tell the truth. Always such a lot to spend money on. Reading, for instance. I expect you're an omnivorous reader, if you're a journalist. What digests do you take?'

At first I thought he referred to some sort of medical treatment, harping back to the conversation of the chaplains the night before, then realized the question had something to do with reading. I had to admit I did not take any digests. Bithel seemed disappointed at this answer.

'I don't really buy a lot of digests myself,' he admitted. 'Perhaps not as many as I should. They have interesting articles in them sometimes. About sex, for instance. Sex psychology, I mean. Do you know about that?'

'I've heard of it.'

'I don't mean the cheap stuff just to catch the eye, girls and legs, all that. There are abnormal sides you'd never guess. It's wiser to know about such things, don't you think?'

'Certainly.'

Bithel moved nearer as we walked, lowering his voice again. There was a faint suggestion of scented soap at this close, too close, range.

'Did they say anything about me before I arrived?' he asked in a troubled tone.

'Who?'

'Anybody in the Battalion?'

'How do you mean?'

34

'Any details about my family?'

'Somebody said you were a brother of the VC.'

'They did?'

'Yes.'

'What did you say when they told you that?'

'I thought you must be too young to be his brother – more likely his nephew.'

'Quite right. I'm not Bithel VC's brother.'

'You are his nephew?'

'I never said so, did I? But don't let's talk any more about that. There was something else I wanted to ask you. Did they say anything about games?'

'What sort of games?'

'Did they say I played any special game?'

'There was some talk of your having played rugger for Wales.'

Bithel groaned.

'There was talk of that?' he asked, as if to make sure he had heard right.

'Yes.'

'I knew there'd been a misunderstanding,' he said.

'What about?'

'Why, about my playing football – about rugger. You know what it is when you've had a few drinks. Very easy to give a wrong impression. I must have done that when I phoned that officer dealing with TA Reservists. Talked too much about local matters, sport, other people of the name of Bithel and so on.'

'So the VC is no relation, and you didn't play rugger for Wales?'

'I wouldn't go so far as to say he was no relation. Never know who you may be related to in this part of the world. He's not a brother or uncle anyway. I must have managed to mislead that fellow completely if he got that idea into his head. He didn't sound very bright on the phone. I thought so at the time. One of these old dug-outs, I suppose. Colonel Blimp type. But it isn't Bithel VC who worries me so much. It's this rugger misunderstanding.'

'How did it arise?'

'God knows. Something misheard on the phone too, I should think. I believe there was a merchant called Bithel in the Welsh Fifteen one year. Perhaps there was a Bithel who played cricket for Glamorgan and I've muddled it. One or the other, I'm sure. It was a few years back anyway. I must have mentioned it for some reason.'

'It doesn't really matter, does it?'

'It would if we had to play rugger.'

'That isn't very likely.'

'The fact is I've never played rugger in my life,' said Bithel. 'Never had the chance. Not particularly keen to either. Do you think we shall have to play?'

'Not much time with all the training, I should imagine.'

'I hope not,' he said, rather desperately. 'There's a rumour we're going to move almost at once in any case.'

'Any idea where?'

'People seem to think Northern Ireland. I say, this parade ground is a long way off, isn't it. Hope we shan't be inspected too closely, I'm not all that well shaved. I cut myself this morning. Hand shaky, for some reason'

'That dance was a splendid affair.'

'What dance?'

'The dance you did round the dummy in your bed last night.'

'Ah,' said Bithel laughing, 'I've heard that one before – having somebody on by pretending he made a fool of himself the night before. I know when I'm having my leg pulled. As a matter of fact I was rather relieved when everyone went off quietly to bed last night. I thought there might be some ragging, and I was feeling tired after the journey. They used to rag a lot when I was in Territorial camp years ago. I never liked it. Not cut out for that sort of thing. But to get back to razors – what shaving soap do you use? I'm trying a new kind. Saw it advertized in *Health and Strength*. Thought I'd experiment. I like a change of soaps from time to time. It freshens you up.'

By that time we had reached the parade ground. Kedward was already there. He took me off to the platoon I was to command. Bithel disappeared in another direction. Kedward explained certain matters, then we marched up and down side by side until officers were ordered to fall in. The service was held in one of the parish churches of the town. Later, from the pulpit, Popkiss, transformed now from the pale, embarrassed cleric of the saloon bar, orated with the ease and energy shared by officers and men throughout the Battalion. His text was from Ezekiel. Popkiss read the passage at length:

'The hand of the Lord was upon me, and carried me out in the spirit of the Lord, and set me down in the midst of the valley which was full of bones, and caused me to pass them round about: and, behold, there were very many in the open valley: and, lo, they were very dry. And he said unto me, Son of man, can these bones live? And I answered, O Lord God thou knowest. Again he said unto me, Prophesy upon these bones, and say unto them, O ye dry bones, hear the word of the Lord. Thus saith the Lord God unto these bones; Behold, I will cause breath to enter into you, and ye shall live. And I will lay sinews upon you, and cover you with skin, and put breath into you, and ye shall live; and ye shall know that I am the Lord. So I prophesied as I was commanded; and as I prophesied there was a noise, and behold a shaking, and the bones came together, bone to bone. And when I beheld, lo, the sinews and the flesh came

37

upon them, and the skin covered them above; and there was no breath in them. Then he said unto me, Prophesy unto the wind, prophesy, son of man, and say to the wind, Thus saith the Lord God; Come from the four winds, O breath, and breathe upon these slain that they may live. So I prophesied as he commanded me, and the breath came unto them and they lived, and stood up upon their feet, an exceeding great army . . .'

Popkiss paused, looked up from his Testament, stretched out his arms on either side. The men were very silent in the pitch-pine pews.

'. . . Oh, my brethren, think on that open valley, think on it with me . . . a valley, do I picture it, by the shaft of a shut-down mine, where, under the dark mountain side, the slag heaps lift their heads to the sky, a valley such as those valleys in which you yourselves abide . . . Journey with me, my brethren, into that open valley, journey with me . . . Know you not those same dry bones? . . . You know them well. . . . Bones without flesh and sinew, bones without skin or breath . . . They are our bones, my brethren, the bones of you and of me, bones that await the noise and the mighty shaking, the gift of the four winds of which the prophet of old did tell . . . Must we not come together, my brethren, everyone of us, as did the bones of that ancient valley, quickened with breath, bone to bone, sinew to sinew, skin to skin . . . Unless I speak falsely, an exceeding great army . . .'

2

THE MOVEMENT ORDER CAME NOT MUCH more than a week afterwards, before I had properly awakened from the dream through the perspectives of which I ranged, London as remote from me as from Kedward, Isobel's letters the only residuum of a world occupied by other matters than platoon training or turning out the guard. As if by the intoxication of a drug, or compulsive hypnotic influences on the will, another world had been entered by artificial means, through which one travelled irresistibly, ominously, like Dr Trelawney and his fellow magicians, borne by their spells out on to the Astral Plane. Now, at last, I was geared to the machine of war, no longer an extraneous organism existing separately in increasingly alien conditions. For the moment, routine duties scarcely allowed thought. There was a day frantically occupied with packing. Then the whole Battalion was on parade. Orders were shouted. We moved off in column of route, leaving behind us Sardis, one of the Seven Churches of Asia, where the garments were white of those few who remained undefiled. The men, although departing from their own neighbourhoods and country, were in a fairly buoyant mood. Something was beginning at last. They sang softly:

'Guide me, O thou great Jehovah,
Pilgrim through this barren land:
I am weak, but thou art mighty,
Hold me with thy powerful hand,

39

Bread of heaven,
Bread of heaven
Feed me till I want no more . . .'

This singing on the march, whatever form it took, always
affirmed the vicissitudes of life, the changes, so often for
the worse, that beset human existence, especially in the
army, especially in time of war. After a while they abandoned the hymn, though not those accustomed themes of
uncertainty, hardship, weariness, despondency, vain effort,
contemplation of which gives such support to the soldier:

'We had ter join,
We had ter join,
We had ter join Belisha's army:

Ten bob a week,
Bugger all to eat,
Great big boots and blisters on yer feet.

We had ter join,
We had ter join,
We had ter join Belisha's army:

Sitting on the grass,
Polishing up the brass,
Great black spiders running up yer – back.

We had ter join – we had ter join—
We had ter join – we had ter join . . .'

Gwatkin was in a state of unconcealed excitement. He
bawled out his commands, loud as if through a megaphone,
perpetually checking Kedward, Breeze and myself about

minor matters. I could just see Bithel plodding along with his platoon at the rear of the company immediately ahead of us. He had turned up on parade carrying a small green leather dressing-case, much battered, which he grasped while he marched.

'Didn't like to trust it with the heavy baggage,' he said, adjusting the worn waterproof cover, while we stood easy at the railway station. 'The only piece of my mother's luggage I have left. She's gone to a Better Place now, you know.'

The train set out towards the north. This was the beginning of a long journey to an unknown destination. Night fell. Hours later, we detrained in stygian darkness. Here was a port. Black craft floated on a pitchy, infernal lake. Beyond the mouth of the harbour, the wash of waves echoed. The boat on which the Battalion embarked was scarcely large enough to accommodate our strength. The men were fitted in at last, sitting or lying like the cargo of a slave ship. The old steamer chugged away from the jetty, and into open sea. Wind was up. We heaved about in choppy waters. There was not going to be much sleep for anyone that night. After much scurrying about on the part of officers and NCOs, Sergeant Pendry reported at last that all was correct. He was accompanied by Corporal Gwylt, one of the Company's several wits, tiny, almost a dwarf, with a huge head of black curly hair; no doubt a member of that primitive race of which the tall, fair Celt had become overlord. Not always to be relied upon to carry out purely military duties to perfection, Gwylt was acceptable as an NCO because he never stopped talking and singing, so that his personality, though obtrusive, helped the Platoon through some of the tedium inseparable from army life.

'Has everyone had their cocoa issue, Sergeant Pendry?'

'That they have, sir, very good it was.'

'Some of the boys was too sick to drink their cocoa, sir,' said Corporal Gwylt, who felt his comment always required.

'Are a lot of the Platoon sea-sick?'

'I told them to lie still and it would pass,' said Sergeant Pendry. 'They do make a lot of fuss, some of them.'

'Oh, bloody sick, some of them,' said Corporal Gwylt, like a Greek chorus. 'That fair boy, Jones, D., bloody sick he has been.'

The boat ploughed through wind and wave. Was this the night journey on the sea of a thousand dreams loaded with hidden meaning? Certainly our crossing was no less mysterious than those nocturnal voyages of sleep. Towards morning I retired below to shave, feeling revived when I returned to deck. The sky was getting lighter and land was in sight. An easterly breeze was blowing when we went ashore, which sprayed about a gentle drizzle. Beyond the harbour stretched a small town, grey houses, factory chimneys. In the distance, mountains were obscured by cloud. Everything looked mean and down-at-heel. There was nothing to make one glad to have arrived in this country.

'March your men ashore promptly when the order comes, platoon commanders,' said Gwatkin. 'Show initiative. Don't hang about. Get cracking.'

He looked rather green in the face, as if, like Jones, D., he too had been sick during the crossing, himself far from the condition required for 'getting cracking'. The companies filed down the gangway, one by one, forming up later by a railway line. There were the usual delays. The rain, borne towards us on a driving wind, was increasing in volume. The Battalion stood easy, waiting for word from the Embarkation Staff. Girls with shawls over their heads were on their way to work. Disregarding the rain, they stopped and watched us from the side of the road, standing huddled together, talking and laughing.

'Aigh-o, Mary,' shouted Corporal Gwylt. 'Have you come to see the foreigners?'

The girls began to giggle purposefully.

'It's no brave day ye've brought with ye,' one of them called back.

'What was that you said, Mary, my love?'

'Why did ye not bring a braver day with ye, I'm asking. 'Tis that we've been wanting since Sunday, sure.'

'What kind of a day, Mary, my own?'

'Why a brave day. 'Tis prosperous weather we're needing.'

Corporal Gwylt turned to Sergeant Pendry and made a gesture with his hand to convey absolute incredulity at such misuse of language.

'*Brave* day?' he said. 'Did you hear what she called it, Sergeant Pendry?'

'I did that, Corporal Gwylt.'

'So that's a funny way to talk.'

'That it is.'

'Now you can tell the way people speak we're far from home.'

'You'll be getting many surprises in this country, my lad,' said Sergeant Pendry. 'You may be sure of that.'

'Will some of them be nice surprises, Sergeant?'

'Ask not that of me.'

'Oh, don't you think I'll be getting some nice surprises, Sergeant Pendry,' said Corporal Gwylt in a soft wheedling tone, 'like a plump little girl to keep me warm at night.'

CSM Cadwallader was pottering about nearby, like a conscientious matron at a boys' school determined to make sure all was well. He had the compact professional feeling of the miner, which he combined with a rather unusual

43

taste for responsibility, so that any company commander was lucky to claim his services.

'We'll be keeping you warm, Corporal Gwylt,' he said. 'Make no mistake. There'll be plenty of work for you, I'll tell you straight. Do not worry about the night-time. Then you will want your rest, not little girls, nor big ones neither.'

'But a plump little girl, Sergeant-Major? Do not yourself wish to meet a plump little girl?'

'Put not such ideas into the Sergeant-Major's head, Corporal Gwylt,' said Sergeant Pendry. 'He does not wish your dirty things.'

'Nor me, the *dirty* girls,' said Corporal Gwylt. 'I never said the dirty ones.'

'Nor then the clean ones, understand.'

'Oh, does he not?' said Corporal Gwylt, in feigned astonishment. 'Not even the clean ones? Do you think that indeed, Sergeant Pendry?'

'I do think that, I tell you.'

'And why, whatever?'

'The Sergeant-Major is a married man, you must know.'

'So you think girls are just for young lads like me, Sergeant-Major? That is good for me, I'm sure.'

'Never mind what I think, Corporal.'

'He is a lucky man, the Sergeant Major,' said Sergeant Pendry sententiously. 'You will be glad when you reach his age, no longer foolish and running after girls.'

'Oh, dear me, is it true what Sergeant Pendry says, Sergeant-Major, that girls are for you no longer? I am that sorry to hear.'

CSM Cadwallader allowed himself a dry smile.

'Have you never heard, Corporal Gwylt, there's those to find many a good tune played on old fiddles?' he said benevolently.

The Embarkation Staff Officer turned up at that moment

with a sheaf of papers. The Battalion was on the move again. Corporal Gwylt had just time to blow a kiss to the girls, who waved frantically, redoubling their gigglings. The Company tramped off towards the train in a siding.

'Now then, there,' shouted the Sergeant-Major, 'pick up the step in the rear files. Left – left – left, right, left . . .'

We steamed through bare, dismal country, wide fields, white cabins, low walls of piled stones, stretches of heather, more mountains far away on the horizon.

'This will give us better training areas than back home,' said Gwatkin.

He had recovered from his sea sickness and the tension brought on by the move. Now he was relatively calm.

'We shall be more like soldiers here,' he said with satisfaction.

'What happens when we arrive, Rowland?' Breeze asked. 'I hope there'll be something to eat.'

Breeze's questions were usually aimed to score the textbook answer from Gwatkin.

'The second echelon of the supply column will have preceded us,' said Gwatkin sharply.

'And what do they do?'

'They will have broken bulk and be ready to issue to units. You should spend more time on your *Field Service Pocket Book*, Yanto.'

We arrived at a small, unalluring industrial town. Once more the Battalion formed up. By now the men were tired. Singing was sombre as we marched in:

'My lips smile no more, my heart loses its lightness,
No dream of the future my spirit can cheer,
I only would brood on the past and its brightness,
The dead I have mourned are again gathered here.
From every dark nook they press forward to meet me,

45

I lift up my eyes to the broad leafy dome.
And others are there looking downward to greet me,
The ashgrove, the ashgrove, alone is my home . . .'

Gwatkin was right about being more like soldiers in these new surroundings. Barracks had been created from a disused linen factory, the long narrow sheds in which the flax had formerly been treated offering barrack-rooms stark as a Foreign Legion film set. Officers were billeted in a forlorn villa on the outskirts of the town, a house that had no doubt once belonged to some successful local businessman. It was a mile or more away from the barracks. There, I still shared a room with Kedward, Breeze and Pumphrey, the last of whom had not yet achieved his RAF transfer. Another subaltern, Craddock, was in with us too, brother of the girl to whom Kedward was engaged. Craddock, fat and energetic, was Messing Officer, which meant he returned to billets in the middle of the night several times a week, when he would either turn on the light, or blunder about the room in the dark, falling over other people's camp-beds in a fruitless effort to find his own. Both methods were disturbing. There was, in any case, not much room to manœuvre round the beds, even when the light was on. Craddock's midnight arrivals were not the only inconvenience. Breeze left old razor blades about in profusion, causing Pumphrey to cut his foot one morning. Kedward talked in his sleep throughout the night, shouting commands, as if he were drilling a company: 'At the halt – on the left – form close column of – platoons . . .'

Pumphrey, inclined to bicker, would throw towels about and sponges. A window pane was broken, which no one ever seemed responsible for mending, through which the night wind whistled, while cold struck up insistently from the floor, penetrating the canvas of a camp-bed. Snow had returned. I record these conditions not as particularly formidable in the circumstances, but to indicate they were sufficiently far from ideal to encourage a change, when, as it happened, opportunity arose. This came about through Gwatkin in an unexpected manner. During the weeks that followed our arrival in these new surroundings, I began to know him better. He was nearer my own age than the other subalterns, except Bithel. Even the captains tended to be younger than Gwatkin and myself, as time went on, some of the older ones being gradually shifted, as insufficiently proficient at their job, to Holding Battalions or the Infantry Training Centre.

'We're getting rid of the dead wood,' said Gwatkin. 'Just as well.'

His own abrupt manner of speaking continued, and he loved to find fault for its own sake. At the same time, he evidently wanted to be friendly, while fearing that too easy a relationship with a subordinate, even one of similar age, might be unmilitary. There were unexpected sides to Gwatkin, sudden displays of uncertainty under a façade meant to be very certain. Some of his duties he carried out very well; for others, he had little or no natural talent.

'A company commander,' said Dicky Umfraville, when we met later that year, 'needs the qualifications of a ringmaster in a first-class circus, and a nanny in a large family.'

Gwatkin aspired to this dazzling combination of gifts – to become (as Pennistone later said) a military saint. Somehow he always fell short of that coveted status. His imperfections never derived from any willingness to spare himself. On the contrary, inability to delegate authority, insistence that he must do everything himself, important or unimportant, was one of Gwatkin's chief handicaps in achieving his high aim. For example, he instituted a 'Company Officer of the Day', one of whose duties was to make

47

sure all was well at the men's dinners. This job, on the whole redundant, since the Orderly Officer of necessity visited all Mess Rooms to investigate 'any complaints', was made additionally superfluous by Gwatkin himself appearing as often as not at dinners, in order to make sure the Company Officer of the Day was not shirking his rounds. In fact, he scarcely allowed himself any time off at all. He seemed half aware that this intense keenness was not, in final result, what was required; at least not without more understanding on his own part. Besides, Gwatkin had none of that faculty, so necessary in the army, of accepting rebuke – even unjust rebuke – and carrying on as if nothing had happened. Criticism from above left him dreadfully depressed.

'It's no good letting the army get you down,' the Adjutant, Maelgwyn-Jones, used to say. 'Just remember, when you're worrying about the Brigadier's inspection, that day will pass, as other days in the army pass.'

Maelgwyn-Jones himself did not always act upon this teaching. He was an efficient, short-tempered Regular, whose slight impediment of speech became a positive stutter when he grew enraged. He wanted to get back to the battalion he came from, where there was more hope of immediate action and consequent promotion. Thoroughly reliable as an officer, hard working as an adjutant, Maelgwyn-Jones did not share – indeed was totally unapprehending of – Gwatkin's resplendent vision of army life. When he pulled up Gwatkin for some such lapse as unpunctual disposal of the Company's swill, Gwatkin would behave as if his personal honour had been called into question; then concentrate feverishly on more energetic training, smarter turn-out. In a sense, of course, that was correct enough, but the original cause of complaint was not always put right in the most expeditious manner. The fact was

48

Gwatkin lacked in his own nature that grasp of 'system' for which he possessed such admiration. This deficiency was perhaps connected in some way with a kind of poetry within him, a poetry which had somehow become a handicap in its efforts to find an outlet. Romantic ideas about the way life is lived are often to be found in persons themselves fairly coarse-grained. This was to some extent true of Gwatkin. His coarseness of texture took the form of having to find a scapegoat after he himself had been in trouble. The scapegoat was usually Breeze, though any of the rest of the Company might suffer. Bithel, usually in hot water of some kind, would have offered an ever available target for these punitive visitations of Gwatkin's, but Bithel was in another company. All the same, although no concern of his in the direct sense, Bithel's appearance and demeanour greatly irked Gwatkin in a general way. He spoke of this one afternoon, when Bithel, wearing one of his gaiters improperly adjusted, crossed our path on the way back from afternoon training.

'Did you ever see such an unsoldierly type?' Gwatkin said. 'And his brother a VC too.'

'Is it certain they're brothers, not just fairly distant relations?'

I was not sure whether Bithel's words to me on that earlier occasion had been spoken in confidence. The tone he had adopted suggested something of the sort. Besides, Bithel might suddenly decide to return to the earlier cycle of legends he had apparently disseminated about himself to facilitate his Reserve call-up; or at least he might not wish to have them specifically denied on his own authority. However, Gwatkin showed no wish to verify the truth, or otherwise, of Bithel's alleged kinships.

'Even if they are not brothers, Bithel is a disgrace for a man with a VC in the family,' Gwatkin said severely. 'He should be ashamed. That VC ought to give him a pride in himself. I wish a relative of mine had won the VC, won an MC even. And it is my belief, I am telling you, Nick, that all about Bithel's rugger is tommy-rot.'

That last conviction was unanswerable by this time. No one who had seen Bithel proceeding at the double could possibly suppose his abilities in the football field had ever been more than moderate.

'Do you know when Idwal was Orderly Officer last week,' said Gwatkin, 'he found Bithel in his dressing-gown listening to the gramophone with the Mess waiters. Bithel said he was looking for Daniels, that servant of his I don't much like either. And then we are expected to keep discipline in the unit.'

'That bloody gramophone makes a frightful row at all hours.'

'So it does, too, and I'm not going to stay in those billets any longer. I have had enough. My camp-bed was taken down to the Company Office this morning. That is the place for a company commander to be. Half the day is lost in this place walking backwards and forwards from billets to barracks. We are lucky enough to have an office next door to the Company Store. The bed can be folded up and go into the store for the day.'

We had reached a fork in the road. One way led to barracks, the other to billets. Gwatkin seemed suddenly to come to a decision.

'Why don't you come down to the Company Office too?' he asked.

He spoke roughly, almost as if he were demanding why I had disobeyed an order.

'Would there be room?'

'Plenty.'

'We're pretty thick on the ground where I am at present,

even though Idwal is on the Anti-gas course at the moment.'

'It won't be so lively sleeping in the office.'

'I can stand that.'

'The great thing is you're on the spot. Near the men. Where every officer should be.'

I was flattered by the suggestion. Kedward was at the Corps School of Chemical Warfare at Castlemallock – usually known as the Anti-gas School – so that Breeze and I were Gwatkin's only subalterns at that moment, and there was a lot of work to do. As I have said, accommodation at the billets had little to recommend it. The Company Office was at least no worse a prospect. To be in barracks would be convenient, not least in its reduction of continual trudging backwards and forwards to the billets.

'I'll have my kit taken down this evening.'

That was the beginning of my comparative intimacy with Gwatkin. Sharing with him the Company Office at night altered not only our mutual relationship, but also the whole tempo of night and morning. Instead of the turmoil of Kedward, Breeze, Pumphrey and Craddock getting dressed, talking, scuffling, singing, there was only the occasional harsh, serious, professional comment of Gwatkin; his tense silences. He slept heavily, often dropping off before the electric light was out and the blackout down; never, like myself, lying awake listening to the talk in the Company Store next door. The partition between the store and the office did not reach all the way to the ceiling, so that conversation held in the store after Lights Out, although usually carried out in comparatively low tones – in contrast with the normal speech of the unit – was often audible. Only the storeman, Lance-Corporal Gittins, was supposed to sleep in the store at night, but, in practice, the room usually housed several others; semi-official assistants of Gittins, friends, relations, Company personalities, like Corporal Gwylt. These would gather in the evening, if not on guard duties, and listen to the wireless; several of those assembled later staying the night among the crates and piles of blankets, to slumber in the peculiar, musty smell of the store, an odour somewhere between the Natural History Museum and an oil-and-colour shop. Lance-Corporal Gittins was CSM Cadwallader's brother-in-law. He was a man not always willing to recognise the artificial and temporary hierarchy imposed by military rank.

'Now, see it you must, Gareth,' I heard the Sergeant-Major's voice once insisting on the other side of the partition. 'In time of peace – in the mine – you are above me, Gareth, and above Sergeant Pendry. Here, that is not. No longer is it the mine. In the Company we are above you. It would be good you remember that, Gareth.'

Gittins was a figure of some prestige in the Company, not only on account of dominion over valuable stock-in-trade, but also for his forcible character. Dark, stocky, another strongly pre-Celtic type, he could probably have become sergeant – even sergeant-major – without difficulty, had he wished for promotion. Like many others, he preferred to avoid such responsibilities, instead ruling the store, where he guarded every item as if it were his own personal property acquired only after long toil and self-denial. Nothing was more difficult than to extort from him the most insignificant replacement of kit.

'I tell you, not without the Skipper's direct order,' was his usual answer to such requests. This circumspection was very generally respected. To coax anything from Gittins was considered a triumph. One of the attractions of the store was its wireless, which would sometimes be tuned in to Haw-Haw's propaganda broadcast from Germany. These came on just after midnight:

'. . . This is *Chairmany* calling . . . *Chairmany* calling . . . These are the stations Köln, Hamburg and DJA . . .

Here is the news in English . . . Fifty-three more British aircraft were shot down over Kiel last night making a total of one hundred and seventeen since Tuesday . . . One hundred and seventeen more British aircraft have been shot down in forty-eight hours . . . The British people are asking their Government why British pilots cannot stay in the air . . . They are asking why British aircraft is inferior to *Chairman* aircraft . . . The British people are asking themselves why they have lost the war in the air . . . They are asking, for example, what has happened to the Imperial Airways Liner *Ajax* . . . Why is the Imperial Airways Liner *Ajax* three weeks overdue, they are asking . . . We can tell you . . . The Imperial Airways Liner *Ajax* is at the bottom of the sea . . . The fishes are swimming in and out of the wreckage of the Imperial Airways Liner *Ajax* . . . The Imperial Airways Liner *Ajax* and her escort were shot down by *Chairman* fighter planes . . . The British have lost the war in the air . . . They have lost the war in the air . . . It is the same on the water . . . The Admiralty is wondering about the *Resourceful* . . . They are worried at the Admiralty about the *Resourceful* . . . They need not worry about the *Resourceful* any more . . . We will tell them about the *Resourceful* . . . The *Resourceful* is at the bottom of the sea with the Imperial Airways Liner *Ajax* . . . The *Resourceful* was sunk by a *Chairman* submarine . . . The Admiralty is in despair at *Chairman* command of the sea . . . Britain has lost the war on the sea . . . One hundred and seventy-five thousand *gross registered* tons of British shipping was sent to the bottom last week . . . The British Government is in despair at these losses in the air and on the water . . . That is not the only thing that makes the British Government despair . . . Not by any means . . . The food shortage in Britain is becoming acute . . . The evacuated women and children are living in misery . . . Instead of food, they are being fed on lies . . . Government lies . . . Only *Chairmany* can tell you the truth . . . The *Chairman* radio speaks the truth . . . The *Chairman* radio gives the best and latest news . . . *Chairmany* is winning the war . . . Think it over, Britain, think it over . . . *Chairmany* is winning the war . . . Listen, Britain . . . Listen, Britain . . . We repeat to all listeners in the Far East . . . Listen, South America . . .'

Someone in the store turned the button. The nagging, sneering, obsessive accents died away with a jerk, as if a sack had been advantageously thrust over the speaker's head, bestowing an immediate sense of relief at his extinction. There was a long pause next door.

'I do wonder he can remember all that,' said a voice, possibly that of Williams, W.H., one of the singers of Sardis, now runner in my platoon.

'Someone writes it down for him, don't you see,' said another voice that could have been Corporal Gwylt's.

'And do they give him all those figures too?'

'Of course they do.'

'So that is it.'

'You must know that, lad.'

'What a lot he do talk.'

'That's for they pay him.'

'Bloody sure he is Germany will win the war. Why does he call it like that – *Chairmany* – it's a funny way to speak to be sure.'

'Maybe that's the way they say it there.'

'If Hitler wins the war, I tell you, lad, we'll go down the mine for sixpence a day.'

No one in the store attempted to deny this conclusion. There was another pause and some coughing. It was not easy to tell how many persons were collected there. Gittins himself appeared to have gone to sleep, only Gwylt and Williams, W. H., unable to bring the day to a close. I

54

thought they too must have nodded off, when suddenly Williams's voice sounded again.

'How would you like to go up in an aircraft, Ivor?'

'I would not mind that so much.'

'I hope I do not have to do that.'

'We are not in the RAF, lad, what are you thinking?'

'I would not like it up there I am sure too.'

'They will not put you up there, no worry.'

'You do not know what they will do, look at those parachutists, indeed.'

'You make me think of Dai and Shoni when they went up in a balloon.'

'And what was that, I wonder.'

'They took two women with them.'

'Did they, then?'

'When the balloon was in the sky, the air began to leak something terrible out of it, it did, and Dai was frightened, so frightened Dai was, and Dai said to Shoni, Look you, Shoni, this balloon is not safe at all, and the air is leaking out of it terrible, we shall have to jump for it, and Shoni said to Dai, But, Dai, what about the women? and Dai said, Oh, fook the women, and Shoni said, But have we time?'

'We shall not have any time to sleep till morning break, I am telling you, if you will jaw all through the night,' spoke another voice, certainly Lance-Corporal Gittins, the storeman, this time. 'How many hundred and hundred of those Dai and Shoni stories have I in all my days had to hear, I should like to know, and most of them said by you, Ivor. Is tarts never out of your thought.'

'Why, Gareth, you talk about tarts too,' said Williams, W. H. 'What was that you was telling my butty of Cath Pendry yesterday?'

'What about her?'

Gittins sounded more truculent this time.

'Her and Evans the checkweighman.'

'You was not meant to hear that, I tell you, Williams, W. H.'

'Come on, Gareth,' said Gwylt.

'Never mind you, Ivor.'

'Oh, that do sound something I would like to hear.'

No one answered Gwylt. There was a lot more coughing, some throat clearing, then silence. They must all have gone to sleep. I was on the point of doing the same, had even reached a state of only semi-consciousness, when there was a sudden exclamation from the direction of Gwatkin's bed. He had woken with a start and was feeling for his electric torch. He found the torch at last and, clambering out of bed, began to put up the blackout boards on the window frame.

'What is it, Rowland?'

'Turn the light on,' he said, 'I've got this board fixed now.'

I switched on the light, which was nearer my bed than his.

'I've just thought of something,' Gwatkin said agitatedly. 'Do you remember I said units had been issued with a new codeword for intercommunication within the Brigade?'

'Yes.'

'What did I do with it?'

He seemed almost to be talking in his sleep.

'You put it in the box, didn't you?'

Gwatkin's usual treatment of the flow of paper that entered the Company Office daily was to mark each item with the date in the inked letters of the Company's rubber-stamp, himself initialling the centre of its circular mauve impression. He would treat the most trivial printed matter in this way, often wryly smiling as he remarked: 'This becomes a habit.' The click of the instrument on an official document, together with his own endorsement 'R. G.' – written with a flourish – seemed to give him a feeling of having settled that matter once and for all, a faint but distinct sense of absolute power. If classified as 'Secret' or 'Confidential', the stuff was put in a large cashbox, of which Gwatkin himself kept the key. The Company's 'Imprest Account' was locked away in this box, together with all sorts of other papers which had taken Gwatkin's fancy as important. The box itself was kept in a green steel cupboard, the shape of a wardrobe, also locked, though its key was considered less sacred than that of the cashbox.

'Are you sure I put it in the box?'

'Pretty sure.'

'Codewords are vital.'

'I know.'

'I'd better make certain.'

He put on a greatcoat over his pyjamas, because the nights were still fairly cold. Then he began fumbling about with the keys, opening the cupboard and bringing out the cashbox. There was not much room in the Company Office at the best of time, when both beds were erected, scarcely any space at all in which to operate, so that the foot of my own bed was the only convenient ledge on which to rest the box while Gwatkin went through its contents. He began to sort out the top layer of papers, arranging them in separate piles over the foot of my bed, all over my greatcoat, which was serving as eiderdown. I sat up in bed, watching him strew my legs with official forms and instructional leaflets of one kind or another. He dealt them out with great care, as if diverting himself with some elaborate form of Patience, military pamphlets doing duty for playing cards. The deeper he delved into the cashbox, the more meticulously he arranged the contents. Among other items, he turned out a small volume bound in faded red cloth. This book, much tattered, was within reach. I picked it up. Opening at the fly-leaf: I read: R. Gwatkin, Capt.', together with the designation of the Regiment. The title-page was that of a pocket edition of *Puck of Pook's Hill*. Gwatkin gave a sudden grunt. He had found whatever he was seeking.

'Here it is,' he said. 'Thank God. I remember now. I put it in a envelope in a special place at the bottom of the box.'

He began to replace the papers, one by one, in the elaborate sequence he had ordained for them. I handed him *Puck of Pook's Hill*. He took the book from me, still apparently pondering the fearful possibilities consequent on failure to trace the codeword. Then he suddenly became aware I had been looking at the Kipling stories. He took the little volume from me, and pushed it away under a *Glossary of Military Terms and Organization in the Field*. For a second he seemed a shade embarrassed.

'That's a book by Rudyard Kipling,' he said defensively, as if the statement explained something.

'So I see.'

'Ever read anything by him?'

'Yes.'

'Read this one?'

'Ages ago.'

'What did you think of it?'

'I liked it.'

'You've read a lot of books, haven't you, Nick?'

'I have to in my profession.'

Gwatkin locked the tin box and replaced it in the cupboard.

'Turn the light out,' he said. 'And I'll take the blackout down again.'

I switched out the light. He removed the window boards. I heard him arranging the greatcoat over himself in the bed.

'I don't expect you remember,' he said, 'but there's a story in that book about a Roman centurion.'

'Of course.'

'That was the one I liked.'

'It's about the best.'

'I sometimes read it again.'

He pulled the greatcoat higher over him.

'I've read it lots of times really,' he said. 'I like it. I don't like any of the others so much.'

'The Norman knight isn't bad.'

'Not so good as the centurion.'

'Do you like his other books?'

'Whose?'

'Kipling's.'

'Oh, yes, of course. I know he wrote a lot of other books. I did try one of them. I couldn't get on with it somehow.'

'Which one did you try?'

'I can't remember the name. Can't remember much about it, to tell the truth. I just didn't like it. All written in a special sort of language I didn't understand. I don't read much. Got other things to do. It's not like you, reading more or less as a business.'

He stopped speaking, was almost immediately asleep and breathing heavily. This was the first evidence come to light that anyone in the unit had ever read a book for pleasure, unless Bithel's 'digests' might be thought to have brought him to a public library in search of some work on sexual psychology. This was an interesting discovery about Gwatkin. By now snores were sounding from the store. I rolled over towards the wall and slept too. The following day Gwatkin made no reference to this nocturnal conversation. Perhaps he had forgotten about it. Leaving barracks that evening there was a small incident to illustrate the way in which he took failure to heart. This happened when Gwatkin, Kedward and I were passing the vehicle park, where the bren-carriers stood.

'I'd like to try driving one of those buses,' Kedward said.

'They're easy enough,' said Gwatkin.

He scrambled into the nearest carrier and started up the engine. However, when he put the vehicle in gear, it refused to move, only rocking backwards and forwards on its tracks. Gwatkin's small head and black moustache bobbed up and down at the end of the carrier, so that he seemed part of the chassis, a kind of figurehead, even the front half of an armoured centaur. There was also something that recalled a knight in the game of chess, immensely large and suddenly animated by some inner, mysterious power. For a time Gwatkin heaved up and down there, as if riding one of the cars on a warlike merry-go-round; then completely defeated by the machinery, perhaps out of order, he climbed slowly to the ground and rejoined us.

'I shouldn't have done that,' he said, humiliated.

All the same, this sort of thing did not at all impair his confidence in himself when it came to dealing with the men. Gwatkin prided himself on his relationship with the 'other ranks' in his company. He did not talk about it much, but the conviction was implicit in his behaviour. His attitude towards Sayce provided a good example. That was clear even before I witnessed their great scene together. Sayce was the Company bad character. He had turned up with another couple of throw-outs voided as unsuitable for employment from one of the regular battalions. His previous unit must have been thankful to get rid of him. Small and lean, with a yellow face and blackened teeth, his shortcomings were not to be numbered. Apart from such recurrent items as lateness on parade, deficiency of shaving kit, lack of clean socks, mislaid paybook, filthy rifle, generally unsatisfactory turn-out, Sayce would produce some new, hitherto unthought-of crime most days. Dirty, disobliging, quarrelsome, little short of mutinous, he was heartily disliked by all ranks. Although a near criminal, he possessed none of the charm J. G. Quiggin, as a reviewer, used to attribute to criminals who wrote memoirs. On the contrary, Sayce, immoderately vain, was also stupid and unprepossessing. From time to time, in order to give him a chance to redeem himself from a series of disasters, he would be assigned some individual task, easy to undertake, but within range of conferring credit by its simple discharge. Sayce always made a hash of it; always, too, for the worst of reasons. He seemed preordained for detention.

'It will be the Glasshouse for that bugger Sayce,' Sergeant Pendry, who got along pretty well with almost everyone, used often to remark.

In dealing with Sayce, therefore, it might be thought Gwatkin would assume his favoured role of martinet, imposing a series of punishments that would eventually bring Sayce before the Commanding Officer; and certainly Sayce took his share of CBs from Gwatkin in the Company Office. At the same time, their point of contact, at least on Gwatkin's side, was not entirely unsympathetic. The fact was, Sayce appealed to Gwatkin's imagination. Those stylized pictures of army life on which Gwatkin's mind loved to dwell did not exclude a soldier of Sayce's type. Indeed, a professional bad character was obviously a type from which no army could remain wholly free. Accordingly, Gwatkin was prepared to treat Sayce with what many company commanders would have considered excessive consideration, to tolerate him up to a point, even to make serious efforts to reform him. Gwatkin had spoken to me more than once about these projects for Sayce's reformation, before he finally announced that he had planned a direct appeal to Sayce's better feelings.

'I'm going to have a straight talk with Sayce,' he said one day, when Sayce's affairs had reached some sort of climax. 'I'd like you to be present, Nick, as he's in your platoon.'

Gwatkin sat at the trestle table with the army blanket over

it. I stood behind. Sayce, capless, was marched in by CSM Cadwallader and a corporal.

'You and the escort can leave the room, Sergeant-Major,' said Gwatkin. 'I want to have a word with this soldier in private – that is to say myself and his Platoon Commander, Mr Jenkins.'

The Sergeant-Major and other NCO withdrew.

'You can stand easy, Sayce,' said Gwatkin.

Sayce stood easy. His yellow face showed distrust.

'I want to speak to you seriously, Sayce,' said Gwatkin. 'To speak to you as man to man. Do you understand what I mean, Sayce?'

Sayce made some inaudible reply.

'It is not my wish, Sayce, to be always punishing you,' said Gwatkin slowly. 'Is that clear? I do not like doing that at all.'

Sayce muttered again. It seemed very doubtful that he found Gwatkin's statement easy to credit. Gwatkin leant forward over the table. He was warming up. Within him were deep reserves of emotion. He spoke now with that strange cooing tone he used on the telephone.

'You can do better, Sayce. I say you can do better.'

He fixed Sayce with his eye. Sayce's own eyes began to roll.

'You're a good fellow at heart, aren't you, Sayce?'

All this was now beginning to tell on Sayce. I had to admit to myself there was nothing I should have liked less than to be grilled by Gwatkin in this fashion. A week's CB would be infinitely preferable. Sayce began swallowing.

'You are, Sayce, aren't you?' Gwatkin repeated more pressingly, as if time were becoming short for Sayce to reveal that unexpected better side of himself, and gain salvation.

'Yes, sir,' said Sayce, very low.

He spoke without much conviction. That could scarcely be because there was doubt in his mind of his own high qualifications. He probably suspected any such information, freely given, might be a dangerous admission, lead to more work.

'Well, Sayce,' said Gwatkin, 'that is what I am going to believe about you. Believe you are a good fellow. You know why we are all here?'

Sayce did not answer.

'You know why we are all here, Sayce,' said Gwatkin again, louder this time, his voice shaking a little with his own depths of feeling. 'Come on, Sayce, you know.'

'Don't know, sir.'

'Yes, you do.'

'Don't, sir.'

'Come on, man.'

Sayce made a great effort.

'To give me CB for being on a charge,' he offered wretchedly.

It was a reasonable hypothesis, but Gwatkin was greatly disturbed at being so utterly misunderstood.

'No, no,' he said, 'I don't mean why we are in the Company Office at this moment. I mean why we are all in the army. You must know that, Sayce. We are here for our country. We are here to repel Hitler. You know that as well as I do. You don't want Hitler to rule over you, Sayce, do you?'

Sayce gulped again, as if he were not sure.

'No, sir,' he agreed, without much vigour.

'We must all, every one of us, do our best,' said Gwatkin, now thoroughly worked up. 'I try to do my best as Company Commander. Mr Jenkins and the other officers of the Company do their best. The NCOs and privates do their best. Are you going to be the only one, Sayce, who is not doing his best?'

Sayce was now in almost as emotional a state as Gwatkin

himself. He continued to gulp from time to time, looking wildly round the room, as if for a path of escape.

'Will you do your best in future, Sayce?'

Sayce began sniffing frantically.

'I will, sir.'

'Do you promise me, Sayce.'

'All right, sir.'

'And we're agreed you're a good chap, aren't we?'

'Yes, sir.'

Indeed, Sayce seemed moved almost to tears by the thought of all his own hitherto unrevealed goodness.

'Never had a chance since I've been with the unit,' he managed to articulate.

Gwatkin rose to his feet.

'We're going to shake hands, Sayce,' he said.

He came round to the front of the table and held out his palm. Sayce took it gingerly, as if he still suspected a trick, a violent electric shock, perhaps, or just a terrific blow on the ear administered by Gwatkin's other hand. However, Gwatkin did no more than shake Sayce's own hand heartily. It was like the termination of some sporting event. Gwatkin continued to shake hands for several seconds. Then he returned to his seat behind the table.

'Now,' he said, 'I'm going to call in the escort again, so stand to attention, Sayce. All right? Get them in, Mr Jenkins.'

I opened the door and said the word. CSM Cadwallader and the corporal returned to their places, guarding Sayce.

'Prisoner admonished,' said Gwatkin, in his military voice.

The Sergeant-Major was unable to conceal a faint tightening of the lips at the news of Sayce escaping all punishment. No doubt he had supposed it would be a matter for the Commanding Officer this time.

'Prisoner and escort – about turn – quick march – left wheel—'

They disappeared into the passage, like comedians retiring in good order from their act, only music lacking, CSM Cadwallader, with an agility perfected for such occasions, closing the door behind him without either pausing or turning.

Gwatkin sat back in his chair.

'How was that?' he asked.

'All right. Jolly good.'

'You thought so?'

'Certainly.'

'I think we shall see a change in Sayce,' he said.

'I hope so.'

This straight talk to Sayce on the part of Gwatkin had a stimulating effect, as it turned out, on Gwatkin, rather than Sayce. It cheered up Gwatkin greatly, made him easier to work with; Sayce, on the other hand, remained much what he had been before. The fact was Gwatkin needed drama in his life. For a brief moment drama had been supplied by Sayce. However, this love of the dramatic sent Gwatkin's spirits both up and down. Not only did his own defeats upset him, but also, vicariously, what he considered defeats for the Battalion. He felt, for example, deeply dishonoured by the case of Deafy Morgan, certainly an unfortunate incident.

'Somebody ought to have been shot for it,' Gwatkin said at the time.

When we had arrived on this side of the water, Maelgwyn-Jones had given a talk to all ranks on the subject of internal security.

'This Command is very different from the Division's home ground,' he said. 'The whole population of this island is not waging war against Germany – only the North. A few miles away from here, over the Border, is a neutral state where German agents abound. There and on our side too elements exist hostile to Britain and her Allies. There have been cases of armed gangs holding up single soldiers separated from their main body, or trying to steal weapons by ruse. You may have noticed, even in this neighbourhood, that some of the corner boys look sullen when we pass and the children sing about hanging up washing on the Maginot – rather than the Siegfried – Line.'

Accordingly, rifles were checked and re-checked, and Gwatkin was given additional opportunity for indulging in those harangues to the Company which he so greatly enjoyed delivering:

'Stand the men easy, Sergeant-Major,' he would say. 'No talking. Move up a little closer at the back so that you can hear me properly. Right. Now I want you all to attend very clearly to what I have to say. The Commanding Officer has ordered me to tell you once again you must all take care of your rifles, for a man's rifle is his best friend in time of war, and a soldier is no longer a soldier when his weapon is gone from him. He is like a man who has had that removed which makes him a man, something sadder, more useless, than a miner who has lost his lamp, or a farmer his plough. As you know, we are fighting Hitler and his hordes, so this Company must show the stuff she is made of, and you must all take care of your rifles or I will put you on a serious charge which will bring you before the Colonel. There are those not far from here who would steal rifles for their own beastly purpose. That is no funny matter, losing a rifle, not like long hair nor a dirty button. There is a place at Alder-shot called the Glasshouse, where men who have not taken proper care of their rifles do not like to visit a second time. Nevertheless, I would not threaten you. That is not how I wish to lead you. It is for the honour of the Regi-

66

ment that you should guard your rifles, like you would guard your wife or your little sister. Moreover, it may be some of the junior NCOs have not yet a proper sense of their own responsibilities in the matter of rifles and others. You Corporals, you Lance-Corporals, consider these things in your hearts. All rifles will be checked at Pay Parade each week, so that a man will bring his rifle to the table when he receives his due, and where you must remember to come smartly to attention and look straight in front of you without moving. That is the way we shall all pull together, and, as we heard the Rev. Popkiss, our Chaplain, read out at Church Parade last Sunday, so may it be said of this Company: Arise Barak, and lead thy captivity captive, thou son of Abinoam. So let your rifles be well guarded and be the smartest company of the Battalion both on parade and in the field. All right, Sergeant-Major . . .'

I was impressed by the speech, though there were moments when I thought Gwatkin's listeners might deride the images he conjured up, such as a man losing what made him a man, or little sisters who had to be protected. On the contrary, the Company listened spellbound, giving a low grunt of emphasis when the Glasshouse was mentioned, like a cinema audience gasping aloud in pleasurable appreciation of some peculiarly agonising sequence of horror film. I remembered Bracey, my father's soldier-servant, employing that very same phrase about his rifle being the soldier's best friend. After twenty-five years, that sentiment had stood up well to the test of time and the development of more scientific weapons of war.

'It does the lads good to be talked to like that,' said CSM Cadwallader afterwards. 'Captain does know how to speak. Very excellent would he have been to preach the Word.'

Even Gittins, whose inherent strain of scepticism was as strong as any in the Battalion, had enjoyed Gwatkin's talk.

He told me so when I came to the Store later, to check supplies of web equipment held there.

'A fine speech that was, the Skipper's,' said Gittins. 'That should make the boys take care of their rifles proper, it should. And the rest of their stuff, too, I hope, and not come round here scrounging what they've lost off me, like a present at Christmas, it was.'

Kedward was less impressed

'Rowland doesn't half love jawing,' he said, 'I should just say so. But what's he going to be like when we get into action, I wonder, he is so jumpy. Will he keep his head at that?'

The doubts Kedward felt about Gwatkin were to some extent echoed by Gwatkin himself in regard to Kedward.

'Idwal is a good reliable officer in many ways,' he confided his opinion to me, 'but I'm not sure he has just the quality for leading men.'

'The men like him.'

'The men can like an officer without feeling he inspires them. Yanto told me the other day he thought the men liked Bithel. You wouldn't say Bithel had the quality of leadership, would you?'

Gwatkin's dislike of Bithel was given new impetus by the Deafy Morgan affair, which followed close on the homily about rifles. Deafy Morgan, as his cognomen – it was far more than a mere nickname – implied, was hard of hearing. In fact, he was as deaf as a post. Only in his middle to late thirties, he gave the impression – as miners of that age often do – of being much older than his years. His infirmity, in any case, set him apart from the hurly-burly of the younger soldiers' life, giving him a mild, even beatific cast of countenance, an expression that seemed for ever untroubled by moral turmoil or disturbing thought. It was probably true to say that Deafy Morgan did not have many thoughts, disturbing or otherwise, because he was not outstandingly bright, although at the same time possessing all sorts of other good qualities. In short, Deafy Morgan was the precise antithesis of Sayce. Always spick and span, he was also prepared at all times to undertake boring or tedious duties without the least complaint – in what could only be called the most Christlike spirit. Even among good soldiers, that is a singular quality in the army. No doubt it was one of the reasons why Deafy Morgan had not been relegated to the Second Line before the Division moved. Not at all fit, he would obviously have to be transferred sooner or later to the rear echelons. However, his survival was mainly due not so much to this habit of working without complaint, rare as that might be, as to the fact that everyone liked him. Besides, he had served as a Territorial longer than any other soldier in the ranks, wanted to remain with his friends – he was alleged to possess at home a nagging wife – so that no one in authority had had the heart to put Deafy Morgan's name on whatever Army Form was required to effect his removal. He was in Bithel's platoon.

Bithel himself had recently been appointed Musketry Officer. This was not on account of any notable qualifications for that duty, simply because the Battalion was short of officers on the establishment, several being also absent on courses. By this time Bithel's individual status had become more clear to me. He was a small-town misfit, supporting himself in peacetime by odd jobs, preferably those on the outskirts of the theatrical world, living a life of solitude and toping, always on the verge of trouble, always somehow managing to extricate himself from anything serious. In the Battalion, there had been no repetition of the dance of love round the dummy, not anything comparable with that in exoticism. All the same, I suspected such expressions of Bithel's personality were dormant rather than totally suppressed. He was always humble, even subservient, in manner, but this demeanour seemed to cloak a good opinion of himself, perhaps even delusions of grandeur.

'Have you ever been interested in the Boy Scout movement?' he asked. 'I was keen about it at one time. Wonderful thing for boys. Gives them a chance. I threw it up in the end. Some of them are little brutes, you know. You'd never guess the things they say. I was surprised they knew about such matters. And their language among themselves. You wouldn't credit it. I was told I was greatly missed after my resignation. They have a great deal of difficulty in getting *suitable* fellows to help. There are some nasty types about.'

The army is at once the worst place for egoists, and the best. Thus it was in many ways the worst for Bithel, always being ordered about and reprimanded, the best for Gwatkin, granted – anyway up to a point – the power and rank he desired. Nevertheless, in the army, as elsewhere, nothing is for ever. Maelgwyn-Jones truly said: 'That day will pass, like other days in the army.' Gwatkin's ambition – the satisfaction of his 'personal myth', as General Conyers would have called it – might be temporarily realized, but there was always the danger that a re-posting, promotion, minor adjustment of duties, might alter everything. Even the obstacles set in the way of Bithel indulging the pottering he loved, could, for the same reasons, be alleviated, if not removed entirely. For instance, Bithel was tremendously pleased at being appointed Musketry Officer. There were several reasons for this. The job gave him a certain status, which he reasonably felt lacking, although there was probably less to do at the range than during the day by day training of a platoon. In addition, Bithel's soldier-servant, Daniels, was on permanent duty at the butts.

'I call him the priceless jewel,' Bithel used to say. 'You know how difficult it is to get a batman in this unit. They just don't want to do the job, in spite of its advantages. Well, Daniels is a little marvel. I don't say he's always on time, or never forgets things. He fails in both quite often. But what I like about him is that he's always got a cheerful word in all weathers. Besides, he's as clean as a whistle. A real pleasure to look at when he's doing PT, which is more than you can say for some of them in early morning. In any case, Daniels is not like all those young miners, nice boys as they are. He is more used to the world. You're not boots for three months at the Green Dragon in my home town without hearing some gossip.'

Others took a less favourable view of Daniels, who, although skilled in juggling with dummy grenades, was in general regarded as light-fingered and sly. There was, I found in due course, nothing unusual in an officer being preoccupied – one might almost say obsessed – by the personality of his servant, though on the whole that was apt to occur in ranks senior to subaltern. The relationship seems to develop a curious state of intimacy in an unintimate society; one, I mean, far removed from anything to be thought of as overstepping established limits of propriety or everyday discipline. Indeed, so far from even approaching the boundaries of sexual aberration or military misconduct, the most normal of men, and conscientious of officers, often provided the most striking instances. Even my father, I remembered, had possessed an almost mystic bond with Bracey, certainly a man of remarkable qualities. It was a thing not easily explicable, perhaps demanded by the emotional conditions of an all-male society. Regular officers, for example, would sometimes go to great pains to prevent their servants suffering some deserved minor punishment for an infringement of routine. Such things made Bithel's eulogies of Daniels no cause for comment. In any case, even if Bithel enjoyed the presence of Daniels at the range, it was not Daniels, but Deafy Morgan, who was source of all the trouble.

'Why on earth did Bith ever send Deafy back there and then?' said Kedward afterwards. 'That bloody rifle could perfectly well have waited an hour or two before it was mended.'

The question was never cleared up. Perhaps Bithel was thereby given opportunity for a longer hob-nob with Daniels. Even if that were the object, I am sure nothing dubious took place between them, while the 'musketry details' were still at the butts. Anything of the sort would have been extremely difficult, even if Bithel had been prepared to take such a risk. Much more likely – Deafy Morgan being one of his own men – Bithel had some idea of avoiding, by immediate action, lack of a rifle in his platoon. Whatever the reason, Bithel sent Deafy Morgan back to barracks by himself with a rifle that had developed some defect requiring the attention of the Sergeant-Armourer. The range, where musketry instruction took place, was situated in a deserted stretch of country, two or three miles by road from the town. This distance could be reduced by taking a short cut across the fields. In wet weather the path across the fields was apt to be muddy, making the journey heavy going. Rain was not falling that day – something of a rarity – and Deafy Morgan chose the path through the fields.

'I suppose I ought to have ordered him to go by road,' Bithel said later. 'But it takes such a lot of shouting to explain anything to the man.'

The incident occurred in a wood not far from the outskirts of the town. Deafy Morgan, by definition an easy victim to ambush, was surrounded by four young men, two of whom threatened him with pistols, while the other two possessed themselves of his rifle. Deafy Morgan struggled, but it was no good. The four of them made off at a run, disappearing behind a hedge, where, so the police reported later, a car had been waiting. There was nothing for Deafy Morgan to do but return to barracks and report the incident. Sergeant Pendry, as it happened, was Orderly Sergeant that day. He handled the trouble with notable competence. Contact was made with the Adjutant, who was touring the country in a truck in the course of preparing a 'scheme': the Constabulary, who handled such matters of civil subversion, were at once informed. Deafy Morgan was, of course, put under arrest. There was a considerable to-do. This was just such an incident as Maelgwyn-Jones outlined in his 'internal security' talk. The Constabulary, perfectly accustomed to ambuscades of this type, corroborated the presence of four suspects in the neighbourhood, who had later withdrawn over the Border. It was an unhappy episode, not least because Deafy Morgan was so popular a figure. Gwatkin, as I have said, was particularly disturbed by it. His mortification took the form of blaming all on Bithel.

'The CO will have to get rid of him,' Gwatkin said. 'It can't go on. He isn't fit to hold a commission.'

'I don't see what old Bith could have done about it,' said Breeze, 'even though it was a bit irregular to send Deafy back on his own like that.'

'It may not have been Bithel's fault directly,' said Gwatkin sternly, 'but when something goes wrong under an officer's command, the officer has to suffer. That may be unjust. He has to suffer all the same. In my opinion, there would be no injustice in this case. Why, I shouldn't wonder if the Colonel himself was not superseded for this.'

That was true enough. Certainly the Commanding Officer was prepared for the worst, so far as his own appointment was concerned. He said so in the Mess more than once. However, in the end nothing so drastic took place. Deafy Morgan was courtmartialled, getting off with a reprimand, together with transfer to the Second Line and his nagging wife. He had put up some fight. In the circumstances, he could hardly be sent to detention for losing his weapon and failing to capture four youngish assailants for whom he had been wholly unprepared; having been certainly too deaf to hear either their approach, or, at an earlier stage, the substance of Maelgwyn-Jones's security talk. The findings of the court-martial had just been promulgated, when the Battalion was ordered to prepare for a thirty-six-hour Divisional exercise, the first of its kind in which the unit had been concerned.

'This is the new Divisional Commander making himself felt,' said Kedward. 'They say he is going to shake us up, right and proper.'

'What's he called?'

To those serving with a battalion, even brigadiers seem infinitely illustrious, the Divisional Commander, a remote, godlike figure.

'Major-General Liddament,' said Gwatkin. 'He's going to ginger things up, I hope.'

It was at the start of this thirty-six-hour exercise – reveille at 4.30 a.m., and the first occasion we were to use the new containers for hot food – that I noticed all was not well with Sergeant Pendry. He did not get the Platoon on parade at the right time. That was very unlike him. Pendry had, in fact, shown no sign of breaking down after a few weeks energetic work, in the manner of Breeze's warning about NCOs who could not perform their promise. On the contrary, he continued to work hard, and his good temper had something of Corporal Gwylt's liveliness about it. No one could be expected to look well at that hour of the morning, but Sergeant Pendry's face was unreasonably greenish at breakfast, like Gwatkin's after the crossing, something more than could be attributed to early rising. I thought he must have been drinking the night before, a foolish thing to do as he knew the early hour of reveille. On the whole, there was very little drinking throughout the Battalion – indeed, small opportunity for it with the pressure of training – but Pendry had some reputation in the Sergeants' Mess for capacity in sinking a pint or two. I thought perhaps the moment had come when Breeze's prediction was now going to be justified, that Pendry had suddenly reached the point when he could no longer sustain an earlier efficiency. The day therefore opened badly, Gwatkin justifiably angry that my Platoon's unpunctuality left him insufficient time to inspect the Company as thoroughly as he wished, before parading with the rest of the Battalion. We were to travel by bus to an area some way from our base, where the exercise was to take place.

'Oh, I do like to ride in a smart motor-car,' said Corporal Gwylt. 'A real pleasure it is to spin along.'

Sergeant Pendry, usually as noisy as any of them, sat silent at the back of the bus, looking as if he might vomit at any moment. Outside, it was raining as usual. We drove across a desolate plain set against a background of vast grey skies, arriving at our destination an hour or two later. Gwatkin had gone ahead in his Company Commander's truck. He was waiting impatiently by the road when the platoons arrived.

'Get the men off the buses at once,' he said, 'and on to the other side of the road – and get some ack-ack defence out, and an anti-gas scout – and have the buses facing up the lane towards that tree, with No. 2 Platoon's vehicle at the head, not where it is now. Do that right away. Then send a runner to B Company to cancel the earlier message that we are going to recce the country on the left flank between us. That order has been changed to the right flank. Now, I want to say a word of warning to all Platoon Commanders before

I attend the Commanding Officer's conference for Company Commanders. I wish to make clear that I am not at all satisfied so far today. You've none of you shown any drive up to date. It's a bad show. You've got to do better, or there will be trouble. Understand? Right. You can rejoin your platoons.'

He had draped a rubber groundsheet round him like a cloak, which, with his flattish-brimmed steel helmet, transformed him into a figure from the later Middle Ages, a captain-of-arms of the Hundred Years War, or the guerrilla campaigning of Owen Glendower. I suddenly saw that was where Gwatkin belonged, rather than to the soldiery of modern times, the period which captured his own fancy. Rain had wetted his moustache, causing it to droop over the corners of the mouth, like those belonging to effigies on tombs or church brasses. Persons at odds with their surroundings not infrequently suggest an earlier historical epoch. Gwatkin was not exactly at odds with the rest of the world. In many ways, he was the essence of conventional behaviour. At the same time, he never mixed with others on precisely their own terms. Perhaps people suspected – disapproved – his vaulting dreams. The platoons had by this time, after much shouting and commanding, unwillingly withdrawn from the comfort of the buses into the pouring rain, and were gloomily forming up.

'Rowland is in a bloody rotten temper this morning,' said Breeze. 'What did he want to bite our heads off for?'

'He's in a state,' said Kedward. 'He nearly left his maps behind. He would have done, if I had not reminded him. Why were you late, Nick? That started Rowland being browned off.'

'Had some trouble with Sergeant Pendry. He doesn't seem well today.'

'I heard the Sergeant-Major say something about Pendry

last night,' said Breeze. 'Did you hear what it was, Idwal?'

'Something about his leave,' said Kedward. 'Just like old Cadwallader to tackle Rowland about an NCO's leave when he was in the middle of preparing for the exercise.'

Gwatkin returned some minutes later, the transparent talc surface of his map-cover marked all over with troop dispositions shown in chinagraph pencil of different colours. 'The Company is in support,' he said. 'Come over here, Platoon Commanders, and look at the map.'

He started to explain what we had to do, beginning with a few general principles regarding a company 'in support'; then moving on to the more specific technical requirements of the moment. These two aspects of the operation merged into an interwoven mass of instruction and disquisition, no doubt based, in the first instance, on sound military doctrine, but not a little confusing after being put through the filter of Gwatkin's own complex of ideas. He had obviously pondered the theory of being 'in support', poring in his spare time over the pages of *Infantry Training*. In addition, Gwatkin had also memorized with care phrases used by the Commanding Officer in the course of his issue of orders ... start-line ... RVs ... forming-up areas ... B echelon ... These milestones in the efficiency of the manœuvre were certainly intended to be considered in relation to ground and other circumstances; in short, left largely to the discretion of the junior commander himself. However, that was not the way Gwatkin looked at things. Although he liked saying that he wanted freedom to make his own tactical arrangements, he always found it hard to disregard the words of the textbook, or those of a comparatively senior officer. By the time he had finished talking, it was clear the Company was to be put through every movement possible to associate with the state of being 'in support'.

'Right,' said Gwatkin. 'Any questions?'

There were no questions; chiefly because of the difficulty in disentangling one single item from the whole. We checked map references; synchronised watches. Rain had stopped falling. The day was still grey, but warmer. When I returned to my platoon trouble was in progress. Sayce, the near criminal, was having an altercation with Jones, D., who carried the anti-tank rifle. As usual, Sayce was morally in the wrong, though technically perhaps on this occasion in the right. That was if Sayce were telling the truth, in itself most improbable. The row was something to do with a case of ammunition. In ordinary circumstances, Sergeant Pendry would have cleared up in a moment anything of this sort. In his present state, higher authority had to be brought in. I adjudicated, leaving both contestants with a sense of grievance. We moved off across open country. At first I closely followed Gwatkin's instructions; then, finding my Platoon lagging behind Breeze and his men, took them on at greater speed. Even so, when we arrived, later in the morning, at the field where the Company was to reassemble, much time had been lost by the formality of the manœuvring. The men were 'stood easy', then allowed to lie on the grass with groundsheets beneath them.

'Wait orders here,' said Gwatkin.

He was still in that tense state which desire to excel always brought about in him. However, his temper was better than earlier in the day. He spoke of the ingenuity of the tactical system as laid down in the book, the manner in which the Company had put this into practice.

'It's all worked out to the nearest minute,' he said.

Then he strolled away, and began to survey the country through field-glasses.

'That's bloody well wrong,' said Kedward, under his breath. 'We ought to be a mile further on at least, if we're going to be any use at the Foremost Defended Localities when the moment comes.'

Holding no strong views on the subject myself, I was inclined to think Kedward right. All was confusion. I had only a very slight idea what was happening by now, and what role the Company should rightly play. I should have liked to lie on the ground and stretch my legs out like the men, instead of having to be on the alert for Gwatkin's next order and superintend a dozen small matters. Some minutes later a runner came up with a written message for Gwatkin.

'Good God,' he said.

Something had evidently gone badly amiss. Gwatkin took off his helmet and shook the rain from it. He looked about him hopelessly.

'It hasn't worked out right,' he said agitatedly.

'What hasn't?'

'Fall in your men at once,' he said. 'It's long past the time when we should have been in position. That's what the message says.'

Instead of being close up behind the company we were supposed to support, here we were, in fact, hanging about miles away; still occupied, I suppose, with some more preliminary involution of Gwatkin's labyrinthine tactical performance. Kedward was right. We ought to have been advancing at greater speed. Gwatkin had done poorly. Now, he began to issue orders right and left. However, before anything much could happen, another runner appeared. This one carried an order instructing Gwatkin to halt his company for the time being, while we 'let through' another company, by now close on our heels. Like golfers who have lost their ball, we allowed this company to pass between our deployed ranks. They were on their way to do the job assigned to ourselves. Bithel was one of their platoon commanders. He

79

trotted by quite near me, red in the face, panting like a dog. As he came level, he paused for a moment.

'Haven't got an aspirin about you?' he asked.

'Afraid not.'

'Forgot to bring mine.'

'Sorry.'

'That's all right,' he said, loosening the helmet from his forehead for a moment, 'just felt an aspirin might be the answer.'

His teeth clicked metallically. He hurried on again to catch up his men, rejoining the platoon as they were already beginning to disappear from sight. We 'stood by' for ages, awaiting an order.

'Can the men sit down again?' asked Breeze.

'No,' said Gwatkin.

He was deeply humiliated by these circumstances, standing silent, fidgeting with his revolver holster. At last the order came. Gwatkin's company was to proceed by road to Battalion Headquarters in the field. He was himself to report to the Commanding Officer forthwith.

'I've let the whole Battalion down,' he muttered, as he went off towards his Company Commander's truck.

Kedward thought the same.

'Did you ever see such frigging about,' he said. 'Why, even as it was, I was behindhand in bringing my platoon up level with the main body of the Company, and by then I'd cut out at least half the things Rowland had told me to do. If I'd done them all, it would have taken a week. We wouldn't even have got as far as that field where we had a breather.'

We set off for Battalion HQ. By the time I brought my platoon in, it was late in the afternoon. Rain had begun to fall again. The place was a clearing in some woods where field kitchens had been set up. At last there was prospect of something to eat, a subject much on the men's minds, scarcely less on my own. I was very ready for a meal, breakfast soon after 5 a.m. by now a long way off. For some reason, probably because it was becoming hard to obtain, I carried no chocolate in my haversack. Gwatkin was waiting for us when we arrived. From his appearance it was clear he had been hauled pretty roughly over the coals by the Commanding Officer for failure to bring up the Company in time earlier that day. His face was white.

'You are to take your platoon out at once on patrol,' he said.

'But they've had no dinner.'

'The men just have time for a mouthful, if they're quick. You can't. I've got to go over the map with you. You are to make a recce, then act as a Standing Patrol. It can't be helped that you haven't eaten yourself.'

He gave the impression of rather enjoying this opportunity for working off his feelings. There seemed no necessity to underline the fact that I was to starve until further notice. Whatever the Commanding Officer had said had certainly not improved Gwatkin's state of mind. He was thoroughly upset. His hand shook when he pointed his pencil at names on the map. He was in a vile temper.

'You will take your men up to this point,' he said. 'There you will establish an HQ. Here is the canal. At this map reference the Pioneers have thrown a rope bridge across. You will personally cross by the rope bridge and make a recce of the far bank from here to here. Then return to your platoon and carry out the duties of a Standing Patrol as laid down in *Infantry Training*, having reported the map reference of your HQ by runner to me at this point here. In due course I shall come and inspect the position and receive your report. All right?'

'Yes.'

He handed over some map references.

'Any questions?'

'None.'

Gwatkin strode off. I returned to my platoon, far from pleased. The fact that missing a meal or two in the army must be regarded – certainly by an officer – as all in the day's work, makes these occasions no more acceptable. Sergeant Pendry was falling in the men when I returned to the area of the wood that had been allotted to the Platoon. They were grumbling at the hurried nature of dinner, complaining the stew had 'tasted' from being kept in the new containers. The only bright spot was that we were to be transported by truck some of the distance towards the place where we were to undertake these duties. Thirty men take an age to get on, or off, a vehicle of any kind. Jones, D., slipped while climbing up over the wheel, dropping the anti-tank rifle – that inordinately heavy, already obsolete weapon – on the foot of Williams, W. H., the platoon runner, putting him temporarily out of action. Sayce now began a long story about feeling faint, perhaps as a result of eating the stew, and what the MO had said about some disease he, Sayce, was suffering from. These troubles were unwillingly presented to me through the sceptical medium of Corporal Gwylt. I was in no mood for pity. If the meal had made Sayce feel queasy, that was better than having no meal at all. Such was my answer. All these things obstructed progress for about ten minutes. I feared Gwatkin might return to find reasonable cause for complaint in this delay, but Gwatkin had disappeared, bent on making life uncomfortable for someone else, or perhaps anxious only to find a quiet place where he could himself mope for a short period, while recovering his own morale. Sergeant Pendry was still showing less than his usual vigour in keeping things on the move. There could be no doubt Breeze had been right about Pendry, I thought, unless he turned out to be merely unwell, sickening for some illness, rather than suffering from a hangover. He dragged his feet when he walked, hardly able to shout out a command. I took him aside as the last man settled into the truck.

'Are you feeling all right, Sergeant?'

He looked at me as if he did not understand.

'All right, sir?'

'You got something to eat with the others just now?'

'Oh, yes, sir.'

'Enough?'

'Plenty there, sir. Didn't feel much like food, it was.'

'Are you sick?'

'Not too good, sir.'

'What's wrong?'

'Don't know just what, sir.'

'But you must know if you're feeling ill.'

'Had a bit of a shock back home, it was.'

This was no time to go into the home affairs of the platoon's personnel, now that at last we were ready and I wanted to give the driver the order to move off.

'Have a word with me when we get back to barracks.'

'All right, sir.'

I climbed into the truck beside the driver. We travelled several miles as far as some crossroads. There we left the truck, which returned to its base. Platoon HQ was set up in a dilapidated cowshed, part of the buildings of a small farm that lay not far away across the fields. When everything was pretty well established in the cowshed, including the siting of the imaginary 2-inch mortar which travelled round with us, I went off to look for the rope bridge over the canal. This was found without much difficulty. A corporal was in charge. I explained my mission, and enquired about the bridge's capacity.

'It do wobble a fair trifle, sir.'

'Stand by while I cross.'

'That I will, sir.'

I started to make the transit, falling in after about three or four yards. The water might have been colder for the time of year. I swam the rest of the way, reaching the far bank not greatly wetter than the rain had left me. There I wandered about for a time, making notes of matters to be regarded as important in the circumstances. After that, I came back to the canal, and, disillusioned as to the potentialities of the rope bridge, swam across again. The canal banks were fairly steep, but the corporal helped me out of the water. He did not seem in the least surprised to find that I had chosen this method of return in preference to his bridge.

'Very shaky, those rope bridges,' was all he said.

By now it was dark, rain still falling. I returned to the cow-shed. There a wonderful surprise was waiting. It appeared that Corporal Gwylt, accompanied by Williams, W. H., had visited the neighbouring farm and managed to wheedle from the owners a jug of tea.

'We saved a mug for you, sir. Wet you are, by Christ, too.'

I could have embraced him. The tea was of the kind Uncle Giles used to call 'a good sergeant-major's brew'. It tasted like the best champagne. I felt immediately ten years younger, hardly wet at all.

'She was a big woman that gave us that jug of tea, she was,' said Corporal Gwylt.

He addressed Williams, W. H.

'Ah, she was,' agreed Williams, W. H.

He looked thoughtful. Good at running and singing, he was otherwise not greatly gifted.

'She made me afraid, she did,' said Corporal Gwylt. 'I would have been afraid of that big woman in a little bed.'

'Indeed, I would too that,' said Williams, W. H., looking as if he were sincere in the opinion.

'Would you not have been afraid of her, Sergeant Pendry, a great big woman twice your size?'

'Shut your mouth,' said Sergeant Pendry, with unexpected force. 'Must you ever be talking of women?'

Corporal Gwylt was not at all put out.

'I would be even more afeared of her in a *big* bed,' he said reflectively.

We finished our tea. A runner came in, brought by a sentry, with a message from Gwatkin. It contained an order to report to him at a map reference in half an hour's time. The place of meeting turned out to be the crossroads not far from the cowshed.

'Shall I take the jug back, Corporal?' asked Williams, W. H.

'No, lad, I'll return that jug,' said Corporal Gwylt. 'If I have your permission, sir?'

'Off you go, but don't stay all night.'

'I won't take long, sir.'

Gwylt disappeared with the jug. The weather was clearing up now. There was a moon. The air was fresh. When the time came, I went off to meet Gwatkin. Water dripped from the trees, but a little wetness, more or less, was by then a matter of indifference. I stood just off the road while I waited, expecting Gwatkin would be late. However, the truck appeared on time. The vehicle drew up in the moonlight just beside me. Gwatkin stepped out. He gave the driver instructions about a message he was to take and the time he was to return to this same spot. The truck drove off. Gwatkin began to stride slowly up the road. I walked beside him.

'Everything all right, Nick?'

I told him what we had been doing, giving the

results of the reconnaissance on the far side of the canal.

'Why are you so wet?'

'Fell off the rope bridge into the canal.'

'And swam?'

'Yes.'

'That was good,' he said, as if it had been a brilliant idea to swim.

'How are things going in the battle?'

'The fog of war has descended.'

That was a favourite phrase of Gwatkin's. He seemed to derive support from it. There was a pause. Gwatkin began to fumble in his haversack. After a moment he brought out quite a sizeable bar of chocolate.

'I brought this for you,' he said.

'Thanks awfully, Rowland.'

I broke off a fairly large portion and handed the rest back to him.

'No,' he said. 'It's all for you.'

'All this?'

'Yes.'

'Can you really spare it?'

'It's meant for you. I thought you might not have any chocolate with you.'

'I hadn't.'

He returned to the subject of the exercise, explaining, so far as possible, the stage things had reached, what our immediate movements were to be. I gnawed the chocolate. I had forgotten how good chocolate could be, wondering why I had never eaten more of it before the war. It was like a drug, entirely altering one's point of view. I felt suddenly almost as warmly towards Gwatkin as to Corporal Gwylt, though nothing would ever beat that first sip of tea. Gwatkin and I had stopped by the side of the road to look at his map in the moonlight. Now he closed the case, buttoning down its flap.

'I'm sorry I sent you off like that without any lunch,' he said.

'That was the order.'

'No,' said Gwatkin. 'It wasn't.'

'How do you mean?'

'There would have been lots of time for you to have had something to eat,' he said.

I did not know what to answer.

'I had to work off on someone that rocket the CO gave me,' he said. 'You were the only person I could get at – anyway the first one I saw when I came back from the Colonel. He absolutely took the hide off me. I'd have liked to order the men off, too, right away, without their dinner, but I knew I'd only get another rocket – an even bigger one – if it came out they'd missed a meal unnecessarily through an order of mine.'

I felt this a handsome apology, a confession that did Gwatkin credit. Even so, his words were nothing to the chocolate. There were still a few remains clinging to my mouth. I licked them from the back of my teeth.

'Of course you've got to go,' said Gwatkin vehemently. 'lunch or no lunch, if it's an order. Go and get caught up on a lot of barbed wire and be riddled by machine-gun fire, stabbed to death with bayonets against a wall, walk into a cloud of poison gas without a mask, face a flame-thrower in a narrow street. Anything. I don't mean that.'

I agreed, at the same time feeling no immediate necessity to dwell at length on such undoubtedly valid aspects of military duty. It seemed best to change the subject. Gwatkin had made amends – one of the rarest things for anyone to attempt in life – now he must be distracted from cataloguing further disagreeable potentialities to be encountered in the course of a soldier's life.

'Sergeant Pendry hasn't been very bright today,' I said. 'I think he must be sick.'

'I wanted to talk to you about Pendry,' said Gwatkin.

'You noticed he was in poor shape?'

'He came to me last night. There wasn't time to tell you before, with all the preparations going on for the exercise – or at least I forgot to tell you.'

'What's wrong with Pendry?'

'His wife, Nick.'

'What about her?'

'Pendry had a letter from a neighbour saying she was carrying on with another man.'

'I see.'

'You keep on reading in the newspapers that the women of this country are making a splendid war effort,' said Gwatkin, speaking with all that passion which would well up in him at certain moments. 'If you ask me, I think they are making a splendid effort to sleep with as many other men as possible while their husbands are away.'

Even if that were an exaggeration, as expressed by Gwatkin, it had to be admitted letters of this kind were common enough. I remembered my brother-in-law, Chips Lovell, once saying: 'The popular Press always talk as if only the rich committed adultery. One really can't imagine a more snobbish assumption.' Certainly no one who administered the Company's affairs for a week or two would make any mistake on that score. I asked Gwatkin if details were known about Pendry's case. None seemed available.

'It makes you sick,' Gwatkin said.

'I suppose the men have some fun too. It isn't only the women. Not that any of us are given much time for it here – except perhaps Corporal Gwylt.'

'It's different for a man,' said Gwatkin. 'Unless he gets mixed up with a woman who makes him forget his duty.'

These words recalled a film Moreland and I had seen together in days before the war. A Russian officer – the story had been set in Tsarist times – had reprimanded an unpunctual subordinate with just that phrase: 'A woman who causes a man to neglect his duty is not worth a moment's consideration.' The young lieutenant in the film, so far as I could remember, had arrived late on parade because he had been spending the night with the Colonel's mistress. Afterwards, Moreland and I had often quoted to each other that stern conclusion.

'It's just the way you look at it,' Moreland had said. 'I know Matilda, for instance, would take the line that no woman was worth a moment's consideration unless she were capable of making a man neglect his duty. Barnby, on the other hand, would say no duty was worth a moment's consideration if it forced you to neglect women. These things depend so much on the subjective approach.'

I wondered if Gwatkin had seen the film too, and memorized that scrap of dialogue as a sentiment which appealed to him. On the whole it was unlikely that the picture, comparatively highbrow, had penetrated so deep in provincial distribution. Probably Gwatkin had simply elaborated the idea for himself. It was a high-minded, but not specially original one. Widmerpool, for example, when involved with Gypsy Jones, had spoken of never again committing himself with a woman who took his mind from his work. Gwatkin rarely spoke of his own wife. He had once mentioned that her father was in bad health, and, if he died, his mother-in-law would have to come and live with them.

'What are you going to do about Pendry?' I asked.

'Arrange for him to have some leave as soon as possible. I'm afraid that will deprive you of a platoon sergeant.'

'Pendry will have to go on leave sooner or later in any case. Besides, he's not much use in his present state.'

'The sooner Pendry goes, the sooner he will bring all this trouble to a stop.'

'If he can.'

Gwatkin looked at me with surprise.

'Everything will come right when he gets back home,' he said.

'Let's hope so.'

'Don't you think Pendry will be able to deal with his wife?'

'I don't know anything about her.'

'You mean she might want to go off with this other man?'

'Anything might happen. Pendry might do her in. You can't tell.'

Gwatkin hesitated a moment.

'You know that Rudyard Kipling book the other night?'

'Yes.'

'There are sort of poems at the beginning of the stories.'

'Yes?'

'One of them always stuck in my head – at least bits of it. I can never remember all the words of anything like that.'

Gwatkin stopped again. I feared he thought he had already said too much, and was not going to admit the verse of his preference.

'Which one?'

'It was about – was it some Roman god?'

'Oh, Mithras.'

'You remember it?'

'Of course.'

'Extraordinary.'

Gwatkin looked as if he could scarcely credit such a mental feat.

'As you said, Rowland, it's my profession to read a lot. But what about Mithras?'

'Where it says "Mithras also a soldier—" '

Gwatkin seemed to think that sufficient clue, that I must be able to guess by now all he hoped to convey. He did not finish the line.

'Something about helmets scorching the forehead and sandals burning the feet. I can't imagine anything worse than marching in sandals, especially on those cobbled Roman roads.'

Gwatkin disregarded the logistic problem of sandal-shod infantry. He was very serious.

' "—keep us pure till the dawn",' he said.

'Oh, yes.'

'What do you make of that?'

'Probably a very necessary prayer for a Roman legionary.'

Again, Gwatkin did not laugh.

'Does that mean women?' he asked, as if the notion had only just struck him.

'I suppose so.'

I controlled temptation to make flippant suggestions about other, more recondite vices, for which, with troops of such mixed origin as Rome's legions, the god's hasty moral intervention might be required. That sort of banter did not at all fit in with Gwatkin's mood. Equally point-less, even hopelessly pedantic, would be a brief exegesis explaining that the Roman occupation of Britain, historic-ally speaking, was rather different from the picture in the book. At best one would end up in an appalling verbal tangle about the relationship of fact and poetry.

'Those lines make you think,' said Gwatkin slowly.

'About toeing the line?'

'Make you glad you're married,' he said. 'Don't have to bother any more about women.'

He turned back towards the place where we had first met. There was the sound of a car further up the road. The truck came into sight again. Gwatkin abandoned further speculations about Mithras. He became once more the Company Commander.

'We've talked so much I haven't inspected your platoon position,' he said. 'There's nothing special I ought to see there?'

'Nothing.'

'Bring your men right away to the place I showed you on the map. We've got some farm buildings for a billet tonight. It's not far from here. Everyone will have a bit of a rest. Nothing much expected of us until midday tomorrow. All right?'

'All right.'

He climbed into the truck. It drove off again. I returned to the platoon. Sergeant Pendry came forward to report. He looked just as he had looked that morning; no better, no worse.

'Captain Gwatkin just had a word with me about your leave, Sergeant. We'll arrange that as soon as the exercise is over.'

'Thank you very much, sir.'

He spoke tonelessly, as if the question of leave did not interest him in the least.

'Fall the platoon in now. We're billeted in a farm near here. There's prospect of some sleep.'

'Right, sir.'

As usual, the distance to march turned out further than expected. Rain came on again. However, the farm buildings were pretty comfortable when we arrived. The platoon was accommodated in a thatched barn where there was plenty of straw. Corporal Gwylt, as always, was unwilling to believe that agricultural surroundings could ever be tolerable.

'Oh, what nasty smells there are here,' he said. 'I do not like all these cows.'

I slept like a log that night. It must have been soon after

92

breakfast the following morning, when I was checking sentry duties with Sergeant Pendry, that Breeze hurried into the barn to issue a warning.

'A staff car flying the Divisional Commander's pennon has just stopped by the road,' Breeze said. 'It must be a snap inspection by the General. Rowland says get all the men cleaning weapons or otherwise usefully occupied forthwith.'

He rushed off to warn Kedward. I set about generating activity in the barn. Some of the platoon were at work removing mud from their equipment. Those not so obviously engaged on a useful task were found other commendable occupations. All was in order within a few minutes. This was not a moment too soon. There was the sound of a party of people approaching the barn. I looked out, and saw the General, his ADC and Gwatkin slopping through the mud of the farmyard.

'They're coming, Sergeant Pendry.'

They entered the barn. Sergeant Pendry called those assembled to attention. It was at once obvious that General Liddament was not in the best of tempers. He was a serious looking man, young for his rank, cleanshaven, with the air of a scholar rather than a soldier. His recent taking over of the Division's command was already to be noticed in small matters of routine. Though regarded by regular soldiers as something of a military pedant – so Maelgwyn-Jones had told Gwatkin – General Liddament was said to be an officer with ideas of his own. Possibly in order to counteract this reputation for an excessive precision in approach to his duties, an imperfection of which he was probably aware and hoped to correct, the General allowed himself certain informalities of dress and turn-out. For example, he carried a long stick, like the wand of a verger in a cathedral, and wore a black-and-brown check scarf thrown carelessly about his neck. A hunting horn was thrust between the buttons of his battle-dress blouse. Maelgwyn-Jones also reported that two small dogs on a lead sometimes accompanied General Liddament, causing great disturbance when they squabbled with each other. Today must have been too serious an occasion for these animals to be with him. The presence of dogs would have increased his air of being a shepherd or huntsman, timeless in conception, depicted in the idealized pastoral scene of some engraving. However, General Liddament's manner of speaking had none of this mild, bucolic tone.

'Tell them to carry on,' he said, pointing his long stick at me. 'What's the name of this officer?'

'Second-lieutenant Jenkins, sir,' said Gwatkin, who was under great strain.

'How long have you been with this unit, Jenkins?'

I told the General, who nodded. He asked some further questions. Then he turned away, as if he had lost all interest in me, all interest in human beings at all, and began rummaging furiously about the place with his stick. After exploring the corners of the barn, he set about poking at the roof.

'Have your men been dry here?'

'Yes, sir.'

'Are you sure?'

'Yes, sir.'

'There is a leak in the thatch here.'

'There is a leak in that corner, sir, but the men slept the other end.'

The General, deep in thought, continued his prodding for some seconds without visible effect. Then, as he put renewed energy into the thrusts of his stick, which penetrated far into the roofing, a large piece of under-thatch all at once descended from above, narrowly missing General Liddament himself, completely overwhelming his ADC with debris of

94

dust, twigs and loam. At that, the General abandoned his activities, as if at last satisfied. Neither he nor anyone else made any comment, nor was any amusement expressed. The ADC, a pink-faced young man, blushed hotly and set about cleaning himself up. The General turned to me again.

'What did your men have for breakfast, Jenkins?'

'Liver, sir.'

I was impressed by his retention of my name.

'What else?'

'Jam, sir.'

'What else?'

'Bread, sir – and margarine.'

'Porridge?'

'No, sir.'

'Why not?'

'No issue, sir.'

The General turned savagely on Gwatkin, who had fallen into a kind of trance, but now started agonisingly to life again.

'No porridge?'

'No porridge, sir.'

General Liddament pondered this assertion for some seconds in resentful silence. He seemed to be considering porridge in all its aspects, bad as well as good. At last he came out with an unequivocal moral judgment.

'There ought to be porridge,' he said.

He glared round at the platoon, hard at work with their polishing, oiling, pulling-through, whatever they were doing. Suddenly he pointed his stick at Williams, W. H., the platoon runner.

'Would you have liked porridge?'

Williams, W.H., came to attention. As I have said, Williams, W.H., was good on his feet and sang well. Otherwise, he was not particularly bright.

'No, sir,' he said instantly, as if that must be the right answer.

The General was taken aback. It would not be too much to say he was absolutely staggered.

'Why not?'

General Liddament spoke sharply, but seriously, as if some excuse like religious scruple about eating porridge would certainly be accepted as valid.

'Don't like it, sir.'

'You don't like porridge?'

'No, sir.'

'Then you're a foolish fellow – a very foolish fellow.'

After saying that, the General stood in silence, as if in great distress of mind, holding his long staff at arm's length from him, while he ground it deep into the earthy surface of the barnhouse floor. He appeared to be trying to contemplate as objectively as possible the concept of being so totally excluded from the human family as to dislike porridge. His physical attitude suggested a holy man doing penance vicariously for the sin of those in his spiritual care. All at once he turned to the man next to Williams, W. H., who happened to be Sayce.

'Do *you* like porridge?' he almost shouted.

Sayce's face, obstinate, dishonest, covered with pock-marks showed determination to make trouble if possible, at the same time uncertainty as how best to achieve that object. For about half a minute Sayce turned over in his mind the pros and cons of porridge eating, just as he might reflect on the particular excuse most effective in extenuation of a dirty rifle barrel. Then he spoke.

'Well, sir—' he began.

General Liddament abandoned Sayce immediately for Jones, D.

'—and you?'

96

'No, sir,' said Jones, D., also speaking with absolute assurance that a negative answer was expected of him.

'—and you?'

'No, sir,' said Rees.

Moving the long stick with feverish speed, as if he were smelling out witches, the General pointed successively at Davies, J., Davies, E., Ellis, Clements, Williams, G.

No one had time to answer. There was a long pause at the end of the line. Corporal Gwylt stood there. He had been supervising the cleaning of the bren. General Liddament, whose features had taken on an expression of resignation, stood now leaning forward, resting his chin on the top of the stick, his head looking like a strange, rather malignant totem at the apex of a pole. He fixed his eyes on Gwylt's cap badge, as if ruminating on the history of the Regiment symbolized in the emblems of its design.

'And you, Corporal,' he asked, this time quite quietly. 'Do you like porridge?'

An enormous smile spread over Corporal Gwylt's face.

'Oh, yes, yes, sir,' he said, 'I do like porridge. I did just wish we had had porridge this morning.'

Slowly General Liddament straightened himself. He raised the stick so that its sharp metal point almost touched the face of Corporal Gwylt.

'Look,' he said, 'look, all of you. He may not be the biggest man in the Division, but he is a sturdy fellow, a good type. There is a man who eats porridge. Some of you would do well to follow his example.'

With these words, the Divisional Commander strode out of the barn. He was followed by Gwatkin and the ADC, the last still covered from head to foot with thatch. They picked their way through the mud towards the General's car. A minute later, the pennon disappeared from sight. The inspection was over.

'The General is a funny-looking chap,' said Breeze afterwards. 'But there's not much he misses. He asked where the latrines were constructed. When I showed him, he told me dig them downwind next time.'

'Just the same with me,' said Kedward. 'He made some of the platoon turn up the soles of their boots to see if they wanted mending. I was glad I had checked them last week.'

We returned from the exercise to find Germany had invaded Norway and Denmark.

'The war's begining now,' said Gwatkin. 'It won't be long before we're in it.'

His depression about failing to provide 'support' in the field was to some extent mitigated by the Company tying for first place in a practice march across country. In fact, at the time when Sergeant Pendry returned from his leave, Gwatkin certainly felt his prestige as a Company Commander in the ascendant. Pendry on the other hand – who had left for home almost immediately after the termination of the thirty-six-hour exercise – came back looking almost as gloomy as before. He returned, however, far more capable of carrying out his duties. No one knew how, if at all, he had settled his domestic troubles. I had never seen a man so greatly changed in the course of a few weeks. From being broad and heavily built, Pendry had become thin and haggard, his formerly glittering blue eyes sunken and glassy. All the same, he could be relied upon once more as Platoon Sergeant. His energy was renewed, though now all the cheerfulness that had once made him such a good NCO was gone. There was no more lateness on parade or forgetting of orders: there was also no more good-natured bustling along of the platoon. Pendry nowadays lost his temper easily, was morose when things went wrong. In spite of this change, there was little to complain of in his work. I told Gwatkin of this improvement.

'I expect Pendry put his foot down,' Gwatkin said. 'It's the only way with women. There should be no more difficulty with him now.'

I felt less certain. However, Pendry's troubles were forgotten. There were other things to think about. He simply settled down as a different sort of person. That happened long before the incident at the road-blocks, by which time everyone was used to Pendry in his new character.

'When Cadwallader goes, which he'll have to, sooner or later,' Gwatkin said, 'Pendry will have to be considered for CSM.'

The road-blocks were concrete pill-boxes constructed throughout the Command to impede an enemy, should the Germans decide to invade this island in the first instance. In addition to normal guard routines, road-blocks were manned after dark, the Orderly Officer inspecting them in turn throughout the night. This inspection continued, until dawn, when there was time for him to have a couple of hours sleep before coming on parade. Breeze had been Orderly Officer that day: Sergant Pendry, NCO in charge of road-blocks. By one of the anomalies of Battalion arrangements, Pendry had been on quarter-guard, followed by a Brigade night exercise, so that 'road-blocks' made his third night running with little or no sleep. It was bad luck, but for some reason – probably chronic shortage of sergeants – there was no avoiding this situation. I spoke a word of condolence on the subject.

'Do not worry, sir,' Pendry said. 'I do not seem to want much sleep now, it is.'

That was a surprising answer. In the army, sleep is prized more than anything else; beyond food, beyond even tea. I decided to speak again to Gwatkin about Pendry, find out whether, as Company Commander, he thought all was well. I felt guilty about having allowed Pendry's situation to slip from my mind. He might be on the verge of a breakdown. Disregard for sleep certainly suggested something of the sort. Trouble could be avoided by looking into matters. However, such precautions, even if they had proved effective, were planned too late in the day. The rest of the story came out at the Court of Inquiry. Its main outlines were fairly clear. Breeze had made his inspection of the pill-box where Pendry was on duty, found all correct, moved on in the Orderly Officer's truck to the next post. About ten minutes after Breeze's departure, the sentry on duty in the pill-box noticed suspicious movements by some tumbledown sheds and fences further up the road. That is, the sentry thought he saw suspicious movements. This may have been his imagination. The Deafy Morgan affair had shown the possibility of hostility from other than German sources. What was going on in the shadows might indicate preparations for some similar aggression. Sergeant Pendry said he would investigate these activities himself. His rifle was loaded. He approached the sheds, where he disappeared from sight. Nothing was seen in that direction for some minutes; then a dog ran across the road. This dog, it was said afterwards, could have been the cause of the original disturbance. Sergeant Pendry could still not be seen. Then there was the echo of a shot; some said two shots. Pendry did not return. After a while, two men from the pill-box went to look for him. His body was found in a pit or ditch among the shacks. Pendry was dead. His rifle had been fired. It was never cleared up for certain whether an assailant caused his death; whether, in tripping and falling into the pit, his own weapon killed him; whether, alone in that dark gloomy place, oppressed with misery, strung up with lack of sleep, Pendry decided to put an end to himself.

'He always meant to do it,' Breeze said.

'It was murder,' said Gwatkin, 'Pendry's the first. There'll be others in due course.'

The Court of Inquiry expressed the opinion that Pendry would have acted more correctly in taking a man with him to conduct the investigation. It was doubtful, too, whether he should have loaded his rifle without direct order from an officer. In this respect, standing instructions for road-block NCOs showed a certain ambiguity. The whole question of ammunition supervision in relation to road-block guards was re-examined, the system later overhauled. Breeze had a trying time while the Court was taking evidence. He was exonerated from all blame, but when opportunity arose, he volunteered for service with one of the anti-tank companies which were being organized on a Divisional basis. Breeze understandably wanted to get away from the Battalion and disagreeable associations. Perhaps he wanted to get away from Gwatkin too. Gwatkin himself, just as he had blamed Bithel for the Deafy Morgan affair, was unwilling to accept the findings of the Court of Inquiry in its complete clearing of Breeze.

'Yanto was just as responsible for Sergeant Pendry's death as if he had shot him down from the German trenches,' Gwatkin said.

'What could Yanto have done?'

'Yanto knew, as we all did, that Pendry had talked of such a thing.'

'I never knew, and Pendry was my own Platoon-Sergeant.'

'CSM Cadwallader knows more than he will say.'

'What does the Sergeant-Major think?'

'He just spoke about Pendry once or twice,' said Gwatkin moodily. 'It's only now I see what he meant. I blame myself too. I should have foreseen it.'

This was another of Gwatkin's ritual sufferings for the

ills of the Battalion. Maelgwyn-Jones took a more robust, more objective view, when I went to see him about arrangements for Pendry's funeral.

'These things happen from time to time,' he said. 'It's just the army. Surprising there aren't more cases. Here's the bumph about the firing party to give Rowland.'

'Almost every man in the Company volunteered for it.'

'They love this sort of thing,' said Maelgwyn-Jones. 'By the way, you're going to Aldershot on a course next week. Tell Rowland that too.'

'What sort of a course?'

'General training.'

I remarked to Gwatkin, when we were turning in that night, how the men had almost fought to be included in the firing party.

'Nothing brings a company together like death,' he said sombrely. 'It looks as though there might be one in my family too. My wife's father isn't at all well.'

'What does he do?'

'In a bank, like the rest of us,' said Gwatkin.

He had been thoroughly upset by the Pendry incident. Over the partition, in the store, Lance-Corporal Gittins was still awake. When last seen, he had been sorting huge piles of Army Form 'ten-ninety-eight', and was probably still thus engaged. He, too, seemed preoccupied with thoughts of mortality, for, while he sorted, he sang quietly to himself:

'When I tread the verge of Jordan,
Bid my anxious fears subside,
Death of Death and hell's destruction,
Land me safe on Canaan's side:
     Songs of praises,
     Songs of praises
I will ever give to thee . . .'

102

3

THE TRAIN, LONG, GRIMY, CLOSELY PACKED, subject to many delays *en route*, pushed south towards London. Within the carriage cold fug stiflingly prevailed, dimmed bulbs, just luminous, like phosphorescent molluscs in the eddying backwaters of an aquarium, hovering above photographic views of Blackpool and Morecambe Bay: one of those interiors endemic to wartime. At a halt in the Midlands, night without still dark as the pit, the Lancashire Fusilier next to me, who had remarked earlier he was going on leave in this neighbourhood, at once guessed the name of the totally blacked-out station, collected his kit and quitted the compartment hurriedly. His departure was welcome, even the more crowded seat now enjoying improved legroom. The grey-moustached captain, whose leathery skin and several medal ribbons suggested a quartermaster, eased himself nearer to where I occupied a corner seat, while he grunted irritably under his breath, transferring from one pocket to another thick sheaves of indents classified into packets secured by rubber bands. Additional space offered hope of less fitful sleep, but, when the engine was getting up steam again, the carriage door slid open. A figure wearing uniform looked in.

'Any room?'

There was no definite denial of the existence of a spare place, but the reception could not be called welcoming. The light grudgingly conceded by the fishy globules flickering in the shallows was too slight to distinguish more than a tall man wearing a British Warm, the shoulder straps of which displayed no badges of rank. The voice was authoritative, precise, rather musical, a voice to be associated with more agreeable, even more frivolous circumstances than those now on offer. One might even have heard it against the thrumming of a band a thousand years before. If so, the occasion was long forgotten. While he shook himself out of his overcoat, the new passenger made a certain amount of disturbance before he settled down, among other things causing the quartermaster to move his kit a few necessary inches along the rack, where it was certainly taking up more than a fair share of room. The quartermaster made some demur at this. His reluctance was confronted with absolute firmness. The man in the British Warm had his way in the end. The kit was moved. Having disposed of his own baggage, he took the place next to me.

'Last seat on the train,' he said.

He laughed; then apparently passed into sleep. We rumbled on for hours through the night. I slept too, beset with disturbing dreams of administrative anxieties. The quartermaster left his seat at five, returning after an age away, still muttering and grumbling to himself. Morning came, a sad, pale light gently penetrating the curtains. Some hidden agency extinguished the blue lamps. It grew warmer. People began to stretch, blow noses, clear throats, light cigarettes, move along the corridor to shave or relieve themselves. I examined the other occupants of the carriage. Except for the middle-aged captain, all had one pip, including the new arrival next to me. I took a look at him while he was still asleep. His face was thin, rather distinguished, with a hook nose and fairish hair. The collar badges were 'Fortnum & Mason' General Service. The rest of the compartment was filled by two officers of the Royal Corps of Signals, a Gunner, a Green Howard (Ted Jeavons's first regiment in the previous war, I remembered) and a Durham Light Infantryman. The thin man next to me began to wake up, rubbing his eyes and gently groaning.

'I think I shall wait till London for a shave,' he said.

'Me too.'

'No point in making a fetish of elegance.'

'None.'

We both dozed again. When it was light enough to read, he took a book from his pocket. I saw it was in French, but could not distinguish the title. Again, his manner struck me as familiar; again, I could not place him.

'Is there a breakfast car on this train?' asked the Green Howard.

'God, no,' said the Durham Light Infantryman. 'Where do you think you are – the Ritz?'

One of the Signals said there was hope of a cup of tea, possibly food in some form, at the next stop, a junction where the train was alleged to remain for ten minutes or more. This turned out to be true. On arrival at this station, in a concerted move from the carriage, I found myself walking along the platform with the man in General Service badges. We entered the buffet together.

'Sitting up all night catches one across the back,' he said.

'It certainly does.'

'I once sat up from Prague to the Hook and swore I'd never do it again. I little knew one was in for a lifetime of journeys of that sort.'

'Budapest to Vienna by Danube can be gruelling at night too,' I said, not wishing to seem unused to continental discomforts. 'Do you think we are in a very strategic position for getting cups of tea?'

'Perhaps not. Let's try the far end of the counter. One might engage the attention of the lady on the second urn.'

'Also stand a chance of buying one of those faded, but still beautiful, sausage rolls, before they are all consumed by Other Ranks.'

We changed our position with hopeful effect.

'Talking of Vienna,' he said, 'did you ever have the extraordinary experience of entering that gallery in the Kunsthistorisches Museum with the screen across the end of it? On the other side of the screen, quite unexpectedly, you find those four staggering Bruegels.'

'The *Hunters in the Snow* is almost my favourite picture.'

'I am also very fond of the *Two Monkeys* in the Kaiser Friedrich in Berlin. I've just been sharing a room with a man in the Essex Regiment who looked exactly like the ape on the left, the same shrewd expression. I say, we're not making much headway with the tea.'

There were further struggles at the counter, eventually successful. The reward was a sausage roll apiece.

'Should we return to the train now? I don't feel absolutely confident about that corner seat.'

'In that case I shall take this sausage roll with me.'

Back in the carriage, the quartermaster went to sleep again; so did the two Signals and the Gunner. Both the Durham Light Infantryman and the Green Howard brought out button-sticks, tins of polish, cloths, brushes. Taking off their tunics, they set to work energetically shining themselves up, while they discussed allowances.

'Haven't we met before somewhere?' I asked.

'My name is Pennistone – David Pennistone.'

I knew no one called that. I told him my own name, but we did not establish a connexion sufficiently firm to suggest a previous encounter. Pennistone said he liked Moreland's music, but did not know Moreland personally.

'Are you going on leave?'

'To a course – and you?'

'I've just come from a course,' he said. 'I'm on leave until required.'

'That sounds all right.'

'I'm an odd kind of soldier in any case. Certain specific qualifications are my only excuse. It will be rather nice to be on one's own for a week or two. I'm trying to get something finished. A case of earn while you learn.'

'What sort of thing?'

'Oh, something awfully boring about Descartes. Really not worth discussing. *Cogito ergo sum*, and all that. I feel quite ashamed about it. By the way, have you ever read this work? I thought one might profit by it in one's new career.'

He held out to me the book he had been reading. I took it from his hand and read the title on the spine: *Servitude et Grandeur Militaire: Alfred de Vigny.*

'I thought Vigny was just a poet – *Dieu! que le son du Cor est triste au fond des bois!* . . .'

'He also spent fourteen years of his life as a regular soldier. He ended as a captain, so there is hope for all of us.'

'In the Napoleonic wars?'

'Too young. Vigny never saw action. Only the most irksome sort of garrison duty, spiced with a little civil disturbance – having to stand quietly in the ranks while demonstrators threw bricks. That kind of thing.'

'I see.'

'In some ways the best viewpoint for investigating army life. Action might have confused the issue by proving too exciting. Action is, after all, exciting rather than interesting. Anyway, this book says what Vigny thought about soldiering.'

'What were his conclusions?'

'That the soldier is a dedicated person, a sort of monk of war. Of course he was speaking of the professional armies

107

of his day. However, Vigny saw that in due course the armed forces of every country would be identified with the nation, as in the armies of antiquity.'

'When the bombing begins here, clearly civilians will play as dangerous a role as soldiers, if not more dangerous.'

'Of course. Even so, Vigny would say those in uniform have made the greater sacrifice by losing the man in the soldier – what he calls the warrior's abnegation, his renunciation of thought and action. Vigny says a soldier's crown is a crown of thorns, amongst its spikes none more painful than passive obedience.'

'True enough.'

'He sees the role of authority as essentially artificial, the army a way of life in which there is as little room for uncontrolled fervour as for sullen indifference. The impetuous volunteer has as much to learn as the unwilling conscript.'

I thought of Gwatkin and his keenness; of Sayce, and his recalcitrance. There was something to be said for this view of the army. By this time, Pennistone and I were the only ones awake in the compartment. The button cleaners had abandoned their paraphernalia, resumed their tunics and nodded off like the rest. The quartermaster began to snore. He did not look particularly saintly, nor even dedicated, though one never could tell. Probably Vigny knew what he was talking about after fourteen years of it.

'All the same,' I said, 'it's a misapprehension to suppose, as most people do, that the army is inherently different from all other communities. The hierarchy and discipline give an outward illusion of difference, but there are personalities of every sort in the army, as much as out of it. On the whole, the man who is successful in civilian life, all things being equal, is successful in the army.'

'Certainly – and there can be weak-willed generals and strong-willed privates.'

'Look, for example, at the way you yourself compelled my neighbour to move his kit last night.'

Pennistone laughed.

'One can just imagine Vigny romanticising that fat sod,' he said, 'but that is by the way. Probably Vigny, while emphasising that we are back with the citizen army of classical times which he himself envisaged, would agree with what you say. He was certainly aware that nothing is absolute in the army – least of all obeying orders. Take my own case. I was instructed to wait until this morning for a train, as there had been local complaints of army personnel overcrowding the railways over weekends to the detriment of civilian travel facilities. I made careful enquiries, found chances of retribution remote and started the night before, thus saving a day of my journey.'

'In other words, the individual still counts, even in the army.'

'Although consigned to circumstances in which, theoretically, no individuality – though much will-power – exists.'

'What would Vigny have thought of your disobeying that order?'

'I could have pleaded that the army was not my chosen profession, that my ill-conduct was a revulsion from uniform, drum, drill, the ritual of the parade ground, the act of an unworthy, amateur neophyte of war.'

We both went to sleep after that. When the train reached London, I said goodbye to Pennistone, who was making his way to the country and his home, there to stay until recalled to duty.

'Perhaps we'll meet again.'

'Let's decide to anyway,' he said. 'As we've agreed, these things are largely a matter of will.'

He waved, and disappeared into the crowds of the railway station. Later in the morning, while attending to the many odd jobs to be done during my few hours in London, I was struck by a thought as to where I might have seen Pennistone before. Was it at Mrs Andriadis's party in Hill Street ten or twelve years ago? His identity was revealed. He was the young man with the orchid in his buttonhole with whom I had struck up a conversation in the small hours. This seemed our characteristic relationship. Stringham had taken me to the party, Pennistone informed me that the house itself belonged to the Duports. Pennistone had told me, too, that Bob Duport had married Peter Templer's sister, Jean. It was Pennistone, that same evening – when all was confusion owing to Milly Andriadis's row with Stringham – whom she had pushed into an armchair when he had tried to tell her an anecdote about Prince Theodoric and the Prince of Wales. By then Pennistone was rather tight. It all seemed centuries ago: the Prince of Wales now Duke of Windsor, Prince Theodoric, buttress of pro-Allied sentiment in a country threatened by German invasion, Pennistone and myself second-lieutenants in our middle thirties. I wondered what had happened to Stringham, Mrs Andriadis and the rest. However, there was no time to ponder long about all that. Other matters required attention. I was glad – overjoyed – to be back in England even for a month or so. There would be weekend leaves from the course, when it should be possible to get as far as my sister-in-law Frederica Budd's house, where Isobel was staying until the child was born. The London streets, empty of traffic, looked incredibly bright and sophisticated, the tarts in Piccadilly dazzling nymphs. This was before the blitz. I knew how Persephone must have felt on the first day of her annual release from the underworld. An RAF officer of unconventional appearance advancing up the street turned out to be Barnby. He recognised me at the same moment.

'I thought you were a war artist.'

'I was for a time,' he said. 'Then I got sick of it and took a job doing camouflage for this outfit.'

'Disguising aerodromes as Tudor cottages?'

'That sort of thing.'

'What's it like?'

'Not bad. If I'm not able to paint in the way I want, I'd as soon do this as anything else.'

'I thought war artists were allowed to paint whatever they wanted.'

'They are in a way,' said Barnby, 'I don't know. I prefer this for some reason, while there's a war on. They let me go on an occasional operational flight.'

I felt a pang. Barnby was a few years older than myself. I had nothing so lively to report. He looked rather odd in his uniform, thick, square, almost as if he were still wearing the blue overalls in which he was accustomed to paint.

'Where are you, Nick?' he asked.

I gave him some account of my life.

'It doesn't sound very exciting.'

'It isn't.'

'I've got a wonderful new girl,' he said.

I thought how, war or peace, nothing ever really changes in such aspects.

'How long are you in London?' he said. 'I'd like to tell you about her. She's got one extraordinary trait. It would amuse you to hear about it. Can't we dine together tonight?'

'I've got to report to Aldershot this afternoon. I've been sent there on a course. Are you stationed in London?'

'Up for the night only. I have to see a man in the Air Ministry about some special camouflage equipment. How's Isobel?'

'Having a baby soon.'

'Give her my love. What happened to the rest of the Tolland family?'

'George is in France with a Guards battalion. He was on the Regular Reserve, of course, now a captain. Robert, always a mysterious figure, is a lance-corporal in Field Security, believed to be on his way to getting a commission. Hugo doesn't want to be an officer. He prefers to stay where he is as a gunner on the South Coast – bombardier now, I believe. He says you meet such awful types in the Officers' Mess.'

'What about those chaps Isobel's sisters married?'

'Roddy Cutts – as an MP – had no difficulty about getting into something. His own county Yeomanry, I think. I don't know his rank, probably colonel by now. Susan is with him. Chips Lovell has joined the Marines.'

'That's an unexpected arm. Is Priscilla with him?'

'So far as I know.'

We spoke of other matters, then parted. Talking to Barnby increased the feeling that I had been released from prison, at the same time inducing a new sensation, that prison life was all I was fit for. Barnby's conversation, everything round about, seemed hopelessly unreal. There was boundless relief in being free, even briefly free, from the eternal presence of Gwatkin, Kedward, Cadwallader, Gwylt and the rest of them; not to have to worry whether the platoon was better occupied digging themselves in or attacking a hill; whether Davies, G., should have a stripe or Davies, L., lose one; yet, by comparison, the shapes of Barnby and Pennistone were little more than figments of the imagination, shadows flickering on the slides of an old-fashioned magic-lantern. I had scarcely arrived in London, in any case, before it was time to leave for Aldershot. In the train on the way there, I reflected on the ideas Pennistone had put forward: the 'occasional operational flights' of Barnby. How would one feel on such aerial voyages? It might be like Dai and Shoni in their balloon. In the army, as up to now experienced, danger, although it might in due course make appearance, at present skulked out of sight in the background; the foreground for ever cluttered with those moral obligations outlined by Vigny. I envied Pennistone, who could turn from war to Descartes, and back again, without perceptible effort. I knew myself incapable of writing a line of a novel – by then I had written three or four – however long released from duty. Whatever inner processes are required for writing novels, so far as I myself was concerned, war now utterly inhibited. That was one of the many disagreeable aspects of war. It was not only physically inescapable, but morally inescapable too. Why did one envy Barnby his operational flights? That was an absorbing question. Certainly not because one wanted to be killed, nor yet because the qualities of those who excel in violent action were the qualities to which one had any claim. For that matter, such qualities were not specially Barnby's. There was perhaps the point. Yet it was absurd to regard war as a kind of competition of just that sort between individuals. If that was the aim in war, why not in peace? No doubt there were plenty of individuals who felt that sort of emulation in peacetime too, but their preoccupations were not one's own. Looked at calmly, war created a situation in which the individual – if he wished to be on the winning side – was of importance only in so much as he contributed to the requirements of the machine, not according to the picturesque figure he cut in the eyes of himself and others. It was no more reasonable, if you were not that sort of person, to aspire to lead a cavalry charge, than, without financial gifts, to dream of cornering the pepper market; without scientific training, split the atom. All the same, as Pennistone had said, these things are largely a matter of the will. I thought of Dr Trelawney, the magician, the night Duport and I had helped him to bed after his asthma attack, when he had quoted as all that was necessary: 'To know, to dare, to will, to be silent.' Armed with those emblems of strength, one might, however out of character, lead a cavalry charge, perhaps even corner the pepper market and split the atom too. Anyway, I thought, it would be a dull world if no one ever had dreams of glory. Moreland was fond of quoting Nietzsche's opinion that there is no action without illusion. Arrival at Aldershot brought an end to these reflections. Most of the train's passengers turned out to be officers on their way to the same course as myself. After reporting to the Orderly Room, we were shown the lines where we were to sleep, a row of small redbrick houses built round a sort of square. Their interiors were uninviting.

'Former married quarters,' said the gloomy C.3 lance-corporal guiding my group. 'Condemned in 1914, don't half wonder.'

I did not wonder either. 1914 was, in fact, the year when, as a child, I had last set eyes on these weary red cantonments, my father's regiment stationed at a hutted camp between here and Stonehurst, the remote and haunted bungalow where my parents lived at that time. I remembered how the Battalion, polished and blancoed, in scarlet and spiked helmets, had marched into Aldershot for some ceremonial parade, drums beating, colours cased, down dusty summer roads. Afterwards, my father had complained of a sore heel caused by the rub of his wellington boot, an abrasion scarcely cured before it was time to go to war. That war, too, had been no doubt the reason why these ramshackle married quarters had never been demolished and replaced. When peace came, there were other matters to think about. Here we were accommodated on the ground floor, a back and front room. Of the five others who were to share this billet, four – two from the Loyals, two from the Manchesters –

were in their late twenties. They did their unpacking and went off to find the Mess. The remaining subaltern, from a Midland regiment, was much younger. He was short and square, with dark skin, grey eyes and very fair curly hair.

'Those Lancashire lads in here with us are a dumb crowd,' he remarked to me.

'What makes you think so?'

'Do you know they thought I talked so broad I must come from Burton-on-Trent,' he said.

He spoke as if he had been mistaken for a Chinese or Ethiopian. There was something of Kedward about him; something, too, which I could not define, of my brother-in-law, Chips Lovell. He did not have a smudgy moustache like Kedward's, and his personality was more forceful, more attractive too.

'We're going to be right cooped up in here,' he said. 'Would you be satisfied if I took over this area of floor space, and left you as far as the wall?'

'Perfectly.'

'My name is Stevens,' he said, 'Odo Stevens.'

I told him my own name. He spoke with a North Country or Midland intonation, not unlike that Quiggin used to assume in his earlier days, when, for social or literary reasons, he chose to emphasize his provincial origins and unvarnished, forthright nature. Indeed, I could see nothing inherently absurd in the mistake the 'Lancashire lads' had made in supposing Stevens a native of Burton-on-Trent. However, I laughed and agreed it was a ludicrous error. I was flattered that he considered me a person to take into his confidence on the subject; glad, too, that I was housed next to someone who appeared agreeable. In the army, the comparative assurance of your own unit, whatever its failings, is at once dissipated by changed circumstances, which threaten fresh conflicts and induce that terrible, recurrent army dejection, the sensation that no one cares a halfpenny whether you live or die.

'Where *do* you come from?'

'Brum, of course.'

'Birmingham?'

'What do you think,' he said, as if it were almost insulting to suppose the matter in the smallest doubt. 'Can't you tell the way I say it? But I've managed to keep out of my home town for quite a while, thank God.'

'Don't you like it there?'

'Finest city in the world,' he said, laughing again, 'but something livelier suits me. As a matter of fact, I was on the continent for the best part of six months before I joined the army.'

'Whereabouts?'

'Holland, Belgium. Even got as far afield as Austria.'

'Doing what?'

'There was an exchange of apprentices for learning languages. I pick up languages pretty easily for some reason. They were beginning to think I'd better come home and do some work just at the moment war broke out.'

'What's your job?'

'Imitation jewellery.'

'You sell it?'

'My pa's in a firm that makes it. Got me into it too. A business with a lot of foreign connexions. That's how I fixed up getting abroad.'

'Sounds all right.'

'Not bad, as jobs go, but I don't want to spend a lifetime at it. That's why I wasn't sorry to make a change. Shall we push along to the Mess?'

We sat next to each other at dinner that night. Stevens asked me what I did for a living.

'You're lucky to have a writing job,' he said, 'I've tried

writing myself. Sometimes think I might take it up, even though peddling costume jewellery is a good trade for putting yourself over with the girls.'

'What sort of writing?'

'Spot of journalism in the local paper – "Spring comes to the Black Country" – "Sunset on Armistice Day" – that sort of thing. I knock it off easily, just as I can pick up languages.'

I saw Stevens would go far, if he did not get killed. He was aware of his own taste for self-applause and prepared to laugh at it. The journalistic streak was perhaps what recalled Chips Lovell, whom he did not resemble physically.

'Did you volunteer for the Independent Companies?' he asked.

'I didn't think I'd be much good at them.'

The Independent Companies – later called Commandos – were small guerilla units, copiously officered. They had been employed with some success in Norway. Raising them had skimmed off the best young officers from many battalions, so that they were not popular with some Commanding Officers for that reason.

'I was in trouble with my CO the time they were recruiting them,' said Stevens. 'He bitched up my application. It was really because he thought me useful to him where I was. All the same, I'll get away into something. My unit are a lot of louts. They're not going to prevent me from having what fun the army has to offer.'

Here were dreams of military glory very different from Gwatkin's. After all this talk, it was time to go to bed. The following morning there was drill on the square. We were squadded by a stagey cluster of glengarry-capped staff-sergeants left over the Matabele campaign, with Harry Lauder accents and eyes like poached eggs. Amongst a couple of hundred students on the course, there was hope

117

of an acquaintance, but no familiar face showed in the Mess the previous night. However, slow-marching across the asphalt I recognised Jimmy Brent in another squad moving at right-angles to our own, a tallish, fat, bespectacled figure, forgotten since Peter Templer had brought him to see Stringham and myself when we were undergraduates. Brent looked much the same. I had not greatly liked him at the time. Nothing heard about him since caused me, in a general way, to want to see more of him. Here, however, any face from the past was welcome, especially so veteran a relic as Brent. After the parade was dismissed, I tackled him.

'We met years ago, when you came over in Peter Templer's second-hand Vauxhall, and he drove us all into the ditch.'

I told him my name. Brent clearly did not recognise me. There was little or no reason why he should. However, he remembered the circumstances of Templer's car accident, and seemed pleased to find someone on the course who had known him in the outside world.

'There were some girls in the car, weren't there,' he said, his face lighting up at that happy memory, 'and Bob Duport too. I knew Peter took us to see a couple of friends he'd been at school with, but I wouldn't be able to place them at this distance of time. So you were one of them? What a memory you've got. Well, it's nice to find a pal in this god-forsaken spot.'

'Do you ever see Peter now? I'd like to hear what's happened to him.'

'Peter's all right,' said Brent, speaking rather cautiously, 'wise enough not to have mixed himself up with the army like you and me. Got some Government advisory job. Financial side. I think Sir Magnus Donners had a hand – Donners hasn't got office yet, I'm surprised to see – Peter always did a spot of prudent sucking-up in that direction.

Peter knows which side his bread is buttered. He's been quite useful to Donners on more than one occasion.'

'I met Peter once there – at Stourwater, I mean.'

'You know Donners too, do you. I've done a little business with him myself. I'm an oil man, you know. I was in the South American office before the war. Did you ever meet Peter's sister, Jean? I used to see quite a bit of her there.'

'I knew her ages ago.'

'She married Bob Duport,' said Brent, 'who was with us on the famous occasion when the Vauxhall heeled over.'

There was a perverse inner pleasure in knowing that Brent had had a love affair with Jean Duport, which he could scarcely guess had been described to me by her own husband. Even though I had once loved her myself – to that extent the thought was painful, however long past – there was an odd sense of power in possessing this secret information.

'I ran into Duport just before war broke out. I never knew him well. I gather they are divorced now.'

'Quite right,' said Brent.

He did not allow the smallest suggestion of personal interest to colour the tone of his voice.

'I heard Bob was in some business mess,' he said. 'Chromite, was it? He got across that fellow Widmerpool, another of Donners's henchmen. Widmerpool is an able fellow, not a man to offend. Bob managed to rub him up the wrong way. Somebody said Bob was connected with the Board of Trade now. Don't know whether that is true. The Board of Trade wanted me to stay in Latin America, as a matter of fact.'

'You'd have had a safe billet there.'

'Glad to leave the place as it happened, though I was doing pretty well.'

'How do you find yourself here?'

'Managed to get into this mob through the good offices of

our Military Attaché where I was. His own regiment. Never heard of them before.'

I supposed that Brent had been relieved to find this opportunity of moving to another continent after Jean had abandoned him. That disappointment, too, might explain his decision to join the army as a change of occupation. He was several years older than myself, in fact entering an age group to be reasonably considered beyond the range of unfriendly criticism for remaining out of uniform; especially if, as he suggested, his work in South America was officially regarded as of some national importance. I remembered Duport's story clearly now. After reconciliation with Jean, they had sailed for South America. Brent had sailed with them. At that time Jean's affair with Brent had apparently been in full swing. Indeed, from what Duport said, there was every reason to suppose that affair had begun before she told me of her own decision to return to her husband. So far as that went, Jean had deceived me as much as she had deceived Duport. Fortunately Brent was unaware of that.

'How do you like the army?'

'Bloody awful,' he said, 'but I'd rather be in than out.'

'Me, too.'

The remaining students of the course were an unexceptional crowd, most of the usual army types represented. We drilled on the square, listened to lectures about the German army, erected barbed wire entanglements, drove 3-ton lorries, map read. One evening, preceding a night exercise in which one half of the course was arrayed in battle against the other half, Stevens showed a different side of himself. The force in which we were both included lay on the ground in a large semi-circle, waiting for the operation to begin. The place was a clearing among the pine woods of heathery, Stonehurst-like country. Stevens and I were on the extreme right flank of the semi-circle. On the extreme left, exactly opposite us, whoever was disposed there continually threw handfuls of gravel across the area between, which landed chiefly on Stevens and myself.

'It must be Croxton,' Stevens said.

Croxton was a muscular neurotic of a kind, fairly common, who cannot stop talking or creating a noise. He sang or ragged joylessly all the time, without possessing any of those inner qualities – like Corporal Gwylt's, for example – required for making such behaviour acceptable to others. He was always starting a row, playing tricks, causing trouble. There could be little doubt that Croxton was responsible for the hail of small stones that continued to spatter over us. The moon had disappeared behind clouds, rain threatening. There seemed no prospect of the exercise beginning.

'I think I'll deal with this,' Stevens said.

He crawled back into the cover of the trees behind us, disappearing in darkness. Some minutes elapsed. Then I heard a sudden exclamation from the direction of the gravel thrower. It was a cry of pain. More time went by. Then Stevens returned.

'It was Croxton,' he said.

'What did you do?'

'Gave him a couple in the ribs with my rifle butt.'

'What did he think about that?'

'He didn't seem to like it.'

'Did he put up any fight?'

'Not much. He's gasping a bit now.'

The following day, during a lecture on the German Division, I saw Croxton, who was sitting a few rows in front, rub his back more than once. Stevens had evidently struck fairly hard. This incident showed he could be disagreeable, if so disposed. He also possessed the gift of isolating himself from his surroundings. These lectures on the

German army admittedly lacked light relief – after listening to many of them, I have preserved only the ornamental detail that the German Reconnaissance Corps carried a sabre squadron on its establishment – and one easily dozed through the lecturer's dronings. On the other hand, to remain, as Stevens could, slumbering like a child, upright on a hard wooden chair, while everyone else was clattering from the lecture room, suggested considerable powers of self-seclusion. Another source of preservation to Stevens – unlike Gwatkin – was an imperviousness to harsh words. He and I had been digging a weapon pit together one afternoon without much success. An instructor came up to grumble at our efforts.

'That's not a damned bit of use,' he said. 'Wouldn't give protection to a cat.'

'We've just reached a surface of rock, sir,' said Stevens, 'but I think I can say we've demonstrated the dignity of labour.'

The instructor sniggered and moved on, without examining the soil. Not everyone liked this self-confident manner of Stevens. Among those who disapproved was Brent.

'That young fellow will get sent back to his unit,' Brent said. 'Mark my words. He's too big for his boots.'

When the whole course was divided into syndicates of three for the purposes of a 'tactical exercise without troops', Brent and I managed to be included in the same trio. To act with an acquaintance on such occasions is an advantage, but it was at the price of having Macfaddean as the third partner. However, although Macfaddean, a schoolmaster in civilian life, was feverishly anxious to make a good impression on the Directing Staff, this also meant that he was prepared to do most of the work. In his middle to late thirties, Macfaddean would always volunteer for a 'demonstration', no matter how uncomfortable the prospect of crawling for miles through mud, for instance, or exemplifying the difficulty of penetrating dannert wire. When the task was written work, Macfaddean would pile up mountains of paper, or laboriously summarize, whichever method he judged best set him apart from the other students. He was so tireless in his energies that towards the end of the day, when we had all agreed on the situation report to be presented and there was some time to spare, Macfaddean could not bear these minutes to be wasted.

'Look here, laddies,' he said, 'why don't we go back into the woods and produce an alternative version? I'm not happy, for instance, about concentration areas. It would look good if we handed in two plans for the commander to choose from, both first-rate.'

There could be no doubt that the anonymity of the syndicate system irked Macfaddean. He felt that if another report were made, the second one might be fairly attributed to his own unaided afforts, a matter that could be made clear when the time came. That was plain enough to both Brent and myself. We told Macfaddean that, for our part, we were going to adhere to the plan already agreed upon; if he wished to make another one, that was up to him.

'Off you go, Mac, if you want to,' said Brent. 'We'll wait for you here. I've done enough for today.'

When Macfaddean was gone, we found a place to lie under some withered trees, blasted, no doubt, to their crumbling state by frequent military experiment. We were operating over the dismal tundra of Laffan's Plain, battlefield of a million mock engagements. The sky above was filled with low-flying aircraft, of outlandish colour and design, camouflaged perhaps by Barnby in a playful mood. Lumbering army reconnaissance planes buzzed placidly backwards and forwards through grey puffs of cloud, ancient machines garnered in from goodness knows what forgotten repository of written-off Governmental stores, now sent aloft again to meet a desperate situation. The heavens looked like one of those pictures of an imagined Future to be found in old-fashioned magazines for boys. Brent rolled over on his back and watched this rococo aerial pageant.

'You know Bob Duport is not a chap like you and me,' he said suddenly.

He spoke as if he had given much thought to Duport's character; as if, too, my own presence allowed him at last to reach certain serious conclusions on that subject. Regarded by Templer, and Duport himself, as something of a butt – certainly a butt where women were concerned – Brent possessed a curious resilience in everyday life, which his exterior did not reveal. This was noticeable on the course, where, unlike Macfaddean, he was adept at avoiding work that might carry with it the risk of blame.

'What about Duport?'

'Bob's *really* intelligent,' said Brent earnestly. 'No intention of minimising your qualifications in that line, or even my own, but Bob's a real wonder-boy.'

'Never knew him well enough to penetrate that far.'

'Terrific gifts.'

'Tell me more about him.'

'Bob can do anything he turns his hand to. Wizard at business. Pick up any job in five minutes. If he were on this course, he'd be the star-turn. Then, girls. They simply lie down in front of him.'

'I see.'

'But he's not just interested in business and women.'

'What else?'

'You wouldn't believe what he knows about art and all that.'

'He never gave the impression of being that sort.'

'You've got to know him well before he lets on. Have to keep your eyes open. Did you ever go to that house the Duports had in Hill Street?'

'Years ago, when they'd let it to someone else. I was taken to a party there.'

'That place was marvellously done up,' said Brent. 'Absolute perfection in my humble opinion. Bob's got taste. That's what I mean. All the same, he isn't one of those who go round gushing about art. He keeps it to himself.'

I did not immediately grasp the point of this great build-up of Duport. It certainly shed a new light on him. I did not disbelieve the picture. On the contrary, in its illumination, many things became plainer. Duport's professional brutality of manner, thus interpreted in Brent's rough and ready style, might indeed conceal behind its façade sensibilities he was unwilling to reveal to the world at large. There was nothing unreasonable about that supposition. It might to some extent explain Duport's relationship with Jean, even if Brent's own connexion with her were thereby made less easy to understand. I thought of the views of my recent travelling companion, Pennistone, so plainly expressed at Mrs Andriadis's party:

'. . . these appalling Italianate fittings – and the pictures – my God, the pictures . . .'

However, such things were a matter of opinion. The point at issue was Duport's character: was he, in principle, regardless of personal idiosyncrasy, what Sir Gavin Walpole-Wilson used to call a 'man of taste'? It was an interesting question. Jean herself had always been rather apologetic about that side of her married life, so that presumably Brent was right: Duport, rather than Jean, had been responsible for the Hill Street decorations and pictures. This was a new angle on Duport. I saw there were important sides of him I had missed.

'When you last met Bob,' said Brent, using the tone of one about to make a confidence, 'did he mention my name to you?'

'He said you and he had been in South America together.'

'Did he add anything about me and Jean?'

'He did, as a matter of fact. I gather there was an involved situation.'

Brent laughed.

'There was,' he said. 'I thought Bob would go round shooting his mouth off. Just like him. It's Bob's one weakness. He can't hold his tongue.'

He sighed, as if Duport's heartless chatter about his own matrimonial situation had aroused in Brent himself a despair for human nature. He gave the impression that he thought it too bad of Duport. I was reminded of Barnby, exasperated at some woman's behaviour, saying: 'It's enough to stop you ever committing adultery again.' The deafening vibrations of an insect-like Lysander just above us, which seemed unable to decide whether or not to make a landing, put a stop to conversation for a minute or two. When it sheered off, Brent spoke once more.

'You said you knew Jean, didn't you?'

'Yes.'

'Wonderful girl in her way.'

'Very nice to look at.'

'For a while we were lovers,' said Brent.

He spoke in that reminiscent, unctuous voice men use when they tell you that sort of thing more to savour an enjoyable past situation, than to impart information which might be of interest. It must have been already clear to him that Duport had already revealed that fact.

'Oh, yes.'

'Bob said that?'

'He put it more bluntly.'

Brent laughed again, very good-naturedly. The way he set about telling the story emphasised his least tolerable side. I tried to feel objective about the whole matter by recalling one of Moreland's favourite themes, the attraction exercised over women by men to whom they can safely feel complete superiority.

'Are you hideous, stunted, mentally arrested, sexually maladjusted, marked with warts, gross in manner, with a cleft palate and an evil smell?' Moreland used to say. 'Then, oh boy, there's a treat ahead of you. You're all set for a promising career as a lover. There's an absolutely ravishing girl round the corner who'll find you irresistible. In fact her knickers are bursting into flame at this very moment at the mere thought of you.'

'But your description does not fit in with most of the lady-killers one knows. I should have thought they tended to be decidedly good-looking, as often as not, together with a lot of other useful qualities as well.'

'What about Henri Quatre?'

'What about him?'

'He was impotent and he stank. It's in the histories. Yet he is remembered as one of the great lovers of all time.'

'He was a king – and a good talker at that. Besides, we don't know him personally, so it's hard to argue about him.'

'Think of some of the ones we do know.'

'But it would be an awful world if no one but an Adonis, who was also an intellectual paragon and an international athlete, had a chance. It always seems to me, on the contrary, that women's often expressed statement, that male good looks don't interest them, is quite untrue. All things being equal, the man who looks like a tailor's dummy stands a better chance than the man who doesn't.'

'All things never are equal,' said Moreland, always impossible to shake in his theories, 'though I agree that to be no intellectual strain is an advantage where the opposite sex is concerned. But you look into the matter. Remember Bottom and Titania. The Bard knew.'

Brent, so far as he had been a success with Jean, seemed to strengthen Moreland's argument. I wondered whether I wanted to hear more. The Jean business was long over, but even when you have ceased to love someone, that does not necessarily bring an indifference to a past shared together. Besides, though love may die, vanity lives on timelessly. I knew that I must be prepared to hear things I should not like. Yet, although where unfaithfulness reigns, ignorance may be preferable to knowledge, at the same time, once knowledge is brutally born, exactitude is preferable to uncertainty. To learn at what precise moment Jean had decided to take on Brent, in preference to myself, would be more acceptable than to allow the imagination continually to range unhindered through boundless fields of disagreeable supposition. Even so, I half hoped Macfaddean would return, full of new ideas about terrain and lines of communication. However, the choice did not lie with me. The narrative rested in Brent's own hands. Whether I wanted to listen or not, he was determined to tell his story.

'You'd never guess,' he said apologetically, 'but Jean fell for me first.'

'Talk about girls lying down for Bob Duport.'

'Shall I tell you how it happened?'

'Go ahead.'

'Peter Templer asked me to dine with him to meet a couple called Taylor or Porter. He could never remember which. Peter subsequently went off with Mrs Taylor, whoever she was, but that was later. He also invited his sister, Jean, to the party, and a woman called Lady McReith. I didn't much take to the latter. We dined at the Carlton Grill.'

Brent paused. I remembered perfectly the occasion of which he spoke. One evening when we were out together, Jean had remarked she was dining with her brother the following night. The fact that the dinner party was to be at the Carlton Grill pinpointed the incident in my mind. I had noted at the time, without soreness, that Peter Templer, as a result of his exertions in the City, could afford to entertain at restaurants of that sort, while I frequented Foppa's and the Strasbourg. It was one of several differences that had taken shape between us. I remembered thinking that. Then the whole matter had passed from my mind until Jean and I next met, when she had made rather a point of emphasising what a boring evening she had had to endure with her brother and his friends. In fact the party at the Carlton Grill appeared to have been so tedious she could not keep off the subject.

'Who was there?'

'Two businessmen you'd never have heard of, one of them married to a very pretty, silly girl, whom Peter obviously has his eye on. Then there was a rather older woman I've met before, who might be a lesbian.'

'What was she called?'

'You wouldn't know her either.'

'What made you think she was a lesbian?'

'Something about her.'

Jean knew perfectly well I had met Lady McReith when, as a boy, I had stayed at the Templers' house. Even had she forgotten that fact, Lady McReith was an old friend of the Templer family, especially of Jean's sister, Babs. It was absurd to speak of her in that distant way. By that time, too, Jean must have made up her mind whether or not Gwen McReith was a lesbian. All this mystification was impossible to ascribe to any rational form of behaviour. Possibly the emphasis on an unknown lesbian was to distract attention from the unmarried businessman – Brent. Jean wanted to talk about the party simply because Brent had had interested her, yet instinct told her this fact must be concealed. It was rather surprising that she had never before met Brent with her brother. Certainly, if she had named him, I should have had no suspicion of what was to follow. If that were the reason – a desire to talk about the party, but at the same time not to mention Brent by name – she could have stated quite simply that Lady McReith was present, gossiped in a straightforward way about Lady McReith's past, present and future. In short, this utterly unnecessary, irrational lie was a kind of veiled attack on our own relationship, a deliberate deceiving of me for no logical reason, except that, by telling a lie of that kind, truth was suddenly undermined between us; thus even though I was unaware of it, moving us inexorably apart. It was a pre-liminary thrust that must have satisfied some strange inner urge.

'Poor Peter,' Jean had said, 'he really sees the most dreary people. One of the men at dinner had never heard of Chaliapin.'

That musical ignoramus was no doubt Brent too. I made up my mind to confirm later his inexperience of opera, even if it meant singing the 'Song of the Volga Boatmen' to him to prove that point. At the moment, however, I did no more than ask for his own version of the dinner party at the Carlton Grill.

'Well, I thought Mrs Duport an attractive piece,' Brent said, 'but I'd never have dreamt of carrying things further, if she hadn't rung me up the next day. You see, it was obvious Peter had just given the dinner because he wanted to talk to the other lady – the one he ran away with. The rest of us had been got there for that sole purpose. Peter's an old friend of mine, so I just did the polite as required, chatted about this and that. Talked business mostly, which Mrs Duport seemed to find interesting.'

'What did she say when she rang up?'

'Asked my opinion about Amparos.'

'Who is Amparos?'

'An oil share.'

'Just that?'

'We talked for a while on the phone. Then she suggested I should give her lunch and discuss oil investments. She knows something about the market. I could tell at once. In her blood, I suppose.'

'And you gave her lunch?'

'I couldn't that week,' said Brent, 'too full of business. But I did the following week. That was how it all started. Extraordinary how things always happen at the same time. That was just the moment when the question opened up of my transfer to the South American office.'

I saw the whole affair now. From the day of that luncheon with Brent, Jean had begun to speak with ever-increasing seriousness of joining up again with her husband; chiefly, she said, for the sake of their child. That seemed reasonable enough. Duport might have behaved badly; that did not mean I never suffered any sensations of guilt.

'How did it end?'

Brent pulled up a large tuft of grass and threw it from him.

'Rather hard to answer that one,' he said.

He spoke as if the conclusion of this relationship with Jean required much further reflection than he had at present been able to allow the subject.

'The fact is,' he said, 'I liked Jean all right, and naturally I was pretty flattered that she preferred me to a chap like Bob. All the same, I always felt what you might call uneasy with her, know what I mean. You must have come across that with girls. Feel they're a bit too good for you. Jean was too superior a wench for a chap of my simple tastes. That was what it came to. Talked all sorts of stuff I couldn't follow. Did you ever go to that coloured night-club called the Old Plantation?'

'Never, but I know it by name.'

'A little coloured girl sold cigarettes there. She was more in my line, though it cost me a small fortune to get her.'

'So the thing with Jean Duport just petered out?'

'With a good deal of grumbling on her side, believe me, before it did. I think she'd have run away with me if I'd asked her. Didn't quite see my way to oblige in that respect. Then one day she told me she didn't want to see me again. As a matter of fact we hadn't met for quite a time when she said that.'

'Why not?'

'Don't know. Suppose I hadn't done much about it. There'd been some trouble at one of our places up the river. Production dropped from forty or fifty, to twenty-five barrels a day. I had to go along there and take a look at things. That was one of the reasons why she hadn't heard from me for some time.'

'Fact was you were tired of it.'

'Jean seemed to think so, the way she carried on. She was bloody rude when we parted. Anyway, she had the consolation of feeling she broke it off herself. Women like that.'

So it appeared, after all, the love affair had been brought to an end by Brent's apathy, rather than Jean's fickleness. Even Duport had not known that. He had supposed Brent to have been, in his own words, 'ditched'. It had certainly never occurred to Duport, as a husband, that Brent, his own despised hanger-on, had actually been pursued by Jean, had himself done the 'ditching'. I, too, had little cause for self-congratulation, if it came to that.

'How did Duport find out about yourself and his wife?'

'Through their dear little daughter.'

'Good God – Polly? I suppose she must be twelve or thirteen by now.'

'Quite that,' said Brent. 'Fancy you're remembering. I expect Bob spoke of her when you saw him. He's mad about that kid. Not surprising. She's a very pretty little girl. Will need keeping an eye on soon – perhaps even now.'

'Did Bob find out while it was still going on?'

'Just before the end. Polly let out something about a meeting between Jean and me. Bob remarked that if it had been anyone else he'd have been suspicious. Then Jean flew off the handle and told him everything. Bob couldn't believe it at first. Didn't think I was up to it. He always regarded me as an absolute flop where women were concerned. It was quite a blow to him in a way. To his pride, I mean.'

In this scene between the Duports, I saw a parallel to the occasion when I had myself made a slighting remark about Jimmy Stripling, and Jean, immediately furious, had told me of her former affair with him. The pattern was, as ever, endlessly repeated. There was something to be admired in Brent's lack of vanity in so absolutely accepting Duport's low estimate of his own attractions, even after causing Duport's wife to fall in love with him. Whatever other reason Brent might have had for embarking on the matter, a cheap desire to score off Jean's husband had played no part whatever. That was certain. Duport, cuckolded or no, remained Brent's ideal of manhood.

'I think it's just as well Bob finally got rid of her,' Brent said. 'Now he'll probably find a wife who suits him better. Work Jean out of his system. Anyway he'll have a freer hand to live the sort of life he likes.'

The tramp of men and sound of singing interrupted us. A detachment of Sappers were marching by, chanting their song, voices harsh and tuneless after those of my own Regiment:

> 'You make fast, I make fast, make fast the dinghy,
> Make fast the dinghy, make fast the dinghy,
> You make fast, I make fast, make fast the dinghy,
> Make fast the dinghy pontoon.
> For we're marching on to Laffan's Plain,
> To Laffan's Plain, to Laffan's Plain,
> Yes we're marching on to Laffan's Plain,
> Where they don't know mud from shit . . .'

The powerful rhythms, primitive, incantatory, hypnotic, seemed not only the battle hymn of warring tribes, but also a refrain with obscure bearing on what Brent had just told me, a general lament for the emotional conflict of men and women. The Sappers disappeared over the horizon, their song dying away with them. From the other direction, Macfaddean approached at the double. He was breathless when he arrived beside us.

'Sorry to keep you laddies waiting,' he said, still panting, 'but I've found a wizard alternative concentration area. Here, look at the map. We won't revise our earlier plan, just show up this as a second choice. It means doing the odd spot of collating. Give me the coloured pencils. Now, take down these map references. Look sharp, old man.'

Meanwhile, the problem of how best to reach Frederica's house when leave was granted remained an unsolved one. I asked Stevens whether he were going to spend the weekend in Birmingham.

'Much too far,' he said, 'I'm getting an aunt and uncle to put me up. It won't be very exciting, but it's somewhere to go.'

He named a country town not many miles from Frederica's village.

'That's the part of the world I'm trying to reach myself. It's not going to be too easy to get there and back in a week-end. Trains are rotten.'

'Trains are hopeless,' said Stevens. 'You'll spend the whole bloody time going backwards and forwards. Look here, I've got a broken-down old car I bought with the proceeds of my writing activities. It cost a tenner, but it should get us there and back. I can put my hand on some black market petrol too. Where exactly do you want to go?'

I named the place.

'I've heard of it,' said Stevens. 'My uncle is an estate agent in those parts. I've probably heard him talk of some house he's done a deal with in the neighbourhood – your sister-in-law's perhaps. I can drop you there easily, if you like. Then pick you up on Sunday night, when we're due back here.'

So it was arranged. The day came. Stevens's car, a Morris two-seater, started all right. We set off. It was invigorating to leave Aldershot. We drove along, while Stevens talked about his family, his girls, his ambitions. I heard how his mother was the daughter of a detective-inspector who had had to leave the force on account of drink; why he thought his sister's husband, a master in a secondary school, was rather too keen on the boys; what a relief it had been when he had heard, just before taking leave of his unit for the Aldershot course, that he had not got a local girl in the family way. Such confidences are rare in the army. Narcissistic, Stevens was at the same time – if the distinction can be made – not narrowly egotistical. He was interested in everything round him, even though everything must eventually lead back to himself. He asked about Isobel. It is hard to describe your wife. Instead I tried to give some account of Frederica's household. He seemed to absorb it all pretty well.

'Good name, "Frederica",' he said, 'I was christened "Herbert", but a hieroglyphic like "Odo" was put on an envelope addressed to me when I was abroad, and I saw at once that was the thing to be called. I was getting fed up with being "Bert" as it was.'

Apart from the unexpected circumstance that Stevens and I should be driving across country together, the war seemed far away. Frederica had lived in her house, a former vicarage, for a year or two. A widow, she had moved to the country for her children's sake. Not large, the structure was splayed out and rambling, so that the building looked as if its owners had at some period taken the place to pieces, section by section, then put it together again, not always in correct proportions. A white gate led up a short drive with rose bushes on either side. The place had that same air of intense respectability Frederica's own personality conveyed. In spite of war conditions, there was no sign of untidiness about the garden, only an immediate sense of having entered a precinct where one must be on one's best behaviour. Stevens stopped in front of the porch. Before I could ring or knock, Frederica herself opened the door.

'I saw you coming up the drive,' she said.

She wore trousers. Her head was tied up in a handkerchief. I kissed her, and introduced Stevens.

'Do come in for a moment and have a drink,' she said. 'Or have you got to push on? I'm sure not at once.'

Frederica was not usually so cordial in manner to persons she did not already know; often, not particularly cordial to those she knew well. I had not seen her since the outbreak of war. The war must have shaken her up. That was the most obvious explanation of this new demeanour. The trousers and handkerchief were uncharacteristic. However, it was not so much style of dress that altered her, as something within herself. Robin Budd her husband had been killed in a fall from his horse nine or ten years before. By now not far from forty, she had never – so far as her own family knew –

136

considered remarriage, still less indulged in any casual love affair; although those rather deliberately formidable, armour-plated good looks of hers were of the sort to attract quite a lot of men. Her sister, Priscilla, had some story about Jack Udney, an elderly courtier whose wife had died not long before, getting rather tight at Ascot after a notable win, and proposing to Frederica while the Gold Cup was actually being run, but the allegation had never been substantiated. It was true Frederica had snapped out total disagreement once, when Isobel met Jack Udney somewhere and said she thought him a bore. In short, Frederica's most notable characteristic was what Molly Jeavons called her 'dreadful correctness'. Now, total war seemed slightly to have dislodged this approach to life. Frederica's reception of Stevens showed that. Stevens himself did not need further pressing to come in for a drink.

'Nothing I'd like better,' he said. 'It'll help me to face Aunt Doris's woes about shortages and ration cards. Half a sec, I'll back the car to a place where I'm not blocking your front door.'

He started up the car again.

'How's Isobel?'

'Pretty well,' said Frederica. 'She's resting. She'll be down in a moment. We're rather full here. Absolutely packed to the ceiling, as a matter of fact.'

'Who have you got?'

'Priscilla is here – with Caroline.'

'Who is Caroline?'

'Priscilla's daughter, our niece. You ought to know that.'

'Ah, yes, I'd forgotten her name.'

'Then Robert turned up unexpectedly on leave.'

'I'll be glad to see Robert.'

Frederica laughed.

'Robert has brought a lady with him.'

'No?'

'But *yes*. One of my own contemporaries, as a matter of fact, though I never knew her well.'

'What's she called?'

'She married an American, now deceased, and has the unusual name of Mrs Wisebite. She was *née* Stringham. I used to see her at dances.'

'Charles Stringham's sister, in fact.'

'Yes, you knew him, didn't you. I remember now. Well, Robert has brought her along. What do you think of that? Then the boys are home for the holidays – and there's someone else you know.'

'Who is that?'

'Wait and see.'

Frederica laughed shrilly again, almost hysterically. That was most unlike her. I could not make out what was happening. Usually calm to the point of iciness, rigidly controlled except when she quarrelled with her sister, Norah, Frederica seemed now half excited, half anxious about something. It could hardly be Robert's morals she was worrying about, although she took family matters very seriously, and the fact that Robert had a woman in tow was certainly a matter for curiosity. That Robert should be associated with Stringham's sister was of special interest to myself. I had never met this sister, who was called Flavia, though I had seen her years before at Stringham's wedding. Chips Lovell, our brother-in-law, Priscilla's husband, had always alleged that Robert had a taste for 'night-club hostesses old enough to be his mother'. Mrs Wisebite, though not a night-club hostess, was certainly appreciably older than Robert. By this time, after several changes of position, Stevens had parked the car to his own satisfaction. As he joined us, another possible explanation of Frederica's jumpiness suddenly occurred to me.

'Isobel hasn't had the baby yet without anyone telling me?'

'Oh, no, no, no.'

However, something about the way I asked the question must have indicated to Frederica herself that her manner struck me as unaccustomed. While we followed her through the hall, she spoke more quietly.

'It's only that I'm looking forward to your meeting an old friend, Nick,' she said.

Evidently Robert was not the point at issue. We entered a sitting-room full of people, including a lot of children. These younger persons became reduced, in due course, to four only; Frederica's two sons, Edward and Christopher, aged about ten and twelve respectively, together with a couple of quite little ones, who played with bricks on the floor. One of these latter was presumably Priscilla's daughter, Caroline. Priscilla herself, blonde and leggy, quite a beauty in her way, was also lying on the floor, helping to build a tower with the bricks. Her brother, Robert Tolland, wearing battle-dress, sat on the sofa beside a tall, good-looking woman of about forty. Robert had removed his gaiters, but still wore army boots. The woman was Flavia Wisebite. Not noticeably like her brother in feature, she had some of Stringham's air of liveliness weighed down with melancholy. In her, too, the melancholy predominated. There was something greyhound-like about her nose and mouth. These two, Robert and Mrs Wisebite, seemed to have arrived in the house only a very short time before Stevens and myself. Tall, angular, Robert wore Intelligence Corps shoulder titles, corporal's stripes on his arm. The army had increased his hungry, even rather wolfish appearance. He jumped up at once with his usual manner of conveying that the last person to enter the room was the one he most wanted to see, an engaging social gesture that often caused people to exaggerate Robert's personal interest in his fellow human beings, regarding whom, in fact, he was inclined to feel little concern.

'Nick,' he said, 'it's marvellous we should have struck just the moment when you've been able to get away for a weekend. I don't think you've ever met Flavia, but she knows all about you from her brother.'

I introduced Odo Stevens to them.

'How do you do, sir,' said Robert.

'Oh, blow the sir, chum,' said Stevens. 'You can keep that for when we're on duty. I'm rather thick with the lance-corporal in your racket who functions with my Battalion. I've borrowed his motor bike before now. Where are you stationed?'

'Mytchett,' said Robert, 'but I hope to move soon.'

'My God, so do I,' said Stevens. 'They train your I. Corps personnel at Mytchett, don't they?'

He seemed perfectly at ease in this rather odd gathering. Before I had time to say much to Mrs Wisebite, a middle-aged man rose from an armchair. He had a tanned face, deep blue eyes, a very neat grey moustache. The sweater worn over a pair of khaki trousers seemed very natural clothes for him, giving somehow the impression of horsy elegance. It was Dicky Umfraville. Frederica was right. His presence was certainly a surprise.

'You didn't expect to find me here, old boy, did you?' said Umfraville. 'You thought I could only draw breath in night-clubs, a purely nocturnal animal.'

I had to agree that night-clubs seemed the characteristic background for our past encounters. There had been two of these at least. Umfraville had turned up at Foppa's that night, ages before, when I had taken Jean Duport there to play Russian billiards; then, a year or two later, Ted Jeavons had brought me to the club Umfraville himself had been running, where Max Pilgrim had sung his songs, Heather Hopkins played the piano:

'Di, Di, in her collar and tie . . .'

I had not set eyes on Umfraville since that occasion, but he seemed determined that we were the oldest of friends. I tried to recall what I knew of him: service in the earlier war with the Foot Guards, I could not remember which; some considerable reputation as gentleman-rider; four wives. Like many men who have enjoyed a career of more than usual dissipation, he had come to look notably distinguished in middle years, figure slim, eyes bright, face brown with Kenya sun. This bronzed skin, well brushed greying hair emphasised the blue of his eyes, which glistened like Peter Templer's, as Sergeant Pendry's had done before his disasters. I could not recall whether or not Umfraville's moustache was an addition. If so, it scarcely altered him at all. His face, in repose, possessed that look of innate sadness which often marks the features of those habituated to the boundless unreliability of horses. I asked him how he was employed in the army.

'On the staff of London District, old boy.'

He spoke with an exaggerated dignity, squaring his chest and coming to attention. Frederica, who was handing round drinks, now joined us. Once more she began to laugh helplessly.

'Dicky's got a very grand job,' she said, 'haven't you?'

She slipped her arm through Umfraville's. This was unheard-of licence for Frederica, something to be regarded as indicating decay of all the moral and social standards she had defended so long.

'It's certainly one of the bigger stations,' Umfraville agreed modestly.

'Of course it is, darling.'

'And should lead to promotion,' he said.

'Without doubt.'

'Collecting the tickets perhaps.'

'Dicky is an RTO,' said Frederica.

She was quite unable to control her laughter, which seemed not so much attributable to the thought of Umfraville being a Railway Transport Officer, as to the sheer delight she took in him for himself.

'He's got a cosy little office at one of those North London stations,' she said. 'I can never remember which, but I've visited him there. I say, Dicky, we'd better tell Nick, hadn't we?'

'About us?'

'Yes.'

'The fact is,' said Umfraville speaking slowly and with gravity, 'the fact is Frederica and I are engaged.'

Isobel came through the door at that moment, so the impact of this unexpected piece of news was to some extent lessened by other considerations immediately presenting themselves. Then and there, no more was said than a few routine congratulations, with further gigglings from Frederica. Isobel looked pale, though pretty well. I had not seen her for months, it seemed years. We went off to a corner together.

'How have you been?'

'All right. There was a false alarm about ten days ago, but it didn't get far enough to inform you.'

'And you're feeling all right?'

'Most of the time – but rather longing for the little brute to appear.'

We talked for a while.

'Who is the character on the floor playing bricks with the children and Priscilla?'

'He's called Odo Stevens. He's on the course and brought me over in his car. Come and meet him.'

We went across the room. Stevens got to his feet and shook hands.

'Look here,' he said, 'I must go. Otherwise Aunt Doris will be upset something's happened to me.'

'Don't rush off, Mr Stevens,' said Priscilla, still prone on the carpet, 'hullo, Nick, I've only had a wave from you so far. How are you?'

Frederica joined us.

'Another drink,' she said.

'No, thank you, really,' said Stevens, 'I must be moving on.'

He turned to say goodbye to Priscilla.

'I say,' he said, 'you'll lose your brooch, if you're not careful.'

She looked down. The brooch hung from its pin. It was a little mandoline in silver-gilt, ornamented with musical symbols on either side, early Victorian keepsake in style, pretty, though of no special value. Priscilla used to wear it before she married Chips. I had always supposed it a present from Moreland in their days together, that the reason for the musical theme of its design. While she glanced down, the brooch fell to the ground. Stevens stooped to pick it up.

'The clasp is broken,' he said. 'Look, if I can take it with me now, I'll put it right in a couple of ticks. I can bring it back on Sunday night, when I turn up with the car.'

'But that would be wonderful,' she said. 'Do you know about brooches?'

'All about costume jewellery. In the business.'

'Oh, do tell me about it.'

'I must be off now,' he said. 'Some other time.'

He turned to me, and we checked the time he would

143

bring the car for our return to Aldershot. Then Stevens said goodbye all round.

'I'll come to the door with you,' said Priscilla. 'I want to hear more about costume jewellery, my favourite subject.'

They went off together.

'What a nice young man,' said Frederica. 'He really made one feel as if one were his own age.'

'Take care,' said Umfraville. 'That's just what I was like when I was young.'

'But that's in his favour,' she said, 'surely it is.'

'Barely twenty,' said Umfraville, in reminiscence. 'Blind with enthusiasm. Fighting like a hero on Flanders fields.'

'Oh, rot,' said Frederica. 'You said you were nearly twenty-four when you went to the war.'

'Well, anyway, look at me now,' said Umfraville. 'A lot of good my patriotism did me, a broken-down old RTO.'

'Cheer up, my pet.'

'Ah,' said Umfraville, 'the heroes of yesterday, they're the *maquereaux* of tomorrow.'

'Well, you're my *maquereau* anyway,' said Frederica, 'so shut up and have another drink.'

Later, when we were alone together upstairs, Isobel gave a fuller account of herself. There was a lot to talk about. The doctor thought everything all right, the baby likely to arrive in a couple of weeks' time. There were, indeed, far more things to discuss than could be spoken of at once. They would have to come out gradually. Instead of dealing with myriad problems in a businesslike manner, settling all kind of points that had to be settled, making arrangements about the future – if it could be assumed there was to be a future – we talked of more immediate, more amusing matters.

'What do you think about Frederica?' Isobel asked.

'Not a bad idea.'

'I think so too.'

'When did she break the news?'

'Only yesterday, when he arrived on leave. I was a bit staggered when told. She's mad about him. I've never seen Frederica like that before. The boys get on well with him too, and seem to approve of the prospect.'

Frederica and Dicky Umfraville getting married was something to open up hitherto unexplored fields of possibility. The first thought, that the engagement was grotesque, bizarre, changed shape after a time, developing until one saw their association as one of those emotional hook-ups of the very near and the very far, which make human relationships easier to accept than to rationalize or disentangle. I remembered that if Frederica's husband, Robin Budd, had lived, his age would not have been far short of Umfraville's. I asked Isobel if the two of them had ever met.

'Just saw each other, I think. Rob looked a little like Dicky too.'

'Where did Frederica pick him up?'

'With Robert. Dicky Umfraville knew Flavia Wisebite in Kenya. Her father farms there – or did, he died the other day – but of course you know that.'

'Do you suppose Flavia and Dicky—'

'I shouldn't wonder. Anyway, it was an instantaneous click so far as Frederica was concerned.'

'Frederica is aware, I suppose, that the past is faintly murky.'

'One wife committed suicide, another married a jockey. Then there was the wife no one knows about – and finally Anne Stepney, who lasted scarcely more than a year, and is now, I hear, living with J. G. Quiggin.'

'That's as many as are recorded. But where did Robert contract Mrs Wisebite? That is even more extraordinary.'

'One never knows with Robert. Tell me about her. She

is sister of your old school pal, Charles Stringham. What else?'

'Charles never saw much of her after they were grown up. She first married a notorious character called Flitton, who lost an arm in the war before this one. A great gambler, also a Kenya figure. Dicky must know him well. Flitton ran away with Baby Wentworth, but refused to marry her after the divorce. Flavia had a daughter by Flitton who must be eighteen or nineteen by now.'

'Flavia told me the late Mr Wisebite, her second husband, came from Minneapolis, and died of drink in Miami.'

'Is she sharing a room with Robert?'

'Not here. There isn't one to share. The beds are too narrow. But, in principle, they seem to be living together. How did you think Priscilla was looking?'

'All right. She was being a bit standoffish, except to Stevens. Who was the other child playing bricks? The Lovells have only Caroline, haven't they?'

'That's Barry.'

'Who is Barry?'

'A slip-up of Frederica's maid, Audrey. Audrey had to bring him along with her, owing to war circumstances. Barry comes in very useful as an escort for Caroline. You know how difficult it always is to find a spare man, especially in the country.'

'Does Barry's mother do the cooking?'

'No, Frederica. She found herself without a cook and no prospect of getting one. She's always been rather keen on cooking, you know. Now she could get a job in any but the very best houses.'

I had an idea, from the way she spoke, that all this talk about Barry, and Frederica's cooking, was, on Isobel's part, a means of temporarily evading the subject of Priscilla. I could tell, from the way she had mentioned her sister, that, for some reason, Priscilla was on Isobel's mind. She was worried about her.

'Any news of Chips?'

'Priscilla isn't very communicative. Where do Marines go? Is he on a ship? She seems to hold it against him that he hasn't been able to arrange for them to have a house or a flat somewhere. I don't think that's Chips's fault. It's all this bloody war. That's why Priscilla is here. She is very restless.'

'Is she having a baby too?'

'Not that I know of. Audrey is, though.'

'Audrey sounds a positive Messalina.'

'Not in appearance. She is a good-natured, dumpy little thing with spectacles.'

'A bit too good-natured, or her lenses need adjusting. Is it Barry's father again?'

'On the contrary, but we understand it may lead to marriage this time.'

'I suppose Frederica will be the next with a baby. What about Robert and Mrs Wisebite?'

'No doubt doing their best. Robert, by the way, is on embarkation leave. He's only spending some of it here. He arrived with Flavia just before you did.'

'Where is he going?'

'He doesn't know – or won't say for security reasons – but he thinks France.'

'How on earth has he managed that?'

'He decided to withdraw his name from those in for a commission, as there was otherwise no immediate hope of a posting overseas.'

'I see.'

'Hardly what one would expect of Robert,' Isobel said.

His own family regarded Robert as one of those quietly self-indulgent people who live rather secret lives because they find themselves thereby less burdened by having to

147

think of others. No one knew much, for example, about his work in an export house dealing with the Far East. The general idea was that Robert was doing pretty well there, though not because he himself propagated any such picture. He would naturally be enigmatic about a situation such as that which involved him with Mrs Wisebite. It was fitting that he should find himself in Field Security. Enterprise must have been required to place himself there too. I wondered what the steps leading to the Intelligence Corps had been. At one moment he had contemplated the navy. No less interesting was this attempt on Robert's part to move closer to a theatre of war at the price of immediately postponing the chance of becoming an officer.

'The war seems to have altered some people out of recognition and made others more than ever like themselves,' said Isobel.

'Have you ever heard of someone called David Pennistone? He was a man in the army I talked to on a train. He said he was writing an article on Descartes.'

'Haven't I seen the name at the end of reviews?'

'That's what I thought. We didn't manage to find anyone we knew in common, but I believe I met him years ago for a minute or two at a party.'

'Didn't the Lovells talk about someone called Pennistone when they came back from Venice? I remember Chips explaining that he was no relation to the Huntercombes, because the name was spelt with a double-n. I have an idea Pennistone lives in Venice – some story of a *contessa*, beautiful but not very young. That's how I'm beginning to feel myself.'

'Anyway, it's nice to meet again, darling.'

'It's been a long time.'

'A bloody long time.'

'It certainly has.'

Later that weekend, when I found him pacing the lawn, Umfraville himself supplied some of the background wanting in his own story.

'Look here, old boy,' he said, when I joined him, 'how do you think you and the others are going to stand up to having me as a brother-in-law?'

'A splendid prospect.'

'Not everyone would think so,' he said. 'You know I must be insane to embrace matrimony again. Stark, staring mad. But not half as mad as Frederica to take me on. Do you realize she'll be my fifth? Something wrong with a man who keeps marrying like that. Must be. But I really couldn't resist Frederica. That prim look of hers. All the same, fancy her accepting me. You'd never expect it, would you. All that business of her emptying the royal slops. She'll have to give up that occupation of course. No good trying to be an Extra Woman of the Bedchamber with me in the offing. Not a bloody bit of use. You can just picture H.M. saying: "Why's that fellow turned up again? I remember him. He used to be a captain in my Brigade of Guards. I had to get rid of him. He's a no-gooder. What does he mean by showing his ugly face again at Buck House? I won't stand it. Off with his head." You agree, don't you?'

'I see what you mean.'

Umfraville stared at me with bloodshot eyes. When we had first met at Foppa's, I had wondered whether he was not a little mad. The way he spoke now, even though it made me laugh, created the same disquieting impression. He nodded his head, smiling to himself, still contemplating his own characteristics with absolute absorption. I suddenly saw that Umfraville had been quite right when he said he was like Odo Stevens. Here again was an almost perfect narcissism, joined in much the same manner to a great acuteness of observation and relish for life.

'You're going to have a professional cad for a brother-in-law, old boy,' he said, 'make no mistake about that. Just to show you I know what I'm talking about when I apply that label to myself, I'll confide a secret. I was the one who took our little friend Flavia's virginity in Kenya years ago. Still, if that were the worst thing that ever happened to poor Flavia, she wouldn't have had much to complain about. Fancy being married to Cosmo Flitton and Harrison F. Wisebite in one lifetime.'

'Isobel and I had already discussed whether you and Mrs Wisebite had ever been in bed together.'

'You had? That shows you're a discerning couple. She's a bright girl, your wife. Well, the answer is in the affirmative. You knew Flavia's brother Charles, didn't you?'

'I used to know him well. I haven't seen him for years.'

'Met Charles Stringham in Kenya too. Came out for a month or two when he was quite a boy. I liked him very much. Then he took to drink, like so many other good chaps. Flavia says he has recovered now, and is in the army. Charles used to talk a lot about that bastard, Buster Foxe, whom their mother married when she and Boffles Stringham parted company. Charles hated Buster's guts.'

'I haven't seen Commander Foxe for ages.'

'Neither have I, thank God, but I hear he's in the neighbourhood. At your brother-in-law, Lord Warminster's home, in fact. He'll soon be my brother-in-law, too. Then there'll be hell to pay.'

'But what on earth is Buster, a sailor, doing at Thrubworth? I thought it was a Corps Headquarters.'

'Thrubworth isn't an army set-up any longer. It's still requisitioned, but they turned the place into one of those frightfully secret inter-service organisations. Buster has dug himself in there.'

150

'Are they still letting Erry and Blanche inhabit their end of the house.'

'Don't object, so far as I hear.'

No very considerable adjustment had been necessary when Thrubworth had been taken over by the Government at the beginning of the war. Erridge, in any case, had been living in only a small part of the mansion (seventeenth-century brick, fronted in the eighteenth century with stone), his sister, Blanche, housekeeping for him. Although the place was only twenty or thirty miles from Frederica's village, there was little or no communication between Erridge and the rest of his family. Since the outbreak of war he had become, so Isobel told me, less occupied than formerly with the practical side of politics, increasingly devoting himself to books about the Anabaptists and revolutionary movements of the Middle Ages.

'Buster's a contemporary of mine,' said Umfraville, 'a son-of-a-bitch in the top class. I've never told you my life story, have I?'

'Not yet.'

'You'll hear it often enough when we become brothers-in-law,' he said, 'so I'll start by revealing only a little now.'

Once more I thought of Odo Stevens.

'My father bred horses for a living,' said Umfraville. 'It was a precarious vocation and his ways were improvident. However, he had the presence of mind to marry the daughter of a fairly well-to-do manufacturer of machinery for the production of elastic webbing. That allowed for a margin of unprofitable deals in bloodstock. If I hadn't learnt to ride as a boy, I don't know where I should have been. There was some crazy idea of turning me into a land-agent. Then the war came in 1914 and I got off on my own. Found my way into one of the newly formed Guards battalions. There had been terrific expansion and they didn't turn up their noses at me and many another like me. In fact some of my brother officers were heels such as you've never set eyes on. I never looked back after that. Not until I fell foul of Buster Foxe. If it hadn't been for Buster, I might have been major-general now, commanding London District, instead of counting myself lucky to be a humble member of its Movement Control staff.'

'You remained on after the war with a regular commission?'

'That was it,' said Umfraville. 'I expect you've heard of a French marshal called Lyautey. Pacified North Africa and all that. Do you know what Lyautey said was the first essential of an officer? Gaiety. That was what Lyautey thought, and he knew his business. His own ideas of gaiety may not have included the charms of the fair sex, but that's another matter. Well, how much gaiety do you find among most of the palsied crackpots you serve under? Precious little, you can take it from me. It was my intention to master a military career by taking a leaf out of Lyautey's book – not as regards neglecting the ladies, but in other respects. First of all it worked pretty well.'

'But what has Buster Foxe to do with Marshal Lyautey?'

'I'm coming to that,' said Umfraville. 'Ever heard of a girl called Dolly Braybrook?'

'No.'

'Dolly was my first wife. Absolute stunner. Daughter of a fellow who'd formerly commanded the Regiment. Bloody Braybrook, her father was universally termed throughout the army, and with reason. She wouldn't have me at first, and who should blame her. Asked her again and again. The answer was always no. Then one day she changed her mind, the way women do. That pertinacity of mine has gone now. All the same, its loss has confirmed my opinion that the older I get, the more attractive I am to women.'

'It certainly looks like it.'

'Formerly, there was all that business of "Not tonight, darling, because I don't love you enough", then "Not tonight, darling, because I love you too much" – Christ, I've been through the whole range of it. The nearest some women get to being faithful to their husband is making it unpleasant for their lover. However, that's by the way. The point is that Dolly married me in the end.'

'How long did it last?'

'A year or two. Happy as the day's long, at least I was. I'd been appointed adjutant too. Then Buster Foxe appeared on the horizon. He was stationed at Greenwich at the time – the Naval College. I used to play an occasional game of cards with him and other convivial souls when he came up west. What should happen but under my very nose Dolly fell in love with Buster.'

The exaggerated dramatic force employed by Umfraville in presenting his narrative made it hard to know what demeanour best to adopt in listening to the story. Tragedy might at any moment give way to farce, so that the listener had always to keep his wits about him. When I first met Umfraville I had noticed some resemblance to Buster Foxe, now revealed as that similarity companionship in early life confers on people.

'It was just the moment when the Battalion was moving from Buckingham Gate to Windsor,' Umfraville said. 'I had to go with them, of course, while Dolly stayed in London, until we could find somewhere to live. I went up to see her one day. Arrived home. The atmosphere was a shade chilly. The next thing was Dolly told me she wanted a divorce.'

'A complete surprise?'

'Old boy, you could have knocked me down with a swizzle-stick. Always the way, of course. Nothing I could say was any good. Dolly was set on marriage to Buster. In the end I agreed. There was no way out. I suppose I might have shot Buster through the head, if I'd got close enough to him, even though it is only the size of a nut. What the hell good would that have done? Besides, I'd have run quite a chance of swinging in this country. It's not like France, where they expect you to react strongly. So I settled down to do the gentlemanly thing, and provide evidence for Dolly to divorce me. I was quite well ahead with that when Buster found Amy Stringham, Flavia's mama, was just as anxious to marry him as Dolly was. Now it didn't take Buster long to work out that marriage to a lady with some very warm South African gold holdings, not to mention a life interest in her first husband Lord Warrington's estate, stud and country mansion, would be more profitable than a wife like Dolly, one of a large family without a halfpenny to bless herself with. Mrs Stringham was a few years older than Buster, it's true, but she was none the less a beauty. We all had to admit that.'

Umfraville paused.

'Next thing I heard,' he said, 'was that Dolly had taken an overdose of sleeping pills.'

'Divorce proceedings had started?'

'Not so far as that they couldn't have been put in reverse gear. I suppose Dolly thought it too late in the day to suggest return, though there's nothing I'd have liked better.'

'But why did that prevent you from Commanding London District?'

'That's a sensible question, old boy. The reason was this. I had to leave the service – abandon my gallant and glorious Regiment. I'll explain. You see I wasn't feeling too good after my poor wife Dolly decided to join the angels, and naturally I looked about for someone to console me. Found several, as a matter of fact. The one I liked best was a girl I met one night at the Cavendish called Joy Grant – at

154

least that was her professional name, and a very suitable one too – so I thought I might as well marry her. Of course, there couldn't be any question of staying in the Regiment, if I married Joy. To begin with, I should have been hard put to it to name a brother officer who hadn't shared the same idyllic experiences as myself in that respect. I sent in my papers and made up my mind to up stumps and emigrate with my blushing bride. Thought I'd try Kenya, the great open spaces where men are men, as Charles Stringham used to say. Well, Joy and I had scarcely arrived in the hotel at Nairobi when it became abundantly clear we had made a mistake in becoming man and wife. We were already living what's called a cat-and-dog life. In short, it wasn't long before she went off with a fellow called Castlemallock, twice her age, who looked like an ostler suffering from a dose of clap.'

'The Corps School of Chemical Warfare is at a house called Castlemallock.'

'That's the family. They used to live there until they lost all their money a generation or two ago. Castlemallock himself, marquess or not, was a common little fellow, but what was much worse, so far as he himself was concerned, was the fact that he found he couldn't perform with Joy in Kenya. He thought it might have something to do with the climate, the altitude, so he took her back to England to see if he could make better going there, or at least consult a competent medical man about getting a shot of something to liven him up occasionally. However, he took too long to find the right specialist, and meanwhile Joy went off with Jo Breen, the jockey, the chap who was suspended one year at Cheltenham for pulling Middlemarch. They keep a pub together now in one of those little places in the Thames Valley, and overcharge you most infamously if you ever drop in for a talk about old times.'

Umfraville paused again. He took out a cigarette case and offered it to me.

'Now this business of wives departing was beginning to get me down,' he said. 'It seemed to be becoming a positive habit. This time, I thought, I'll be the one to do the cattle rustling, so I removed from him the wife of a District Commissioner. There was no end of trouble about that. When I previously found myself in that undignified position, I'd behaved like a gent. This fellow, the husband, didn't see things in that light at all. I found myself in a perfect rough-house.'

He lit a cigarette and sighed.

'How did it end?'

'We got married,' he said, 'but she died of enteric six months later. You see I don't have much luck with wives. Then you were present yourself when I met little Anne Stepney at Foppa's. You know the end of the story. That was a crazy thing to do, to marry Anne, if ever there was. Anyway, it didn't last long. Least said, soonest mended. But now I've turned over a new leaf. Frederica is going to be my salvation. The model married couple. I'm going to find my way out of Movement Control, and once more set about becoming a general, just as I was before being framed by Buster. Frederica is going to make a first-class general's wife. Don't you agree? My God, I never dreamed I'd marry one of Hugo Warminster's daughters, and I don't expect he did either.'

By then, it was time for luncheon. I found myself sitting next to Flavia Wisebite. She had a quiet, rather sad manner, suggesting one of those reserved, well behaved, fairly peevish women, usually of determined character, often to be found as wives, or ex-wives, of notably dissipated men like Flitton or Wisebite. Their peevishness appears to derive not so much from a husband's ill behaviour, as to be a trait

156

natural to them, which attracts men of that kind. Such was mere conjecture, since I knew little or nothing of Flavia's private life, except that Stringham had more than once implied that his sister's matrimonial troubles were largely of her own choosing. In that she would have been, after all, not unlike himself. I asked for news of her brother.

'Charles?' she said. 'He's in a branch of the army called the RAOC – Royal Army Ordnance Corps. I expect you know about it. According to Charles, they look after clothes and boots and blankets, all that sort of thing. Is it true?'

'Perfectly true. What rank?'

'Private.'

'I see.'

'And likely to remain so, he says.'

'He's – all right now?'

'Oh, yes,' she said. 'Hardly touches a drop. In fact, so cured he can even drink a glass of beer from time to time. That's a great step. I always said it was just nerves, not real addiction.'

Familiar herself with alcoholics, she took her brother's former state in a very matter-of-fact way; also his circumstances in the army, which did not sound very enviable. Stringham as a private in the RAOC required an effort of imagination even to picture.

'How does Charles like it?'

'Not much.'

'I'm not surprised.'

'He says it's rather hell, in fact, but he was bent on getting into something. For some reason, the RAOC were the only people who seemed to want him. I think Charles is having a more uncomfortable time than Robert. You rather enjoy the I. Corps, don't you, dear?'

'Enjoy is rather a strong word,' said Robert. 'Things might be worse at Mytchett. I always like prying into other people's business, and that's what Field Security is for.'

Flavia Wisebite's manner towards Robert was almost maternal. She was nearer in age to Robert than to Umfraville, but gave the impression, although so different an example of it, of belonging much more to Umfraville's generation. Both she and Umfraville might be said to represent forms of revolt, and nothing dates people more than the standards from which they have chosen to react. Robert and Flavia's love affair, if love affair it were, took a very different shape from Frederica's and Umfraville's. Robert and Flavia gave no impression that, for the moment at least, they were having the time of their lives. On the contrary, they seemed very subdued. By producing Flavia at his sister's house, Robert was at last to some extent showing his hand, emotionally speaking, something he had never done before. Perhaps he was in love. The pressures of war were forcing action on everyone. Were his efforts to get to France part of this will to action, or an attempt to escape? The last might also be true. The telephone bell rang as we were rising from table. Frederica went to answer it. She returned to the room.

'It's for you, Priscilla.'

'Who is it?'

'Nick's friend, Mr Stevens.'

'Oh, yes, of course,' said Priscilla. 'About the brooch.'

She went rather pink.

'Priscilla's made a hit,' said Umfraville.

I asked Flavia whether she ever saw her mother's former secretary, Miss Weedon, who had married my parents' old acquaintance, General Conyers.

'Oh, Tuffy,' she said. 'She used to be my governess, you know. Yes, I visited her only the other day. It is all going very well. The General read aloud to us an article he had written about heightened bi-sexuality in relation to early religiosity. He is now much more interested in psycho-analysis than in his 'cello playing.'

'What does he think about the war?'

'He believed a German offensive would start any moment then, probably in several places at once.'

'In fact this Norwegian and Danish business was the beginning.'

'I suppose so.'

'It doesn't sound as if things are going too well,' Umfraville said, 'I think we've taken some knocks.'

Priscilla returned.

'It was about the brooch,' she said. 'Mr Stevens can't do it himself, as one of the stones has come out, but he has arranged for someone he knows to mend it. He just wanted to warn me that he wouldn't have it for me when he came to pick up Nick in the car.'

'I said he was a very polite young man,' remarked Frederica, giving her sister rather a cold look.

The rest of the weekend passed with the appalling rapidity of wartime leave, melting away so quickly that one seemed scarcely to have arrived before it was time to go. Dinner was a trifle gloomy on that account, conversation fragmentary, for the most part about the news that evening.

'I wonder whether this heavy bombing is a prelude to a move in France,' said Robert. 'What do you think, Dicky?'

'That will be the next thing.'

Towards the end of the meal, the telephone bell sounded.

'Do answer it, Nick,' said Frederica. 'You're nearest the door.'

She spoke from the kitchen, where she was making coffee. The telephone was installed in a lobby off the hall. I went out to it. A man's voice asked if he were speaking to Frederica's number.

'Yes.'

'Is Lance-Corporal Tolland there?'

'Who is speaking?'

He named some army unit. As I returned to the dining-room, a knocking came from the front door. I told Robert he was wanted on the telephone.

'Shall I answer the door, Frederica?'

'It's probably the vicar about a light showing,' she said. 'He's an air-raid warden and frightfully fussy. Bring him in, if it is. He might like a cup of coffee.'

However, a tall naval officer was on the step when I opened the door. He had just driven up in a car.

'This is Lady Frederica Budd's house?'

'Yes.'

'I must apologize for calling at this hour of the night, but I believe my step-daughter, Mrs Wisebite, is staying here.'

'She is.'

'There are some rather urgent business matters to talk over with her. I heard she was here for a day or two, and thought Lady Frederica would not mind if I dropped in for a moment. I am stationed in the neighbourhood – at her brother, Lord Warminster's house, as a matter of fact.'

'Come in. You're Commander Foxe, aren't you. I'm Nicholas Jenkins. We've met once or twice in the past.'

'Good God, of course we have,' said Buster. 'This is your sister-in-law's house?'

'Yes.'

'You were a friend of Charles's, weren't you. This is splendid.'

Commander Foxe did not sound as if he thought finding me at Frederica's was as splendid as all that, even though he seemed relieved that his arrival would be cushioned by an introduction. Another sponsor would certainly be preferable, since any old friend of Stringham's was bound to have heard many stories to his own discredit. However, Buster, although he had that chronic air some men possess of appearing to consider all other men potential rivals, put a reasonably good face on it. For my own part, I suddenly thought of what Dicky Umfraville had told me. He would hardly welcome this arrival. There was nothing to be done about that. I took Buster along to the sitting-room, where the rest of the party were now sitting. Buster had evidently planned a fairly dramatic entry.

'I really must apologize, Lady Frederica—' he began to say, as he came through the door.

Following him into the room, I saw at once something disagreeable had happened. Robert appeared to be the centre of attention. He had evidently just announced news consequent on his telephone call. Everyone looked disturbed. Flavia Wisebite seemed near tears. When she saw Commander Foxe, her distress turned to furious annoyance.

'Buster,' she said sharply, 'where on earth have you come from?'

She sounded very cross, so cross that for a moment she forgot how upset she was. Commander Foxe must have grasped that his arrival was not altogether welcome at the moment. He was plainly taken aback by that. Smiling uneasily, he glanced round the room, as if to recover himself by finding some friendly face. His eyes rested first on Dicky Umfraville. Umfraville held out his hand.

'Hullo, Buster,' he said, 'a long time since we met.'

When people really hate one another, the tension within them can sometimes make itself felt throughout a room, like atmospheric waves, first hot, then cold, wafted backwards and forwards, as if in an invisible process of air conditioning, creating a pervasive physical disturbance. Buster Foxe and Dicky Umfraville, between them, brought about that state. Their really overpowering mutual detestation dominated for a moment all other local agitations. The fact that neither party was going to come out in the open at this stage made the currents of nervous electricity generated by suppressed emotion even more powerful. At the same time, to anyone who did not know what horrors linked them together, they might have appeared a pair of old friends, met after an age apart. Their distinct, though imprecise, physical similarity increased this last impression. Before Buster could do more than make a gesture of acknowledgment in Umfraville's direction, Frederica came forward. Buster began once more to apologize, to explain he wanted only a brief word with Flavia, then be gone. Frederica listened to him.

'We're all in rather a stew here at the moment,' she said. 'My brother Robert has just heard his leave is cancelled. He has to go back as soon as possible.'

Buster was obviously put out at finding himself in the disadvantageous position of having to listen to someone else's troubles, when he had come with the express object of stating his own. It had to be admitted he looked immensely distinguished, more so even than Umfraville. I had never before seen Commander Foxe in naval uniform. It suited him. His iron-grey hair, of which he still possessed plenty, was kept short on a head almost preternaturally small, as Umfraville had pointed out. Good looks, formerly of a near film-star quality, had settled down in middle-age to an appearance at once solid and forcible, a bust of the better type of Roman senator. A DSC was among his medal ribbons. I thought of Umfraville's lament that the heroes of yesterday are the *maquereaux* of tomorrow. Something had undoubtedly vexed Commander Foxe a great deal. He attempted, without much success, to assume a sympathetic expression about the subject of Robert's leave cancellation. Clearly ignorant of any connexion between Flavia and Robert, he was at a loss to understand why Flavia was so disturbed. After her first outburst, she had forgotten about Buster again, and was gazing at Robert, her eyes full of tears.

'Surely you can take a train tomorrow,' she said. 'You don't have to leave tonight, darling. What trains are there, Frederica?'

'Not very good ones,' said Frederica. 'But they'll get you there sooner or later. Why don't you do that, Robert?'

'Aren't you taking the army too seriously, Robert?' said Umfraville. 'Having just sent you on leave, they can't expect you to go back at a moment's notice. Your unit doesn't know Nick is going back by car tonight. Even if you are a bit late, there's nothing the authorities can do to you, if they countermand their own orders in this way.'

'That's not the point,' said Robert.

This was the only time I had ever seen Robert fairly near to what might be called a state of excitement. He was knocking his closed fists together gently.

'If I don't get back before tomorrow night,' he said, 'I may miss the overseas draft. My name is only included in the list on sufferance anyway. If they've got an excuse, they'll remove it. That was the Orderly Room Sergeant on the line. He's rather a friend of mine, and was giving me warning about that. Of course he couldn't say it straight out, but he made his meaning quite clear to me. There are rows of other corporals they can send, if a party has been ordered to move forthwith. That's what it looks like. Besides, I don't want to have to make all my arrangements about packing and so on at the very last moment. That was why I thought your friend Stevens might be able to fit me into his car, Nick. You could then disgorge me somewhere in the neighbourhood of Mytchett. I could walk the last lap, if you landed me reasonably near.'

'It won't be very comfortable in the car, but I don't see why you shouldn't come with us.'

'When is Stevens arriving?'

'Any time now.'

'I'll go and get my things ready,' said Robert.

He went off upstairs. Flavia began to dab her eyes with a rolled-up handkerchief. Buster must have remembered he had met Priscilla before – at the party his wife had given for Moreland's symphony – and he filled in the time during this discussion about Robert's affairs by talking to her. That was also perhaps a method of avoiding Dicky Umfraville's eye. Buster was accompanying this conversation with a great display of middle-aged masculine charm. From time to time, he glanced in Flavia's direction to see if she were sufficiently calm to be tackled about whatever he hoped to speak. Now, Flavia, making an effort to recover herself, moved towards Buster of her own volition.

'What's happened?' she said. 'I was going to ring you up, but I've been dreadfully entangled with other things. Besides, I've only just arrived here. Now all this has upset everything.'

If Buster did not already know about Robert, that was not very enlightening, but he was probably sharp enough to have grasped the situation by this time.

'It's about your mother,' he said. 'It's all damned awkward. I thought the sooner you knew the better. There was a lot of difficulty in getting hold of your address. When I found by a lucky chance you were in the neighbourhood of Thrubworth, I decided to try and see you, in case I lost the opportunity for months.'

'But what is it?'

'Your mother is behaving in a very extraordinary way. There are serious money difficulties for one thing. They may affect you and Charles. Your settlements, I mean.'

'She's always quite reckless about money. You must have learnt that by now.'

164

'She has been unwise about all kind of matters. I had no idea what was going on.'

'Where is she now?'

'That's one of the points. She has closed both houses and gone to live in a workman's cottage to be near Norman.'

'Norman Chandler?'

'Of course.'

'But I thought Norman had joined the army.'

'He has. He has been sent to a camp in Essex. That's why your mother has gone there. What's more, she wants to divorce me.'

This news certainly surprised Flavia a lot.

'But—'

'I've nowhere to go,' said Buster, speaking with great bitterness. 'When I was last in London, I had to stay at my club. Now this news about a divorce is sprung on me. Your mother went off without a word. All kinds of arrangements have to be made about things. It is too bad.'

'But does she want to marry Norman?'

'How do I know what she wants to do?' said Buster. 'I'm the last person she ever considered. I think Norman, too, has behaved very badly to allow her to act in this way. I always liked Norman. I did not in the least mind his being what he is. I often told him so. I thought we were friends. Many men in my position would have objected to having someone like Norman about the house, doing the flowers and dancing attendance upon their wife. Norman pleased your mother. That was enough for me. What thanks do I get for being so tolerant? Your mother goes off to Essex with Norman, taking the keys with her, so that I can't even get at my own suits and shirts. On top of all that, I'm told I'm going to be divorced.'

At that point there was another loud knock on the front

door. This must be Stevens. I went to let him in. Umfraville followed me into the hall.

'Look here,' he said, 'tell me quickly what's happened to Buster to upset him so.'

'Mrs Foxe had a friend called Norman Chandler – a little dancer she adored, who was always about her house. He was quite a good actor too. It looks as if she has got fed up at last and kicked Buster out.'

'Buster is going to get me into this secret set-up at Thrubworth. I've decided that.'

'How's it going to be managed?'

'I once took a monkey off Buster at poker. Apart from his other misdemeanours, I've never seen my money. I know where I can make things unpleasant, if Buster doesn't jump to it and get me fixed up. Boffles Stringham once said: "Mark my words, Dicky, the day will come when Amy will have to get rid of that damned polo-playing sailor." That day has come. There are some other reckonings for Buster to pay too.'

Another knock came on the door. Umfraville went back to the sitting-room. I admitted Stevens.

'I'm a bit late,' he said, 'we'll have to bustle back.'

'There's rather a commotion going on here. My brother-in-law, Robert Tolland, has just had his leave cancelled. He wants to get back to Mytchett tonight. Will it be all right if he comes with us? We pass near his unit and can drop him on the way.'

'Of course. If he doesn't mind having his balls crushed in the back of the car. Is he ready?'

'He's just gone off to pack. Then there's a naval officer making a scene with his step-daughter.'

'Bring 'em all on,' said Stevens. 'We oughtn't to delay too long. I'd just like to have word with that lady about her brooch.'

We went into the sitting-room. By that time things had quietened down. Buster, especially, had recovered his poise. He was now talking to Frederica, having presumably settled with Flavia whatever he had hoped to arrange. Flavia and Robert had retired to a sofa and were embracing. Stevens said a word of greeting to Frederica, then made at once for Priscilla. Frederica turned again to Buster.

'I'm glad to hear Erry is behaving himself,' she said.

'I agree we were all prepared to find your brother rather difficult,' said Buster, 'but on the contrary – anyway so far as I am personally concerned – he has done everything in his power to make my life agreeable. He has, if I may say so, the charm of all your family, though in a different manner to the rest of you.'

Umfraville interrupted them.

'Come and talk shop with me for a moment, Buster,' he said.

They went into a corner of the room together. Isobel and I went into another one. It was clearly time to get under way. If we did not set out without further delay, we should not be back by the required hour. Then Isobel went rather white.

'Look here,' she said, 'I'm sorry to have to call attention to myself at this moment, but I'm feeling awfully funny. I think perhaps I'd better go to my room – and Frederica or someone can ring up the doctor.'

That was the final touch. In a state of the utmost confusion and disquiet we left them at last, arriving in Aldershot just in time, having dropped Robert on the way.

'Not feeling much like going on the square tomorrow, are you?' said Stevens. 'Still it was the hell of a good weekend's leave. I had one of the local girls under a hedge.'

4

WHEN, DURING THOSE RARE, INTOXICATING
moments of solitude, I used to sit in a window seat at
Castlemallock, reading *Esmond*, or watching the sun go
down over the immense brick rampart of the walled garden,
the Byronic associations of the place made me think of *Don
Juan*:

> I pass my evenings in long galleries solely,
> And that's the reason I'm so melancholy . . .

The long gallery at Castlemallock, uncarpeted, empty of
furniture except for a few trestle tables and wooden chairs,
had these built-in seats all along one side. Here one could be
alone during the intervals between arrival and departure of
Anti-Gas students, when Kedward and I would be Duty
Officer on alternate days. That meant little more than
remaining within the precincts of the castle in the evening,
parading 'details' – usually a couple of hundred men – at
Retreat, sleeping at night by the telephone. We were
Gwatkin's only subalterns now, for this was the period of
experiment, later abandoned as unsatisfactory, when one
platoon in each company was led by a warrant-officer. If an
Anti-Gas course were in progress, we slept alternate nights
in the Company Office, in case there was a call from
Battalion. I often undertook Kedward's tour of duty, as he
liked to 'improve his eye', when training was over for the
day, by exploring the neighbouring country with a view to
marking down suitable sites for machine-gun nests and

anti-tank emplacements. Lying in the window-seat, I would think how it felt to be a father, of the times during the latter part of the Aldershot course when I had been able to see Isobel and the child. She and the baby, a boy, were 'doing well', but there had been difficulty in visiting them, Stevens's car by then no longer available. Stevens, as Brent prophesied, had been 'Returned to Unit'.

'I shan't be seeing you lads after tomorrow,' he said one afternoon.

'Why not?'

'I've been RTU-ed.'

'Whatever for?'

'I cut one of those bloody lectures and got caught.'

'Sorry about this.'

'I don't give a damn,' he said. 'All I want is to get abroad. This may start me on the move. I'll bring it off sooner or later. Look here, give me your sister-in-law's address, so I can keep in touch with her about that brooch.'

There was a certain bravado about all this. To get in the army's black books is something always to be avoided; as a rule, no help to advancement in any direction. I gave Stevens the address of Frederica's house, so that he could send Priscilla back her brooch. We said goodbye.

'We'll meet again.'

'We will, indeed.'

The course ended without further incident of any note. On its last day, I had a word with Brent, before our ways, too, parted.

'Pleased we ran into each other,' he said. 'To tell the truth, I was glad to spill all that stuff about the Duports for some reason. Don't quite know why. You won't breathe a word, will you?'

'Of course not. Where are you off to now?'

'The ITC – for a posting.'

I sailed back across the water. Return, like the war news, was cheerless. The Battalion had been re-deployed further south, in a new area nearer the border, where companies were on detachment. Gwatkin's, as it turned out, was quartered at the Corps School of Chemical Warfare, the keeps, turrets and castellations of which also enclosed certain Ordnance stores of some importance, which came under Command. For these stores, Gwatkin's company provided security guards, also furnishing men, if required, for Anti-Gas demonstrations. When the Battalion operated as a unit, we operated with the rest, otherwise lived a life apart, occupied with our own training or the occasional demands of the School.

Isobel wrote that her aunt, Molly Jeavons – as a rule far from an authority on such matters – had lent her a book about Castlemallock, its original owner, a Lord Chief Justice (whose earldom had been raised to a marquisate for supporting the Union) having been a distant connexion of the Ardglass family. His heir – better known as Hercules Mallock, friend of d'Orsay and Lady Blessington – had sold the place to a rich linen manufacturer, who had pulled down the palladian mansion and built this neo-gothic castle. The second Lord Castlemallock died unmarried, at a great age, in Lisbon, leaving little or nothing to the great-nephew who inherited the title, father or grandfather of the Castlemallock who had run away with Dicky Umfraville's second wife. Like other houses of similar size throughout this region, Castlemallock, too large and inconvenient, had lain un-tenanted for twenty or thirty years before its requisition-ing. The book also quoted Byron's letter (a fragment only, said to be of doubtful authenticity) written to Caroline Lamb who had visited the house when exiled from England by her family on his account. Isobel had copied this out for me:

'. . . even though the diversions of Castlemallock may exceed those of Lismore, I perceive you are ignorant of one matter – that he to whose *Labours* you appear not insensible was once known to your humble servant by the chaste waters of the Cam. Moderate, therefore, your talent for novel writing, My dear Caro, or at least spare me an account of his protestations of affection & recollect that your host's namesake preferred *Hylas* to the *Nymphs*. Learn, too, that the theme of assignations in romantick groves palls on a man with a cold & quinsy & a digestion that lately suffered the torment of supper at Ld Sleaford's . . .'

This glade in the park at Castlemallock was still known as 'Lady Caro's Dingle', and thought of a Byronic interlude here certainly added charm to grounds not greatly altered at the time of the rebuilding of the house. An air of thwarted passion could be well imagined to haunt these grass-grown paths, weedy lawns and ornamental pools, where moss-covered fountains no longer played. However, such memories were not in themselves sufficient to make the place an acceptable billet. At Castlemallock I knew despair. The proliferating responsibilities of an infantry officer, simple in themselves, yet, if properly carried out, formidable in their minutiae, impose a strain in wartime even on those to whom they are a lifelong professional habit; the excruciating boredom of exclusively male society is particularly irksome in areas at once remote from war, yet oppressed by war conditions. Like a million others, I missed my wife, wearied of the officers and men round me, grew to loathe a post wanting even the consolation that one was required to be brave. Castlemallock lacked the warmth of a regiment, gave none of the sense of belonging to an army that exists in any properly commanded unit or formation. Here was only cursing, quarrelling, complaining, inglorious officers of the instructional and administrative staff, Other Ranks – except for Gwatkin's company – of low medical category. Here, indeed, was the negation of Lyautey's ideal, though food enough for the military resignation of Vigny.

However, there was an undoubted aptness in this sham fortress, monument to a tasteless, half-baked romanticism, becoming now, in truth, a military stronghold, its stone walls and vaulted ceilings echoing at last to the clatter of arms and oaths of soldiery. It was as if its perpetrators had re-created the tedium, as well as the architecture of mediaeval times. At fourteenth-century Stourwater (which had once caused Isobel to recall the *Morte d'Arthur*), Sir Magnus Donners was far less a castellan than the Castle-mallock commandant, a grey-faced Regular, recovering from appendicitis; Sir Magnus's guests certainly less like feudatories than the seedy Anti-Gas instructors, sloughed off at this golden opportunity by their regiments. The Ordnance officers, drab seneschals, fitted well into this gothic world, most of all Pinkus, Adjutant-Quartermaster, one of those misshapen dwarfs who peer from the battlements of Dolorous Garde, bent on doing disservice to whomsoever may cross the drawbridge. This impression – that one had slipped back into a nightmare of the Middle Ages – was not dispelled by the Castlemallock 'details' on parade. There were warm summer nights at Retreat when I could scarcely proceed between the ranks of these cohorts of gargoyles drawn up for inspection for fear of bursting into fits of uncontrollable demoniac laughter.

'Indeed, they are the maimed, the halt and the blind,' CSM Cadwallader remarked more than once.

In short, the atmosphere of Castlemallock told on the nerves of all ranks. Once, alone in the Company Office, a former pantry set in a labyrinth of stone passages at the back of the house, I heard a great clatter of boots and a frightful wailing like that of a very small child. I opened the door to see what was happening. A young soldier was standing there, red faced and burly, tears streaming down his cheeks, his hair dishevelled, his nose running. He looked at the end of his tether. I knew him by sight as one of the Mess waiters. He swayed there limply, as if he might fall down at any moment. A sergeant, also young, followed him quickly up the passage, and stood over him, if that could be said of an NCO half the private's size.

'What the hell is all this row?'

'He's always on at me,' said the private, sobbing convulsively.

The sergeant looked uncomfortable. They were neither of them Gwatkin's men.

'Come along,' he said.

'What's the trouble?'

'He's a defaulter, sir,' said the sergeant. 'Come along now, and finish that job.'

'I can't do it, my back hurts,' said the private, mopping his eyes with a clenched hand.

'Then you should report sick,' said the sergeant severely, 'see the MO. That's what you want to do, if your back hurts.'

'Seen him.'

'See him again then.'

'The Adjutant-Quartermaster said if I did any more malingering he'd give me more CB.'

The sergeant's face was almost as unhappy as the private's. He looked at me as if he thought I might be able to offer some brilliant solution to their problems. He was wrong about that. I saw no way out. Anyway, they were neither of them within my province.

'Well, go away, and don't make a disturbance outside here again.'

'Sorry, sir.'

The two of them went off quietly, but, as they reached the far end of the stone passage, I heard it all starting up again. They were not our men, of course, amongst whom such a scene would have been inconceivable, even when emotions were allowed full rein, which sometimes happened. In such circumstances the display would have taken a far less dismal form. This sort of incident lowered the spirits to an infinitely depressed level. Even though there might be less to do here than with the Battalion, no road-blocks to man, for example, there were also no amusements in the evening, beyond the grubby pubs of a small, down-at-heel town a mile or two away.

'There isn't a lot for the lads to do' said CSM Cadwallader.

He was watching, unsmilingly, a Red Indian war-dance a group of men were performing, led by Williams, I. G., whose eccentric strain probably accounted for his friendship with Lance-Corporal Gittins, the storeman. The dancers, with tent-peg mallets for tomahawks, were moving slowly round in a small circle, bowing their heads to the earth and up again, as they gradually increased the speed of their rotation. I thought what a pity that Bithel was not there to lead them in this dance.

'What about organising some football?'

'No other company there is to play, sir.'

'Does that matter?'

'Personnel of the School, C.3., they are.'

'But there are plenty of our own fellows. Can't they make up a game among themselves?'

'The boys wouldn't want that.'

'Why not?'

'Another company's what they like to beat.'

That was a good straightforward point of view, no pretence that games were anything but an outlet for power and aggression; no stuff about their being enjoyable as such. You played a game to demonstrate that you did it better than someone else. If it came to that, I thought, how few people do anything for its own sake, from making love to practising the arts.

'How do they amuse themselves when not doing Indian war-dances?'

'Some of the lads has found a girl.'

The Sergeant-Major smiled quietly to himself, as if he might have been of that number.

'Corporal Gwylt?'

'Indeed, sir, Corporal Gwylt may have a girl or two.'

Meanwhile, since my return from Aldershot, I was aware of a change that had taken place in Gwatkin, though precisely what had happened to him, I could not at first make out. He had been immensely gratified, so Kedward told me, to find himself more or less on his own as a junior commander, keenly jealous of this position in relation to the Castlemallock Commandant, always making difficulties with him when men were wanted for demonstrational purposes. On the other hand, Gwatkin had also developed a new vagueness, even bursts of apparent indolence. He would pass suddenly into a state close to amnesia, sitting at his table in the Company Office, holding in the palm of his hand, lettering uppermost, the rubber-stamp of the Company, as if it were an orb or other symbol of dominion, while he gazed out on to the cobbled yard, where outbuildings beyond had been transformed into barrack rooms. For several minutes at a time he would stare into space, scanning the roofs as if he could descry beyond the yard and stables vision of battle, cavalry thundering down, long columns of infantry advancing through the smoke, horse artillery bringing up the guns. At least, that was what I supposed. I thought Gwatkin had at last 'seen through' the army as he had formerly imagined it, was experiencing a casting out of devils within himself, the devils of his old military ideas. Gwatkin seemed himself to some extent aware of these visitations, because, so soon as they were passed, his 'regimental' manner would become more obtrusive than ever. On such occasions he would indulge in tussles with the Commandant, or embark on sudden explosions of energy and extend hours of training. However, side by side with exertions that insisted upon an ever-increased standard of efficiency, he became no less subject to these lethargic moods. He talked more freely, too, abandoning all pretence of being a 'man of few words', formerly one of his favourite roles. Again, these bursts of talkativeness alternated with states of the blackest, most silent gloom.

'Anything wrong with Rowland?' I asked Kedward.

'Not that I know of.'

'He doesn't seem quite himself.'

'All right, so far as I've heard.'

'Just struck me as a bit browned off.'

'Has he been on your tail?'

'Not specially.'

'I thought he'd been better tempered lately. But, my God, it's true he's always forgetting things. We nearly ran out of Acquittance Rolls last Pay Parade owing to Rowland having shoved a lot of indents the CQMS gave him into a drawer. Perhaps you're right, Nick, and he's not well.'

For some reason, the matter of the *Alarm* brought home to me these developments in Gwatkin. Command had issued one of their periodic warnings that all units and formations were to be on their guard against local terrorist action of the Deafy Morgan sort, which, encouraged by German successes in the field, had recently become more common. A concerted attack by subversive elements was thought likely to take shape within the next week or two in the Castlemallock area. Accordingly, every unit was instructed to devise its own local *Alarm* signal, in addition to the normal *Alert*. The *Alert* was, of course, based on the principle that German invasion had taken place south of the Border, where British troops would consequently move forthwith. For training purposes, these *Alerts* were usually issued in code by telephone or radio – in the case of Gwatkin's company, routine procedure being to march on the main body of the Battalion. For merely local troubles, however – to which the warning from Command referred – different action would be required, therefore a different warning given. At Castlemallock, for example, the Commandant decided that any such outbreak should be made known by blowing the *Alarm* on the bugle. All ranks were paraded to hear the *Alarm* sounded, so that its notes should at once be recognised, if need arose. Afterwards, Gwatkin, Kedward, CSM Cadwallader and I assembled in the Company Office to check arrangements. The question obviously arose of those men insufficiently musical to register in the head the sound they had just heard.

'All those bugle calls have words to them,' said Kedward. 'What are the ones for the *Alarm*?'

'That's it,' said Gwatkin, pleased at this opportunity to make practical use of military lore, *Cookhouse,* for instance:

> Come to the cookhouse door, boys,
> Come to the cookhouse door,
> Officers' wives have puddings and pies,
> Soldiers' wives have skilly.

How does the *Alarm* go, Sergeant-Major? That must have words too.'

It was the only time I ever saw CSM Cadwallader blush. 'Rather vulgar words they are, sir,' he said.

177

'Well, what are they?' said Gwatkin.

The Sergeant-Major seemed still for some reason unwilling to reveal the appropriate assonance.

'Think most of the Company know the call now, sir,' he said.

'That's not the point,' said Gwatkin. 'We can't take any risks. There may be even one man only who won't recognise it. He'll need the rhyme. What are the words?'

'Really want them, sir?'

'I've just said so,' said Gwatkin.

He was half irritated at the Sergeant-Major's prevarication, at the same time half losing interest. He had begun to look out of the window, his mind wandering in the manner I have described. CSM Cadwallader hesitated again. Then he pursed his lips and gave a vocalized version of the bugle blaring the *Alarm*:

> 'Sergeant-Major's-got-a-horn!
> Sergeant-Major's-got-a-horn! . . .'

Kedward and I burst out laughing. I expected Gwatkin to do the same. He was normally capable of appreciating that sort of joke, especially as a laugh at CSM Cadwallader's expense was not a thing to be missed. However, Gwatkin seemed scarcely to have heard the words, certainly not taken in their import. At first I thought he had been put out by receiving so broadly comic an answer to his question, feeling perhaps his dignity was compromised. That would have been a possibility, though unlike Gwatkin, because he approved coarseness of phrase as being military, even though he might be touchy about his own importance. It was then I realized he had fallen into one of his trances in which all around was forgotten: the *Alarm*, the Sergeant-Major, Kedward, myself, the Battalion, the army, the war itself.

'Right, Sergeant-Major,' he said, speaking abruptly, as if he had just woken from a dream. 'See those words are promulgated throughout the Company. That's all. You can fall out.'

By this time it was summer and very hot. The Germans had invaded the Netherlands, Churchill become Prime Minister. I read in the papers that Sir Magnus Donners had been appointed to the ministerial post for which he had long been tipped. The Battalion was required to send men to reinforce one of the Regular Battalions in France. There was much grumbling at this, because we were supposed to be something more than a draft-finding unit. Gwatkin was particularly outraged by this order, and the loss of two or three good men from his company. Otherwise things went on much the same at Castlemallock, the great trees leafy in the park, all water dried up in the basins of the fountains. Then, one Saturday evening, Gwatkin suggested he and I should walk as far as the town and have a drink together. There was no Anti-Gas course in progress at that moment. Kedward was Duty Officer. As a rule, Gwatkin was rarely to be seen in the Mess after dinner. No one knew what he did with himself during those hours. It was possible that he retired to his room to study the *Field Service Pocket Book* or some other military manual. I never guessed he might make a practice of visiting the town. However, that was what his next remark seemed to suggest.

'I've found a new place – better than M'Coy's,' he said rather challengingly. 'The porter there is bloody marvellous. I've drunk it now several times. I'd like to have your opinion.'

I had once visited M'Coy's with Kedward. It was, in fact, the only pub I had entered since being stationed at Castle-mallock. I found no difficulty in believing M'Coy's could be improved upon as a drinking resort, but it was hard to guess why Gwatkin's transference of custom from M'Coy's to this new place should be an important issue, as Gwatkin's manner seemed to suggest. In any case, it was unlike him to suggest an evening's drinking. I agreed to make the trip. It would have been unfriendly, rather impolitic, to have refused. A walk into the town would be a change. Besides, I was heartily sick of *Esmond*. When dinner was at an end, Gwatkin and I set off together. We tramped along the drive in silence. We had almost reached the road, when he made an unexpected remark.

'It won't be easy to go back to the Bank after all this,' he said.

'All what?'

'The army. The life we're leading.'

'Don't you like the Bank?'

As Kedward had explained at the outset, most of the Battalion's officers worked in banks. This was one of the aspects of the unit which gave a peculiar sense of uniformity, of existing almost within a family. Even though one was personally outside this sept, its homogeneous character in itself offered a certain cordiality, rather than the reverse, to an intruder. Until now, no one had given the impression he specially disliked that employment, over and above the manner in which most people grumble about their own job, whatever it is. Indeed, all seemed to belong to a caste, clearly defined, powerful on its home ground, almost a secret society, with perfect understanding between its members where outward things were concerned. The initiates might complain about specific drawbacks, but never in a way to imply hankering for another occupation. To hear absolute revolt expressed was new to me. Gwatkin seemed to relent a little when he spoke again.

'Oh, the bloody Bank's not that bad,' he said laughing, 'but it's a bit different being here. Something better to do than open jammed Home Safes and enter the contents in the Savings Bank Ledger.'

'What's a Home Safe, and why does it jam?'

'Kids' money-boxes.'

'Do the children jam them?'

'Parents, usually. Want a bit of ready. Try to break into the safe with a tin-opener. The bloody things arrive back at the office with the mechanism smashed to pieces. When the cashier gets in at last, he finds three pennies, a halfpenny and a tiddlywink.'

'Still, brens get jammed too. It's traditional for machine-guns – you know, the Gatling's jammed and the Colonel's dead. Somebody wrote a poem about it. One might do the same about a Home Safe and the manager.'

Gwatkin ignored such disenchantment.

'The bren's a soldier's job,' he said.

'What about Pay Parades and Kit Inspection? They're soldiers' jobs. It doesn't make them any more enjoy-able.'

'Better than taking the Relief Till to Treorchy on a market day, doling out the money from a bag in old Mrs Jones-the-Milk's front parlour. What sort of life is that for a man?'

'You find the army more glamorous, Rowland?'

'Yes,' he said eagerly, 'glamorous. That's the word. Don't you feel you want to do more in life than sit in front of a row of ledgers all day long? I know I do.'

'Sitting at Castlemallock listening to the wireless announcing the German army is pushing towards the Channel ports isn't particularly inspiring either – especially after an hour with the CQMS trying to sort out the Company's sock situation, or searching for a pair of battle-dress trousers to fit Evans, J., who is such an abnormal shape.'

'No, Nick, but we'll be in it soon. We can't stay at Castle-mallock for ever.'

'Why not?'

'Anyway, Castlemallock's not so bad.'

He seemed desperately anxious to prevent me from speaking hardly of Castlemallock.

'I agree the park is pretty. That is about the best you can say for it.'

'It's come to mean a lot to me,' Gwatkin said.

His voice was full of excitement. I had been quite wrong in supposing him disillusioned with the army. On the contrary, he was keener than ever. I could not understand why his enthusiasm had suddenly risen to such new heights. I did not for a moment, as we walked along, guess what the answer was going to be. By that time we had reached the pub judged by Gwatkin to be superior to M'Coy's. The façade, it had to be admitted, was remarkably similar to M'Coy's, though in a back alley, rather than the main street of the town. Otherwise, the place was the usual large cottage, the ground floor of which had been converted to the purposes of a tavern. I followed Gwatkin through the low door. The interior was dark, the smell uninviting. No one was about when we entered, but voices came from a room beyond the bar. Gwatkin tapped the counter with a coin.

'Maureen . . .' he called.

He used that same peculiar cooing note he employed when answering the telephone.

'Hull-ooe . . . hull-ooe . . .' he would say, when he spoke into the instrument. Somehow that manner of answering seemed quite inappropriate to the rest of his character.

'I wonder whether what we call politeness isn't just weakness,' he had once remarked.

This cooing certainly conveyed no impression of ruthless moral strength, neither on the telephone, nor at the counter of this pub. No one appeared. Gwatkin pronounced the name again.

'Maur-een . . . Maur-een . . .'

Still nothing happened. Then a girl came through the door leading to the back of the house. She was short and thick-set, with a pale face and lots of black hair. I thought her good-looking, with that suggestion of an animal, almost a touch of monstrosity, some men find very attractive. Barnby once remarked: 'The Victorians saw only refinement in women, it's their coarseness makes them irresistible to me.' Barnby would certainly have liked this girl.

'Why, it would be yourself again, Captain Gwatkin,' she said.

She smiled and put her hands on her hips. Her teeth were very indifferent, her eyes in deep, dark sockets, striking.

'Yes, Maureen.'

Gwatkin did not seem to know what to say next. He glanced in my direction, as if to seek encouragement. This speechlessness was unlike him. However, Maureen continued to talk herself.

'And with another military gentleman too,' she said. 'What'll ye be taking this evening now? Will it be porter, or is it a wee drop of whiskey this night, I'll be wondering, Captain?'

Gwatkin turned to me.

'Which, Nick?'

'Guinness.'

'That goes for me too,' he said. 'Two pints of porter, Maureen. I only drink whiskey when I'm feeling down. Tonight we're out for a good time, aren't we, Nick?'

He spoke in an oddly self-conscious manner. I had never seen him like this before. We seated ourselves at a small table by the wall. Maureen began to draw the stout. Gwatkin watched her fixedly, while she allowed the froth to settle,

183

scraping its foam from the surface of the liquid with a saucer, then returning the glass under the tap to be refilled to the brim. When she brought the drinks across to us, she took a chair, refusing to have anything herself.

'And what would be the name of this officer?' she asked.

'Second-Lieutenant Jenkins,' said Gwatkin, 'he's one of the officers of my company.'

'Is he now. That would be grand and all.'

'We're good friends,' said Gwatkin soberly.

'Then why haven't ye brought him to see me before, Captain Gwatkin, I'll be asking ye?'

'Ah, Maureen, you see we work so hard,' said Gwatkin. 'We can't always be coming to see you, do you understand. That's just a treat for once in a while.'

'Get along with ye,' she said, smiling provocatively and showing discoloured teeth again, 'yourself's down here often enough, Captain Gwatkin.'

'Not as often as I'd like, Maureen.'

Gwatkin had now recovered from the embarrassment which seemed to have overcome him on first entering the pub. He was no longer tongue-tied. Indeed, his manner suggested he was, in fact, more at ease with women than men, the earlier constraint merely a momentary attack of nerves.

'And what would it be you're all so busy with now?' she asked. 'Is it drilling and all that? I expect so.'

'Drilling is some of it, Maureen,' said Gwatkin. 'But we have to practise all kind of other training too. Modern war is a very complicated matter, you must understand.'

This made her laugh again.

'I'd have ye know my great-uncle was in the Connaught Rangers,' she said, 'and a fine figure of a man he was, I can promise ye. Why, they say he was the best-looking young fellow of his day in all County Monaghan. And brave too.

184

Why, they say he killed a dozen Germans with his bayonet when they tried to capture him. The Germans didn't like to meet the Irish in the last war.'

'Well, it's a risk the Germans won't have to run in this one,' said Gwatkin, speaking more gruffly than might have been expected in the circumstances. 'Even here in the North there's no conscription, and you see plenty of young men out of uniform.'

'Why, ye wouldn't be taking all the young fellows away from us, would ye?' she asked, rolling her eyes. 'It's lonely we'd be if they all went to the war.'

'Maybe Hitler will decide the South is where he wants to land his invasion force,' said Gwatkin. 'Then where will all your young men be, I'd like to know.'

'Oh God,' she said, throwing up her hands. 'Don't say it of the old blackguard. Would he do such a thing? You think he truly may, Captain Gwatkin, do ye?'

'Shouldn't be surprised,' said Gwatkin.

'Do you come from the other side of the Border yourself?' I asked her.

'Why, sure I do,' she said smiling. 'And how were you guessing that, Lieutenant Jenkins?'

'I just had the idea.'

'Would it be my speech?' she said.

'Perhaps.'

She lowered her voice.

'Maybe, too, you thought I was different from these Ulster people,' she said, 'them that is so hard and fond of money and all.'

'That's it, I expect.'

'So you've guessed Maureen's home country, Nick,' said Gwatkin. 'I tell her we must treat her as a security risk and not go speaking any secrets in front of her, as she's a neutral.'

Maureen began to protest, but at that moment two young men in riding breeches and leggings came into the pub. She rose from the chair to serve them. Gwatkin fell into one of his silences. I thought he was probably reflecting how odd was the fact that Maureen seemed just as happy talking and laughing with a couple of local civilians, as with the dashing officer types he seemed to envisage ourselves. At least he stared at the young men, an unremarkable pair, as if there were something about them that interested him. Then it turned out Gwatkin's train of thought had returned to dissatisfaction with his own peacetime employment.

'Farmers, I suppose,' he said. 'My grandfather was a farmer. He didn't spend his time in a stuffy office.'

'Where did he farm?'

'Up by the Shropshire border.'

'And your father took to office life?'

'That was it. My dad's in insurance. His firm sent him to another part of the country.'

'Do you know that Shropshire border yourself?'

'We've been up there for a holiday. I expect you've heard of the great Lord Aberavon?'

'I have, as a matter of fact.'

'The farm was on his estate.'

I had never thought of Lord Aberavon (first and last of his peerage) as a figure likely to go down to posterity as 'great', though the designation might no doubt reasonably be applied by those living in the neighbourhood. His name was merely memorable to myself as deceased owner of Mr Deacon's *Boyhood of Cyrus,* the picture in the Walpole-Wilsons' hall, which always made me think of Barbara Goring when I had been in love with her in pre-historic times. Lord Aberavon had been Barbara Goring's grandfather; Eleanor Walpole-Wilson's grandfather too. I wondered what had happened to Barbara, whether her husband,

Johnny Pardoe (who also owned a house in the country of which Gwatkin spoke) had been recalled to the army. Eleanor, lifelong friend of my sister-in-law, Norah Tolland, was now, like Norah herself, driving cars for some women's service. Gwatkin by his words had certainly conjured up the past. He looked at me rather uncomfortably, as if he could read my mind, and knew I felt suddenly carried back into an earlier time sequence. He also had the air of wanting to elaborate what he had said, yet feared he might displease, or, at least, not amuse me. He cleared his throat and took a gulp of stout.

'You remember Lord Aberavon's family name?' he asked.

'Why, now I come to think of it, wasn't it "Gwatkin"?'

'It was – same as mine. He was called Rowland too.'

He said that very seriously.

'I'd quite forgotten. Was he a relation?'

Gwatkin laughed apologetically.

'No, of course he wasn't,' he said.

'Well, he might have been.'

'What makes you think so?'

'You never know with names.'

'If so, it was miles distant,' said Gwatkin.

'That's what I mean.'

'I mean so distant, he wasn't a relation at all,' Gwatkin said. 'As a matter of fact my grandfather, the old farmer I was talking about, used to swear we were the same lot, if you went back far enough – right back, I mean.'

'Why not, indeed?'

I remembered reading one of Lord Aberavon's obituaries, which had spoken of the incalculable antiquity of his line, notwithstanding his own modest start in a Liverpool shipping firm. The details had appealed to me.

'Wasn't it a very old family?'

'So they say.'

187

'Going back to Vortigern – by one of his own daughters? I'm sure I read that.'

Gwatkin looked uncertain again, as if he felt the discussion had suddenly got out of hand, that there was something inadmissible about my turning out to know so much about Gwatkin origins. Perhaps he was justified in thinking that.

'Who was Vortigern?' he asked uneasily.

'A fifth-century British prince. You remember – he invited Hengist and Horsa. All that. They came to help him. Then he couldn't get rid of them.'

It was no good. Gwatkin looked utterly blank. Hengist and Horsa meant nothing to him; less, if anything, than Vortigern. He was unimpressed by the sinister splendour of the derivations indicated as potentially his own; indeed, totally uninterested in them. Thought of Lord Aberavon's business acumen kindled him more than any steep ascent in the genealogies of ancient Celtic Britain. His romanticism, though innate, was essentially limited – as often happens – by sheer lack of imagination. Vortigern, I saw, was better forgotten. I had deflected Gwatkin's flow of thought by ill-timed pedantry.

'I expect my grandfather made up most of the stuff,' he said. 'Just wanted to be thought related to a man of the same name who left three-quarters of a million.'

He now appeared to regret ever having let fall this confidence regarding his own family background, refusing to be drawn into further discussion about his relations, their history or the part of the country they came from. I thought how odd, how typical of our island – unlike the Continent or America in that respect – that Gwatkin should put forward this claim, possibly in its essentials reasonable enough, be at once attracted and repelled by its implications, yet show no wish to carry the discussion further. Was it surprising that,

in such respects, foreigners should find us hard to understand? Odd, too, I felt obstinately, that the incestuous
Vortigern should link Gwatkin with Barbara Goring and
Eleanor Walpole-Wilson. Perhaps it all stemmed from that
ill-judged negotiation with Hengist and Horsa. Anyway, it
linked me, too, with Gwatkin in a strange way. We had
some more stout. Maureen was now too deeply involved in
local gossip with the young farmers, if farmers they were,
to pay further attention to us. Their party had been increased by the addition of an older man of similar type, with
reddish hair and the demeanour of a professional humorist.
There was a good deal of laughter. We had to fetch our
drinks from the counter ourselves. This seemed to depress
Gwatkin still further. We talked rather drearily of the affairs
of the Company. More customers came in, all apparently on
the closest terms with Maureen. Gwatkin and I drank a fair
amount of stout. Finally, it was time to return.

'Shall we go back to barracks?'

This designation of Castlemallock on Gwatkin's part
added nothing to its charms. He turned towards the bar as
we were leaving.

'Good night, Maureen.'

She was having too good a joke with the red-haired
humorist to hear him.

'Good night, Maureen,' Gwatkin said again, rather
louder.

She looked up, then came round to the front of the bar.

'Good night to you, Captain Gwatkin, and to you,
Lieutenant Jenkins,' she said, 'and don't be so long in
coming to see me again, the pair of ye, or it's vexed with you
both I'd be.'

We waved farewell. Gwatkin did not open his mouth
until we reached the outskirts of the town. Suddenly he
took a deep breath. He seemed about to speak; then, as if he

could not give sufficient weight to the words while we walked, he stopped and faced me.

'Isn't she marvellous?' he said.

'Who, Maureen?'

'Yes, of course.'

'She seemed a nice girl.'

'Is that all you thought, Nick?'

He spoke with real reproach.

'Why, yes. What about you? You've really taken a fancy to her, have you?'

'I think she's absolutely wonderful,' he said.

We had had, as I have said, a fair amount to drink – the first time since joining the unit I had drunk more than two or three half-pints of beer – but no more than to loosen the tongue, not sufficient to cause amorous hallucination. Gwatkin was obviously expressing what he really felt, not speaking in an exaggerated manner to indicate light desire. The reason of those afternoon trances, that daydreaming while he nursed the Company's rubber-stamp, were now all at once apparent, affection for Castlemallock also explained. Gwatkin was in love. All love affairs are different cases, yet, at the same time, each is the same case. Moreland used to say love was like sea-sickness. For a time everything round you heaved about and you felt you were going to die – then you staggered down the gangway to dry land, and a minute or two later could hardly remember what you had suffered, why you had been feeling so ghastly. Gwatkin was at the earlier stage.

'Have you done anything about it?'

'About what?'

'About Maureen.'

'How do you mean?'

'Well, taken her out, something like that.'

'Oh, no.'

'Why not?'

'What would be the good?'

'I don't know. I should have thought it might be enjoyable, if you feel like that about her.'

'But I'd have to tell her I'm married.'

'Tell her by all means. Put your cards on the table.'

'But do you think she'd come?'

'I shouldn't wonder.'

'You mean – try and seduce her?'

'I suppose that was roughly the line indicated – in due course.'

He looked at me astonished. I felt a shade uncomfortable, rather like Mephistopheles unexpectedly receiving a hopelessly negative reaction from Faust. Such an incident in opera, I thought, might suggest a good basis for an *aria*.

'Some of the chaps you meet in the army never seem to have heard of women,' Odo Stevens had said. 'You never know in the Mess whether you're sitting next to a sex-maniac of nineteen or a middle-aged man who doesn't know the facts of life.'

In Gwatkin's case, I was surprised by such scruples, even though I now recalled his attitude towards the case of Sergeant Pendry. In general, the younger officers of the Battalion were, like Kedward, engaged, or, like Breeze, recently married. They might, like Pumphrey, talk in a free and easy manner, but it was their girl or their wife who clearly preoccupied them. In any case, there had been no time for girls for anyone, married or single, before we reached Castlemallock. Gwatkin was certainly used to the idea of Pumphrey trying to have a romp with any barmaid who might be available. He had never seemed to disapprove of that. I knew nothing of his married life, except what Kedward had told me, that Gwatkin had known his wife all their lives, had previously wanted to marry Breeze's sister.

'But I'm married,' Gwatkin said again.

He spoke rather desperately.

'I'm not insisting you should take Maureen out. I only asked if you had.'

'And Maureen isn't that sort of girl.'

'How do you know?'

He spoke angrily this time. Then he laughed, seeing, I suppose, that was a silly thing to say.

'You've only met Maureen for the first time, Nick. You don't realize at all what she's like. You think all that talk of hers means she's a bad girl. She isn't. I've often been alone with her in that bar. You'd be surprised. She's like a child.'

'Some children know a thing or two.'

Gwatkin did not even bother to consider that point of view.

'I don't know why I think her quite so wonderful,' he admitted, 'but I just do. It worries me that I think about her all the time. I've found myself forgetting things, matters of duty, I mean.'

'Do you go down there every night?'

'Whenever I can. I haven't been able to get away lately owing to one thing and another. All this security check, for instance.'

'Does she know this?'

'Know what?'

'Does Maureen know you're mad about her?'

'I don't think so,' he said.

He spoke the words very humbly, quite unlike his usual tone. Then he assumed a rough, official voice again.

'I thought it would be better if I told you about it all, Nick,' he said. 'I hoped the thing wouldn't go on inside me all the time so much, if I let it out to someone. Unless it stops a bit, I'm frightened I'll make a fool of myself in some way to do with commanding the Company. A girl like Maureen makes everything go out of your head.'

'Of course.'

'You know what I mean.'

'Yes.'

Gwatkin still did not seem entirely satisfied.

'You really think I ought to take her out?'

'That's what a lot of people would do – probably a lot of people are doing already.'

'Oh, no, I'm sure they're not, if you mean from the School of Chemical Warfare. I've never seen any of them there. It was quite a chance I went in myself. I was looking for a short cut. Maureen was standing by the door, and I asked her the way. Her parents own the pub. She's not just a barmaid.'

'Anyway, there's no harm in trying, barmaid or not.'

During the rest of the walk back to Castlemallock, Gwatkin did not refer again to the subject of Maureen. He talked of routine matters until we parted to our rooms.

'The Mess will be packed out again tomorrow night,' he said. 'Another Anti-Gas course starts next week. I suppose all that business will begin again of wanting to take my men away from me for their bloody demonstrations. Well, there it is.'

'Good night, Rowland.'

'Good night, Nick.'

I made for the stables, where I shared a groom's room with Kedward, rather like the sleeping quarters of Albert and Bracey at Stonehurst. As Duty Officer that night, Kedward would not be there and I should have the bedroom to myself, always rather a treat. I was aware now that it had been a mistake to drink so much stout. Tomorrow was Sunday, so there would be comparatively little to do. I thought how awful Bithel must feel on parade the mornings after his occasional bouts of drinking. Reflecting on people often portends their own appearance. So it was in the case of Bithel. He was among the students to arrive at the School the following week. We should, indeed, all have been prepared for Bithel to be sent on an Anti-Gas course. It was a way of getting rid of him, pending final banishment from the Battalion, which, as Gwatkin said, was bound to come sooner or later. I was sitting at one of the trestle tables of the Mess, addressing an envelope, when Bithel peered through the door. He was fingering his ragged moustache and smiling nervously. When he saw me, he made towards the table at once.

'Nice to meet again,' he said, speaking as usual as if he expected a rebuff. 'Haven't seen you since the Battalion moved.'

'How have you been?'

'Getting rockets, as usual,' he said.

'Maelgwyn-Jones?'

'That fellow's got a positive down on me,' Bithel said, 'but I don't think it will be for long now.'

'Why not?'

'I'm probably leaving the Battalion.'

'Why's that?'

'There's talk of my going up to Division.'

'On the staff?'

'Not exactly – a command.'

'At Div HQ?'

'Only a subsidiary command, of course. I shall be sorry to leave the Regiment in some ways, if it comes off, but not altogether sorry to see the back of Maelgwyn-Jones.'

'What is it? Or is that a secret?'

Bithel lowered his voice in his accustomed manner when speaking of his own affairs, as if there were always a hint of something dubious about them.

'The Mobile Laundry Unit,' he said.

'You're going to command it?'

'If I'm picked. There are at least two other names in for it from other units in the Division, I happen to know – one of them very eligible. As it happens, I have done publicity work for one of the laundries in my own neighbourhood, so I have quite a chance. In fact, that should stand very much in my favour. The CO seems very anxious for me to get the appointment. He's been on the phone to Division about it himself more than once. Very good of him.'

'What rank does the job carry?'

'A subaltern's command. Still, it's promotion in a way. What you might call a step. The war news doesn't look very good, does it, since the Belgian Government surrendered.'

'What's the latest? I missed the last news.'

'Fighting on the coast. One of our Regular Battalions has been in action, I was told this morning. Got knocked about pretty badly. Do you remember a rather good-looking boy called Jones, D. Very fair.'

'He was in my platoon – went out on the draft.'

'He's been killed. Daniels, my batman, told me that. Daniels gets all the news.'

'Jones, D. was killed, was he. Anyone else from our unit?'

'Progers, did you know him?'

'The driver with a squint?'

'That's the fellow. Used to bring the stuff up to the Mess sometimes. Dark curly hair and a lisp. He's gone too. Talking of messing, what's it like here?'

'We've had beef twice a day for just over a fortnight – thirty-seven times running, to be precise.'

'What does it taste like?'

'Goat covered with brown custard powder.'

We settled down to talk about army food. When I next saw CSM Cadwallader, I asked if he had heard about Jones, D. Corporal Gwylt was standing nearby.

'Indeed, I had not, sir. So a bullet got him.'

'Something did.'

'Always an unlucky boy, Jones, D.,' said CSM Cadwallader.

'Remember how sick he was when we came over the water, Sergeant-Major?' said Corporal Gwylt, 'terrible sick.'

'That I do.'

'Never did I see a boy so sick,' said Corporal Gwylt, 'nor a man neither.'

This was the week leading up to the withdrawal through Dunkirk, so Jones, D. and Progers were not the only fatal casualties known to me personally at that period. Among these, Robert Tolland, serving in France with his Field Security Section, was also killed. The news came in a letter from Isobel. Nothing was revealed, then or later, of the circumstances of Robert's death. So far as it went, he died as mysteriously as he had lived, like many other young men to whom war put an end, an unsolved problem. Had Robert, as Chips Lovell alleged, lived a secret life with 'night-club hostesses old enough to be his mother?' Would he have made a lot of money in his export house trading with the Far East? Might he have married Flavia Wisebite? As in musical chairs, the piano stops suddenly, someone is left without a seat, petrified for all time in their attitude of that particular moment. The balance-sheet is struck there and then, a matter of luck whether its calculations have much bearing, one way or the other, on the commerce conducted. Some die in an apparently suitable manner, others like Robert on the field of battle with a certain incongruity. Yet Fate had ordained this end for him. Or had Robert decided for himself? Had he set aside the chance of a commission to fulfil a destiny that required him to fall in France; or was Flavia's luck so irredeemably bad that her association with him was sufficient – as Dr Trelawney might have said – to summon the Slayer of Osiris, her pattern of life, rather than Robert's, dominating the issue of life and death? Robert could even have died to escape her. The potential biographies of those who die young possess the mystic dignity of a headless statue, the poetry of enigmatic passages in an unfinished or mutilated manuscript, unburdened with contrived or banal ending. These were disturbing days, lived out in suffocating summer heat. While they went by, Gwatkin, for some reason, became more cheerful. The war increasingly revealed persons stimulated by disaster. I thought Gwatkin might be one of this fairly numerous order. However, there turned out to be another cause for his good spirits. He revealed the reason one afternoon.

'I took your advice, Nick,' he said.

We were alone together in the Company Office.

'About the storage of those live Mills bombs?'

Gwatkin shook his head, at the same time swallowing uncomfortably, as if the very thought of live grenades and where they were to be stored, brought an immediate sense of guilt.

'No, not about the Mills bombs,' he said, 'I'm still thinking over the best place to keep them – I don't want any interference from the Ordnance people. I mean about Maureen.'

For a moment the name conveyed nothing. Then I remembered the evening in the pub: Maureen, the girl who had so greatly taken Gwatkin's fancy. Thinking things over the next day, I had attributed his remarks to the amount of stout we had drunk. Maureen had been dismissed from my mind.

'What about Maureen?'

'I asked her to come out with me.'

'You did?'

'Yes.'

'What did she say?'

197

'She agreed.'

'I said she would.'

'It was bloody marvellous.'

'Splendid.'

'Nick,' he said, 'I'm serious. Don't laugh. I really want to thank you, Nick, for making me take action – not hang about like a fool. That's my weakness. Like the day we were in support and I made such a balls of it.'

'And Maureen's all right?'

'She's wonderful.'

That was all Gwatkin said. He gave no account of the outing. I should have liked to hear a little about it, but clearly he regarded the latest development in their relationship as too sacred to describe in detail. I saw that Kedward, in some matters no great psychologist, had been right in saying that when Gwatkin took a fancy to a girl it was 'like having the measles'. This business of Maureen could be regarded only as a judgment on Gwatkin for supposing Sergeant Pendry's difficulties easy of solution. Now, he had himself been struck down by Aphrodite for his pride in refusing incense at her altars. The goddess was going to chastise him. In any case, there was nothing very surprising in this sort of thing happening, when, even after an exhausting day's training, the camp-bed was nightly a rack of desire, where no depravity of the imagination was unbegotten. No doubt much mutual irritation was caused by this constraint, particularly, for example, something like Gwatkin's detestation of Bithel.

'God,' he said, when he set eyes on him at Castlemallock, 'that bloody man has followed us here.'

Bithel himself was quite unaware of the ferment of rage he aroused in Gwatkin. At least he showed no sign of recognising Gwatkin's hatred, even at times positively thrusting himself on Gwatkin's society. Some persons feel drawn towards those who dislike them, or are at least determined to overcome opposition of that sort. Bithel may have regarded Gwatkin's unfriendliness as a challenge. Whatever the reason, he always made a point of talking to Gwatkin whenever opportunity arose, showing himself equally undeterred by verbal rebuff or crushing moroseness. However, Gwatkin's attitude in repelling Bithel's conversational advances was not entirely based on a simple brutality. Their relationship was more complicated than that. The code of behaviour in the army which Gwatkin had set himself did not allow his own comportment with any brother officer to reach a pitch of unfriendliness he would certainly have shown to a civilian acquaintance disliked as much as he disliked Bithel. This code – Gwatkin's picture of it, that is – allowed, indeed positively kindled, a blaze of snubs directed towards Bithel, at the same time preventing, so to speak, any final dismissal of him as a person too contemptible to waste time upon. Bithel was a brother officer; for that reason always, in the last resort, handed a small dole by Gwatkin, usually in the form of an incitement to do better, to pull himself together. Besides, Gwatkin, with many others, could never finally be reconciled to abandoning the legend of Bithel's VC brother. Mythical prestige still hung faintly about Bithel on that account. Such legends, once taken shape, endlessly proliferate. Certainly I never heard Bithel himself make any public effort to extirpate the story. He may have feared that even the exacerbated toleration of himself Gwatkin was at times prepared to show would fade away, if the figure of the VC brother in the background were exorcised entirely.

'Coming to sit with the Regiment tonight, Captain Gwatkin,' Bithel would say when he joined us; then add in his muttered, confidential tone: 'Between you and me, there're not much of a crowd on this course. Pretty second-rate.'

Bithel always found difficulty in addressing Gwatkin as 'Rowland'. In early days, Gwatkin had protested once or twice at this formality, but I think he secretly rather enjoyed the respect implied by its use. Bithel, like everyone else, possessed one or more initial, but no one ever knew, or at least seemed to have forgotten, the name or names for which they stood. He was always called 'Bith' or 'Bithy', in some ways a more intimate form of address, which Gwatkin, on his side, could never bring himself to employ. The relaxation Bithel styled 'sitting with the Regiment' took place in an alcove, unofficially reserved by Gwatkin, Kedward and myself for our use as part of the permanent establishment of Castlemallock, as opposed to its shifting population of Anti-Gas students. The window seat where I used to read *Esmond* was in this alcove, and we would occasionally have a drink there. Since the night when he had first joined the Battalion, Bithel's drinking, though steady when drink was available, had not been excessive, except on such occasions as Christmas or the New Year, when no great exception could be taken. He would get rather fuddled, but no more. Bithel himself sometimes referred to his own moderation in this respect.

'Got to keep an eye on the old Mess bill,' he would say. 'The odd gin-and-orange adds up. I have had the CO after me once already about my wine bill. Got to mind my p's and q's in that direction.'

As things turned out at Castlemallock, encouragement to overstep the mark came, unexpectedly, from the army authorities themselves. At least that was the way Bithel himself afterwards explained matters.

'It was all the fault of that silly old instruction,' he said. 'I was tired out and got absolutely misled by it.'

Part of the training on the particular Castlemallock course Bithel was attending consisted in passing without a mask through the gas-chamber. Sooner or later, every rank in the army had to comply with this routine, but students of an Anti-Gas course naturally experienced a somewhat more elaborate ritual in that respect than others who merely took their turn with a unit. A subsequent aspect of the test was first-aid treatment, which recommended, among other restoratives, for one poisonous gas sampled, 'alcohol in moderate quantities'. On the day of Bithel's misadventure, the gas-chamber was the last item on the day's programme for those on the course. When Bithel's class was dismissed after this test, some took the advice of the text-book and had a drink; others, because they did not like alcohol, or from motives of economy, confined themselves to hot sweet tea. Among those who took alcohol, no one but Bithel neglected the manual's admonition to be moderate in this remedial treatment.

'Old Bith's having a drink or two this evening, isn't he,' Kedward remarked, even before dinner.

Bithel always talked thickly, and, like most people who habitually put an unusually large amount of drink away, there was in general no great difference between him drunk or sober. The stage of intoxication he had reached made itself known only on such rare occasions as his dance round the dummy. At Castlemallock that night, he merely pottered about the ante-room, talking first to one group of anti-gas students, then to another, when, bored with him, people moved away. He did not join us in the alcove until the end of the evening. Everyone used to retire early, so that Gwatkin, Kedward and myself were alone in the room by the time Bithel arrived there. We were discussing the German advance. Gwatkin's analysis of the tactical situation had continued for some time, and I was making preparations to move off to bed, when Bithel came towards us. He sat down heavily, without making his usual rather apologetic request to Gwatkin that he might be included in the party. For a time he listened to the conversation without speaking. Then he caught the word 'Paris'.

'Ever been to Paris, Captain Gwatkin?' he asked.

Gwatkin shot out a glance of profound disapproval.

'No,' he said sharply.

The answer conveyed that Gwatkin considered the question a ridiculous one, as if Bithel had asked if he had ever visited Lhasa or Tierra del Fuego. He continued to lecture Kedward on the principles of mobile warfare.

'I've been to Paris,' said Bithel.

He made a whistling sound with his lips to express a sense of great conviviality.

'Went there for a weekend once,' he said.

Gwatkin looked furious, but said nothing. A Mess waiter appeared and began to collect glasses on a tray. He was, as it happened, the red-faced, hulking young soldier, who, weeping and complaining his back hurt, had made such a disturbance outside the Company Office. Now, he seemed more cheerful, answering Bithel's request for a final drink with the information that the bar was closed. He said this with the satisfaction always displayed by waiters and barmen at being in a position to make that particular announcement.

'Just one small Irish,' said Bithel. 'That's all I want.'

'Bar's closed, sir.'

'It can't be yet.'

Bithel tried to look at his watch, but the figures evidently eluded him.

'I can't believe the bar's closed.'

'Mess Sergeant's just said so.'

'Do get me another, Emmot – it is Emmot, isn't it?'

'That's right, sir.'

202

'Do, do get me a whiskey, Emmot.'

'Can't sir. Bar's closed.'

'But it can be opened again.'

'Can't, sir.'

'Open it just for one moment – just for one small whiskey.'

'Sergeant says no, sir.'

'Ask him again.'

'Bar's closed, sir.'

'I beseech you, Emmot.'

Bithel rose to his feet. Afterwards, I was never certain what happened. I was sitting on the same side as Bithel and, as he turned away, his back was towards me. He lurched suddenly forward. This may have been a stumble, since some of the floorboards were loose at that place. The amount he had drunk did not necessarily have anything to do with Bithel's sudden loss of balance. Alternatively, his action could have been deliberate, intended as a physical appeal to Emmot's better feelings. Bithel's wheedling tone of voice a minute before certainly gave colour to that interpretation. If so, I am sure Bithel intended no more than to rest his hand on Emmot's shoulder in a facetious gesture, perhaps grip his arm. Such actions might have been thought undignified, bad for discipline, no worse. However, for one reason or another, Bithel lunged his body forward, and, either to save himself from falling, or to give emphasis to his request for a last drink, threw his arms round Emmot's neck. There, for a split second, he hung. There could be no doubt about the outward impression this posture conveyed. It looked exactly as if Bithel were kissing Emmot – in farewell, rather than in passion. Perhaps he was. Whether or not that were so, Emmot dropped the tray, breaking a couple of glasses, at the same time letting out a discordant sound. Gwatkin jumped to his feet. His face was white. He was trembling with rage.

'Mr Bithel,' he said, 'consider yourself under arrest.'

I had begun to laugh, but now saw things were serious. This was no joking matter. There was going to be a row. Gwatkin's eyes were fanatical.

'Mr Kedward,' he said, 'go and fetch your cap and belt.'

The alcove where we had been sitting was not far from the door leading to the great hall. There, on a row of hooks, caps and belts were left, before entering the confines of the Mess, so Kedward had not far to go. Afterwards, Kedward told me he did not immediately grasp the import of Gwatkin's order. He obeyed merely on the principle of not questioning an instruction from his Company Commander. Meanwhile, Emmot began picking up fragments of broken glass from the floor. He did not seem specially surprised by what had happened. Indeed, considering how far I knew he could go in the direction of hysterical loss of control, Emmot carried off the whole situation pretty well. Perhaps he understood Bithel better than the rest of us. Gwatkin, who now seemed to be in his element, told Emmot to be off quickly, to clear up the rest of the debris in the morning. Emmot did not need further encouragement to put an end to the day's work. He retired from the ante-room at once with his tray and most of the broken glass. Bithel still stood. As he had been put under arrest, this position was no doubt militarily correct. He swayed a little, smiling to himself rather foolishly. Kedward returned, wearing his cap and buckling on his Sam Browne.

'Escort Mr Bithel to his room, Mr Kedward,' said Gwatkin. 'He will not leave it without permission. When he does so, it will be under the escort of an officer. He will not wear a belt, nor carry a weapon.'

Bithel gave a despairing look, as if cut to the quick to be forbidden a weapon, but he seemed to have taken in more or less what was happening, even to be extracting a certain masochistic zest from the ritual. Gwatkin jerked his head towards the door. Bithel turned and made slowly towards it, moving as if towards immediate execution. Kedward followed. I was relieved that Gwatkin had chosen Kedward for this duty, rather than myself, no doubt because he was senior in rank, approximating more nearly to Bithel's two pips. When they were gone, Gwatkin turned to me. He seemed suddenly exhausted by this output of disciplinary energy.

'There was nothing else I could do,' he said.

'I wasn't sure what happened.'

'You did not see?'

'Not exactly.'

'Bithel *kissed* an Other Rank.'

'Are you certain?'

'Haven't you got eyes?'

'I could only see Bithel's back. I thought he lost his balance.'

'In any case, Bithel was grossly drunk.'

'That's undeniable.'

'To put him under arrest was my duty. It was the only course I could follow. The only course any officer could follow.'

'What's the next step?'

Gwatkin frowned.

'Cut along to the Company Office, Nick,' he said in a rather calmer tone of voice. 'You know where the *Manual of Military Law* is kept. Bring it to me here. I don't want Idwal to come back and find me gone. He'll think I've retired to bed. I must have a further word with him.'

When I returned with the *Manual of Military Law*, Gwatkin was just finishing his instructions to Kedward. At the end of these he curtly said good night to us both. Then he went off, the Manual under his arm, his face stern. Kedward looked at me and grinned. He was evidently surprised, not absolutely staggered, by what had taken place. It was all part of the day's work to him.

'What a thing to happen,' he said.

'Going to lead to a lot of trouble.'

'Old Bith was properly pissed.'

'He was.'

'I could hardly get him up the stairs.'

'Did you have to take his arm?'

'Heaved him up somehow,' said Kedward. 'Felt like a copper.'

'What happened when you arrived in his room?'

'Luckily the other chap there went sick and left the course yesterday. Bith's got the room to himself, so things weren't as awkward as they might have been. He just tumbled on to the bed, and I left him. Off to bed myself now. You're for the Company Office tonight, aren't you?'

'I am.'

'Good night, Nick.'

'Good night, Idwal.'

The scene had been exhausting. I was glad to retire from it. Confused dreams of conflict pursued throughout the night. I was in the middle of explaining to the local builder at home – who wore a long Chinese robe and had turned into Pinkus, the Castlemallock Adjutant-Quartermaster – that I wanted the front of the house altered to a pillared façade of Isobel's own design, when a fire-engine manned by pygmies passed, ringing its bell furiously. The bell continued in my head. I awoke. It had become the telephone. This was exceptional in the small hours. There were no curtains to the room, only shutters for the blackout, which were down, so that, opening my eyes, I saw the sky was already getting light above the outbuildings of the yard. I grasped the instrument and gave the designation of the unit and my name. It was Maelgwyn-Jones, Adjutant of our Battalion.

'Fishcake,' he said.

I was only half awake. It was almost as if the dream continued. As I have said, Maelgwyn-Jones's temper was not of the best. He began to get very angry at once, as it turned out, with good reason.

'Fishcake . . .' he repeated. 'Fishcake – fishcake – fishcake . . .'

Obviously 'Fishcake' was a codeword. The question was: what did it mean? I had no recollection ever of having heard it before.

'I'm sorry, I—'

'Fishcake!'

'I heard Fishcake. I don't know what it means.'

'Fishcake, I tell you . . .'

'I know Leather and Toadstool . . .'

'Fishcake has taken the place of Leather – and Bathwater of Toadstool. What the hell are you dreaming about?'

'I don't think—'

'You've bloody well forgotten.'

'First I've heard of Fishcake.'

'Rot.'

'Sure it is.'

'Do you mean to say Rowland hasn't told you and Kedward? I gave him Bathwater a week ago – in person – when he came over to the Orderly Room to report.'

'I don't know about Fishcake or Bathwater.'

'Oh, Christ, is this one of Rowland's half-baked ideas about security? I suppose so. I told him the new code came into force in forty-eight hours from the day before yesterday. Didn't he mention that?'

'Not a word to me.'

"Oh, Jesus. Was there ever such a bloody fool command-ing a company. Go and get him, and look sharp about it.'

I went off with all speed to Gwatkin's room, which was in the main part of the house. He was in deep sleep, lying on his side, almost at the position of attention. Only the half of his face above the moustache appeared over the grey-brown of the blanket. I agitated his shoulder. As usual, a lot of shaking was required to get him awake. Gwatkin always slept as if under an anaesthetic. He came to at last, rubbing his eyes.

'The Adjutant's on the line. He says it's Fishcake. I don't know what that means.'

'Fishcake?'

'Yes.'

Gwatkin sat upright in his camp-bed.

'Fishcake?' he repeated, as if he could hardly believe his ears.

'Fishcake.'

'But we were not to get Fishcake until we had been sig-nalled Buttonhook.'

'I've never heard of Buttonhook either – or Bathwater. All I know are Leather and Toadstool.'

Gwatkin stepped quickly out of bed. His pyjama trousers fell from him, revealing sexual parts and hairy brown thighs. The legs were small and boney, well made, their nakedness suggesting something savage and untaught, yet congruous to his nature. He grabbed the garments to him and held them there, standing scratching his head with the other hand.

'I believe I've made a frightful balls,' he said.

'What's to be done?'

'Didn't I mention the new codes to you and Idwal?'

'Not a word.'

'God, I remember now. I thought I'd leave it to the last

208

moment for security reasons – and then I went out with Maureen, and forgot I'd never told either of you.'

'Well, I should go along to the telephone now, or Maelgwyn-Jones will have apoplexy.'

Gwatkin ran off quickly down the passage, still holding up with one hand the untied pyjama trousers, his feet bare, his hair dishevelled. I followed him, also running. We reached the Company Office. Gwatkin took up the telephone.

'Gwatkin . . .'

There was the hum of the Adjutant's voice at the other end. He sounded very angry, as well he might.

'Jenkins didn't know . . .' Gwatkin said, 'I thought it best not to tell junior officers until the last moment . . . I didn't expect to get a signal the first day it came into operation . . . I was going to inform them this morning . . .'

This answer must have had a very irritating effect on Maelgwyn-Jones, whose voice crepitated for several minutes. I could tell he had begun to stutter, a sure sign of extreme rage with him. Whatever the Adjutant was asserting must have taken Gwatkin once more by surprise.

'But Bathwater was to take the place of Walnut,' he said, evidently appalled.

Once more the Adjutant spoke. While he listened, Gwatkin's face lost its colour, as always when he was agitated.

'To take the place of Toadstool? Then that means—'

There was another burst of angry words at the far end of the line. By the time Maelgwyn-Jones had ceased to speak, Gwatkin had recovered himself sufficiently to reassume his parade ground manner.

'Very good,' he said, 'the Company moves right away.'

He listened for a second, but Maelgwyn-Jones had hung up. Gwatkin turned towards me.

'I had to tell him that.'

'Tell him what?'

'That I had confused the codewords. The fact is, I forgot, as I said to you just now.'

'Forgot to pass on the new codewords to Idwal and me?'

'Yes – but not only are the codewords new, the instructions that go with them are amended in certain respects too. But what I said was partly true. I had muddled them in my own mind. I've been thinking of other things. God, what a fool I've made of myself. Anyway, we mustn't stand here talking. The Company is to march on the Battalion right away. Wake Idwal and tell him that. Send the duty NCO to CSM Cadwallader, and tell him to report to me as soon as the men are roused – he needn't bother to be properly dressed. Get your Platoon on parade, Nick, and tell Idwal to do the same.'

He hurried off, shaking up NCOs, delivering orders, amplifying instructions altered by changed arrangements. I did much the same, waking Kedward, who took this disturbance very well, then returning to the Company Office to dress as quickly as possible.

'This is an imperial balls-up,' Kedward said, as we were on the way to inspect our platoons. 'What the hell can Rowland have been thinking about?'

'He had some idea of keeping the codeword up his sleeve till the last moment.'

'There'll be a God Almighty row about it all.'

I found my own Platoon pretty well turned out considering the circumstances. With one exception, they were clean, shaved, correctly equipped. The exception was Sayce. I did not even have to inspect the Platoon to see what was wrong. It was obvious a mile off. Sayce was in his place, no dirtier than usual at a casual glance, even in other respects properly turned out, so it appeared, but without a helmet. In short, Sayce wore no headdress at all. His head was bare.

'Where's that man's helmet, Sergeant?'

Sergeant Basset had replaced Sergeant Pendry as Platoon Sergeant, since Corporal Gwylt, with his many qualities, did not seriously aspire to three stripes. Basset, basically a sound man, had a mind which moved slowly. His small pig eyes set in a broad, flabby face were often puzzled, his capacities included none of Sergeant Pendry's sense of fitness. Sergeant Pendry, even at the time of worst depression about his wife, would never have allowed a helmetless man to appear on parade, much less fall in. He would have found a helmet for him, told him to report sick, put him under arrest, or devised some other method of disposing of him out of sight. Sergeant Basset, bull-necked and worried, began to question Sayce. Time was getting short. Sayce, in a burst of explanatory whining, set forth a thousand reasons why he should be pitied rather than blamed.

'Says somebody took his helmet, sir.'

'Tell him to fall out and find it in double-quick time, or he'll wish he'd never been born.'

Sayce went off at a run. I hoped that was the last we should see of him that day. He could be dealt with on return. Anything was better than the prospect of a helmetless man haunting the ranks of my platoon. It would be the last straw as far as Gwatkin was concerned, no doubt Maelgwyn-Jones too. However, while I was completing the inspection, Sayce suddenly appeared again. This time he was wearing a helmet. It was too big for him, but that was an insignificant matter. This was no time to be particular, still less to ask questions. The platoon moved off to take its place with the rest of the Company. Gwatkin, who looked worried, but had now recovered his self-possession, made a rapid inspection and found nothing to complain of. We marched down the long drives of Castlemallock, out on to the road, through the town. As we passed the alley leading to Maureen's pub, I saw Gwatkin cast an eye in that direction, but it was too early in the morning for Maureen herself, or anyone else much, to be about.

'Something awful are the girls of this town,' said Corporal Gwylt to the world at large, 'never did I see such a way to go on.'

When we reached Battalion Headquarters, there was a message to say the Adjutant wanted an immediate word with Captain Gwatkin. Gwatkin returned from this interview with a set face. It looked as if subordinates might be in for a bad time, such as that after the Company's failure to provide 'support'. However, Gwatkin showed no immediate desire to get his own back on somebody, though he must have had an unenjoyable ten minutes with Maelgwyn-Jones. We set out on the day's scheme, marching and counter-marching across the mountains, infiltrating the bare, tree-less fields. From start to finish, things went badly. In fact, it was a disastrous day. Still, as Maelgwyn-Jones had said, it passed, like other days in the army, and we returned at length to Castlemallock, bad-tempered and tired. Kedward and I were on the way to our room, footsore, longing to get our boots off, when we met Pinkus, the Adjutant-Quarter-master, the malignant dwarf from the *Morte d'Arthur*. His pleased manner showed there was trouble in the air. He had a voice of horrible refinement, which must have taken years to perfect, and somewhat recalled that of Howard Craggs, the left-wing publisher.

'Where's your Company Commander?' asked Pinkus. 'The Commandant wants him pronto.'

'In his room, I suppose. The Company's just been dis-missed. He's probably changing.'

'What's this about putting one of the officers of the course under arrest? The Commandant's bloody well brassed off about it, I can tell you – and, what's more, the Commandant's own helmet is missing, too, and he thinks one of your fellows has taken it.'

'Why on earth?'

'Your Platoon falls in just outside his quarters.'

'Much more likely to be one of the permanent staff on Fire Picquet. They pass just by the door.'

'The Commandant doesn't think so.'

'I bet one of the Fire Picquet pinched it.'

'The Commandant says he doesn't trust your mob an inch.'

'Why not?'

'That's what he says.'

'If he wants to run down the Regiment, he'd better take it up with our Commanding Officer.'

'Make enquiries, or there'll be trouble. Now, where's Gwatkin?'

He went off, mouthing refinedly to himself. I saw what had happened. In the stresses following realization that he had forgotten about the changed codewords, Gwatkin had also forgotten Bithel. During the exertions of the day in the field, I, too, had given no thought to the events of the previous night, at least none sufficient to consider how best the situation should be handled on our return. Now, back at Castlemallock, the Bithel problem loomed up ominously. Bad enough, in any case, to leave the matter unattended made it worse than ever. Even Kedward had no copybook solution.

'My God,' he said, 'I suppose old Bith ought to have been under escort all day. Under my escort, too, if it comes to that. It was Rowland's last order to me.'

'Anyway, Bithel should have been brought up before the Commandant within twenty-four hours and charged,

213

as a matter of routine. That's the regulation, isn't it?'

'Twenty-four hours isn't up yet.'

'Still, it's a bit late in the day.'

'Rowland's going to find this one tough to sort out.'

'There's nothing we can do about it.'

'Look, Nick,' said Kedward, 'I'll go off right away and see exactly what's happened before I take my boots off. Christ, my feet feel like balloons.'

After a while, Kedward returned, saying Gwatkin was already with the Castlemallock Commandant, straightening out the Bithel affair. When I saw Gwatkin later, he looked desperately worried.

'That business of Bithel last night,' he said harshly.

'Yes?'

'We'd better forget about it.'

'OK.'

'This Anti-Gas course is almost at an end.'

'Yes.'

'Bithel goes back to the Battalion.'

'He may be going up to Division.'

'Bithel?'

'Yes.'

'What on earth for?'

'To command the Mobile Laundry.'

'I hadn't heard that,' said Gwatkin. 'How do you know?'

'Bithel himself told me.'

Gwatkin did not look best pleased, but he reserved judgment.

'The CO will be glad to be rid of him,' he said, 'no doubt about that. The point of what I'm saying now is that Bithel may have made a bloody swine of himself last night, but it's going to be too much of a business to see he gets his deserts.'

'I can understand that.'

'I suspect that Bithel himself got hold of the Mess waiter

214

concerned. Between the two of them, they are prepared to swear that the whole thing was an accident. Bithel stayed in bed all day, saying he had 'flu.'

'How did the Commandant know about the arrest?'

'It leaked out. He seemed to think I'd been officious. I suppose he was just waiting to get something back on me for trying to prevent him from standing between me and my own men and their training. He said Bithel may have had a few drinks, even too many, but, after all, he'd been through the gas-chamber, and, as it turned out, was also sickening for 'flu. The Commandant said, too, he didn't want a row of that undesirable sort at his School of Chemical Warfare. He'd already had trouble about that particular Mess waiter, and, if it came up for court-martial, there might be a real stink.'

'Probably just as well to drop the whole affair.'

Gwatkin sighed.

'Do you think that too, Nick?'

'I do.'

'Then you really don't care about discipline either,' said Gwatkin. 'That's what it means. You're like the rest. Well, well, few officers seem to these days – or even decent behaviour.'

He spoke without bitterness, just regret. All the same, it was perhaps a relief to him – as it certainly was to everyone else – that the Bithel charge should be dropped. However, matters had gone too far at the outset for the whole story to be suppressed. Its discussion throughout the Castlemallock garrison eventually spread to the Battalion; no doubt, in due course, to the ears of the Commanding Officer. Bithel himself, as usual, took the whole business in his stride.

'I made a proper fool of myself that night,' he said to me, just before he left Castlemallock. 'Ought to stick to beer really. Whiskey is always a mistake on top of gin-and-

215

orange. Might have messed up my chances of getting that command. Captain Gwatkin does go off the deep-end, though. Never know what he's going to do next. The Commandant was very decent. Saw my side. War news doesn't look too good, does it? What do you think about Italy coming in? Just a lot of ice-creamers, that's my opinion.'

Then, one sweltering afternoon, returning with the Platoon after practising attack under cover of a smoke-screen, I found several things had happened which altered the pattern of life. When I went into the Company Office, Gwatkin and Kedward were both there. They were standing facing each other. Even as I came through the door and saluted, disturbance was in the air. In fact tension could be described as acute. Gwatkin was pale, Kedward rather red in the face. Neither of them spoke. I made some casual remark about the afternoon's training. This was ignored by Gwatkin. There was a pause. I wondered what had gone wrong. Then Gwatkin spoke in his coldest, most military voice.

'There will be some changes announced in Part II Orders next week, Nick,' he said.

'Yes?'

'You'll like to know them before they appear officially.'

I could not imagine why all this to-do should be made; why, if there were to be changes, Gwatkin could not quite simply state what the changes were, instead of behaving as if about to notify me that the British Government had surrendered, and Kedward and I were to make immediate arrangements for our platoons to become prisoners-of-war. He paused again. Behaviour like this was hard on the nerves.

'Idwal is your new Company Commander,' Gwatkin said.

Everything was explained in a flash. There was nothing to do but remain silent.

'There have been other promotions too,' said Gwatkin. He spoke as if this fact, that there were other promotions, was at least some small consolation. I looked at Kedward. Then I saw, what I had missed before, that he was in an ecstasy of controlled delight. I had not at first noticed this to be the reason for his tense bearing. The air of strain had been imposed by an effort not to grin too much. Even Kedward must have realized this was a painful moment for Gwatkin. Now, the presence of a third party slightly easing the situation, he allowed a slight smile to appear on his face. It spread. He could no longer limit its extent. The grin, by its broadness, almost concealed his little moustache.

'Congratulations, Idwal.'

'Thanks, Nick.'

'And what about you, Rowland?'

I could hardly imagine Gwatkin was to be promoted major. If that were to happen, he would be looking more cheerful. There was a possibility he might be going to command Headquarter Company, an appointment he was known to covet. I doubted myself whether he were wholly qualified to deal with Headquarter Company's many components, remembering, among other things, the incident with the bren-carrier. All the same, I was not prepared for the answer I received, even though I knew, as soon as I heard it, that the sentence pronounced on him should have been guessed at the first indication of upheaval.

'I'm going to the ITC,' said Gwatkin.

'Pending—'

'To await a posting,' Gwatkin said abruptly.

He could not conceal his own mortification. The corner of his mouth worked a little. It was not surprising he was upset. There was no adequate comment at hand to offer in condolence. Gwatkin had been relieved of his Company. There was nothing more or less to it than that. He was

217

being sent to the Regimental Depot – the Infantry Training Centre – whence he would emerge, probably posted to a Holding Battalion finding drafts for the First Line. His career as a military paragon was at an end, though not perhaps his visions as a monk of war, after the echoes and dreams of action died away. Gwatkin might get a company again, he might not. His Territorial captaincy at least was substantive, so that he could not, like holders of an emergency commission, be reduced in rank. However, a captaincy was not in every respect an advantage for someone who hoped to repair this catastrophe. An unreducible captain could find himself in some dead-end where three pips were by convention required, ship's adjutant, for example, or like Pinkus at Castlemallock. That would not be much of fate for a Stendhalian hero, a man bent on making a romantic career in arms, the sort of figure I had supposed Gwatkin only a few months before; in Stendhal, I thought this fate would be attributed to malign political intrigue, the work of Ultras or Freemasons.

'You can fall out, both of you, now,' said Gwatkin, speaking with forced cheerfulness. 'I'll straighten out the papers for you, Idwal. We'll go through them together tomorrow.'

'What about the Imprest Account?' asked Kedward.

'I'll bring it up to date.'

'And the other Company accounts?'

'Them, too.'

'I only mention that, Rowland, because you're sometimes a bit behindhand with them. I don't want to have to waste a lot of time on paper work. There's too much to do about the Company without that.'

'We'll check everything.'

'Has that bren been returned we lent to the Anti-Gas School?'

'Not yet.'

'I shall want it formally handed over again, before I sign for the Company's weapons.'

'Of course.'

'Then Corporal Rosser's promotion.'

'What about it?'

'Did you decide to make him up?'

'Yes.'

'Have you told him?'

'Not yet.'

'Then don't tell him, Rowland.'

'Why not?'

'I want to see more of Rosser before I decide he's to have a third stripe,' said Kedward. 'I shall think about it further.'

Gwatkin's face took on a shade more colour. These were forcible reminders of Kedward's changed position. I was myself a little surprised at the manner in which Kedward accepted the Company as his undoubted right. In one sense, he could have behaved in a more tactful manner about the take-over, anyway leave such questions until they were going through the papers together; in another, as Company Commander designate, he was there to arrange matters in the Company's best interests – by Gwatkin's own definition – not to be polite or spare Gwatkin's feelings. Nevertheless, Gwatkin had not cared for being treated in this manner. He tapped with his knuckles on the blanket covering the trestle table, played with his beloved symbol, the rubber stamp. Gwatkin was deeply humiliated, even though keeping himself under control.

'I want to be alone now, boys,' he said.

He began to rustle papers. Kedward and I retired. We went along the passage together, Kedward deep in thought.

'Rowland is taking this pretty hard,' I said.

Kedward showed surprise.

'Losing the Company?'

'Yes.'

'Do you think so?'

'I do.'

'He must have seen it coming.'

'I don't think he did for a moment.'

'Rowland has been getting less and less efficient lately,' Kedward said. 'You must have noticed that. You said yourself something was wrong, when you came back from the Aldershot course.'

'I somehow didn't expect him to be unstuck just like this.'

'The Company needs a thorough overhaul,' said Kedward. 'There are one or two points I shall want altered in your own Platoon, Nick. It is far from satisfactory. I've noticed there's no snap about them when they march in from training. That's always a good test of men. They are the worst of the three platoons at musketry, too. You'll have to give special attention to the range. And another thing, Nick, about your own personal turn-out. Do get that anti-gas cape of yours properly folded. The way you have it done is not according to regulations.'

'I'll see to all that, Idwal. Who are you getting as another subaltern?'

'Lyn Craddock. He'll go in senior to you, of course. I think Lyn should help pull the Company together.'

'When do you put your pips up?'

'Monday. By the way, did I tell you Yanto Breeze is to become a captain too – in the Traffic Control Company. I just heard that this afternoon from one of the drivers who brought some stuff here. It isn't like getting a company in a battalion, but it's promotion all the same.'

'Does Rowland know about Yanto?'

'I was just telling him when you came into the Company

Office – saying it was funny two of his subalterns should become captain at the same moment.'

'How did Rowland take it?'

'Didn't seem much interested. Rowland never liked Yanto. I don't know whether all that about his sister rankled. I say, Nick, do you know what?'

'What?'

'I'm going to write tonight and arrange about the wedding on my next leave.'

'When's that going to be?'

'Getting the Company may mean a postponement, but even then it won't be too far off. By the way, I've got a new snap of my fiancée. Like to see it?'

'Of course.'

We gazed at the photograph.

'She's altered her hair,' Kedward said.

'So I see.'

'I'm not sure I like it the new way,' he said.

Nevertheless, he gave the photograph its routine kiss before putting it away. His promotion, his fiancée, the wedding in prospect, were matters of fact to him, not, as to Gwatkin, dreams come true. When Gwatkin was given the Company, that must have seemed the first important step in a glorious career; when he first took out Maureen, entry into an equally glorious romance. Kedward, it was true, accepted accession of rank with enthusiasm, but without the smallest romanticism, military or otherwise. As Moreland would have said, it is just the way you look at things. We crossed the hall. Emmot, the Mess waiter, appeared from a doorway. The whole Bithel affair had greatly cheered him up. He looked positively a new man. It was hard to believe he had been sobbing like a child only a few weeks before.

'You're wanted on the phone, sir,' he said, grinning, as if

221

he and I had shared most of the fun of the Bithel incident, 'your unit.'

I went to the telephone in the Duty Officer's room.

'Jenkins here.'

It was the Adjutant.

'Hold on a moment,' he said.

I held on. At the other end of the line Maelgwyn-Jones began to talk to someone in the Orderly Room. I waited. He returned at last.

'Who is that?'

'Jenkins.'

'What do you want?'

'You rang up for me.'

'What was it? Oh, yes. Here's the chit. Second-Lieutenant Jenkins. You will report to Divisional Headquarters, DAAG's office, by 1700 hrs tomorrow, taking all your kit with you.'

'Do you know what I'm to do there?'

'No idea.'

'For how long?'

'No idea of that either.'

'What's the DAAG's name?'

'Also unknown. He's a new appointment. Old Square-arse got bowler-hatted.'

'How shall I get to Div HQ?'

'There's a truck going up tomorrow with some details for hospital treatment. I'll tell it to pick you up at Castle-mallock on the way. I expect you've heard about certain changes in your Company.'

'Yes.'

'Strictly speaking, this instruction should have been issued by me through your Company Commander, but, to avoid confusion, I thought I'd tell you direct. There was another reason, too, why I wanted to speak personally. If the new DAAG is an approachable chap, find out about that Intelligence course I'm supposed to be going on. Also about those two officer reinforcements we've been promised. All right?'

'All right.'

'Report what I've just told you about yourself to the two officers concerned – Rowland and Idwal – right away. Tell them they'll get it in writing tomorrow. All right?'

'Yes.'

Maelgwyn-Jones hung up. Castlemallock was to be left behind. I heard the news without regret; although in the army – as in love – anxiety is an ever-present factor where change is concerned. I returned to Kedward and told him what was happening to me.

'You're leaving right away?'

'Tomorrow.'

'What are you going to do at Div?'

'No idea. Could be only temporary, I suppose. I may reappear.'

'You won't if you once go.'

'You think not?'

'As I've said before, Nick, you're a bit old for a subaltern in an operational unit. I want to make the Company more mobile. I was a little worried anyway about having you on my hands, to tell the truth.'

'Well, you won't have to worry any longer, Idwal.'

These words of mine expressed, on my own part, no more, no less, than what they were, a mere statement of fact. They did not convey the smallest reverberation of acerbity at being treated so frankly as a more than doubtful asset. Kedward dealt in realities. There is much to be said for persons who traffic in this corn, provided it is always borne in mind that so-called realities present, as a rule, only a small part of the picture. On this occasion, however, I was myself in complete

223

agreement with Kedward's view about my departure, feeling even stimulated by a certain excitement at the thought of being on the move.

'You'd better tell Rowland right away.'

'I'm going to.'

I returned to the Company Office. Gwatkin was surrounded with papers. He looked as if he were handing over an Army in the field, rather than a Company on detachment for security duties. He glared when I came through the door at this disobeying of an order that he should be left undisturbed. I repeated Maelgwyn-Jones's words. Gwatkin pushed back his chair.

'So you're leaving the Battalion too, Nick?'

'The Adjutant didn't say for how long.'

'You won't come back, if you go to Division.'

'That's what Idwal said.'

'What can it be? They'd hardly give you a staff appointment. It's probably something like Bithel. I hear he's going to the Mobile Laundry. The CO must have rigged that.'

I saw that even Bithel's new command was painful to Gwatkin, destined himself for the ITC. My own unexplained move was scarcely less disturbing to him. He frowned.

'This must be part of a general shake-up,' he said. 'CSM Cadwallader is leaving the Battalion too.'

'Why is the Sergeant-Major going?'

'Age. I don't understand why Maelgwyn-Jones did not pass the order about yourself to me in the first instance.'

'He said he spoke to me personally because he wanted to explain about some questions I was to put to the new DAAG.'

'He should have done that through me.'

'He said you would get it in writing tomorrow.'

'If the Adjutant ignores the correct channels, I don't

know what he expects other officers to do,' said Gwatkin.

He laughed, as if he found some relief in the thought that the whole framework of the Company, as we had known it together, was now to be broken up; not, so to speak, given over unimpaired to the innovations of Kedward. There was no doubt, I saw now, that Gwatkin would have preferred almost anyone, rather than Kedward, to succeed him.

'Idwal will get either Phillpots or Parry in your place, I expect,' he said.

He began to fiddle with his papers again. I turned to go. Gwatkin looked up suddenly.

'Doing anything special tonight?' he said.

'No.'

'Come for a stroll in the park.'

'After Mess?'

'Yes.'

'All right.'

I went off to pack, and make such other preparations as were required for departure the following day. Gwatkin came into dinner late. I was already sitting in the ante-room when he joined me.

'Shall we go?'

'Right.'

We left the house by the steps leading to what remained of the lawn, its turf criss-crossed now with footpaths worn by the feet of soldiers taking short cuts. Shrubberies divided the garden from the park. When we were among the trees, Gwatkin took the way leading to Lady Caro's Dingle. After the heat of the afternoon, these woods were wonderfully cool and peaceful. The moon was full, the sky almost as light as day. Now that I was about to leave Castlemallock, I began to regret having spent so little time in this park. All I knew was the immediate neighbourhood of the house.

225

To have frequented its woods and glades would perhaps have only increased the melancholy inherent in the place.

'Do you know, Nick,' said Gwatkin, 'although the Company used to mean everything to me, it's leaving the Battalion that's the real blow. Of course there will be up-to-date training at the ITC, opportunity to get to know the latest weapons and tactics thoroughly, not just rush through them and instruct, as we have to here.'

I did not know what to say to that, but Gwatkin was just getting it off his chest. He did not require answers.

'Idwal is pretty pleased with himself now,' he said. 'Let him see what it's like to be skipper. Perhaps it isn't as easy as he thinks.'

'Idwal certainly enjoys the idea of being a company commander.'

'Then there's Maureen,' Gwatkin said. 'This means leaving her. That was what I wanted to talk to you about.'

I had supposed that to be the reason for our coming to the park.

'You'll at least have time to say goodbye to her.'

That did not sound much consolation. It seemed to me he was well rid of Maureen, if she really was disturbing him to the extent that it appeared; but being judicious about other people's love affairs is easy, often merely a sign one has not understood their force or complexity.

'I'm going to try and get down there tomorrow,' he said, 'take her out for the evening.'

'Have you been seeing much of her?'

'Quite a bit.'

'It's bad luck.'

'I know I've made a bloody fool of myself,' Gwatkin said, 'but I don't know that I'd do different if I started again. Anyway, it isn't quite over.'

'What isn't?'

'Maureen.'

'In what way?'

'Nick—'

'Yes?'

'She's pretty well said – you know—'

'She has?'

'I believe if I can manage to see her tomorrow – but I don't want to talk about it. She can't make up her mind, you see. I understand that.'

I thought of Dicky Umfraville's comment: 'Not tonight, darling, I don't love you enough – not tonight, darling, I love you too much . . .' It sounded as if Gwatkin had had his share of such reservations. As we walked, his mind continually jumped from one aspect of his vexations to another.

'If I'm at the ITC and there's an invasion,' he said, 'I'll at least be nearer the scene of action than here. I don't think the Germans will try this country, do you? There'd be no difficulty in landing here, but it would mean mounting another operation after their arrival.'

'Hardly worth it, I'd have thought.'

'Idwal didn't take long to get hold of the idea he was to command the Company.'

'He certainly did not.'

'Do you remember my saying what we call good manners are just a form of weakness?'

'Very well.'

'I suppose if that's true, Idwal was right to speak as he did.'

'There's a lot to be said for going straight to the point.'

'But that's what I've always tried to do since I've been in the army,' Gwatkin said. 'It doesn't seem to have worked in my case. Here I am being sent back to the ITC as a dud. It's not because I haven't been keen, or slacked in any way –

except I know I forgot about those bloody codewords – and other people make balls-ups too.'

He spoke without self-pity, just lack of understanding, deep desire to know the answer why, so far as he was concerned, things had gone so wrong. It would be no good attempting to explain. I was not even sure I knew the explanation myself. All Gwatkin said was true. He had worked hard. In many respects he was a good officer, so far as he went. He was even conscious of such moral aspects of military life as the fact that the army is a world of the will, accordingly, if the will is weak, the army is weak. I could see, however, that one of the fallacies that made him so vulnerable was the supposition that manners, good or bad, had anything to do with the will as such.

'I loved commanding the Company,' Gwatkin said. 'Don't you enjoy your Platoon, Nick?'

'I might have once. I don't know. It's too late now. That's certain. Thirty men are merely a responsibility without the least compensatory feeling of power. They only need everlasting looking after.'

'Do you really feel that?' he said, astonished. 'When the war broke out, I was thrilled at the thought I might lead men into action. I suppose I may yet. This could be only a temporary set-back.'

He laughed unhappily. By this time we were approaching the dingle, a glade enclosed by a kind of shrubbery. A large stone seat was on one side of it, ornamental urns set on plinths at either end. All at once there was a sound of singing.

> 'Arm in arm together,
> Just like we used to be,
> Stepping out along with you
> Meant all the world to me . . .'

228

It was a man's voice, a familiar one. The song, recalling old fashioned music-hall tunes of fifty years before, was, in fact, contemporary to that moment, popular among the men, perhaps, on account of such nostalgic tones and rhythm. The singing stopped abruptly. A woman began giggling and squeaking. Gwatkin and I paused.

'One of our fellows?' he said.

'It sounds to me like Corporal Gwylt.'

'I believe you're right.'

'Let's have a look.'

We skirted the dingle by way of a narrow path among the bushes, stepping quietly through the undergrowth that surrounded the glade. On the stone seat a soldier and a girl were sprawled in a long embrace. The soldier's arm bore two white stripes. The back of the huge head was unmistakably that of Corporal Gwylt. We watched for a moment. Suddenly Gwatkin gave a start. He drew in his breath.

'Christ,' he said very quietly.

He began to pick his way with great care through the shrubs and laurels. I followed him. I was not at first aware why he was moving so soon, nor that something had upset him. I thought his exclamation due to the scratch of a thorn, or remembrance of some additional item to be supervised before handing over the Company. When we were beyond the immediate outskirts of the dingle, he began walking quickly. He did not speak until we were on the path leading back to the house.

'You saw who the girl was?'

'No.'

'Maureen.'

'God, was she?'

There was absolutely no comment to make. This was even more unanswerable than the news that Gwatkin had been superseded in his command. If you are in love with a woman – and Gwatkin was undoubtedly in love – you can recognise her a mile off. The fact that I myself had failed to identify Maureen in the evening light did not make Gwatkin's certainty in the least suspect. The statement could be accepted as correct.

'Corporal Gwylt,' he said. 'Could you believe it?'

'It was Gwylt all right.'

'What do you think of it?'

'There's nothing to say.'

'Rolling about with him.'

'They were certainly in a clinch.'

'Well, say something.'

'Gwylt ought to pray more to Mithras.'

'What do you mean?'

'You know – the Kipling poem – "keep us pure till the dawn".'

'My God,' said Gwatkin, 'you're bloody right.'

He began to laugh. That was one of the moments when I felt I had not been wrong in thinking there was some style about him. We reached the house, parting without further discussion on either side, though Gwatkin had again laughed loudly from time to time. I made my way up the rickety stairs of the stable. The light was out in the bedroom, the blackout down from the window, through which moonlight shone on to the floor. This would usually have meant Kedward was asleep. However, as I came through the door, he sat up in bed.

'You're late, Nick.'

'I went for a walk in the park with Rowland.'

'Is he browned off?'

'Just a shade.'

'I couldn't get to sleep,' Kedward said. 'Never happened to me before. I suppose I'm so bloody pleased to get command of the Company. I keep on having new ideas about running it. I was thinking, I'll probably get Phillpots or Parry in your place, now that you're going up to Div.'

'Phillpots is a nice chap to work with.'

'Parry is the better officer,' said Kedward.

He turned over, in due course going to sleep, I suppose, in spite of these agitations induced by the prospect of power. For a time I thought about Gwatkin, Gwylt and Maureen, then went to sleep myself. The following day there were farewells to be said. I undertook these in the afternoon.

'I hear you're leaving the Battalion too, Sergeant-Major.'

'That I am, sir.'

'I expect you're sorry to go.'

'I am that, sir, and then I'm not. Nice to see home again, that will be, but there needs promotion for these younger lads that must be getting on.'

'Who is going to take your place?'

'It will be Sergeant Humphries, I do believe.'

'I hope Humphries does the job as well as you have.'

'Ah, well, sir, Humphries is a good NCO, and he should be all right, I do think.'

'Thank you for all your help.'

'Oh, it was a pleasure, sir . . .'

Before CSM Cadwallader could say more – not a man to take lightly opportunity to speak at length on the occasion of such a leave-taking, he was certainly going to say more, much more – Corporal Gwylt came running up. He saluted perfunctorily. Evidently I was not the object of his approach. He was tousled and out of breath.

'Excuse me, sir, may I speak to the Sergeant-Major?'

'Go ahead.'

Gwylt could hardly contain his indignation.

'Somebody's broke in and stole the Company's butter, Sergeant-Major, and the lock's all bust and the wire ripped out of the front of the meat-safe where it was put, and the

Messing Corporal do think it be that bugger Sayce again that has taken the butter to flog it, so will you come and see right away, the Messing Corporal says, that we have your witness, Sergeant-Major, if there's a Summary of Evidence like there was those blankets . . .'

CSM Cadwallader shortened his speech in preparation to a mere goodbye and grip of the hand. There was no alternative in the circumstances. He looked disappointed, but characteristically put duty before even the most enjoyably sententious of valedictions. He and Corporal Gwylt hurried off together. By this time the truck that was to take me to Divisional Headquarters had driven up. An NCO was parading the men who were to travel up in it for medical treatment. Gwatkin appeared. He had been busy all the morning, but had promised he would turn up to see me off. We talked for a minute or two about Company arrangements, revisions proposed by Kedward. Gwatkin had resumed his formality of manner.

'Perhaps you'll arrive at the ITC yourself, Nick,' he said, 'on the way to something better, of course, but it's used as a place of transit. I trust I'll be gone by then, but it would be good to meet.'

'We may both turn up on the same staff,' I said, without great seriousness.

'No,' he said gravely, 'I'll never get on the staff. I don't mind that. All I want is to carry out regimental duties properly.'

He tapped his gaiter with the swagger stick he carried. Then his tone changed.

'I had some rather bad news from home this morning,' he said.

'You're not in luck.'

'My father-in-law passed away. I think I told you he had been ill for some time.'

'You did. I'm sorry. Did you get on very well with him?'

'Pretty well,' said Gwatkin, 'but this will mean Blodwen's mother will have to move in with us. I like her all right, but I'd rather that didn't have to happen. Look, Nick, you won't speak to anyone about last night.'

'Of course not.'

'It was bloody awful,' he said.

'Of course.'

'But a lesson to me.'

'One never takes lessons to heart. It's just a thing people talk about – learning by experience and all that.'

'Oh, but I do take lessons to heart,' he said. 'What do you think then?'

'That one just gets these knocks from time to time.'

'You believe that?'

'Yes.'

'You really believe that everyone has that sort of thing happen to them?'

'In different ways.'

Gwatkin considered the matter for a moment.

'I don't know,' he said, 'I can't help thinking it was just because I was such a bloody fool, what with Maureen and making a balls of the Company too. I thought at least I was being some good as a soldier, but I was bloody wrong.'

I thought of Pennistone and his quotations from Vigny.

'A French writer who'd been a regular officer said the whole point of soldiering was its bloody boring side. The glamour, such as it was, was just a bit of exceptional luck if it came your way.'

'Did he?' said Gwatkin.

He spoke without a vestige of interest. I was impressed for the ten thousandth time by the fact that literature illuminates life only for those to whom books are a necessity. Books are unconvertible assets, to be passed on only to those who possess them already. Before I could decide whether it was worth making a final effort to ram home Vigny's point, or whether further energy thus expended was as wasteful of Gwatkin's time as my own, Kedward crossed the yard.

'Rowland,' he said, 'come to the cookhouse at once, will you. It's serious.'

'What's happened?' said Gwatkin, not pleased by this interruption.

'The Company butter's been flogged. So far as I can see, storage arrangements have been quite irregular. I'd like you to be present while I check facts with the CQMS and the Messing Corporal. Another thing, the galantine that's just arrived is bad. It's disposal must be authorized by an officer. I've got to straighten out this butter business before I do anything else. Nick, will you go along and sign for the galantine. Just a formality. It's round at the back by the ablutions.'

'Nick's just off to Div HQ,' said Gwatkin.

'Oh, are you, Nick?' said Kedward. 'Well best of luck, but you will sign for the galantine first, won't you?'

'Of course.'

'Goodbye, then.'

'Goodbye, Idwal, and good luck.'

Kedward hastily shook my hand, then rushed off to the scene of the butter robbery, saying: 'Don't be long, Rowland.'

Gwatkin shook my hand too. He smiled in an odd sort of way, as if he dimly perceived it was no good battling against Fate, which, seen in right perspective, almost always provides a certain beauty of design, sometimes even an occasional good laugh.

'I leave you to your galantine, Nick,' he said. 'Best of luck.'

I gave him a salute for the last time, feeling he deserved it. Gwatkin marched away, looking a trifle absurd with his little moustache, but somehow rising above that. I went off in the other direction, where the burial certificate of the galantine awaited signature. A blazing sun was beating down. For this, my final duty at Castlemallock, Corporal Gwylt, who was representing the Messing Corporal, elsewhere engaged in the butter investigation, had arranged the galantine, an immense slab of it, in its wrappings on a kind of bier, looking like a corpse in a mortuary. Beside the galantine, he had placed a pen and the appropriate Army Form.

'Oh, that galantine do smell something awful, sir,' he said. 'Sign the paper without smelling it, I should, sir.'

'I'd better make sure.'

I inclined my head with caution, then quickly withdrew it. Corporal Gwylt was absolutely right. The smell was appalling, indescribable. Shades of the *Potemkin*, I thought, wondering if I were going to vomit. After several deep breaths, I set my name to the document, confirming animal corruption.

'I'm leaving now, Corporal Gwylt. Going up to Division. I'll say goodbye.'

'You're leaving the Company, sir?'

'That I am.'

The Battalion's form of speech was catching.

'Then I'm sorry, sir. Good luck to you. I expect it will be nice up at Division.'

'Hope so. Don't get into too much mischief with the girls.'

'Oh, those girls, sir, they never give you any peace, they don't.'

'You must give up girls and get a third stripe. Then you'll be like the Sergeant-Major and not think of girls any longer.'

'That I will, sir. It will be better, though I'll not be the man the Sergeant-Major is, I haven't the height. But don't you believe the Sergeant-Major don't like girls. That's just his joke. I know they put something in the tea to make us not want them, but it don't do boys like me no good, it seem, nor the Sergeant-Major either.'

We shook hands on it. Any attempt to undermine the age-old army legend of sedatives in the tea would be as idle as to lecture Gwatkin on Vigny. I returned to the truck, and climbed up beside the driver. We rumbled through the park with its sad decayed trees, its Byronic associations. In the town, Maureen was talking to a couple of corner-boys in the main street. She waved and blew a kiss as we drove past, more as a matter of routine, I thought, than on account of any flattering recognition of myself, because she seemed to be looking in the direction of the men at the back of the truck, who, on passing, had raised some sort of hoot at her. Now they began to sing:

'She'll be wearing purple socks,
And she's always in the pox,
And she's Mickey McGilligan's daughter,
    Mary-Anne . . .'

There were no villages in the country traversed, rarely even farms or hovels. One mile looked like another, except when once we passed a pair of stone pillars, much battered by the elements, their capitals surmounted by heraldic animals holding shields. Here were formerly gates to some mansion, the gryphons, the shields, the heraldry, nineteenth century in design. Now, instead of dignifying the entrance to a park, the pillars stood starkly in open country, alone among wide fields: no gates; no wall; no drive; no park; no house. Beyond them, towards the far horizon, stretched hedgeless ploughland, rank grass, across the expanses of which, like the divisions of a chess-board, squat walls of piled stone were beginning to rise. The pillars marked the entrance to Nowhere. Nothing remained of what had once been the demesne, except these chipped, over-elaborate coats of arms, emblems probably of some lord of the Law, like the first Castlemallock, or business magnate, such as those who succeeded him. Here, too, there had been no heirs, or heirs who preferred to live elsewhere. I did not blame them. North or South, this country was not greatly sympathetic to me. All the same, the day was sunny, there was a vast sense of relief in not being required to settle the Company butter problem, nor take the Platoon in gas drill. Respite was momentary, but welcome. At the back of the vehicle the hospital party sang gently:

'Open now the crystal fountain,
Whence the healing stream doth flow:
Let the fire and cloudy pillar
Lead me all my journey through:
Strong Deliverer,
Strong Deliverer
Be thou still my strength and shield . . .'

Gwatkin, Kedward and the rest already seemed far away. I was entering another phase of my war. By this time we had driven for an hour or two. The country had begun to change its character. Mean dwellings appeared more often, then the outer suburbs of a large town. The truck drove up a long straight road of grim houses. There was a crossroads where half a dozen ways met, a sinister place such as that where Oedipus, refusing to give passage, slew his father, a locality designed for civil strife and street fighting. Pressing on, we reached a less desolate residential quarter. Here, Divisional Headquarters occupied two or three adjacent houses. At one of these, a Military Policeman stood on duty.

'I want the DAAG's office.'

I was taken to see a sergeant-clerk. No one seemed to have heard I was to arrive. The truck had to move on. My kit was unloaded. The DAAG's office was consulted from the switchboard, a message returned that I was to 'come up'. A soldier-clerk showed the way. We passed along passages, the doors of which were painted with the name, rank and appointment of the occupants, on one of them:

Major-General H. de C. Liddament, DSO, MC.
Divisional Commander

The clerk left me at a door on which the name of the former DAAG – 'Old Square-arse', as Maelgwyn-Jones designated him – was still inscribed. From within came the drone of a voice apparently reciting some endless chant, which rose and fell, but never ceased. I knocked. No one answered. After a time, I knocked again. Again there was no answer. Then I walked in, and saluted. An officer, wearing major's crowns on his shoulder, was sitting with his back to the door dictating, while a clerk with pencil and pad was taking down letters in shorthand. The DAAG's back was fat and humped, a roll of flesh at the neck.

'Wait a moment,' he said, waving his hand in the air, but not turning.

He continued his dictation while I stood there.

'. . . It is accordingly felt . . . that the case of the officer in question – give his name and personal number – would be more appropriately dealt with – no – more appropriately regulated – under the terms of the Army Council Instruction quoted above – give reference – of which para II, sections (d) and (f), and para XI, sections (b) and (h), as amended by War Office Letter AG 27/9852/73 of 3 January, 1940, which, it would appear, contemplate exceptional cases of this kind . . . It is at the same time emphasised that this formation is in no way responsible for the breakdown in administration –

238

no, no, better not say that – for certain irregularities of routine that appear to have taken place during the course of conducting the investigation of the case, *vide* page 23, para 17 of the findings of the Court of Inquiry, and para VII of the above quoted ACI, section (e) – irregularities which it is hoped will be adjusted in due course by the authorities concerned . . .'

The voice, like so many other dictating or admonitory voices of even that early period of the war, had assumed the timbre and inflexions of the Churchill broadcast, slurred consonants, rhythmical stresses and prolations. These accents, in certain circumstances, were to be found imitated as low as battalion level. Latterly, for example, Gwatkin's addresses to the Company could be detected, by an attentive ear, to have veered away a little from the style of the chapel elder, towards the Prime Minister's individualities of delivery. In this, Gwatkin's harangues lost not a little of their otherwise traditional charm. If we won the war, there could be no doubt that these rich, distinctive tones would be echoed for a generation at least. I was still thinking of this curious imposition of a mode of speech on those for whom its manner was totally incongruous, when the clerk folded his pad and rose.

'Will you sign these, sir?' he asked.

' "For Major General",' said the DAAG, 'I'll sign them "for Major-General".'

He turned in his chair.

'How are you?' he said.

It was Widmerpool. He brought his large spectacles to bear on me like searchlights, and held out his hand. I took it. I felt enormously glad to see him. One's associations with people are regulated as much by what they stand for, as by what they are, individual characteristics becoming from time to time submerged in more general implications. At that moment, although I had never possessed anything approaching a warm relationship with Widmerpool, his presence brought back with a rush all kinds of things, more or less desirable, from which I had been cut off for an eternity. I wondered how I could ever have considered him in the disobliging light that seemed so innate since we had been at school together.

'Sit down,' he said.

I looked about. The shorthand clerk had been sitting on a tin box. I chose the edge of a table.

'Anyway, between these four walls,' said Widmerpool, 'don't feel rank makes a gulf between us.'

'How did you know it was me when I came into the room?'

Widmerpool indicated a small circular shaving-mirror, which stood on his table, almost hidden by piles of documents. He may have thought this question already presumed too far on our difference in rank, because he stopped smiling at once, and began to tap his knee. His battle-dress, like his civilian clothes, seemed a little too small for him. At the same time, he was undeniably a somewhat formidable figure in his present role.

'I'll put you in the picture right away,' he said. 'In the first place, I do not mean to stay on this staff long. That is between ourselves, of course. The Division is spoken of as potentially operational. So far as I am concerned, it is a backwater. Besides, I have to do most of the work here. Ack-and-Quack, a Regular, is a good fellow, but terribly slow. He is not too bad on supply, but possesses little or no grasp of personnel.'

'What about the General?'

Widmerpool took off his spectacles. He leant towards me. His face was severe under his blinking. He spoke in a low voice.

'I despair of the General,' he said.

'I thought everyone admired him.'

'Quite a wrong judgment.'

'As bad as that?'

'Worse.'

'He has a reputation for efficiency.'

'Mistakenly.'

'They like him in the units.'

'People love buffoonery,' said Widmerpool, 'soldiers like everyone else. Incidentally, I don't think General Liddament cares for me either. However, that is by the way. I make sure he can find nothing to complain of in my work. As a result, he contents himself with adopting a mock-heroic style of talk whenever I approach him. Very undignified in a relatively senior officer. I repeat, I do not propose to stay with this formation long.'

'What job do you want?'

'That's my affair,' said Widmerpool, 'but in the meantime, so long as I remain, the work will be properly done. Now it happens lately there has been a spate of courtsmartial, none of special interest, but all requiring, for one reason or another, a great deal of work from the DAAG. With his other duties, it has been more than one man can cope with. It was too much for my predecessor. That was to be expected. Now I thrive on work, but I saw at once that even I must have assistance. Accordingly, I have obtained War Office authority for the temporary employment of a junior officer to aid me in such matters as taking Summaries of Evidence. Various names were put forward within the Division, yours among them. I noticed this. I had no reason to suppose you would be the most efficient, but, since none of the others had any more legal training than yourself, I allowed the ties of old acquaintance to prevail. I chose you – subject to your giving satisfaction, of course.'

Widmerpool laughed.

'Thanks very much.'

'I take it you did not find yourself specially cut out to be a regimental officer.'

'Not specially.'

'Otherwise, I doubt if your name would have been submitted to me. Let's hope you will be better adapted to staff duties.'

'We can but hope.'

'I remember when we last met, you came to see me with a view to getting help in actually entering the army. How did you get in?'

'In the end I was called up. As I told you at the time, my name was already on the Emergency Reserve. I merely consulted you as to the best means of speeding up that process.'

I saw no reason to give Widmerpool further details about that particular subject. It had been no thanks to him that the calling-up process had been accelerated. By now he had succeeded in dispelling, with extraordinary promptness, my earlier apprehension that army contacts were necessarily preferable with people one knew in civilian life. I began to wonder whether I was not already regretting Gwatkin and Kedward.

'Like so many units and formations at this moment,' said Widmerpool, 'the Division is under-establishment. You will be expected to help while you are here in other capacities than purely "A" duties. When in the field – on exercises, I mean – you will be something of a dogsbody, to use a favourite army phrase, with which you are no doubt familiar. You understand?'

'Perfectly.'

'Good. You will be in F Mess. F is low, but not the final dregs of the Divisional Headquarters staff, if they can be so called. The Mobile Bath Officer, and his like, are in E Mess.

By the way, a body from your unit, one Bithel, is coming up to command the Mobile Laundry.'

'So I heard.'

'Brother of a VC, I understand, and was himself a notable sportsman when younger. Pity they could not find him better employment, for he should be a good type. But we must get on with the job, not spend our time coffee-housing here. Your kit is downstairs?'

'Yes.'

'I will give orders for it to be taken round to your billet – you had better go with it to see the place. Come straight back here. I will run through your duties, then take you back to the Mess to meet some of the staff.'

Widmerpool picked up the telephone. He spoke for some minutes about my affairs. Then he said to the operator: 'Get me Major Farebrother at Command.'

He hung up the receiver and waited.

'My opposite number at Command is one, Sunny Farebrother, a City acquaintance of mine – rather a slippery customer to deal with. He was my Territorial unit's Brigade-Major at the beginning of the war.'

'I met him years ago.'

The telephone bell rang.

'Well, get cracking,' said Widmerpool, without commenting on this last observation. 'The sooner you go, the sooner you'll be back. There's a good deal to run through.'

He had already begun to speak on the telephone when I left the room. I saw that I was now in Widmerpool's power. This, for some reason, gave me a disagreeable, sinking feeling within. On the news that night, motorized elements of the German army were reported as occupying the outskirts of Paris.

The Soldier's Art

for
Roy Fuller

1

WHEN, AT THE START OF the whole business, I bought an army greatcoat, it was at one of those places in the neighbourhood of Shaftesbury Avenue, where, as well as officers' kit and outfits for sport, they hire or sell theatrical costume. The atmosphere within, heavy with menace like an oriental bazaar, hinted at clandestine bargains, furtive even if not unlawful commerce, heightening the tension of an already novel undertaking. The deal was negotiated in an upper room, dark and mysterious, draped with skiing gear and riding-breeches, in the background of which, behind the glass windows of a high display case, two headless trunks stood rigidly at attention. One of these effigies wore Harlequin's diagonally spangled tights; the other, scarlet full-dress uniform of some infantry regiment, allegorical figures, so it seemed, symbolising dualisms of the antithetical stock-in-trade surrounding them . . . Civil and Military . . . Work and Play . . . Detachment and Involvement . . . Tragedy and Comedy . . . War and Peace . . . Life and Death . . .

An assistant, bent, elderly, bearded, with the congruous demeanour of a Levantine trader, bore the greatcoat out of a secret recess in the shadows and reverently invested me within its double-breasted, brass-buttoned, stiffly pleated khaki folds. He fastened the front with rapid bony fingers, doing up the lapels to the throat; then stepped back a couple of paces to judge the effect. In a three-sided full-length looking-glass nearby I, too, critically examined the back view of the coat's shot-at-dawn cut, aware at the same time that soon, like Alice, I was to pass, as it were by virtue of these habiliments, through its panes into a world no less enigmatic.

'How's that, sir?'

'All right, I think.'

'Might be made for you.'

'Not a bad fit.'

Loosening now quite slowly the buttons, one by one, he paused as if considering some matter, and gazed intently.

'I believe I know your face,' he said.

'You do?'

'Was it *The Middle Watch*?'

'Was what the middle watch?'

'The show I saw you in.'

I have absolutely no histrionic talent, none at all, a constitutional handicap in almost all the undertakings of life; but then, after all, plenty of actors possess little enough. There was no reason why he should not suppose the Stage to be my profession as well as any other. Identification with something a shade more profound than a farce of yesteryear treating boisterously of gun-room life in the Royal Navy might have been more gratifying to self-esteem, but too much personal definition at such a point would have been ponderous, out of place. Accepting the classification, however sobering, I did no more than deny having played in that particular knockabout. He helped me out of the sleeves, gravely shaking straight their creases.

'What's this one for?' he asked.

'Which one?'

'The overcoat—if I might make bold to enquire?'

'Just the war.'

'Ah,' he said attentively. '*The War* . . .'

It was clear he had remained unflustered by recent public events, at the age he had reached perhaps disillusioned with the commonplaces of life; too keen a theatre-goer to spare time for any but the columns of dramatic criticism, however indifferently written, permitting no international crises from the news pages to cloud the keenness of aesthetic consideration. That was an understandable outlook.

'I'll bear the show in mind,' he said.

'Do, please.'

'And the address?'

'I'll take it with me.'

Time was short. Now that the curtain had gone up once more on this old favourite—*The War*—in which, so it appeared, I had been cast for a walk-on part, what days were left before joining my unit would be required for dress rehearsal. Cues must not be missed. The more one thought of it, the more apt seemed the metaphor. Besides, clothes, if not the whole man, are a large part of him, especially when it comes to uniform. In a minute or two the parcel, rather a bulky one, was in my hands.

'Tried to make a neat job of it,' he said, 'though I expect the theatre's only round the corner from here.'

'The theatre of war?'

He looked puzzled for a second, then, recognising a mummer's obscure quip, nodded several times in appreciation.

'And I'll wish you a good run,' he said, clasping together his old lean hands, as if in applause.

'Thanks.'

'Good day, sir, and thank *you*.'

I left the shop, allowing a final glance to fall on the pair

3

of flamboyantly liveried dummies presiding from their glass prison over the sombre vistas of coat-hangers suspending tweed and whipcord. On second thoughts, the headless figures were perhaps not antithetical at all, on the contrary, represented 'Honour and Wit, fore-damned they sit', to whom the Devil had referred in the poem. Here, it was true, they stood rather than sat, but precise posture was a minor matter. The point was that their clothes were just right; while headlessness—like depicting Love or Justice blindfold—might well signify the inexorable preordination of twin destinies that even war could not alter. Indeed, war, likely to offer both attributes unlimited range of expression, would also intensify, rather than abate, their ultimate fatality. Musing on this surmise in the pale, grudging sunshine of London in December, a light wan yet intimate, I recognised the off-licence ever memorable for the bottle of port—could the fluid be so designated—that Moreland and I, centuries before, had bought with such high hopes that Sunday afternoon, later so dismally failed to drink.

Looking back from a disturbed, though at the same time monotonous present, those Moreland days seemed positively Arcadian. Even the threatening arbitrament of war (the Prime Minister's rather ornate phrase in his broadcast) had lent a certain macabre excitement to the weeks leading up to the purchase of the greatcoat. Now, some fourteen months later, that day seemed scarcely less remote than the immolation of the port bottle. The last heard of Moreland —from one of Isobel's letters—was that a musical job had taken him to Edinburgh. Even that information had been sent long ago, soon after my own arrival at Division. Since then I had served a million years at these Headquarters, come to possess no life but the army, no master but Widmerpool, no table companions but Biggs and Soper.

4

Meanwhile, the war itself had passed through various phases, some of them uncomfortable enough: France in defeat: Europe overrun: invasion imminent: the blitz opened over London. In this last aspect—more specifically—Isobel reported, too, a direct hit on Barnby's frescoes in the Donners-Brebner Building, a pictorial memory dim as Barnby himself, now Camouflage Officer on some distant RAF station. Latterly, things had looked up a trifle, in the Western Desert, for example, but in general the situation remained capable of considerable improvement before being regarded as in the least satisfactory. F Mess—defined by Widmerpool as 'low, though not the final dregs of the Divisional Staff'—did not at all alter a sense that much was wrong with the world.

After our first local blitz—when they killed a thousand people, at that stage of the war regarded as quite a large number for a provincial city in a single night—Major-General Liddament, the Divisional Commander, ordered the Defence Platoon (of which I had temporary charge) to mount brens within the billeting area between the sounding of Air-raid Warning and All Clear. This was just a drill, in practice no shooting envisaged, unless exceptional circumstances—dive-bombing, for example—were to arise; Command, of course, operating normal anti-aircraft batteries. Announced by the melancholy dirge of sirens, like ritual wailings at barbarous obsequies, the German planes used to arrive shortly before midnight—it was a long way to come—turning up in principle about half an hour after sleep had descended. They would fly across the town at comparatively high altitude, then, wheeling lower, hum fussily back on their tracks, sometimes dropping an incendiary or two, for luck, in the immediate neighbourhood of the Mess, before passing on to the more serious business of

5

lodging high explosive on docks and shipyards. These circlings over the harbour lasted until it was time to return. On such nights, after weapons were back in the armoury, sections dismissed to the barrack-room, not much residue of sleep was to be recaptured.

The last jerky, strangled notes of the Warning, as it died away, always recalled some musical instrument inadequately mastered; General Conyers, for example, rendering Gounod or Saint-Saëns on his 'cello, or that favourite of Moreland's (also inclined to play Saint-Saëns), the pirate-like man with an old-fashioned wooden leg and patch over one eye, who used to scrape away at a fiddle in one of the backstreets off Piccadilly Circus. Still sleepy, I began to dress in the dark, since switching on the light in the curtain-less bedroom would entail the trouble of rearranging the window's blackout boards. Musical variations of different forms of Air-raid Warning might repay study. Where Isobel was living in the country, the vicar, as chief warden, issued the local Warning in person by telephone. Either to instil the seriousness of the notification, or because intoning came as second nature to one of his calling, he always enunciated the words imitatively, ululating his voice from high to low in paraphrase of a siren:

'. . . Air-raid Warning . . . *Air-raid Warning* . . . Air-raid Warning . . . *Air-raid Warning* . . . Air-raid Warning . . . *Air-raid Warning* . . .'

Such reveries floated out of the shadows of the room, together with the hope that the Luftwaffe, bearing in mind the duration of their return journey, would not protract with too much Teutonic conscientiousness the night's activities. Tomorrow, a Command three-day exercise opened, when, so far as the Defence Platoon was concerned, sleep might be equally hard to come by. Outside in the street the air was sharp, although by now meagre signs of the spring were appearing in the surrounding countryside, the hedgeless fields partitioned one from another by tumbledown stone walls. The moonlight had to compete with a rapidly increasing range of artificial illumination that made blackout nugatory. Section posts were to be inspected in turn. The guns were already setting up a good deal of noise. Once a minute fragment of shrapnel pattered with a tinny rattle, like attack from a pea-shooter, against the metal of my helmet. The bren section at the corner of the sports field, last to be visited, had their weapon mounted for aircraft action already and revealed, rather apologetically, they had just discharged a burst.

'Got tired of hanging about watching them drop those things,' said Corporal Mantle, 'so we shot down a flare, for goodness' sake.'

His spectacles gave him a learned, scholarly air, out of keeping with such impatience and violent action. He was a young, energetic NCO, whose name was to go in as candidate for a commission, unless the process were thwarted by Colonel Hogbourne-Johnson, recently showing signs of obstruction in that quarter.

'We'll have to account for the rounds.'

'I'll remember that, sir. Had a few in hand, as a matter of fact. Always just as well, in case there's one of those snap inspections of ammo.'

A shapeless, dumpy figure in a mackintosh came towards us out of the night, the garment so long it reached almost to his heels. This turned out to be Bithel. It was impossible to guess why he should be wandering about at this hour of the night in the middle of a raid. As officer in charge of the Mobile Laundry, his duties could scarcely be required at this moment. He came close to us.

7

'You can't sleep with this noise going on,' he said.

He spoke peevishly, as if remedy, easily applicable, had been for some reason disregarded by the authority responsible.

'I've run out of those pills of mine,' he went on. 'Not even sure I'll be able to get them any longer. Gone off the market, like so many other useful commodities these days. Thought it wiser to put on a helmet. Regulation about that anyway, I expect. I didn't know you or any of the rest of Div HQ were on duty on these occasions. Don't Command organise the pom-poms? That's what they're called, I believe. Then there's a Bofors gun. That's ack-ack too, isn't it? Swedish. I ought to know much more about the Royal Artillery and their functions. Don't come your way as an infantryman, though I've picked up a bit since being at Div.'

He smiled uncomfortably, looking, as always, as if he expected a rebuff. Some months before, he had shaved off the untidy moustache worn when—from some forlorn hope of the Territorial Army Reserve—he had first joined our former Battalion. The physical change, more in keeping with his other natural characteristics, additionally emphasised, in a large moonlike face, the unbelievably inexpert adjustment of his false teeth. That Bithel had lasted so comparatively long in charge of the Mobile Laundry was little short of a miracle. Survival was chiefly due to the fact that this unit was attached only for purposes of administrative convenience, never officially part of the Divisional establishment, therefore liable to be removed at short notice. Accordingly, it never received quite the same disciplinary attention; and, in any case, he was lucky in having Sergeant Ablett as subordinate, who probably did most of the administration. Another reason, too, may have played a

8

part in delaying Bithel's dislodgement, ultimately inevitable. He was accustomed to speak enthusiastically of his own affiliations with the theatrical world, boasts reduced on closer examination to having worked as 'front of the House', for a few months, at the theatre of the provincial capital where for a time he had existed precariously. The job had come to an end when that playhouse had been transformed into a cinema, but some shreds of Thespian prestige still clung to Bithel, anyway in his own eyes, so that when the officer in charge of the Mobile Bath Unit—traditional impresario of the Divisional Concert Party—went sick in the middle of rehearsal, the enterprise was handed over to Bithel, who, as producer and director, mounted a very tolerable show.

All the same, ejection sooner or later could not be in doubt. Widmerpool, as DAAG conveniently placed for furthering this measure, was anxious to oust Bithel at the first opportunity; undoubtedly would have done so long before had the Laundry been of our own establishment. Widmerpool's disapproval was not only on understandable general grounds, but, in addition, because he had—rather uncharacteristically, since usually well informed on such matters—swallowed Bithel's intermittently propagated myth about being brother of an officer of the same name and regiment who had won a VC in the '14-'18 war. There seemed no reason why even a VC's younger brother should not fall short in commanding a Mobile Laundry, but for some reason, at an earlier stage, Widmerpool's imagination had been temporarily captured by the legend, so that he felt bitterly about it when the story was shown to be patently untrue. Now, Bithel stood gazing at the bren with close attention, as if he had never before seen such a weapon.

'So far as Div HQ are concerned, only the Defence

Platoon stands-to when there's a raid—one of the General's ideas to keep everyone on their toes,' I said.

Bithel nodded gravely at this explanation of why we were on guard over the sports field. As it happened, he and I had hardly spoken since the night when, in his own phrase, he had 'taken a glass too much' after traversing the gas-chamber at the Castlemallock School of Chemical Warfare. The peregrinations of the Laundry, by definition, kept its officer, a subaltern, in a state of almost permanent circuit throughout the formation's area, while my own duties, however trivial, were too numerous and dispersed to offer much time for hobnobbing with other branches of HQ. We had therefore done no more up to that moment than exchange an odd word together, usually as neighbours at periodical assemblies of all Headquarters officers to attend a lecture or listen to harangues delivered from time to time by the General. This was the first occasion we had met without a crowd of other people round about.

'Bit of a sweat to have to get up like this night after night,' he said. 'Shall we take a turn up the field?'

His sympathy was not without a touch of despair. Few officers could have looked less on their toes than himself at that moment.

'Wait till I've checked this bren.'

The section was found correct. Bithel and I strolled across the grass towards a broken-down cricket pavilion or changing room, a small wooden structure, not much more than a hut. The place had been the cause of trouble lately, because Biggs, Staff Officer Physical Training, had mislaid the key just at the moment when the civilian owners of the requisitioned sports field wanted to store benches or garden seats there. Widmerpool had complained greatly of time wasted on this matter, and, with justice, had been very cross with Biggs, to whom the hut and its key had become almost an obsession. I tried the door to see if it had been properly locked again after the key had been found and the seats moved there. It would not open. Biggs must have seen to that.

The noise of the cannonade round about was deepening. An odour like smouldering rubber imposed a rank, unsavoury surface smell on lesser exhalations of soot and smoke. Towards the far side of the town—the direction of the harbour—thin greenish rays of searchlight beam rapidly described wide intersecting arcs backwards and forwards against the eastern horizon, their range ever reducing, ever extending, as they sliced purposefully across each other's tracks. Then, all at once, these several zigzagging angles of light would form an apex on the same patch of sky, creating a small elliptical compartment through which, once in a way, rapidly darted a tiny object, moving like an angry insect confined in a bottle. As if reacting in deliberately regulated unison to the searchlights' methodical fluctuations, shifting masses of cloudbank alternately glowed and faded, constantly redesigning by that means half-a-dozen intricately pastelled compositions of black and lilac, grey and saffron, pink and gold. Out of this resplendent firmament—which, transcendentally speaking, seemed to threaten imminent revelation from on high—slowly descended, like Japanese lanterns at a fête, a score or more of flares released by the raiding planes. Clustered together in twos and threes, they drifted at first aimlessly in the breeze, after a time scarcely losing height, only swaying a little this way and that, metamorphosed into all but stationary lamps, apparently suspended by immensely elongated wires attached to an invisible ceiling. Suddenly, as if at a prearranged signal for the climax of the spectacle—a set-piece at midnight—high swirling clouds of inky smoke rose from below to meet these flickering airborne torches. At ground level, too, irregular knots of flame began to blaze away like a nest of nocturnal forges in the Black Country. All the world was dipped in a livid, unearthly refulgence, theatrical yet sinister, a light neither of night nor day, the penumbra of Pluto's frontiers. The reek of scorched rubber grew more than ever sickly. Bithel fidgeted with the belt of his mackintosh.

'There's been a spot of bother about a cheque,' he said.

'Yours?'

'I think that's what was really keeping me awake as much as lack of those pills. Things may work out all right because I've paid up—borrowed a trifle from the Postal Officer, as a matter of fact—but cheques are always a worry. They ought to be abolished.'

'Perhaps they will after the war.'

'That'll be too late for me,' said Bithel.

He spoke quite seriously.

'Large sum?'

'Matter of a quid or two—but it did bounce.'

'Can't you keep it quiet?'

'I don't think the DAAG knows up to date.'

That was an important factor from Bithel's point of view. Otherwise Widmerpool might find the opportunity for which he was waiting. I was about to commiserate further, when a deep, rending explosion, that seemed to split the earth, sounded above the regular thud-thud-thud of the guns, vibrations of its crash echoing back in throbbing, shuddering waves from the surrounding hills. Bithel shook his head, his attention distracted for the moment from his own troubles, no doubt worrying enough.

'That must have got home,' he said.

'Sounded like it.'

He began to speak again, then for some reason stopped, apparently changing his mind about the way he was going to put a question. Having evidently decided to frame it in a different form, he made the enquiry with conscious diffidence.

'Told me you were a reader—like me—didn't you?'

'Yes, I am. I read quite a lot.'

I no longer attempted to conceal the habit, with all its undesirable implications. At least admitting to it put one in a recognisably odd category of persons from whom less need be expected than the normal run.

'I love a good book when I have the time,' said Bithel. 'St John Clarke's *Match Me Such Marvel*, that sort of thing. Something serious that takes a long time to get through.'

'Never read that one, as it happens.'

Bithel seemed scarcely aware of my answer. St John Clarke's novel was evidently a side issue, not at all the goal at which these ranging shots were aimed. Though rarely possible to guess, when in a mood for intimate conversation, what he would say next, such pronouncements of Bithel's were always worth attention. Something special was on his mind. When he put the next question, there was a kind of fervour in his voice.

'Ever buy magazines like *Chums* and the *Boy's Own Paper* when you were a nipper?'

'Of course—used to read them in bound annuals as a rule. I've a brother-in-law who still does.'

It was Erry's only vice, though one he tried to keep dark, as showing in himself a lack of earnestness and sense of social obligation. Bithel made some reply, but a sudden concentrated burst of ack-ack fire, as if discharged deliberately for that purpose, drowned his utterance.

'What was that you said?'

Bithel spoke again.

'Still can't hear.'

He came closer.

'. . . hero . . .' he shouted.

'You feel a hero?'

'No . . . I . . .'

The noise lessened, but he still had to yell at the top of his voice to make himself heard.

'. . . always imagined myself the hero *of those serials.*'

The shouted words were just audible above the clatter of guns. He seemed to think they offered a piece of unparalleled psychological revelation on his own part.

'Every boy does,' I yelled back.

'Everyone?'

He was disappointed at that answer.

'I'm sure my brother-in-law does to this day.'

Bithel was not at all interested in my own, or anyone else's, brother-in-law's tendency to self-identification while reading fiction. That was reasonable, because he knew nothing of Erridge's existence. Besides, he wanted only to talk about himself. Although wholly concentrated on that subject, he remained at the same time apologetic as well as intense.

'Only I was thinking the other night—when Jerry first came over—that I was having the very experience I used to read about as a lad.'

'How do you mean?'

' "Coming under fire for the first time"—that was always a great moment in the hero's career. You must remember. Where he "showed his mettle", as the story usually put it.'

He laughed, as if trying to excuse such reckless flights

of fancy, in doing so displaying the double row of Low Comedy teeth.

' "The rattle of musketry from distant hills"—"a little shower of sand churned up by a bullet in front of the redoubt"?'

These conventional phrases from boys' adventure stories might encourage Bithel to plunge further into observations about life. The clichés did indeed stir him.

'That's it,' he said, speaking with much more animation than usual, 'that's just what I meant. Wonderful memory you've got. What you said brings those yarns right back. I was a great reader as a lad. One of those thoughtful little boys. Never kept it up as I should.'

This was all a little reminiscent of Gwatkin, my former Company Commander, poring secretly in the Company office over the *Hymn to Mithras*; but, whereas Gwatkin had meditated such literary material as a consequence of his own infatuation with the mystique of a soldier's life, Bithel's ruminations were quite other. In Bithel, memory of his former partiality for tales of military prowess merely gave rise to a very natural surprise that he was not himself more personally frightened at this moment of comparative danger.

'Strictly speaking, one experienced raids—coming under fire, if you like—when still reading the *Boy's Own Paper*. During the earlier war, I mean.'

'Oh, I didn't,' said Bithel. 'The Zeppelins never came near any of the places we lived when I was a kid. That's just why I was surprised not to mind this sort of thing more. I'm the nervy type, you see. I once had to give evidence in court, rather a nasty case—nothing to do with me, I'm glad to say, just a witness—and I thought my legs were going to give way under me. But this business we're

15

listening to now really doesn't worry me. Worst moment's when the Warning goes, don't you think?'

The question of fear inevitably propounds itself from time to time if a state of war exists. Will circumstances arise when its operation on the senses might become uncomfortably hard to control? Like Bithel, I, too, had thought a certain amount about that subject, reaching the very provisional conclusion that fear itself was less immediately related to unavoidable danger than might at first be supposed; although no doubt that danger, more or less indefinitely increased in motive power, might—indeed certainly would—cause the graph to rise steeply. In bed at night, months before the blitz struck the locality, I would occasionally feel something like abject fear, turning this way and that in my sleeping-bag, for no special reason except that life seemed so utterly out of joint. That was a kind of nervous condition—as Bithel had said of himself—perfectly imaginable in time of peace; perhaps even experienced then, now forgotten, like so much else of that lost world. In the same way, I would sometimes lie awake enduring torments of thwarted desire, depraved fantasies hovering about the camp-bed, reveries of concupiscence that seemed specifically generated by unprepossessing military surroundings. Indeed, it was often necessary to remind oneself that low spirits, disturbed moods, senses of persecution, were not necessarily the consequence of serving in the army, or being part of a nation at war, with which all-inclusive framework depressive mental states now seemed automatically linked.

The raid in progress at that moment was, as Bithel had indicated, more spectacular than alarming, even a trifle stimulating now one was fully awake and dressed; so long as the mind did not dwell on the tedium of a three-day exercise the following day, undertaken after a missed night's sleep. On the other hand, if bombs began to fall in the sports field, such light-hearted impressions might easily deteriorate, especially if the bren were knocked out, removing chance of retaliation. (It might be added that all sense of excitement was to evaporate from air-raids three or four years later.) However, Bithel had ceased to require comment on his own meditations about 'baptism of fire'. He now returned to those personal worries, predominantly financial, which were never far from his mind.

'I do hope things will be OK about that cheque,' he said. 'It all started with the Pay Department being late that month in paying Field Allowance into my banking account.'

This situation did, indeed, arise from time to time, owing to absence of method, possibly downright incompetence, on the part of the Financial Branch of the War Office concerned; possibly due to economic ineptitudes, or ingrained malice, of what Pennistone used later to call the 'cluster of highly educated apes' ultimately in charge of such matters at the Treasury. Whatever the cause, the army from time to time had to forego its wages; sometimes such individual disasters as Bithel's resulting.

'I can see there'll be a fuss,' he said, 'but with any luck it won't come to a court-martial.'

Two or three lesser reports, each thunderous enough, had followed the last big explosion. Now noise was diminishing, the barrage gradually, though appreciably, reducing its volume. Quite suddenly the guns fell entirely silent, like dogs in the night, which, after keeping you awake for hours by their barking, suddenly decide to fall asleep instead. There was a second or two of absolute stillness. Then in the far distance the bell of a fire-engine or ambulance clanged desperately for a time, until the echoes died sadly away on the wind. This discordant ringing was followed by a great clamour, shouts, starting-up of trucks, hooting . . . *the sound of horns and motors, which shall bring Sweeney to Mrs Porter in the spring.* . . . Huge smuts, like giant moths exploring the night air, pervaded its twilight. The smell of burning rubber veered towards a scent more specifically chemical in character, in which the fumes of acetylene seemed recognisable. The consolatory, long drawn out drone came at last. At its first note, as if thus signalled, large drops of rain began to fall. In a minute or two the shower was coming down in buckets, the freshness of the newly wet grass soon obtruding on the other scents.

'Buck up and get that bren covered, Corporal.'

'Shall we pack it in now, sir?'

'Go ahead.'

'Think I'll return to bed too,' said Bithel. 'Doubt if I'll get much sleep. Glad I brought a mac with me now. Need it more than a helmet really. Awful climate over here. Makes you swill down too much of that porter, as they call it. More than you can afford. Just to keep the damp out of your bones. Come and see us in G Mess some time. You'd like Barker-Shaw, the Field Security Officer. He's a professor—philosophy, I think—at one of the 'varsities. Can't remember which. Clever face. The bloke in charge of the Hygiene Section is a bright lad too. You should hear him chaffing the Dental Officer about sterility.'

Our several ways parted. Corporal Mantle marched off his men to the barrack-room. I completed the rounds of the other bren sections, dismissed them, made for bed.

F Mess was only a few minutes' walk from the last of these posts. The Mess was situated in a redbrick, semi-detached villa, one of the houses of a side-street sloping away towards the perimeter of the town. Entering the front

18

door, you were at once assailed by a nightmare of cheer-lessness and squalor, all the sordid melancholy, at its worst, of any nest of bedrooms where only men sleep; a prescript of nature unviolated by the character of solely male-infested sleeping quarters established even in buildings hallowed by age and historical association. F Mess was far from such; at least any history to be claimed was in the making. From its windows in daytime, beyond the suburbs, grey, stony hills could be seen, almost mountains; in another direction, that of the docks over which the blitz had been recently concentrating, rose cranes and factory chimneys beyond which inland waters broadened out towards the sea—'the unplumb'd, salt, estranging sea.' About half a mile away from the Mess, though still in the same predominantly residential area, two or three tallish houses accommodated all but the ancillary services of Divisional Headquarters. A few scattered university buildings in the same neighbour-hood failed to impart any hint of academic flavour.

'No room in this bloody Mess as it is,' said Biggs, Staff Officer Physical Training, expressing this opinion when I first turned up there. 'Now you come along and add to the crowd, Jenkins, making an extra place at that wretched rickety table we've been issued with to eat off, and another body to occupy the tin sink on the top floor they call a bath—no shaving in the bathroom, remember, absolutely *verboten*. What are you supposed to be doing at Div any-way?'

A captain with '14–'18 ribbons, bald as an egg, he had perhaps been good-looking in a heavy classical manner when younger; anyway, had himself so supposed. Now, with chronically flushed cheeks, he was putting on flesh, his large bulbous nose set between fierce frightened eyes and a small cupid's bow mouth that kept twitching open and shut like a rubber valve. Muscular over-development of chest, shoulder and buttock gave him the air of a strong man at a circus—a strong woman almost—or professional weight-lifter about to present an open-air act to a theatre queue. His voice, harsh and unsure, registered the persecution mania that beset him, that condition, not uncommon in the army, of for ever expecting a superior to appear—bursting like the Demon King out of a trapdoor in the floor—and find fault. In civilian life sports organiser at a seaside resort, Biggs, so I learnt later, was in process of divorcing his wife, a prolonged undertaking, troublesome and expensive, of which he would often complain.

'I'm attached to the DAAG's office.'

'How long for?'

'Don't know.'

'How's Major Widmerpool got authority for an assistant, I should like to know?'

'War Office Letter.'

'Go on.'

'It's to help clear up a lot of outstanding stuff like court-martial proceedings and requisition claims.'

'I've got a lot of outstanding stuff too,' said Biggs. 'A bloody lot. I'm not given an assistant. Well, I don't envy you, Jenkins. It's a dog's life. And don't forget this. Don't forget it. There's nothing lower in the whole bloody army than a second-lieutenant. Other Ranks have got their rights, a one-pipper's none. That goes especially for a Div HQ, and what's more Major Widmerpool is a stickler for having things done the right way. He's been on my own track before now, I can tell you, about procedure he didn't consider correct. He's a devil for procedure.'

After that Biggs lost interest in what was not, indeed, a very interesting subject, except in the light indicated, that to acquire an understrapper at all was, on Widmerpool's part, an achievement worthy of respect. No one but a tireless creator of work for its own sake would have found an assistant necessary in his job, nor, it could be added, in the ordinary course of things been allowed one, even if required. Widmerpool had brought that off. As it happened, a junior officer surplus to establishment was to some extent justified additionally, not long before my arrival at Division, by Prothero, commanding the Defence Platoon, falling from his motor-bicycle and breaking his leg. While he was in hospital I was allotted some of Prothero's duties as well as those delegated by Widmerpool.

'You'll find there's a lot of work to do here,' said Widmerpool, on my first morning. 'A great deal. We shall be at it to a late hour most nights.'

This warning turned out to be justified. There were, as it happened, several courts-martial pending, and another, convened in the past, the findings of which Widmerpool considered unsatisfactory in law. A soldier, who had temporarily gone off his head and assaulted two civilians, had been acquitted at his trial. Widmerpool was engaged in a complicated correspondence on this matter with the Judge Advocate General's Department. Such things took up time, as most of the week was spent out of doors on exercises. Although, since days when we had been at school together, I had been seeing him on and off—very much on and off— for more than twenty years by this time, I found when I worked under him there were still comparatively unfamiliar sides to Widmerpool. Like most persons viewed through the eyes of a subordinate, his nature was to be appreciated with keener insight from below. This new angle of observation revealed, for example, how difficult he was to work with, particularly on account of a secretiveness that derived from perpetual fear, almost obsession, that tasks completed by himself might be attributed to the work of someone else. On that first morning at Division, Widmerpool spoke at length of his own methods. He was already sitting at his table when I arrived in the room. Removing his spectacles, he began to polish them vigorously, assuming at the same time a manner of hearty military geniality.

'No excuses required,' he said, before I could speak. 'Your master is always the first staff officer to arrive at these Headquarters in the morning, and, apart from those on night duty, the last to leave after the sun has gone down. Now I want to explain certain matters before I go off to attend A & Q's morning conference. The first thing is that I never turn work away, neither in the army nor anywhere else. To turn work away is always an error. Never let me find you doing that—unless, of course, it is work another branch is wrongly trying to foist on us, for which they themselves will ultimately reap the credit. A man fond of stealing credit for other people's work is Farebrother, my opposite number at Command. I do not care for Farebrother. He is too smooth. Besides, he is always trying to get even with me about a certain board-meeting in the City we both once attended.'

'I met Farebrother years ago.'

'So you keep on telling me. You mentioned the fact at least once last night. Twice, I think.'

'Sorry.'

'I hope previous acquaintance will prevent you being taken in by his so-called charm, should you have dealings with him as my representative.'

Widmerpool's feud with Sunny Farebrother, so I found, was of old standing, dating back to long before this, though, militarily speaking, in especial to the period when

22

Farebrother had been brigade-major to Widmerpool's Territorials soon after the outbreak of war. The work of the 'A' staff, which Widmerpool (under 'A & Q', Colonel Pedlar) represented at Division, comprised administration of 'personnel' and 'interior economy', spheres in which, so it appeared, Farebrother had more than once thwarted Widmerpool, especially in such matters as transfers from one unit to another, candidates for courses and the routine of disciplinary cases. Farebrother was, for example, creating difficulties about Widmerpool's correspondence with the Judge Advocate's Department. There were all kind of ways in which an 'opposite number' at Corps or Command could make things awkward for a staff officer at Division. As Command Headquarters were established in one of the blocks of regular army barracks on the other side of the town, I had no contact with Farebrother in the flesh, only an occasional word on the telephone when the DAAG was not available; so the matter of our having met before had never arisen. It was hard to estimate how justly, or otherwise, Widmerpool regarded this mutual relationship. Farebrother's voice on the line never showed the least trace of irritation, even when in warm conflict as to how some order should be interpreted. That quiet demeanour was an outstanding feature of Sunny Farebrother's tactic. On the whole, honours appeared fairly evenly divided between the two of them where practical results were concerned.

'Right, Sunny, right,' Widmerpool would mutter, gritting his teeth when he had sustained a defeat.

'It's gone the way Kenneth wants,' was Farebrother's formula for accepting the reverse situation.

Then there were my own hopes and fears. Though by now reduced to the simplest terms, these were not without complication. In the first place, I desired to separate myself from Widmerpool; at the same time, if possible, achieve material improvement in my own military condition. However, as the months went by, no prospect appeared of liberation from Widmerpool's bottle-washing, still less of promotion. After all, I used to reflect, the army was what you wanted, the army is what you've got—in terms of Molière, *le sous-lieutenant Georges Dandin*. No use to grumble, not to mention the fact that a great many people, far worse off, would have been glad of the job. This was a change, of course, from taking pride in the thought that only luck and good management had brought a commission at all at a moment when so many of my contemporaries were still failing to achieve that. However, to think one thing at one moment, another at the next, is the prescriptive right of every human being. Besides, I recognised the fact that those who desire to share the faint but perceptible inner satisfaction of being included, however obscurely, within the armed forces in time of war, must, if in their middle thirties and without any particular qualifications for practising its arts, pay for that luxury, so far as employment is concerned, by taking what comes. Consolation was to be found, if at all, in Vigny's views (quoted that time in the train by David Pennistone) on the theme of the soldier's 'abnegation of thought and action'.

All the same, although the soldier might abnegate thought and action, it has never been suggested that he should abnegate grumbling. There seemed no reason why I alone, throughout the armies of the world, should not be allowed to feel that military life owed me more stimulating duties, higher rank, increased pay, simply because the path to such ends was by no means clear. Even if Widmerpool left Divisional Headquarters for what he himself used to call 'better things', my own state, so far from improving, would almost certainly be worsened. The Battalion, made up to strength with a flow of young officers increasingly available, would no longer require my services as platoon commander, still less be likely to offer a company. Indeed, those services, taking them all in all, were not to be exaggerated in value to a unit set on streamlining its efficiency. I was prepared to admit that myself. On the other hand, without ordination by way of the War Intelligence Course, or some similar apostleship, there was little or no likelihood of capturing an appointment here or on any other staff. For a course of that sort I should decidedly not be recommended so long as Widmerpool found me useful. When, for one reason or another, that subjective qualification ceased to be valid—when, for example, Widmerpool went to 'better things'—it looked like pretty certain relegation to the Regiment's Infantry Training Centre, a fate little to be desired, and one unlikely to lead to name and fame. Widmerpool himself was naturally aware of these facts. Once, in an expansive mood, he had promised to arrange a future preferable to assignment—as an object to be won, rather than as a competitor—to the lucky-dip provided by an ITC.

'I look after people who've been under me,' Widmerpool said, in the course of cataloguing some of his own good qualities. 'I'll see you get fixed up in a suitable job when I move up the ladder myself. That shouldn't be long now, I opine. At very least I'll get you sent on a course that will make you eligible for the right sort of employment. Don't worry, my boy, I'll keep you in the picture.'

That was a reasonable assurance in the circumstances, and, I felt, not undeserved. 'Putting you in the picture', that relentlessly iterated army phrase, was a special favourite of Widmerpool's. He had used it when, on my first arrival at Headquarters, he had sketched in for me the characteristics of the rest of the Divisional staff. Widmerpool had begun with General Liddament himself.

'Those dogs on a lead and that hunting horn stuck in the blouse of his battle-dress are pure affectation,' he said. 'Come near to being positively undignified in my opinion. Still, of the fifteen thousand men in the Division, I can think of only one other fit to command it.'

'Who is?'

'Modesty forbids my naming him.'

Widmerpool allowed some measure of jocularity to invest his tone when he said that, which increased, rather than diminished, the impression that he spoke with complete conviction. The fact was he rather feared the General. That was partly on account of General Liddament's drolleries, some of which were indeed hard to defend; partly because, when in the mood, the Divisional Commander liked to tease his officers. Widmerpool did not like being teased. The General was not, I think, unaware of Widmerpool's qualities as an efficient, infinitely industrious DAAG, while at the same time laughing at him as a man. In this Widmerpool was by no means his only victim. Generals are traditionally represented as stupid men, sometimes with good reason; though Pennistone, when he talked of such things later, used to argue that the pragmatic approach of the soldier in authority—the basis of much of this imputation—is required by the nature of military duties. It is an approach which inevitably accentuates any individual lack of mental flexibility, an ability, in itself, to be found scarcely more among those who have risen to eminence in other vocations; anyway when operating outside their own terms of reference. In General Liddament, so I was to discover, this pragmatic approach, even if paramount, was at the same time modified by notable powers of observation. A bachelor, devoted to his profession, he was thought to have a promising future ahead of him. Earlier in the war he had been wounded in action with a battalion, a temporary disability that probably accounted for his not already holding a command in the field.

When the General himself was present, Widmerpool was prepared to dissemble his feelings about the two attendant dogs (he disliked all animals), which could certainly become a nuisance when their double-leashed lead became entangled between the legs of staff officers and their clerks in the passages of Headquarters. All the same, Widmerpool was not above saying 'wuff-wuff' to the pair of them, if their owner was in earshot, which he would follow up by giving individual, though unconvincing, pats of encouragement.

'Thank God, the brutes aren't allowed out on exercise,' he said. 'At least the General draws the line there. I think Hogbourne-Johnson hates them as much as I do. Now Hogbourne-Johnson is a man you must take care about. He is bad-tempered, unreliable, not more than averagely efficient and disliked by all ranks, including the General. However, *I* can handle him.'

Hogbourne-Johnson, a full colonel with red tabs, was in charge of operational duties, the staff officer who represented the General in all routine affairs. A Regular, decorated with an MC from the previous war, he was tall, getting decidedly fat, with a small beaky nose set above a pouting mouth turning down at the corners. He somewhat resembled an owl, an angry, ageing bird, recently baulked of a field-mouse and looking about for another small animal to devour. The MC suggested that he was presumably a brave man, or, at very least, one who had experienced enough active service to make that term almost beside the point. Widmerpool acknowledged these earlier qualities.

'Hogbourne-Johnson's had a disappointing career up to date,' he said. 'Unrealized early hopes. At least that's his own opinion. Sword of Honour at Sandhurst, all that sort of thing. Then he made a balls-up somewhere—in Palestine, I think—just before the war. However, he hasn't by any means given up. Still thinks he'll get a Division. If he asked me, I could tell him he's bound for some administrative backwater, and lucky if he isn't bowler-hatted before the cessation of hostilities. The General's going to get rid of him as soon as he can lay hands on the particular man he wants.'

'But the General could sack him tomorrow.'

'For some reason it doesn't suit him to do that. Hogbourne-Johnson is also given to putting on a lot of swank about being a Light Infantryman. To tell the truth, I'm surprised any decent Line regiment could put up with him. They might at least have taught him not to announce himself to another officer on the telephone as "*Colonel* Hogbourne-Johnson". I know Cocksidge says, "This is *Captain* Cocksidge speaking", if he's talking to a subaltern. You expect that from Cocksidge. Hogbourne-Johnson is supposed to know better. The CRA doesn't say, "This is *Brigadier* Hawkins", he says "Hawkins here". However, I suppose I shouldn't grumble. I can manage the man. That's the chief thing. If he hasn't learn how to behave by now, he never will.'

All this turned out to be a pretty just description of Colonel Hogbourne-Johnson and his demeanour, from which in due course I saw no reason to dissent. The army is a place where simple characterisation flourishes. An officer or man is able, keen, well turned out; or awkward, idle, dirty. He is popular or detested. In principle, at any rate, few intermediate shades of colour are allowed to the military spectrum. To some extent individuals, by the very force of such traditional methods of classification, fall into these hard and fast categories. Colonel Hogbourne-Johnson was one of the accepted army types, disappointed, sour, on the look-out for trouble; except by his chief clerk, Diplock, not much loved. On the other hand, although he may have had his foolish moments as well as his disagreeable ones, Hogbourne-Johnson was not a fool. Where Widmerpool, as it turned out, made a mistake, was in supposing he had Colonel Hogbourne-Johnson eating out of his hand. The Colonel's failings, such as they were, did not include total lack of grasp of what Widmerpool himself was like in his dealings. Indeed, Hogbourne-Johnson showed comparatively deep understanding of Widmerpool eventually, when the titanic row took place about Diplock, merging—so far as Widmerpool and Hogbourne-Johnson were concerned—into the question of who was to command the Divisional Reconnaissance Regiment.

The Reconnaissance Unit, then in process of generation, was one in which Colonel Hogbourne-Johnson took a special interest from the start, though not an entirely friendly interest.

'These Recce fellows are doing no more than we Light Bobs used to bring off on our flat feet,' he would remark. 'Nowadays they want a fleet of armoured vehicles for their blasted operations and no expense spared. There's a lot of damned nonsense talked about this so-called Recce Battalion.'

The Reconnaissance Corps—as in due course it emerged

—was indeed, on first coming into being, a bone of considerable contention among the higher authorities. Some pundits thought like Colonel Hogbourne-Johnson; others, just the opposite. One aspect of the question turned on whether the Recce Corps—to some extent deriving in origin from the Anti-tank Companies of an earlier phase of the war—should be used as a convenient limbo for officers, competent, but judged, for one reason or another, less than acceptable in their parent unit; or, on the other hand, whether the Corps should be moulded into one of the élites of the army, having its pick of the best officers and men available. Yanto Breeze, for example, of my former Battalion, had transferred to an Anti-tank Company after the never-explained death—suicide or murder—of Sergeant Pendry. Breeze had been implicated only to the extent of being Orderly Officer that night, sufficient contact—bringing the unpleasantness of a Court of Inquiry—to make him want to leave the Battalion. A good, though not particularly ornamental officer, he was felt to be entirely suitable for the Anti-tank Company. Adherents of a more stylish Recce Corps might, rightly or wrongly, have required rather more outward distinction from their officer in-take than Breeze could show. That was much how things stood. The whole question also appealed greatly to Widmerpool, both as an amateur soldier in relation to tactical possibilities, and, as a professional trafficker in intrigue, a vehicle offering all sorts of opportunity for personal interference.

'Hogbourne-Johnson is playing a double game about the Recce Corps,' he said. 'I happen to know that. The Divisional Commander is very keen on this new unit. The Generals at Corps and Command, on the other hand, are neither of them enthusiastic on the subject, not helpful about speeding things up. Hogbourne-Johnson thinks—in my opinion rightly—that General Liddament plans to get rid of him. Accordingly, he is doing his best to suck up to the other two Generals by backing their policy. He'll then expect help if relieved of his appointment.'

'Like the Unjust Steward.'

'Who was he?'

'In the Bible.'

'I thought you meant an officer of that name.'

'The one who said write ten, when it ought to have been fifty.'

'There's nothing unjust about it,' said Widmerpool, always literal-minded. 'Naturally Hogbourne-Johnson has to obey his own Divisional Commander's orders. I do not for a moment suggest he is overstepping the bounds of discipline. After all, Recce developments are a matter of opinion. A regular officer of his standing has a perfect right to hold views. However, what our General would not be specially pleased to hear is that Hogbourne-Johnson is also moving heaven and earth to get a friend from his own regiment appointed to this new unit's command.'

'How do you know?'

'Because I too have my candidate.'

'To command the Recce Corps?'

'Going into the matter, I discovered Hogbourne-Johnson's tracks. However, I can circumvent him.'

Widmerpool smiled and nodded in a manner to indicate extreme slyness.

'Who?'

'No one you would have met. An excellent officer of my acquaintance called Victor Upjohn. Knew him as a Territorial. First-rate man.'

'Won't they appoint a cavalryman, in spite of Hog-bourne-Johnson and yourself?'

'They'll appoint my infantryman—and be glad of him.'

'If the General is likely to be annoyed about Hogbourne-Johnson messing about behind his back as to appointments to command in his Division, he'll be even less pleased to find you at the same game.'

'He won't find out. Neither will Hogbourne-Johnson. Upjohn will simply be gazetted. In the meantime, so far as it goes, I am prepared to play ball with Hogbourne-Johnson up to a point. After all, if I know the right man to command the Recce Corps, it's surely my duty to get him there.'

There was something to be said for this view. If you want your own way in the army, or elsewhere, it is no good following the rules too meticulously, a canon all great military careers—and most civil ones—abundantly illustrate. What Widmerpool had not allowed for, as things turned out, was a sudden deterioration of his own relations with Colonel Hogbourne-Johnson. No doubt one reason for his assurance about that, in spite of the Colonel's uncertain temper, was that most of Widmerpool's dealings were with his own immediate superior, Colonel Pedlar, so less likelihood of friction existed in the other more explosive quarter. Naturally he was in touch with Colonel Hogbourne-Johnson from time to time, but there was no day-to-day routine, during which Hogbourne-Johnson was likely, sooner or later, to make himself disagreeable as a matter of principle.

Colonel Pedlar, as 'A & Q', set no problem at all. Also a regular full colonel with an MC, he had little desire to be unaccommodating for its own sake. A certain stiffness of manner in official transactions was possibly due to apprehension that more might be required of him than he had to offer, rather than an innate instinct, like Hogbourne-Johnson's, to be unreasonable in all his dealings. Colonel Pedlar seemed almost surprised to have reached the rank he had attained; appeared to possess little or no ambition to rise above it, or at least small hope that he would in due course be promoted to a brigade. The slowness of his processes of thought sometimes irked his subordinate, Widmerpool, even though these processes were on the whole reliable. If Colonel Hogbourne-Johnson looked like an owl, Colonel Pedlar resembled a retriever, a faithful hound, sound in wind and limb, prepared to tackle a dog twice his size, or swim through a river in spate to collect his master's game, but at the same time not in the top class for picking up a difficult scent.

Trouble with Colonel Hogbourne-Johnson might never have arisen, as it did at that particular moment, had not Colonel Pedlar been, quite by chance, out of the way. When it came, sudden and violent, the cause was a far more humdrum matter than the clandestine guiding of appointments. Indeed, the incident itself was such a minor one, so much part of the day's work, that, had I not myself witnessed it—owing to the exceptional occurrence of Advance Headquarters and Rear Headquarters being brought together in one element at the close of the three-day exercise—I should always have believed some essential detail to have been omitted from the subsequent story; guessed that nothing so trivial in itself could have so much discomposed Widmerpool. That incredulity was due, I suppose, to underestimation, even after the years I had known him, of Widmerpool's inordinate, almost morbid, self-esteem.

During 'schemes', the Defence Platoon was responsible

33

for guarding the Divisional Commander's Advance Head-quarters. This meant, on these occasions, accommodation for myself in the General's Mess; accordingly, temporary disengagement from Widmerpool, whose duties as DAAG focussed on Rear Headquarters. On the last evening of this particular exercise, the Command three-day one, Advance HQ had been established, as usual, in a small farmhouse, one of the scattered homesteads lying in the forbidding countryside of the Command's north-western area, right up in the corner of the map. The first fifty-six hours had been pretty active—as foreseen by me the night before we set out—giving little chance of sleep. However, by the time the General and his operational staff sat down to a late meal at the end of the third day, there was a feeling abroad that the main exertions of the exercise might reasonably be regarded as at an end. Everyone could take things easy for a short time. The General himself was in an excellent temper, the battle against the Blue Force to all intents won.

A single oil lamp threw a circle of dim light round the dining table of the farm parlour where we ate, leaving the rest of the room in heavy shadow, dramatising by its glow the central figures of the company present. Were they a group of conspirators—something like the Gunpowder Plot —depicted in the cross-hatchings of an old engraved illus-tration? It was not exactly that. At the same time the hard lights and shades gave the circle of heads an odd, mys-terious unity. The faces of the two colonels, bird and beast, added a note deliberately grotesque, surrealist, possibly indicating a satirical meaning on the part of the artist, a political cartoonist perhaps. The colonels were placed on either side of General Liddament, who sat at the head of the table, deep in thought. His thin, cleanshaven, ascetic features, those of a schoolmaster or priest—also a touch of Sir Magnus Donners—were yellowish in complexion. Perhaps that tawny colour clarified the imagery, for now it became plain.

Here was Pharaoh, carved in the niche of a shrine between two tutelary deities, who shielded him from human approach. All was manifest. Colonel Hogbourne-Johnson and Colonel Pedlar were animal-headed gods of Ancient Egypt. Colonel Hogbourne-Johnson was, of course, Horus, one of those sculptured representations in which the Lord of the Morning Sun resembles an owl rather than a falcon; a bad-tempered owl at that. Colonel Pedlar's dog's muzzle, on the other hand, was a milder than normal version of the jackal-faced Anubis, whose dominion over Tombs and the Dead did indeed fall within A & Q's province. Some of the others round about were less easy to place in the Egyptian pantheon. In fact, one came finally to the conclusion, none of them were gods at all, mere bondsmen of the temple. For example, Cocksidge, officer responsible for Intelligence duties, with his pale eager elderly-little-boy expression—although on the edge of thirty—was certainly the lowest of slaves, dusting only exterior, less sacred precincts of the shrine, cleaning out with his hands the priest's latrine, if such existed on the temple premises. Next to Cocksidge sat Greening, the General's ADC, pink cheeked, fair haired, good-natured, about twenty years old, probably an alien captive awaiting sacrifice on the altar of this anthropomorphic trinity. Before anyone else could be satisfactorily identified, Colonel Pedlar spoke.

'How went the battle, Derrick?' he asked.

There had been silence until then. Everyone was tired. Besides, although Colonel Hogbourne-Johnson and Colonel Pedlar were not on notably good terms with each other, they felt rank to inhibit casual conversation with subordinates. Both habitually showed anxiety to avoid a junior officer's eye at meals in case speech might seem required. To make sure nothing so inadvertent should happen, each would uninterruptedly gaze into the other's face across the table, with all the fixedness of a newly engaged couple, eternally enchanted by the charming appearance of the other. The colonels were, indeed, thus occupied when Colonel Pedlar suddenly put his question. This was undoubtedly intended as a form of expressing polite interest in his colleague's day, rather than to show any very keen desire for further tactical information about the exercise, a subject with which Colonel Pedlar, and everyone else present, must by now be replete. However Colonel Hogbourne-Johnson chose to take the enquiry in the latter sense.

'Pretty bloody, Eric,' he said. 'Pretty bloody. If you want to know about it, read the sit-rep.'

'I've read it, Derrick.'

The assonance of the two colonels' forenames always imparted a certain whimsicality to their duologues.

'Read it again, Eric, read it again. I'd like you to. There are several points I want to bring up later.'

'Where is it, Derrick?'

Colonel Pedlar seemed to possess no intellectual equipment for explaining that he had absolutely no need, even less desire, to re-read the situation report. Perhaps, having embarked on the subject, he felt a duty to follow it up.

'Cocksidge will find it for you, Eric, writ in his own fair hand. Seek out the sit-rep, Jack.'

In certain moods, especially when he teased Widmerpool, the General was inclined to frame his sentences in a kind of Old English vernacular. Either because the style appealed equally to himself, or, more probably, because use of it implied compliment to the Divisional Commander, Colonel Hogbourne-Johnson also favoured this mode of speech. At his words, Cocksidge was on his feet in an instant, his features registering, as ever, deference felt for those of higher rank than himself. Cocksidge's demeanour to his superiors always recalled a phrase used by Odo Stevens when we had been on a course together at Aldershot:

'Good morning, Sergeant-Major, here's a sparrow for your cat.'

Cocksidge was, so to speak, in a chronic state of providing, at a higher level of rank, sparrows for sergeant-majors' cats. His own habitual incivility to subordinates was humdrum enough, but the imaginative lengths to which he would carry obsequiousness to superiors displayed something of genius. He took a keen delight in running errands for anyone a couple of ranks above himself, his subservience even to majors showing the essence of humility. He had made a close, almost scientific study of the likes and dislikes of Colonel Hogbourne-Johnson and Colonel Pedlar, while the General he treated with reverence in which there was even a touch of worship, of deification. In contact with General Liddament, so extreme was his respect that Cocksidge even abated a little professional boyishness of manner, otherwise such a prominent feature of his all-embracing servility, seeming by its appealing tone to ask forbearance for his own youth and immaturity. Widmerpool, to do him justice, despised Cocksidge, an attitude Cocksidge seemed positively to enjoy. The two colonels, on the other hand, undoubtedly approved his fervent attentions, appeared even appreciative of his exaggeratedly juvenile mannerisms. In addition, it had to be admitted Cocksidge did his job competently, apart from

37

such elaborations of his own personality. Now he came hurriedly forward with the situation report.

'Thanks, Jack,' said Colonel Pedlar.

He studied the paper, gazing at it with that earnest, apparently uncomprehending stare, of which Widmerpool had more than once complained.

'I've seen this,' he said. 'Seems all right, Derrick. Take it back where it belongs, Jack.'

'Glad it seems all right to you, Eric,' said Colonel Hogbourne-Johnson, 'because I rather flatter myself the operational staff, under my guidance, did a neat job.'

The bite in his tone should have conveyed warning. He terminated this comment, as was his habit, by giving a smirk, somehow audibly extruded from the left-hand side of his mouth, a kind of hiss, intended to underline the aptness or wit of his words. Unless in a bad humour he would always give vent to this muted sound after speaking. The fact was Colonel Hogbourne-Johnson did not attempt to conceal his own sense of superiority over a brother officer, inferior not only in appointment, regiment and mental equipment, but also in a field where Colonel Hogbourne-Johnson felt himself particularly to shine, that is to say in the arena where men of the world sparklingly perform. The play of his wit was often directed against the more leisurely intellect of Colonel Pedlar, whose efforts to keep up with all this parade of brilliance occasionally landed him in disaster. It was so on that night. After giving a glance at the situation report, he handed it back to Cocksidge, who received the document with bent head, as if at Communion or in the act of being entrusted with a relic of supreme holiness. There could be no doubt that the sit-rep had at least confirmed Colonel Pedlar in the belief that nothing remained to worry about where the exercise was concerned. At such moments as this one he was inclined to overreach himself.

'Going to finish up with a glass of port tonight, Derrick,' he asked, 'now that our exertions are almost at an end?'

'Port, Eric?'

A wealth of meaning attached to the tone given by Colonel Hogbourne-Johnson to the name of the wine. Widmerpool's mother, years before, had pronounced 'port' with a similar interrogative inflexion in her voice, though probably to imply her guests were lucky to get any port at all, rather than for the reasons impelling Colonel Hogbourne-Johnson so precisely to enunciate the word.

'Yes, Derrick?'

'Not tonight, Eric. Port don't do the liver any good. Not the sort of port we have in this Mess anyway. I shall steer clear of port myself, Eric, and I should advise you to do the same.'

'You do?'

'I do, Eric.'

'Well, I think I'll have a small glass nevertheless, Derrick. I'm sorry you won't be accompanying me.'

Colonel Pedlar gave the necessary order. Colonel Hogbourne-Johnson shook his head in disapproval. He was known to favour economy; it was said, even to the extent of parsimony. A glass of port was brought to the table. Colonel Pedlar, looking like an advertisement for some well known brand of the wine in question, held the glass to the lamp-light, turning the rim in his hand.

'Fellow in my regiment was telling me just before the war that his grandfather laid down a pipe of port for him to inherit on his twenty-first birthday,' he remarked.

Colonel Hogbourne-Johnson grunted. He did this in a manner to imply observation of that particular custom, even the social necessity of such a provision, was too well accepted in decent society for any casual commendation of the act to be required; though the tradition might be comparatively unfamiliar in what he was accustomed to describe as 'Heavy' infantry; and, it might be added, not much of a regiment at that.

'Twelve dozen bottles,' said Colonel Pedlar dreamily. 'Pretty good cellar for a lad when he comes of age.'

Colonel Hogbourne-Johnson suddenly showed attention. He began to bare a row of teeth under the biscuit-coloured bristles and small hooked nose.

'Twelve dozen, Eric?'

'That's it, isn't it, Derrick?'

Colonel Pedlar sounded nervous now, already aware no doubt that he had ventured too far in claiming knowledge of the world; had made, not for the first time, an elementary blunder.

'*Twelve dozen?*' repeated Colonel Hogbourne-Johnson.

He added additional emphasis to the question, carrying the implication that he himself must have misheard.

'Yes.'

'You're wide of the mark, Eric. Completely out of the picture.'

'I am, Derrick?'

'You certainly are, Eric.'

'What is a pipe then, Derrick? I'm not in the wine trade.'

'Don't have to be in the wine trade to know what a pipe of port is, old boy. Everyone ought to know that. Nothing to do with being a shopman. *More than fifty dozen.* That's a pipe. You're absolutely out in your calculations. Couldn't be more so. Mismanaged your slide-rule. Landed in an altogether incorrect map-square. Committed a real bloomer.

Got off on the wrong foot, as well as making a false start.'

'Is that a pipe, by Jove?'

'That's a pipe, Eric.'

'I got it wrong, Derrick.'

'You certainly did, Eric. You certainly got it wrong. You did, by Jove.'

'You've shaken me, Derrick. I'll have to do better next time.'

'You will, Eric, you will—or we won't know what to think of you.'

General Liddament seemed not to hear them. It was as if he had fallen into a cataleptic sleep or was under the influence of some potent drug. After this exchange between the two colonels, another long silence fell, one of those protracted abstinences from all conversation so characteristic of army Messes—British ones, at least—during which, as every moment passes, you feel someone is on the point of giving voice to a startling utterance, yet, for no particular reason, that utterance is always left pending, for ever choked back, incapable, from inner necessity, of being finally brought to birth. An old tin alarm-clock ticked away noisily on the dresser, emphasising the speedy passing of mortal life. Colonel Pedlar sipped away at his port, relish departed after his blunder. Cocksidge, with the side of his palm, very quietly scraped together several crumbs from the surface of the table cloth, depositing them humbly, though at the same time rather coyly, on his own empty plate, as if to give active expression, even in the sphere of food, to his perpetual dedication in keeping spick and span the surroundings of those set in authority over him, doing his poor best in making them as comfortable as possible. Only that morning, in the dim light at an early hour in the farmhouse kitchen, I had tripped over him, nearly fallen

41

headlong, as he crouched on his knees before the fire, warming the butter ration so that its consistency might be appropriately emulsified for the General to slice with ease when he appeared at the breakfast table. No doubt, during all such silences as the one that now had fallen on the Mess, the mind of Cocksidge was perpetually afire with fresh projects for self-abasement before the powerful. By now there was no more to hope for, so far as food was concerned. It seemed time to withdraw from the board, in other respects unrewarding.

'May I go and see how the Defence Platoon is getting on, sir?'

General Liddament appeared not to have heard. Then, with an effort, he jerked himself from out of his deep contemplation. It was like asking permission from one of the supine bodies in an opium den. He took a few seconds more to come to, consider the question. When he spoke it was with almost biblical solemnity.

'Go, Jenkins, go. No officer of mine shall ever be hindered from attending to the needs of his men.'

A sergeant entered the room at that moment and approached the General.

'Just come through on the W/T, sir, enemy planes over the town again.'

'Right—take routine action.'

The sergeant retired. I followed him out into a narrow passage where my equipment hung from a hook. Then, buckling on belt and pouches, I made for the outbuildings. Most of the platoon were pretty comfortable in a loft piled high with straw, some of them snoring away. Sergeant Harmer was about to turn in himself, leaving things in the hands of Corporal Mantle. I ran through the matter of sentry duties. All was correct.

'Just come through they're over the town again, Sergeant.'

'Are they again, the buggers.'

Harmer, a middle-aged man with bushy eyebrows, largely built, rather slow, given to moralising, was in civilian life foreman in a steel works.

'We haven't got to wake up for them tonight.'

'It's good that, sir, besides you never know they won't get you.'

'True enough.'

'Ah, you don't, life's uncertain, no mistake. Here today, gone tomorrow. After my wife went to hospital last year the nurse met me, I asked how did the operation go, she didn't answer, said the doctor wanted a word, so I knew what he was going to say. Only the night before when I'd been with her she said "I think I'll get some new teeth". We can't none of us tell.'

'No, we can't.'

Even the first time I had been told the teeth story, I could think of no answer than that.

'I'll be getting some sleep. All's correct and Corporal Mantle will take over.'

'Good night, Sergeant.'

Corporal Mantle remained. He wanted to seize this opportunity for speaking a word in private about the snag arisen about his candidature for a commission. Colonel Hogbourne-Johnson had decided to make things as difficult as possible. Mantle was a good NCO. Nobody wanted to lose him. Indeed, Colonel Hogbourne-Johnson had plans to promote him sergeant, eventually perhaps sergeant-major, when opportunity arose to get rid of Harmer, not young enough or capable of exceptional energy, even if he did the job adequately. Widmerpool, through whom such matters to some extent circulated, was not interested either way in what happened to Mantle. He abetted Hogbourne-Johnson's obstructive tactics in that field, partly as line of least resistance, partly because he was himself never tired of repeating the undeniable truth that the army is an institution directed not towards the convenience of the individual, but to the production of the most effective organisation for an instrument designed to win wars.

'At the present moment there are plenty of young men at OCTUs who are potentially good officers,' Widmerpool said. 'Good corporals, on the other hand, are always hard to come by. That situation could easily change. If we get a lot of casualties, it *will* change so far as officers are concerned—though no doubt good corporals will be harder than ever to find. In the last resort, of course, officer material is naturally limited to the comparatively small minority who possess the required qualifications—and do not suppose for one moment that I presume that minority to come necessarily, even primarily, from the traditional officer class. On the contrary.'

'But Mantle doesn't come from what you call the traditional officer class. His father keeps a newspaper shop and he himself has some small job in local government.'

'That's as may be,' said Widmerpool, 'and more power to his elbow. Mantle's a good lad. At the same time I see no reason for treating Mantle's case with undue bustle. As I've said before, I have no great opinion of Hogbourne-Johnson's capabilities as a staff officer—on that particular point I find myself in agreement with the General—but Hogbourne-Johnson is within his rights, indeed perfectly correct, in trying to delay the departure of an NCO, if he feels the efficiency of these Headquarters will be thereby diminished.'

There the matter rested. Outside the barn I had a longish

talk with Mantle about his situation. By the time I returned to the house, everyone appeared to have gone to bed; at least the room in which we had eaten seemed at first deserted, although the oil lamp had not been extinguished. It had, however, been moved from the dinner table to the dresser standing on the right of the fireplace. Then, as I crossed the room to make for a flight of stairs on the far side, I saw General Liddament himself had not yet retired to his bedroom. He was sitting on a kitchen chair, his feet resting on another, while he read from a small blue book that had the air of being a pocket edition of some classic. As I passed he looked up.

'Good night, sir.'

'How goes the Defence Platoon?'

'All right, sir. Guards correct. Hay to sleep on.'

'Latrines?'

'Dug two lots, sir.'

'Down wind?'

'Both down wind, sir.'

The General nodded approvingly. He was rightly keen on sanitary discipline. His manner showed he retained the unusually good mood of before dinner. There could be no doubt the day's triumph over the Blue Force had pleased him. Then, suddenly, he raised the book he had been reading in the air, holding it at arm's length above his head. For a moment I thought he was going to hurl it at me. Instead, he waved the small volume backwards and forwards, its ribbon marker flying at one end.

'Book reader, aren't you?'

'Yes, sir.'

'What do you think of Trollope?'

'Never found him easy to read, sir.'

The last time I had discussed books with a general had

been with General Conyers, a much older man than General Liddament, one whose interests were known to range from psychoanalysis to comparative religion; and in many other directions too. Long experience of the world of courts and camps had given General Conyers easy tolerance for the opinions of others, literary as much as anything else. General Liddament, on the other hand, seemed to share none of that indulgence for those who did not equally enjoy his favourite authors. My answer had an incisive effect. He kicked the second chair away from him with such violence that it fell to the ground with a great clatter. Then he put his feet to the floor, screwing round his own chair so that he faced me.

'*You've never found Trollope easy to read?*'

'No, sir.'

He was clearly unable to credit my words. This was an unhappy situation. There was a long pause while he glared at me.

'Why not?' he asked at last.

He spoke very sternly. I tried to think of an answer. From the past, a few worn shreds of long forgotten literary criticism were just pliant enough to be patched hurriedly together in substitute for a more suitable garment to cover the dialectic nakedness of the statement just made.

'. . . the style . . . certain repetitive tricks of phrasing . . . psychology often unconvincing . . . sometimes downright dishonest in treating of individual relationships . . . women don't analyse their own predicaments as there represented . . . in fact, the author does more thinking than feeling . . . of course, possessor of enormous narrative gifts . . . marshalling material . . . all that amounting to genius . . . certain sense of character, even if stylised . . . and naturally as a picture of the times . . .'

46

'Rubbish,' said General Liddament.

He sounded very angry indeed. All the good humour brought about by the defeat of the Blue Force had been dissipated by a thoughtless expression of literary prejudice on my own part. It might have been wiser to have passed some noncommittal judgment. Possibly I should be put under arrest for holding such mutinous views. The General thought for a long time, perhaps pondering that question. Then he picked up the second chair from the floor where it had fallen on its side. He set it, carefully, quietly, at the right distance and angle in relation to himself. Once more he placed his feet on the seat. Giving a great sigh, he tilted back his own chair until its joints gave a loud crack. This physical relaxation seemed to infuse him with a greater, quite unexpected composure.

'All I can say is you miss a lot.'

He spoke mildly.

'So I've often been told, sir.'

'Whom do you like, if you don't like Trollope?'

For the moment, I could not remember the name of a single novelist, good or bad, in the whole history of literature. Who was there? Then, slowly, a few admired figures came to mind—Choderlos de Laclos—Lermontov—Svevo. . . . Somehow these did not have quite the right sound. The impression given was altogether too recondite, too eclectic. Seeking to nominate for favour an author not too dissimilar from Trollope in material and method of handling, at the same time in contrast with him—not only in being approved by myself—in possessing greater variety and range, the *Comédie Humaine* suddenly suggested itself.

'There's Balzac, sir.'

'*Balzac!*'

General Liddament roared the name. It was impossible

47

to know whether Balzac had been a very good answer or a very bad one. Nothing was left to be considered between. The violence of the exclamation indicated that beyond argument. The General brought the legs of the chair down level with the floor again. He thought for a moment. Fearing cross-examination, I began to try and recall the plots of all the Balzac books, by no means a large number in relation to the whole, I had ever read. However, the next question switched discussion away from the sphere of literary criticism as such.

'Read him in French?'

'I have, sir.'

'Get along all right?'

'I'm held up with occasional technical descriptions—how to run a provincial printing press economically on borrowed money, what makes the best roofing for a sheepcote in winter, that sort of thing. I usually have a fairly good grasp of the narrative.'

The General was no longer listening.

'You must be pretty bored with your present job,' he said.

He pronounced these words deliberately, as if he had given the matter much thought. I was so surprised that, before I could make any answer or comment, he had begun to speak again; now seeming to have lost all his former interest in writers and writing.

'When's your next leave due?'

'In a week's time, sir.'

'It is, by God?'

I gave the exact date, unable to imagine what might be coming next.

'Go through London?'

'Yes, sir.'

'And you'd like a change from what you're doing?

48

'I should, sir.'

It had never struck me that General Liddament might be sufficiently interested in the individuals making up Divisional Headquarters to have noticed any such thing. Certainly, as a general, he was exceptional enough in that respect. He was also, it occurred to me, acting in contrast with Widmerpool's often propagated doctrines regarding the individual in relation to the army. His next remark was even more staggering.

'You've been very patient with us here,' he said.

Again I could think of no reply. I was also not sure he was not teasing. In one sense, certainly he was; in another, he seemed to have some project in mind. This became more explicit.

'The point is,' he said, 'people like you may be more useful elsewhere.'

'Yes, sir.'

'It's not a personal matter.'

'No, sir.'

'We live such a short time in the world, it seems a pity not to do the jobs we're suited for.'

These sentences were closer to Widmerpool's views, though more sanely interpreted; their reminder that life was dust had a flavour, too, of Sergeant Harmer's philosophy.

'I'm going to send a signal to Finn.'

'Yes, sir.'

'Ever heard of Finn?'

'No, sir.'

'Finn was with me at the end of the last war—a civilian, of course—in the City in those days.'

'Yes, sir.'

General Liddament mentioned 'the City' with that faint touch of awe, a lowering of the voice, somewhere between reverence and horror, that regular soldiers, even exceptional ones like himself, are apt to show for such mysterious, necromantic means of keeping alive.

'But he put up a good show when he was with us.'

'Yes, sir.'

'An excellent show.'

'Yes, sir.'

'Got a VC.'

'I see, sir.'

'Then, after the war, Finn gave up the City. Went into the cosmetic business—in Paris.'

'Yes, sir.'

'Made a good thing out of it.'

'Yes, sir.'

'Now he's come back here with the Free French.'

'I see, sir.'

'I understand Finn's looking for suitable officers for the work he's doing. I suggest you drop in on him during your leave. Give him my compliments. Robin will issue you with an instruction when we get back to base.'

'Robin' was Greening, the ADC.

'Shall I mention this to the DAAG, sir?'

General Liddament thought for a moment. For a split second he looked as if he were going to smile. However, his mouth finally remained at its usual enigmatically set position when in repose.

'Keep it under your hat—keep it under your hat—just as well to keep it under your hat.'

Before I could thank him, or indeed any more might be said between us, the door of the room opened violently. Brigadier Hawkins, Commanding the Divisional artillery, came in almost at a run. Tall, lean, energetic, the CRA was the officer Widmerpool had commended for 'knowing how to behave when speaking on the telephone', in contrast with Colonel Hogbourne-Johnson. Widmerpool was right about that. Brigadier Hawkins, who had seen to it the Gunner Mess was the best run in the Division, was one of the few members of its staff who set about his duties with the 'gaiety', which, according to Dicky Umfraville, Marshal Lyautey regarded as the first requirement of an officer. Both Colonel Hogbourne-Johnson and Colonel Pedlar had to be admitted to fall unequivocally short in that respect. Not so, in his peculiar way, the General, whose old friend the Brigadier was said to be.

'Glad to find you still up, sir,' he said. 'Sorry to disturb you at this hour, but you should see a report at once they've just brought in. I thought I'd come myself, to cut out a lot of chat. The Blue Force we thought encircled is moving men in driblets across the canal.'

General Liddament once more kicked away the chair from his feet, sending it sliding across the room. He picked up a map-case lying beside him, and began to clear a space on the table, littered with a pipe, tobacco, other odds and ends. Trollope—I could not see which novel he had been reading—he slipped into the thigh pocket of his battle-dress. Brigadier Hawkins began to outline the situation. I made a move to retire from their conference together.

'Wait . . .' shouted the General.

He scribbled some notes on a pad, then pointed towards me with his finger.

'Wake Robin,' he said. 'Tell him to come down at once —before dressing. Then go and alert the Defence Platoon to move forthwith.'

I went quickly up the stairs to Greening's room. He was asleep. I shook him until he was more or less awake. Greening was used to that sort of thing. He jumped out of bed as if it were a positive pleasure to put an end to sleep, be on the move again. I gave him the General's orders, then returned to the Defence Platoon in the loft. They were considerably less willing than Greening to be disturbed. In fact there was a lot of grousing. Not long after that the Movement Order was issued. Advance Headquarters set off to a new location. This was the kind of thing General Liddament thoroughly enjoyed, unexpected circumstances that required immediate action. Possibly, in its minuscule way, my own case had suggested itself to him in some such terms.

'They do never want us to have no sleep,' said Sergeant-Major Harmer, 'but at least it's all on the way home.'

The Blue Force was held in check before the time limits of the exercise ran out. In short, the battle was won. It was nearly morning when Advance Headquarters were again ordered to move, this time in preparation for our return to base. We were on this occasion brought, contrary to habit in such manœuvres, into direct contact with our own Rear Headquarters; both branches of the staff being assembled together in a large farm building, cowshed or barn, waiting there while transport arrangements went forward. It was here that the episode took place which so radically altered Widmerpool's attitude towards Colonel Hogbourne-Johnson.

Cars and trucks were being marshalled along a secondary road on the other side of a ploughed field on which drizzle was falling. A short time earlier, a message had come through from base stating that the raid during the night had done damage that would affect normal administration on return to the town. Accordingly, Colonel Pedlar had driven back at once to arrange any modification of routine that might be required. Colonel Pedlar's presence with the rest of the staff could possibly, though by no means certainly, have provided a buffer between Widmerpool and Colonel Hogbourne-Johnson. As things fell out, those two came into direct impact just before we moved off. Widmerpool, with the two other officers who normally shared the same staff car, was about to leave the cowshed where we were hanging about, sleepless and yawning, when Colonel Hogbourne-Johnson came suddenly through the doorway. He was clearly very angry, altogether unable to control the rage surging up within him. Even for a professionally bad-tempered man, he was in a notably bad temper. 'Where's the DAAG?' he shouted at the top of his voice.

Widmerpool came forward with that serious, self-important air of his, which, always giving inadequate impression of his own capabilities, was often calculated to provoke irritation in people he dealt with, even if not angry already.

'Here I am, sir.'

Colonel Hogbourne-Johnson turned on Widmerpool as if he were about to strike him.

'What the bloody hell do you think of yourself?' he asked, still speaking very loudly.

'Sir?'

Widmerpool was not in the least prepared at that moment for such an onslaught. Only a few minutes before he had been congratulating himself aloud on how successfully had gone his share of the exercise. Now he stood staring at Colonel Hogbourne-Johnson in a way that was bound to make matters worse rather than better.

'Traffic circuits!' shouted Colonel Hogbourne-Johnson. 'What in God's name have you done about them? Don't you know that's a DAAG's job? I suppose you don't. You're not fit to organise an outing for a troop of Girl Guides in the vicarage garden. Divisional Headquarters

53

has been ordered to move back to base forthwith. Are you aware of that?'

'Certainly, sir.'

'You've read the Movement Order? Have you got as far as that?'

'Of course, sir.'

'And made appropriate arrangements?'

'Yes, sir.'

'Then why is the Medium Field Regiment coming in at right angles across our route? That's not all. It has just been reported to me that Divisional Signals, and all their technical equipment, are being held up at another cross-roads half a mile up the same road by the Motor Ambulance Convoy making a loop and entering the main traffic artery just ahead of them.'

'I talked with the DAPM about distributory roads, sir—' began Widmerpool.

'I don't want to hear who you talked to,' said Colonel Hogbourne-Johnson, his voice rising quite high with fury. 'I want an immediate explanation of the infernal muddle your incompetence has made.'

If Widmerpool were not allowed to mention recommendations put forward by Keef, Captain Commanding Military Police at Div HQ, also to some extent responsible for traffic control, it was obviously impossible for him to give a clear picture of what arrangements had been made for moving the column back. Brigadier Hawkins used to advocate two sovereign phrases for parrying dissatisfaction or awkward interrogation on the part of a superior: 'I don't know, sir, I'll find out', and its even more potent alternative: 'the officer/man in question has been transferred to another unit'. On this occasion, neither of those great international army formulae of exorcism were applicable. Matters were in any case too urgent. For once, those powerful twin spells were ineffective. However, Widmerpool, as it turned out, could do far better than fall back on such in-decisive rubric, however magical, to defend his own position. He possessed chapter and verse. Instead of answer-ing at once, he allowed Colonel Hogbourne-Johnson to fume, while he himself drew from the breast pocket of his battle-dress blouse a fat little notebook. After glancing for a second or two at one of its pages, he looked up again, and immediately began to recite a detailed account of troop movements, unit by unit, throughout the immediate area of Divisional activities.

'. . . Medium Field Regiment proceeding from . . . on the move at . . . must have reached . . . in fact, sir, should already have passed that point on the road twenty minutes ago . . . Motor Ambulance Convoy . . . shouldn't be any-where near the Royal Signals route . . . proceeding to base via one of the minor roads parallel to and south of our main body . . . I'll show you on the map in a second, sir . . . only thing I can think of is some trouble must have occurred on that narrow iron bridge crossing the canal. That bridge wasn't built for heavy traffic. I'll send a DR right away . . .'

These details showed commendable knowledge of local transport conditions. Widmerpool recapitulated a lot more in the same vein, possessing apparently the movement-tables of the entire Division, an awareness that certainly did him credit as DAAG. The information should have satisfied Colonel Hogbourne-Johnson that, whatever else could have happened, Widmerpool, at least on the face of it, was not to blame for any muddle that might have taken place. However, Colonel Hogbourne-Johnson was in no state of mind to give consideration to any such possi-bility; nor, indeed, to look at the problem, or anything else, in the light of reason. There was something to be said for this approach. It is no good being too philosophical about such questions as a column of troops in a traffic jam. Action is required, not explanation. Such action may have to transcend reason. Historical instances would not be difficult to find. That concept provided vindication for Colonel Hogbourne-Johnson's method, hard otherwise to excuse.

'You've made a disgraceful mess of things,' he said. 'You ought to be ashamed of yourself. I know we have to put up these days with a lot of amateur staff officers who've had little or no experience, and possess even less capacity for learning the ABC of military affairs. Even so, we expect something better than this. Off you go now and find out immediately what's happened. When you've done so, report back to me. Look sharp about it.'

Widmerpool's face had gone dark red. It was an occasion as painful to watch as the time when Budd had hit him between the eyes full-pitch with an overripe banana; or that moment, even more portentous, when Barbara Goring poured sugar over his head at a ball. Under the impact of those episodes, Widmerpool's bearing had indicated, under its mortification, masochistic acceptance of the assault—'that slavish look' Peter Templer had noted on the day of the banana. Under Colonel Hogbourne-Johnson's tirade, Widmerpool's demeanour proclaimed no such thing. Perhaps that was simply because Hogbourne-Johnson was not of sufficiently high rank, in comparison with Budd (then captain of the Eleven), not a person of any but local and temporary importance in the eyes of someone like Widmerpool, who thought big—in terms of the Army Council and beyond—while Barbara had invoked a passion in him which placed masochism in love's special class. All the same, the difference is worth recording.

56

'Right, sir,' he said.

He saluted, turned smartly on his heel (rather in the manner of one of Bithel's boyhood heroes), and tramped out of the cowshed. Colonel Hogbourne-Johnson showered a hail of minor rebukes on several others present, then went off to raise hell elsewhere. In due course, not without delays, matters were sorted out. The dispatch-rider sent by Widmerpool returned with news that one of the field ambulances, skidding in mud churned up by the passing and repassing of tanks, had wedged its back wheels in a deep ditch. Meanwhile, the Light Aid Detachment, occupied some miles away with an infantry battalion's damaged carrier tracks, was not allowed—as too heavy in weight—to cross the iron bridge mentioned by Widmerpool. The LAD had therefore been forced to make a detour. The blocked road necessitated several other traffic diversions, which resulted in the temporary hold-up. That had already been cleared up by the time the DR reached the crossroads. No one was specially to blame, certainly not Widmerpool, such accidents as that of the ambulance representing normal wear-and-tear to be expected from movement of most of the available Command transport across country where roads were few and bad.

At the same time, to be unjustly hauled over the coals about such a matter is in the nature of things, certainly military things. Incidents like this must take place all the time in the army. In due course, I was to witness generals holding impressive appointments receiving a telling-off in the briskest manner imaginable, from generals of even greater eminence, all concerned astronomically removed from the humble world of Hogbourne-Johnson and Widmerpool. All the same, it was true Colonel Hogbourne-Johnson had been violent in his denunciation, conveying strictures on what he believed to be inefficiency with a kind of personal contempt that was unfitting, something over and above an official reprimand for supposed administrative mishandling. In addition, Hogbourne-Johnson, as a rule, seemed thoroughly satisfied with Widmerpool, as Widmerpool himself had often pointed out.

Whatever the rights and wrongs of the case, Widmerpool was very sore about it. He took it as badly as my former Company Commander, Rowland Gwatkin, used to take his tickings-off from the adjutant, Maelgwyn-Jones. In fact this comparatively trivial exchange between them transformed Widmerpool from an adherent of Colonel Hogbourne-Johnson—even if, in private, a condescending one—to becoming the Colonel's most implacable enemy. As it turned out, opportunity to make himself awkward arose the day we returned from the exercise. In fact, revenge was handed to Widmerpool, as it were, on a plate. This came about in connexion with Mr Diplock, Colonel Hogbourne-Johnson's chief clerk.

'Diplock may be an old rascal,' Colonel Hogbourne-Johnson himself had once commented, 'but he knows his job backwards.'

Repeating the remark later, Widmerpool had indulged in one of his rare excursions into sarcasm.

'We all know Diplock's a rascal,' he had remarked, 'and also knows his job backwards. The question is—does he know it forwards? In my own view, Diplock is one of the major impediments to the dynamic improvement of this formation.'

Mr Diplock (so styled from holding the rank of Warrant Officer, Class One) was a Regular Army Reservist, recalled to the colours at the outbreak of war. As indicating status bordering on the brink of a commissioned officer's (more

58

highly paid than a subaltern), he was entitled to service dress of officer-type cloth (though high-collared) and shoes instead of boots. His woolly grey hair, short thick body, air of perpetual busyness, suggested an industrious gnome conscripted into the service of the army; a gnome who also liked to practise considerable malice against the race of men with whom he mingled, by making as complicated as possible every transaction they had to execute through himself. Diplock was totally encased in military obscurantism. Barker-Shaw, the FSO—as Bithel mentioned, a don in civil life—had cried out, in a moment of exasperation, that Diplock, with education behind him, could have taken on the whole of the Civil Service, collectively and individually, in manipulation of red tape; and emerged victorious. He would have outdone them all, Barker-Shaw said, in pedantic observance of regulation for its own sake to the detriment of practical requirement. Diplock's answer to such criticism was always the same: that no other way of handling the matter existed. Filling in forms, rendering 'states', the whole process of documentation, seemed to take the place of religion in his inner life. The skill he possessed in wielding army lore reached a pitch at which he could sabotage, or at least indefinitely protract, almost any matter that might have earned the disapproval of himself or any superior of whom he happened to be the partisan—in practice, Colonel Hogbourne-Johnson—while at the same time, if something administratively unusual had to be arranged, Diplock always said he knew how to arrange it. This self-confidence, on the whole justified, was perhaps the main reason why Colonel Hogbourne-Johnson was so well affected towards his chief clerk. The other was no doubt the parade of deference—of a deeper, better understood sort than Cocksidge's—that Diplock, in return, offered to

Colonel Hogbourne-Johnson. Diplock's methods had always irritated Widmerpool, although himself no enemy to formal routine as a rule.

'I told Hogbourne-Johnson in so many words this morning that we should never get anything done here so long as we had a chief clerk who was such an old woman. Do you know what he said?'

Although Widmerpool prided himself on his own grasp of army life, he had not been able wholly to jettison the more civilian approach, that you are paid to give advice to your superiors in whatever happens to be a specialised aspect of your particular job; that such advice should be presented in the plainest, most forceful terms. He never quite became accustomed to a tradition that aims at total self-effacement in the subordinate, more especially when his professional recommendations are controversial.

'What was the answer?'

' "Diplock wasn't an old woman when he won the Military Medal".'

'How does he know?—some old women are very tough.'

'I replied in the most respectful manner that Diplock won the MM a long time ago,' said Widmerpool, ignoring this facetiousness. 'That I was only referring to his present fumbling about with ACIs, Ten-Ninety-Eights, every other bit of bumph he can lay his hands on, especially when something is needed in a hurry. I suppose Hogbourne-Johnson thought he was snubbing me. He gave that curious snarling laugh of his.'

This slight brush had taken place before Widmerpool's more disastrous encounter with the Colonel. It illustrated not only Widmerpool's retention, in certain respects, of civilian values, but also his occasional lack of grasp of some quite obvious matter. Even in civilian life, a frontal attack would have been ill-judged in approaching a relationship in a business firm such as Hogbourne-Johnson's with Diplock. It was not going to alter the stranglehold Diplock enjoyed on Hogbourne-Johnson. At the same time, the fact that Widmerpool felt it possible to offer that remark about Diplock at all, absolved him from any suggestion of later deliberately assailing the Colonel through insidious attack by way of his own chief clerk. Widmerpool had already decided Diplock was unsatisfactory. When the time came, of course, he was not blind to pleasure derived from that method, but he did not contrive it of sheer malice. Once the ball was rolling, as DAAG, he had no alternative but to follow up suspicions aroused.

That even the lightest of such suspicions should have come into being on the subject of Mr Diplock behaving in an irregular manner might seem out of the question; far less, that there should be indications he was embezzling government funds. However, that was how things began to look. Possibly so much rectitude in observing the letter of the law in matters of daily routine required, psychologically speaking, release in another direction. General Conyers had been fond of expatiating on something of the sort. Anyway, the affair opened by Widmerpool saying one day, soon after the three-day exercise, that he was not satisfied with the financial administration of the HQ Sergeants' Mess.

'Something funny is going on there,' he said. 'Diplock is at the bottom of it, I'm sure. I've told those Mess treasurers time and again to take the bottle from the cellar account and charge it to the bar account. They never seem to understand. In Diplock's case, it looks to me as if he *won't* understand.'

These doubts were not set at rest as the weeks passed.

Not long after Widmerpool made this comment, several small sums of money disappeared from places where they had been deposited.

'I've recommended that cash-boxes be screwed to the floor,' said Widmerpool. 'At least you know then where they've been left. Diplock put all sorts of difficulties in the way, but I insisted.'

'Have you mentioned these losses higher up?'

'I had a word with Pedlar, who didn't at all agree with what I am beginning to wonder—I try to have as few direct dealings as possible now with Hogbourne-Johnson. I am well aware I should not receive a sympathetic hearing there. It will be a smack in the eye for him if my suspicions turn out to be correct.'

Then it appeared, in addition to the Sergeants' Mess, something unsatisfactory was afoot in connexion with the Commuted Ration Allowance.

'Mark my words,' said Widmerpool. 'This is all going to link up. What I require is evidence. As a start, you will go out to the Supply Column tomorrow and make a few enquiries. I must have facts and figures. As you are to be travelling in that direction, it will be a good opportunity to explain those instructions I have here just issued to RASC sub-units. You can go on to the Ammunition Company and the Petrol Company, after you've gathered the other information. Take haversack rations, as they're some distance apart, and the other thing will need some little time to extract. There may be lack of co-operation. CRASC has been difficult ever since the business of those trucks, which I was, in fact, putting to a perfectly legitimate use.'

At one time or another, Widmerpool had quarrelled with most of the officers at Divisional Headquarters. The row with CRASC—Commanding Royal Army Service Corps at

HQ, a lieutenant-colonel—had been about employment of government transport on some occasion when interpretation of regulations was in doubt. It had been a drawn battle, like that with Sunny Farebrother. Widmerpool's taste for conflict seemed to put him less at a disadvantage than might be supposed. His undoubted reputation for efficiency had indeed been to some extent built up on being regarded as a difficult man to deal with; rather than on much more deserved respect for the plodding away at unspectacular work to which he used to devote himself every night in his own office. Personal popularity is an asset easy to exaggerate in the transaction of practical affairs. Possibly it can even be a handicap. The fact that Widmerpool was brusque with everyone he met, even actively disobliging to most, never seemed in the last resort to weaken his position. However the Diplock affair was rather a different matter.

Enquiries at the quarters of the Supply Column indicated that, as Widmerpool supposed, all was not well. His feud with CRASC had certainly penetrated there, if unwillingness to spare time to impart information was anything to judge by. I left the place with a clearer understanding of my father's strictures, in the distant past, regarding Uncle Giles's transference to the Army Service Corps. However, certain essential details were now to some extent available. There could be no doubt that, at best, existing arrangements, so far as the Sergeants' Mess was concerned, were in disorder; at worst, something more serious was taking place in which Diplock might be involved. I brought back the material required by Widmerpool that evening.

'Just as I thought,' he said, 'I'll go and have a word with A & Q right away.'

Widmerpool stayed a long time with Colonel Pedlar. He had told me to wait until his return, in case further information collected during the day might be needed. When he came back to the room his expression immediately showed that he regarded the interview to have been unsatisfactory.

'Things will have to be looked into further,' he said. 'Pedlar's still unwilling to believe anything criminal is taking place. I don't agree with him. Just run through what they told you again.'

It was nearly dinner time when I arrived back that night at F Mess. I went to the bedroom to change into service dress. When I came down the stairs, the rest of them were going into the room where we ate.

'Buck up, Jenkins,' said Biggs, 'or you'll miss all the lovely bits of gristle Sopey's been collecting from the swill tubs all the afternoon for us to gnaw. Wonder he has the cheek to put the stuff he does in front of a man.'

He was in one of his noisy moods that night. When Biggs felt cheerful—which was not often—he liked to shout and indulge in horseplay. This usually took the form of ragging Soper, the Divisional Catering Officer. Soper, also a captain with '14–'18 ribbons, was short and bandy-legged, which, with heavy eyebrows and deep-set shifty eyes, gave him a simian appearance that for some reason suggested a professional comedian. In civil life one of the managers, on the supply side, of a chain of provincial restaurants, he was immersed in his work as DCO, never in fact making a remark that in the least fitted in with his promisingly slapstick appearance, or even one to be classed as a joke. Off duty he talked of scarcely any subject but army allowances. Biggs and Soper to some extent reproduced, at their lower level, the relationship of Colonel Hogbourne-Johnson and Colonel Pedlar in the General's Mess; that is to say they grated on each other's nerves, but, as twin veterans of the earlier war, maintained some sort of uneasy alliance. This bond was strengthened by a fellow feeling engendered by the relatively unexalted nature of their own appointments, both being much on their dignity where the 'G' staff—'operational' in duties—was concerned. There was, however, this important deviation in their reflection of the two colonels' relationship, for, although Biggs, aggressive and strident, so to speak bullied Soper (like Colonel Hogbourne-Johnson oppressing Colonel Pedlar), it was Soper who, vis-à-vis Biggs, enjoyed the role of man of the world, pundit of a wider sophistication. For example, Soper's knowingness about food—albeit army food—impressed Biggs, however unwillingly.

'How are the diet sheets, Sopey?' said Biggs, belching as he sat down. 'When are you going to give us a decent bit of beefsteak for a change? Can you tell me that?'

Soper showed little or no interest in this enquiry, certainly predominantly rhetorical in character. He had picked up a fork, from which he was removing with his thumbnail a speck of dried vegetable matter that adhered to the handle.

'Wouldn't you like to know,' was all he replied, adding to the table in general, 'Suppose if I complain about the washing up, we'll just be told there's not enough water.'

The raid that had taken place while we were on the Command exercise had damaged one of the local mains, so that F Mess was suffering from a water shortage; produced as excuse for every inadequacy in the kitchen.

'What do you say, Doc?' said Biggs, turning in the other direction. 'Couldn't you do with a nice cut of rump steak with a drop of blood on it? I know I could. Makes my mouth water, the thought. I'd just about gobble it up.'

Macfie, DADMS, a regular Royal Army Medical Corps

major, who had seen some pre-war service in India, gaunt, glum, ungenial, rarely spoke at meals or indeed at any other time. Now, glancing at Biggs with something like aversion, he made no answer beyond jerking his head slightly a couple of times before returning to the type-written report he was thumbing over. No one among the two or three others at the table seemed any more disposed to comment.

'Come on, Doc, give the VD stats a rest at mealtimes,' said Biggs, who had perhaps drunk more beer than usual before dinner. 'God, I'm looking forward to some grub. Feel as empty as a bloody drum.'

He began stamping his feet loudly on the bare boards of the floor, at the same time banging with his clenched fists on the table.

'Buck up, waiter!' he shouted. 'When are we going to get something to eat, you slow bugger?'

'I want to swop night duty tomorrow,' said Soper. 'Take it on, Jenkins?'

'Mine's next Friday.'

'That'll do me.'

'They won't change the system again?'

'I'll act for you even if they do.'

'OK.'

Soper had caught me out once on a reorganised Duty Roster, avoiding my turn for night duty as well as his own. He was sharp on matters of that kind. I did not want to fall for a second confidence trick. Biggs ceased his tattoo on the surface of the table.

'Couldn't get a bloody staff car all day,' he said. 'I've a good mind to put in a report to A & Q.'

'Fat lot of good that would do,' said Soper.

He seemed satisfied now the fork was fairly clean, replacing it by the side of his plate. A spoon now attracted his attention.

'Organising that bloody boxing next week's going to be a bugger,' said Biggs. 'Don't have an easy life like you, Sopey, you old sod, driving round the units in state and tasting the sea-pie and Bisto. Hope this bloody beef isn't as tough tonight as it was yesterday. I'll be after you, Sopey, if it is. God, what a day it's been. A & Q on my tail all the time about that bloody boxing, and Colonel H-J giving me the hell of a rocket about a lot of training pamphlets I'd never heard of. He came through on the blower after I'd locked the safe and was looking forward to downing a pint. I'm just about brassed off, I can tell you. Went to see Bithel of the Mobile Laundry this afternoon. He's a funny bugger, if ever there was one. We had a pint together all the same. He soaks up that porter pretty easy. It was about one of his chaps that's done a bit of boxing. Might represent Div HQ, if he's the right weight. We could win that boxing compo, you know. That would put me right with Colonel H-J. Command's best welterweight had a bomb dropped on him in the blitz the other night, when they hit the barracks. Gives us a chance.'

Plates of meat were handed round by a waiter.

'Potatoes, sir?'

I was thinking of other things; thinking, to be precise, that I could do with a bottle of wine, then and there, however rough or sour. The Mess waiter was holding a dish towards me. I took a potato; then, for some reason, looked up at him. His enquiry, though quietly made, had penetrated incisively into these fantasies of the grape, cutting a neat channel, as it were, through both vinous daydreams and a powerful conversational ambience generated

67

by Biggs in his present mood. I glanced at the waiter's face for a second, then looked away, feeling, as I took a second potato, faintly, indeterminately uneasy. The soldier was tall and thin, about my own age apparently, with a pale, washed-out complexion, high forehead, dark hair receding at the temples and slightly greying. Bloodshot eyes, with dark, bluish rims, were alive, but gave at the same time an impression of poor health, this vitiated look increased by the fact of a battle-dress blouse with a collar too big in circumference for a long thin neck. I replaced the spoon in the potato dish, still aware of a certain inner discomfort. The waiter moved on to Biggs, who took four potatoes, examining each in turn, as, one after another, they rolled on to his plate, splashing gravy on the cloth. I followed the waiter with my eyes, while he offered the dish to Macfie.

'Spuds uneatable again,' said Biggs. 'Like bloody golf balls. They haven't been done long enough. That's all about it. Here, waiter, tell the chef, with my compliments, that he bloody well doesn't know how to cook water.'

'I will, sir.'

'And he can stick these spuds up his arse.'

'Yes, sir.'

'Repeat to him just what I've said.'

'Certainly, sir.'

'Where's he to stick the spuds?'

'Up his arse, sir.'

'Bugger off and tell him.'

So far as cooking potatoes went, I was wholly in agreement with Biggs. However, purely gastronomic considerations were submerged in confirmation of a preliminary impression; an impression upsetting, indeed horrifying, but correct. There could no longer be any doubt of that.

What I had instantaneously supposed, then dismissed as inconceivable, was, on closer examination, no longer to be denied. The waiter was Stringham. He was about to go through to the kitchen to deliver Biggs's message to the cook, when Soper stopped him.

'Half a tick,' said Soper. 'Who laid the table?'

'I did, sir.'

'Where's the salt?'

'I'll get some salt, sir.'

'Why didn't you put any salt out?'

'I'm afraid I forgot, sir.'

'Don't forget again.'

'I'll try not to, sir.'

'I didn't say try not to, I said don't.'

'I won't, sir.'

'Haven't they got any cruets in the Ritz?' said Biggs. 'Hand the pepper and salt round personally to all the guests, I suppose.'

'Mustard, sir—French, English, possibly some other more obscure brands—so far as I remember, sir, rather than salt and pepper,' said Stringham, 'but handing round the latter too could be a good idea.'

He went out of the room to find the salt, and tell the cook what Biggs thought about the cooking. Soper turned to Biggs. He was plainly glad of this opportunity to put the SOPT in his place.

'Don't show your ignorance, Biggy,' he said. 'Handing salt round at the Ritz. I ask you. You'll be going into the Savoy next for a plate of fish and chips or baked beans and a cup o' char.'

'That's no reason why we shouldn't have any salt here, is it?' said Biggs.

He spoke belligerently, disinclined for once to accept

69

Soper as social mentor, even where a matter so familiar to the DCO as restaurant administration was in question.

'Something wrong with that bloke,' he went on. 'Man's potty. You can see it. Hear what he said just now? Talks in that la-di-da voice. Why did he come to this Mess? What happened to Robbins? Robbins wasn't much to look at, but at least he knew you wanted salt.'

'Gone to hospital with rupture,' said Soper. 'This one's a replacement for Robbins. Can't be much worse, if you ask me.'

'This one'll have to be invalided too,' said Biggs. 'Only got to look at him to see that. Bet I'm right. No good having a lot of crazy buggers about, even as waiters. Got to get hold of blokes who are fit for something. Jesus, what an army.'

'Always a business finding a decent Mess waiter,' said Soper. 'Can't be picking and choosing all the time. Have to take what you're bloody well offered.'

'Don't like the look of this chap,' said Biggs. 'Gets me down, that awful pasty face. Can't stick it. Reckon he tosses off too much, that's what's wrong with him, I shouldn't wonder. You can always tell the type.'

From the rubber valve formed by pressure together of upper and lower lip, he unexpectedly ejected a small morsel of fat, discharging this particle with notable accuracy of aim on to the extreme margin of his plate, just beyond the potatoes left uneaten. It was a first-rate shot of its kind.

'When did the new waiter arrive?' I asked.

Nothing was to be gained by revealing previous acquaintance with Stringham.

'Started here at lunch today,' said Soper.

'I've run across him before,' said Biggs.

'At Div HQ?'

'One of the fatigue party fixing up the boxing ring,' said Biggs. 'Ever so grand the way he talks, you wouldn't believe. Needs taking down a peg or two in my opinion. That's why I asked him about the Ritz. Don't expect he's ever been inside the Ritz more than I have.'

Soper did not immediately comment. He stared thoughtfully at the scrap of meat rejected by Biggs, either to imply censure of too free and easy table manners, or, in official capacity as DCO, professionally assessing the nutritive value of that particular cube of fat—and its waste—in wartime. Macfie also gave Biggs a severe glance, rustling his typewritten report admonishingly, as he propped the sheets against the water jug, the better to absorb their contents while he ate.

'He'll do as a waiter so long as we keep him up to the mark,' said Soper, after a while. 'You're always grousing about something, Biggy. If it isn't one thing, it's another. Why don't you put a bloody sock in it?'

'There's enough to grouse about in this bloody Mess, isn't there?' said Biggs, his mouth full of beef and cabbage, but still determined to carry the war into Soper's country. 'Greens stewed in monkeys' pee and pepper as per usual.'

Stringham had returned by this time with the salt. Dinner proceeded along normal lines. Food, however unsatisfactorily cooked, always produced a calming effect on Biggs, so that his clamour gradually died down. Once I caught Stringham's eye, and thought he gave a faint smile to himself. Nothing much was said by anyone during the rest of the meal. It came to an end. We moved to the anteroom. Later, when preparing to return to the DAAG's office, I saw Stringham leave the house by the back door. He was accompanied by a squat, swarthy lance-corporal, no doubt the cook so violently stigmatised by Biggs. At Headquarters, when I got back there, Widmerpool was already in his room, going through a pile of papers. I told him about the appearance of Stringham in F Mess. He listened, showing increasing signs of uneasiness and irritation.

'Why on earth does Stringham want to come here?'

'Don't ask me.'

'He might easily prove a source of embarrassment if he gets into trouble.'

'There's no particular reason to suppose he'll get into trouble, is there? The embarrassment is for me, having him as a waiter in F Mess.'

'Stringham was a badly behaved boy at school,' said Widmerpool. 'You must remember that. You knew him much better than I did. He took to drink early in life, didn't he? I recall at least one very awkward incident when I myself had to put him to bed after he had had too much.'

'I was there too—but he is said to have been cured of drink.'

'You can never be sure with alcoholics.'

'Perhaps he could be fixed up with a better job.'

'But being a Mess waiter is one of the best jobs in the army,' said Widmerpool impatiently. 'It's not much inferior to sanitary lance-corporal. In that respect he has nothing whatever to grumble about.'

'So far as I know, he isn't grumbling. I only meant one might help in some way.'

'In what way?'

'I can't think at the moment. There must be something.'

'I have always been told,' said Widmerpool, '—and rightly told—that it is a great mistake in the army, or indeed elsewhere, to allow personal feelings about individuals to affect my conduct towards them professionally. I mentioned this to you before in connexion with

72

Corporal Mantle. Mind your own business is a golden rule for a staff officer.'

'But you're not minding your own business about who's to command the Recce Corps.'

'That is quite different,' said Widmerpool. 'In a sense the command of the Recce Corps *is* my business—though perhaps someone like yourself cannot see that. The point is this. Why should Stringham have some sort of preferential treatment just because you and I happen to have been at school with him? That is exactly what people complain about—and with good reason. You must be aware that such an attitude of mind—that certain persons have a right to a privileged existence—causes a lot of ill feeling among those less fortunately placed. War is a great opportunity for everyone to find his level. I am a major—you are a second-lieutenant—he is a private. I have no doubt that you and I will achieve promotion. So far as you are concerned, you will in any case receive a second pip automatically at the conclusion of eighteen months' service as an officer, which in your case cannot be far off by now. I think I can safely say that my own rank will not much longer be denoted by a mere crown. Of Stringham, I feel less certain. A private soldier he is, and, in my opinion, a private soldier he will remain.'

'All the more reason for trying to find him a suitable billet. It can't be much fun handing round the vegetables in F Mess twice a day.'

'We are not in the army to have fun, Nicholas.'

I accepted the rebuke, and said no more about Stringham. However, that night in bed, I reflected further on his arrival at Div HQ. We had not met for years; not since the party his mother had given for Moreland's symphony—where all the trouble had started about

Moreland and my sister-in-law, Priscilla. Priscilla, as it happened, was in the news once more, from the point of view of her family. Rumours were going round that, separated from Chips Lovell by the circumstances of war, she was not showing much discretion about her behaviour. A 'fighter-pilot' was said often to be seen with her, this figment, in another version, taking the form of a 'commando', loose use of the term to designate an individual, rather the unit's collective noun. However, all that was by the way. The last heard of Stringham himself had been from his sister, Flavia Wisebite, who had described her brother as cured of drink and serving in the army. At least the second of these two statements was now proved true. It was to be hoped the first was equally reliable. Meanwhile, there could be no doubt it was best to conceal the fact that we knew each other. Widmerpool also agreed on this point, when he himself brought up the subject again the following day. He too appeared to have pondered the matter during the night.

'So you think something else should be found for Stringham?' he asked that afternoon.

'I do.'

'I'll give my mind to it,' he said, speaking more soberly than on the earlier occasion. 'In the meantime, we are none of us called upon to do more than fulfil the duties of our respective ranks and appointments, vegetables or no vegetables. Now go and find out from the DAPM whether he has proceeded with the enquiries to be made in connexion with Diplock and his dealings. Get cracking. We can't talk about Stringham all day.'

So far as Stringham's employment in F Mess was concerned, nothing of note happened during the next day or two. On the whole he did what was required of him with competence—certainly better than Robbins—though he would sometimes unsmilingly raise his eyebrows when waiting on me personally. For one reason or another, circumstances always prevented speech between us. I began to think we might not be able to find an opportunity to talk together before I went on leave. Then one evening, on the way back to F Mess from Headquarters, I saw Stringham coming towards me in the twilight. He saluted, looking straight ahead of him, was going to pass on, when I put out a hand.

'Charles.'

'Hullo, Nick.'

'This is extraordinary.'

'What is?'

'Your turning up here.'

'What makes you think so?'

'Let's get off the main road.'

'If you like.'

We went down into a kind of alley-way, leading to a block of office buildings or factory works, now closed for the night.

'What's been happening to you, Charles?'

'As you see, I've become a waiter in F Mess. I always used to wonder what it felt like to be a waiter. Now I know with immense precision.'

'But how did it all come about?'

'How does anything come about in the army?'

'When did you join, for instance?'

'Too long ago to remember—right at the beginning of the Hundred Years War. After enlisting in my first gallant and glorious corps, and serving at their depot, I managed to exchange into the infantry, and got posted to this melancholy spot. You know how—to use a picturesque army phrase—one gets arsed around. I don't expect that happens any less as an officer. When the Royal Army Ordnance Corps took me to its stalwart bosom, I was not medically graded A.1.—which explains why in the past one's so often woken up feeling like the wrath of God—so I got drafted to Div HQ, a typical example of the odds and sods who fetch up at a place like that. Hearing there was a job going as waiter in F Mess, I applied in triplicate. My candidature was graciously confirmed by Captain Soper. That's the whole story.'

'But isn't—can't we find something better for you?'

'What sort of thing?'

That had been Widmerpool's question too. Stringham asked it without showing the smallest wish for change, only curiosity at what might be put forward.

'I don't know. I thought there might be something.'

'Don't you feel I'm quite up to the mark as waiter?' he said. 'Nick, you fill me with apprehension. Surely you are not on the side of Captain Biggs, who, I realise, does not care for my personality. I thought I was doing so well. I admit failure about the salt. I absolutely acknowledge the machine broke down at that point. All the same, such slips befall the most practised. I remember when the Duke of Connaught lunched with my former in-laws, the Bridgnorths, the butler, a retainer of many years' standing, no mere neophyte like myself, offered him macaroni cheese without having previously provided His Royal Highness with a plate to eat it off. I shall never forget my ex-father-in-law's face, richly tinted at the best of times—my late brother-in-law, Harrison Wisebite, used to say Lord Bridgnorth's complexion recalled Our Artist's Impression of the Hudson in the Fall. On that occasion it was more like the Dutch bulb fields in bloom. No, forget about the salt,

76

Nick. We all make mistakes. I shall improve with habit.'

'I don't mean——'

'Between you and me, Nick, I think I have it in me to make a first-class Mess waiter. The talent is there. It's just a question of developing latent ability. I never dreamed I possessed such potentialities. It's been marvellous to release them.'

'I know, but——'

'You don't like my style? You feel I lack polish?'

'I wasn't——'

'After all, you must agree it's preferable to hand Captain Biggs his food, and retire to the kitchen with Lance-Corporal Gwither, rather than sit with the Captain throughout the meal, to have to watch him masticate, day in day out. Gwither, on the other hand, is a delightful companion. He was a plasterer's mate before he joined the army, and, whatever Captain Biggs may say to the contrary, is rapidly learning to cook as an alternative. In addition to that, Nick, I understand you yourself work for our old schoolmate, Widmerpool. You're not going to try and swop jobs, are you? If so, it isn't on. How did your Widmerpool connexion come about, anyway?'

I explained my transference from battalion to Div HQ had been the result of Widmerpool applying for me by name as his assistant. Stringham listened, laughing from time to time.

'Look, Charles, let's fix up dinner one night. A Saturday, preferably, when most of the stuff at the DAAG's office has been cleared up after the week's exercise. We've a mass of things to talk about.'

'My dear boy, are you forgetting our difference in rank?'

'No one bothers about that off duty. How could they? London restaurants are packed with officers and Other

77

Ranks at the same table. Life would be impossible otherwise. My own brothers-in-law, for example, range from George, a major, to Hugo, a lance-bombardier. We needn't dine at the big hotel, such as it is, if you prefer a quieter place.'

'I didn't really mean that, Nick. I know perfectly well, in practice, we could dine together—even though you would probably have to pay, as I'm not particularly flush at the moment. It isn't that. I just don't feel like it. Dining with you would spoil the rhythm so far as I'm concerned. I wouldn't go so far as to say I'm actively enjoying what I'm doing at the moment—but then how little of one's life has ever been actively enjoyable. At the same time, what I'm doing is what I've chosen to do. Even what I want to do, if it comes to that. Up to a point it suits me. I've become awfully odd these days. Perhaps I always was odd. Anyway, that's beside the point. How I drone on about myself. Talking of your relations, though, I heard your brother-in-law, Robert Tolland, was killed.'

'Poor Robert. In the fighting round the Channel ports.'

'Awfully chic to be killed.'

'I suppose so.'

'Oh, yes, of course. You can't beat it. Smart as hell. Fell in action. I'm always struck by that phrase. Seems absolutely no chance of action here, unless Captain Biggs draws a gun on me for handing him the brussels sprouts the wrong side, or spilling gravy on that bald head of his. You know Robert Tolland was running round with my sister, Flavia, before he went to France and his doom. You never met Flavia, did you?'

'Saw her and Robert together when I was on leave last year.'

'Flavia never has any luck with husbands and lovers.

Think of being married to Cosmo Flitton and Harrison Wisebite in quick succession. Why, I'd make a better husband myself. No doubt you heard at the same time that my mother's parted company with Buster Foxe. She's having money troubles at the moment. One of the reasons why Buster packed up. I'm feeling the draught myself. Decided shortage of ready cash. My father left what halfpence he had to that French wife of his, supposing, quite mistakenly, Mama would always be in a position to shell out.'

'Your mother's at Glimber?'

'Good God, no. Glimber has some ministry evacuated there, so that's one problem off her hands. She's living in a labourer's cottage near a camp in Essex to be near Norman —you remember, her little dancer. At one moment she was getting up at half-past five every morning to cook his breakfast. There's devotion for you. Norman's going to an OCTU. Won't he look wonderful in a Sam Browne belt—that waist. Of course by the nature of things he can only be a son to her—a better son than her own, I fear— and in any case living with Norman in a cottage must be infinitely preferable to Buster in a castle, even allowing for the early rising. How sententious one gets. Just the sort of conclusion Tennyson was always coming to. You know, talking of the Victorians, I've taken to reading Browning.'

'Our General reads Trollope—the Victorians are obviously the fashion in this Division.'

'It was Tuffy who started me off on him. Rather a surprising taste for her in a way. You remember Tuffy? Nick, you make me talk of old times.'

'Miss Weedon—of course.'

'Tuffy cured me of the booze. Then, having done that,

79

she got bored with me. I see the point, there was nothing more to do. I mean I was going to prove absolutely impossible to set up as a serious member of civilised society. Stopping drinking alone was sufficient to ensure that. Even I myself grasped I'd become the most desperate of bores by being permanently sober. Then the war came along and I began to develop all sorts of martial ambitions. Tuffy didn't really approve of them, although the fact they were even within the bounds of possibility so far as I was concerned was a considerable tribute to herself. She saw, all the same, one way or another, I was going to escape her clutches. The long and the short of it was, I entered the army, while Tuffy married an octogenarian—perhaps by now even nonagenarian—general. Just the age when you get into your stride as a soldier. They'll probably appoint him CIGS.'

'You're out of touch. Generals are frightfully young nowadays. Widmerpool will be one at any moment. Anyway, they might do worse than employ General Conyers. I've known him for years.'

'My dear Nick, you know everybody. Not a social item escapes you. I myself can no longer keep up with births, marriages and deaths—well, deaths now and then perhaps, but not births and marriages. That's why being in the ranks suits me. No strain in that particular respect. Nobody asks you if you read in this morning's *Times* that so-and-so's engaged or somebody else is getting a divorce. All that had begun to get me down for some reason. Make me tired. Anyway, to hark back to the long and wearisome story of my own life, the point was that Tuffy, like everyone else, had had enough of me. She wanted another sphere in which to exercise her tireless remedial activities. That was why I took the shilling:

I 'listed at home for a lancer,
Oh who would not sleep with the brave?

I am not, as your familiarity with military insignia will
already have proclaimed, strictly speaking a lancer—just as
well, for these days I couldn't possibly take part in those
musical rides lancers are always performing at the Military
Tournament and places like that . . . haven't sat on a
horse for years . . .'

Stringham paused a moment, beginning now to hum a
bar or two of a jerky tune, the sort to which riders at a
Horse Show might canter round the paddock.

'So-let-each-cavalier-who-loves-honour-and-me
Come-follow-the-bonnets-of-Bonny-Dundee . . .'

He curled his wrists slightly, lifting them in the air as
if holding reins. He seemed far away, to have forgotten
completely that we were talking. I wondered how sane he
remained. Then he came suddenly back to himself.

'. . . What was I saying? Oh, yes, A. E. Housman, of
course . . . not my favourite poet, as a matter of fact, but
that was just what happened . . . though I hasten to add
I sleep with the brave only in the sense of dormitory
accommodation. To tell the truth, Nick, I had the greatest
difficulty in extracting the metaphorical shilling from an
equally metaphorical Recruiting Sergeant. No magnificent
figure with a bunch of ribbons in his cap, but several rather
seedy characters in a stuffy office drinking cups of tea.
Even so, they wouldn't look at me when I first breezed in.
Then the war took a turn for the worse, in Norway and
elsewhere, and they saw they'd need Stringham after all.
One of the reasons I left the RAOC is that they have a

peculiarly trying warrant rank called Conductor—just as if you were on a bus—so I made the exchange I spoke of. What a fascinating place the army is. Before I joined, I thought all you had to do when you fired a rifle was to get your eye and the sights and the target all in one line and then blaze away. The army has produced a whole book about it, a fat little volume. But my egotism is insufferable, Nick. Tell me about yourself. What have you been doing? How are you reacting to it all? You look a trifle harassed, if I may say so. Not surprising, working with Widmerpool.'

Stringham himself looked ill, though not in the least harassed.

'On top of everything else,' he said, 'one's getting frightfully old. Do you think I shall qualify as a Chelsea pensioner after the war? I'd like one of those red frockcoats, though I've never cared for Chelsea as a neighbourhood. No leanings whatever towards bohemian life. However, one may come to both before one's finished—residence in Chelsea and a bohemian to boot. You know I've been thinking a lot about myself lately, when scrubbing the floors and that sort of thing—an activity for some reason I often find myself quite enjoying—and I've come to the conclusion I'm narcissistic, mad about myself. That's why my marriage went wrong. I really was awfully glad when it was over.'

'Do you do anything about girls now?'

'Seem to have lost all interest. Isn't that strange? You know how it is. My great amusement now is trying to get things straight in my own mind. That takes me all my time, as you can imagine. The more I think, the less I know. Funny, isn't it? Talking of girls, what happened to our old pal, Peter Templer? Do you remember how he used to go on about girls?'

'Peter's said to have some government job to do with finance.'

'Not in the army?'

'Not so far as I know.'

'How like Peter. Always full of good sense, in his own way, though many people never guessed that at first. Married?'

'First wife ran away—second one, he appears to have driven mad.'

'Has he?' said Stringham. 'Well, I daresay I might have driven Peggy mad, had we not gone our separate ways. Talking of separate ways, I'll have to be getting back to my cosy barrack-room, or I'll be on a charge. It's late.'

'Won't you really dine one night?'

'No, Nick, no. Better not, on the whole. I won't salute, if you'll forgive such informality, as no one seems to be about. Nice to have had a talk.'

He moved away before there was time even to say good-night, walking quickly up the path leading to the main thoroughfare. I followed at less speed. By the time I reached the road at the top of the alley, Stringham was already out of sight in the gloom. I turned again in the direction of F Mess. This reunion with an old friend had been the reverse of enjoyable, indeed upsetting, painful to a degree. I tried to imagine what Stringham's present existence must be like, but could reconstruct in the mind only superficial aspects, those which least disturbed, probably even stimulated him. I felt more than ever glad a week's leave lay ahead of me, one of those curious escapes that in wartime punctuate army life, far more than a 'holiday', comparable rather with brief and magical entries into another incarnation.

Widmerpool did not like anyone going on leave, least of

all his own subordinates. In justice to this attitude, he appeared to treat his own leaves chiefly as opportunities for extending freedom of contact with persons who might further his military career, working scarcely less industriously than when on duty. I should be in no position to criticise him in that respect, if General Liddament fulfilled his promise in relation to this particular leave, during which I too hoped to better my own condition. However, it was probable the General had forgotten about his remarks during the exercise. The tactical upheaval which immediately followed our talk would certainly have justified that. I had begun to wonder whether I ought to remind him, and, if so, how this should be effected. However, by the morning after the encounter with Stringham, I had still taken no step in that direction; nor had I mentioned the meeting to Widmerpool, who was, as it happened, in a peevish mood.

'When do you begin this leave of yours?' he asked.

'Tomorrow.'

'I thought it was the day after.'

'Tomorrow.'

'If you see your relations, the Jeavonses, it's as well for you to know their sister-in-law staying as a paying guest in my mother's cottage wasn't a success. My mother decided she'd rather have evacuees.'

'Has she got evacuees?'

'She had some for a short time,' said Widmerpool, 'then they went back to London. They were absolutely ungrateful.'

He talked of his mother less than formerly, even giving an impression from time to time that Mrs Widmerpool's problems had begun to irritate him, that he felt she was becoming a millstone round his neck. Widmerpool had been on edge for several days past owing to the Diplock affair turning out to be so much more complicated than appeared on first examination. Diplock had brought all his own notable powers of causing confusion to bear, darkening the waters round him like a cuttlefish, so that evidence was hard to collect. Colonel Hogbourne-Johnson, for his part, made no secret of regarding Widmerpool's attempted impeachment of his chief clerk as nothing more nor less than a personal attack on himself. Indeed, Widmerpool could not have hit on a more wounding method of revenging himself on the Colonel, if his suspicions about Diplock were in due course to be substantiated. On the other hand, there was likely to be trouble if nothing more could be proved than that Diplock had been in the habit of keeping rather muddled accounts. Greening, the General's ADC, came into the DAAG's room at that moment. He handed me a small slip of paper.

'His Nibs says you know about this,' he said.

Greening, although he blushed easily, was otherwise totally unselfconscious. He was inclined to express himself in a curious, outdated schoolboy slang that sounded as if it had been picked up from some favourite book in childhood. Probably this habit appealed to General Liddament's taste for a touch of the exotic in his entourage. He may even have encouraged Greening in vagaries of speech, an extension of his own Old English. The piece of paper was inscribed with the typewritten words 'Major L. Finn, VC', followed by the name of a Territorial regiment and a telephone number. I saw I had underrated General Liddament's capacity for detail.

'Not much he forgets about,' said Greening, with artless curiosity. 'What is it?'

ADCs are a category of officer usually disparaged in

popular scrutiny of military matters. On the whole, they are no worse than most, better than many; while the job they do is the best possible training, if they are likely to rise in the world. Greening was, of course, not the sort likely to rise very far.

'Just a message to be delivered in London.'

Widmerpool looked up from the file in which he was writing away busily.

'What is that?'

'Something for the General.'

'What are you to do?'

'Telephone this officer.'

'What officer?'

'A Major Finn.'

'And say what?'

'Give him the General's compliments.'

'Nothing else?'

'See what he says.'

'Sounds odd.'

'That's what the General said.'

'Let me see.'

I handed him the paper.

'Finn?' he said. 'It's a Whitehall number.'

'So I see.'

'A VC.'

'Yes.'

'I seem to know the name—Finn. Sure I know it. When did the General tell you to do this?'

'On the last Command exercise.'

'At what moment?'

'After dinner on the last night.'

'Did he say anything else?'

'He talked about Trollope—and Balzac.'

'The authors?'

I was tempted to reply, 'No—the generals,' but discretion prevailed.

'You seem to be on very intimate terms with the Divisional Commander,' said Widmerpool sourly. 'Well, let me tell you that you will return from leave to find a pile of work. Are you waiting for something, Greening?'

'The General bade me discourse fair words to you, sir, anent traffic circuits.'

'What the hell do you mean?'

'I don't know, sir,' said Greening. 'That's exactly how the General put it.'

Widmerpool did not answer. Greening went away. He was one of the most agreeable officers at those Headquarters. I never saw him much except on exercises. Towards the end of the war, I heard, in a roundabout way, that, after return to his regiment, he had been badly wounded at Anzio as a company commander and—so my informant thought—might have died in hospital.

2

SULLEN REVERBERATIONS of one kind or another—blitz in England, withdrawal in Greece—had been providing the most recent noises-off in rehearsals that never seemed to end, breeding a wish that the billed performance would at last ring up its curtain, whatever form that took. However, the date of the opening night rested in hands other than our own; meanwhile nobody could doubt that more rehearsing, plenty more rehearsing, was going to be needed for a long time to come. Although these might be dispiriting thoughts, an overwhelming sense of content descended as the train reached the outskirts of London. Spring seas had been rough the night before, the railway carriage as usual overcrowded, while we threaded a sluggish passage through blackness towards the south; from time to time entering—pausing in—then vacating—areas where air-raid warnings prevailed. Viewed from the windows of the train, the deserted highways and gutted buildings of outlying districts created to the eye the semblance of an abandoned city. Nevertheless, I felt full of hope.

London contacts had to be sorted out. A letter from Chips Lovell, received only the day before, complicated an arrangement to dine with Moreland that evening. Lovell had heard I was coming on leave, and wanted to talk about 'family affairs'. That was a motive reasonable enough in principle; in practice, a disturbing phrase, when considered in relation to rumoured 'trouble' with Priscilla. Lovell was a Marine. He had been commissioned into the Corps at the time of its big expansion at the beginning of the war, soon after this being posted to a station on the East Coast. Evidently he had moved from there, because he gave a London telephone exchange (with extension) to find him, though no indication of what his new employment might be.

First, I called up the number Greening had consigned from General Liddament. The voice of Major Finn on the line was quiet and deep, persuasive yet firm. I began to tell my story. He cut me short at once, seeming already aware what was coming, another tribute to the General's powers of transmuting thought to action. Instructions were to report later in the day to an address in Westminster. This offered breathing space. A hundred matters of one sort or another had to be negotiated before going down to the country. After speaking with Major Finn, I rang Lovell.

'Look, Nick, I never thought you'd get in touch so soon,' he said, before there was even time to suggest anything. 'Owing to a new development, I'm booked for dinner tonight—first date for months—but that makes it even more important I see you. I'm caught up in work at lunchtime—only knocking off for about twenty minutes—but we can have a drink later. Can't we meet near wherever you're dining, as I shan't get away till seven at the earliest.'

'The Café Royal—with Hugh Moreland.'

'I'll be along as soon as I can.'

'Hugh said he'd turn up about eight.'

It seemed required to emphasise that, if Lovell stayed too long over our drink, he would encounter Moreland.

89

This notification was in Moreland's interest, rather than Lovell's. Lovell had never been worried by the former closeness of Priscilla and Moreland. Priscilla might or might not have told her husband the whole affair with Moreland had been fruitless enough, had never taken physical shape; if she had, Lovell might or might not have believed her. It was doubtful whether he greatly minded either way. I myself accepted they had never been to bed, because Moreland had told me that in one of his few rather emotional outbursts. It was because Moreland was sensitive, perhaps even touchy about such matters, that he might not want to meet Lovell. Besides, if Priscilla were now behaving in a manner to cause Lovell concern, he too might well prefer to remain unreminded of a former beau of his wife's; a man with whom he had in any case not much in common, apart from Priscilla. This turned out to be a wrong guess on my own part. Lovell showed no sign whatever of wanting to avoid Moreland. On the contrary, he was disappointed the three of us were not all dining together that evening.

'What a relief to meet someone like Hugh Moreland again,' he said. 'Pity I can't join the party. I can assure you it would be more fun than what faces me. Anyway, I'll go into *that* when we meet.'

Lovell was an odd mixture of realism and romanticism; more specifically, he was, like quite a lot of people, romantic about being a realist. If, for example, the suspicion ever crossed his mind that Priscilla had married him 'on the rebound', any possible pang would have been allayed, in his philosophy, by the thought that he had in the end himself 'got the girl'. He might also have argued, of course, that the operation of the rebound is unpredictable, some people thwarted in love, shifting, bodily and totally, on to another person the whole weight of a former strong emotion. Lovell was romantic, especially, in the sense of taking things at their face value—one of the qualities that made him a good journalist. It never struck him anyone could think or do anything but the perfectly obvious. This took the practical form of disinclination to believe in the reality of any matter not of a kind to be ventilated in the press. At the same time, although incapable of seeing life from an unobvious angle, Lovell was prepared, when necessary, to vary the viewpoint—provided obviousness remained unimpeded, one kind of obviousness simply taking the place of another. This relative flexibility was owed partly to his own species of realism—when his realism, so to speak, 'worked'—partly forced on him by another of his firm moral convictions: that every change which took place in life—personal—political—social—was both momentous and for ever; a system of opinion also stimulating to the practice of his profession.

Once Lovell's way of looking at the world was allowed, he could be subtle about ways and means. With the additional advantages of good looks and plenty of push, these methods were bringing fair success in his chosen career by the time war broke out. In marrying Priscilla, he had not, it is true, consummated a formerly voiced design to 'find a rich wife'; but then that project had never, in fact, assumed the smallest practical shape. Its verbal expression merely illustrated another facet of Lovell's romanticism— in this case, romanticism about money. He had, in any case, taken a keen interest in Priscilla even back in the days when he and I had been working on film scripts together (none of which ever appeared on any screen), so there was no surprise when the two of them married. At first he lost jobs and they were hard up. Priscilla, who had some taste for living dangerously, never seemed to mind these lean stretches. Lovell himself used to present an equally unruffled surface to the world where shortage of money was concerned, though underneath he certainly felt guilty regarding lack of it. He looked upon lack of money as a failing in himself; or, for that matter, in anyone else. From time to time, though without any strong force behind it, his romanticism would take moral or intellectual turns too. He would indulge, for instance, in fits of condemning material things and all who pursued them. These moods were sometimes accompanied by reading potted philosophies: the Wisdom of the East in one volume, Marx Without Tears, the Treasury of Great Thought. Like everyone else of his kind he was writing a play, an undertaking that progressed never further than the opening pages of the First Act.

'I never get time to settle down to serious writing,' he used to say, thereby making what almost amounted to a legal declaration in defining his own inclusion within an easily recognisable category of non-starting literary apprenticeship.

These were some of the thoughts about Lovell that passed through my head while I sat on a bench in the hall waiting to see Major Finn. The address in Westminster to which I had been told to report turned out to be a large house converted to the use of military headquarters. After a while a Free French corporal, his arm in a sling, joined me on the bench; then two members of the Free French women's service. Soon the three of them began an argument together in their own language. I re-read Moreland's postcard—a portrait of Wagner in a kind of tam-o'-shanter—confirming our dinner that night. Enigmatic in tone, its wording indefinably lacked the liveliness of manner usual in this, Moreland's habitual mode of communication.

We had not met since the first week of the war, soon after Matilda had left him. Matilda's subsequent marriage to Sir Magnus Donners had been effected with an avoidance of publicity remarkable even at a time when all sorts of changes, public and private, many of these revolutionary enough, were being quietly brought about. Muting the news of the ceremony was no doubt to some extent attributable to controls Sir Magnus found himself in a position to exercise in certain fields. The wedding of the divorced wife of a musician, well known even if not particularly prosperous, to a member of the Government rated in general more attention, even allowing for the paper shortage, than the few scattered paragraphs that appeared at the time. People said the break-up of Moreland's marriage had at first so much disturbed him that he seemed likely to go to pieces entirely, giving himself up increasingly to drink, while living as best he could from one day to the next. However, a paradox of that moment in the war was an excess, rather than deficiency, of musical employment; so that, in fact, Moreland found himself immersed in work of one sort or another, which, even if not very inspiring professionally, kept him alive and busy. That, at any rate, was what I had heard. Inevitably we had lost touch with each other since I had been in the army. Friendship, popularly represented as something simple and straightforward—in contrast with love—is perhaps no less complicated, requiring equally mysterious nourishment; like love, too, bearing also within its embryo inherent seeds of dissolution, something more fundamentally destructive, perhaps, than the mere passing of time, the all-obliterating march of events which had, for example, come between Stringham and myself.

These rather sombre speculations were interrupted by a door opening nearby. A Free French officer in a képi appeared. Middle-aged, with spectacles, rather red in the face, he was followed from the room by a youngish, capless captain, wearing Intelligence Corps badges.

'Et maintenant, une dernière chose, mon Capitaine,' said the Frenchman, 'maintenant que nous avons terminé avec l'affaire Szymanski. Le Colonel s'est arrangé avec certains membres du Commandement pour que quelques jeunes officiers soient placés dans le Génie. Il espère que vous n'y verrez pas d'inconvenient.'

'Vous n'avez pas utilisé la procédure habituelle, Lieutenant?'

'Mon Capitaine, le Colonel Michelet a pensé que pour une pareille broutille on pouvait se dispenser des voies hierarchiques.'

'Nous aurons des ennuis.'

'Le Colonel Michelet est convaincu qu'ils seront négligeables.'

'Ça m'étonnerait.'

'Vous croyez vraiment?'

'J'en suis sûr. Il nous faut immédiatement une liste de ces noms.'

'Très bien, mon Capitaine, vous les aurez.'

The English officer shook his head to express horror at what had been contemplated. They both laughed a lot.

'Au revoir, Lieutenant.'

'Au revoir, mon Capitaine.'

The Frenchman retired. The captain turned to me.

'Jenkins?'

'Yes.'

'Finn told me about you. Come in here, will you.'

I followed into his room, and sat opposite while he turned the pages of a file.

'What have you been doing since you joined the army?'

Reduced to narrative form, my military career up to date did not sound particularly impressive. However, the captain seemed satisfied. He nodded from time to time. His manner was friendly, more like the good-humoured approach of my old Battalion than the unforthcoming demeanour of most of the officers at Div HQ. The story came to an end.

'I see—how old are you?'

I revealed my age. He looked surprised that anyone could be so old.

'And what do you do in civilian life?'

I indicated literary activities.

'Oh, yes,' he said. 'I believe I read one.'

However, he showed none of General Liddament's keen interest in the art of the novel, made no effort to explore further this aspect of my life.

'What about French?'

It seemed simplest to furnish the same descriptive phrases offered to the General.

'I can read a book as a rule, but get held up with slang or something like the technical descriptions of Balzac.'

The captain laughed.

'Well,' he said, 'suppose we come back to that later. Are you married?'

'Yes.'

'Children?'

'One.'

'Prepared to go abroad?'

'Of course.'

'Sure?'

'Yes.'

He seemed almost surprised at this rather minimal acceptance of military obligation.

'We're looking for liaison officers with the Free French,' he said. 'At battalion level. They're not entirely easy to find. Speaking another language tolerably well seems so often to go with unsatisfactory habits.'

The captain smiled sadly, a little archly, across the desk at me.

'Whilst our Allies expect nothing less than one hundred per cent service,' he said, 'and quite right too.'

He fixed me with his eye.

'Care to take the job on?'

'Yes—but, as I explained, I'm no great master of the language.'

He did not reply. Instead, he opened a drawer of the desk from which he took a document. He handed this to me. Then he rose and went to a door on the other side of the room. It gave on to a smaller room, almost a cupboard, surrounded by dark green metal safes. In one corner was a little table on which stood a typewriter in its rubber cover. A chair was beside it.

'Make a French translation of these instructions,' he said. 'Subsistence Allowance is *frais d'alimentation*. Here is paper—and a typewriter, should you use one. Alternatively, here too is *la plume de ma tante*.'

Smiling not unkindly, he shut me in. I settled down to examine the printed sheet handed to me. It turned out to be an Army Form, one specifying current regulations governing issue, or non-issue, of rations to troops in the field. At first sight the prose did not seem to make much sense in English; I saw at once there was little hope of my own French improving it. Balzac on provincial type-setting was going to be nothing to this. However, I sat down and worked away, because I wanted the job badly.

Outside, on cornices and parapets of government buildings, starlings in thousands chattered and quarrelled. I was aware of that dazed feeling that is part of the impact of coming on leave. I read through the document again, trying to compose my mind to its meaning. This was like being 'kept in' at school. '. . . the items under (i) are obtainable on indent (A.B.55) which is the ordinary requisition of supplies . . . the items under (iii) and other items required to supplement the ration so as to provide variety and admit of the purchase of seasonable produce, and which are paid for with money provided by the Commuted Ration Allowance and Cash Allowance (iii above) . . . the officer i/c Supplies renders a return (A. F. B. 179), which shows the quantities and prices of rations actually issued in kind to the unit during the month, from which their total value is calculated . . .'

The instruction covered a couple of foolscap pages. I remembered being told never to write 'and which', but the mere grammar used by the author was by no means his most formidable side. It was not the words that were difficult. The words, on the whole, were fairly familiar. Giving them some sort of conviction in translation was the problem; conveying that particular tone sounded in official manifestos. Through the backwoods of this bureaucratic jungle, or the like, Widmerpool was hunting down Mr Diplock, in relentless safari. Such distracting thoughts had to be put from the mind. I chose *la plume de ma tante* in preference to the typewriter, typescript imparting an awful bareness to language of any kind, even one's own. For a time I sweated away. Some sort of a version at last appeared. I read it through several times, making corrections. It did not sound ideally idiomatic French; but then the original did not sound exactly idiomatic English. After embodying a few final improvements, I opened the door a crack.

'Come in, come in,' said the captain. 'Have you finished? I thought you might have succumbed. It's dreadfully stuffy in there.'

He was sitting with another officer, also a captain, tall, fair, rather elegant. A blue fore-and-aft cap lay beside him with the lion-and-unicorn General Service badge. I passed my translation across the desk to the I. Corps captain. He took it, and, rising from his chair, turned to the other man.

'I'll be back in a moment, David,' he said—and to me: 'Take a seat while I show this to Finn.'

He went out of the room. The other officer nodded to me and laughed. It was Pennistone. We had met on a train during an earlier leave of mine and had talked of Vigny. We had talked of all sorts of other things, too, that seemed to have passed out of my life for a long time. I remembered now Pennistone had insisted his own military employments were unusual. No doubt the Headquarters in which I now found myself represented the sort of world in which he habitually functioned.

'Splendid,' he said. 'Of course we agreed to meet as an exercise of the will. I'm ashamed to say I'd forgotten until now. Your own moral determination does you credit. I congratulate you. Or is it just one of those eternal recurrences of Nietzsche, which one gets so used to? Have you come to work here?'

I explained the reason for my presence in the building.

'So you may be joining the Free Frogs.'

98

'And you?'

'I look after the Poles.'

'Do they have a place like this too?'

'Oh, no. The Poles are dealt with as a Power. They have an ambassador, a military attaché, all that. The point about France is that we still recognise the Vichy Government. The other Allied Governments are those in exile over here in London. That is why the Free French have their own special mission.'

'You've just come to see them?'

'To discuss some odds and ends of Polish affairs that overlap with Free French matters.'

We talked for a while. The other captain returned.

'Finn wants to see you,' he said.

I followed him along the passage into a room where an officer was sitting behind a desk covered with papers. The I. Corps captain announced my name and withdrew. I had left my cap in the other office, so, on entering, could not salute, but, with the formality that prevailed in the area where I was serving, came to attention. The major behind the desk seemed surprised at this. He rose very slowly from his desk, and, keeping his eye on me all the time, came round to the front and shook hands. He was small, cleanshaved, almost square in shape, with immensely broad shoulders, large head, ivory-coloured face, huge nose. His grey eyes were set deep back in their sockets. He looked like an enormous bird, an ornithological specimen very different from Colonel Hogbourne-Johnson, kindly but at the same time immensely more powerful. I judged him in his middle fifties. He wore an old leather-buttoned service-dress tunic, with a VC, Légion d'Honneur, Croix de Guerre avec palmes, and a couple of other foreign decorations I could not identify.

'Sit down, Jenkins,' he said.

He spoke quietly, almost whispered. I sat down. He began to fumble among his papers.

'I had a note from your Divisional Commander,' he said. 'Where is it? Draw that chair a bit nearer. I'm rather deaf in this ear. How is General Liddament?'

'Very well, sir.'

'Knocking the Division into shape?'

'That's it, sir.'

'Territorial Division, isn't it?'

'Yes, sir.'

'He'll get a Corps soon.'

'You think so, sir?'

Major Finn nodded. He seemed a little embarrassed about something. Although he gave out an extraordinary sense of his own physical strength and endurance, there was also something mild, gentle, almost undecided, about his manner.

'You know why you've been sent here?' he asked.

'It was explained, sir.'

He lowered his eyes to what I now saw was my translation. He began to read it to himself, his lips moving faintly. After a line or two of doing this, it became clear to me what the answer was going to be. The only question that remained was how long the agony would be drawn out. Major Finn read the whole of my version through to himself; then, rather nobly, read it through again. This was either to give dramatic effect, or to rouse himself to the required state of tension for making an unwelcome announcement. Those, at least, were the reasons that occurred to me at the time, because he must almost certainly have gone through the piece when the captain had first brought it to him. I appreciated the gesture, which indicated he was doing the best he could for me, including not sparing himself. When he came to the end for the second time, he looked across the desk, and, shaking his head, sighed and smiled.

'Well . . .' he said.

I was silent.

'Won't do, I'm afraid.'

'No, sir?'

'Not as your written French stands.'

He took up a pencil and tapped it on the desk.

'We'd have liked to have you . . .'

'Yes, sir.'

'Masham agrees.'

'Masham' I took to be the I. Corps captain.

'But this translation . . .'

He spoke for a second as if I might have intended a deliberate insult to himself and his uniform by the botch I had made of it, but that he was prepared magnanimously to overlook that. Then, as if regretting what might have appeared momentary unkindness, in spite of my behaviour, he rose and shook hands again, gazing into the middle distance of the room. The vision to be seen there was certainly one of total failure.

'. . . not sufficiently accurate.'

'No, sir.'

'In fact, doesn't begin to be.'

'I see, sir.'

'You understand me?'

'Of course, sir.'

'A pity.'

We stared at each other.

'Otherwise I think you would have done us well.'

Major Finn paused. He appeared to consider this

hypothesis for a long time. There did not seem much more to be said. I hoped the interview would end as quickly as possible.

'Perfectly suitable . . .' he repeated.

His voice was far away now. There was another long pause. Then a thought struck him. His face lighted up.

'Perhaps it's only written French you're shaky in.'

He wrinkled his broad, ivory-coloured forehead.

'Now let us postulate the 9th Regiment of Colonial Infantry are on the point of mutiny,' he said. 'They may be prepared to abandon Vichy and come over to the Allies. How would you harangue them?'

'In French, sir?'

'Yes, in French.'

He spoke eagerly, as if he expected something enjoyably dramatic.

'I'm afraid I should have to fall back on English, sir.'

His face fell again.

'I feared that,' he said.

Failure was certainly total. I had been given a second chance, had equally bogged it. Major Finn stroked the enormous bumpy contours of his nose.

'Look here,' he said, 'I'll tell you what I'll do. I'll make a note of your name.'

'Yes, sir?'

'There may be certain changes taking place in the near future. Not here, elsewhere. But don't count on it. That's the best I can say. I don't question anything General Liddament suggests. It's just the language.'

'Thank you, sir.'

He smiled.

'You're on leave, aren't you?'

'Yes, sir.'

'Wouldn't mind some leave myself.'

'No, sir?'

'And my respects to General Liddament.'

'I'll convey them, sir.'

'A great man.'

I made a suitable face and left the room, disappointed and furious with myself. The fact that such an eventuality was in some degree to be expected made things no better. To have anyone in the army—let alone a general—show interest in your individual career is a rare enough experience. To fall at the language hurdle—just the field in which someone like myself, anyway in the eyes of General Liddament, might be expected to show reasonable proficiency—seemed to let down the General too. There would be little hope of his soliciting further candidatures in my interest. Why should he? I wondered why I had never taken the trouble in the past to learn French properly; as a boy, for instance, staying with the Leroys at La Grenadière, or in the course of innumerable other opportunities. At the same time, I was aware that a liaison officer at battalion level would be required to show considerable fluency. Perhaps it was just Fate. As for having a note made of my name, that was to be regarded as a polite formula on the part of Major Finn—an unusually likeable man—an echo of civilian courtesies from someone who took a pride in possessing good manners as well as a VC; a gesture to be totally disregarded for all practical purposes.

I returned to the captain's room. Pennistone was still there. He was about to leave, standing up, wearing his cap.

'Well then,' he was saying. 'On the first of next month Szymanski ceases to serve under the Free French authority, and comes under the command of the Polish Forces in Great Britain. That's settled at last.'

Masham, the I. Corps captain, turned to me. I explained the deal was off. He knew, of course, already.

'Sorry,' he said. 'Thanks for looking in. I hear you and David know each other.'

After taking leave of him, Pennistone and I went out together into the street. He asked what had happened. I outlined the interview with Major Finn. Pennistone listened with attention.

'Finn seems to have been well disposed towards you,' he said.

'I liked him—what's his story?'

'Some fantastic episode in the first war, when he got his VC. After coming out of the army, he decided to go into the cosmetics business—scent, face powder, things like that, the last trade you'd connect him with. He talks very accurate French with the most outlandish accent you ever heard. He's been a great success with the Free French— liked by de Gaulle, which is not everyone's luck.'

'Surprising he's not got higher rank.'

'Finn could have become a colonel half-a-dozen times over since rejoining the army,' said Pennistone. 'He always says he prefers not to have too much responsibility. He has his VC, which always entails respect—and which he loves talking about. However, I think he may be tempted at last to accept higher rank.'

'To what?'

'Very much in the air at the moment. All I can say is, you may be more likely to hear from him than you think.'

'Does he make money at his cosmetics?'

'Enough to keep a wife and daughter hidden away somewhere.'

'Why are they hidden away?'

'I don't know,' said Pennistone, laughing. 'They just are. There are all kinds of things about Finn that are not explained. Keeping them hidden away is part of the Finn system. When I knew him in Paris, I soon found he had a secretive side.'

'You knew him before the war?'

'I came across him, oddly enough, when I was in textiles, working over there.'

'Textiles are your job?'

'I got out in the end.'

'Into what?'

Pennistone laughed again, as if that were an absurd question to ask.

'Oh, nothing much really,' he said. 'I travel about a lot —or used to before the war. I think I told you, when we last met, that I'm trying to write something about Descartes.'

All this suggested—as it turned out rightly—that Pennistone, as well as Finn, had his secretive side. When I came to know him better, I found what mattered to Pennistone was what went on in his head. He could rarely tell you what he had done in the past, or proposed to do in the future, beyond giving a bare statement of places he had visited or wanted to visit, books he had read or wanted to read. On the other hand, he was able to describe pretty lucidly what he had thought—philosophically speaking— at any given period of his life. While other people lived for money, power, women, the arts, domesticity, Pennistone liked merely thinking about things, arranging his mind. Nothing else ever seemed to matter to him. It was the aim Stringham had announced now as his own, though Pennistone was a very different sort of person from

Stringham, and better equipped for perfecting the process. I only found out these things about him at a later stage.

'Give me the essential details regarding yourself,' Pennistone said. 'Unit, army number, that sort of thing—just in case anything should crop up where I myself might be of use.'

I wrote it all down. We parted company, agreeing that Nietzschean Eternal Recurrences must bring us together soon again.

Even by the time I reached the Café Royal that evening, I was still feeling humiliated by the failure of the Finn interview. The afternoon had been devoted to odd jobs, on the whole tedious. The tables and banquettes of the large tasteless room looked unfamiliar occupied by figures in uniform. There was no one there I had ever seen before. I sat down and waited. Lovell did not arrive until nearly half-past seven. He wore captain's pips. It was hard not to labour under a sense of being left behind in the military race. I offered congratulations.

'You don't get into the really big money until you're a major,' he said. 'That should be one's aim.'

'Vaulting ambition.'

'Insatiable.'

'Where do you function?'

'Headquarters of Combined Operations,' he said, 'that curious toy fort halfway down Whitehall. It's a great place for Royal Marines. A bit of luck your being on leave, Nick. One or two things I want to talk about. First of all, will you agree to be executor of my will?'

'Of course.'

'Perfectly simple. Whatever there is—which isn't much, I can assure you—goes to Priscilla, then to Caroline.'

'That doesn't sound too complicated.'

One never knows what may happen to one.'

'No, indeed.'

The remark echoed Sergeant Harmer's views. There was a pause. I had the sudden sense that Lovell was going to broach some subject I should not like. This apprehension turned out to be correct.

'Another small matter,' he said.

'Yes?'

'It would interest me to hear more of this fellow Stevens. You seem to be mainly responsible for bringing him into our lives, Nick.'

'If you mean someone called Odo Stevens, he and I were on a course together at Aldershot about a year ago. I didn't know he was in our lives. He isn't in mine. I haven't set eyes on him since then.'

I had scarcely thought of Stevens since he had been expelled from the course. Now the picture of him came back forcibly. Lovell's tone was not reassuring. It was possible to guess something of what might be happening.

'You introduced him into the family,' said Lovell.

He spoke calmly, not at all accusingly, but I recognised in his eye the intention to stage a dramatic announcement.

'One weekend leave from Aldershot Stevens gave me a lift in his very brokendown car as far as Frederica's. Then he took me back on Sunday night. Isobel was staying there. It was just before she had her baby. In fact, the birth started that night. Stevens got RTU-ed soon after we got back on the course. I haven't seen or heard of him since.'

'You haven't?'

'Not a word.'

'Priscilla was at Frederica's then.'

'I remember.'

'She met Stevens.'

'She must have done.'

'She's been with him lately up in a hotel in Scotland,' said Lovell, 'living more or less openly, so there's no point in not mentioning it.'

There was nothing to be said to that. Stevens had certainly struck up some sort of an acquaintance with Priscilla on that occasion at Frederica's. I could recall more. Some question of getting a piece of jewellery mended for her had arisen. Such additional consequences as Lovell outlined were scarcely to be foreseen when I took Stevens to the house. Nevertheless, it was an unfortunate introduction. However, this merely confirmed stories going round. No doubt Stevens, by now, was a figure with some sort of war career behind him. That could happen in the matter of a few weeks. That Stevens might be the 'commando', or whatever shape Priscilla's alleged fancy-man took, had never suggested itself to me. Lovell lit a cigarette. He puffed out a cloud of smoke. His evident inclination to adopt a stylised approach—telling the story as we might have tried to work it out together in a film script years before—was some alleviation of immediate embarrassments caused by the disclosure. The dramatic manner he had assumed accorded with his own conception of how life should be lived. I was grateful for it. By this means things were made easier.

'When did all this start?'

'Pretty soon after they first met.'

'I see.'

'I was down at that godforsaken place on the East Coast. There was nowhere near for her to live. It wasn't my fault we weren't together.'

'Is Stevens stationed in Scotland?'

'So far as I know. He did rather well somewhere—was

it the Lofoten raid? That sort of thing. He's a hero on top of everything else. I suppose if I were to do something where I could get killed, instead of composing lists of signal equipment and suchlike, I might make a more interesting husband.'

'I don't think so for a moment.'

In giving this answer, I spoke a decided opinion. To assume such a thing was a typical instance of Lovell's taste, mentioned earlier, for the obvious. It was a supposition bound to lead to a whole host of erroneous conclusions— that was how the conjecture struck me—regarding his own, or anyone else's, married life.

'You may be right,' he said.

He spoke as if rather relieved.

'Look at it the other way. Think of all the heroes who had trouble with their wives.'

'Who?'

'Agamemnon, for instance.'

'Well, that caused enough dislocation,' said Lovell. 'What's Stevens like, apart from his heroism?'

'In appearance?'

'Everything about him.'

'Youngish, comes from Birmingham, traveller in costume jewellery, spot of journalism, good at languages, short, thickset, very fair hair, easy to get on with, keen on the girls.'

'Sounds not unlike me,' said Lovell, 'except that up to date I've never travelled in costume jewellery—and I still rather pride myself on my figure.'

'There is a touch of you about him, Chips. I thought so at Aldershot.'

'You flatter me. Anyway, he seems more of a success than I am with my own wife. If he is keen on the girls, I suppose making for Priscilla would be a matter of routine?'

'So I should imagine.'

'You liked him?'

'We got on pretty well.'

'Why was he Returned-to-Unit?'

'For cutting a lecture.'

Lovell seemed all at once to lose interest in Stevens and his personality. His manner changed. There could be no doubt he was very upset.

'So far as I can see there was nothing particularly wrong with our marriage,' he said. 'If I hadn't been sent to that God-awful spot, it would have gone on all right. At least that's how things appeared to me. I don't particularly want a divorce even now.'

'Is there any question of a divorce?'

'It isn't going to be much fun living with a woman who's in love with someone else.'

'Lots of people do it, and *vice versa*.'

'At best, it's never going to be the same.'

'Nothing ever remains the same. Marriage or anything else.'

'I thought your theory was that everything did always remain the same?'

'Everything alters, yet does remain the same. It might even improve matters.'

'Do you really think so?'

'Not really.'

'Neither do I,' said Lovell, 'though I see what you mean. That's if she's prepared to come back and live with me. I'm not even sure of that. I think she wants to marry Stevens.'

'She must be mad.'

'Mad she may be, but that's the way she's talking.'

'Where's Caroline?'

'My parents are looking after her.'

'And Priscilla herself?'

'Staying with Molly Jeavons—though I only found out that by chance yesterday. She's been moving about among various relations, is naturally at times rather vague about her whereabouts, so far as keeping me informed is concerned.'

'You've dished all this up with her?'

'On my last leave—making it a charming affair.'

'But lately?'

'Since then, we've been out of touch more than once. We are at this moment, until I found, quite by chance, she was at the Jeavonses'. I'm hoping to see her tonight. That's why I can't dine with you.'

'You and Priscilla are dining together?'

'Not exactly. You remember Bijou Ardglass, that gorgeous mannequin, one-time girl-friend of Prince Theodoric? I ran into her yesterday on my way to Combined Ops. She's driving for the Belgians or Poles, one of the Allied contingents—an odd female organisation run by Lady McReith, whom Bijou was full of stories about. Bijou asked me to a small party she is giving for her fortieth birthday, about half-a-dozen old friends at the Madrid.'

'Bijou Ardglass's fortieth birthday.'

'Makes you think.'

'I only knew her by sight, but even so—and Priscilla will be there?'

'Bijou found her at Aunt Molly's. Of course Priscilla told Bijou I was on the East Coast. I was when we last exchanged letters. I explained to Bijou I'd just been posted to London at short notice—which was quite true—and hadn't managed to get together with Priscilla yet.'

'You haven't called up Priscilla at the Jeavonses'?'

'I thought it would be best if we met at Bijou's party—without Priscilla knowing I was going to be there. I have a reason for that. The Madrid was the place we celebrated our engagement. The Madrid might also be the place where we straightened things out.'

That was just like Lovell. Everything had to be staged. Perhaps he was right, and everything does have to be staged. That is a system that can at least be argued as the best. At any rate, people must run their lives on their own terms.

'I mean it's worth making an effort to patch things up,' he said, 'don't you think, Nick?'

He asked the question as if he had no idea what the answer would be, possibly even expecting a negative rather than affirmative one.

'Yes, of course—every possible effort.'

'You can imagine what all this is like going on in one's head, round and round for ever, while you're trying to sort out a lot of bloody stuff about radios and landing-craft. For instance, if she goes off with Stevens, think of all the negotiations about Caroline, all that kind of thing.'

'Chips—Hugh Moreland has appeared at the door on the other side of the room. Is there anything else you want to say that's urgent?'

'Nothing. I've got it all off my chest now. That was what I needed. You understand?'

'Of course.'

'The point is, you agree it's worth taking trouble to get on an even keel again?'

'Can't say it too strongly.'

Lovell nodded several times.

'And you'll be my executor?'

'Honoured.'

'I'll write to the solicitors then. Marvellous to have got that fixed. Hullo, Hugh, how are you? Ages since we met.'

Dressed in his familiar old blue suit, looking more than ever as if he made a practice of sleeping in it, dark grey shirt and crimson tie, Moreland, hatless, seemed an improbable survival from pre-war life. He was flushed and breathing rather hard. This gave the impression of poorish health. His face, his whole person, was thinner. The flush increased when he recognised Lovell, who must at once have recalled thoughts of Priscilla. Even after this redness had died down, a certain discoloration of the skin remained, increasing the suggestion that Moreland was not well. There was a moment of awkwardness, in spite of Lovell's immediate display of satisfaction that they should have met again. This was chiefly because Moreland seemed unwilling to commit himself by sitting at our table; an old habit of his, one of those characteristic postponements of action for which he was always laughing at himself, like his constitutional inability in all circumstances to decide from a menu what he wanted to eat.

'I shall be taken for a spy if I sit with you both,' he said. 'Somehow I never expected you'd really be wearing uniform, Nick, even though I knew you were in the army. I must tell you of rather a menacing thing that happened the other day. Norman Chandler appeared on my doorstep to hear the latest musical gossip. He's also become an officer, and we went off to get some lunch at Foppa's, where neither of us had been since the beginning of the war. The downstairs room was shut, because the window had been broken by a bomb, so we went upstairs, where the club used to be. There we found a couple of seedy-looking characters who said the restaurant was closed. We asked where Foppa was to be found. They said they didn't know. They weren't at all friendly. Positively disagreeable. Then I suddenly grasped they thought we were after Foppa for being an Italian—wanted to intern him or something. An army type and a member of the Special Branch. It was obvious as soon as one thought of it.'

'The Special Branch must have changed a lot if they now dress like you, Hugh.'

'Not more than army officers, if they now look like Norman.'

'Anyway, take a seat,' said Lovell. 'What are you going to drink? How's your war been going, Hugh? Not drearier than mine, I feel sure, if you'll excuse the self-pity.'

Moreland laughed, now more at ease after telling the story about Chandler and himself; Foppa's restaurant, even if closed, providing a kind of frame to unite the three of us.

'I seem to have neutralised the death-wish for the moment,' he said. 'Raids are a great help in that. I was also momentarily cheered just now by finding the man with the peg-leg and patch over one eye still going. He was behind the London Pavilion this evening, playing *Softly Awakes My Heart*. Rather an individual version. One of the worst features of the war is the dearth of itinerant musicians, indeed of vagrants generally. For example, I haven't seen the cantatrice on crutches for years. As I seem equally unfitted for warlike duties, I've thought of filling the gap and becoming a street musician myself. Unfortunately, I'm such a poor executant.'

'There's a former music critic in our Public Relations

branch,' said Lovell. 'He says the great thing for musicians now is the RAF band.'

'Doubt if they'd take me,' said Moreland, 'though the idea of massed orchestras of drum and fife soaring across the sky is attractive. Which is your PR man's paper?'

Lovell mentioned the name of the critic, who turned out to be an admirer of Moreland's work. The two of them began to discuss musical matters, of which Lovell possessed a smattering, anyway as far as personalities were concerned, from days of helping to write a column. No one could have guessed from Lovell's manner that inwardly he was in a state of great disturbance. On the contrary, it was Moreland who, after a preliminary burst of talkativeness, reverted to an earlier uneasiness of manner. Something was on his mind. He kept shifting about in his seat, looking towards the door of the restaurant, as if expecting an arrival that might not be exactly welcome. This apparent nervousness brought to mind the unaccustomed tone of his postcard. It looked as if something had happened, which he lacked the will to explain.

'Are you dining with us?' he suddenly asked Lovell.

There was no reason why that enquiry should not be made. The tone was perfectly friendly. All the same, a touch of abruptness added to this sense of apprehension.

'Chips is going to the Madrid—I didn't realise places like that still functioned.'

'Not many of them do,' said Lovell. 'In any case I'm never asked to them. I've no doubt it will be a very sober affair compared with the old days. The only thing to be said is that Max Pilgrim is doing a revival there of some of his old songs—*Tess of Le Touquet, Heather, Heather, she's under the weather*, all those.'

'Max is our lodger now,' said Moreland unexpectedly.

'He may be looking in here later after his act. He's been with ENSA entertaining the forces—by his own account enjoying a spot of entertainment himself—and has been released to do this brief season at the Madrid as a kind of rest.'

I was curious to know who was included when Moreland spoke of 'our' lodger. A question on this subject might be more tactfully put after Lovell's withdrawal. It sounded as if someone had taken Matilda's place. Lovell spoke a word or two about the party ahead of him. He seemed unwilling to leave us.

'I've never been to the Madrid as a client,' said Moreland. 'I once went there years ago, so to speak to the stage door, to collect Max after his act, because we were having supper together. I remember his talking about your friend Bijou Ardglass then. Wasn't she mistress of some Balkan royalty?'

'Theodoric,' said Lovell, 'but they can't have met for years. That Scandinavian princess he married keeps Theodoric very much in order. They were both lucky to get away when they did. He's always been very pro-British and would have been in a bad way had the Germans got him when they overran the country. There's a small contingent of his own people over here now. They were training in France when the war came, and crossed at the time of Dunkirk. I say, I hope there'll be something to drink tonight. The wine outlook becomes increasingly desperate since France went. One didn't expect to have to fight a war on an occasional half-pint of bitter, and lucky if you find that. Well, it's been nice seeing you both. I'll keep in touch, Nick, about those various points.'

We said goodbye to him. Lovell left for the Madrid. Moreland showed signs of relief that he was no longer with us. At first I thought this was still, as it were, on account of Priscilla; or, like some people—amongst whom several of his own relations were included—he simply found Lovell's company tedious. As it turned out, both possibilities were incorrect. Quite another matter was on Moreland's mind. This was only revealed when I suggested it was time to order dinner. Moreland hesitated.

'Do you mind if we wait a minute or two longer?' he said. 'Audrey thought she'd probably get away in time to join us for some food.'

'Audrey who?'

'Audrey Maclintick—you know her.'

He spoke sharply, as if the question had been a silly one to ask.

'Maclintick's wife—the one who went off with the violinist?'

'Yes—Maclintick's widow, rather. I always assume everyone is familiar with the rough outlines of my own life, such as they are. I suppose, as a gallant soldier, you live rather out of the world of rank and fashion. Audrey and I are running steady now.'

'Under the same roof?'

'In my old flat. I found I could get back there, owing to the blitz and it being left empty, so took the opportunity to move in again.'

'And Max Pilgrim is your lodger?'

'Has been for some months.'

Moreland had been embarrassed by having to explain so specifically that he was now living with Mrs Maclintick, but seemed glad this fact was made plain. There had been no avoiding a pointblank enquiry about the situation; nor was all surprise possible to conceal. He must certainly have been conscious that, to any friend not already aware he and Mrs Maclintick had begun to see each other frequently, the news must come as an incalculable reversal of former circumstances and feelings.

'Life became rather impossible after Matilda left me,' he said.

He spoke almost apologetically, at the same time seemed to find relief in expressing how the present situation had come about. The statement that life for him had become 'impossible' after Matilda's departure was easy to believe. Without Matilda, the organisation of Moreland's day was hard to imagine. Formerly she had arranged almost all the routine of those affairs not immediately dictated by his profession. In that respect, unless she had greatly changed, Mrs Maclintick could hardly be proving an adequate substitute. On the one or two occasions when, in the past, I had myself encountered Mrs Maclintick, she had appeared to me, without qualification, as one of the least sympathetic of women. So far as that went, in those days she had been in the habit of showing towards Moreland himself sentiments not much short of active dislike. He had been no better disposed to her, though, as an old friend of Maclintick's, always doing his best to keep the peace between them as husband and wife. When she had left Maclintick for Carolo, Moreland's sympathies were certainly on Maclintick's side. In short, this was another of war's violent readjustments; possibly to be revealed under close investigation as more logical than might appear at first sight. Indeed, as Moreland began to expand the story, as so often happens, the unthinkable took on the authoritative tone of something that had to be.

'After Audrey bolted with Carolo, they kept company till the beginning of the war—surprising in a way, knowing them both, it went on so long. Then he left her for a girl in a repertory company. Audrey remained on her own. She was working in a canteen when we ran across each other—still is. She's coming on from there tonight.'

'I never heard a word about you and her.'

'We don't get on too badly,' said Moreland. 'I haven't been specially well lately. That bloody lung. Audrey's been very good about looking after me.'

He still seemed to feel further explanation, or excuse, was required; at the same time he was equally anxious not to appear dissatisfied with the new alignment.

'Maclintick doing himself in shook me up horribly,' he said. 'Of course, there can be no doubt Audrey was partly to blame for that, leaving him flat as she did. All the same, she was fond of Maclintick in her way. She often talks of him. You know you get to a stage, especially in wartime, when it's a relief to hear familiar things talked about, whatever they are, and whoever's saying them. You don't care what line the conversation takes apart from that. For instance, Maclintick's unreadable book on musical theory he was writing. It was never finished by him, much less published. His last night alive, as a final gesture against the world, Maclintick tore the manuscript into small pieces and stopped up the lavatory with it. That was just before he turned the gas on. You'd be surprised how much Audrey knows about what Maclintick said in that book— on the technical side, I mean, which she's no training in or taste for. In an odd way, I like knowing about all that. It's almost as if Maclintick's still about—though if he were, of course, I shouldn't be living with Audrey. Here she is, anyway.'

Mrs Maclintick was moving between the tables, making in our direction. She wore a three-quarter length coat over trousers, a rather notably inelegant form of female dress popular at that moment in circumstances where no formality was required. I remembered that Gypsy Jones—La Passionaria of Hendon Central, as Moreland himself had called her—had heralded in her own person the advent of this mode, when Widmerpool and I had seen her addressing a Communist anti-war meeting from a soapbox at a street corner. The clothes increased Mrs Maclintick's own air of being a gipsy, one in fact, rather than just in name. Moreland's nostalgia for vagrancy was recalled, too, by her appearance, which immediately suggested telling fortunes if her palm was crossed with silver, selling clothes-pegs, or engaging in any other traditional Romany activity. By way of contrast with this physical exterior, she entirely lacked any of the ingratiating manner commonly associated with the gipsy's role. Small, wiry, aggressive, she looked as ready as ever for a row, her bright black eyes and unsmiling countenance confronting a world from which perpetual hostility was not merely potential, but presumptive. Attack, she made clear, would be met with counter-attack. However, in spite of this embattled appearance, discouraging to anyone who had ever witnessed her having a row with Maclintick, she seemed disposed at this particular moment to make herself agreeable; more agreeable, at any rate, than on earlier occasions when we had run across each other.

'Moreland told me you would be here,' she said. 'We don't get out to this sort of place much nowadays—can't afford it—but when we do we're glad to meet friends.'

She spoke as if I had a trifle blatantly imposed myself on a party of their own, rather than herself converged on a meeting specially arranged between Moreland and myself. At the same time her tone was not antagonistic; indeed, by her pre-war standards, in as much as I knew them, it was positively amiable. It occurred to me she perhaps saw her association with Moreland as a kind of revenge on Maclintick, who had so greatly valued him as a friend. Now, Maclintick was underground and Moreland belonged to her. Moreland himself, whose earlier state of nerves had certainly been provoked by the prospect of having to present himself and Mrs Maclintick as a ménage, now looked relieved, the immediate impact manoeuvred without disaster. Characteristically, he began to embark on one of those dissertations about life in which he was habitually inclined to indulge after some awkwardness had arisen. It had been just the same when he used to feel with Matilda that the ice was thin for conversational skating and would deliberately switch from the particular to the general.

'Since war prevents any serious work,' he said, 'I have been trying to think out a few things. Make my lymphatic brain function a little. All part of my retreat from perfectionism. Besides, one really must hold one or two firm opinions on matters before one's forty—a doom about to descend before any of us know where we are. I find war clears the mind in a few respects. At least that can be said for it.'

I was reminded how Stringham, too, had remarked that he was thinking things out, though it was hard to decide whether 'perfectionism' played much part in Stringham's problems. Perhaps it did. That was one explanation. In Moreland's case, there could be no doubt Mrs Maclintick herself was an element in this retreat. In her case, indeed, so far as Moreland was concerned, withdrawal from perfectionism had been so unphased as to constitute an operation reasonably to be designated a rout. Perhaps Mrs Maclintick herself, even if the awareness remained undefined in her mind, felt she must be regarded as implicit in this advertised new approach—therefore some sort of protest should be made—because, although she spoke without savagery, her next words were undoubtedly a call to order.

'The war doesn't seem to clear your mind quite enough, Moreland,' she said. 'I only wish it stopped you dreaming a bit. Guess where that lost ration card of yours turned up, after I'd looked for it up hill and down dale. *In the toilet*. Bettter than nowhere, I suppose. Saved me from standing in a queue at the Town Hall for a couple of hours to get you another one—and when was I going to find time for that, I wonder.'

She might have been addressing a child. Since she herself had never given birth—had, I remembered, expressed active objection to being burdened with offspring—Moreland may to some extent have occupied a child's role in her eyes; possibly even in her needs, something she had sought in Maclintick and never found. Moreland, so far as it went, seemed to accept this status, receiving the complaint with a laugh, though no denial of its justice.

'I must have dropped it there before fire-watching,' he said. 'How bored one gets on those nights. It's almost worse, if there isn't a raid. I began to plan a work, last time, called *The Fire-watcher's March*, drums, you know, perhaps triangle and oboe. I was feeling particularly fed up that night, not just displeased with the war, or certain social or political conditions from which one suffers, but tired of the whole thing. That is one of the conceptions most difficult for stupid people to grasp. They always suppose some ponderable alteration will make the human condition more bearable. The only hope of survival is the realisation that no such thing could possibly happen.'

'Never mind what goes through your head when you're

fire-watching, Moreland,' said Mrs Maclintick. 'You order some dinner. We don't want to starve to death while you hold forth. It won't be much when it comes, if I'm any prophet.'

These words were another reminder of going out with Moreland and Matilda, though Matilda's remonstrance would have been less downright. The plea for food was reasonable enough. We got hold of a waiter. There was the usual business of Moreland being unable to decide, even from the limited choice available, what he wanted to eat. In due course dinner arrived. Moreland, now back on his accustomed form, discoursed about his work and people we knew. Mrs Maclintick, grumbling about domestic difficulties, showed herself in general amenable. The evening was turning out a success. One change, however, was to be noticed in Moreland's talk. When he dwelt on the immediate past, it was as if all that had become very distant, no longer the matter of a year or two before. For him, it was clear, a veil, a thick curtain, had fallen between 'now' and 'before the war'. He would suddenly become quite worked up about people we had known, parties we had been to, subjects for amusement we had experienced together, laughing at moments so violently that tears ran down his cheeks. One felt he was fairly near to other, deeper emotions, that the strength of his feelings was due to something in addition to a taste for mulling over moments in retrospect enjoyable or grotesque.

'You must admit funny things did happen in the old days,' he said. 'Maclintick's story about Dr Trelawney and the red-haired succubus that could only talk Hebrew.'

'Oh, don't go on about the old days so,' said Mrs Macklintick. 'You make me feel a hundred. Try and live in the present for a change. For instance, it might interest

123

you to know that a one-time girl friend of yours is about to sit down at a table over there.'

We looked in the direction she had indicated by jerking her head. It was perfectly true. Priscilla Lovell and an officer in battle-dress were being shown to a table not far from our own. The officer was Odo Stevens. For a moment they were occupied with a waiter, so that a brief suspension of time was offered to consider how best to deal with this encounter, superlatively embarrassing, certainly soon unavoidable. At first it struck me as a piece of quite undeserved, almost incredible ill chance that they should turn up like this; but, on consideration, especially in the light of what Lovell himself had told me, there was nothing specially odd about it. Probably Stevens was on leave. This was an obvious enough place to dine, though certainly not one to choose if you wanted to be discreet.

'Adulterers are always asking the courts for discretion,' Peter Templer used to say, 'when, as a rule, discretion is the last thing they've been generous with themselves.'

If Priscilla thought her husband still stationed on the East Coast, she would of course not expect to meet him here. On the face of it, there was no reason why she should not dine with Stevens, if he happened to be passing through London. A second's thought showed that what seemed a piece of preposterous exhibitionism only presented that appearance on account of special knowledge acquired from Lovell. All the same, if Priscilla were dining here, that meant she had cut the Bijou Ardglass party. So unpredictably do human beings behave, she might even plan to take Stevens on there later.

'Is that her husband with her?' asked Mrs Maclintick. 'I've never had the pleasure of meeting him. I suppose you look on him as the man who cut you out, Moreland?'

124

I was surprised she knew about Moreland's former entanglement with Priscilla. No doubt Maclintick had spoken of it in the past. As Moreland himself had remarked, she and Maclintick must, at least some of the time, have enjoyed a closer, more amicable existence together than their acquaintances inclined to suppose. The Maclinticks could even have met Moreland and Priscilla at some musical event. Anyway, Mrs Maclintick had turned out to know Priscilla by sight, had evidently gathered scraps of her story, at least so far as Moreland was concerned. That was all. She could not also be aware of other implications disturbing to myself. So far as Mrs Maclintick's knowledge went, therefore, Priscilla's presence might be regarded as merely personally displeasing, in her capacity as a former lover of Moreland's. However, so developed was Mrs Maclintick's taste for malice, like everyone of her kind, that she seemed to know instinctively something inimical to myself, too, was in the air. Moreland, on the other hand, having talked with Lovell only a short time before, could not fail to suspect trouble of one sort or another was on foot. Never very good at concealing his feelings, he went red again. This change of colour was no doubt chiefly caused by Mrs Maclintick's not too delicate reference to himself, but probably he guessed something of my own sentiments as well.

'The girl's Nick's sister-in-law,' he said. 'You seem to have forgotten that. I don't know who the army type is.'

'Oh, yes, she's your sister-in-law, isn't she,' said Mrs Macklintick. 'Now I remember. Not bad looking. Got herself up for the occasion too, hasn't she?'

Mrs Maclintick did not elaborate why she thought Priscilla's clothes deserved this comment, though they were certainly less informal than her own outfit. Priscilla's appearance, at its most striking, made her not far short of a 'beauty'. She looked striking enough now, though not in the best of humours. Her fair hair was longer than at Frederica's, her face thinner. There was about her that taut, at the same time supple air, the yielding movement of body women sometimes display when conducting a love affair, like the physical pose of an athlete observed between contests. She had a high colour. Stevens, apparently in the best of spirits, was talking noisily. No escape was offered, even though they were the last people I wanted to run into at that moment. It seemed wise to prepare the ground with some explanation of why these two might reasonably be out together. This was perhaps instinctive, rather than logical, because Lovell himself had spoken as if the whole world knew about the affair.

'The man's called Odo Stevens. I was on a course with him.'

'Oh, you know him, do you?' said Mrs Maclintick. 'He looks a bit . . .'

She did not finish the sentence. Although her comment was never revealed, one had the impression she grasped pretty well the essential aspects of Odo Stevens, even if only the superficial ones. No great psychological powers were required to make a reasonably accurate guess at these, anyway for immediate practical purposes, whatever might be found deeper down. At that moment Stevens caught sight of us. He waved. Then, at once, he spoke to Priscilla, who herself looked in our direction. She too waved, at the same time began to say something to Stevens. Whatever that was, he disregarded it. Jumping up, he came towards our table. The only hope now was that Mrs Maclintick's uncompromising manner might save the situation by causing Stevens to feel himself unwelcome; if not drive him off entirely, at least discourage a long conversation. She could easily make matters more bizarre than embarrassing. I felt suddenly grateful for her presence. However, as things fell out, Mrs Maclintick was not placed in the position of exercising an active role. This was on account of Stevens himself. I had completely underestimated the change that had taken place in him. Never lacking in self-confidence, at Aldershot he had at the same time been undecided how best to present himself; how, so to speak, to get the maximum value from his own personality. He held various cards in his hand—as I had tried to explain to Lovell—most of them good ones. At different times he would vary the line he took: rough diamond: ambitious young provincial salesman: journalist on the make: soldier of fortune: professional womaniser. Those were just a few of them, all played with a reasonable lightness of touch. Stevens was certainly aware, too, of possibility to charm by sheer lack of any too exact a definition of personality or background. Some of this vagueness of outline may have had a fascination for Priscilla. Now, however, he had enormously added to the effectiveness of his own social attack, immediately giving the impression, as he approached our table, that he was prepared to take on this, or any other party of people, off his own bat. He himself was going to do the entertaining. No particular co-operation from anyone else was required. He had put up an additional pip since we last met, but, although still only a lieutenant, he wore the mauve and white ribbon of an MC, something of a rarity in acquisition at this comparatively early stage of the war.

'Well, old cock,' he said. 'Fancy meeting you here. This is a bit of luck. What are you up to? On leave, or stationed in London?'

Before I could answer, Priscilla herself came up to the table. She had followed Stevens almost at once. There was not much else for her to do. Even if she might have preferred to postpone a meeting, in due course inevitable, or, like myself, hoped to reduce contacts to no more than a nod or brief word at the end of the evening, Stevens had given her no chance to impede his own renewal of acquaintance. His principle was to work on impulse. Nothing could have prevented him from making the move he had. Now that had taken place, she no doubt judged the best tactical course was to ally herself with this explosive greeting; as good a way of handling the situation as any other, if it had to be handled at all. Besides, Priscilla may have felt that, by joining us, she could keep an eye on Stevens; modify, if necessary, whatever he might say.

'Yes, why are you here, Nick?' she asked, speaking challengingly, as if I, rather than her, found myself in doubtful company. 'I thought you were miles away across the sea. And Hugh—how marvellous to see you again after so long. I was listening to something of yours in a BBC programme last week.'

She was perfectly self-possessed. If aware of rumours afloat about herself and Stevens—of which she could hardly be ignorant, had she bothered to give a moment's thought to the matter—Priscilla was perfectly prepared to brazen these out. The two of them could not know, of course, how narrowly they had missed Lovell himself. Perhaps, again, neither cared. Lovell's taste for drama would certainly have been glutted, had they arrived an hour or so earlier. In the group we now formed, Moreland was the one who seemed most embarrassed. Conventionally speaking, he had not risen to the occasion very successfully. His highly developed intuitive faculties had instantly registered something was amiss; while the mere fact he had himself once been in love with Priscilla was, in any case, enough to agitate him, when unexpectedly confronted with her. No doubt he was also piqued at her coming on him in circumstances which must reveal sooner or later he and Mrs Maclintick were making a life together. He muttered something or other about whatever composition Priscilla had heard on the radio, but seemed unable to pursue any coherent conversation. Mrs Maclintick stared at Stevens without friendliness, though a good deal of curiosity, a reception that seemed perfectly to satisfy him.

'Look here,' he said. 'Are you all having a very special private party? If not, couldn't we come and sit with you? This is the chance of a lifetime to make a jolly evening of my last night in London for a long time—who knows, perhaps for ever. I'm on embarkation leave, you know, have to catch a train back to my unit tonight.'

He began addressing this speech to me, but, halfway through, turned towards Mrs Maclintick, as if to appeal to her good nature. She did not offer much encouragement; at the same time issued no immediate refusal.

'Anything you like,' she said. 'I'm too tired to care much what happens. Been on my feet all day doling out shepherd's pie made of sausage meat and stale swiss roll all minced up together. But don't expect Moreland to pay. I've let him have enough out of the house-keeping money to cover our share of dinner—and an extra round of drinks if we can get that.'

Moreland made some sort of protest at this, half amused, half ashamed. Stevens, obviously assessing Mrs Maclintick's measure at a glance (just as Stringham had, at the

129

party years before after Moreland's symphony), laughed loudly. She glared at him for treating her self-pity so lightly, but, although fierce in expression, her stare was not entirely one of dislike.

'We'll be absolutely self-supporting, I promise that,' said Stevens. 'I've only got a quid or two left myself, but Priscilla cashed a cheque earlier in the day, so we'll have to prise it out of her if necessary.'

'You may not find that so easy,' said Priscilla, laughing too, though perhaps not best pleased at this indication of being permanently in the company of Stevens. 'In the end Nick will probably have to fork out, as a relation. Will it really be all right if we join you, Nick?'

Although she said this lightly, in the same sort of vein used by Stevens himself, she spoke now with less assurance than he. Certainly she would, in any case, have preferred no such suggestion to be made. Once put, she was not going to run counter to it. She was determined to support her lover, show nothing was going to intimidate her. No doubt she had hoped to spend the evening tête-à-tête with him, especially if this were his last night in England. Even apart from that, there was, from her own point of view, nothing whatever to be said for deliberately joining a group of people that included a brother-in-law. On the other hand, she had perhaps already learnt the impossibility of dissuading Stevens from doing things the way he wanted them done. Perhaps, again, that was one of the attractions he exercised, in contrast with Lovell, usually amenable in most social matters. Stevens clearly possessed one of those personalities that require constant reinforcement for their egotism and energy by the presence and attention of other people round them, an audience to whom they can 'show off'. Such men are attractive to women, at the same time hard for women to keep at heel. For my own part, I would much rather have prevented the two of them from sitting with us, but, short of causing what might almost amount to a 'scene', there seemed no way of avoiding this. Even assuming I made some more or less discouraging gesture, that was likely to prove not only rather absurd, but also useless from Lovell's point of view; perhaps even undesirable where Lovell's interests were in question.

'I mean you look a bit uncertain, Nick?' said Priscilla, laughing again.

Obviously the thoughts going through my head were as clear as day to her.

'Don't be silly.'

'Half a minute,' said Stevens, 'I'll try and find a waiter and get another chair. We can't all cram together on the banquette.'

He went off. Mrs Maclintick began some complicated financial computation with Moreland. This was going to hold the attention of the pair of them for a minute or two. Priscilla had sat down, and, perhaps because she felt herself more vulnerable without Stevens, had her head down, fumbling in her bag, as if she wanted to avoid my eye. I felt some statement should be made which might, at least to some small extent, define my own position. It was now or never. Any such 'statement' was, I thought, to be conceived of as the term is made use of by the police, for the description of an accident or crime, a brief summary of what happened, how and why it took place or was committed.

'I had a drink with Chips this evening.'

She looked up.

'*Chips?*'

131

'Here—just before dinner. He thought he might see you at Bijou Ardglass' party at the Madrid.'

That information would at least prevent her from taking Stevens to the restaurant, had the thought been in her mind, though, at the same time, could prejudice any faint chance of herself looking in at the Ardglass party after Stevens had left to catch his train. Such a possibility had to be faced. A chance must be taken on that. It was, in any case, unlikely she would go later to the Madrid. Everything would close down by midnight at the latest, probably before that.

'Oh, but is Chips in London?'

She was plainly surprised.

'At Combined Ops.'

'On the Combined Ops staff?'

'Yes.'

'That was only a possibility when I last heard.'

'It's happened.'

'Chips thought the move wouldn't be for a week or two, even if it came off. His last letter only reached me this morning. It chased all over the country after me. I'm at Aunt Molly's.'

'I'll give you the Combined Ops number and extension.'

'I had to put Bijou off,' she said quite calmly. 'I'll get in touch with Chips tomorrow.'

'He thought you might be at the Jeavonses'.'

'Why didn't he ring up then?'

'He hoped he was going to see you at the Madrid—make a surprise of it.'

She did not rise to that.

'The Jeavons house is more of a shambles than ever,' she said. 'Eleanor Walpole-Wilson is there—Aunt Molly usen't to like her, but they're great buddies now—and then there are two Polish officers whose place was bombed and had nowhere to go, and a girl who's having a baby by a Norwegian sailor.'

'Who's having a baby by a Norwegian sailor?' asked Stevens. 'No one we know, I hope.'

He had come back to the table at that moment. Such as it was, my demonstration had been made, was now, of necessity, over. There was nothing more to be said. The situation could only be accepted, until, in one field or another, further action might be required. That, at least, was so far as I myself was concerned. Recognition of this as a fact seemed unavoidable. The return of Stevens brought about a reshuffle of places, resulting in Mrs Maclintick finding herself next him on the banquette with me on the other side of her. Priscilla and Moreland were opposite. This seating had been chiefly organised by Stevens himself, possibly with no more aim than a display of power. I congratulated him on his MC.

'Oh, that?' he said. 'Pretty hot stuff to have one of those, isn't it? I really deserved it—we both did—for putting up with that Aldershot course where we first met. It was far more gruelling than anything expected of me later—those lectures on the German army. Christ, I dream about them. Are you at the War House or somewhere?'

'On leave—going down to the country tomorrow.'

'Hope you have as much fun on it as I've had on mine,' he said.

He seemed totally unaware that, among members of Priscilla's family—myself, for example—conventional reservations might exist regarding the part he was at that moment playing; that at least they might not wish to hear rubbed in what an enjoyable time he had been having as her lover. All the same, shamelessness of any kind, perhaps

133

rightly, always exacts a certain respect. Lovell himself was
no poor hand at displaying cheek. As usual, a kind of
poetic justice was observable in what was happening.

'I suppose your destination is secret?'

'Don't quote me, but there's been a tropical issue.'

'Middle East?'

'That's my opinion.'

'Might be the Far East.'

'You never know. I think the other myself.'

Until then Moreland had been sitting in silence, apparently unable, or unwilling, to cope with the changed composition of the party at the table. This awkwardness with
new arrivals had always been a trait of his, and probably
had little or nothing to do with the comparatively unfamiliar note struck by the personality and conversation
of Stevens. A couple of middle-aged music critics he had
known all his life might have brought about just the same
sort of temporary stoppage in Moreland's conversation.
Later, he would recover; talk them off their feet. Now,
this change took place, he spoke with sudden animation.

'My God, I wish I could be transplanted to the Far
East without further delay,' he said. 'I'd be prepared to be
like Brahms and play the piano in a brothel—even play
Brahms's own compositions in a brothel, part of the
Requiem would be very suitable—if I could only be
somewhere like Saigon or Bangkok, leave London and
the blackout behind.'

'A naval officer I talked to on a bus the other day, just
back from Hong-Kong, reported life there as bloody amusing,' said Stevens. 'But look, Mr Moreland, there's something I must tell you before we go any further. Of course,
I wanted to see Nicholas again, that was why I came over,
but another pretty considerable item was that I had recog-

nised you. I saw a chance of telling you personally what a fan of yours I am. Hearing your *Tone Poem Vieux Port* performed at Birmingham was one of the high spots of my early life. I was about sixteen, I suppose. You've probably forgotten Birmingham ever had a chance of hearing it, or you yourself ever came there. I haven't. I've always wanted to meet you and say how much it thrilled me.'

This was an unexpected trump card for Stevens to play. Moreland, always modest about his own works, showed permissible signs of pleasure at this sudden hearty praise from such an unexpected source. Music was an entirely new line from Stevens, so far as I knew him, until this moment. Obviously it constituted a weapon in his armoury, perhaps a formidable one. He had certainly opened up operations on an extended front since our weeks together at Aldershot. Mrs Maclintick broke in at this point.

'*Vieux Port*'s the one Maclintick always liked,' she said. 'He used to go on about that piece of music until I told him never to mention the thing to me again.'

'When it was performed at Birmingham, Maclintick was about the only critic who offered any praise,' said Moreland. 'Even that old puss Gossage was barely civil. The rest of the critics buried my music completely and me with it. I feel now like Nero meeting in Hades the unknown mourner who strewed flowers on his grave.'

'You're not in your grave yet, Moreland,' said Mrs Maclintick, 'nor even in Hades, though you always talk as if you were. I never knew such a morbid man.'

'I meant the grave of my works rather than my own,' said Moreland. 'That's what it looked like that year at Birmingham. Anyway, not being dead's no argument against feeling like Nero. Quite the reverse.'

'Not much hope of a Roman orgy here,' said Stevens. 'Even the food's hard to wallow in, don't you agree, Mrs Maclintick?'

He turned his attention to her, in the manner of his particular brand of narcissism, determined to make a conquest, separate and individual, of everyone sitting at the table.

'From the way you talk,' he said, 'you don't sound as great a Moreland fan as you should be. Fancy saying you got tired of hearing *Vieux Port* praised. I'm surprised at you.'

'I'm a fan all right,' said Mrs Maclintick. 'Not half, I am. You should see him in bed in the morning before he's shaved. You couldn't help being a fan then.'

There was some laughter at that, in which Moreland himself joined loudly, though he would probably have preferred his relationship with Mrs Maclintick to have been expressed less explicitly in the presence of Priscilla. At the same time, Mrs Maclintick's tone had been not without affection of a kind. The reply she had made, whether or not with that intention, hindered Stevens from continuing to discuss Moreland's music more or less seriously, an object he seemed to have in view. However, this did not prevent him from increasing, if only in a routine manner, his own air of finding Mrs Maclintick attractive, a policy that was beginning to make a good impression on her. This behaviour, however light-hearted, was perhaps displeasing to Priscilla, no doubt unwilling to admit to herself that, for Stevens, one woman was, at least up to a point, as good as another; anyway when sitting in a restaurant. She may reasonably have felt that no competition should be required of her to keep him to herself. There was, of course, no question of Stevens showing any real interest in Mrs Maclintick, but, in circumstances prevailing, Priscilla probably regarded all his attention as belonging to herself alone. Whether or not this was the reason, she had become quite silent. Now she interrupted the conversation.

'Listen . . .'

'What?'

'I believe there's a blitz on.'

We all stopped talking for a moment. A faint suggestion of distant gunfire merged into the noise of traffic from the street, the revving up of a lorry's engine somewhere just outside the back of the building. No one else at the other tables round about showed any sign of noticing indications of a raid.

'I don't think so,' said Moreland. 'Living in London all the time, one gets rather a good ear for the real thing.'

'Raids when I'm on leave make me bloody jumpy,' said Stevens. 'Going into action you've got a whole lot of minor responsibilities to keep your mind off the danger. A gun, too. In an air-raid I feel they're after me, and there's nothing I can do about it.'

I asked how much hand-to-hand fighting he had been engaged in.

'The merest trifle.'

'What was it like?'

'Not too bad.'

'Hard on the nerves?'

'Difficult to describe,' he said. 'You feel worked up just before, of course, rather like going to school for the first time or the morning of your first job. Those prickly sensations, but exciting too.'

'Going back to school?' said Moreland. 'You make warfare sound most disturbing. I shouldn't like that at all.

In London, it's the sheer lack of sleep gets one down. However, there's been quite a let-up the last day or two. Do you have raids where you are, Nick?'

'We do.'

'I thought it was all very peaceful there.'

'Not always.'

'I have an impression of acute embarrassment when bombed,' said Moreland. 'That rather than gross physical fear—at present anyway. It's like an appalling display of bad manners one has been forced to witness. The utter failure of a party you are giving—a friend's total insensitiveness about some delicate matter—suddenly realising you've lost your note-case, your passport, your job, your girl. All those things combined and greatly multiplied.'

'You didn't like it the other night when the glass shattered in the bathroom window,' said Mrs Maclintick. 'You were trembling like a leaf, Moreland.'

'I don't pretend to be specially brave,' said Moreland, put out by this comment. 'Anyway, I'd just run up three flights of stairs and nearly caught it in the face. I was just trying to define the sensation one feels—don't you agree, Nick, it's a kind of embarrassment?'

'Absolutely.'

'Depends on such a lot of different things,' said Stevens. 'People you're with, sleep, food, drink, and so on. This show I was in——'

He did not finish the sentence, because Priscilla interrupted. She had gone rather white. For a second one saw what she would be like when she was old.

'For God's sake don't talk about the war all the time,' she said. 'Can't we sometimes get away from it for a few seconds?'

This was quite different from her earlier detached tone.

She seemed all at once in complete despair. Stevens, not best pleased at having his story wrecked, mistook the reason, whatever it was, for Priscilla's sudden agitation. He thought she was afraid, altogether a misjudgment.

'But it isn't a blitz, sweetie,' he said. 'There's nothing to get worked up about.'

Although, in the light of his usual manner of addressing people, he might easily have called Mrs Maclintick 'sweetie', this was, in fact, the first time he had spoken to Priscilla with that mixture of sharpness and affection that can suddenly reveal an intimate relationship.

'I know it isn't a blitz,' she said. 'We long ago decided that. I was just finding the conversation boring.'

'All right. Let's talk of something else,' he said.

He spoke indulgently, but without grasping that something had gone badly wrong.

'I've got rather a headache.'

'Oh, sorry, darling. I thought you had the wind up.'

'Not in the least.'

'Why didn't you say you had a head?'

'It's only just started.'

She was looking furious now, furious and upset. I knew her well enough to be fairly used to Priscilla's quickly changing moods, but her behaviour was now inexplicable to me, as it obviously was to Stevens. I imagined that, having decided a mistake had been made in allowing him to join our table, she had now settled on a display of bad temper as the best means of getting him away.

'Well, what would you like to do?' he said. 'We've got nearly an hour still. Shall I take you somewhere quieter? It is rather airless and noisy in here.'

He seemed anxious to do anything he could to please her. Up till now they might have been any couple having

139

dinner together, no suggestion of a particularly close bond, Stevens's ease of manner concealing rather than emphasising what was happening. Now, however, his voice showed a mixture of concern and annoyance that gave more away about the pair of them. This change of tone was certainly due to incomprehension on his part, rather than any exhibitionistic desire to advertise that Priscilla was his mistress; although he might well have been capable of proclaiming that fact in other company.

'Where?' she said.

This was not a question. It was a statement to express the truth that no place existed in this neighbourhood where they could go, and be likely to find peace and quiet.

'We'll look for somewhere.'

She fixed her eyes on him. There was silence for a moment.

'I think I'll make for home.'

'But aren't you coming to see me off—you said you were.'

'I've got a splitting headache,' she said. 'I've suddenly begun to feel perfectly awful, too, for some reason. Simply dreadful.'

'Not up to coming to the station?'

'Sorry.'

She was nearly in tears. Stevens plainly had no idea what had gone wrong. I could not guess either, unless the comparative indifference of his mood—after what had no doubt been a passionate interlude of several days—had upset her. However, although young, and, until recently, probably not much accustomed to girls of Priscilla's type, he was sufficiently experienced with women in general to have certain settled principles in dealing with situations of this kind. At any rate, he was now quite decisive.

'I'll take you back then.'

Faced with the prospect of abandoning a party where he had begun to be enjoyably the centre of attention, Stevens spoke without a great deal of enthusiasm, at the same time with complete sincerity. The offer was a genuine one, not a polite fiction to be brushed aside on the grounds he had a train to catch. He intended to go through with the proposal. Certainly it was the least he could do, but, at the same time, considering Priscilla's demeanour and what I knew of his own character, even this minimum was to display magnanimity of a sort. He accepted her sudden decision with scarcely any demur. Priscilla seemed to appreciate that.

'No.'

She spoke quite firmly.

'Of course I will.'

'You've got all your stuff here. You can't lug it back to Kensington.'

'I'll pick it up here again after I've dropped you.'

'You can't do that.'

'Of course I can.'

'No . . .' she said. 'I'd much rather you didn't . . . I don't quite know . . . I just feel suddenly rather odd . . . I can't think what it is . . . I mean I'd rather be alone . . . Must be alone . . .'

The situation had become definitely very painful. Even Mrs Maclintick was silenced, awed by this interchange. Moreland kept on lighting cigarettes and stubbing them out. It all seemed to take hours of time.

'I'm going to take you back.'

'No, really no.'

'But——'

'I can take you back, Priscilla,' I said. 'Nothing easier.'

That settled things finally.

'I don't want anybody to take me back,' she said. 'I'll say goodbye now.'

She waved her hand in the direction of Stevens.

'I'll write,' she said.

He muttered something about getting a taxi for her, began to try and move out from where he was sitting. People leaving or arriving at the next table penned him in. Priscilla turned and made quickly for the glass doors. Just before she went through them, she turned and blew a kiss. Then she disappeared from sight. By the time Stevens had extracted himself, she was gone. All the same, he set off across the room to follow her.

'What a to-do all of a sudden,' said Mrs Maclintick. 'Did she behave like this when you knew her, Moreland?'

I thought it possible, though not very likely, that Priscilla had gone to look for Lovell at the Madrid. That surmise belonged to a way of life more dramatic than probable, the sort of development that would have greatly appealed to Lovell himself; in principle, I mean, even had he been in no way personally concerned. However, for better or worse, things like that do not often happen. At the same time, even though sudden desire to make it up with her husband might run contrary to expectation, I was no nearer conjecturing why Priscilla had gone off in this manner, leaving Stevens cold. The fact she might be in love with him was no reason to prevent a sudden display of capricious temper, brought on, likely as not, by the many stresses of the situation. Stevens himself was no doubt cynical enough in the way he was taking the affair, although even that was uncertain, since Lovell had supposed marriage could be in question. Lovell might be right. Stevens's false step, so far as Priscilla was concerned, seemed to be marked by the moment he had suggested her fear about the supposititous air-raid warning. That had certainly made her angry. Even allowing for unexpected nervous reactions in wartime, it was much more likely she heard an air-raid warning—where none existed—because of her highly strung state, rather than from physical fear. Stevens had shown less than his usual grasp in suggesting such a thing. Possibly this nervous state stemmed from some minor row; possibly Priscilla's poorish form earlier in the evening suggested that she was beginning to tire of Stevens, or feared he might be tiring of her. On the other hand, the headache, the thought of her lover's departure, could equally have upset her; while the presence of the rest of the party at the table, the news that her husband was in London, all helped to discompose her. Reasons for her behaviour were as hard to estimate as that for giving herself to Stevens in the first instance. If she merely wanted amusement, while Lovell's physical presence was removed by forces over which he had no control, why make all this trouble about it, why not keep things quiet? Lovell, at worst, appeared a husband preferable to many. Even if less indefatigably lively than Stevens, he was not without his own brand of energy. Was 'trouble', in fact, what Priscilla required? Was her need—the need of certain women—to make men unhappy? There was something of the kind in her face. Perhaps she was simply tormenting Stevens now for a change; so to speak, varying the treatment. If so, she might have her work cut out to disturb him in the way she was disturbing Lovell; had formerly disturbed Moreland. The fact that he was able to look after himself pretty well in that particular sphere was implicit in the manner Stevens made his way back across the room. He looked politely worried, not at all shattered.

'Did she get a taxi?'

'She must have done. She'd disappeared into the black-out by the time I got to the door on the street. There were several cabs driving away at that moment.'

'She did take on,' said Mrs Maclintick.

'It's an awful business,' said Stevens. 'The point is I'm so immobile myself at this moment. There's a lot of junk in the cloakroom here, a valise, God knows what else—odds and ends they wanted me to get for the Mess—all of which I've got to hump to the station before long.'

He looked at his watch; then sat down again at the table.

'Let's have some more to drink,' he said, 'that's if we can get it.'

For a short time he continued to show some appearance of being worried about Priscilla, expressing anxiety, asserting she had seemed perfectly all right earlier that evening. He reproached himself for not being able to do more to help her get home, wanting our agreement that there was anyway little or nothing he could have done. After repeating these things several times, he showed himself finally prepared to accept the fact that what had happened was all in the day's work where women were concerned.

'I'll ring up when I get to the station,' he said.

Priscilla's behaviour had positively stimulated Mrs Mac-lintick, greatly cheered her up.

'Whatever's wrong with the girl?' she said. 'Why does she want to go off like that? I believe she didn't approve of me wearing these filthy old clothes. Got to, doing the job I do. No good dressing up as if you were going to a wedding. You know her, Moreland. What was it all about?'

'I haven't the least idea,' said Moreland sharply.

144

He showed no wish to discuss Priscilla's behaviour further. If, once or twice that evening, he had already brought a reminder of his behaviour when out with Matilda, now, by the tone he used, he recalled Maclintick out with Mrs Maclintick. She may have recognised that herself, because she pursed her lips.

'Wonder what's happened to Max,' she said. 'He should have been along by now. That turn must be over. It's a short one anyway, and he comes on early at the Madrid.'

'Probably gone to bed,' said Moreland.

Mrs Maclintick agreed that must have happened.

'More sense than sitting about in a place like this,' she added, 'especially if you've got to get up early in the morning like I have.'

'That's not Max Pilgrim you're talking about?' asked Stevens.

'He's our lodger,' said Moreland.

Stevens showed interest. Moreland explained he had known Pilgrim for years.

'I've always hoped to see him do his stuff,' said Stevens. 'There was a chance at this revival of his old songs at the Madrid—I suppose that's what he was coming on here from. I read about it in the paper and wanted to go, but Priscilla wouldn't hear of it. I can see now she hasn't been herself all day. I ought to have guessed she might be boiling up for a scene. You should know how girls are going to behave after you've been with them for a bit. I see I was largely to blame. She said she'd seen Pilgrim before and he bored her to hell. I told her I thought his songs marvellous. In fact I used to try and write stuff like that myself.'

I asked if he had ever sold anything of that sort to magazines.

'Only produced it for private consumption,' he said,

laughing. 'The sole verses I ever placed was sentimental stuff in the local press. They wouldn't have liked my Max Pilgrim line, if it could be called that.'

'Let's hear some of it,' said Moreland.

He had evidently taken a fancy to Stevens, who possessed in his dealings that energetic, uninhibited impact which makes its possessor master of the immediate social situation; though this mastery always requires strong consolidating forces to keep up the initial success. Mr Deacon used to say nothing spread more ultimate gloom at a party than an exuberant manner which has roused false hopes. Stevens did not do that. He could summon more than adequate powers of consolidation after his preliminary attack. The good impression he had made on Moreland was no doubt helped, as things stood, by Priscilla's departure. Moreland wanted to forget about her, start off on a new subject. Stevens was just the man for that. Mention of his verse offered the channel. There were immediate indications that Stevens would not need much pressing about giving an example of his own compositions.

'For instance, I wrote something about my first unit when I was with them,' he said.

'Recite it to us.'

Stevens laughed, a merely formal gesture of modesty. He turned to me.

'Nicholas,' he said, 'were you ever junior subaltern in your battalion?'

'For what seemed a lifetime.'

'And proposed the King's health in the Mess on guest nights?'

'Certainly.'

'*Mr Vice, the Loyal Toast*—then you rose to your feet and said: *Gentlemen, the King.*'

146

'Followed by *The Allied Regiments*—such-and-such a regiment of Canada and such-and-such a regiment of Australia.'

'Do you mean to say this actually happened to you yourself, Nick?' asked Moreland. 'You stood up and said *Gentlemen, the King?*'

He showed total incredulity.

'I used to love it,' said Stevens. 'Put everything I had into the words. It was the only thing I liked about the dump. I only asked all this because I wrote some lines called *Guest Night.*'

'Shoot them off,' said Moreland.

Stevens cleared his throat, then, without the least self-consciousness, began his recitation in a low, dramatic voice:

> 'On Thursday it's a parade to dine,
> The Allied Regiments and the King
> Are pledged in dregs of tawny wine,
> But now the Colonel's taken wing.
>
> Yet subalterns still talk and tease
> (Wide float the clouds of Craven A
> Stubbed out in orange peel and cheese)
> Of girls and Other Ranks and pay.
>
> If—on last night-scheme—B Coy broke
> The bipod of the borrowed bren:
> The Sergeants' Mess is out of coke:
> And Gordon nearly made that Wren.
>
> Along the tables of the Mess
> The artificial tulips blow,
> Tired as a prostitute's caress
> Their crimson casts no gladdening glow.

Why do those phallic petals fret
The heart, till coils—like Dannert wire—
Concentrically expand regret
For lost true love and found desire?

While Haw-Haw, from the radio,
Aggrieved, insistent, down the stair,
With distant bugles, sweet and low,
Commingles on the winter air.'

Stevens ceased to declaim. He smiled and sat back in his seat. He was certainly unaware of the entirely new conception of himself his own spoken verses had opened up for me. Their melancholy revealed quite another side of his nature, one concealed as a rule by aggressive cheerfulness. This melancholy was no doubt a logical counterpart, the reverse surface of the coin, one to be expected from high spirits of his own particular sort, bound up as they were with a perpetual discharge of personality. All the same, one never learns to expect the obvious. This contrast of feeling in him might have been an element that attracted Priscilla, something she recognised when they first met at Frederica's; something more fundamentally melodramatic, even, than Lovell himself could achieve. We all expressed appreciation. Moreland was, I think, almost as surprised as myself.

'Not much like Max's stuff though,' he said.

'All the same, Max Pilgrim was the source.'

'Nor very cheerful,' said Mrs Maclintick. 'I do believe you're as morbid as Moreland is himself.'

Although she spoke in her accustomed spirit of depreciation, Stevens must have achieved his aim in making more or less of a conquest, because she smiled quite kindly at him after saying that. Moved by her complaisance, or, more likely, by the repetition of his own lines, his face registered self-pity.

'I wasn't feeling very cheerful at the time,' he said. 'That unit I went to as a one-pipper fairly got me down.'

Then, immediately, one of those instantaneous changes of mood, that were so much a part of him, took place.

'Would you like to hear one of the bawdy ones?' he asked.

Before anyone could reply, another officer, a big captain with a red face and cropped hair, like Stevens also wearing battle-dress, passed our table. Catching sight of Stevens, this man began to roar with laughter and point.

'Odo, my son,' he yelled. 'Fancy seeing your ugly mug here.'

'God, Brian, you old swine.'

'I suppose you've been painting the town red, and, like me, have got to catch the night train back to the bloody grind again. I've been having a pretty wet weekend, I can tell you.'

'Come and have a drink, Brian. There's lots of time.'

'Not going to risk being cashiered for WOASAWL.'

'What on earth's that he said?' asked Mrs Maclintick.

'While-On-Active-Service-Absent-Without-Leave,' said Stevens, characteristically not allowing her even for a second out of his power by disregarding the question. 'Oh, come on, Brian, no hurry yet.'

The red-faced captain was firm.

'Got to find a taxi, for one thing. Besides, I've baggage to pick up.'

Stevens looked at his watch.

'I've got baggage too,' he said, 'a valise and a kit bag

149

and some other junk. Perhaps you're right, Brian, and I'd do well to accompany you. Anyway it would halve the taxi fare.'

He rose from the table.

'Then I'll be bidding you all goodbye,' he said.

'Do you really have to go?' said Mrs Maclintick. 'We're just beginning to get to know you. Are you annoyed about something, like the girl you were with?'

In the course of her life she could rarely have gone further towards making an effort to show herself agreeable. It was a triumph for Stevens. He laughed, conscious of this, pleased at his success.

'Duty calls,' he said. 'I only wish I could stay till four in the morning, but they're beginning to shut down here as it is, even if I hadn't a train to catch.'

We said goodbye to him.

'Wonderful to have met you, Mr Moreland,' said Stevens. 'Here's to the next performance of *Vieux Port* on the same programme as your newest work—and may I be there to hear. Goodbye, Nicholas.'

He held out his hand. From being very sure of himself, he had now reverted a little to that less absolute confidence of the days when I had first known him. He was probably undecided as to the most effective note to strike in taking leave of us. It may at last have dawned on him that all the business of Priscilla could include embarrassments of a kind to which he had hitherto given little or no thought. The hesitation he showed possibly indicated indecision as to whether or not he should make further reference to her sudden withdrawal from the party. If, for a second, he had contemplated speaking of that, he must have changed his mind.

'We'll be meeting again,' he said.

'Goodbye.'

'And Happy Landings.'

'Come on, Odo, you oaf,' said the red-faced captain, 'cut out the fond farewells, or there won't be a cab left on the street. We've got to get cracking. Don't forget there'll be all that waffle with the RTO.'

They went off together, slapping each other on the back.

'He's a funny boy,' said Mrs Maclintick.

Stevens had made an impression on her. There could be no doubt of that. The way she spoke showed it. Although his presence that night had been unwelcome to myself—and the other two at first had also displayed no great wish to have him at the table—a distinct sense of flatness was discernible now Stevens was gone. Even Moreland, who had fidgeted when Mrs Maclintick had expressed regrets at this departure, seemed aware that the conviviality of the party was reduced by his removal. I said I should have to be making for bed.

'Oh, God, don't let's break it all up at once,' Moreland said. 'We've only just met. Those others prevented our talking of any of the things we really want to discuss—like the meaning of art, or how to get biscuits on the black market.'

'They won't serve any more drink here.'

'Come back to our place for a minute or two. There might be some beer left. We'll get old Max out of bed. He loves a gossip.'

'All right—but not for long.'

We paid the bill, went out into Regent Street. In the utter blackness, the tarts, strange luminous form of nocturnal animal life, flickered the bulbs of their electric torches. From time to time one of them would play the light against her own face in self-advertisement, giving the effect of candles illuminating a holy picture in the shadows of a church.

'Ingenious,' said Moreland.

'Don't doubt Maclintick would have found it so,' said Mrs Maclintick, not without bitterness.

A taxi set down its passengers nearby. We secured it. Moreland gave the address of the flat where he used to live with Matilda.

'I've come to the conclusion the characteristic women most detest in a man is unselfishness,' he said.

This remark had no particular bearing on anything that had gone before, evidently giving expression only to one of his long interior trains of thought.

'They don't have to put up with much of it,' said Mrs Maclintick. 'It's passed me by these forty years, but perhaps I'm lucky.'

'How their wives must have hated those saintly kings in the Middle Ages,' Moreland said. 'Still, as you truly remark, Audrey, one's speaking rather academically.'

The taxi had already driven off, and Moreland was putting the key in the lock of the front-door of the house, when the Air-raid Warning began to sound.

'Just timed it nicely,' Moreland said. 'That's the genuine article, not like the faint row when we were at dinner. No doubt at all allowed to remain in the mind. Are the flat's curtains drawn? I was the last to leave and it's the sort of thing I always forget to do.'

'Max will have fixed them,' said Mrs Maclintick.

We climbed the stairs, of which there were a great number, as they occupied the top floor flat.

'I hope Max is all right,' she said. 'I never like the idea of him being out in a raid. There's bound to be trouble if he spends the night in a shelter. He's always talking about giving the Underground a try-out, but I tell him I won't have him doing any such thing.'

If Moreland was one of Mrs Maclintick's children, clearly Max Pilgrim was another. We entered the flat behind her. Moreland did not turn on the switch until it was confirmed all windows were obscured. In the light, the apartment was revealed as untidier than in Matilda's day, otherwise much the same in outward appearance and decoration.

'Max . . .' shouted Mrs Maclintick.

She uttered this call from the bedroom. A faint answering cry came from another room further up the short passage. Its message was indeterminate, the tone, high and tremulous, bringing back echoes of a voice that had twittered through myriad forgotten night-clubs in the small hours.

'We've got a visitor, Max,' shouted Mrs Maclintick again.

'I hope there'll turn out to be some beer left,' said Moreland. 'I don't feel all that sure.'

He went into the kitchen. I remained in the passage. A door slowly opened at the far end. Max Pilgrim appeared, a tall willowy figure in horn-rimmed spectacles and a green brocade dressing gown. It was years since I had last seen him, where, I could not even remember, whether in the distance at a party, or, less likely, watching his act at some cabaret show. For a time he had shared a flat with Isobel's brother, Hugo, but we had not been in close touch with Hugo at that period, and had, as it happened, never visited the place. There had been talk of Pilgrim giving up his performances in those days and joining Hugo in the decorating business. Even at that time, Pilgrim's songs had begun to 'date', professionally speaking. However, that project had never come off, and, whatever people might say about being old-fashioned, Pilgrim continued to find himself in demand right up to the outbreak of war. Now, of course, he expressed to audiences all that was most nostalgic. Although his hair was dishevelled—perhaps because of that—he looked at this very moment as if about to break into one of his songs. He moved a little way up the passage, then paused.

'Here you are at last, my dears,' he said. 'You don't know how glad I am to see you. You must forgive what I'm looking like, which must be a perfect sight. I took off my slap before going to bed and am presenting you with a countenance natural and unadorned, something I'm always most unwilling to do.'

He certainly appeared pale as death. I had thought at first he was merely looking much older than I remembered. Now I accepted as explanation what he had said about lack of make-up. I noticed, too, that his right hand was bandaged. The voice was fainter than usual. He looked uncertainly at me, disguised in uniform. I explained I was Hugo's brother-in-law; that we had met once or twice in the past. Pilgrim took my right hand in his left.

'My dear . . .'

'How are you?'

'I've been having a most unenjoyable evening,' he said.

He did not at once release my hand. For some reason I felt a sudden lack of ease, an odd embarrassment, even apprehension, although absolutely accustomed to the rather unduly fervent social manner he was employing. I tried to withdraw from his grasp, but he held on tenaciously, almost as if he were himself requiring actual physical support.

154

'We hoped you were coming on from the Madrid to join us at dinner,' I said. 'Hugh tells me you were doing some of the real old favourites there.'

'I was.'

'Did you leave the Madrid too late?'

Then Max Pilgrim let go my hand. He folded his arms. His eyes were fixed on me. Although no longer linked to him by his own grasp, I continued to feel indefinably uncomfortable.

'You knew the Madrid?' he asked.

'I've been there—not often.'

'But enjoyed yourself there?'

'Always.'

'You'll never do that again.'

'Why not?'

'The Madrid is no more,' he said.

'Finished?'

'Finished.'

'The season or just your act?'

'The place—the building—the tables and chairs—the dance-floor—the walls—the ceiling—all those gold pillars. A bomb hit the Madrid full pitch this evening.'

'Max . . .'

Mrs Maclintick let out a cry. It was a reasonable moment to give expression to a sense of horror. Moreland had come into the passage from the kitchen, carrying a bottle of beer and three glasses. He stood for a moment, saying nothing; then we all went into the sitting-room. Pilgrim at once took the armchair. He nursed his bound hand, rocking himself slowly forward and back.

'In the middle of my act,' he said. 'It was getting the bird in a big way. Never experienced the like before, even on tour.'

'So there *was* a blitz earlier in the evening,' said Moreland.

'There was,' said Pilgrim. 'There certainly was.'

No one spoke for some seconds. Pilgrim continued to sit in the chair, looking straight in front of him, holding his wounded hand with the other. I knew there was a question I ought to ask, but felt almost physically inhibited from forming the words. In the end, Mrs Maclintick, not myself, put the enquiry.

'Anybody killed?'

Pilgrim nodded.

'Many?'

Pilgrim nodded again.

'Helped to get some of them out,' he said.

'There were a lot?'

'Of course it's a ghastly muddle on these occasions,' he said. 'Frenzied. Like Dante's Inferno. All in the black-out too. The wardens and I carried out six or seven at least. Must have. They'd all had it. I knew some of them personally. Nasty business, I can assure you. I suppose a few got away with it—like myself. They tried to persuade me to go with them and have some treatment, but after I'd had my hand bound up, all I wanted was home, sweet home. It's only a scratch, so I came back and tucked up. But I'm glad you're all here. Very glad.'

There was no escape now. So far as possible, certainty had to be established. An effort must be made.

'Bijou Ardglass was there with a party.'

Pilgrim looked at me with surprise.

'You knew that?' he said.

'Yes.'

'Were you asked? If so, you were lucky to have another engagement.'

'They were—'

'Bijou's table was just where it came through the ceiling.'

'So—'

'I'm afraid it was Bijou's last party.'

Pilgrim glanced away, quickly passing the bandaged hand across his eyes. It was an instinctive, not in the least dramatised, gesture.

'But the rest of them?'

'No one survived from that corner. That was where the worst of the damage was done. My end of the room wasn't so bad. That's why I'm here now.'

'You're sure all the Ardglass party—'

'They were the ones I helped carry out,' said Pilgrim. He spoke quite simply.

'Chips Lovell—'

'He'd been at the table.'

Moreland looked across at me. Mrs Maclintick took Pilgrim's arm.

'How did you get back yourself, Max?' she asked.

'I got a lift on one of the fire-engines. Can you imagine?'

'Here,' said Moreland. 'Have some beer.'

Pilgrim took the glass.

'I'd known Bijou for years,' he said. 'Known her when she was a little girl with a plait trying to get a job in the chorus. Wasn't any good for some reason. Can't think why, because she had the Theatre in her blood both sides. Do you know, Bijou's father played Abanazar in *Aladdin* when my mother was Principal Boy in the same show? Anyway, it all turned out best for Bijou in the end. Did much better as a mannequin than she'd ever have done on the boards. Met richer men, for one thing.'

There was a pause. Moreland cleared his throat uncom-

fortably. Mrs Maclintick sniffed. In the far distance, unexpectedly soon, the All Clear droned. It was followed, an
instant later, by a more local siren.

'That one didn't take long,' Moreland said.

'Another tip-and-run raider,' said Pilgrim. 'The fashion
of the moment.'

'It was a single plane caught the Madrid?'

'That's it.'

'I'll make some tea,' said Mrs Maclintick. 'Do us good.'

'Just what I need, Audrey, my dear,' said Pilgrim, sigh-
ing. 'I couldn't think what it was. Now I know it's tea—
not beer at all.'

He drank the beer all the same. Mrs Maclintick went
off to the kitchen. It became clear that an unpleasant duty
must be performed. There was no avoiding it. Priscilla
would have to be told about the Madrid as soon as possible.
If I called up the Jeavonses' house right away, the telephone, with any luck, would be answered by Molly
Jeavons herself. I could tell her what had happend. She
could break the news. So far as that went, even to make
the announcement to Molly would be bad enough. It
might be hard on her to have to tell Priscilla, but at least
Molly was, by universal consent, a person adapted by
nature to such harrowing tasks; warm-hearted, not over
sensitive, grasping immediately the needs of the bereaved,
saying just what was required, emotional yet never in-
capacitated by emotion. Molly, if I were lucky, would do
the job. There was always the chance Priscilla herself
might be at the other end of the line. That was a risk that
had to be taken into consideration. In a cowardly way, I
delayed action until Mrs Maclintick had returned with the
tea. After finishing a cup, I asked if I might use the telephone.

'By the bed,' said Moreland.

Pilgrim began to muse aloud.

'Strange those young Germans up there trying to kill me,' he murmured to himself. 'Ungrateful too. I've always had such good times in Berlin.'

The bedroom was more untidy than would ever have been allowed in Matilda's day. I sat on the edge of the bed and dialled the Jeavons number. There was no buzz. I tried again. After several unsuccessful attempts, none of which even achieved the 'number unobtainable' sound, I rang the Exchange. There were further delays. Then the operator tried the Jeavons number. That, too, was unproductive. No sound of ringing came. The line was out of order. I gave it up and returned to the sitting room.

'I can't get through. I'll have to go.'

'Stay the night, if you like,' said Mrs Maclintick. 'You can sleep on the sofa. Maclintick often did in our Pimlico place. Spent almost more time there than he did in bed.'

The offer was unexpected, rather touching in the circumstances. I saw she was probably able to look after Moreland better than I thought.

'No—thanks all the same. As I failed on the telephone, I'll have to go in person.'

'Priscilla?' said Moreland.

'Yes.'

He nodded.

'What a job,' he said.

Max Pilgrim gathered his dressing gown round him. He yawned and stretched.

'I wonder when the next one will arrive,' he said. 'Worse than waiting for the curtain to go up.'

I said goodnight to them. Moreland came to the door.

'I suppose you've really got to do this?' he said.

'Not much avoiding it.'

'Glad it's not me,' he said.

'You're right to be.'

There seemed no more taxis left in London. I walked for a time, then, totally unlooked for at that hour, a bus stopped by the place I was passing. Without any very clear idea of doing more than move in a south-westerly direction, I boarded it, in this way travelled as far as a stop in the neighbourhood of Gloucester Road. Here the journey had to be resumed on foot. The pavements were endless, threading a way down them like those interminable rovings pursued in dreams. Cutting through several side turnings, I at last found myself among a conjunction of dark red brick Renaissance-type houses. In one of these the Jeavonses had lived for twenty years or more, an odd centre of miscellaneous hospitality to which Chips Lovell himself had first taken me. In the lower reaches of their street, two fire-engines were drawn up. By the light of electric torches, firemen and air-raid wardens were passing in and out of one of the front-doors. This particular house turned out to be the Jeavonses'. In the dark, little was to be seen of what was happening. Apart from these dim figures going to and fro, like the trolls in *Peer Gynt*, nothing seemed abnormal about the façade. There was no sign of damage to the structure. One of the wardens, in helmet and overalls, stopped by the steps and lit a cigarette.

'Did this house get it?'

'About an hour ago,' he said, 'that last tip-and-run raider.'

'Anybody hurt?'

He took the cigarette from his mouth and nodded.

'I know the people—are they about?'

'You know Mr Jeavons and Lady Molly?'

'Yes.'

'You've only just arrived here?'

'That's it.'

'Mr Jeavons and me are on the same warden-post,' he said. 'They've taken him down there. Giving him a cup of tea.'

'Was he injured?'

'It was her.'

'Badly?'

The warden looked at me as if I should not have asked that question.

'You hadn't heard?' he said.

'No.'

'Didn't survive.'

He went on speaking at once, as if from a kind of embarrassment at having to announce such a thing.

'She and the young lady,' he said. 'It was all at the back of the house. You wouldn't think there was a jot of damage out here in front, but there's plenty inside, I can tell you. Dreadful thing. Used to see a lot of them. Always very friendly people. Got their newspapers from me, matter of fact. If you know them, there's a lady inside can tell you all about it.'

'I'll go in.'

He threw away the stub of his cigarette and trod on it.

'So long,' he said.

'So long.'

He was right about there being a mess inside. A woman in some sort of uniform was giving instructions to the people clearing up. She turned out to be Eleanor Walpole-Wilson.

'Eleanor.'

She looked round.

'Hullo, Nick,' she said. 'Thank goodness you've come.'

She did not seem at all surprised to see me. She came across the hall. Now in her middle thirties, Eleanor was less unusual in appearance than as a girl. No doubt uniform suited her. Though her size and shape had also become more conventional, she retained an air of having been never properly assimilated to either sex. At the same time, big and broad-shouldered, she was not exactly a 'mannish' woman. Her existence might have been more viable had that been so.

'You've heard what's happened?' she said abruptly.

Her manner, too, so out of place in ordinary social relations, had equally come into its own.

'Molly's . . .'

'And Priscilla.'

'God.'

'One of the Polish officers too—the nice one. The other's pretty well all right, just a bang over the head. That wretched girl who got into trouble with the Norwegian has been taken to hospital. She'll be all right, too, when she's recovered from the shock. I don't know whether she'll keep the baby.'

It was clear all this briskness was specifically designed to carry Eleanor through. She must have been having a very bad time indeed.

'A man at the door—one of the wardens—said Ted was down at the post.'

'He was there when it happened. They may have taken him on to the hospital by now. How did you hear about it? I didn't know you were in London.'

'I'm passing through on leave.'

'Is Isobel all right?'

'She's all right. She's in the country.'

Just for the moment I felt unable to explain anything very lucidly, to break through the barricade of immediate action and rapid talk with which Eleanor was protecting herself. It was like trying to tackle her in the old days, when she had been training one of her dogs with a whistle, and would not listen to other people round her. She must have developed early in life this effective method of shutting herself off from the rest of the world; a weapon, no doubt, against parents and early attempts to make her live a conventional sort of life. Now, while she talked, she continued to move about the hall, clearing up some of the debris. She was wearing a pair of green rubber gloves that made me think of the long white ones she used to draw on at dances.

'We shall have to have a talk as to who must be told about all this—and in what order. Are you in touch with Chips?'

'Eleanor—Chips has been killed too.'

Eleanor stopped her tidying up. I told her what had happened at the Madrid. She began to take off the green gloves. People were passing through the passage all the time. Eleanor put the rubber gloves on the top of the marquetry cabinet Molly's sister had left her when she died, the one Ted Jeavons had never managed to move out of the hall.

'Let's go upstairs and sit down for a bit,' she said. 'I've had just about as much as I can take. We can sit in the drawing room. That was one of the rooms that came off least badly.'

We went up to the first floor. The drawing room, thick in dust and fallen plaster, had a long jagged fissure down one wall. There were two rectangular discoloured spaces where the Wilson and the Greuze had hung. These pictures had presumably been removed to some safer place at the outbreak of war. So, too, had a great many of the oriental bowls and jars that had formerly played such a part in the decoration. They might have been valuable or absolute rubbish; Lovell had always insisted the latter. The pastels, by some unknown hand, of Moroccan types remained. They were hanging at all angles, the glass splintered of one bearing the caption *Rainy Day at Marrakesh*. Eleanor and I sat on the sofa. She began to cry.

'It's all too awful,' she said, 'and I was so fond of Molly. You know, she usen't to like me. When Norah and I first shared a flat together, Molly didn't approve. She put out a story I wore a green pork-pie hat and a bow tie. It wasn't true. I never did. Anyway, why shouldn't I, if I wanted to? There I was in the country breeding labradors and bored to death, and all my parents wanted was for me to get married, which I hadn't the least wish to do. Norah came to stay and suggested I should join her in taking a flat. There it was. Norah was always quite good at getting jobs in shops and that sort of thing, and I found all the stuff I knew about dogs could be put to some use too when it came to the point. Besides, I'd always adored Norah.'

I had sometimes wondered how Eleanor's ménage with Norah Tolland had begun. No one ever seemed to know. Now it was explained.

'Where's Norah now?'

'In Scotland, driving for the Poles.'

She dried her eyes.

'Come on,' she said. 'We must get out some sort of plan. No good just sitting about. I'll find a pencil and paper.'

She began to rummage in one of the drawers.

'Here we are.'

We made lists of names, notes of things that would have to be done. One of the wardens came up to say that for the time being the house was safe to stay in, they were going home.

'Where are you spending the night, Nick?'

'A club.'

'There might be someone who could take you part of the way. The chief warden's got a car.'

'What about you?'

'I shall be all right. There's a room fitted up with a bed in the basement. Ted used it sometimes, if he had to come in very late.'

'Will you really be all right?'

She dismissed the question of herself rather angrily. The ARP official with the car was found.

'Goodbye, Eleanor.'

I kissed her, which I had never done before.

'Goodbye, Nick. Love to Isobel. It was lucky I was staying here really, because there'll be a lot that will have to be done.'

The fire-engines had driven away. The street was empty. I thought how good Eleanor was in a situation like this. Molly had been good, too, when it came to disaster. I wondered what would happen to Ted. The extraordinary thing about the outside of the house was that everything looked absolutely normal. Some sort of a notice about bomb damage had been stuck on the front-door by the wardens; otherwise there was nothing to indicate the place had been subjected to an attack from the air, which had killed several persons. This lack of outward display was comparable with the Madrid's fate earlier that evening, when a lot of talking in a restaurant had been sufficient to drown the sound of the Warning, the noise of the guns.

This must be what Dr Trelawney called 'the slayer of Osiris and his grievous tribute of blood'. I wondered if Dr Trelawney himself had survived: when Odo Stevens would receive the news: whether the Lovells' daughter, Caroline, would be brought up by her grandparents. Reflecting on these things, it did not seem all that long time ago that Lovell, driving back from the film studios in that extraordinary car of his, had suggested we should look in on the Jeavonses', because 'the chief reason I want to visit Aunt Molly is to take another look at Priscilla Tolland, who is quite often there.'

3

THE FIRST MEAL EATEN IN Mess after return from leave is
always dispiriting. Room, smell, food, company, at first
seemed unchanged; as ever, unenchanting. On taking a
seat at table I remembered with suddenly renewed sense
of internal discomfort that Stringham would be on duty.
In the pressure of other things that had been happening,
I had forgotten about him. However, when the beef
appeared, it was handed round by a red-haired gangling
young soldier with a hare-lip and stutter. There was no
sign of Stringham. The new waiter could be permanent,
or just a replacement imported to F Mess while Stringham
himself was sick, firing a musketry course, temporarily
absent for some other routine reason. Opportunity to enquire why he was gone, at the same time to betray no
exceptional interest in him personally, arose when Soper
complained of the red-haired boy's inability to remember
which side of the plate, as a matter of common practice,
were laid knife, fork and spoon.

'Like animals, some of them,' Soper said. 'As for getting
a message delivered, you're covered with spit before he's
halfway through.'

'What happened to the other one?'

If asked a direct question of that sort, Soper always
looked suspicious. Finding, after a second or two, no

grounds for imputing more than idle curiosity to this one, he returned a factual, though reluctant, reply.

'Went to the Mobile Laundry.'

'For the second time of asking, Soper,' said Macfie, 'will you pass the water jug?'

'Here you are, Doc. Those tablets come in yet?'

Macfie was gruff about the tablets, Soper persuasive. The Cipher Officer remarked on the amount of flu about. There was general agreement, followed by some discussion of prevalent symptoms. The subject of Stringham had to be started up again from scratch.

'Did you sack him?'

'Sack who?'

'The other Mess waiter.'

'What's he got to do with you?'

'Just wondered.'

'He was transferred to the Laundry from one day to the next. Bloody inconvenient for this Mess. He'd have done the job all right if Biggy hadn't been on at him all the time. I complained to the DAAG about losing a waiter like that, but he said it had got to go through.'

Biggs, present at table, but in one of his morose moods that day, neither denied nor confirmed his own part in the process of Stringham's dislodgement. He chewed away at a particularly tough piece of meat, looking straight in front of him. Soper, as if Biggs himself were not sitting there, continued to muse on the aversion felt by Biggs for Stringham.

'That chap drove Biggy crackers for some reason,' he said. 'Something about him. Wasn't only the way he talked. Certainly was a dopey type. Don't know how he got where he was. Had some education. I could see that. You'd think he'd have found better employment than a Mess waiter. Got a bad record, I expect. Trouble back in Civvy Street.'

That Stringham had himself engineered an exchange from F Mess to avoid relative persecution at the hands of Biggs was, I thought, unlikely. In his relationship with Biggs, even a grim sort of satisfaction to Stringham might be suspected, one of those perverse involutions of feeling that had brought him into the army in the first instance. Such sentiments were hard to unravel. They were perhaps no more tangled than the rest of the elements that made up Stringham's life—or anybody else's life when closely examined. Not only had he disregarded loopholes which invited avoidance of the Services—health, and, at that period, age too—but, in face of much apparent discouragement from the recruiting authorities, had shown uncharacteristic persistence to get where he was. One aspect of this determination to carry through the project of joining the army was no doubt an attempt to rescue a self-respect badly battered during the years with Miss Weedon; however much she might also have accomplished in setting Stringham on his feet. An innate restlessness certainly played a part too; taste for change, even for adventure of a sort; all perhaps shading off into a vague romantic patriotism that especially allured by its own ironic connotations, its very lack, so to speak, of what might be called contemporary intellectual prestige.

'Awfully chic to be killed,' he had said.

Death was a prize, at least on the face of it, that war always offered. Lovell's case had demonstrated how the unexpected could happen within a few hours to those who deplored a sedentary job. Thinking over Stringham's more immediate situation, it seemed likely that, hearing of a vacancy in the ranks of the Mobile Laundry, he had decided on impulse to explore a new, comparatively exotic field of army life in his self-imposed military pilgrimage. Bithel could even have marked down Stringham as a man likely to do credit to the unit he commanded. That, I decided, was even more probable. These speculations had taken place during one of the Mess's long silences, less nerve-racking than those at the general's table, but also, in most respects, even more dreary. Biggs suddenly, unexpectedly, returned to the subject.

'Glad that bugger's gone,' he said. 'Got me down. It's a fact he did. I've got worries enough as it is, without having him about the place.'

He spoke as if it were indeed a great relief to him. I had to admit to myself that Stringham's physical removal was a great relief to me too. This sense of deliverance, of moral alleviation, was at the same time tempered with more than a trace of guilt, because, so far as potential improvement in his state was in question, Stringham had left F Mess without the smallest assistance from myself. I dispelled such twinges of conscience by reflecting that the Mobile Laundry, at least while Bithel remained in command, led for the moment a raggle-taggle gipsy life, offering, at least on the face of it, a less thankless daily prospect than being a Mess waiter. If absorbed into the Divisional Concert Party, he might even bring off a vocalist's stage debut, something he used to talk of on the strength of having been briefly in the choir at school. In short, the problem seemed to me to resolve itself—after an honourable, even quixotic gesture on Stringham's part—to finding the least uncongenial niche available in the circumstances. That supposition was entirely my own. It was probably far removed from Stringham's personal ambitions, if these were at all formulated.

'What's on your mind, Biggy?' said Soper. 'You're not yourself today.'

'Oh, stuff it up,' said Biggs, 'I've got a pile of trouble. Those lawyers are going to skin me.'

When I saw Widmerpool that afternoon I spoke about Stringham going to the Mobile Laundry.

'It was my idea to send him there.'

'A very good one.'

'It seemed the solution.'

Widmerpool did not elaborate what he had done. I was surprised, rather impressed, by the speed with which he had taken action, especially after earlier remarks about leaving Stringham where he was. It looked as if Widmerpool had thought things over and decided there was something to be said for trying to make Stringham's existence more agreeable, however contrary that might be to a rule of life that taught disregard for the individual. I felt I had for once misjudged Widmerpool, too readily accepted the bleak façade displayed, which, anyway in Stringham's case, might screen a complex desire to conceal good nature, however intermittent.

General Liddament had to be faced on the subject of my own missed Free French opportunities. The matter was not one of sufficient importance—at the General's end—to ask for an interview through Greening, so I had to wait until the Divisional Commander was to be found alone. As I rarely saw him during daily routine, this took place once again on an exercise. Defence Platoon duties usually brought me to breakfast first on those mornings, even before Cocksidge, otherwise in the vanguard of the rest of the staff. The General varied in his habits, sometimes early, sometimes late. That morning, he had appeared at table before Cocksidge himself, who, as it turned out later, had been delayed by breaking a bootlace or cutting his rubber-like face shaving. When the General had drunk some tea, I decided to tackle him.

'I saw Major Finn in London, sir.'

'Finn?'

'Yes, sir.'

'How was he?'

'Very well, sir. Sent his respects. He said my French was not up to liaison work at battalion level.'

'Ah.'

That was General Liddament's sole comment. He drank more tea in huge gulps, while he studied a map. The fact that Cocksidge entered the room a minute or two later did not, I think, affect the conversation in any way; I mean so far as further discussion of my own affairs by the General might have taken place. That was already at an end. Cocksidge was quite overcome by finding the Divisional Commander already almost at the end of breakfast.

'Excuse me, sir,' he said, 'but I do believe they've given you the chipped cup. I'll change it at once, sir. I wonder how often I've spoken to the Mess Sergeant about that cup, sir, and told him never to give it to a senior officer, and above all not yourself, sir. I'll make sure it never happens again, sir.'

Military action in Syria had been making it clear why there had been call for more British liaison officers with the Free French overseas. I thought of the 9th Regiment of Colonial Infantry being harangued by someone with better command of the language—and more histrionic talent—than myself. Then the Germans attacked in Crete. The impression was that things were not going too well there. Meanwhile, the Division continued to train; policies, units, began to take more coherent shape, to harden: new weapons were issued: instructors improved. The Commanding Officer of the Reconnaissance Unit remained unappointed. I asked Widmerpool if he had progressed further in placing his own candidate. The question did not please him.

'Difficulties have arisen.'

'Someone else getting the command?'

'I can't quite understand what is happening,' said Widmerpool. 'There has been no opportunity to go into the matter lately. This Diplock case has been taking up so much of my time. The more I investigate, the more incriminated Diplock seems to be. There's going to be hell to pay. Hogbourne-Johnson is behaving very badly, making himself offensive to me personally, and doing his best to shield the man and cause obstruction. That is quite useless. I am confident I shall be able to show that Diplock's behaviour has been not merely irregular, but criminal. Pedlar is almost equally unwilling to believe the worst, but at least Pedlar approaches the matter with a reasonably open mind, even if a slow one.'

'Does the General know about Diplock?'

'Hogbourne-Johnson says there is not sufficient evidence yet to lay before him.'

In the matter of Diplock, I believed Widmerpool to be on the right track. Few things are more extraordinary in human behaviour than the way in which old sweats like this chief clerk Warrant Officer will suddenly plunge into serious misdoing—usually on account of a woman. Diplock might well have a career of petty dishonesty behind him, but this looked like something far more serious.

'Talking of the Recce Unit,' said Widmerpool, 'there's still some sorting out to be done about the officer establishment. At least one of the captaincies assigned to that unit, before it came into existence, is still—owing to some whim of the General's—in use elsewhere as a local rank. That is one of the things I want you to go into among the stuff I am leaving tonight.'

'Establishments without troops always make one think of *Dead Souls*. A military Chichikov could first collect battalions, then brigades, finally a Division—and be promoted major-general.'

I said that to tease Widmerpool, feeling pretty certain he had never read a line of Gogol, though he would rarely if ever admit to failure in recognising an allusion, literary or otherwise. On this occasion he merely nodded his head several times; then returned to the fact that, contrary to his usual practice, he would not be working after dinner that evening.

'For once I shall cut office hours tonight,' he said. 'I'm giving dinner to that fellow—for the moment his name escapes me—from the Military Secretary's branch, who is doing a tour of duty over here.'

'Is this in the interests of the Recce Unit appointment?'

Widmerpool winked, a habit of his only when in an exceptionally good temper.

'More important than that,' he said.

'Yourself?'

'Dinner may put the finishing touches to something.'

'Promotion?'

'Who knows? It's been in the air for some time, as a matter of fact.'

Widmerpool rarely allowed himself a night off in this manner. He worked like an automaton. Work, civil or military, was his sole interest. If it came to that, he never gave his assistant a night off either, if he could help it, because everyone who served under him was expected to do so to the fullest extent of his powers, which was no doubt reasonable enough. The result was that a great deal of work was completed in the DAAG's office, some useful, some less useful. On the whole the useful work, it had to be admitted, made up for a fair percentage of time and energy wasted on Widmerpool's pet projects, of which there were several. I was thinking of such things while stowing away papers in the safe that night, preparatory to leaving Headquarters for bed. I shut the safe and locked it. The time was ten o'clock or thereabouts. The telephone bell began to ring.

'DAAG's office.'

'Nick?'

The voice was familiar. All the same, I could not immediately place it. No officer at Div HQ used just that intimate inflexion when pronouncing my name.

'Speaking.'

'It's Charles.'

That took me no further. So far as I could remember, none of the local staff were called 'Charles'. It must be someone recently arrived in the place, who knew me.

'Charles who?'

'Private Stringham, sir—pardon the presumption.'

'Charles—yes—sorry.'

'Bit of luck catching you in.'

'I'm just leaving, as a matter of fact. How did you know I was here?'

'I rang up F Mess first—in the character of General Fauncefoot-Fritwell's ADC.'

'Who on earth is General Fauncefoot-Fritwell?'

'Just a name that occurred to me as belonging to the sort of officer of senior rank who would own an ADC—so

175

don't worry if Captain Biggs, who I think answered the telephone, mentions the General to you. He will say there was no message. Captain Biggs, if it was indeed he, sounded quite impressed, even rather frightened. He told me you were probably still working, unless on your way back now. I must say, you officers are kept at it.'

'But, Charles, what is all this about?'

I thought he must be drunk, and began to wonder how best to deal with him. This was just the sort of embarrassment Widmerpool had envisaged. It could be awkward. I experienced one of those moments—they cropped up from time to time—of inwardly agreeing there was something to be said for Widmerpool's point of view. However Stringham sounded perfectly sober; though to sound sober was not unknown as one of the characteristics he was apt to display after a great deal to drink. That was especially true of the period immediately preceding his going under entirely. I felt apprehensive.

'Yes, I must come to the point, Nick,' he said. 'I'm getting dreadfully garrulous in old age. It's barrack-room life. Look, forgive me for ringing up at this late hour, which I know to be contrary to good order and discipline. The fact is I find myself with a problem on my hands.'

'What's happened?'

'You know my officer, Mr Bithel?'

'Of course.'

'You will therefore be aware that—like my former unregenerate self—he is at times what our former mentor, Mr Le Bas, used to call a devotee of Bacchus?'

'Bithel's drunk?'

'Got it in one. Rather overdone the Dionysian rites.'

'Passed out?'

'Precisely.'

'Whereabouts?'

'I've just tripped over his prostrate form on the way back to bed. When I was suddenly, quite unexpectedly, whisked away from F Mess, and enlisted under Mr Bithel's gallant command, he behaved very kindly to me on arrival. He has done so ever since. I therefore feel grateful towards him. I thought—to avoid further danger to himself, physical or moral—you might have some idea of the best way of getting him back without undue delay to wherever he belongs. Otherwise some interfering policeman, civil or military, will feel it his duty to put the Lieutenant in the cooler. I'm not sure where he's housed. G Mess, is it? Anyway, I can't manage him all on my own-io, as the Edwardian song used to say. I wondered if you had any suggestions.'

This emergency had noticeably cheered Stringham. That was plain, even on the telephone. There was only one thing to do.

'I'll come along. What about yourself? Are you all right for time?'

'I'm on a late pass.'

'And where are you exactly?'

Stringham described a spot not far from where we had met in the street on that earlier occasion. The place was about ten minutes' walk from Headquarters; rather more from G Mess, where Bithel slept.

'I'll stand guard over Mr B. until you arrive,' Stringham said. 'At the moment he's propped up out of harm's way on the steps of a bombed house. Bring a torch, if you've got one. It's as dark as hell and stinks of something far worse than cheese.'

By some incredibly lucky concatenation of circumstances, Bithel had managed, though narrowly, to escape court-martial over the affair of the bouncing cheque that had worried him the night of the biggish raid of several weeks before. However, Widmerpool had now stated categorically he was on the point of removing Bithel from the Mobile Laundry command as soon as he could negotiate that matter satisfactorily with the authority to whom the Laundry was ultimately responsible. That might be a judgment from which there was no appeal, but, even so, gave no reason to deny a hand in getting Bithel as far as his own bed that night, rather than leave him to be picked up by the Provost Marshal or local constabulary. It was even possible that definite official notification of his final sacking might have brought about this sudden alcoholic downfall; until now kept by Bithel within reasonable bounds. He would certainly be heartbroken at losing the command of the Mobile Laundry, of which he was, indeed, said to have made a fair success. If this intimation had reached him, he might be additionally upset because dismissal would almost certainly mark the first stage of final ejection from the army. Bithel was proud of being in the army; it also brought him a livelihood. Apart from any of that, Stringham had to be backed up in undertaking Bithel's rescue. That was how things looked. I made a last inspection of the office to make sure no papers had been left outside the safe that should have been locked away, then left Headquarters.

Outside in the street, it was impossible to see a yard ahead without a torch. In spite of that, I found the place without much difficulty. Stringham, hands in his pockets, was leaning against the wall of a house that had been burnt out by an incendiary bomb a week or two before. He was smoking a cigarette.

'Hullo, Nick.'

'Where's Bithel?'

'At the top of these steps. I pulled him up there out of the way. He seemed to be coming-to a moment ago. Then he sank back again. Let's go and have a look at him.'

Bithel was propped up under a porch against the front-door of the house, his legs stretched down the steps, head sunk on one shoulder. This was all revealed by a flash of the torch. He was muttering a little to himself. We examined him.

'Where's he got to go?' asked Stringham.

'G Mess. That's not too far from here.'

'Can we carry him feet first?'

'Not a very tempting prospect in the blackout. Can't we wake him up and force him to walk? Everyone must realize they have to make a special effort in wartime. Why should Bithel be absolved from that?'

'How severe you always are to human weakness, Nick.'

We shook Bithel, who was again showing slight signs of revival, at least in so much that protests were wrung from him by this rough treatment.

'. . . Don't shake us, old man . . . don't shake us like that . . . whatever are you doing it for? . . . makes me feel awful . . . I'll throw up . . . I will really . . .'

'Bith, you've got to pull yourself together, get back to your billet.'

'What's that you're saying . . .'

'Can you stand up? If so, we'll hold you on either side.'

'. . . Can't remember your name, old man . . . didn't see you in that last pub . . . couldn't see any officers there . . . rather glad of that . . . prefer talking to those young fellows without a lot of majors poking their noses in . . . keep in touch with the men . . . never go far wrong if

179

you do that . . . take an interest in them off duty . . . then it got late . . . couldn't find the way home . . .'

'It *is* late, Bith. That's why we've got to take you back to bed. It's Nick Jenkins. We're going to pilot you to G Mess.'

'Nick Jenkins . . . in the Regiment together. . . . Do you remember . . . *Mr Vice—the Loyal Toast* . . . then, you . . .'

'That's it.'

'*The King* . . .'

Bithel shouted the words, turning on one elbow and making as if to raise a glass in the air.

'*The King*, Bith.'

'Loved the old Regiment. . . . Give you *The Regiment* . . . no heelers. . . . Age shall not . . . something . . . nor the years condemn . . .'

'Come on, Bith, make an effort.'

'. . . at the going down of the sun . . . that's it . . . we shall remember them . . .'

He suddenly began to sing in a thin piping voice, not unlike Max Pilgrim's.

'Fol-low, fol-low, we will fol-low Davies—
We will follow Davies, everywhere he leads . . .'

'Bith.'

'Remember how we went romping all over the house that Christmas night after dinner . . . when the Mess was in those former bank premises . . . trailing along behind Colonel Davies . . . under the tables . . . over the chairs . . . couldn't do it this moment for five pounds . . . God, I do really believe I'm going to throw up . . .'

We got him to his feet with a tremendous heave. This

sudden change of posture was too much for Bithel, who had rightly judged his own digestive condition. After much vomiting, he seemed appreciably more sober. We had allowed him to sink on all fours to the ground while relieving his stomach. Now we raised him again on his feet to prepare for the journey back to G Mess.

'If you can walk, Bith, we'll take you home now. Stringham, one of your own chaps, is here to help.'

'String . . .'

'Here, sir,' said Stringham, who had begun to laugh a lot. 'Stringham of the Mobile Laundry, present and correct.'

The name, coupled with that of his command, faintly animated Bithel. Perhaps it suggested to him the title of one of those adventure stories he had enjoyed as a boy; certainly the picaresque operation of a Mobile Laundry would have made an enthralling Henty volume.

'That 'varsity man the DAAG sent to me?'

'That's the one, sir.'

'Only good turn Major Widmerpool's ever done me . . .'

Stringham was now laughing so much we had to lower Bithel to the ground again.

'I know just how you're feeling, sir,' said Stringham. 'Nobody better.'

'Stringham's a 'varsity man, like yourself, Nick. . . . Did you know that? . . . good type . . . got some fine boys in the Laundry . . . proud to command them . . . Sergeant Ablett . . . splendid type. . . . You should hear him sing *The Man who broke the Bank at Monte Carlo* . . . brings back the old music halls . . . but Stringham's the only 'varsity man . . .'

The access of emotion that had now descended on Bithel was in danger of changing once more to stupor. He

181

began to breathe heavily. We tried to lift him again from the pavement.

'One of the things I like about him,' said Stringham, 'is the fact there's so little difference when he's sober. Drink doesn't make him turn nasty. On the contrary. How well one knows the feeling of loving the whole world after downing a few doubles. As I no longer drink, I no longer love the whole world—nor, if it comes to that, even a small part of it.'

'All the same, you took the trouble to be a Good Samaritan on this occasion.'

'After all, he is my Commanding Officer—and has been very gracious to me. I still have some gratitude, even if no general goodwill towards mankind. I like gratitude, because it's the rarest of virtues and a very difficult one to cultivate. For example, I never feel nearly grateful enough to Tuffy. In some respects, I'm ashamed to say I'm even conscious of a certain resentment towards her. Tonight's good deed was just handed me on a plate. Such a conscience have I now developed, I even feel grateful to Widmerpool. That does me credit, doesn't it? Do you know, Nick, he went out of his way to get me moved from F Mess to the Mobile Laundry—just as an act of pure kindness. Who'd have thought that of Widmerpool? I learnt the fact from Mr Bithel himself, who was equally surprised at the DAAG finding suitable personnel for him. I must say I was at once attracted by the idea of widening my military experience. Besides, there are some real treasures in the Laundry. I don't know how I can show Widmerpool gratitude. Keep out of the way, I suppose. The one thing I can't understand is Mr Bithel's obsession with university life. I explained to him, when he brought up the subject, that my own college days had been among the most melancholic of a life not untinged by shadow.'

All the time Stringham had been speaking, we were trying to galvanise Bithel from his spell of total collapse into a state of renewed awareness. We achieved this, finally bringing him into actual motion.

'Now, if you'll guide us, Nick, we'll have the Lieutenant tucked up between sheets in no time.'

Once we had Bithel traversing the pavement between us, the going was quite good in spite of Stygian darkness. In fact, we must have been within a hundred and fifty yards of G Mess before anything inopportune occurred. Then was disaster. The worst happened. Stringham and I were rounding a corner, Bithel mumbling incomprehensibly between us, when a figure, walking hurriedly from the other direction, collided violently with our party. The effect of this strong oncoming impact was for Stringham to let go of Bithel's arm, so that, taken by surprise and unable to support the full weight alone, I too became disengaged from Bithel, who sank heavily to the ground. The person who had obstructed us also stumbled and swore, a moment later playing a torch on my face, so that I could not see him or anything else.

'What the hell is happening?'

The voice was undoubtedly Widmerpool's, especially recognisable when angry. His quarters were also in this neighbourhood. He was on his way back to B Mess after dinner with his acquaintance from the Military Secretary's branch. This was a most unfortunate encounter. The only thing to do was to fabricate as quickly as possible some obvious excuse for Bithel's condition, and hope for the best.

'This officer must have tripped in the black-out,' I said.

183

'He had knocked himself out. We're taking him back to his billet.'

Widmerpool played his torch on each of us in turn.

'Nicholas . . .' he said, 'Bithel . . . Stringham . . .'

He spoke Stringham's name with surprise, not much approval. Since identities were now revealed, there was now no hope of proceeding without further explanation.

'Charles Stringham found Bithel lying stunned. He got in touch with me. We're taking him back to G Mess.'

That might have sounded reasonably convincing, if only Bithel himself had kept quiet. However, the last fall seemed, if not to have sobered him, at least to have shaken off the coma into which he had sunk at an earlier stage. Now, without any help from the rest of us, he picked himself up off the pavement. He took Widmerpool by the arm.

'Ought to go home . . .' he said. 'Ought to go home . . . had too much of that bloody porter . . . sickly stuff when you mix it with gin-and-italian . . . never do if we run into the APM . . .'

Then he began to sing again, though in a lower key than before.

'Fol-low, fol-low, we will follow Davies . . .'

The words of the rest of the song were drowned at that moment by the sudden note of the Air-raid Warning. For me, the ululating call registered a routine summons not to be disregarded. Bithel's troubles, however acute, must now be accepted as secondary to overseeing that the Defence Platoons reported for duty, without delay mounted their brens for aircraft action. A chance remained that this diversion might distract Widmerpool's attention from the business of getting Bithel home. There was no reason for Widmerpool to hang about in the streets after the Warning had gone. His orderly mind might indicate that correct procedure for him was to take shelter. However, he made no such move, only disengaging himself from Bithel by pushing him against the wall. He must have grasped the situation perfectly, seen at once that the first thing to do was to get Bithel himself out of the way. Certainly he retained no doubts as to why Bithel had been found lying on the pavement, but accepted at the same time the fact that there was no point in making a fuss then and there. Disciplinary action, if required, was to be attended to later. This was neither the time nor the place.

'I'll have to leave him on your hands now. I've got to get those bren posts distributed forthwith.'

'Yes, get off to the Defence Platoon right away,' said Widmerpool. 'Look sharp about it. Stringham and I will get this sot back to bed. I'll see this is the last time the army's troubled with him. It will only be a matter of expediting matters already in hand. Take one side, Stringham.'

Bithel was still leaning against the wall. Stringham once more took him by the arm. At the same time, he turned towards Widmerpool.

'It's interesting to recall, sir,' he said, 'the last time we met, I myself was the inert frame. It was you and Mr Jenkins who so kindly put me to bed. It shows that improvement is possible, that roles can be reversed. I've turned over a new leaf. Stringham is enrolled in the ranks of the sober, as well as the brave.'

I did not wait to hear Widmerpool's reply. The guns had started up. A helmet had to be collected before doing the rounds of the sections. After acquiring the necessary equipment, I set about my duties. The Defence Platoon got off the mark well that night.

'They always come a Wednesday,' said Sergeant Harmer. 'Might as well sit up for them.'

As blitzes went, that night's was not too bad a one. They went home early. We were in bed by half-past twelve.

'No more news about me, I suppose, sir?' asked Corporal Mantle, before he marched away his section.

I told him I would have another word with the DAAG. As it happened, the following morning had to be devoted to Defence Platoon affairs, so I did not see Widmerpool until the afternoon. I was not sorry about that, because it gave a time for cooling off. After the Bithel affair, an ill humour, even a downright row, was to be expected. However, this turned out to be a wrong appraisal. When I arrived in the room Widmerpool gave the impression of being more than usually pleased with himself. He pushed away the papers in front of him, evidently intending to speak at once of what had happened the night before, rather than get through the afternoon's routine, and institute a disagreeable post mortem on the subject at the end of the day's work, a rather favourite practice of his when he wanted to make a fuss about something.

'Well,' he said.

'Did you deal with Bithel?'

'I did.'

'What happened?'

I meant, by that question, to ask what had taken place over the next hundred yards or so of pavement leading to G Mess, how Bithel had been physically conveyed to his room. Widmerpool chose to understand the enquiry as referring to the final settlement of Bithel as a local problem.

'I had a word with A & Q this morning,' he said.

'Bithel's been sent on immediate leave. He will shortly be removed from the army.'

'By court-martial?'

'Unnecessary—purely administrative relegation to civilian life will save both time and trouble.'

'That can be done?'

'Bithel himself agrees it is the best way.'

'You've seen him?'

'I sent for him first thing this morning.'

'How was he feeling?'

'I have no idea. I am not concerned with the state of his health. I simply offered him the alternative of court-martial or acceptance of the appropriate report declaring him unsuitable for retention as an officer. The administrative documents releasing him from the army in the shortest possible period of time are now in motion. He wisely concurred, though not without an extraordinary scene.'

'What sort of scene?'

'Tears poured down his cheeks.'

'He was upset?'

'So it appeared.'

The episode plainly struck Widmerpool as of negative interest. That he should feel no pity for Bithel was reasonable enough, but it was a mark of his absolute lack of interest in human beings, as such, that the several implications of the interview—its sheer physical grotesqueness, for example, in the light of what Bithel must have drunk the night before—had made no impression on him he thought worth repeating. On the other hand, the clean-cut line of action he had taken emphasised his ability in dealing decisively with a problem of the kind Bithel raised by his very existence. Widmerpool's method was a contrast with that of my former Company Commander, Rowland Gwatkin, earlier confronted with Bithel in another of his unsatisfactory incarnations. When Bithel had drunk too much at the Castlemallock Gas School, Gwatkin had profitlessly put him under close arrest. Then he had omitted to observe the required formalities in relation to army arrest, with the result that the whole procedure collapsed. That, it was true, had not been entirely Gwatkin's fault; nevertheless, from Gwatkin's own point of view, the action had totally miscarried. With Widmerpool, on the other hand, there was no melodrama; only effective disposal of the body. The Bithel problem was at an end. If Bithel handicapped the war effort further, that would be in a civilian capacity.

'A pity the Warning went off like that last night,' said Widmerpool, speaking rather savagely. 'We could have frog-marched the brute back to his billet. I've seen it done with three.'

'Who will command the Laundry?'

'Another officer is already under orders. He will arrive this evening—may even have got here by now. I shall want to see him. There's a slight flap on, as a matter of fact.'

'What kind?'

'The Mobile Laundry have been ordered to stand in readiness to move at forty-eight hours' notice. This needs immediate attention with a new officer taking over only tonight. I was expecting the order in a week or two's time, not quite so soon as it has come. As usual, things will have to be done in a hurry.'

'Bithel was going anyway?'

'Of course—but only to the ITC. Now he will leave the army.'

'Is the Div moving?'

'The Laundry's orders have nothing to do with this formation, as such. There's been a call for Mobile Laundries. Between ourselves, I have reason to suppose this one is for the Far East, but naturally the destination is secret— and you are certainly not to mention that I hold that opinion.'

'You've known for some time they were going to move?'

'It came through to me when you were on leave.'

'You knew when you transferred Stringham?'

'That was precisely why I posted him to the Laundry.'

'So he'll go to the Far East?'

'If that's where the Laundry's bound.'

This was certainly arbitrary treatment of an old acquaintance.

'Will he want to go?'

'I have no idea.'

Widmerpool looked at me blankly.

'I suppose he could get out of it on grounds of age.'

'Why should he want to get out of it?'

'Well, he doesn't look as if his health is too good. As you said the other day, he's put away a good deal of drink in his time.'

'But it was you who suggested shifting him from his job as Mess Waiter,' said Widmerpool, not without impatience. 'That's one of the reasons I acted in the matter. I thought it over and decided, on balance, that you were right in feeling Stringham should not be there—in fact should not be at these Headquarters at all. Now you seem dissatisfied at what has happened. Why should it be your job—still less mine—to keep Stringham wrapped in cotton-wool? In any case, you surely don't envisage him remaining here after he and two of Div HQ's officers, one of them its DAAG, have been collectively concerned in putting another officer to bed because he has been found drunk in the street. You assured me Stringham would not be an embarrassment to us. That is exactly what has taken place.'

'But Stringham is quite used to the idea of drunks being put to bed. As he said last night, the pair of us once had to put him to bed ourselves. It couldn't conceivably affect Stringham's behaviour that he helped with Bithel—especially as Bithel's gone.'

'That has nothing to do with it.'

'What has then?'

'Nicholas, have you never heard of the word discipline?'

'But nobody knows except us—or was Biggs or somebody about when you got Bithel to G Mess?'

'No one—as it fortunately turned out. But that makes no difference whatever. Stringham could certainly not remain here after an incident of that kind. I applaud my own forethought in making the arrangement about him I did. So far as these Headquarters are concerned, the further afield he is sent the better. Let me add that all this is entirely a matter of principle. Stringham's presence would no longer affect me personally.'

'Why not?'

'Because I am leaving this formation.'

That piece of information brought a new, disturbing element into the conversation. I was annoyed, even disgusted, by Widmerpool's attitude towards Stringham, this utter disregard for what might happen to him, posted away to God knows where. However, worse now threatened. Self-interest, equally unattractive in outer guise and inner essence, is, all the same, a necessity for individual survival. It should perhaps not be too much despised, if only for that reason. Despised or not, its activities are rarely far from the surface. Now, at Widmerpool's words about leaving, I was unwelcomely conscious of self-interested anxieties throbbing hurriedly into operation. What was Widmerpool's present intention towards myself, if he were to go elsewhere? Would my fate be as little of interest to him as Stringham's? That was my instant thought.

'You've got promotion?'

'In the sense of immediate accession of rank—no. With the connotation that my employment will now be established in a more lofty—an incalculably more lofty—sphere than a Divisional Headquarters—yes.'

'The War Office?'

Widmerpool raised his hand slightly, at the same time allowing a brief smile to lighten his face in indication of the superiority, stratospheric in degree, towards which he was about to soar beyond the range of any institution so traditionally prosaic, not to say sordid in function, as the War Office. He folded his arms.

'No,' he said, 'not the War Office, I am thankful to say.'

'Where, then?'

'The Cabinet Offices.'

'I'm rather vague about them.'

'An admission that does not surprise me.'

'It's the top thing of all?'

'You might describe it that way.'

'How else?'

'The Cabinet Offices comprise, in one aspect, the area of action where the Ministry of Defence—the Chiefs of Staff, if you prefer—are in immediate contact with each other and with the Government of this country—with the Prime Minister himself.'

'I see.'

'So you will appreciate the fact that my removal of Stringham from these Headquarters will not affect me in the smallest way.'

'You go at once?'

'I have only heard unofficially at present. I imagine it will be the matter of a week, perhaps less.'

'Have you any idea what will happen to me when you're gone?'

'None.'

There was something impressive in his total lack of interest in the fate of all persons except himself. Perhaps it was not the lack of interest in itself—common enough to many people—but the fact that he was at no pains to conceal this within some more or less hypocritical integument.

'I shall be left high and dry?'

'I certainly doubt if my successor will be allocated an assistant. My own particular methods, more energetic than most, led to an abnormal amount of work for a mere DAAG. Even so, there has been recent pressure from above to encourage me to dispense with your services.'

'You haven't anything in mind for me?'

'Nothing.'

'You said you might try and fix something.'

'I have no recollection of doing so—and, anyway, what could I fix?'

'So it will be the Infantry Training Centre?'

'I should imagine.'

'Not much of a prospect.'

'The army more often than not offers uninviting prospects,' said Widmerpool. 'Look at the months I have been stuck here, wasting my time, and, if I may say so, my abilities. We are not soldiers just to enjoy ourselves. We are waging a war. You seem aggrieved. Let me point out

there is nothing startlingly brilliant in your own work—
your industry and capabilities—to make me press for a
good appointment for you. In addition to what can only
be regarded as mediocre qualities as a staff officer, it was
you, and no other, who saw fit to involve me in the whole
Bithel–Stringham hash. That might well have turned out
very awkwardly for me. No, Nicholas, if you examine
your conscience, you will find you have very little to
grumble at.'

He sighed, whether at my own ingratitude or human
frailty in general, I was uncertain. Cocksidge appeared in
the doorway.

'A & Q wants to see you, sir,' he said. 'Right away. Very
urgent. He's got the DAPM with him.'

'Right.'

'I hear you may be leaving us, sir,' said Cocksidge.

He spoke more with unction than servility.

'It's got round, has it?' said Widmerpool approvingly.

I had the impression he had put the rumour round himself. He went off down the passage. Cocksidge turned towards me, at the same time sharply adjusting his manner
from that of lower-middle-grade obsequiousness to a major
and staff officer, to one more in keeping for employment
towards a second-lieutenant not even a member of the
staff.

'The night you were last Duty Officer, Jenkins, the Field
Park Company received their routine telephone contact five
minutes later than the time noted on your report.'

'It went out in the normal manner with the others.'

'What happened then?'

'I suppose the Sapper Duty Officer didn't note it down
immediately or else his watch was wrong.'

'I shall have to look into this,' said Cocksidge.

He spoke threateningly, as if expecting further explanation. I remembered now I had indeed effected the Field Park contact a few minutes later than the others for some trivial reason. However, I stuck to my guns. The matter was not of the smallest practical importance. If Cocksidge wanted to make trouble, he would have to undertake researches at some considerable labour to himself. That was unlikely with such meagre advantages in view. He left the room, slamming the door behind him. The telephone bell rang.

'Major Farebrother, from Command, downstairs, sir. Wants to see the DAAG.'

'Send him up.'

This was the first time Sunny Farebrother had ever paid a visit to Divisional Headquarters. Recently, he and Widmerpool had been less in conflict, less even in direct contact. Either old enmities had died down, or, I supposed, other more important matters had been occupying both of them. The news about himself Widmerpool had just released, in his own case confirmed that view. Farebrother was likely to have been similarly engaged, unless he had greatly changed. At that moment he came through the door, stopping short for a second, while he saluted with parade ground formality. Military psychology could to some extent be gauged by this business of saluting when entering a room. Officers of field rank would sometimes omit the convention, if, on entering, they immediately sighted only a subaltern there. These officers, one noticed, were often wanting when more serious demands were made on their capacity. However, few, even of those who knew how to behave, brought out the movement with such a click and snap as Farebrother had done. When he had relaxed, I explained Widmerpool had been summoned by Colonel

Pedlar and might be away from the office for some little time.

'I'm in no particular hurry,' said Farebrother. 'I had another appointment in the neighbourhood and thought I would look in on Kenneth. I'll wait, if I may.'

He accepted a chair. His manner was kindly but cold. He did not recognise me. There was little reason why he should after nearly twenty years, when we had travelled together to London after staying with the Templers. I remembered the taxi piled high with miscellaneous luggage and sporting equipment, as our ways had parted at the station. There had been a gun-case, a cricket bat and a fishing rod; possibly two squash racquets.

'You must come and lunch with me one of these days,' he had said, giving one of his very open smiles.

He was surprisingly unchanged from that moment. A suggestion of grey threaded, here and there, neat light-coloured hair. This faint powdering of silver increased the air of distinction, even of moral superiority, which his outward appearance always conveyed. The response he offered —that he was a person of self-denying, upright life—had nearly been allowed to become tinged with a touch of self-righteousness. Any such outgrowth was kept within bounds by the soldierly spruceness of his bearing. I judged him now to be in his early fifties. Middle-age caused him to look more than ever like one's conception of Colonel New-come, though a more sophisticated, enterprising prototype of Thackeray's old warrior. Sunny Farebrother could never entirely conceal his own shrewdness, however much he tried. He was a Colonel Newcome who, instead of collapsing into bankruptcy, had become, on retirement from the army, a brisk business executive; offered a seat on the East India Company's Board, rather than mooning round the precincts of the Charterhouse. At the same time, Farebrother would certainly know the right phrase to express appreciation of any such historic buildings or sentimental memories with which he might himself have been associated. One could be sure of that. He was not a player to overlook a useful card. Above all, he bestowed around him a sense of smoothness, ineffable, unstemmable smoothness, like oil flowing ever so gently from the spout of a vessel perfectly regulated by its pourer, soft lubricating fluid, gradually, but irresistibly, spreading; and spreading, let it be said, over an unexpectedly wide, even a vast area.

'What's your name?'

'Jenkins, sir.'

'Ah, we've spoken sometimes together on the telephone.'

Uniform—that of a London Territorial unit of Yeomanry cavalry—hardly changed Farebrother at all, unless to make him seem more appropriately clad. Cap, tunic, trousers, all battered and threadbare as his former civilian suits, had obviously served him well in the previous war. Frayed and shiny with age, they were far from making him look down-at-heel in any inadmissible way, their antiquity according a patina of impoverished nobility—nobility of the spirit rather than class—a gallant disregard for material things. His Sam Browne belt was limp with immemorial polishing. I recalled Peter Templer remarking that Farebrother's DSO had been 'rather a good one'; of the OBE next door to it, Farebrother himself had commented: 'told them I should have to wear it on my backside, as the only medal I've ever won sitting in a chair.' Whether or not he had in fact said any such thing, except in retrospect, he was well able to look after himself and his business in that un-warlike position, however assured he might also be in combat. It was not surprising Widmerpool hated him.

Leaning forward a little, puckering his face, as if even at this moment he found a sedentary attitude unsympathetic, he gazed at me suddenly as if he were dreadfully sorry about something.

'I've got some rather bad news for Kenneth, I'm afraid,' he said, 'but I expect I'd better keep it till he returns. I'd better tell him personally. He might be hurt otherwise.'

He spoke in a tone almost of misery. I thought the point had arrived when it should be announced that we had met before. Farebrother listened, with raised eyebrows and a beaming smile, while I briefly outlined the circumstances.

'That must have been seventeen or eighteen years ago.'

'Just after I'd left school.'

'Peter Templer,' he said. 'That's a curious coincidence.'

'You've heard about him lately?'

'I have, as a matter of fact. Of course I often used to run across him in the City before the war.'

'He's attached to some ministry now in an advisory capacity, isn't he?'

'Economic Warfare,' said Farebrother.

He fixed his very honest blue eyes on me. There was something a bit odd about the look.

'He told me he wasn't very happy where he was,' he said, 'and hearing I was making a change myself, thought I might be able to help.'

I did not see quite how Farebrother could help, but assumed that might be through civilian contacts, rather than from his own military status. Farebrother seemed to decide that he wanted to change the subject from Templer's immediate career, giving almost the impression that he felt he might himself have been indiscreet. He spoke quickly again.

'The old man died years ago, of course,' he said. 'He was an old devil, if ever there was one. Devil incarnate.'

I was a little surprised to hear Farebrother describe Peter Templer's father in such uncomplimentary terms, because, when we had met before, he had emphasised what a 'fine old man' he had thought Mr Templer; been positively sentimental about his good qualities, not to mention having contributed a laudatory footnote of personal memoir to the official obituary in *The Times*. I was more interested to talk of Peter than his father, but Farebrother would allow no further details.

'Said more than I should already. You surprised it out of me by mentioning the name so unexpectedly.'

'So you're leaving Command yourself, sir?'

'As I've begun being indiscreet, I'll continue on that line. I'm going to one of the cloak-and-dagger shows.'

From time to time one heard whispers of these mysterious sideshows radiating from out of the more normal activities of the Services. In a remote backwater like the Divisional Headquarters where I found myself, they were named with bated breath. Farebrother's apparent indifference to the prospect of becoming part of something so esoteric seemed immensely detached and nonchalant. Nevertheless, the manner in which he made this statement, in itself not in the least indiscreet, was at the same time perhaps a shade self-satisfied.

'Getting a step too,' he said. 'About time at my age.'

It was all at once clear as day that one of his reasons for coming round to Div HQ was to inform Widmerpool of this promotion to lieutenant-colonel. The discovery that we had known each other in the past had removed all coolness from Farebrother's manner. Now, he seemed, for some reason, even anxious to acquire me as an ally.

'How do you get on with our friend Kenneth?' he asked. 'A bit difficult at times? Don't you find that?'

I made no effort to deny the imputation. Widmerpool was grading low in my estimation at that moment. I saw no reason to conceal hard feelings about him. Farebrother was pleased at getting this affirmative reaction.

'I've no objection to a fellow liking to do things his own way,' he said, 'but I don't want a scrimmage about every new Army Council Instruction as soon as it appears. Don't you agree? In that sort of respect Kenneth doesn't know where to stop. Not only that, I found he's behaved rather badly behind my back with your Corps' MGA.'

It was news that Widmerpool's activities behind the scenes had taken him as far up in the hierarchy as so relatively august a personage as the Major-General in charge of Administration at Corps HQ.

'I mention that in confidence, of course,' said Farebrother, 'and for your own guidance. Kenneth can be a little thoughtless at times about his own subordinates. I daresay you've found that. Not that I would say a word against Kenneth as a man or a staff officer. In many ways he's wasted in this particular job.'

'He's leaving it.'

'He is?'

In spite of a conviction that Widmerpool's gifts were not being given sufficient scope, Farebrother did not sound altogether pleased to hear this matter was going to be put right. He asked the question with more open curiosity than he had showed until then.

'I don't think it's a secret.'

'Even if it is, it will go no further with me. What's ahead of him?'

'The Cabinet Offices, he told me, though I believe it's not official yet.'

Farebrother whistled, one of those crude expressions of feeling he would allow himself from time to time, which seemed hardly to accord with the dignity of the rest of his demeanour. I remembered him making a similar popping sound with his lips, at the same time snapping his fingers, when some beautiful woman's name had come into the conversation staying at the Templers'.

'The Cabinet Offices, by God,' he said. 'Has he been promoted?'

'I gather he goes there in his present rank, but thinks there's a good chance of going up pretty soon.'

'I see.'

Farebrother showed a little relief at Widmerpool's promotion being delayed, if only briefly. He had plainly been disturbed by what he had heard.

'*The Cabinet Offices,*' he repeated with emphasis. 'Well, that's very exalted. I only hope what I've come to tell him won't make any difference. However, as I said before, better not refer to that until I've seen him.'

He shook his head. Widmerpool came back to the room at that moment. He was fidgeting with the collar of his battle-dress, always a sign he was put out. It looked as if the interview with A & Q had not gone too well. Seeing Farebrother sitting there was not welcome to him either.

'Oh, hullo, Sunny,' he said, without much warmth.

'I came along to bid you farewell, Kenneth, and now I hear from Nicholas you're on the move like myself.'

Widmerpool showed a touch of surprise at Farebrother using my first name, then remembered we had formerly known each other.

'I forgot you'd both met,' he said. 'Yes, I'm going. Did Nicholas tell you where?'

'Scarcely revealed anything,' said Farebrother.

Not for the first time, I noted his caution, and was grateful for it, though Widmerpool seemed to want his destination known.

'The Cabinet Offices.'

Widmerpool could not conceal his own satisfaction.

'I say, old boy.'

The comparative enthusiasm Farebrother managed to infuse into this comment was something of a masterpiece in the exercise of dissimulation.

'It will mean work, morning, noon and night,' said Widmerpool. 'But there'll undoubtedly be interesting contacts.'

'There will, old boy, I bet there will—and promotion.'

'Possibly.'

'Quite soon.'

'Oh, you never know in the bloody army,' said Widmerpool, thought of his new job inducing a better humour, marked as usual by the assumption of his hearty military manner, 'but what's happening to you, Sunny, if you say you're going too?'

'One of these secret shows.'

'Baker Street?'

'I shouldn't be surprised.'

'Promotion too?'

Farebrother nodded modestly.

'That's the only reason I'm taking it. Need the pay. Much rather do something straightforward, if I had the choice.'

Widmerpool could not have been pleased to hear that Farebrother was about to become a lieutenant-colonel, while he himself, however briefly, remained a major. Indeed, it probably irritated him that Farebrother should be promoted at all. At the same time, a display of self-control rare with him, he contrived to show no concern, his manner being even reasonably congratulatory. This was no doubt partly on account of the satisfactory nature of his own promised change of employment, but, as he revealed on a later occasion, also because of the low esteem in which he held the organisation which Farebrother was about to join.

'A lot of scallywags, in my opinion,' he said later.

Farebrother was certainly acute enough to survey their respective future situations from much the same point of view, that is to say appreciating the fact that, although he might himself be now ahead, Widmerpool's potentialities for satisfying ambition must be agreed to enjoy a wider scope. Indeed, in a word or two, he openly expressed some such conclusion. Farebrother could afford this generosity, because, as it turned out, he had another trick up his sleeve. He brought this trump card out only after they had talked for a minute or two about their new jobs. Farebrother opened his attack by abruptly swinging the subject away from their own personal affairs.

'You've been notified Ivo Deanery's going to get the Recce Unit?' he asked suddenly.

Widmerpool was taken aback by this question. He began to look angry again.

'Never heard of him,' he said.

The answer sounded as if it were intended chiefly to gain time.

'Recently adjutant to my Yeomen,' said Farebrother. 'As lively a customer as you would meet in a day's march. Got an MC in Palestine just before the war.'

Widmerpool was silent. He did not show any interest at

all in Ivo Deanery's juvenile feats of daring, whatever they might have been. I supposed he did not want to admit to Farebrother that he himself had been running a candidate for the Recce Unit's Commanding Officer; and that candidate, from what had been said, must have been unsuccessful.

'Knew you were interested in the Recce Regiment command,' said Farebrother, speaking very casually.

'Naturally.'

'I mean specially interested.'

'There was nothing special about it,' said Widmerpool.

'Oh, I understood there was,' said Farebrother, assuming at once a puzzled expression, as if greatly worried at Widmerpool's denial of special interest. 'In fact that was the chief reason I came round to see you.'

'Look here,' said Widmerpool, 'I don't know what you're getting at, Sunny. How could you be DAAG of a formation and not take a keen interest in who's appointed to command its units?'

He was gradually losing his temper.

'The MGA thinks you were a bit too interested,' said Farebrother, speaking now with exaggerated sadness. 'Old boy, there's going to be the hell of a row. You've put your foot in it.'

'What do you mean?'

Widmerpool was thoroughly disturbed now, frightened enough to control his anger. Farebrother looked interrogatively at me, then his eyes travelled back to Widmerpool. He raised his eyebrows. Widmerpool shook his head vigorously.

'Say anything you like in front of him,' he said. 'He knows I had a name in mind for the Recce Unit command. Nothing wrong with that. Naturally I regret my chap hasn't got it. That's all there is to it. What's the MGA beefing about?'

Farebrother too shook his head, but slowly and more lugubriously than ever.

'I understand from the MGA that you were in touch with him personally not long ago about certain matters with which I myself was concerned.'

Widmerpool went very red.

'I think I know what you mean,' he said, 'but they were just as much my concern as yours.'

'Wouldn't it have been better form, old boy, to have mentioned to me you were going to see him?'

'I saw no cause to do so.'

Widmerpool was not at all at ease.

'Anyway,' said Farebrother mildly, 'the MGA, rightly or wrongly, feels you misled him about various scraps of unofficial information you tendered, especially as he had no idea at the time that you were pressing in other quarters for a certain officer to be appointed to a command then still vacant.'

'How did he find that out?'

'I told him,' said Farebrother, simply.

'But look here . . .' said Widmerpool.

He was too furious to finish the sentence.

'The long and the short of it was the MGA said he was going to get in touch with your General about the whole matter.'

'But I behaved in no way incorrectly,' said Widmerpool. 'There is not the smallest reason to suggest . . .'

'Believe me, Kenneth, I'm absolutely confident you did nothing to which official exception could possibly be taken,' said Farebrother. 'On my heart. That's why I thought it best to put my own cards on the table. The MGA is sometimes hasty. As you know well, amateur soldiers like you and me tend to go about our business in rather a different way from the routine a Regular gets accustomed to. We like to get things done expeditiously. I just thought it was a pity myself you went and told the MGA all those things about me. That was why I decided he ought to know more about you and your own activities. I'm sure everything will be all right in the end, but I believed it right to warn you—as I was coming to say goodbye anyway—simply that my General might be getting in touch with your General about all this.'

Farebrother's quiet, reassuring tone did not at all soothe Widmerpool, who now looked more disturbed than ever. Farebrother rose to his feet. He squared his shoulders and smiled kindly, pleased, as well he might be, with the devastation his few minutes' conversation had brought about in the promotion of Widmerpool's plans. In his own way, as I learnt later, Farebrother was an efficient operator when he wanted something done; very efficient indeed. Widmerpool had made a mistake in trying to double-cross him in whatever matter the visit to the MGA had concerned. He should have guessed that Farebrother, sooner or later, would find out. Perhaps he had disregarded that possibility, ruling out the risk of Farebrother turning to a formidable weapon at hand. However, with characteristic realism, Widmerpool grasped that something must be done quickly, if trouble, by now probably inevitable, was to be reduced in magnitude. He was not going to waste time in recrimination.

'I'll come with you to the door, Sunny,' he said. 'I can explain all that business about going to the MGA. It wasn't really aimed at you at all, though now I see it must look like that.'

Farebrother turned towards me. He gave a nod.

'Goodbye, Nicholas.'

'Goodbye, sir.'

They left the room together. The situation facing Widmerpool might be disagreeable, almost certainly was going to be. One thing at least was certain: whomsoever he had been trying to jockey into the position of commanding the Recce Unit would have done the job as well, if not better, than anyone else likely to be appointed. Widmerpool's candidate—if only for Widmerpool's own purposes—would, from no aspect, turn out unsuitable. If his claims were pressed by Widmerpool, he would be a first-class officer, not a personal friend whose competence was no more than adequate. That had to be said in fairness to Widmerpool methods, though I had no cause to like them. So far as that went, Farebrother's man, Ivo Deanery, as it turned out, made a good job of the command too. He led the Divisional Recce Corps, with a great deal of dash, until within a few days of the German surrender; then was blown up when his jeep drove over a landmine. However, that is equally by the way. The immediate point was that Widmerpool, even if his machinations had not actually transgressed beyond what were to be regarded as the frontiers of discipline, could, at the same time, well have allowed himself liberties with the established scope permissible to an officer of his modest rank, which, if brought to light, would seriously affront higher authority. Probably his original contact with the Major-General at Corps had been on the subject of a petty contention with Farebrother; something better not arranged—certainly better not arranged behind Farebrother's back; at the same time trivial enough. Widmerpool had no scruples about conduct of that sort.

'No good being too gentlemanly,' he had once said.

The next stage might be guessed. Having gained access to the MGA on this pretext, opportunity had been found to link the subject in hand with matters relating to the Recce Unit. Possibly the MGA was even glad to be provided with one or other of those useful items of miscellaneous private information which Widmerpool was so pre-eminent in storing up his sleeve for use at just that sort of interview. Then, so it seemed, something had gone wrong. The MGA had allowed Farebrother to find out, or at least make a good guess, that Widmerpool had been brewing up trouble for him. Like so many individuals who believe in being 'ungentlemanly', Widmerpool did not allow sufficiently for the eventuality of other people practising the same doctrine. Indeed, he used to complain bitterly if they did. Farebrother was an example of a man equally unprejudiced by scruple. No doubt he had pointed out to the MGA that Widmerpool's suggested line included contrivances that, when examined in the light of day, revealed—perhaps only to an over-fastidious sense of how things should be done—shreds of what might be regarded as the impertinent intrigue of a junior officer. That, at least, seemed to have been just how the MGA had seen the matter. He had become angry. Now, as Farebrother said, there was going to be the hell of a row; this at a most awkward juncture in Widmerpool's career. He was evidently having a longish talk with Farebrother on the doorstep. Before he returned Greening looked in.

'DAAG about?'

'Just gone down the stairs to have a final word with his opposite number from Command. He'll be back in a second.'

'His Nibs wants Major Widmerpool at once.'

'Shall I tell him?'

'I'll wait. His Nibs is far from pleased. Absolutely cheesed off, in fact. I don't dare go back without my man —like the North-West Mounted Police.'

'What's happened?'

'No idea.'

It looked as if the trouble in question was about to begin. Greening and I had a game of noughts and crosses. Widmerpool returned. Greening delivered his summons. Widmerpool, who was looking worried already, gave a slight twitch, but made no comment. He and Greening went off together in the direction of the General's room. In the army, long tracts of time when nothing whatever seems to happen are punctuated by sudden unexpected periods of upheaval and change. That is traditional. We had been all at once sucked into one of those whirlpools. Colonel Hogbourne-Johnson was the next person to enter the room. This was a rare occurrence, of which the most likely implication was that some sudden uncontrollable rage was too great to allow him to remain inactive while Widmerpool was summoned by telephone to his own presence. He must have come charging up the passage to prevent it boiling over without release, thereby perhaps doing him some internal injury. However, that turned out to be a wrong guess. The Colonel was, on the contrary, in an unusually good humour.

'Where's the DAAG?'

'With the Divisional Commander, sir.'

Colonel Hogbourne-Johnson took the chair on which Farebrother had been sitting a moment before. To remain was as unexpected as arrival here. There could be no doubt he was specially pleased about something. It might well be he already knew Widmerpool was in hot water. He pulled at his short, bristly, dun-coloured moustache.

'Aren't you some sort of a literary bloke in civilian life?' he asked.

I agreed that was the case.

'The General said something of the kind the other day.'

Colonel Hogbourne-Johnson emitted that curious sound, a kind of hissing gulp issuing from the corner of his mouth, after this comment, apparently, on this occasion, to express the ease he himself felt in the presence of the arts.

'I once wrote rather a good parody myself,' he said.

'You did, sir?'

'On Omar Khayyám.'

I indicated respectful interest.

'Quite amusing, it was,' said Colonel Hogbourne-Johnson, without apology.

I was about to entreat him to recite, if not all, at least a few quatrains of what promised to be an essay in pastiche well worth hearing, when Widmerpool's return prevented further exploration of the Colonel's Muse.

'Ah, Kenneth,' said Colonel Hogbourne-Johnson, assuming his most unctuous manner, 'I was hoping you would spare me a moment of your valuable time.'

Widmerpool looked even less pleased to see Hogbourne-Johnson than at Farebrother's visit. He was by now showing a good deal of wear and tear from the blows raining down on him.

'Yes, sir?' he answered tonelessly.

'Mr Diplock . . .' said Colonel Hogbourne-Johnson. 'No, you need not go, Nicholas.'

He sat on the chair banging his knees with his clenched fists, taking his time about what he wanted to say. It looked as if he desired a witness to be present at what was to be his humiliation of Widmerpool over the Diplock affair.

Use of my own christian name indicated an exceptionally good humour.

'Yes, sir?' repeated Widmerpool.

'I'm afraid you're going to be proved to have made a big mistake, my son,' said Colonel Hogbourne-Johnson.

He snapped the words out like an order on the parade ground. Widmerpool did not speak.

'Barking up the wrong tree,' said Colonel Hogbourne-Johnson.

Widmerpool pursed his lips and raised his eyebrows. Even in the despondent state to which he had been reduced, he was still capable of anger.

'You brought a series of accusations against an old and tried soldier,' said Colonel Hogbourne-Johnson, 'by doing so causing a great deal of unpleasantness, administrative dislocation and unnecessary work.'

Widmerpool began to speak, but the Colonel cut him short.

'I had a long talk with Diplock yesterday,' he said, 'and I am now satisfied he can clear himself completely. With that end in view, I sanctioned a day's leave for him to collect certain evidences. Now, I understand you may be leaving us?'

'I . . .'

Widmerpool hesitated. Then he pulled himself together.

'Yes, sir,' he said. 'I'm certainly leaving the Division.'

'Before you go,' said Colonel Hogbourne-Johnson, 'I consider it will be necessary for you to make an apology.'

'I don't yet know, sir,' said Widmerpool, 'the new facts which have come to light that should so much alter what appeared to be incontrovertible charges. I have been with A & Q earlier this afternoon, who told me you had made the arrangement you mention. He had informed the

DAPM, thinking Diplock should be kept under some general supervision.'

Even though he said that in a fairly aggressive tone, Widmerpool's manner still gave the impression that his mind was on other things. No doubt—his own fate in the balance—he found difficulty in concentrating on the Diplock case. It looked as if Colonel Hogbourne-Johnson, like a cat with a mouse, wanted to play with Widmerpool for a while before releasing information, because, instead of communicating anything he might know that had fresh bearing on Diplock and his goings-on, he changed the subject.

'Then there's another matter,' he said. 'Certain moves made with regard to the Reconnaissance Battalion.'

'The General has just been speaking on that subject too,' said Widmerpool.

Hogbourne-Johnson was plainly surprised at this admission. His expression showed he had no knowledge of the disturbance proceeding, at a higher level than his own, on the subject of Widmerpool's Recce Unit intrigues.

'To you?'

'Yes,' said Widmerpool bluntly. 'The General told me a Major—now, of course, Lieutenant-Colonel—Deanery has been appointed to that command.'

If he had hoped to score off Widmerpool in the Recce Unit sphere, it seemed Hogbourne-Johnson had overreached himself. He reddened. No doubt he knew Widmerpool had been fishing in troubled waters, but was not up to date as to the outcome. If Widmerpool's candidate had been turned down, so too, it now appeared, had his own. This fact was most unacceptable to the Colonel. His manner changed from a peculiar assertive, sneering self-assurance, to mere everyday bad temper.

'Ivo Deanery?'

'A cavalryman.'

'That's the one.'

'He's got the command.'

'I see.'

For the moment, Colonel Hogbourne-Johnson had nothing to say. He was absolutely furious, but could not very well admit he had just heard news that showed his own secret plans, whatever they were, had miscarried. That Widmerpool, whom he had come to harass, should be the vehicle of this particular item of information must have been additionally galling. However, something much worse from Hogbourne-Johnson's point of view, also much more dramatic, happened a second later. The door opened and Keef, the DAPM, came into the room. He was excited about something. Clearly looking for Widmerpool, not at all expecting to find Colonel Hogbourne-Johnson there, Keef appeared taken aback. A gnarled, foxy little man— like most DAPMs, not a particularly agreeable figure—he was generally agreed to handle soundly his section of Military Police, always difficult personnel of whom to be in charge. Now, he hesitated for a moment, trying to decide, so it seemed, whether, there and then, to make some disclosure he had on his mind, or preferably concoct an excuse, and retire until such time as he could find Widmerpool alone. Keef must have come to the conclusion that immediate announcement of unwelcome tidings would be best, because, straightening himself almost to the position of attention, he addressed Colonel Hogbourne-Johnson, as if it were Colonel Hogbourne-Johnson himself he had been looking for all the time. The reason for his momentary reluctance was revealed only too soon.

'Excuse me, sir.'

'Yes?'

'A serious matter has come through on the telephone, sir.'

'Well, what is it?'

'Diplock's deserted, sir.'

This message was so unexpected that Colonel Hogbourne-Johnson, already sufficiently provoked by the appointment of Ivo Deanery to the command of the Recce Unit, could find no words at first to register the fact that he fully comprehended what Keef had to report. The awfulness of the silence that followed must have told on Keef's nerves. Still standing almost to attention, it was he who spoke first.

'Just come through, sir,' he repeated. 'A & Q issued an order to keep an eye on him, but it was too late. The man's known to have made his way across the Border. He's in neutral territory by this time.'

To have trusted Diplock, to have stood by him when accused of peculation, was, so far as I knew from my own experience of Colonel Hogbourne-Johnson, the only occasion when he had ever shown a generous impulse. Of course that was speaking from scarcely any knowledge of him at all. In private life he may have displayed qualities concealed during this brief observation of his professional behaviour. Even if that were not so, and he were as unengaging to his friends and family as to his comrades in arms, even if, with regard to Diplock, his conduct had been dictated by egoism, prejudice, pig-headedness, the fact remained that he had believed in Diplock, had trusted him. He had, for example, called Widmerpool to order for describing the chief clerk as an old woman, simply because he respected the fact that Diplock, years before, had been awarded the Military Medal. Now he had been thoroughly let down. The climax had not been altogether deserved. Widmerpool had been wrong too. Diplock might be an old woman when he fiddled about with Army Forms; not when it came to evading his deserts. Still, that was another matter. It was Colonel Hogbourne-Johnson who had been betrayed. Possibly he felt that himself. He rose to his feet, in doing so managing to sweep to the floor some of the papers from the pile of documents on Widmerpool's table. Giving a jerk of his head to indicate Keef was to follow him, he left the room. Their steps could be heard thudding down uncarpeted passages. Widmerpool shut the door after them. Then he stooped and laboriously recovered several Summaries of Evidence from the floor. Anxiety about his own future was evidently too grave to allow any satisfaction at Hogbourne-Johnson's discomfiture. In fact, I had not seen Widmerpool so upset, so reduced to utter despair, since the day, long past, when he had admitted to paying for Gypsy Jones's 'operation'.

'There's been the devil of a row,' he said.

'What's happened?'

'The General's livid with rage.'

'About what Sunny Farebrother said?'

'That bloody MGA's given him a totally false picture of what I said.'

'What's the upshot?'

'General Liddament says he's going to make further enquiries. If he's satisfied I've behaved in a way of which he disapproves, he won't keep me on his staff. Of course I don't mind that, as I'm leaving anyway. What I'm worried about is he may take it into his head to ruin my chance of this much better job, when he gets official notification. He seemed to have forgotten that was in the air.'

'Does he know Hogbourne-Johnson was playing about with the same matter?'

'Of course not. Hogbourne-Johnson will be able to cover his tracks now.'

'And Diplock?'

'Oh, yes, Diplock,' said Widmerpool, cheering up a little. 'I'd forgotten about Diplock. Well, it was just as I said, though I'd never have guessed he'd go as far as to desert. Perhaps he wouldn't have deserted, if there hadn't been a frontier so conveniently near. This is all very worrying. Still, we must get on with some work. What have you got there?'

'The question of Mantle's name being entered for a commission has come up again.'

Widmerpool thought for a moment.

'All right,' he said, 'we'll by-pass Hogbourne-Johnson and send it in.'

He took the paper from me.

'And Stringham?'

'What about him?'

'If the Mobile Laundry are to be pushed off to the Far East, as you think——'

'Oh, bugger Stringham,' said Widmerpool, his mood suddenly changing. 'Why are you always fussing about Stringham? If he wants to get out of going overseas, he can probably do so at his age. That's his affair. Which reminds me, the officer replacing Bithel in charge of the Mobile Laundry should be reporting in an hour or so. I shall want you to take him round there and give him a preliminary briefing. I'll go into things myself in more detail later. He's called Cheesman.'

Nothing much else happened that afternoon. Widmerpool uttered one or two sighs to himself, but did not discuss

215

his own predicament further. As he had said, there was nothing to be done. He could only wait and see how matters shaped. No one knew better than Widmerpool that, in the army, all things are possible. He might ride the storm. On the other hand, he could easily find himself packed off to a static appointment in West Africa, or another distant post unlikely to lead to the sort of promotion he had at present in mind. When Cheesman appeared later on, it was immediately clear that the Laundry, when proceeding overseas, was to have a very different commander from Bithel.

'I'm afraid I'm not quite so punctual as I intended, sir,' he said, 'but I'm anxious to get to work as soon as possible.'

Cheesman told me later he was thirty-nine. He looked quite ageless. Greying hair and wire spectacles suited his precise, rather argumentative manner of speech, in which he had not allowed the smallest trace of an army tone to alloy indefectibly civilian accents. Indeed, he spoke as if he had just arrived from a neighbouring firm to transact business with our own. He treated Widmerpool respectfully, as if a mere representative was meeting a managing director, but nothing in the least military supervened. Widmerpool might sometimes behave like this, but he also prided himself on the crispness of his own demeanour as a staff officer, and obviously did not greatly take to Cheesman. However, from whatever reports he had received about Cheesman's ability, he had evidently satisfied himself the job would be done in an efficient manner. After exchanging a few sentences regarding the taking-over of the Laundry, he told me to act as guide, after Cheesman's baggage had been delivered to G Mess. No doubt, in the prevailing circumstances, Widmerpool was glad to be left alone for a time to think things over.

'I'll have a word with you tomorrow, Cheesman,' he said, 'when you've a better idea of the Laundry's personnel and equipment, in relation to a move.'

'I shall be glad to have a look round, sir,' said Cheesman.

He and I set off together for the outer confines of the billeting area, where the Mobile Laundry had its being during spells at HQ. Cheesman told me he was an accountant in civilian life. He had done a good deal of work on laundry accounts at one time or another, accordingly, after getting a commission, had put in for a Mobile Laundry command.

'They seemed surprised I wanted to go to one,' he said. 'It struck me as only logical. The OC of my OCTU roared with laughter. He used to do that anyway when I spoke with him. He agreed I was too old for an infantry second-lieutenant and wanted me to go to the Army Pay Corps, or to train as a cipher officer, but in the end I got a Laundry. I hoped to command men. I was transferred to this one because my work seems to have been thought well of. I felt flattered.'

'You've got a first-rate sergeant in Ablett.'

'That's good news. My last one wasn't always too reliable.'

Sergeant Ablett was waiting for us. As Bithel had asserted in his drunken delirium, the Sergeant added to his qualities as an unusually efficient NCO those required for performing as leading comedian at the Divisional Concert, where he would sing forgotten songs, crack antediluvian jokes and dance unrestrainedly about the stage wearing only his underclothes. Ablett's was always the most popular turn. Now, however, this talent for vaudeville had been outwardly subdued, in its place assumed the sober, posi-

217

tively severe bearing of an old soldier, whose cleanshaven upper lip, faintest possible proliferation of side-whisker, perhaps consciously characterised a veteran of Wellington's campaigns. Contact was made between Cheesman and Ablett. It struck me that now would be a good opportunity to try and speak with Stringham.

'There's a man in your outfit I want a word with. May I do that while the Sergeant is showing you round?'

'By all means,' said Cheesman. 'Some personal matter?'

'He's a chap I know in civilian life.'

Cheesman was the sort of person to be trusted with that information. Anyway, the unit was moving. Sergeant Ablett summoned a corporal. I went off with him to find Stringham, leaving Cheesman to get his bearings.

'Last saw Stringy on his bed in the barrack room,' said the corporal, a genial bottle-nosed figure, who evidently did not take military formalities too seriously.

He went off through a door. I waited in a kind of yard, where the Mobile Laundry's outlandish vehicles were parked. In a minute or two the corporal appeared again. He was followed by Stringham, who looked as if the unexpected summons had made him uneasy. He was not wearing a cap. When he saw me, his face cleared. He came to attention.

'Thank you, Corporal.'

'You're welcome, sir.'

The bottle-nosed corporal disappeared.

'You gave me quite a turn, Nick,' Stringham said. 'I was lying on my bed musing about Tuffy and what a strange old girl she is. I was reading Browning, which always makes me think of her. Browning's her favourite poet. Did I tell you that? Of course I did, I'm getting hopelessly

218

forgetful. He always makes me feel rather jumpy. That was why I got in a flap when Corporal Treadwell said I was wanted by an officer.'

'I've just brought your new bloke round who's taken Bithel's place.'

'Poor Bith. That was an extraordinary evening last night. What's happened to him?'

'Widmerpool's shot him out.'

'Dear me. Just as well, perhaps, for the army's sake, but I shall miss him. What's this one like?'

'He's called Cheesman. Should be easy to handle if you stay with him.'

'Why shouldn't I stay with him? I'm wedded to the Laundry by this time. I've really begun to know the meaning of *esprit de corps*, something lamentably lacking in me up to now.'

'I want to talk about all that.'

'*Esprit de corps?*'

'Can't we take a stroll for a couple of minutes while Cheesman deals with your Sergeant?'

'Ablett's a great favourite of mine too,' said Stringham. 'I'm trying to memorise some of his jokes for use at dinner parties after the war, if I'm ever asked to any again—indeed, if any are given *après la guerre*. Ablett's jokes have an absolutely authentic late nineteenth-century ring that fills one with self-confidence. Wait a moment, I'll get a cap.'

When he returned, wearing a side-cap, he carried in his hand a small tattered volume. We walked slowly up an endless empty street of small redbrick houses. The weather, for once, was warm and sunny. Stringham held up the book.

'Before we part, Nick,' he said, 'I must read you some-

219

thing I found here. I can't make out just what all of it means, but some has obvious bearing on army life.'

'Charles, you've got to do some quick thinking. The Mobile Laundry is due to move.'

'So we heard.'

'There've been rumours?'

'One always knows these things first in the ranks. That's one of the advantages. Where's it to be?'

'Of course that's being kept secret, but Widmerpool thinks—for what it's worth—the destination is probably the Far East.'

'We heard that too.'

'Then you know as much as me.'

'We seem to. Of course, security may be so good, it will really turn out to be Iceland. That sort of thing is always happening.'

'The point is, you could probably—certainly—get out of being sent overseas on grounds of age and medical category.'

'I agree I'm older than the rocks amongst which I sit, and have died infinitely more times than the vampire. Even so, I'd quite like to see the gorgeous East—even the Icelandic geysers, if it comes to that.'

'You'll go through with it?'

'Not a doubt.'

'I just thought I ought to pass on what was being said— strictly against all the rules.'

'That shan't go any further. Depend upon it. I suppose Widmerpool saw this coming?'

'So I gather.'

'And all that altruism about F Mess was to get me on the move?'

'That's about it.'

'He couldn't have done me a better turn,' said Stringham. 'The old boy's a marvellous example of one of the
aspects of this passage I want to read you. Like everything
that's any good, it has about twenty different meanings.'

He stopped and began turning the pages of the book he
had brought with him. We stood beside a pillar-box. When
he found the place, he began to read aloud:

'I shut my eyes and turned them on my heart.
As a man calls for wine before he fights,
I asked one draught of earlier, happier sights
Ere fitly I could hope to play my part.
Think first, fight afterwards—the soldier's art;
One taste of the old time sets all to rights.'

'Childe Roland to the Dark Tower came?'
'Childe Stringham—in this case.'
'I'm never sure what I feel about Browning.'
'He always gives the impression of writing about people
who are wearing very expensive fancy dress. All the same,
there's a lot in what he says. Not that I feel in the least
nostalgic about earlier, happier sights. I can't offhand recall many. The good bit is about thinking first and fighting
after.'

'Let's hope the High Command have taken the words
to heart.'

'Odd that Browning should know that was so important.'
'Perhaps he should have been a general.'
'It ought to be equally borne in mind by all ranks. There
might be an Order of the Day on the subject. Can't Widmerpool arrange that?'

'Widmerpool's leaving Div HQ too.'
'To become a colonel?'

'The Divisional Commander may bitch that up. He's tumbled on some of Widmerpool's intriguing and doesn't approve, but Widmerpool will go either way.'

'How very dramatic.'

'Isn't it.'

'Then what will happen to you?'

'God knows. The ITC, I imagine. Look, I shall have to go back to Cheesman soon, but I must tell you about the hell of a business on my leave the other day.'

I gave some account of the bombing of the Madrid and the Jeavons house.

'The Madrid, fancy that. I once took Peggy there in the early days of our marriage. The evening was a total frost. And then where I used to live in that top floor flat with Tuffy looking after me—where I learnt to be sober. Where Tuffy used to read Browning. Is it all in ashes?'

'Not in the least. The outside of the house looks just the same as usual.'

'Poor Lady Molly—she ought to have stayed doing that job at Dogdene.'

'Much too quiet for her.'

'Poor Ted, too. What on earth will he do with himself now? I used to enjoy occasionally sneaking off to the pub with Ted.'

'He's going on as before. Camping out in the house and carrying on as an air-raid warden.'

'I chiefly remember your sister-in-law, Priscilla, as making rather good going with some musician for whom my mother once gave an extraordinary party. Weren't you there, Nick? I associate that night with an odd little woman covered in frills like Little Bo-Peep. I made some sort of dive at her.'

'She was called Mrs Maclintick. She's now living with

the musician for whom your mother gave the party—Hugh Moreland.'

'Moreland, that was the name. She's living with him, is she? What lax morals people have these days. The war, I suppose. I do my best to set an example, but no one follows me in my monastic celibacy. That was a strange night. Tuffy arrived to drive me home. It comes back to me fairly clearly, in spite of a great deal too much to drink. That's a taste of old times, if ever there was one. Makes one ready to fight anybody.'

'Charles, I shall have to get back to Cheesman. You've absolutely decided to stick to the Mobile Laundry, come what may?'

'*Quis separabit?*—that's the Irish Guards, isn't it? The Mobile Laundry shares the motto.'

'Are you returning to the billet?'

'I think I'll go for a stroll. Don't feel like any more poetry reading at the moment. Poetry always rather disturbs me. I think I shall have to give it up—like drink. A short walk will do me good. I'm off duty till nine o'clock.'

'Goodbye, Charles—if we don't meet before the Laundry moves.'

'Goodbye, Nick.'

He smiled and nodded, then went off up the street. He gave the impression of having severed his moorings pretty completely with anything that could be called everyday life, army or otherwise. I returned to Cheesman and Sergeant Ablett. They seemed to have got on well together and were still vigorously discussing vehicle maintenance.

'Find that man all right, sir?' asked the Sergeant.

'Had a word with him. Know him in civilian life.'

'Thought you might, sir. He could have been of use in

the concert, but now it looks as if we're moving and there won't be any concert.'

'I expect you'll put on a show wherever you go. We shall miss your trouserless tap-dance next time, Sergeant.'

'That's always a popular item,' said Sergeant Ablett, without false modesty.

I took Cheesman back to G Mess. His mildness did not prevent him from being argumentative about every subject that arose.

'That's what you think,' he said, more than once, 'but there's another point of view entirely.'

This determination would be useful in running the Laundry, subject, like every small, more or less independent entity, to all sorts of pressures from outside.

'Wait a moment,' he said. 'Before I forget, I'd like to make a note of your name, and the Sergeant's, and the DAAG's.'

He loosened the two top buttons of his service-dress tunic to rummage for a notebook. This movement revealed that he wore underneath the tunic a khaki waistcoat cut like that of a civilian suit. I commented on the unexpectedness of this garment, worn with uniform and made of the same material.

'You're not the first person to mention that,' said Cheesman unsmilingly. 'I can't see why.'

'You just don't see waistcoats as a rule.'

'I've always worn one up to now. Why should I stop because I'm in the army?'

'No reason at all.'

'Even the tailor seemed surprised. He said: "We don't usually supply a vest with service-dress, sir." '

'It's a tailor's war, anyway.'

'What do you mean?'

'That's just a thing people say.'

'Why?'

'God knows.'

Cheesman looked puzzled, but pursued the matter no further.

'See you at Church Parade tomorrow.'

Sunday morning was always concerned with getting the Defence Platoon on parade, together with the Military Police and other miscellaneous troops who make up Divisional Headquarters. This parade was not without its worries, because the Redcaps, most of them ex-guardsmen, marched at a more leisurely pace than the Line troops, some of whom, Light Infantry or fusiliers, were, on the other hand, unduly brisk. Colonel Hogbourne-Johnson, whose sympathies were naturally with the 'Light Bobs' was always grumbling about its lack of progressional uniformity. That day all went well. After these details had been dismissed, I went to the DAAG's office to see if anything had to be dealt with before Monday. As it happened, I had spoken with none of the other officers after church. Widmerpool was not in his room, nor had he been present at the service. It was not uncommon for him to spend Sunday morning working, so that he might already have finished what he wanted to do and gone back to the Mess. Almost as soon as I arrived there the telephone bell rang.

'DAAG's office—Jenkins.'

'It's A & Q. Is the DAAG there?'

'No, sir.'

'Has he been in this morning?'

'Not since I came here from Church Parade, sir.'

Colonel Pedlar sounded in an agitated state, it was hard to tell whether pleased or angry.

'Was the DADMS in church?'

'Yes, sir.'

I had noticed Macfie a few pews in front of where I was sitting.

'I can't get any reply from his room. Tell the man on the switch-board to try and find Major Widmerpool and Major Macfie and send them to me—and come along yourself.'

'Yes, sir.'

Colonel Pedlar was walking up and down his room.

'Have you told them to find the DADMS?'

'Yes, sir.'

'There's not much we can do until he arrives. A very unfortunate thing's happened. A tragedy, in fact. Most unpleasant.'

'Yes, sir?'

'The fact is the SOPT's hanged himself in the cricket pavilion.'

'That hut on the sports field, sir?'

'That's it. The one they lost the key of.'

Colonel Pedlar continued to stride backwards and forwards across his office.

'There's nothing much to be done until the DAAG and the DADMS arrive,' he said.

'When was this discovered, sir?'

'Only a short time ago—by a civilian who had to fetch some benches from the place.'

Colonel Pedlar stopped for a moment. Talking seemed to have relieved his feelings. Then he began to move again.

'What do you think of the news?' he asked.

'Well, it's rather awful, sir. Biggs was in my Mess—'

'Oh, I don't mean Biggs,' he said. 'Haven't you seen a paper or heard the wireless this morning? Germany's invaded Russia.'

226

An immediate, overpowering, almost mystic sense of relief took shape within me. I felt suddenly sure everything was going to be all right. This was something quite apart from even the most cursory reflection upon strategic implications involved.

'I give the Russians three weeks,' said Colonel Pedlar. 'If you haven't heard that the German army's attacked Russia, you probably don't know General Liddament has been given command of a Corps.'

'I didn't, sir.'

'He left this morning to take over at once.'

I had never known Colonel Pedlar so talkative. He was no doubt trying to keep his mind off Biggs by imparting all this information, while he wandered about the room.

'And we're going to lose our DAAG.'

'I'd heard he might be leaving, sir.'

'Though the posting hasn't come through yet.'

'No, sir.'

Colonel Pedlar ceased pacing up and down. He sat in his chair, holding his hand to his head.

'There was something else I wanted to talk to you about,' he said. 'Now what was it?'

I waited. The Colonel began looking among the papers on his table. More than ever his face was reminiscent of a dog sniffing about for a lost scent. Suddenly he picked it up and took hold of a scrap of paper.

'Ah, yes,' he said. 'About your own disposal.'

'Yes, sir?'

'You were going to the ITC.'

'Yes, sir.'

'But I've just had this. It should go through the DAAG, of course, but as you're here, you may as well see it.'

He handed across a teleprint message. It quoted my

227

name, rank, number, instructing me to report to a room, number also quoted, in the War Office the following week.

'I don't know anything about this,' said Colonel Pedlar.

'Nor me, sir.'

'Anyway it solves the problem of what's going to happen to you.'

'Yes, sir.'

At that moment, Widmerpool and Macfie came into the room. Macfie looked as glum as ever, if possible, glummer, but Widmerpool's face showed he had received news of the General's promotion and departure. His manner to Colonel Pedlar indicated that too, when the Colonel began to outline the circumstances of the suicide.

'I don't think Jenkins needs to stay, does he?' Widmerpool asked brusquely.

'I hardly think he does,' said Pedlar. 'You may as well go now. Don't forget to take necessary action about that signal I passed you.'

I went back to F Mess. Soper was discussing with Keef what had happened. His heavy simian eyebrows contorted in agitation, he looked more than ever like a professional comedian.

'A fine kettle of fish,' he said. 'Never thought Biggy would have done that. In the cricket pav, of all places, and him so fond of the game. Worrying about that key did it. More than the wife business, in my opinion. Quite a change it will be, not having him grousing about the food every day.'

That same week the plane was shot down in which Barnby was undertaking a reconnaissance flight with the aim of reporting on enemy camouflage.

The Military Philosophers

for
Georgina

1

Towards morning the teleprinter's bell sounded. A whole night could pass without a summons of that sort, for here, unlike the formations, was no responsibility to wake at four and take dictation—some brief unidentifiable passage of on the whole undistinguished prose—from the secret radio *Spider*, calling and testing in the small hours. Sleep was perfectly attainable when no raid intervened, though recurrent vibration from one or both machines affirmed next door the same restlessness of spirit that agitated the Duty Officer's room, buzzing all the time with desultory currents of feeling bequeathed by an ever changing tenancy. Endemic as ghouls in an Arabian cemetery, harassed aggressive shades lingered for ever in such cells to impose on each successive inmate their preoccupations and anxieties, crowding him from floor and bed, invading and distorting dreams. Once in a way a teleprinter would break down, suddenly ceasing to belch forth its broad paper shaft, the column instead crumpling to a stop in mid-air like waters of a frozen cataract. Jammed works might at this moment account for the call. More probably the bell signified an item of news that could demand immediate action. I went through to investigate.

Grey untidy typescript capitals registered the information that small detachments of Poles were crossing the Russian frontier into Iran, just a few men at a time, but enough to suggest some sort of evacuation had begun. This was very much our concern. It had been long awaited. My first thought was to ring Colonel Finn at once at his flat, but, reconsidering matters, day nearly come, a copy of the cable would be on his desk when he arrived in a few hours' time. Nothing effective could be done until consultations had taken place. Besides, working late the night before—past eleven when last seen heavily descending the stairs with the tread of Regulus returning to Carthage—Finn deserved any repose he could get. I returned to bed. The teleprinters continued to clatter out their incantations, sullen and monotonous, yet not without a threat of sudden uncontrolled frenzy. However, shattered fragments of sleep were no longer to be reconstituted. After a while attempt had to be abandoned, the day faced. On the way to shave I paused in the room of the Section handling incoming signals. For the tour of duty one came under orders, whatever his rank, of their officer in charge for any given period, on this occasion a near-midget, middle-aged and two-pipped, with long arms and short legs attached to a squat frame, who had exacted regulation rights—waived by the easy-going—to assistance in his postal deliveries the evening before. As he had hurried fretfully down the long dark passages, apportioning hot news to swell the in-trays at break of day, he seemed one of the throng from the Goblin Market. Now, opening the door of their room, identification was more precise. The curtain had obviously just risen on the third drama of *The Ring*—Mime at his forge—the wizened lieutenant revealed in his shirtsleeves, crouched over a table, while he scoured away at some object in an absolute fever of energy.

'Good morning.'

There was no concealing a certain peevishness at interruption of the performance at such a crucial juncture, only a

2

matter of seconds before the burst of guttural tenor notes opened the introductory lament:

> 'Labour unending
> Toil without fruit!
> The strongest sword
> That ever I forged . . .'

However, he discontinued his thankless task for a brief space, though still clutching the polishing cloth in claw-like fingers. It was not, in fact, Siegfried's sword to which he was devoting so much attention (trading with the enemy, when one came to think of it), but that by now almost universally adopted—possibly Moghul—contribution to military tailoring, the Sam Browne belt, doubtless his own, the unbuckled brace of which waited treatment on another table.

'Can I see the cable about Poles leaving the USSR?'

The distribution marked at the foot would provide a forecast of immediate contacts on the subject. Rather grudgingly producing the night's harvest, he held the sheaf of telegrams close to his chest, like the cards of a cautious poker player, so that, as he thumbed them through, no other eye should violate their security. The required copy was at the bottom of the pile. Recipients noted, we had a further word together on the subject of the building's least uninviting washing place, agreeing in principle that no great diversity of choice was available. Shaking his head despairingly, either at the thought of rows of grubby basins or his own incessant frustration as swordsmith, or rather leather worker, Mime returned to the Sam Browne. The door closed on sempiternal burnishings. Outside in the corridor, diffused in clouds by the brooms of the cleaners' dawn patrol and smarting to the eye like pepper, rose the dust of eld. Messengers in shabby blue uniforms, a race churlish almost to a man, were beginning to shuffle about,

3

yawning and snarling at each other. Theoretically, night duty continued until 9 a.m., but the Nibelung allowing fealty to himself and his clan by now sufficiently discharged, I dressed, and, not sorry to be released once again from this recurrent nocturnal vassalage, went out to find some breakfast. As well as stimulating teleprinter news, there were things to think over that had happened the previous day.

An unfriendly sky brooded over lines of overcrowded buses lumbering up Whitehall. Singapore had fallen five or six weeks before. Because of official apprehension of a lowering effect on public morale, Japanese excesses there had been soft-pedalled, though those in touch with documents of only relatively restricted circulation knew the sort of thing that had been going on. Withdrawal in Burma was about to take shape. In London the blitz, on the whole abated, would from time to time break out again like an incurable disease. The news about the Poles being at last allowed to leave Russia was good. Something cheering was welcome. The matter had particular bearing on my own changed circumstances.

Nine or ten months before, a posting had come to a small, rather closed community of the General Staff, the Section's establishment—including Finn himself, a lieutenant-colonel —something less than a dozen officers. Gazetted captain, after a brief period of probation, I had been transferred to the Intelligence Corps 'for purposes of administrative convenience'. Like most of those who could claim an earlier military incarnation, I continued to wear the badges, deemed for no particular reason to carry an enhanced prestige, of my former line regiment. Pennistone, for example, recently promoted major, would not even abandon his anonymous lion-and-unicorn under which he had first entered the army. I was Pennistone's assistant in Polish Liaison. The rest of the Section were concerned either with the other original Allies —Belgium, the Netherlands, Luxembourg, Norway,

4

Czechoslovakia—or the Neutrals—some of whom from time to time were metamorphosed into Allies or enemies—running to nearly twenty in number who boasted a military attaché.

A military attaché was the essential point. He provided the channel through which work was routed for all but three of the Allied forces. Exceptions were the Free French, the Americans, the Russians. Only matters innate to the particular appointment of military attaché as such—routine invitations to exercises and the like—involved Finn with this trio. They were, for their part, dealt with by special missions: Americans and Russians, on account of sheer volume of work involved; Free French, for the good reason they lacked an embassy to which a military attaché could be attached. The Vichy administration, unlike German-established puppet regimes in other occupied countries, was still recognized by Great Britain as the government of France, though naturally unrepresented diplomatically at the Court of St James's. Pennistone had explained much of this when we met a year before at the Free French Mission itself, where Finn, then a major, had interviewed me for a job to which I was not appointed. That interview had in due course brought me to the Section, though whether it would have done so had not Finn himself decided to accept the promotion he had so often in the past refused is another matter. Pennistone might have got me into the Section anyway. There seems no avoiding what has to be.

'Finn's good nature makes him vulnerable,' Pennistone said. 'But he can always fall back on his deafness and his VC.'

Finn was certainly prepared to use either or both these attributes to their fullest advantage when occasion required, but he had other weapons too, and took a lot of bypassing when it came to conflict. Quite why he had changed his mind about accepting promotion, no one knew. If, until

5

that moment, he had preferred to avoid at his age (what that age was remained one of his secrets) too heavy responsibilities, too complex duties, he now found himself assailed by work as various as it was demanding. There was perhaps a parallel with Lance-Corporal Gittins, storeman in my former Battalion, a man of similarly marked character, who, no doubt to the end, preferred a job he liked and knew thoroughly to the uncertainty of rising higher. Possibly a surface picturesqueness about the duties, the people with whom he was now brought in contact, had tempted Finn more than he would have admitted. That would be easy, for Finn admitted to nothing but the deafness and the VC; not even the 'L' of his own initial, though he would smile if the latter question arose, as if he looked forward one day to revealing his first name at the most effective possible moment.

'Finn's extraordinary French is quite famous in Paris,' said Pennistone. 'He has turned it to great advantage.'

Pennistone, capable, even brilliant, at explaining philosophic niceties or the minutiae of official dialectic, was entirely unable to present a clear narrative of his own daily life, past or present, so that it was never discoverable how he and Finn had met in Paris in the first instance. Probably it had been in the days before Pennistone had abandoned commerce for writing a book about Descartes—or possibly Gassendi—and there had been some question of furnishing Finn's office with Pennistone's textiles. In peace or war, Finn was obviously shrewd enough, so he might have ferreted out Pennistone as assistant even had he not been already one of the Section's officers, but, on the contrary, concealed in the innermost recesses of the military machine. He enjoyed a decided prominence in Finn's councils, not by any means only because he spoke several languages with complete fluency.

'Why did Finn leave the City for the cosmetics business?'

6

'Didn't he inherit some family interest? I don't know. His daughter is married to a Frenchman serving with the British army—as a few are on account of political disinclinations regarding de Gaulle—but Finn keeps his wife and family hidden away.'

'Why is that?'

Pennistone laughed.

'My theory is because presence of relations, whatever they were like, would prejudice Finn's own operation as a completely uncommitted individual, a kind of ideal figure—anyway to himself in his own particular genre—one to whom such appendages as wives and children could only be an encumbrance. Narcissism, perhaps the best sort of narcissism. I'm not sure he isn't right to do so.'

I saw what Pennistone meant, also why he and Finn got on so well together, at first sight surprising, since Finn had probably never heard of Descartes, still less Gassendi. He was not a great reader, he used to say. Such panache as he felt required by his own chosen persona had immense finish of style, to which even the most critical could hardly take offence. Possibly Mrs Finn had proved the exception in that respect, lack of harmony in domestic life resulting. Heroes are notoriously hard to live with. When Finn conversed about matters other than official ones, he tended on the whole to offer anecdotal experiences of the earlier war, old favourites like the occasion when, during a halt on the line of march, he had persuaded the Medical Officer to pull a troublesome molar. Copious draughts of rum were followed by the convulsions as of earthquake. Finn would make appropriate gestures and mimings during the recital, quite horrifying in their way, and undeniably confirming latent abilities as an actor. The climax came almost in a whisper.

'The MO made a balls of it. The tooth was the wrong one.'

Had Finn, in fact, chosen the stage as career, rather than

7

war and commerce, his personal appearance would have restricted him to 'character' parts. Superficial good looks were entirely absent. Short, square, cleanshaven, his head seemed carved out of an elephant's tusk, the whole massive cone of ivory left more or less complete in its original shape, eyes hollowed out deep in the roots, the rest of the protuberance accommodating his other features, terminating in a perfectly colossal nose that stretched directly forward from the totally bald cranium. The nose was preposterous, grotesque, slapstick, a mask from a Goldoni comedy. He had summoned me a day or two before the teleprinter news of the Polish evacuation.

'As David's still in Scotland,' he said. 'I want you to attend a Cabinet Offices meeting. Explain to them how one Polish general can be a very different cup of tea to another.'

The Poles were by far the largest of the Allied contingents in the United Kingdom, running to a Corps of some twenty thousand men, stationed in Scotland, where Pennistone was doing a week's tour of duty to see the army on the ground and make contact with the British Liaison Headquarters attached to it. The other Allies in this country mustered only two or three thousand bodies apiece, though some of them held cards just as useful as soldiers, if not more so: the Belgians, for example, still controlling the Congo, the Norwegians a large and serviceable merchant fleet. However, the size of the Polish Corps, and the fact that the Poles who had reached this country showed a high proportion of officers to that of 'other ranks', inclined to emphasise complexities of Polish political opinion. Some of our own official elements were not too well versed in appreciating the importance of this tricky aspect of all Allied relationships. At misunderstanding's worst, most disastrous, the Poles were thought of as a race not unlike the Russians; indeed, by some, scarcely to be distinguished apart. Even branches more at home in this respect than the

8

Censorship—to whom it always came as a complete and chaotic surprise that Poles wrote letters to each other expressing feelings towards the USSR that were less than friendly—were sometimes puzzled by internal Allied conflicts alien to our own, in many respects unusual, ideas about running an army.

'The Poles themselves have a joke about their generals being either social or socialist,' said Finn. 'Only wish it was as easy as that. I expect you've got the necessary stuff, Nicholas. If you feel you want to strengthen it, apply to the Country Section or our ambassador to them. This is one of Widmerpool's committees. Have you heard of Widmerpool?'

'Yes, sir, I——'

'Had dealings with him?'

'Quite often, I——'

'Some people find him . . .'

Finn paused and looked grave. He must have decided to remain imprecise, because he did not finish the sentence.

'Very active is Widmerpool,' he went on. 'Not everyone likes him—I mean where he is. If you've come across him already, you'll know how to handle things. Have all the information at your finger tips. Plenty of notes to fall back on. We want to deliver the goods. Possibly Farebrother will be there. He has certain dealings with the Poles in these secret games that take place. Farebrother's got great charm, I know, but you must resist it, Nicholas. Don't let him entangle us in any of his people's goings-on.'

'No, sir. Of course not. Is it Colonel Widmerpool?'

'He's a half-colonel—Good God, I've been keeping Hlava waiting all this time. He must come up at once. You'd better ring David in Scotland and tell him you're standing in for him at this Cabinet Office meeting. He may have something to add. Make a good impression, Nicholas. Show them we know our business.'

9

The fact was Finn was rather overawed by the thought of the Cabinet Offices. I was a little overawed myself. The warning about Farebrother, whose name I had already heard mentioned several times as a lieutenant-colonel in one of the secret organizations, expressed a principle of Finn's, almost an obsession, that his own Section should have as distant relations as possible with any of the undercover centres of warfare. He considered, no doubt with reason, that officers concerned in normal liaison duties, if they swam, even had an occasional dip, in waters tainted by the varied and dubious currents liable to be released, sometimes rather recklessly, from such dark and mysterious sources, risked undermining confidence in themselves *vis-à-vis* the Allies with whom they daily worked. Secret machinations of the most outlandish kind might be demanded by total war; they were all the same to be avoided—from the security point of view and every other—by those doing a different sort of job. That was Finn's view. You could take it or leave it as a theory. For his own staff, it had to be observed. All contact with clandestine bodies could not, of course, be prevented, because, where any given Ally was concerned, common areas of administration were bound to exist between routine duties and exceptional ones; for example, transfer of individual or group in circumstances when the change had to be known to the Liaison Officer. Even so, Finn's Section saw on the whole remarkably little of those tenebrous side-turnings off the main road of military operations, and he himself would always give a glance of the deepest disapproval if he ran across any of their representatives, male or female, in uniform or *en civile*, frequenting our room, which did occasionally happen.

The meeting was to take place in one of the large buildings at the Parliament Square end of Whitehall. I had set off there the previous morning, aware of certain trepidations. After the usual security guards at the entrance, Royal

Marines were on duty, either because the Ministry of Defence had been largely shaped in early days by a marine officer, because their bifarious nature was thought appropriate to inter-service affairs, or simply because a corps organized in small detachments was convenient for London. The blue uniforms and red capbands made me think of Chips Lovell.

'I know it's a tailor's war,' he had said, 'but I can't afford that blue get-up. They'll have to accept me for what I am in khaki.'

I asked for Colonel Widmerpool.

'Aye, aye, sir.'

This old-fashioned naval affirmative, recalling so many adventure stories read as a boy, increased a sensation of going between decks in a ship. I followed the marine down flight after flight of stairs. It was like the lower depths of our own building, though more spacious, less shabby. The marine, who had a streaming cold in his head, showed me into a room in the bowels of the earth, the fittings and decoration of which were also less down-at-heel than the general run of headquarters and government offices. A grave grey-haired civilian, evidently a chief clerk, was arranging papers down each side of a long table. I explained my business.

'Colonel Widmerpool will be here shortly,' he said. 'He is with the Minister.'

He spoke with severity, as if some regulation had already been transgressed by too early arrival, which had made it necessary to reveal Widmerpool's impressive engagement. I hung about. The chief clerk, like a verger arranging service papers in a cathedral before a wedding, set out a further selection of documents, adjusting them in some very exact relation to those already on the table. A naval captain and RAF wing-commander came in together, talking hard. Ignoring the chief clerk and myself, they sat down at the far end of the long table, produced more papers from briefcases and continued their conversation. They were followed in a minute by a youngish lieutenant-colonel, with the air of a don in uniform, who this time muttered a faint 'good morning' in my direction, then joined the sailor and airman in whatever they were discussing. It was impossible to remain unaware of an atmosphere of exceedingly high pressure in this place, something much more concentrated, more intense, than that with which one was normally surrounded. This was not because work was unplentiful or disregarded in our own building; nor—some of it—lacking in immediacy or drama. However much those characteristics might there obtain, this ethos was something rather different. In this brightly lit dungeon lurked a sense that no one could spare a word, not a syllable, far less gesture, not of direct value in implementing the matter in hand. The power principle could almost be felt here, humming and vibrating like the drummings of the teleprinter. The sensation that resulted was oppressive, even a shade alarming. I was still kicking my heels, trying to rationalize the sense of tension, when the same marine who had escorted myself, blowing his nose hard, ushered in Sunny Farebrother.

Farebrother came through the door looking as quietly distinguished as ever. He was wearing on his threadbare tunic the badge of a parachutist. This qualification was held desirable for those who, in the course of their administrative duties, had to arrange the 'dropping' of others, usually into destinations of excessive danger. Its acquisition was not to be sneezed at for a man in his fifties. It bore out the rumour that Farebrother's DSO in the previous war had been a 'good one'. I was glad to see someone I knew already, but Farebrother's arrival did not in other respects make the atmosphere of the room substantially more cordial; if anything, the reverse. In fact none of the people at the table even looked up. Farebrother himself was obviously on his best behaviour. He addressed himself to the other half-colonel.

'Hullo, Reggie.'

After this ranging shot, he greeted the rest in a manner precisely to indicate appreciation that the sailor was a rung above him, the airman at the same level, both employed in other arms of the Services, therefore unlikely to have immediate bearing on his own interests and promotion. Farebrother's capacity for conveying such subtleties of official relationship was unrivalled. On this occasion, his civilities were scarcely returned. He seemed to expect no more, accepting his status as small fry in the eyes of people such as these. The others continued their discussion. He came across to me.

'So you've had a move up too, Nicholas.'

'Not long after your own, sir.'

'Have you taken David Pennistone's place? I expected him to be your Section's representative here.'

Pennistone regarded himself as rather an authority on Sunny Farebrother, often laughing about that 'charm' against which Finn had warned me.

'Farebrother himself refers to it,' Pennistone said. 'The other day he remarked that some general had "ordered me to use my famous charm". The extraordinary thing is that he has got a way of getting round people, in spite of boasting about it himself. He does put himself over. A remarkable fellow in his way. Ambitious as hell, stops at nothing. I always enjoy his accounts of his own small economies. "Found a place off Baker Street where you can get a three-course luncheon for three-and-six—second helpings, if you ask—a man of my build needs proper nourishment. It's becoming hard to get nowadays, especially at a reasonable price."'

This taste for saving money, usually to be thought of as a trait threatening to diminish an air of distinction, never seemed to detract from Farebrother's. His blue eyes always smiled out bravely on the world. Parsimony, like the dilapidation of his uniform, the one product of the other, positively enhanced his personality—his 'charm' perhaps—even when you knew he was well off. Indeed, Pennistone, like others before him, took the view that Farebrother was decidedly rich.

'And then when he puts on his holy face and tone of voice,' said Pennistone. 'A sacred subject is mentioned—the Prime Minister, religion, some high decoration—Sunny sucks in his cheeks and drops his eyes.'

Farebrother pointed to the strip lighting with which the underground room was equipped.

'Wish I could afford to install something like that in my peacetime office,' he said. 'What you need, if you're going to get any work done. Can't tell whether it's three o'clock in the morning, or three o'clock in the afternoon. No disturbance from time. I expect you know we're going to meet an old friend here this morning?'

'Kenneth Widmerpool?'

Farebrother laughed. Concealing as a rule his likes and dislikes about most people, he scarcely attempted to hide his hatred of Widmerpool, whom it must have been galling to find once more his equal in rank, after temporarily outstripping him; not to mention the fact that Widmerpool's appointment was of such undeniably superior standing to Farebrother's.

'Oh, Kenneth, of course,' he said. 'No, I didn't mean him. This is certainly Kenneth's bower, a very cosy one, don't you think? No—Peter Templer. I was talking to him yesterday about some matter in which his Ministry was concerned, and he told me the usual man's sick and he himself would be representing Economic Warfare here this morning.'

Templer came into the room at that moment, followed by

another civilian. Sir Magnus Donners—who continued to hold his place in the Cabinet, in spite of a concerted attack for several months from certain sections of the Press—had probably had some hand in finding this job for him in MEW. Catching sight of me, Templer nodded and gave a slight smile, but did not come over and speak. Instead, he sat down with the party at the table, where he too began to produce papers. He seemed to know them all.

'I must have a word with Peter,' said Farebrother.

He went across to Templer and said something. At Stourwater, where I had last seen him, I had been struck by a hardness, even brutality of expression that had changed someone I had once known well. That look had seemed new to Templer, perhaps to be attributed to lack of concord with his second wife, Betty, then showing herself an unassimilable member of Sir Magnus's houseparty; indeed, so near the borderline of sanity that it seemed unwise ever to have brought her into those formidable surroundings. Templer had not lost this rather grim appearance. If anything, it had increased. He was thinner, more resembling himself in his younger days in that respect. To go through his papers he had put on spectacles, which I had never before seen him wear. While I was wondering whether I too ought to go and sit at the table, Widmerpool himself entered the room.

'My apologies, gentlemen.'

Holding up a sheaf of documents in both hands, at the same time making jocular movements with his head and arms in the direction of the small crowd awaiting him, he looked very pleased with himself; like a dog delighted to show ability in carrying a newspaper in his mouth.

'You must excuse me,' he said. 'I was kept by the Minister. He absolutely refused to let me go.'

Grinning at them all through his thick lenses, his tone

15

suggested the Minister's insistence had bordered on sexual importunity.

'Let us be seated.'

Everyone except Farebrother and myself was already sitting down. Widmerpool turned towards me, somewhat abating the geniality of his manner.

'I was not informed by Finn that you were coming here in Pennistone's place, Nicholas. He should have done so.'

'I have the necessary stuff here.'

'I hope you have. Finn is rather slack about such notifications. There are security considerations here of which he may not appreciate the complexity. However, let us begin. This Polish business should not take too long. We must be brisk, as a great many more important matters have to be got through this morning.'

The other civilian, who had entered the room with Templer, turned out to be the Foreign Office representative on this particular committee, a big fat man with a small mouth and petulant manner. He had brought a paper with him which he now read aloud in the tone of one offering up an introductory prayer. There was some general talk, when he had finished, of Pilsudski's *coup d'état* of 1926, from which so many subsequent Polish complications of political relationship had arisen. I consulted my notes.

'The broad outline is that those senior officers who stem from the Carpathian Brigade of Legions tend to be nationalist and relatively right-wing, in contrast with those of the First Brigade—under Pilsudski himself and Sosnokowski—on the whole leftish in outlook.'

'The First Brigade always regarded itself as the *élite*,' said Widmerpool.

He had evidently read the subject up, at least familiarized himself with its salient points. Probably the knowledge was fairly thorough, as his capacity for work was enormous.

'General Sikorski himself was entirely eclipsed after the

16

coup. Henceforth he lived largely abroad. Since taking over, he has shown himself very reasonable, even well disposed, towards most of his former political opponents.'

'Though by no means immune to French flattery,' said Widmerpool.

'Let's hear something about General Anders,' said the sailor.

'He's GOC Polish troops in Russia, I understand. How's he doing at that job?'

'Efficiently, it's thought—insomuch as he's allowed to function with a free hand.'

'Where will Anders fit in, if he comes over here? Will there be friction with the present chap?'

'Up to now, Anders has not been a figure of anything like comparable political stature to Sikorski. There seems no reason to suppose he wishes to compete with him at that level. Unlike Sikorski—although he actively opposed Pilsudski in 'twenty-six—Anders never suffered in his career. In fact he was the first colonel to be promoted general after the change of régime.'

'Anders is a totally different type from Sikorski,' said Widmerpool. 'Rather a swashbuckler. A man to be careful of in certain respects. Ran a racing stable. Still, I'm no enemy to a bit of dash. I like it.'

Widmerpool removed his spectacles to emphasize this taste for ardour in living.

'The Russians kept him in close confinement for two years.'

'So we are aware.'

'Sometimes in atrocious conditions.'

'Yes, yes. Now, let's get on to lesser people like their Chief of Staff, Kielkiewicz, and the military attaché, Bobrowski . . .'

Clarification of the personalities of Polish generals continued for about an hour. The various pairs of hands lying on the table formed a pattern of contrasted colours and shapes. Widmerpool's, small, gnarled, with cracked nails, I remembered from school. Farebrother's, clasped together, as if devotionally, to match his expression, were long fingered, the joints immensely nobbly, rather notably clean and well looked after, but not manicured like Templer's. Those of the Foreign Office representative were huge, with great bulbous fingers, almost purple in colour, like lumps of meat that had been chopped in that shape to make into sandwiches or hot-dogs. The soldier and sailor both possessed good useful hands of medium size, very reasonably clean; the airman's, small again, rather in the manner of Widmerpool's, nails pared very close, probably with a knife.

'That seems to be about all we want to know,' said Widmerpool. 'Is that agreed? Let us get on to more urgent matters. The extraneous personnel can go back to their own work.'

Farebrother, apparently anxious to get away quickly, rose, said some goodbyes and left. Templer also wanted to be on his way.

'I was told you wouldn't need me either after the first session, Kenneth,' he said. 'None of the stuff you're moving on to will concern my people directly and we'll get copies of the paper. There's a particular matter back at the office I'd like to liquidate, if I could be excused—and Broadbent will be back tomorrow.'

'It isn't usual,' said Widmerpool.

'Couldn't an exception be made?'

After a minute or two of sparring, Widmerpool assented ungraciously. I suggested to Templer we should walk a short way up the street together.

'All right,' said Templer indifferently.

This exchange between Templer and myself had the effect of making Widmerpool restive, even irritable. He looked up from the table, round which a further set of papers was being doled out by the chief clerk.

'Do go away, Nicholas. I have some highly secret matters to deal with on the next agenda. I can't begin on them with people like you hanging about the room.'

Templer and I retired. On the first landing of the stairs, the sneezing marine was drying his handkerchief on the air-conditioning plant. We reached the street before Templer spoke. He seemed deeply occupied with his own thoughts.

'What's working at MEW like?'

'Just what you'd imagine.'

His manner was so unforthcoming, so far from recognizing we were old friends who had not met for a long time, that I began to regret suggesting we should have a word together after the meeting.

'Are you often in contact with Sunny Farebrother?'

'Naturally his people are in touch with the Ministry from time to time, though not as a rule with me personally.'

'When I saw him at my former Div HQ he rather indicated his new job might have some bearing on your own career.'

'That was poor security on Sunny's part. Well, you never know. Perhaps it will. I admit I've been looking about for something different. These things take time. The trouble is one's so frightfully old. Kenneth's sitting pretty, isn't he?'

'He thought he'd never get that job. He was in fairly hot water when last seen.'

'Kenneth can winkle his way out of anything,' said Templer. 'God save me from such a grind myself, but, if you like that sort of thing, it's quite a powerful one, properly handled. You can bet Kenneth gets the last ounce out of it.'

'You grade it pretty high?'

'Of course, it's nothing to find yourself working fourteen

hours a day at a stretch, even longer than that, night after night into the small hours, and then back again at 9 a.m. If you can stand up to it physically—get the rest of the committee to agree with what you've written down of their discussion over a period of six or seven hours—you, as their secretary, word the papers that may go right up to the Chiefs of Staff—possibly to the PM himself. You've only seen the merest chicken feed, Nick. A Military Assistant Secretary, like Kenneth, can have quite an influence on policy—in a sense on the whole course of the war—if he plays his hand well.'

Templer had dropped his distant manner. The thought of Widmerpool's potential powers evidently excited him.

'It's only a lieutenant-colonel's appointment.'

'They range from majors to brigadiers—there might even be a major-general. I'm not sure. You see there are quite a lot of them. In theory, they rank equal in their own particular work, but of course rank always carries its own prestige. I say, this possibility has just occurred to me. Do you ever come across Prince Theodoric in your racket?'

'I believe my Colonel has seen him once or twice. I've never run across him myself—except for a brief moment years ago before the war.'

'I just wondered,' said Templer. 'I used to have business dealings with his country. Theodoric's position is a trifle delicate here, politically speaking, his brother, the King, not only in such bad health, but more or less in baulk.'

'Musing upon the King his brother's wreck?'

'And the heir to the throne too young to do anything, and anyway in America. Theodoric himself has always been a hundred per cent anti-Nazi. I'm trying to get Kenneth to put up a paper on the subject. That's all by the way. How's your family?'

The abruptness of transition was clearly to mark a deliberate change of subject. I told him Isobel and our child were living near enough to London to be visited once a fortnight; in return enquiring about Betty Templer. Although curious to hear what had happened to her, I had not asked at first because any question about Templer's women, even wives, risked the answer that they had been discarded or had left. His manner at that moment conveyed that revelation forced on him—if anything of the sort were indeed to be revealed—would be answered in a manner calculated to embarrass. There had been times when he liked to unload personal matters; this did not look like one of them. In any case, I hardly knew Betty, at least no more of her than her state of extreme nervous discomfort at Stourwater. However, enquiry was not to be avoided. Templer did not answer at once. Instead, he looked at me with an odd sardonic expression, preparation for news hardly likely to be good.

'You hadn't heard?'

'Heard what?'

'About Betty?'

'Not ill, I hope.'

It occurred to me she might have been killed in a raid. That could happen to acquaintances and remain unknown to one for months.

'She went off her rocker,' he said.

'You mean . . .'

'Just what I say. She's in the bin.'

He spoke roughly. The deliberate brutality of the statement was so complete, so designed to let no one, least of all myself, off any of its implications, that it could only be accepted as concealing an abyss of painful feeling. At least, correctly or not, such downright language had to be given the benefit of the doubt in that respect.

'Rather a peach, isn't she?'

That was what he had said of her, when I had first seen them together at Umfraville's night-club, a stage in their relationship when Templer could not remember whether his future wife's surname was Taylor or Porter. Now, he made no effort to help out the situation. There was nothing whatever to be said in return. I produced a few conventional phrases, none in the least adequate, at the same time feeling rather aggrieved that Templer himself should choose, first, to carry curtness of manner to the point of seeming positively unfriendly; then change to a tone that only long intimacy in the past could justify. Perhaps— thinking over Betty's demeanour staying with Sir Magnus Donners—this ultimate disaster was not altogether surprising. Having such cares on his mind could to some extent explain Templer's earlier unaccommodating manner.

'Just one of those things,' he said.

He spoke this time as if a little to excuse himself for what might look like an earlier show of heartlessness.

'To tell the truth, I'm feeling a shade fed up about marriage, women, my job, in fact the whole bag of tricks,' he said. 'Then this awful business of one's age. You keep on getting back to that. If it isn't one objection, it's another. "You're not young enough, old boy". I'm always being told that nowadays. On top of it all, a bomb hit my flat the other night. I was on Fire Duty at the Ministry. Everybody said what a marvellous piece of luck. Not sure.'

'Did it wreck the place completely?'

Templer shook his head, indicating not so much lack of damage at the flat, as that he could not bring himself to recapitulate further a subject so utterly tedious and unrewarding.

'You haven't any good idea where I might go temporarily? I'm living from hand to mouth at the moment with anyone who will put me up.'

I suggested the Jeavons house in South Kensington. Ted Jeavons, having somehow managed to find a builder to patch up the roof and back wall—an achievement no one but himself would have brought off at that moment—was still in residence. Only the rear part of the structure had been damaged by the bomb, the front remaining almost untouched. Jeavons ran the house more or less as it had been run when Molly was alive, with a shifting population of visitors, some of whom lived there more or less permanently, paying rent. Lots of households of much that kind existed in wartime London, a matter of luck if, homeless like Templer, you knew where to apply. He wrote down the address, at the same time showing characteristic lack of interest in information about Jeavons.

'I might propose myself,' he said. 'If a bomb's already hit the place, with any luck it won't happen again, though I don't know that there's any real reason to suppose that.'

He paused, then suddenly began to talk about himself in a manner that was oddly apologetic, quite unlike his accustomed style as remembered, or the tone he had been using up till now. Until then, I had felt all contact lost between us, that the picture I retained of him when we had been friends years before had become largely imaginary. Now a closer proximity seemed renewed.

'I've given up girls,' he said. 'I thought you'd be interested to know.'

'Charles Stringham said the same when I ran across him in the ranks. Is this for the war?'

Templer laughed.

'I used to think I was rather a success with the ladies,' he said. 'Now one wife's run away and the other is where I indicated, I'm not so sure. At least I can't be regarded as a great hand at marriage. It's lately been made clear to me I'm not so hot extra-matrimonially either. That's why I was beefing about age.'

He made a dismissive gesture.

'I'll ring your friend Jeavons,' he said.

He strolled away. There was always the slight impression

of which Stringham used to complain—persisting even into the universal shabbiness of wartime—that Templer was too well dressed. I had never before known him so dejected.

While eating breakfast after Night Duty, I reflected that it would be as well to warn Jeavons that Templer might be getting in touch with him. Without some such notification, knowing them both, nothing was more likely than that they would get at cross purposes with each other. Then I put personal matters from my mind and began to think about the day's work that lay ahead.

'You'll be surprised at the decisions one has to take on one's own here.' Pennistone had said when I first joined the Section. 'You might think that applied to the Operational people more than ourselves, but in fact captains and majors in 'I' have to get used to giving snap answers about all sorts of relatively important policy matters.'

When I returned to the building, this time to our own room, Dempster, who looked after the Norwegians and had a passion for fresh air, was trying vainly to open one of the windows, laughing a lot while he did so. He was in the timber business and knew Scandinavia well, spending skiing holidays in Norway when a boy with an aunt who was a remote kinswoman of Ibsen's. Dempster was always full of Ibsen stories. He had won a couple of MCs in '14–'18, the second up at Murmansk during the War of Intervention, an interlude the less inhibited of the Russians would, once in a way, enjoy laughing about, if the subject came up after a lot of drinks at one of their own parties. That did not apply to the Soviet military attaché himself, General Lebedev, who was at all times a stranger to laughter. Dempster was a rather notably accomplished pianist, who had been known to play a duet with Colonel Hlava, the Czech, also a competent performer, though not quite in Dempster's class.

'No good,' said Dempster.

Holding a long pole with a hook on the end with which he had been trying to open the window, he looked like an immensely genial troll come south from the fjords to have a good time. Still laughing, he replaced the pole in its corner. This endlessly repeated game of trying to force open the window was always unsuccessful. The sun's rays, when there was any sun, penetrated through small rectangles in otherwise bricked up glass. The room itself, irregular of shape, was on the first floor, situated in an angle of the building, under one of the domed cupolas that ornamented the four corners of the roof. In winter—it was now early spring—life here was not unlike that lived at the earth's extremities, morning and evening only an hour or two apart, the sparse feeble light of day tailing away in early afternoon, until finally swallowed up into impenetrable outer blackness. Within, lamplight glowed dimly through the shadows and nimbus of cigarette smoke, the drone of dictating voices measuring a kind of plain-song against more brief emphatic exchanges made from time to time on one or more of the seven or eight telephones. This telephonic talk was, as often as not, in some language other than English; just as the badges and insignia of visitors tended, as often as not, to diverge from the common run of uniform.

Pennistone, still wearing a blue side-cap, was sitting in his chair, preparing for action by opening the small gold hunter that always lay on the desk in front of him during working hours, a watch that was wound with a key.

'Good morning, Nick.'

'You came down from Scotland last night?'

'Got a sleeper by a bit of luck. I shared it with an air-commodore who snored. How did the Cabinet Office meeting go?'

'All right—look, I'm just off night duty. What do you

think? A message has come through that a few Poles are trickling over the Persian frontier.'

'No?'

'The Russians have released a driblet.'

'This could mean a Second Polish Corps.'

Pennistone had fair hair with a high-bridged nose over which he could look exceeding severe at people who annoyed him, of whom there were likely to be quite a few in the course of a day's business. Without possessing a conventionally military appearance, a kind of personal authority and physical ease of movement carried off in him the incisive demands of uniform. More basically, he could claim an almost uncanny instinctive grasp of what was required from a staff officer. Indeed, after months of dealing with him from day to day, General Bobrowski, when informed Pennistone was not a Regular, had exploded into a Polish ejaculation of utter astonishment, at the same time bursting into loud laughter, while executing in mid-air one of those snatching, clutching gestures of the fingers, so expressive of his own impatience with life. A major-general, Bobrowski, who was military attaché, had been with the Polish contingent in France at the beginning of the war, where, in contravention of the French Chief of Army Staff's order that no Polish troops were to be evacuated to England, he had mounted brens on locomotives and brought the best part of two brigades to a port of embarkation.

'Bobrowski began his military career in a Russian rifle regiment.' Pennistone had told me. 'He was *praporschik*—ensign, as usually translated—at the same time that Kielkiewicz was an aspirant—always a favourite rank of mine—in the Austro-Hungarian cavalry.'

Hanging his cap on one of the hooks by the door, Pennistone went upstairs at once to get orders from Finn about the news from Iran. Polish GHQ must have received the information simultaneously from their own sources—reports

26

almost always comprehensive, if at times highly coloured—because Michalski, one of General Kielkiewicz's ADCs, came through on the telephone just after Pennistone had left the room, seeking to arrange an interview with everyone from the Chief of the Imperial General Staff downwards. He was followed almost immediately on the line by Horaczko, one of Bobrowski's assistants, with the same end in view for his master. We were on easy terms with both Michalski and Horaczko, so temporizing was not too difficult, though clearly fresh and more urgent solicitations would soon be on the way.

Michalski, now in his late thirties, had served like Bobrowski with the Polish contingent in France. Of large size, sceptical about most matters, he belonged to the world of industrial design—statuettes for radiator caps and such decorative items—working latterly in Berlin, which had left some mark on him of its bitter individual humour. In fact Pennistone always said talking to Michalski made him feel he was sitting in the Romanisches Café. His father had been a successful portrait painter, and his grandfather before him, stretching back to a long line of itinerant artists wandering over Poland and Saxony.

'Painting pictures that are now being destroyed as quickly as possible,' Michalski said.

He was accomplished at providing thumbnail sketches of the personalities at the Titian, the former hotel, subdued, Edwardian in tone, where headquarters of the Polish army in exile was established. Uncle Giles had once stayed there in days gone by, a moment when neither the Ufford nor the De Tabley had been able to accommodate him at short notice. 'I'll be bankrupt if I ever do it again,' he had declared afterwards, a financial state all his relations in those days supposed him to be in anyway.

Horaczko had reached England in a different manner from Michalski, and only after a lot of adventures. As an officer of the Reserve, he had begun the Eastern campaign on horseback, cantering about at the head of a troop of lancers, pennons flying, like one of the sequences of *War and Peace*, to intercept the advancing German armour. Executive in a Galician petroleum plant, he was younger than Michalski, having—as Pennistone and I agreed—some of the air of the junior lead in a drawing-room comedy, the young lover perhaps. When Poland was overrun on two fronts, Horaczko had avoided capture and internment, probably death, by escaping through Hungary. Both he and Michalski held the rank of second-lieutenant. While I was still speaking to Horaczko on the telephone, our clerk, Corporal Curtis, brought in a lot more stuff to be dealt with, additional, that is, to the formidable pile lying on the desk when I came in from breakfast.

'Good morning, Curtis.'

'Good morning, sir.'

'How are things?'

Curtis, a studious-looking young man, whose military career had been handicapped by weak eyesight, was a henchman of notable efficiency and wide interests. He had once confessed to Pennistone that he had read through the whole of Grote's *History of Greece*.

'A rather disturbing letter from the Adjutant-General's branch, sir.'

'Oh, Lord.'

'But not so bad as my first premonition on reading it. In fact, sir, I all but perpetrated a schoolboy howler in that connexion.'

'Impossible.'

'On the subject of redundant Polish officers taking commissions in the King's African Rifles—*Accra*, sir—the AG.10 clerk spoke indistinctly, as well as using what I understand to be an incorrect pronunciation, so that, to cut a long story short, sir, the place was first transcribed by me

28

as *Agra*. The error did not take long to be righted, but it was a disturbing misconstruction.'

By the time I had run through the new lot of papers Pennistone had returned. He reported that Finn—after a word with the more sagacious of the two brigadiers—had been told to consult the Major-General in charge of our Directorate. I reported that Michalski and Horaczko had telephoned.

'Ring Horaczko back, otherwise Bobrowski will make him persecute us all day. Tell him we'll let him know the very moment anything comes through that his general should have. Don't worry about Michalski. I'll be seeing him. I'm off to the Titian at once to get Kielkiewicz's reactions.'

'What were the Colonel's?'

'He's in one of his flaps.'

Sudden pressures of this kind always upset Finn, whose temperament unpredictably fused agitation with calm; violent inner antagonism of these warring characteristics having presumably motivated whatever he had done— killed goodness knows how many enemy machine-gunners with a bayonet?—to be awarded his VC. No doubt the comparative lack of precedent for the situation now arisen in Persia, its eccentric deficiency of warning at the diplo-matic level, general departure from normal routine—even from official good manners so far as the Soviet was con-cerned—discomposed Finn, a man both systematic and courteous. Although not a professional soldier, he had one way and another, seen a good deal of military service, having, like Dempster, stayed on for a while in the army after the Armistice in 1918; then been re-employed in the rank of major as early as 1938. In short, he had enjoyed plenty of opportunity to observe military problems, which on the whole he seemed to prefer to semi-political ones, like the evacuation of the Poles.

'He'll be all right when he's used to the idea,' said Pennistone. 'At first he could consider nothing short of flying out there at once and arranging it all himself.'

He reached for his cap again, unhooking it from the wall with the crook of a walking stick. Then he returned the watch to the breast pocket of his tunic.

'Have a talk with Q (Ops.) Colonel,' he said.

Borrit, who looked after the Netherlands, passed on his way towards the door.

'Borrit . . .'

'Yes, Pennistone?'

'You're not making for the car?'

Borrit's small fair moustache was set in a serious melancholy face, deeply tanned, as if he had spent much of his life under a blazing sun. Perhaps he had. He had come to the Section from employment as one of the Intelligence Officers at Headquarters on the Gold Coast, owing his knowledge of Spanish—at first naturally steering him to duties with the Neutrals—to many years spent on the wholesale side of the fruit trade. Language as usual proving of less consequence than facility for handling an 'opposite number' with tact, he had in due course gravitated to the more responsible job with an Ally. Stebbings, who took Borrit's place with the Spaniards and Latin-Americans, was also, oddly enough, in the fruit business, though on the retail side, where he had a nervous breakdown when his firm went into bankruptcy at the outbreak of war. If addressed sharply, Stebbings's left eyelid twitched, probably in consequence of that collapse. He remained always rather afraid of Finn. All the same, he tackled his duties with judgment. Stebbings was recently married to a Portuguese, a fact that continually worried the Security people. Borrit, on the other hand, was a widower. He must have been forty, perhaps a shade more, because he had seen action in the first war, though only as a result of having falsified his age to the recruiting authorities. During the occasional lulls of work Borrit and Stebbings would talk earnestly of fruit. Pennistone and Borrit had a standing rivalry over the Section's car—a vehicle of inconceivably cramped seating accommodation—for first use in the morning.

'Wait a moment...' said Pennistone.

'I'll drop you,' said Borrit. 'If you're on the way to the Titian.'

Pennistone turned to me again.

'Where was I?'

'Q (Ops.).'

'Ah, yes—the point is there's only the traditional one man and a boy at Meshed.'

'That's the key name?'

'We shall be hearing a lot about Meshed—and resorts like Yangi-yul and Alma Ata. Some sort of a reception centre will have to be rigged up. There may be quite a party to deal with once they start.'

'What am I to say to Q (Ops.)?'

'Just ventilate the question. They may have other ideas to ours.'

'They're presumably prepared for this. They were on the distribution.'

'But will want to be brought up to date from our end—and we'll need their background stuff to tell the London Poles.'

'Do you mind if we go, Pennistone?' said Borrit. 'Otherwise I'll be late for my appointment with Van der Voort.'

Pennistone, never to be hurried, stood in deep thought. He was as likely to be reflecting on Cartesianism as on the best way to approach Q (Ops.). Borrit made another move towards the door.

'What was it? I know—trouble again about Szymanski. You wouldn't think it possible one man could be such a nuisance. There's now doubt whether it's his real name, because a lot of people are called that. MI5 want a word about him. Try and clear it up. Another good deed would be to extract an answer from Blackhead about the supply of straw for stuffing medical establishment palliasses. They're frantic about it in Scotland.'

'Blackhead's not raised objection to that?'

'He says straw comes under a special restrictive order. He should be alerted about the evacuation too, so that he can think up difficulties.'

Borrit opened the door, allowing a sharp current of air to drive in from the passages. This was done as a challenge. He leant on the handle, looking rather aggrieved. There were some shouts from the others requiring that the door be shut at once. Borrit pointed to Pennistone and myself. He would not venture to leave without Pennistone, but, to humour him, we both made a move towards the corridor.

'Come as far as the staff entrance,' said Pennistone. 'In case I think of other urgent problems.'

We followed Borrit down the back staircase. On the first floor, Intelligence, in its profuse forms, mingled with Staff Duties, a grumpy crowd, most of them, especially the Regulars ('If they were any good, they wouldn't be here', Pennistone said) and a few Operational sections, on the whole less immediately active ones, the more vital tending to have rooms on the floor above, close to the generals and higher grade brigadiers. A few civilian *hauts fonction-naires*, as Pennistone called them, were also located here, provided with a strip of carpet as they rose in rank; at the highest level—so it was rumoured—even a cupboard containing a chamber pot. The Army Council Room was on this floor, where three or four colonels, Finn among them, had also managed to find accommodation. The great double staircase leading from the marble hall of the main entrance (over which the porter, Vavassor, presided in a blue frock coat with scarlet facings and top hat with gold band) led directly to these, as it were, state apartments. On the ground floor, technical branches and those concerned with supply rubbed shoulders with all sorts and conditions, internal security contacts of a more or less secret sort, Public Relations, typing pools, dispatch-riders, Home Guard.

'Kielkiewicz has heard of Kafka,' said Pennistone, as we reached the foot of the stairs.

'You put them all through their literary paces as a matter of routine?'

'He laughed yesterday when I used the term Kafka-esque.'

'Wasn't that rather esoteric?'

'It just slipped out.'

Pennistone laughed at the thought. Though absolutely dedicated to his duties with the Poles, he also liked getting as much amusement out of the job as possible.

'In the course of discussing English sporting prints with Bobrowski,' he said, 'a subject he's rather keen on. It turned out the Empire style in Poland is known as "Duchy of Warsaw". That's nice, isn't it?'

'I don't look forward to this tussle with Blackhead about palliasse straw—by the way, what happened in the war about the Air Cooperation Squadron and which command it came under?'

'One of my notable achievements up there was to settle that. But go and see Q (Ops.). That's the big stuff now. Then have a talk with Finn. Where's the driver?'

Borrit gave a shout. An AT came quickly from behind the screen that stood on one side of the untidy cramped little hall, crowded with people showing identity cards as they passed into the building. She glanced at us without interest, then went through the door into the street.

'Not bad,' said Borrit. 'I hadn't seen her before.'

Very young, she was one of those girls with a dead white complexion and black hair, the only colouring capable of rising above the boundlessly unbecoming hue of khaki. Instead of the usual ATS tunic imposed by some higher authority anxious that the Corps should look, if not as masculine as possible, at least as Sapphic, she had managed to provide herself, as some did, with soldier's battledress, paradoxically more adapted to the female figure. It had to be admitted that occasional intrusion at 'official level' of an attractive woman was something rather different from, more exciting than, the intermittent pretty secretary or waitress of peacetime, perhaps more subtly captivating from a sense that you and she belonged to the same complicated organism, in this case the Army. At the same time, Borrit's comment was one of routine rather than particular interest, because, according to himself, he lived a rather melancholy emotional life. His wife, a Canadian, had died about ten years before, and, while Borrit marketed fruit in Europe, their children preferred to live with grandparents in Canada. His own relations with the opposite sex took an exclusively commercial form.

'I've never had a free poke in my life,' he said. 'Subject doesn't seem to arise when you're talking to a respectable woman.'

He had confided this remark to the room in general. In spite of existing in this amatory twilight, he presented a reasonably cheerful exterior to the world, largely sustained by such phrases as 'What news on the Rialto?' or 'Bring on the dancing girls'. He and Pennistone followed the driver to where the Section's car was parked outside. I turned away from the staff entrance and made for Q (Ops.).

The new flight of stairs led down into the bowels of the earth, the caves and potholes of the basement and sub-basement, an underground kingdom comparable with that inhabited by Widmerpool. It might have been thought that Mime and his fellow Nibelungen haunted these murky subterranean regions, but they were in fact peopled by more

34

important, less easily replaceable beings, many of whom practised mysteries too momentous to be exposed (in a target registering already more than a dozen outers, though as yet no bull's eye) to the comparative uncertainties of life at street level or above. Here, for example, the unsleeping sages of Movement Control spun out their lives, sightless magicians deprived eternally of the light of the sun, while, by their powerful arts, they projected armies or individual over land and sea or through the illimitable wastes of the air. The atmosphere below seemed to demand such highly coloured metaphor, thoughts of magic and necromancy bringing Dr Trelawney to mind, and the rumours in the earlier war that he had been executed in the Tower as a spy. I wondered if the Good Doctor, as Moreland used to call him, were still alive. Indiscreet observance of the rites of his cult, especially where these involved exotic drugs, could bring trouble in this war, though retribution was likely to stop short of the firing squad. Moreland himself, with Mrs Maclintick, had left London months before on some governmentally sponsored musical tour of the provinces.

Like a phantasm in one of Dr Trelawney's own narcotically produced reveries, I flitted down passage after passage, from layer to layer of imperfect air-conditioning, finding the right door at last in an obscure corner. Q (Ops.) Colonel was speaking on the scrambler when I entered the room, so I made as if to withdraw. He vigorously beckoned me to stay, continuing to talk for a few seconds about some overseas force. Abyssinia might have been a good guess. He hung up. I explained where I came from and put myself at his disposal.

'Ah, yes . . .'

He began to sort out papers, putting some away in a drawer. He gave an immediate impression, not only of knowing what he was about himself, but also of possessing the right sort of determination to use any information available from other sources. Inefficiency was rare in the building, but there was inevitably the occasional boor or temperamental obscurantist.

'Polish evacuation—here we are—these troops held by our Russian Allies since their invasion of our Polish Allies in 1939. They've retained their own units and formations?'

'We understand some in Central Asia have, or at least certain units have already been brigaded after release from prison camps. General Anders is organizing this.'

'The lot are in Central Asia?'

'At least eight or nine thousand Polish officers remain untraced.'

'Rather a large deficiency.'

'That's a minimum, sir. It's been put as high as fifteen thousand.'

'Any idea where they are?'

'Franz Josef Land's been suggested, sir.'

'Within the Arctic Circle?'

'Yes.'

He looked straight in front of him.

'Unlikely they'll be included in this evacuation, whatever its extent?'

'Seems most unlikely, sir.'

'Just the figures I have here?'

He pushed them over.

'So far as we know at present. On the other hand, anything might happen.'

'Let's have a look at the map again . . . Yangi-yul . . . Alma Ata . . . There's been constant pressure for the release of these troops?'

'All the time—also to discover the whereabouts of the missing officers.'

He wrote some notes.

'Lease-Lend . . .'

'Yes, sir?'

'You see the consignment papers?'

'From time to time some minor item is earmarked for the Polish forces in Russia and the papers pass through our hands.'

Once, when one of these interminable lists of weapons and vehicles, *matériel* of war for the Eastern Front, had come to us, Pennistone had compared the diplomatic representations of the moment directed to obtaining the release of the immobilized Polish army with a very small powder in a very large spoon of Lease-Lend jam. Now, the Germans penetrating into the country on an extended front, these solicitations seemed at last to have attracted official Soviet attention. This must have been four or five months before the siege of Stalingrad. Q (Ops.) Colonel ran through facts and figures, asked a few additional questions, then shook the papers together and clipped them back into their file.

'Right?'

'Right, sir.'

He took up the green telephone again.

'If the London Poles have anything to add to what I have here already, let me know.'

'We will, sir.'

He 'went over' on the scrambler with whomever he was talking to, and, as I withdrew, could have been dealing with Icelandic matters. Like Orpheus or Herakles returning from the silent shades of Tartarus, I set off upstairs again, the objective now Finn's room on the second floor.

Outside the Army Council Room, side by side on the passage wall, hung, so far as I knew, the only pictures in the building, a huge pair of subfusc massively framed oil-paintings, subject and technique of which I could rarely pass without re-examination. The murkily stiff treatment of these two unwontedly elongated canvases, although not in fact executed by Horace Isbister RA, recalled his brushwork and treatment, a style that already germinated a kind of low-grade nostalgia on account of its naïve approach and total disregard for any 'modern' development in the painter's art. The merging harmonies—dark brown, dark red, dark blue—depicted incidents in the wartime life of King George V: *Where Belgium greeted Britain*, showing the bearded monarch welcoming Albert, King of the Belgians, on arrival in this country as an exile from his own: *Merville, December 1st, 1914*, in which King George was portrayed chatting with President Poincaré, this time both with beards, the President wearing a hat somewhat resembling the head-dress of an *avocat* in the French lawcourts. Perhaps it was fur, on account of the cold. This time too busy to make a fresh assessment, aesthetic or sartorial, I passed the pictures by. Finn's door was locked. He might still be with the General, more probably was himself making a round of branches concerned with the evacuation. There was nothing for it but Blackhead, and restrictions on straw for hospital palliasses.

The stairs above the second floor led up into a rookery of lesser activities, some fairly obscure of definition. On these higher storeys dwelt the Civil branches and their subsidiaries, Finance, Internal Administration, Passive Air Defence, all diminishing in official prestige as the altitude steepened. Finally the explorer converged on attics under the eaves, where crusty hermits lunched frugally from paper bags, amongst crumb-powdered files and documents ineradicably tattooed with the circular brand of the teacup. At these heights, vestiges of hastily snatched meals endured throughout all seasons, eternal as the unmelted upland snows. Here, under the leads, like some unjustly confined prisoner of the Council of Ten, lived Blackhead. It was a part of the building rarely penetrated, for even Blackhead himself preferred on the whole to make forays on others, rather than that his own fastness should be invaded.

'You'll never get that past Blackhead,' Pennistone had said, during my first week with the Section.

'Who's Blackhead?'

'Until you have dealings with Blackhead, the word "bureaucrat" will have conveyed no meaning to you. He is the super-*tchenovnik* of the classical Russian novel. Even this building can boast no one else quite like him. As a special treat you can negotiate with Blackhead this afternoon on the subject of the issue of screwdrivers and other tools to Polish civilian personnel temporarily employed at military technical establishments.'

This suggested caricature, Pennistone's taste for presenting individuals in dramatic form. On the contrary, the picture was, if anything, toned down from reality. At my former Divisional Headquarters, the chief clerk, Warrant Officer Class I Mr Diplock, had seemed a fair performer in the field specified. To transact business even for a few minutes with Blackhead was immediately to grasp how pitifully deficient Diplock had, in fact, often proved himself in evolving a really impregnable system of obstruction and preclusion; awareness of such falling short of perfection perhaps telling on his nerves and finally causing him to embezzle and desert.

'Blackhead is a man apart,' said Pennistone. 'Even his colleagues are aware of that. His minutes have the abstract quality of pure extension.'

It was true. Closely 'in touch' with the Finance branch, he was, for some reason, not precisely categorized as one of them. Indeed, all precision was lacking where the branch to which Blackhead belonged was in question, even the house telephone directory, usually unequivocal, becoming all at once vague, even shifty. The phrase 'inspection and collation of governmental civil and economic administration in relation to Allied military liaison' had once been used by a member of one of the Finance branches themselves, then hastily withdrawn as if too explicit, something dangerous for security reasons to express so openly. Such prevarication hinted at the possibility that even his fellows by now could not exactly determine—anyway define to a layman—exactly what Blackhead really did. His rank, too, usually so manifest in every civil servant, seemed in Blackhead's case to have become blurred by time and attrition. To whom was he was responsible? Whom—if anyone—did he transcend? Obviously in the last resort he was subservient to the Permanent Under-Secretary of State for War, and Blackhead himself would speak of Assistant Under Secretaries—even of Principals—as if their ranks represented unthinkable heights of official attainment. On the other hand, none of these people seemed to have the will, even the power, to control him. It was as if Blackhead, relatively humble though his grading might be, had become an anonymous immanence of all their kind, a fetish, the Voodoo deity of the whole Civil Service to be venerated and placated, even if better—safer—hidden away out of sight: the mystic holy essence incarnate of arguing, encumbering, delaying, hair-splitting, all for the best of reasons.

Blackhead might be a lone wolf, a one-man band, but he was a force that had to be reckoned with, from whom there was no court of appeal, until once in a way Operations would cut the Gordian knot, brutally disregarding Blackhead himself, overriding his objections, as it were snapping asunder the skinny arm he had slipped through the bolt-sockets of whatever administrative door he was attempting to hold against all comers. Operations would, as I say, sometimes thrust Blackhead aside, and continue to wage war unimpeded by him against the Axis. However, such a confrontation took place only when delay had become desperate. There was no doubt he would make himself felt by delaying tactics when the evacuation got under way, until something of that drastic sort took place.

'Of course I'm not an officer,' he had once remarked bitterly to Pennistone when a humiliation of just that kind had been visited on him, 'I'm only Mr Blackhead.'

Some years after the war was over—by chance attending a gathering of semi-official character, possibly a *soirée* organized for a fund or charity—I enquired Blackhead's story from a former colleague of his who happened to be present. This personage (even in war days of distinguished rank, one of the *hauts fonctionnaires* on the second floor) would at first do no more than laugh, loudly though a shade uncomfortably. He seemed anxious to evade the question. In fact, all at length recoverable from his answers, such as they were, became reduced to the hypothesis that Blackhead had been deliberately relegated to an appointment peculiar to himself—that in which our Section had dealings with him— chiefly in order to keep him out of the way of more important people. As unique occupant of his individual branch, even if he did not promote the war effort, he did not greatly impede it—so, at least, my informant insisted—while duties almost anywhere else might prove less innocuous. This highly successful person nodded several times when he admitted that. Self-esteem made the reply a little unacceptable to me. Did we matter so little? I argued the point. Why could not Blackhead be eradicated entirely? No such machinery existed. That was definite. Blackhead's former colleague showed himself as nearly apologetic about the fact as anyone of his calling had it in him. He fiddled with the decoration round his neck.

'The process was known afterwards as doing a Blackhead,' he allowed. 'Alternatively, having a Blackhead done on you. The public may think we're a staid crowd, but we have our professional jokes like everyone else. I say, what are your views on liquid refreshment? Would it be acceptable? I wouldn't say no myself. Don't I see a buffet over there? Let's make tracks.'

This subsequent conversation explained why Pennistone and the rest of us, like Jacob and the Angel, had to wrestle with Blackhead until the coming of day, or nearly that. Such was the biblical comparison that came to mind as I climbed the stairs leading to Blackhead's room, the moral exile to which his own kind had banished him emphasized not only by its smallness, but also by the fact that he lived there alone, isolation rare for one of his putatively low degree—if, indeed, his degree was low. I opened the door a crack, but further enlargement of entry was blocked by sheer stowage of paper, the files thickly banked about the floor like wholesale goods awaiting allotment to retailers, or, more credibly, the residue of a totally unsaleable commodity stored up here out of everyone's way. Blackhead himself was writing. He jumped up for a second and fiercely kicked a great cliff of files aside so that I could squeeze into the room. Then he returned to whatever he was at, his right hand moving feverishly across the paper, while his left thumb and forefinger, both stained with ink, rested on the handle of a saucerless cup.

'I'll attend to you in a minute, Jenkins.'

Not only was Blackhead, so to speak, beyond rank, he was also beyond age; beyond or outside Time. He might have been a worn—terribly worn—thirty-five; on the other hand (had not superannuation regulations, no doubt as sacred to Blackhead as any other official ordinances, precluded any such thing), he could easily have achieved threescore years and ten, with a safe prospect for his century. Emaciated, though obviously immensely strong, he was probably in truth approaching fifty. His hair, which formed an irregular wiry fringe over a furrowed leathery brow, was of a metallic shade that could have been natural to him all his life.

'Glad you've come, Jenkins,' he said, putting his face still closer to the paper on which he was writing. 'Pennistone minuted me . . . Polish Women's Corps . . . terms I haven't been able fully to interpret . . . In short don't at all comprehend . . . '

His hand continued to move at immense speed, with a nervous shaky intensity, backwards and forwards across the page of the file, ending at last in a signature. He blotted the minute, read through what he had written, closed the covers. Then he placed the file on an already overhanging tower of similar dockets, a vast rickety skyscraper of official comment, based on the flimsy foundation of a wire tray. At this final burden, the pyramid began to tremble, at first seemed likely to topple over. Blackhead showed absolute command of the situation. He steadied the pile with scarcely a touch of his practised hand. Then, eyes glinting behind his spectacles, he rose jerkily and began rummaging about among similar foothills of files ranged on a side table.

'Belgian Women's Corps, bicycle for . . . Norwegian military attaché, office furniture . . . Royal Netherlands Artillery, second echelon lorries . . . Czechoslovak Field Security, appointment of cook . . . Distribution of Polish Global Sum in relation to other Allied commitments—now we're getting warm . . . Case of Corporal Altmann, legal costs in alleged rape—that's moving away . . . Luxembourg shoulder flashes —right out . . . Here we are . . . Polish Women's Corps, soap issue for—that's the one I wanted a word about.'

'I really came about the question of restrictions on straw for stuffing hospital palliasses in Scotland.'

Blackhead paused, on the defensive at once.

'You can't be expecting an answer on straw already?'

'We were hoping—'

'But look here . . .'

'It must be a week or ten days.'

'Week or ten days? Cast your eyes over these, Jenkins.'

Blackhead made a gesture with his pen in the direction of

the files stacked on the table amongst which he had been excavating.

'Barely had time to glance at the straw,' he said. 'Certainly not think it out properly. It's a tricky subject, straw.'

'Liaison HQ in Scotland hoped for a quick answer.'

'Liaison HQ in Scotland are going to be disappointed.'

'What's so difficult?'

'There's the Ministry of Supply angle.'

'Can't we ignore them for once?'

'Ministry of Agriculture may require notification. Straw interests them ... We won't talk about that now. What I want you to tell me, Jenkins, is what Pennistone means by this ...'

Blackhead held—thrust—the file forward in my direction.

'Couldn't we just cast an eye over the straw file too, if you could find it while I try to solve this one.'

Blackhead was unwilling, but in the end, after a certain amount of search, the file about hospital palliasses was found and also extracted.

'Now it's the Women's Corps I want to talk about,' he said. 'Issue of certain items—soap, to be exact, and regulations for same. There's a principle at stake. I pointed that out to Pennistone. Read this ... where my minute begins ...'

To define the length of a 'minute'—an official memorandum authorizing or recommending any given course—is, naturally, like trying to lay down the size of a piece of chalk. There can be short minutes or long minutes, as there might be a chalk down or a fragment of chalk scarcely perceptible to the eye. Thus a long minute might be divided into sections and sub-headings, running into pages and signed by an authority of the highest rank. On the other hand, just as a piece of chalk might reasonably be thought of as a length of that limestone convenient for writing on a blackboard, the ordinary run of minutes exchanged between

44

such as Pennistone and Blackhead might be supposed, in general, to take a fairly brief form—say two or three, to perhaps ten or a dozen, lines. Blackhead pointed severely to what he had written. Then he turned the pages several times. It was a real Marathon of a minute, even for Blackhead. When it came to an end at last he tapped his finger sharply on a comment written below his own signature.

'Look at this,' he said.

He spoke indignantly. I leant forward to examine the exhibit, which was in Pennistone's handwriting. Blackhead had written, in all, three and a half pages on the theory and practice of soap issues for military personnel, with especial reference to the Polish Women's Corps. Turning from his spidery scrawl to Pennistone's neat hand, two words only were inscribed. They stood out on the file:

Please amplify. D. Pennistone. Maj. GS.

Blackhead stood back.

'What do you think of that?' he asked.

I could find no suitable answer, in fact had nearly laughed, which would have been fatal, an error from which no recovery would have been possible.

'He didn't mention the matter to me.'

'As if I hadn't gone into it carefully,' said Blackhead.

'You'd better have a word with Pennistone.'

'Word with him? Not before I've made sure about the point I've missed. He wouldn't have said that unless he knew. I thought you'd be able to explain, Jenkins. If he thinks I've omitted something, he'd hardly keep it from you.'

'I'm at a loss—but about the palliasse straw—'

'What else can he want to know?' said Blackhead 'It's me that's asking the questions there, not him.'

'You'll have to speak together.'

'Amplify, indeed,' said Blackhead. 'I spent a couple of hours on that file.'

45

Blackhead stared down at what Pennistone had written. He was distraught; aghast. Pennistone had gone too far. We should be made to suffer for this frivolity of his. That was, if Blackhead retained his sanity.

'What would you like me to do about it?'

Blackhead took off his spectacles and pointed the shafts at me.

'I'll tell you what,' he said. 'I could send it to F 17 (b) for comments. They're the *only ones*, in my view, who might take exception to not being consulted. They're a touchy lot. Always have been. I may have slipped up in not asking them, but I'd have never guessed Pennistone would have spotted that.'

'The thing we want to get on with is the straw.'

'Get on with?' said Blackhead. 'Get on with? If Pennistone wants to get on with things, why does he minute me in the aforesaid terms? That's what I can't understand.'

'Why not talk to him when he comes back. He's at Polish GHQ at the moment. Can't we just inspect the straw file?'

Blackhead had been put so far off his balance that his usual obstinacy must have become impaired. Quite unexpectedly, he gave way all at once about the straw. We discussed the subject of palliasses fully, Blackhead noting in the file that 'a measure of agreement had been reached'. It was a minor triumph. I also prepared the way for papers about the evacuation, but this Blackhead could hardly take in.

'I can't understand Pennistone writing that,' he said. 'I've never had it written before—*please amplify*—not in all my service, all the years I've worked in this blessed building. It's not right. It suggests a criticism of my method.'

I left him gulping the chill dregs of his tea. Finn would probably be back in his room now, ready to hear the substance of what Q (Ops.) Colonel had said.

Rounding the corner of the passage just beyond the two

pictures of George V, I saw Finn's door was open. A tall, stoutish officer, wearing khaki and red tabs, though not for some indefinable reason a British uniform, was taking leave of him. It seemed best to let them finish their conversation, then, when the foreign officer, probably a newly appointed military attaché, had left, catch Finn between interviews. This was never easy, because a steady flow perennially occupied him. He looked up the passage at that moment, and, seeing me, jerked his head as a summons. The red-tabbed officer himself turned. Dark complexioned, hook nosed—though that feature was nothing to the size of Finn's —he had something of the air of a famous tenor. More on account of recent photographs in the press, than because of having seen him before, I recognized Prince Theodoric. The story of the escape he had made from his own country at the moment of its invasion (he was said to have shot dead a Gestapo agent) had been given a lot of publicity when he arrived in England.

'Nicholas,' said Finn, 'I want to present you. One of my officers, sir—he will see you to the door, sir.'

Prince Theodoric held out his hand.

'You've been too kind already, Colonel Finn,' he said. 'Allowing me to take up your precious time with our small concerns. I certainly mustn't impose myself further by requisitioning the services of your officers, no doubt as over-worked as yourself. I may have shown myself in the past inexperienced in methods of tactical withdrawal—as you know too well from the newspapers, I left the palace with-out shaving tackle—but at least let me assure you, my dear Colonel, that I can find my way unaided from this build-ing.'

Theodoric talked that precise, rather old-fashioned Eng-lish, which survives mainly outside the country itself. His manner, very consciously royal, had probably been made more assertive and genial by recent hazards undergone, because he had entirely overcome the self-conscious embarrassment I remembered from former brief contacts with him. Now, he added to that total ease and directness of royalties, who have never doubted for a second the validity of their own rank and station, the additional confidence of a man who has made his own way in the world, and a dangerous way at that. Finn began to assure the Prince that we were all at his service at any moment of the day.

'Finn's in many ways an unworldly man,' Pennistone used to say. 'He likes to hobnob with people like Bernhard of the Netherlands, Olaf of Norway, Felix of Luxembourg. Snobbish, if you like, in one sense. On the other hand, he wouldn't for a second allow any such taste to influence an official decision—nor would he walk across the passage to ingratiate himself with anyone, military or civil, for material reasons. In that respect, Finn is quite unlike Farebrother. Farebrother will get right up the arse of anyone he thinks likely to help him on. After all, everyone's got to choose their own approach to life.'

In any case, if Finn were ceremonious in his treatment of Theodoric, the Prince—as Templer had remarked—had always shown himself profoundly anti-Nazi and a friend of this country. There was reason to show courtesy. At this moment Farebrother himself appeared. He had evidently just made some contact required in our building and was marching along the passage, wearing his cap, a stick tucked under his arm. He came to a halt where we stood and saluted, immediately beginning to dispense round him what Stringham used to call 'several million volts of synthetic charm'.

'This is well met, sir,' he said dramatically.

He addressed himself to Theodoric, at the same time putting his hand on Finn's shoulder.

'I was coming to look in on my old friend here, after paying another visit, and now I find Your Royal Highness

48

present too, just when I had made a mental note to telephone your equerry and ask for an interview.'

'Oh, I've nothing so grand as an equerry these days,' said Theodoric. 'But my staff-officer will arrange an appointment, Colonel Farebrother, any time that suits you.'

'There are several things I hoped to discuss, sir.'

'Why, of course, Colonel—'

Finn began to look rather disturbed. However much he might admire Farebrother's 'charm', he was not at all anxious to have some plot hatched on his doorstep. He must now have scented danger of circuitous arrangements being made through himself, because he suddenly assumed the expression of countenance that gave notice his deafness was about to come into play forthwith. At the same time, he twisted round his head and leant forward slightly.

'Can't hear all you say, Sunny, in this passage,' he said. 'Come into my room just for a moment or two. I'd like a word about Belgian arrangements, so far as they affect us both. I can just fit you in before General Asbjørnsen arrives. Don't keep the Prince waiting, Nicholas.'

'Why, Nicholas?' said Farebrother, feigning to recognize me only at that moment. 'You and I must have a talk, too, about yesterday's meeting...'

If Farebrother hoped to prolong this interlude with Prince Theodoric by bringing me in, he underrated Finn's capacity for action. The delaying tactic failed entirely. Finn somehow managed to get behind Farebrother, and, with surprising adroitness, propelled him forward into the room, the door of which was immediately closed.

'Then I shall hear from you, Colonel Farebrother?' Theodoric called.

He had shown every sign of being inquisitive about whatever Farebrother had to offer, but now it was clearly too late to go into matters further. He turned and smiled at me a little uncomprehendingly. We set off together in the direction of the front staircase.

'Your car's at the main entrance, sir?'

'Car? Not a bit of it. I walk.'

It seemed wiser not to refer to the party given by Mrs Andriadis more than a dozen years before, where I had in fact first set eyes on Theodoric, but I mentioned my presentation to him when he had been staying with Sir Magnus Donners at Stourwater, and the Walpole-Wilsons had taken me over to luncheon there. According to Pennistone, Mrs Andriadis herself was living in one room in Bloomsbury, drinking and drugging heavily. Later, one heard, she occupied herself with making propaganda for the so-called 'Second Front'.

'By Jove, those were the days,' said Theodoric. 'We didn't know how lucky we were. Will you believe me, Captain Jenkins, I had at that time only been shot at twice in my life, on each occasion by certified lunatics? And then, of course, marriage makes one more serious. We have become middle-aged, my dear Captain, we have become middle-aged.'

He sighed.

'I saw Sir Gavin Walpole-Wilson the other day,' he went on. 'Of course he is getting on now, older even than ourselves. We discussed a lot of matters—as you remember, he was formerly your country's minister plenipotentiary to my own. Now he stands well to the left politically. I have certain leanings that way myself, but not as far as Sir Gavin. One must not remain embedded in the past, but Sir Gavin does not always understand our difficulties and the ruthless methods of a certain Ally. There are plenty of good young men in my country who want to get rid of the Germans. There are also men not equally good there who play another part—not all of them our own countrymen.'

Theodoric spoke with great earnestness. It was clear he

50

considered not only people like Finn and Farebrother, but even those of my own rank worth sweeping in as supporters of whatever policy he represented.

'In knowing Sir Magnus Donners,' he said, 'I am particularly fortunate. He is personally conversant with our industrial problems, also—perhaps I should not say this—has the ear of a Very Important Person. If something is to be done, Sir Magnus is the man to do it. I need not tell you that I have had more than one long and interesting talk with him. He says we must wait.'

Theodoric stopped on the way down the marble stairs, where the flights divided, left and right, under the elaborately gilded wall clock and bronze bust of Kitchener. His tone suggested my views on the matter were scarcely less important than those of Sir Magnus. In terms of propaganda, that was an effective technique. The persuasiveness of the Prince was something to be reckoned with. This characteristic could have direct bearing on the fate of his country.

'I shall continue to put our case,' he said.

By now we had reached the great hall. Vavassor, the porter, an attendant spirit of some importance in the Section's background, was standing by the door. It was commonly Vavassor's duty to give warning to Finn of the arrival of callers belonging to the higher echelons, some of whom were capable of turning up without previous appointment, and demanding an interview on the spot. Vavassor could hold them in check; in extreme cases, turn them away. He was also, in this office of guarding the door, a key figure in the lives of Pennistone and myself, on account of frequent association with Allied comings and goings, raising no difficulties about our using the main entrance—superstitiously, though uncategorically, apprehended as prerogative of officers of the rank of brigadier and above—when we arrived for duty in the morning. This not only saved several yards of pavement, but, more important, means avoidance of the teeming mob at the staff entrance. It was a good opening to the day's work. Vavassor saluted Theodoric.

'No fire?' said the Prince.

'Don't let us have any coal when the weather's short of freezing,' said Vavassor. 'That grate takes the best part of a hundredweight a day, it's the truth. Wasn't made for rationing.'

He pointed to the huge fireplace. One supposed that at a certain level of rank—say, lieutenant-general—he called officers 'sir', though I had never heard him do so. In any case it was a formality he always considered inappropriate for foreigners, royal or otherwise.

'When I wait to be summoned by Colonel Finn and warm myself beside the fire,' said Theodoric. 'I always feel like St Peter.'

'I hope you won't cut off any ears, sir, when delay has been intolerably long.'

'How reassuring, Captain Jenkins, that your General Staff are brought up on the Scriptures. They are the foundation of knowledge. Now I must say goodbye. Tell Colonel Finn I will check the figures I gave him—persuade him, something I think he is rather nervous about, that I will not involve him in any matter of which he might disapprove.'

Theodoric laughed. He had evidently summed up Finn correctly. I remembered Sillery (who had recently written a long letter to *The Times* in praise of Stalin's declared war aims) speaking of the shrewdness Theodoric inherited from 'that touch of Coburg blood', adding with characteristic malice, 'though I suppose one should not hint at that.' I saw the Prince down the steps. He waved his hand, and set off at a sharp pace in the direction of Trafalgar Square. I returned under the high portal.

'Prince, is he?' asked Vavassor. 'That's what he calls himself when he arrives.'

'That's what he is.'

'Allied or Neutral?'

'So far as he himself is concerned, Allied.'

'See 'em all down here if you wait long enough.'

'I bet you do.'

'I suppose some of 'em help to win the war.'

'Let's hope so.'

'Not too good in the Far East at the moment of speaking.'

'Ever serve there?'

'Eight years to a day.'

'Things may pick up.'

'I worry too much,' said Vavassor. 'Shakespeare's dying words.'

His attention, my own too, was at that moment unequivocally demanded by the hurricane-like imminence of a thickset general, obviously of high rank, wearing enormous horn-rimmed spectacles. He had just burst from a flagged staff-car almost before it had drawn up by the kerb. Now he tore up the steps of the building at the charge, exploding through the inner door into the hall. An extraordinary current of physical energy, almost of electricity, suddenly pervaded the place. I could feel it stabbing through me. This was the CIGS. His quite remarkable and palpable extension of personality, in its effect on others, I had noticed not long before, out in the open. Coming down Sackville Street, I had all at once been made aware of something that required attention on the far pavement and saw him pounding along. I saluted at admittedly longish range. The salute was returned. Turning my head to watch his progress, I then had proof of being not alone in acting as a kind of receiving-station for such rays—which had, morally speaking, been observable, on his appointment to that top post, down as low as platoon commander. On this Sackville Street occasion, an officer a hundred yards or more ahead, had his nose glued to the window of a book-shop. As the CIGS passed (whom he might well have missed in his concentration on the contents of the window), this officer suddenly swivelled a complete about-turn, saluting too. No doubt he had seen the reflection in the plate glass. All the same, in its own particular genre, the incident gave the outward appearance of exceptional mag-netic impact. That some such impact existed, was confirmed by this closer conjunction in the great hall. Vavassor, momentarily overawed—there could be no doubt of it— came to attention and saluted with much more empresse-ment than usual. Having no cap, I merely came to atten-tion. The CIGS glanced for a split second, as if summariz-ing all the facts of one's life.

'Good morning.'

It was a terrific volume of sound, an absolute bellow, at the same time quite effortless. A moment later, he was on the landing halfway up the stairs, where Theodoric had paused. Then he disappeared from sight. Vavassor grinned and nodded. He was without comment for once. I left him to his reflections about the Far East, hurrying myself now, again in the hope of catching Finn, quickly passing Kitchener's cold and angry eyes, haunting and haunted, surveying with the deepest disapproval all who came that way. Finn was free. He made no reference to Farebrother.

'You'll have to be quick, Nicholas,' he said. 'Asbjørnsen's due at any moment, but he's sometimes a second or two late. Now what about Q (Ops.)?'

He had quite set aside his deafness. I ran over the points at speed. Finn made some notes, collating the information with whatever material had emerged from his session with our own General. He was now quite recovered from the phase, reported by Pennistone, of feeling the only hope of

54

getting the thing properly done would be to fly to Persia and himself arrange it singlehanded.

'The civilian elements are now definitely coming out, sir?'

'Anders insisted—no doubt rightly—but the women and children will not make the operation any easier.'

There had been controversy about these camp-followers who had managed to exist in the wake of the army, largely on its shared rations. At first it had seemed they might have to stay behind.

'Some of the boys are old enough to be trained as cadets. The CIGS himself noted that point on the paper with approval.'

Finn's telephone bell rang.

'Ask him to come up,' he said. 'It's Asbjørnsen. We'll return to the evacuation later, Nicholas. I shall have to keep Asbjørnsen from talking too much, as Colonel Chu is due in less than twenty minutes. Did I tell you Chu's latest after his six months course at Sandhurst?'

The Chinese military attaché, well known for the demanding nature of his requests, had just completed an attachment as cadet to the Royal Military College.

'Chu enjoyed the RMC so much he wants to go to Eton.'

'He could see Windsor Castle at the same time, though the state apartments are probably not open.'

'Good God,' said Finn. 'He doesn't just want to visit the place—he hopes to attend the school as a pupil.'

'He's a shade old, sir.'

'I told him thirty-eight is regarded as too mature in this country to be still at school. It was no good. All he said was "I can make myself young." '

Finn sighed.

'I wish I could,' he said.

Sometimes the military attachés dispirited him. Chu's unreasonableness seemed to have achieved that. General

55

Asbjørnsen arrived in the room. Tall, like General Lebedev, not much given to laughter, he always reminded me of Monsieur Ørn, the long craggy Norwegian, who had been at La Grenadière when, as a boy, I had stayed with the Leroys in Touraine. He shook hands with Finn and myself gravely. I withdrew to our room. Corporal Curtis had again increased the pile of stuff on the desk. I was still going through this when Pennistone returned from the Titian.

'What on earth were you about, David, minuting Blackhead *please amplify*?'

'Has it upset him?'

'Beyond description.'

'Good.'

'What were your reasons?'

'Renan says complication is anterior to simplicity. I thought Blackhead would make an interesting experiment for trying out that theory.'

'We can only pray Renan was right.'

'Renan would find prayer charming, but ineffectual. Did you see Q (Ops.)?'

Pennistone went through the points I had cleared with Finn.

'Look, Nick,' he said. 'I shan't be able to collect the Klnisaszewski Report tomorrow afternoon, as there's another meeting about the evacuation. Will you get it? Nothing whatever required, except to receive it from the Polish officer on duty.'

The Klnisaszewski Report was one of those items of Intelligence that fell, as such items sometimes do, in a no-man's-land between normal official channels and those secret services so cautiously handled by Finn. Even Finn saw no harm in our trafficking in this particular exchange of information, which the Operational and 'Country' sections liked to see. For some internal reason, the Polish branch concerned preferred to hand over the report direct, rather than present it, in the normal manner, through the Second Bureau of their GHQ. Pennistone, as it happened, always collected the Klnisaszewski Report, though merely, in the division of our duties, because he had fallen into the habit of doing so.

'Here's the address,' he said. 'It's the north side of the Park. We might discuss some of these evacuation points further at lunch.'

The following day I arranged to collect the report in the afternoon. When I went down to the staff entrance and shouted for our driver, the white-faced girl commended by Borrit again appeared from behind the screen. She was as sulky as ever. The Section's car was just large enough to hold four persons in great discomfort. If you were the only passenger, you could travel at the back or beside the driver, according to whim. I told her the street number and sat in front.

'Can you find your way there?'

'Yes.'

'You know London pretty well?'

She hardly answered. After a few minutes beside her, it was clear this AT possessed in a high degree that power which all women—some men—command to a greater or lesser extent when in the mood, of projecting round them a sense of vast resentment. The girl driving, I noticed, was able to do this with quite superlative effect. Her rankling animosity against the world in general was discharged with adamantine force, comparable with Audrey Maclintick's ill humours when her husband was alive, or Anne Stepney's intimations of rebellion before she had shaken off the trammels of family life. However, those two, although not without their admirers, were hardly in the same class as this girl when it came to looks. Borrit had been right in marking her down. She was very striking. All the same, after another remark received with little or no response, I gave

57

up further talk. Perhaps she had a grievance or the curse. These drivers usually only did duty for a week or two and at the moment inducement was lacking to coax her out of that mood. It occurred to me—one never feels older than in the middle thirties—that she was bored with all but young men or had taken an instantaneous dislike to me. Conversation lapsed. Then, while driving through Hyde Park, she suddenly spoke of her own accord, though even then in a way to suggest that speech was a painful effort to her, every word so far as possible to be conserved.

'You're Captain Jenkins, aren't you?'

'I am.'

'I think you know my mother.'

'What's your mother's name?'

'Flavia Wisebite—but I'm Pamela Flitton. My father was her first husband.'

This was Stringham's niece. I remembered her holding the bride's train at his wedding. She must have been five or six years old then. At one stage of the service there had been a disturbance at the back of the church and someone afterwards said she had been sick in the font. Whoever had remarked that had found nothing surprising in unsatisfactory behaviour from her. Someone else had commented: 'That child's a fiend.' I knew little of her father, Cosmo Flitton—not even whether he were still alive—except for the fact that he had lost an arm in the earlier war, drank heavily, and was said to be a professional gambler. Alleged to be not too scrupulous in business dealings, Flitton had been involved in Baby Wentworth's divorce, later rejecting marriage with her. He had left Pamela's mother when this girl was not much more than a baby. Establishing the sequence of inevitable sameness that pursues individual progression through life, Flavia had married another drunk, Harrison F. Wisebite, son of a Minneapolis hardware millionaire, whose jocularity he had inherited with only a

58

minute fragment of a post-depression fortune. I wondered idly whether Flavia owed her name to *The Prisoner of Zenda*. Mrs Foxe would have been quite capable of that. Mrs Foxe was said to have given her daughter a baddish time. Pamela, an only child, must be at least twenty by now. She looked younger.

'Where is your mother at the moment?'

'She's helping with Red Cross libraries. She gets sent all over the place.'

'I suppose you've no news of your Uncle Charles?'

'Charles Stringham?'

'The last I saw of him, he'd been posted overseas. I don't even know where.'

She began driving the little car very fast and we nearly ran into an army truck coming across the Park from the opposite direction. She did not answer. I repeated the question.

'You've heard nothing?'

'He was at Singapore.'

'Oh, God...'

With that strange instinct that exists in the ranks for guessing a destination correctly, Stringham had supposed himself on the way to the Far East.

'Nothing's known, I suppose?'

'No.'

'Just reported missing?'

'Yes.'

'He used to be a great friend of mine.'

'We were close when I was quite a child.'

She said that in an odd way, as if almost intending to imply something not to be investigated too far. When I thought the remark over later, it seemed to me unlikely she had seen much of Stringham when she was a child and he was being cured of drink in the iron grip of Miss Weedon. Later, I understood that the ambiguity might have been deliberate. Girls of Pamela's sort take pleasure in making remarks like that, true or not.

'Will you tell your mother—how dreadfully sorry . . .'

Again she made no answer. Iciness of manner remained complete. She was perhaps not altogether normal, what Borrit called 'a bit off the beam'. There was no denying she was a striking girl to look at. Many men would find this cosmic rage with life, as it seemed to be, an added attraction. Perhaps all these suppositions were wide of the mark, and she was just in poor form because she considered herself crossed in love or something obvious of that sort. All the same, the impression was of an uneasy personality, one to cause a lot of trouble. The news about Stringham made relations even more difficult. Her demeanour suggested only gross indifference on my own part had kept me in ignorance of what had happened, that she did not wish to speak more about a matter specially painful to herself.

'How did you discover I was in the Section?'

'Oh, I don't know. Your name cropped up somewhere the other night. I was saying what a bloody awful series of jobs I always get, and the next one was to drive for this outfit. Somebody said you were in it.'

'You don't like the ATS?'

'Who wants to be a bloody AT?'

By this time we had entered the confines of Bayswater. Some of the big houses here had been bombed and abandoned, others were still occupied. Several blocks that had formerly housed Victorian judges and merchants now accommodated refugees from Gibraltar, whose tawny skins and brightly coloured shirts and scarves made this once bleak and humdrum quarter of London, with its uncleaned or broken windows and peeling plaster, look like the back streets of a Mediterranean port. Even so, the area was not yet so squalid as it was in due course to become in the period immediately following the end of the war, when squares and crescents over which an aroma of oppressive respectability had gloomily hung, became infested at all hours of day and night by prostitutes of the lowest category.

'What number did you say?'

'It must be the one on the corner.'

She drew up the car in front of a large grey house in the midst of a complex of streets that had on the whole escaped bomb damage. Several steps led up to a sub-palladian porch, the fanlight over the open door daubed with dark paint to comply with black-out regulations. The place had that slightly sinister air common to most of the innumerable buildings hurriedly converted to official use, whether or not they were enclaves of a more or less secret nature.

'Will you wait with the car? I shan't be long.'

After the usual vetting at the door, my arrival being expected, quick admission took place. A guide in civilian clothes led the way to a particular office where the report was to be obtained. We went up some stairs, through a large hall or ante-chamber where several men and women were sitting in front of typewriters, surrounded by walls covered with a faded design of blue and green flowers, enclosed above and below by broad parchment-like embossed surfaces. This was no doubt the double-drawing-room of some old-fashioned family, who had not redecorated their home for decades. I was shown into the office of a Polish lieutenant-colonel in uniform, from whom the report was to be received. We shook hands.

'Good afternoon... Please sit down... *Procze, pana, procze, pana*... I usually see Major Pennistone, yes.'

He unlocked a drawer and handed over the report. We spoke about its contents for a minute or two, and shook hands again. Then he accompanied me back to where I could find my way out, and, after shaking hands for the third time, we parted. Halfway down the stairs, I grasped that I was in the Ufford, ancient haunt of Uncle Giles. The place of typewriters, so far from being the drawing-room of some banker or tea-broker (perhaps that once), was the combined 'lounge' and 'writing-room', in the former of which my Uncle used to entertain me with fishpaste sandwiches and seed cake. There, Mrs Erdleigh had 'set out the cards', foretold the rows about St John Clarke's book on Isbister, my love affair with Jean Duport. The squat Moorish tables of those days had been replaced by trestles: the engraving of *Bolton Abbey in the Olden Time*, by a poster of characteristically Slavonic design announcing an exhibition of Polish Arts and Crafts. On the ledge of the mantelpiece, on which under a glass dome had stood the clock with hands eternally pointing to twenty minutes past five, were photographs of General Sikorski and Mr Churchill. It struck me the Ufford was in reality the Temple of Janus, the doors between the lounge and the writing-room closed in peace, open in war.

Reaching the entrance, I saw the hotel's name had been obliterated over the front door, as had also that of the De Tabley opposite, to which Uncle Giles had once, at least, briefly defected; only to return in penitence—had he been capable of that inner state—to the Ufford. The De Tabley was now the local branch of the Food Office. The name always recalled an incident at school. Le Bas used to make a habit of reading from time to time the works of the lesser-known Victorian poets to his pupils. He had been doing this on some occasion, declaiming with his accustomed guttural enunciation and difficulty with the letter 'R':

> 'Sweet are the ways of death to weary feet,
>   Calm are the shades of men.
> The phantom fears no tyrant in his seat,
>   The slave is master then.'

He asked where the lines came from. Of course no one knew.

'Lord de Tabley's chorus from *Medea*.'

'Never heard of him, sir.'

'A melancholy fellow, but not without merit.'

Stringham, who had previously appeared all but asleep, had asked if he might see the book. Le Bas handed it over. He always rather liked Stringham, although never much at ease with him. Stringham turned the pages for a moment or two, then returned to the poem Le Bas had read aloud. Stringham himself spoke the second verse:

> 'Love is abolished; well that that is so;
> We know him best as Pain.
> The gods are all cast out, and let them go!
> Who ever found them gain?'

Le Bas was prepared, in moderation, to have Death commended, but he never liked references to Love; probably, for that matter, was unwilling to have the Gods so peremptorily dismissed. He had, I suppose, been betrayed into quoting the earlier lines on account of some appositeness they bore to whatever he had been talking about. He must have seen that to allow Stringham to handle the volume itself had been a false step on his own part.

'Love, of course, had a rather different meaning—indeed, two quite separate meanings in Ancient Greece—from what the modern world understands by the term,' he said. 'While railing against the gods was by no means unknown in their mythological stories.'

'Not bad for a peer of the realm, do you think, sir?' said Stringham.

That was rather cheek, but Le Bas had let it pass, probably finding a laugh the easiest channel for moving on to less tricky matters.

As I went down the steps, I saw a uniformed Pole had strolled out of the Ufford—as I now thought of the place— and was chatting with Pamela Flitton. He seemed to be making a better job of it than myself, because, although continuing to look sullen, she was listening with comparative acceptance to what seemed the commonplaces of conversation. At first I thought the Pole was an officer, then saw he was an 'other rank', who wore his battledress, as most of them did, with a tough air and some swagger. He was dark, almost oriental in feature, showing a lot of gold teeth when he smiled and saluted, before withdrawing up the steps. We set off on the return journey. In the far distance sounded the gentle lowing of an Air Raid Warning. They were to be heard intermittently in the daytime. As the car passed once more through the park, the All Clear sounded, equally faint and far.

'Sounds as if they let off the first one by mistake.'

She did not answer. Perhaps she only liked foreigners. In any case, the thought of Stringham put things on an unhappy, uncomfortable basis. I was not sure, in truth, whether she wanted to avoid discussing the subject because she herself felt so deeply, or because she was really scarcely at all interested in anything but her own personality. We reached the staff entrance. I made some further remark about a message to her mother. She nodded, disappearing once more behind the screen. Pennnistone had returned from the meeting.

'How did it go?'

'Finn brought off one of his inimitable French phrases—Kielkiewicz is, as you know, more at ease in French. During a moment's silence, Finn suddenly murmured very audibly: Le Commandant-Chef aime bien les garçons.'

'What provoked this startling revelation?'

'The Polish cadets—a message came down from the top approving of them as potential training material. Thank God, Bobrowski wasn't there. He'd have had a stroke. Even Kielkiewicz went rather red in the face and pretended to blow his nose.'

'You didn't ask Finn to amplify?'

'One was reminded of the French judge comforting the little boy cross-questioned in court. "Ne t'inquiètes-pas, mon enfant, les juges aiment les petits garçons"—then remembering himself and adding: "Pourtant les juges aiment les petites filles."'

A day or two later Pamela Flitton drove me again when I was going to Bobrowski's office. This was in the Harley Street neighbourhood (ten years later I used to sit in a dentist's chair where once I had talked with Horaczko), from where I should proceed to the Titian. Horaczko's business was likely to be completed in a few minutes, so she was told to wait with the car. As it happened, Horaczko himself wanted to visit Polish GHQ and asked for a lift. When we came out together from the military attaché's office, Pamela Flitton was standing by the car, surveying the street with her usual look of hatred and despair. Horaczko, seeing her, lightly touched the peak of his cap. For a moment I thought this just another example of well-applied technique in what was generally agreed to be the eminently successful relationship established by the Polish forces with the opposite sex in the country of their exile, but, although her acknowledgment was of the slightest, it was plain they had met before. As there were two of us, Horaczko and I sat at the back of the car. We talked about official matters all the way to the Titian.

Passing through its glass doors, guarded by Military Police wearing red covers, like our own, on their angular ethnic Polish lancer caps, Eastern Europe was instantaneously attained. A similar atmosphere imposed, though in a less powerful form, on the Ufford, no doubt accounted to some extent for the brief exorcism there, on first arrival, of the ghost of Uncle Giles. At the Titian, this Slav ethos was overwhelming. Some Poles, including Horaczko, who prided himself on assimilation with things British, found his own nation's characteristics, so he said, here rather depressingly caricatured. To me, on the other hand, the Titian offered an exotic change from the deadly drabness of the wartime London backcloth. The effect was to some extent odorously created, an aroma that discreetly blended elements of eau-de-cologne and onions, sweat and leather, the hotel's Edwardian past no doubt contributing its own special Art Nouveau pungency to more alien essences.

'I see you know our driver. She's the daughter of a friend of mine, as it happens.'

Horaczko at once became tremendously diplomatic in manner, as if large issues were raised by this remark, which was certainly the product of curiosity.

'Miss Flitton?' he said. 'Oh, yes. She's—well, a rather delicate situation has been raised by her.'

He smiled and looked rather arch, if that is the right word.

'She is a beautiful girl,' he said.

We shook hands and he went off to whatever duties concerned him. Horaczko was always immensely tactful. For once he had been surprised into giving away more than he was usually prepared to do. It looked as if Pamela Flitton was already quite a famous figure in Polish military circles. I mounted the stairs to General Kielkiewicz's ante-room. One or more of his ADCs was always on duty there, usually in the company of a Polish colonel of uncertain age, probably a good deal older than he looked at first sight, with features resembling those of a death's head, who sat on an upright chair, eternally reading *Dziennik Polski*. This colonel seemed to be awaiting an interview for which the General was never available. Now, he rose, folded his newspaper, shook hands with me and left the room. Michalski was on duty at that moment. We too shook hands.

'I hope the Colonel did not go away on my account?'

'It is to be arranged that he should write a history of

cavalry,' said Michalski. 'The General has not yet found time to break the news to him.'

A week or two later, there was trouble about the Section's car. Finn had specially ordered it for an important meeting and it was not at the door when he went down. One of the other ATS drivers said she thought the vehicle was out on duty, but no one could trace a Section officer who was using it, or had sent it out on an errand. When Driver Flitton was in due course traced, she said she had been given instructions some weeks before to deliver certain routine papers of a non-secret nature to several of the Neutral military attachés. She had been out by herself doing this. The precise degree of truth in that matter was hard to pinpoint. It was alleged, with apparent conviction, that those particular instructions had later been countermanded, the documents being not at all urgent, though some of them had certainly been sent out. Even if correct that Driver Flitton had misunderstood the instruction, she had taken an unusually long time to make the rounds. Rather a fuss took place about the whole matter. Either on account of that, or simply because, quite by chance, she was given another posting, Driver Flitton was withdrawn from duties with the Section.

2

LIKE FINN'S ACHING JAW ON the line of march, the war throbbed on, punctuated by interludes when more than once the wrong tooth seemed to have been hurriedly extracted. Meanwhile, I inhabited a one-room flat on the eighth floor of a prosaic Chelsea tenement. Private life, apparently at a standstill, as ever formed new patterns. Isobel's brother, George Tolland (by then a lieutenant-colonel serving as 'A & Q' on a Divisional staff in the Middle East), badly wounded in the campaign defeating Rommel, was in hospital in Cairo. Her sister Susan's husband, Roddy Cutts, major of Yeomanry transformed into Reconnaissance Corps, had recently written home to say he had fallen in love with one of the girls decoding cables at GHQ Persia/Iraq Force, and, accepting risk of spoiling a promising political career, wanted a divorce. This eventuality, not at all expected by Susan, nor any of the rest of the family, as Roddy had always been regarded as rather unadventurous in that sort of situation, caused a good deal of dismay.

If not required to stay late in the Whitehall area, I used, as a general routine, to come straight back from duty to a nearby pub, dine there, then retire to bed with a book. At that period the seventeenth century particularly occupied me, so that works like Wood's *Athenae Oxonienses* or Luttrell's *Brief Relation* opened up vistas of the past, if not necessarily preferable to one's own time, at least appreciably different. These historical readings could be varied with Proust. The flat itself was not wholly unsympathetic. The block's ever-changing population, a mixed bag consisting largely of persons of both sexes working for the ministries, shaded off on the female side from high-grade secretaries, officers of the women's services, organisers of one thing and another, into a nebulous world of divorcées living on their own and transient types even less definable, probably all but unemployable where 'war work' was concerned, yet for one reason or another prepared to stay in London and face the blitz. On warm evenings these unattached ladies were to be met with straying about on the flat roof of the building, watching the bombers fly out, requesting cigarettes or matches and complaining to each other, or anyone else with whom they made contact, about the shortcomings of Miss Wartstone.

On another floor of the block, Hewetson, the Section's officer with the Belgians and Czechs, also rented a flat. For a time he and I used to set out together every morning; then, deciding to share a larger place with a friend in the Admiralty (who had a hold over a woman who could cook) Hewetson moved elsewhere. He was a solicitor in private life, and, although he did not talk much of such things, gave the impression of being more fortunate than Borrit in chance relationships. He did admit to some sort of an adventure that had arisen from sunning himself on the roof during a period of convalescence after a bout of flu with one of these sirens of the chimney pots. Another told him she could only achieve emotional intimacy with her own sex, so Hewetson probably knew the roof better than one might think. All the same, he could not get on with Miss Wartstone. She was manageress of the flats. Her outward appearance at once prepared residents for an unusually contentious temperament. Miss Wartstone had, indeed, passed into a middle-age of pathological quarrelsomeness, possibly in part legacy of nervous tensions built up during the earlier years of the blitz. Latterly, nothing worse than an occasional window broken by blast had disturbed the immediate neighbourhood, but, as the war progressed, few tempers remained as steady as at the beginning.

Miss Wartstone used to put up notices, like those at school, and, in the same way, people would draw pictures on them and write comments. '*Disgasting Management*', somebody scrawled, probably one of the Allied officers, of whom quite a fair number were accommodated at the flats. Hewetson himself would go white if Miss Wartstone's name was mentioned.

'That woman,' he would say.

When the Eighth Army moved into Tripoli, Hewetson was offered promotion in a new branch of the Judge-Advocate General's department proliferated in North Africa. As things turned out, this resulted in a change of my own position in the Section. It could be dated, more or less, by the fact that, when Hewetson came down from speaking with Finn about his own departure, Colonel Cobb, one of the American assistant military attachés, was in our room at that moment, talking of the capture of the German generals at Stalingrad. Although the Americans had a mission of their own for the bulk of their business, Cobb used to visit Finn from time to time about a few routine matters. He usually dropped in afterwards for a minute or two, chiefly, I think, to satisfy a personal preoccupation with the British Army and its unexpected ways, an interest by now past the stage of mere desire for professional enlightenment and become fairly obsessive. He would endlessly question people, if opportunity arose, about their corps, Regular or Territorial, its special peculiarities and customs: when raised: where served: what worn. In the banter that sometimes followed these interrogations, Cobb rather enjoyed a touch of grimness, smiling with grave acquiescence when, in the course of one such scrutiny, it was by chance revealed that my own Regiment had borne among the Battle Honours of its Colours the names of Detroit and Miami.

'Ah, Detroit?' he said, speaking as if it had happened yesterday. 'An unfortunate affair that . . . Miami . . . The name reminds me of my great-aunt's grandfather, a man not to be trifled with, held a commission from King George in the West Florida Provincials.'

To his own anecdotes, of which he possessed an impressive store, Cobb brought a dignified tranquillity of manner that might have earned a high fee in Hollywood, had he ever contemplated acting a military career, rather than living one. He narrated them in a low unemphasized mumble, drawing the words and sentences right back into his mouth, recalling certain old-fashioned types of Paris American. Like Finn, though in a totally different genre, Cobb indulged these dramatic aptitudes in himself, which, one suspected, could even motivate a deliberate visit—for example, the day after Pearl Harbour—should he feel an affirmation required to be made in public.

'What's America's next step, Colonel?' someone had asked on that occasion.

Cobb did not answer at once. Instead, he threw himself into a relatively theatrical pose, one of those attitudes, stylized yet unforced, in which he excelled; this time in the character of a man giving deep attention to a problem of desperate complexity. Then he spoke a considered judgment.

'The US Navy are prohibited alcohol,' he said. 'We'll have to call in their golf-clubs, I guess.'

Years later in New York, I repeated that comment to Harrison F. Wisebite's nephew, Milton, met at a publisher's party at the St Regis. Milton Wisebite, who worked in the

Time-Life office at that period, had himself served in Europe with his country's expeditionary force.

'Courthouse Cobb?' he said. 'Haven't thought of him in decades.'

'That was his nickname?'

'Throughout the US Army.'

'What did it mean?'

'There was reference to a supposed predilection towards severity in the exercise of discipline.'

That was a side of Colonel Cobb, imaginable, though happily never imperative to encounter. However, Milton Wisebite's words recalled the stern tone in which Cobb had referred to the capitulation of Paulus on that day, endorsing thereby in memory the progress of the war and the moment when Hewetson left the Section. Finn was unwilling to replace him with an officer lacking any previous experience of liaison work. Accordingly the new man, Slade, a schoolmaster by profession, was given to Pennistone as second-string, and I was ordered to take over the Belgians and Czechs.

As it happened, on that evening at the St Regis, when everyone had had a good deal to drink, Milton Wisebite had gone on to ask news of Pamela Flitton, with whom, so it then appeared, he had enjoyed a brief moment of intimacy at some stage of the war. Apparently the episode had been the high peak of romance in his life, more especially as she was a kind of relation of his. Whatever took place between them—he was not explicit—must have been at an appreciably later period than the other surrender at Stalingrad, but, within the year or less that had passed since she had driven for the Section, Pamela Flitton's name had already become fairly notorious for just that sort of adventure.

The stories, as such stories do, came in gradually. For example, the affair of which Horaczko had hinted, when our ways had parted in the hall of the Titian, was confirmed later by Michalski, less reserved in discussing such matters, who said he thought things had ended by a Polish major being brought before one of their army's Courts of Honour. Even if that were an exaggeration, there was much else going round to suggest it might be true. To mention a few of these items: two RAF officers, one from Bomber, the other from Fighter Command, were court-martialled as a consequence of a fight about which was to drive her home after a party. The Naval Police had separated them, and, although a serious view was not taken by the authorities, the episode had made too much disturbance to be disregarded. The Navy was involved again in the person of a paymaster-lieutenant commander, who for some reason received a severe reprimand on her account. He was reported to be a scatterbrained fellow anyway. More ominously, a relatively senior official in the Treasury, a married man with several children, gave her a lift in his car one night at Richmond station—goodness knows what she was doing there in the first instance—starting a trail of indiscretion that led to his transference to a less distinguished ministry. Barker-Shaw, who had been Field Security Officer at my former Division, now at MI 5, hinted there had nearly been an unofficial strike about her down at the docks. These were only some of the tales one heard. No doubt most of them were greatly inflated in the telling, if not positively untrue, but they indicated her range, even if you discounted ones like pouring the wine on the floor when Howard Craggs, the left-wing publisher, now a temporary civil servant of some standing, had given her dinner at an expensive black market restaurant; even less to be believed that—like Barbara Goring discharging the sugar over Widmerpool—she had emptied the bottle over Craggs's head. The latter version was agreed to be untrustworthy if only because he was known still to pursue her.

Even if these highly coloured anecdotes were to be

73

disbelieved, their very existence indicated a troublesome personality. Myth of such pervasive volume does not suddenly arise about a woman entirely without reason. One thing was certain. She had left the ATS. This was said to be due to bad health, trouble with a lung.

'I never yet met a pretty girl who didn't tell you she had TB,' said Dicky Umfraville. 'Probably the least of the diseases she inherited from Cosmo.'

Umfraville had been unsuccessful in his efforts to find a niche in one of the secret organizations, and was now commanding a transit camp with the rank of major.

'Giving men hell is what Miss Flitton likes,' he said. 'I know the sort. Met plenty of them.'

There was something to be said for accepting that diagnosis, because two discernible features seemed to emerge from a large, often widely diversified, canon of evidence chronicling Pamela Flitton's goings-on: the first, her indifference to the age and status of the men she decided to fascinate: the second, the unvarying technique of silence, followed by violence, with which she persecuted her lovers, or those who hoped to be numbered in that category. She appeared, for example, scarcely at all interested in looks or money, rank or youth, as such; just as happy deranging the modest home life of a middle-aged air-raid warden, as compromising the commission of a rich and handsome Guards ensign recently left school. In fact, she seemed to prefer 'older men' on the whole, possibly because of their potentiality for deeper suffering. Young men might superficially transcend their seniors in this respect, but they probably showed less endurance in sustaining that state, while, once pinioned, the middle-aged could be made to writhe almost indefinitely. In the Section her memory remained with Borrit.

'Wonder what happened to that juicy looking AT,' he said more than once. 'The good-lookers never stay. Wouldn't mind spending a weekend with her.'

'Weekends' took place once a fortnight, most people saving up their weekly one day off to make them up. Once in a way Isobel managed to come to London during the week and we went out for a mild jaunt. This was not often, and, when she rang up one day to say Ted Jeavons had got hold of a couple of bottles of gin and was asking a few people in to share them with him, the invitation presented itself as quite an excitement. After Molly's death, Isobel and her sisters used to keep in closer touch with Jeavons than formerly, making something of a duty to see him at fairly regular intervals, on the grounds that, a widower, he needed more attention than before. I had not seen him myself since suggesting Templer should take a room at the Jeavons' house, but heard Templer had done so. Whether he remained, I did not know. Jeavons, keeping up Molly's tradition of always welcoming any member of the family, had shown surprising resilience in recovering from the unhappy night when he had lost his wife. Certainly he had been greatly upset at the time, but he possessed a kind of innate toughness of spirit that carried him through. Norah Tolland, who did not care for any suggestion of sentimentality that concerned persons of the opposite sex—though she tolerated the loves, hates and regrets of her own exclusively feminine world—insisted that Jeavons's recovery was complete.

'Ted's perfectly capable of looking after himself,' she said. 'In some respects—allowing for the war—the place is better run than when Molly was alive. I get a bit sick of those long disjointed harangues he gives about ARP.'

His duties as an air-raid warden had now become Jeavons's sole interest, the whole background of his life. Apart from his period in the Army during the previous war, he must have worked longer and more continuously at air-raid precautions than at any other job. Jeavons, although to be regarded as not much good at jobs, had here found his vocation. No one knew quite how the money situation would resolve itself when Molly died, Jeavons no longer in his first youth, with this admitted lack of handiness at earning a living. It turned out that Molly, with a forethought her noisy manner concealed, had taken steps to compound for her jointure, a financial reconstruction that had included buying the South Kensington house, thereby insuring (air raids unforeseen in that respect) her husband having a roof over his head, if she predeceased him. Although she was older, that possibility seemed unlikely enough in the light of Jeavons's much propagated 'rotten inside', the stomach wound so perpetually reviled by himself. However, the unlikely had come to pass. Chips Lovell, when alive, had never tired of deploring Sleaford stinginess where their widows were concerned, but at least Jeavons had reaped some residue. One felt he deserved that at his age, though what precisely that age was, no one knew. Fifty must be in the offing, if not already attained.

'Norah's bringing a girl-friend with her,' he said. 'Wonder what she's got hold of this time. The last one had a snub nose and freckles with biggish feet.'

Norah Tolland was a driver in one of the several classifications of women's services, a corps which regarded themselves as of rather more consequence than mere ATS, whose officers they were not required to salute. Norah had taken pleasure in explaining that to a very important ATS officer wearing red tabs who had hauled her up for a supposed omission of respect.

'Sorry your friend Templer's gone, Nick,' said Jeavons. 'We got on pretty well. Used to have long talks at odd moments of the night when we'd both come off duty in the small hours. He told me a thing or two. Stories about the ladies, my hat.'

Jeavons's thick dark hair, with its ridges of corkscrew curls, had now turned quite white, the Charlie Chaplin moustache remaining black. This combination of tones for some reason gave him an oddly Italian appearance, enhanced by blue overalls, obscurely suggesting a railway porter at a station in Italy. Jeavons continued to wear these overalls, though by now promoted to an administrative post at the local ARP headquarters. He poured out glasses of gin-and-orange, a drink for ever to recall world war.

'Why did Templer leave?'

'Been fed up for ages. Wanted a more active job. Quite worried him.'

'He told me all that nearly a year ago.'

'There was a woman in the case. Usually is. That's why he wanted to do something more dangerous. London's quite dangerous enough for me. Templer didn't think so.'

'It sounds unlike him.'

'He went off to some training place,' said Jeavons. 'Never know how people will behave. Look at poor Charles Stringham, missing at Singapore. Remember when he lived on the top floor here with Miss Weedon trying to cure him of the booze. He and I used to have one on the sly once in a way. Mrs Conyers, I should call her, not Miss Weedon. Bad luck her husband dropping dead like that, but in your nineties you must be prepared for accidents.'

General Conyers, also an air-raid warden, had collapsed in the street one night, pursuing looters attempting to steal a refrigerator from a bombed house. He died, as he had lived, in active, dramatic, unusual circumstances; such, one felt, as he himself would have preferred.

'Tuffy, as Charles used to call her, is in MI 5 now,' said Jeavons. 'Don't think she has to get into evening dress and jade ear-rings and vamp German agents. Just supervises the girls there. Always looked as if she knew a lot of secrets. Those black dresses and white collars. I expect they want reliable people, and she's reliable all right. This girl of Templer's made him feel he was getting old. He wanted

77

to find out whether that was true or not. Of course, you might argue he oughtn't to have been playing around at all. You've got to remember the circumstances. Wife's in a mental home, as you probably know. Awful thing to happen. It's hard to keep straight, if you're on your own. I remember Smith, that butler of your brother-in-law Erry's, using those very words. Erry used to lend us Smith from time to time, when he was away from Thrubworth. Of course, Smith's wife had been dead for years, luckily for her. I warrant there'd been some high jinks on Smith's part at one time or another. Terrible chap, Smith. Oughtn't to say it, but I'm really glad he's dead. No chance of his ever working here again.'

'Erry said it was a rather ghastly business when Smith pegged out.'

'Ghastly?' said Jeavons. 'Just about. Didn't you know? He was bitten by Maisky, that monkey Molly used to own. It seems Smith tried to take a biscuit away from that tenacious ape. Probably wanted it himself to mop up some of the gin he'd drunk. God, the way that man used to put back our gin. I marked the bottle, but it wasn't a damn bit of use. Silly thing to do, to take issue with Maisky. Of course Smith came off second-best. Perhaps they both reached out for the biscuit at the same moment. Anyway, Maisky wouldn't have any snatching and Smith contracted septicemia with fatal results. Meant the end of Maisky too, which wasn't really just. But then what is just in this life? Still, I suppose some things are, if you think about them. Smith'll be the last butler I'll ever find myself employing— not that there's likely to be many butlers to employ, the way things are going. That fact doesn't break my heart. Taking them all in all, the tall with the short, the fat with the thin, the drunk with the sober, they're not a profession that greatly appeals to me. Of course, I was brought in contact with butlers late in life. Never set eyes on them in the circles I came from. I may have been unlucky in the butlers I've met. There may be the one in a hundred, but it's a long time to wait. Read about butlers in books—see 'em in plays. That's all right. Have 'em in the house—a very different matter. Look what they do to your clothes, apart from anything else. I started without butlers and I'll die without butlers, no less a happy man. There's the bell. No butler, so I'll answer it myself. Probably some of the pals from my ARP dump.'

He went off down the stairs. After the bomb damage, the house had been shored up to prevent collapse, but no interior renovation had taken place. A long, jagged crack still zigzagged across one of the walls, which were in many places covered with large brown patches, like maps showing physical features, or the rather daring ornamental designs of a modernistic decorator. All the pictures, even the Moroccan pastels, had been removed, as well as the oriental bowls and jars that used to clutter the drawing-room. A snapshot of Molly, wearing a Fair Isle jumper and holding Maisky in her arms like a baby, stood on the mantelpiece, curled and yellowing. Maisky, heedless of mortality, looked infinitely self-satisfied. Jeavons returned, bringing with him several ARP colleagues, male and female.

'Room's not looking very smart for a party,' he said.

A minute or two later Norah Tolland arrived. Her companion—'girl-friend', as Jeavons had termed her—turned out to be Pamela Flitton. Norah was in uniform, which suited her. She was, in general, more settled, more sure of herself than when younger, though on this particular occasion the presence of Pamela seemed to make her both elated and nervous.

'Ted, I felt sure you wouldn't mind my bringing Pam,' she said. 'She's having dinner with me tonight. It seemed so much easier than meeting at the restaurant.'

'Most welcome,' said Jeavons.

79

He looked Pamela over. Jeavons examining a woman's points was always in itself worth observing. If good-looking, he stared at her as if he had never before seen anything of the kind, though at the same time determined not to be carried away by his own astonishment. Pamela justified this attention. She was wearing a neat black frock, an improvement on her battledress blouse. It was clear she had established over Norah an absolute, even if only temporary, domination. Norah's conciliatory manner showed that.

'Have a drink?' said Jeavons.

'What have you got?'

Pamela glanced aggressively round the room, catching my eye, but making no sign of recognition.

'Gin-and-orange.'

'No whisky?'

'Sorry.'

'I'll have gin-and-water—no, neat gin.'

I went across to her.

'Escaped from the ATS?'

'Got invalided.'

'A lady of leisure?'

'My job's a secret one.'

Jeavons took her lightly by the arm and began to introduce her to the other guests. She shook his hand away with her elbow, but allowed him to tell her the names of two or three persons who worked with him. When introductions were over, she picked up a paper from the table—apparently some not very well printed periodical—and took it, with her glass of gin, to the furthest corner of the room. There she sat on a stool, listlessly turning the pages. Norah, talking to Isobel, gave an anxious glance, but did not take any immediate steps to join Pamela, or try to persuade her to be more sociable. A talkative elderly man with a red face, one of the ARP guests, engaged me in conversation. He said he was a retired indigo planter. Jeavons himself went across the room and spoke to Pamela, but he must have received a rebuff, because he returned a second or two later to the main body of the guests.

'She's reading our ARP bulletin,' he said.

He spoke with more surprise than disapproval; in fact almost with admiration.

'Read the poem in this number?' asked the indigo planter. 'Rather good. It begins "What do you carry, Warden dear?" Gives a schedule of the equipment—you know, helmet, gas-mask, First Aid, all that—but leaves out one item. You have to guess. Quite clever.'

'Jolly good.'

Norah, evidently not happy about Pamela, separated herself from Isobel soon after this, and went across to where her friend was sitting. They talked for a moment, but, if Norah too hoped to make her circulate with the rest, she was defeated. When she returned I asked her what her own life was like.

'I was with Gwen McReith's lot for a time. Quite fun, because Gwen herself is amusing. I first met Pam with her, as a matter of fact.'

'Pam seems quite a famous figure.'

Norah sighed.

'I suppose she is now,' she said.

'Is she all right over there in the corner?'

'No good arguing with her.'

'I mean we both of us might go over and talk to her.'

'For God's sake not.'

Nothing of any note took place during the rest of the party, until Norah and Pamela were leaving. Throughout that time, Pamela had continued to sit in the corner. She accepted another drink from Jeavons, but ceased to read the ARP bulletin, simply looking straight in front of her. However, before she and Norah went off together, an unexpected thing happened. She came across the room and spoke in her accustomed low, almost inaudible tone.

'Are you still working with the Poles?'

'No—I've switched to the Belgians and Czechs.'

'When you were with the Poles, did you ever hear the name Szymanski?'

'It's a very common Polish name, but if you mean the man who used to be with the Free French, and caused endless trouble, then transferred to the Poles, and caused endless trouble there, I know quite a lot about him.'

She laughed.

'I just wondered,' she said.

'What about him?'

'Oh, nothing.'

'Was he the character you were talking to outside that Polish hide-out in Bayswater?'

She shook her head, laughing softly again. Then they went away. The ARP people left too.

'There's enough for one more drink for the three of us,' said Jeavons. 'I hid the last few drops.'

'What do you think of Pamela Flitton?'

'That's the wench that gave Peter Templer such a time,' said Jeavons. 'Couldn't remember the name. It's come back. He said it all started as a joke. Then he got mad about her. That was the way Templer put it. What he didn't like—when she wasn't having any, as I understand it—was the feeling he was no good any more. How I feel all the time. Nothing much you can do about it. Mind you, he was browned off with the job too.'

'Do men really try to get dangerous jobs because they've been disappointed about a woman?'

'Well, I don't,' Jeavons admitted.

The enquiry about Szymanski was odd, even if he were not the Pole outside the Ufford. Neither Pennistone nor I had ever set eyes on this man, though we had been involved in troubles about him, including a question asked in Parliament. There was some uncertainty as to his nationality, even whether the territory where he was stated to have been born was now Polish or Czechoslovak, assuming he had in truth been born there. Most of his life he had lived on his wits as a professional gambler—like Cosmo Flitton—so it appeared, familiar as a dubious character in France, Belgium and the Balkans; in fact all over the place. He had a row of aliases: Kubitsa: Brod: Groza: Dupont: to mention only a few of them. No one—even MI 5 was vague—seemed to know when and how he had first appeared in this country, but at an early stage he was known to have volunteered for the Belgian forces. This offer was prudently declined. Szymanski then tried the Free French, who, with the self-confidence of their race, took him on the strength; later ceding him with relief to the Poles, who may have wanted to make use of him in some special capacity. The general opinion was that he had a reasonable claim to Polish citizenship. The Czechs raised no objection. There were those who insisted his origins were really Balkan.

'It seems fairly clear he's not Norwegian,' said Pennistone, 'but I've learnt to take nothing on trust about Szymanski. You may have him on your hands before we've finished, Dempster.'

Szymanski was one of those professional scourges of authority that appear sporadically in all armies, a type to which the Allied contingents were peculiarly subject owing to the nature of their composition and recruitment. Like Sayce of my former Battalion, Szymanski was always making trouble, but Sayce magnified to a phantasmagoric degree, a kind of super-Sayce of infinitely greater intelligence and disruptive potential. The abiding fear of the Home Office was that individuals of this sort might, after being found stateless, be discharged

83

from the armed forces and have to be coped with as alien civilians.

As it happened, Szymanski's name cropped up again a day or two later in our room. Masham, who was with the British Mission in liaison with the Free French, was waiting to be summoned by Finn, to whom he was to communicate certain points arising out of Giraud taking over from Darlan in North Africa. Masham asked Pennistone how the Poles were getting on with Szymanski, who had caused a lot of trouble to himself in his Free French days.

'Szymanski's gone a bit too far this time,' Pennistone said. 'They've sent him to detention. It was bound to come.'

There was a barracks, under the control of a British commandant, specially to accommodate delinquent Allied personnel.

I asked how recently that had happened.

'A week or so ago.'

'I'm not surprised,' said Masham. 'Though one's got to admit the man was rather a card. It looks as if this North African switch-over will mean a back place for de Gaulle.'

'Has anyone else hanged himself in his braces in that Free French snuggery behind Selfridge's?' asked Borrit.

'Nobody hanged himself in his braces there or in any other Free French establishment,' said Masham, rather irritably. 'You've got the story wrong.'

Like all his Mission, Masham was, as he himself would have expressed it, *plus catholique que le Pape*, far more Francophil than the Free French themselves, who on the whole rather enjoyed a good laugh at less reputable aspects of their own corporate body. When in due course I had direct dealings with them myself, they were always telling stories about some guerrilla of theirs who divided his time between being parachuted into France to make contact with

84

the Resistance, and returning to London to run a couple of girls on Shaftesbury Avenue.

'What did happen then?'

'There was some fuss about an interrogation.'

'De Gaulle was pretty cross when our people enquired about it.'

'He's got to run his own show, hasn't he?' said Masham. 'Anyway, it looks as if he's on the way out. By the way, Jenkins, the successful candidate for the job you applied to us for caught it at Bir Hakim.'

Kucherman rang up at that moment, and, by the time I had finished with Belgian business, Masham had gone up to see Finn. Transfer to the Belgians and Czechs meant no more physically than ceasing to sit next to Pennistone, though it vitiated a strong alliance in resisting Blackhead. The two Allied contingents with which I was now in liaison were, of course, even in their aggregate, much smaller numerically than the Polish Corps. At first sight, in spite of certain advantages in being one's own master, responsible only to Finn, a loss in other directions seemed threatened by diminution of variety in the general field of activity. A claustrophobic existence offered, in this respect, the consolation of exceptional opportunities for observing people and situations closely in a particular aspect of war. Our Section's viewpoint was no doubt less all embracing than, say, Widmerpool's in his subterranean lair; at the same time could provide keener, more individual savour of things noted at first-hand.

It had been stimulating, for example, to watch the quickly gathering momentum of the apparatus—infinitesimally propelled, among others, by oneself—that reduced to some order the circumstances of the hundred and fifteen thousand Poles permitted to cross the Russian frontier into Iran; assisting, as it were, Pennistone's 'one man and a boy' at the receiving end. Hundreds of thousands were left behind, of course, while those who got out were in poorish shape. All the same, these were the elements to form the Second Polish Army Corps; later so creditably concerned at Monte Cassino and elsewhere. Regarded superficially, the new Belgian and Czech assignments seemed to offer problems less obviously engrossing. However, as matters turned out, plenty of channels for fresh experience were provided by these two. Even the earliest meetings with Major Kucherman and Colonel Hlava promised that.

Precise in manner, serious about detail, Hewetson was judged to perform his duties pretty well, though he possessed no particular qualifications as expert on Belgian affairs, still less those of Czechoslovakia. Before I took over from him, he gave me a briefing about the characteristics of the Allies in question.

'An excellent point about the Belgians,' he said, 'is not caring in the least what they say about each other, or their own national failings. They have none of that painful wish to make a good impression typical of some small nations. It's a great relief. At the same time their standards in certain respects—food and drink, for example—are high ones. They are essentially easy to get on with. Do not believe disobliging propaganda, chiefly French, about them. They are not, it must be admitted, indifferent to social distinction. Their assistant MA, Gauthier de Graef, likes telling a story, no doubt dating from the last war, of an English officer, French officer, and Belgian officer, when a woman rode by on a horse. The Englishman said: "What a fine horse"; the Frenchman, "What a fine woman": the Belgian, "I wonder what she was née". Of course I don't suggest that would happen today.'

'One can't make the classless society retroactive.'

'Another saying of Gauthier's is that when he wakes up in the night in a wagon-lit and hears a frightful row going on in the next compartment, he knows he's back in his own

beloved country—though I must say I haven't been subjected to the smallest ill-humour myself on the part of my
Belgian charges.'

'They sound all right.'

'One small snag—Lannoo was given promotion the
other day, and has already left for his new job. The Belgian
authorities still won't make up their minds whom to
appoint in his place. I've been dealing with Gauthier de
Graef for weeks, who of course can't take the decisions his
boss could. I suppose this delay is the sort of thing the
Belgians themselves grumble about.'

As it turned out, the official appointment of Kucherman
came through only on the day when Hewetson left the
Section. There was some misunderstanding about certain
customary formalities, one of those departmental awkward-
nesses that take place from time to time and can cause
coolness. The fact was Kucherman himself was a figure of
much more standing at home than the average officer likely
to be found in that post. Possibly some of the Belgian
Government thought this fact might overweight the job;
others, that more experience was desirable in purely military
matters. At least that was the explanation given to Hewetson when things were in the air. As he had said, a particular charm possessed by the Belgians was, in a world everyday increasingly cautious about hazarding in public opinions about public affairs, no Belgian minded in the least
criticizing his Government, individually or collectively.

'One of their best points,' Hewetson repeated.

In short, by the time I introduced myself to Kucherman,
a faint sense of embarrassment had been infused into the
atmosphere by interchanges at a much higher level than
Finn's. Kucherman was only a major, because the
Belgians were rather justly proud of keeping their ranks
low.

'After all the heavy weather that's been made, you'll

have to be careful not to get off on the wrong foot, Nicholas,' said Finn. 'Kucherman's own people may have been to blame for some of that, but we've been rather stiff and unaccommodating ourselves. You'll have to step carefully. Kucherman's a well known international figure.'

I repeated these remarks of Finn's to Pennistone.

'Kucherman's a big shot all right,' said Pennistone. 'I used to hear a lot about him and his products when I was still in business. He's head of probably the largest textile firm. That's just one of his concerns. He's also a coal owner on an extensive scale, not to mention important interests in the Far East—if they still survive. We shall expect your manner to alter after a week or two of putting through deals with Kucherman.'

The picture was a shade disconcerting. One imagined a figure, younger perhaps, but somewhat on the lines of Sir Magnus Donners: tall: schoolmasterish: enigmatic. As it turned out, Kucherman's exterior was quite different from that. Of medium height, neat, brisk, with a high forehead and grey hair, he seemed to belong to the eighteenth-century, the latter half, as if he were wearing a wig of the period tied behind with a black bow. This, I found later, was one of the Belgian physical types, rather an unexpected one, even in a nation rich in physiognomies recalling the past.

On the whole, a march-past of Belgian troops summoned up the Middle Ages or the Renaissance, emaciated, Memling-like men-at-arms on their way to supervise the Crucifixion or some lesser martyrdom, while beside them tramped the clowns of Teniers or Brouwer, round rubicund countenances, haled away from carousing to be mustered in the ranks. These latter types were even more to be associated with the Netherlands contingent—obviously a hard and fast line was not to be drawn between these Low Country peoples—Colonel Van der Voort himself an almost perfect example. Van der Voort's features seemed to have parted company completely from Walloon admixtures—if, indeed, it was Walloon blood that produced those mediaeval faces. Van der Voort's air had something faintly classical about it too, something belonging not entirely to domestic pot-house or kermesse scenes, a touch of the figures in the train of Bacchus or Silenus; though naturally conceived in Dutch or Flemish terms. Kucherman's high forehead and regular features—the French *abbé* style—was in contrast with all that, a less common, though a fairly consistent Belgian variant that gave the impression, on such occasions as the parade on their National Day, of the sudden influence of a later school of painting.

The first day at Eaton Square—by then almost a preserve of the Belgian ministries—the name of Sir Magnus Donners did indeed crop up. He had been in the headlines that morning on account of some more or less controversial statement made in public on the subject of manpower. Kucherman referred to this item of news, mentioning at the same time that he had once lunched at Stourwater. We talked about the castle. I asked if, since arrival in England, he had seen Sir Magnus. Kucherman laughed.

'A member of your Cabinet does not want to be bothered by a major in one of the smaller Allied contingents.'

'All the same, it might be worth while letting him know you are here.'

'You think so?'

'Sure of it.'

'Certainly he showed great interest in Belgium when we met—knowledge of Belgian affairs. You know Belgium yourself?'

'I've been there once or twice. When my father was at the War Office, I remember him bringing two Belgian officers to our house. It was a great excitement.'

'Your father was *officier de carrière*?'

'He'd come back from Paris, where he'd been on the staff of the Peace Conference. By the way, several Belgian officers are living at the same block of flats as myself. I don't know any of them.'

Kucherman asked the name of the place.

'Ah, yes,' he said. 'Clanwaert is there. You will be dealing with him about Congo matters. An amusing fellow.'

'I have an appointment with him tomorrow.'

'He was formerly in the Premier Régiment des Guides— like your Life Guards, one might say. I believe he fought his first engagement in 1914 wearing what was almost their parade uniform—green tunic, red breeches, all that. Then a love affair went wrong. He transferred to La Force Publique. A dashing fellow with a romantic outlook. That was why he never married.'

The Force Publique was the Congo army, quite separate from the Belgian army, officered somewhat on the lines, so it seemed, of our own Honourable East India Company's troops in the past.

'Kucherman's going to be all right,' said Finn.

Even Gauthier de Graef, who had all his countrymen's impatience with other people's methods, and would not have hesitated to grumble about his new chief, agreed with that judgment. He was a tall young man with a large moustache, who, after a frantic drive to the coast to catch up the remnant of the Belgian forces embarked for England, had jumped the last yard or so over water, as the boat had already set sail from harbour.

'I needed a drink after that,' he said. 'A long one, let me assure you.'

I was just off to see Kucherman or Hlava one morning, when General Bobrowski was put through on my telephone. Bobrowski, even for himself, was in a tremendous state of excitement. He explained that he had been unable to make contact with Finn, and now he was told that neither Pennistone nor Slade were available. It was a matter of the most urgent importance that he had an appointment with Finn as soon as possible. He appealed to me as Pennistone's former assistant in Polish liaison. Finn was at that moment with one of the brigadiers; Pennistone probably at the Titian—where it was quite likely he would learn of whatever was on Bobrowski's mind—and Slade was no doubt somewhere in the building negotiating with another section. Slade returned at that moment and I handed Bobrowski over to him. I wondered what the trouble was. Bobrowski became easily excited, but this seemed exceptional. Pennistone outlined the enormity on my return.

'Listen to this,' he said. 'Tell me whether you believe it or not.'

He was partly angry himself, partly unable not to laugh.

'Let's go and have lunch. I'll tell you there.'

The story was certainly a strange one.

'Szymanski's out,' said Pennistone.

'Out of where?'

'Jug.'

'He's escaped from the detention barracks?'

'In a rather unusual way.'

'Did he break out?'

'He left by the front door.'

'In disguise?'

'It appears that first of all a certain amount of telephoning took place from the appropriate branches, Polish and British, saying that Szymanski's conviction had been quashed and his case was to be reconsidered. Then two British officers arrived bearing the correct papers to obtain his body. Szymanski was accordingly handed over to their custody.'

'This was bogus?'

'The next thing was, Szymanski himself appeared shortly after at the prison, wearing the uniform of a British second-lieutenant and explaining that he knew the way to get out of anywhere. In fact, the prison hasn't been invented that could keep him inside.'

'Didn't they lock him up again?'

'They couldn't. The documents made him a free man.'

'What had happened?'

'There were those who thought Szymanski's outstanding qualities—not necessarily his most gentlemanly ones—might come in useful for a piece of work required.'

'You mean some of our people?'

'Possibly certain Polish elements were also sympathetic to the scheme. That's not clear yet. It would have been easier to organize, had that been the case. However, one can't be sure. Another country may be in on it too.'

'Was this Sunny Farebrother's crowd?'

'It looks like it.'

'With forged papers?'

'Yes.'

'Won't there be the hell of a row?'

'There will—and is. As liaison officer with the Poles, naturally I can only regard the whole affair as perfectly disgraceful. At the same time, one can't help seeing it has its funny side.'

'Finn must be having a fit.'

'He's beside himself.'

'Is Sunny personally involved?'

'So it's believed—though he did not turn up himself at the prison gates.'

'Is it known who did?'

'One of them was called Stevens. I believe rather a tough nut, quite young, with an MC. He's said to have been wounded in the Middle East, and came back to join Farebrother's show.'

'Odo Stevens?'

'I don't know his first name.'

'Will they re-arrest Szymanski?'

'How can they? He's been disposed of abroad probably. Anyway undergoing training at some secret place.'

'He'll be dropped somewhere?'

'To do something pretty unpleasant, I should imagine.'

'And the Poles are angry?'

'Our ones are livid. Can you blame them? I've never seen Bobrowski in such a state. It's understandable. At one end of the scale, our authorities make a great parade of the letter of the Law. The Home Office, if it possibly can, displays its high-mindedness in hampering the smaller Allies from arresting their deserters—they'd be much too afraid to obstruct the Americans or Russians—then a thing like this happens. All we can do is to grin feebly, and say we hope no offence will be taken.'

Although this incident had its being in the half-light encompassing those under-the-counter activities from which Finn liked to keep his Section so rigorously apart, Finn himself, not to mention Pennistone, had to suffer most of the consequences of what had taken place, so far as the Polish authorities were concerned. They were not at all pleased, saying, not without reason, that a serious blow had been struck against discipline. The episode strongly suggested that the British, when it suited them, could carry disregard of all convention to inordinate lengths; indulge in what might be described as forms of military bohemianism of the most raffish sort. Finn was, of course, entirely on the Polish side in thinking that. It was hard that he himself should have to bear most of the brunt of their complaint. The undertaking was no less remarkable in that Farebrother, outwardly so conventional, was prepared to lend himself to such a plot. It was just another view as to how the war should be won; perhaps the right one.

'A great illusion is that government is carried on by an infallible, incorruptible machine,' Pennistone said. 'Officials

—all officials, of all governments—are just as capable of behaving in an irregular manner as anyone else. In fact they have the additional advantage of being able to assuage their conscience, if they happen to own one, by assuring themselves it's all for the country's good.'

I wondered if Pamela Flitton had known these monkey-tricks were on the way, when she had enquired about Szymanski. Her own exploits continued to be talked about. Clanwaert was the next Ally to mention her. That was a month or two later. We met one evening on the way back to the block of flats. Outwardly, Clanwaert suppressed any indication of the romanticism at which Kucherman had hinted. He had a moustache even larger than Gauthier de Graef's, and an enormous nose to which it seemed attached, as if both were false. The nose was a different shape from Finn's, making one think more of Cyrano de Bergerac. Clanwaert used to tap it, in the old-fashioned traditional gesture, when he knew the answer to some question. Like Kucherman, he talked excellent English, though with a thicker, more guttural accent, a habit of spitting all his words out making most of his remarks sound ironic. Perhaps that was intended. I asked if it were true he had fought his first battle in red breeches.

'Not *red*, my friend—this is important—*amaranthe*. How do you say that in English?'

'Just the same—amaranth.'

'That's the name of a colour?'

'An English writer named St John Clarke called one of his books *Fields of Amaranth*. It was a novel. The flower is supposed to be unfading in legend. The other name for it in English is Love-lies-bleeding. Much play was made about these two meanings in the story.'

'Love-lies-bleeding? That's a strange name. Too good for a pair of breeches.'

'Not if they were unfading.'

94

'Nothing's unfading, my friend,' said Clanwaert. 'Nothing in Brussels, at least.'

'I've enjoyed visits there before the war.'

'It was a different city after '14–'18. Most places were. That was why I transferred to la Force Publique. I can assure you the Congo was a change from la Porte Louise. For a long time, if you believe me, I was Elephant Officer. Something to hold the attention. I would not mind going back there at the termination of this war. Indeed, one may have no choice—be lucky if one reaches Africa. Nevertheless, there are times when the Blacks get on one's nerves. One must admit that. Perhaps only because they look at the world in a different manner from us—maybe a wiser one. I shall be writing you another letter about those officers in the Congo who want a share in this war of ours. As I told you before, they feel out of it, afraid of people saying afterwards—"As for you, gentlemen, you were safe in the Congo." It is understandable. All the same your High Command say they cannot see their way to employ these Congo officers. I understand that too, but I shall be writing you many letters on the subject. You must forgive me. By the way, I met a young lady last night who told me she knew you.'

'Who was that?'

'Mademoiselle Flitton.'

'How was she?'

Clanwaert laughed, evidently aware of the impression the name would make.

'She told me to remind you of the Pole she mentioned when you last met.'

'She did?'

'That was some joke?'

'Some people thought so. I hope Mademoiselle Flitton is in good Belgian hands now.'

'I think she has higher aspirations than that.'

Clanwaert laughed, but revealed no secrets. As it turned out, the implications of the words were clarified through the agency of the Czechs.

'Colonel Hlava is an excellent man.' Hewetson had said. 'More ease of manner than most of his countrymen, some of whom like to emphasise their absolute freedom, as a nation, from the insincere artificialities of social convention. Makes them a bit dour at times. Personally, I find it oils the wheels when there's a drop of Slovak, Hungarian or Jewish blood. Not so deadly serious.'

'Hlava's a flying ace?'

'With innumerable medals for gallantry in the last war—where he served against the Russians, whom he's now very pro—not to mention international awards as a test pilot. He is also rather keen on music, which I know nothing about. For example, he asked me the other day if I didn't get rather tired of Egyptian music. As I'm almost tone deaf, I'd no idea Egypt was in the forefront as a musical country.'

'Tzigane—gipsy.'

'I thought he meant belly-dancing,' said Hewetson. 'By the way, when you're dealing with two Allies at once, it's wiser never to mention one to the other. They can't bear the thought of your being unfaithful to them.'

It was at one of Colonel Hlava's musical occasions that the scene took place which showed what Clanwaert had been talking about. This was at a performance of *The Bartered Bride* mounted by the Czechoslovak civil authorities in the interests of some national cause. I was not familiar with the opera, but remembered Maclintick and Gossage having a music critics' argument about Smetana at Mrs Foxe's party for Moreland's symphony. No recollection remained of the motif of their dispute, though no doubt, like all musical differences of opinion, feelings had been bitter when aroused. I was invited, with Isobel, to attend *The Bartered Bride* in a more or less official capacity. We sat with Colonel Hlava, his staff and their wives.

'The heroine is not really a bride, but a fiancée,' explained Hlava. 'The English title being not literal for German *Die Verkaufte Braut.*'

In most respects very different from Kucherman, the Czech colonel possessed the same eighteenth-century appearance. Perhaps it would be truer to say Hlava recalled the nineteenth century, because there was a look of Liszt about his head and thick white hair, together with a certain subdued air of belonging to the Romantic Movement. This physical appearance was possibly due to a drop of Hungarian blood—one of the allegedly lubricating elements mentioned by Hewetson—though Hlava himself claimed entirely Bohemian or Moravian origins. Quiet, almost apologetic in manner, he was also capable of firmness. His appointment dated back to before the war, and, during the uncertainties of the immediately post-Munich period, he had armed his staff, in case an effort was made to take over the military attaché's office by elements that might have British recognition, but were regarded by himself as traitorous. Hlava liked a mild joke and was incomparably easy to work with.

'Smetana's father made beer,' he said. 'Father wanted son to make beer too, but Smetana instead make Czechoslovak national music.'

These wartime social functions had to take place for a variety of reasons: to give employment: raise money: boost morale. They were rarely very enjoyable. Objection was sometimes aimed at them on the grounds that they made people forget the war. Had such oblivion been attainable, they would, indeed, have provided a desirable form of recuperation. In fact, they often risked additionally emphasizing contemporary conditions, the pursuits of peace, especially the arts, elbowed out of life, being hard to re-establish at short notice. Conversations, on such occasions as this opera, were apt to hover round semi-political or semi-official matters, rather than break away into some aesthetic release.

'Your other great national composer is, of course, Dvořák.'

'Dvořák poor man like Smetana. Dvořák's father poor pork butcher.'

'But a musical pork butcher?'

'Played the bagpipes in the mountains,' said Hlava. 'Like in Scotland.'

Most of the theatre was occupied with Allied military or civil elements, members of the Diplomatic Corps and people with some stake in Czech organizations. In one of the boxes, Prince Theodoric sat with the Huntercombes and a grey-haired lady with a distinguished air, probably one of his household, a countrywoman in exile. Lord Huntercombe, now getting on in age, was shown in the programme as on the board staging this performance. He was closely connected with many Allied causes and charities, and looked as shrewd as ever. He and Theodoric were wearing dark suits, the grey-haired lady in black—by this stage of the war not much seen—beside Lady Huntercombe, in rather a different role from that implied by her pre-war Gainsborough hats, was formidable in Red Cross commandant's uniform.

'Who's the big man with the white moustache three rows in front?' asked Isobel.

'General van Strydonck de Burkel, Inspector-General of the Belgian Army and Air Force—rather a figure.'

The overture began. The curtain had already gone up on the scene of the country fair, when a woman came through one of the doors of the auditorium, paused and looked about her for a moment, then, showing no sign of being embarrassed by her own lateness, made her way to an empty seat beside another woman, in the same row as General van Strydonck, but nearer the middle. In doing this she caused a good deal of disturbance. Several men stood up to let her get by, among them Widmerpool, whom I had not before noticed. It was surprising to see him at a show like this, as he was likely to be working late every night at his particular job. When the lights went on again, he was revealed as being in the company of a youngish major-general. Our party went out during the entr'acte.

'How unpunctual Miss Flitton is,' said Isobel.

Pamela Flitton came into the foyer at that moment. She was wearing a bright scarlet coat and skirt, and accompanied by a woman in uniform, Lady McReith, someone I had not seen for the best part of twenty years.

'She must have blown every coupon she's got on that outfit.'

'Or taken them off some poor chap who received a special issue for overseas.'

Apart from hair now iron-grey, very carefully set, Lady McReith remained remarkably unaltered. She was thinner than ever, almost a skeleton, the blue veins more darkly shaded in on her marble skin. She retained her enigmatic air, that disconcerting half-smile that seemed to be laughing at everyone, although at this moment she did not look in the best of humours. Probably she had paid for Pamela's ticket and was cross at her lateness. If Lady McReith were at the head of a detachment of drivers, she would know about discipline. However, annoyance showed only in her eyes, while she and Pamela stood in a corner watching the crowd. Widmerpool and his general, who was of unknown identity, were behaving as if something important was brewing between them, strolling up and down in a pre-occupied manner like men talking serious business, rather than a couple of opera-lovers having a night off duty. On the way back to our seats, we found ourselves next to them in the aisle. Widmerpool, who had met Isobel in the past, peered closely to make sure I was out with my wife, and said good evening. Then he muttered a question under his breath.

'Do you happen to know the name of the girl in red who came in late? I've seen her before. With some Americans at one of Biddle's big Allied gatherings.'

'Pamela Flitton.'

'So that's Pamela Flitton?'

'She's a niece of Charles Stringham's. You heard he was at Singapore when the Japs moved in?'

'Yes, yes, poor fellow,' said Widmerpool.

He made no reference to the fact that he had been in some measure responsible for sending Stringham there, indeed, there was no time to do so before he went back to his seat. During the second entr'acte he did not appear, possibly having left the theatre with his companion. The Huntercombes, who had remained in their box on this earlier opportunity for the audience to stretch its legs, now entered the foyer with Theodoric and the foreign lady. Theodoric, always very conscious of the social demands imposed by royal rank, began to look about him for people to whom it was a requirement to make himself agreeable. No doubt feeling the disfavour Czechs, in principle, affected for persons of high degree had first claim on his good manners, he came over to shake hands with Hlava's party.

'How is Colonel Finn? Busy as ever?'

'More than ever, sir.'

'I try not to waste his time with our small problems, but I may have to ask for an interview next week.'

I gave a reassuring reply. Theodoric left the Hlava group, crossing the floor for a word with Van Strydonck de Burkel. Huge, with a white curled moustache, the Belgian general, though now rather old to take an active part in the direction of policy, looked everything he should from his picturesque reputation. In the earlier war, at the head of two squadrons of cavalry, he had led an operationally successful charge against a German machine-gun emplacement; a kind of apotheosis of those last relics of horsed warfare represented by Horaczko and Clanwaert. Having spoken a word or two to Van Strydonck, the Prince was on his way to another sector of the foyer, when Pamela Flitton suddenly detached herself from Lady McReith, and moved swiftly through the crowd. On reaching Theodoric, she slipped her arm through his.

'Don't miss Lola Montez,' said Isobel.

Considering the familiarity of the behaviour, its contrast with Pamela's usually icy demeanour, Theodoric accepted the gesture with composure. If he felt whatever intimacy might exist between them were better left unadvertised in a theatre packed with official personages, he did not encourage gossip by showing any sign of that. On the contrary, he took her hand, pressed it earnestly, as if they scarcely knew each other but he wished to show himself specially grateful for some thoughtful action that had gratified his sense of what was right. Then, having spoken a few words to her, he gave a smile of dismissal, and turned towards General Asbjørnsen who was standing nearby. Pamela was at first not prepared to accept this disengaging movement on the part of the Prince, or at any rate preferred to demonstrate that it was for her rather than Theodoric himself to decide when and how the conversation should be terminated. Accordingly, she constituted herself part of the Theodoric-Asbjørnsen axis for a minute or two; then, giving in her turn a nod to Theodoric, at the same time patting his arm, she coolly returned to Lady McReith, who now made no effort to look anything but cross. The bell sounded. We sat down to the Third Act and the man disguised as a bear.

'British gave Smetana musical degree,' said Hlava.

The Bartered Bride was the only occasion, a unique one,

so far as I know, that added any colour to the rumour going round that Pamela Flitton was 'having an affair' with Prince Theodoric. Whether that were true, or whether she merely hoped to create an impression it was true, was never to my knowledge finally cleared up. All that can be said is that later circumstances supplied an odd twist to the possibility. When, subsequently, Jeavons heard the story, he showed interest.

'Sad Molly's gone,' he said. 'She always liked hearing about Theodoric, on account of his having been mixed up years ago with her ex-sister-in-law, Bijou. Looks as if Theodoric falls for an English girl every dozen years or so. Well, his wife's in America and I told you what Smith said, Can't be too cheerful having your country occupied by the Germans either. By all accounts, he's doing what he can to help us get them out. Needs some relaxation. We all do.'

About this time, Jumbo Wilson, in the light-hearted manner of generals, made nonsense of the polite letters Clanwaert and I used to send each other on the subject of the Congo army, by delivering a speech in honour of a visiting Belgian ex-Prime Minister to the effect that the services of La Force Publique would come in very useful in the Middle East. The words were scarcely out of his mouth when they set off with all their vehicles to the field of operation, arriving there very reasonably intact, and, I suppose, justifying Jumbo Wilson's oratory. However, if Clanwaert and I were thereby given something to laugh about, plenty of horrible matters were abroad too.

An announcement was made on the German radio, stating that at a place called Katyn, near the Russian town of Smolensk, an accumulation of communal graves had been found by advancing German troops. These graves were filled with corpses wearing Polish uniform. There were several thousands of bodies. The source of this information was naturally suspect, but, if in any degree to be believed, offered one solution to the mysterious disappearance of the untraced ten or fifteen thousand Polish officers, made prisoners of war by the Soviet army in 1939. 'Rather a large deficiency', as Q (Ops.) Colonel had remarked. The broadcast stated that individual bodies could be identified by papers carried on them, in some cases a tunic still bearing the actual insignia of a decoration, a practice of the Polish army in the case of operational awards. The hands had been tied together and a shot placed in the base of the skull. As a consequence of this radio announcement, the Polish Government in London approached the International Red Cross with a view to instituting an investigation. Exception was at once taken to this step by the USSR, relations with the Polish Government being immediately severed.

'The show-down has come,' said Pennistone.

The day this news was released, I went upstairs to see Finn about a rather complicated minute (to be signed by one of the Brigadiers) on the subject of redundant Czech army doctors being made available for seconding to the Royal Army Medical Corps. There had been difficulty about drafting satisfactory guarantees to make sure the Czechs, should they so require, would be able to recover the services of their MOs. Finn was in one of his unapproachable moods. The Russo-Polish situation had thoroughly upset him.

'It's a bad business,' he kept repeating. 'A bad business. I've got Bobrowski coming to see me this afternoon. What the hell am I to say?'

I tried to get the subject round to Czech medical matters and the views of the RAMC brasshats, but he told me to bring the matter up again that afternoon.

'You've got to go over to the Cabinet Offices now,' he said. 'They've just rung through. Some Belgian papers they want us to see. Something about the King. Nothing of any great importance, I think, but graded "hand of officer", and to be read by those in direct contact with the Belgians.'

The position of the King of the Belgians was delicate. Formally accepted as monarch of their country by the Belgian Government in exile, the royal portrait hanging in Kucherman's office, King Leopold, rightly or wrongly, was not, officially speaking, very well looked on by ourselves. His circumstances had been made no easier by a second marriage disapproved by many of his subjects.

'Have a look at this Belgian file before you bring it up,' said Finn. 'Do a note on it. Then we can discuss it after we've settled the Czech medicos. God, this Polish business.'

I went across to the Ministry of Defence right away. Finn had given the name of a lieutenant-colonel from whom the papers were to be acquired. After some search in the Secretariat, this officer was eventually traced in Widmerpool's room. I arrived there a few minutes before one o'clock, and the morning meeting had begun to adjourn. If they were the same committee as that I had once myself attended, the individual members had all changed, though no doubt they represented the same ministries. The only one known to me was a figure remembered from early London days, Tompsitt, a Foreign Office protégé of Sir Gavin Walpole-Wilson's. Sir Gavin himself had died the previous year. Obituaries, inevitably short in wartime, had none of them mentioned the South American misjudgment that had lead to his retirement. His hopes in Tompsitt, untidy as ever and no less pleased with himself, seemed to have been realized, this job being presumably a respectable one for his age, if not particularly glamorous. Widmerpool, again in a good humour, made a facetious gesture of surprise on seeing me.

'Nicholas? Good gracious me. What is it you want, do you say? Belgian papers? Do you know anything about this, Simon? You do? Then we must let him have them.'

Someone was sent to find the papers.

'We finished early this morning,' said Widmerpool. 'An unheard of thing for us to do. I'm going to allow myself the luxury of lunching outside this building for once. So you're looking after the Belgians now, are you, Nicholas? I thought it was the Poles.'

'I've moved over.'

'You must be glad.'

'There were interesting sides.'

'Just at this moment, I mean. You are well out of the Poles. They are rocking the boat in the most deplorable manner. Our own relations with the USSR are never exactly easy—then for the Poles to behave as they have done.'

The attention of the other civilian, who, with Tompsitt, had been attending the meeting, was caught by Widmerpool's reproachful tone. He looked a rather younger version of our former housemaster, le Bas, distinctly clerical, a thin severe overworked curate or schoolmaster.

'One would really have thought someone at the top of the Polish set-up would have grasped this is not the time to make trouble,' he said. 'Your people must be pretty fed up, aren't they, Tompy?'

Tompsitt shook back his unbrushed hair.

'Fed to the teeth,' he said. 'Probably put everything back to scratch.'

'All the same,' said the sailor, 'it looks a bit as if the Russkis did it.'

He was a heavily built man, with that totally anonymous personality achieved by certain naval officers, sometimes concealing unexpected abilities.

'Not to be ruled out,' said Tompsitt.

'More information's required.'

'Doesn't make it any better to fuss at this moment,' said the curate-schoolmaster.

He stared angrily through his spectacles, his cheeks contorted. The soldier, youngish with a slight stutter, who looked like a Regular, shook his papers together and put them into a briefcase.

'It's quite a crowd,' he said.

'What are the actual figures?' asked the sailor.

'Been put as high as nine or ten thousand,' said the airman.

He was a solid-looking middle-aged man with a lot of decorations, who had not spoken until then.

'How would that compare with our own pre-war army establishment?' asked the sailor. 'Let me see, about . . .'

'Say every third officer,' said the soldier. 'Quite a crowd, as I remarked. Say every third officer in our pre-war army.'

'But it's not pre-war,' said Tompsitt. 'It's war.'

'That's the point,' said Widmerpool. 'It's war. Just because these deaths are very upsetting to the Poles themselves—naturally enough, harrowing, tragic, there isn't a word for it, I don't want to underrate that for a moment—but just because of that, it's no reason to undermine the fabric of our alliances against the Axis. Quarrels among the Allies themselves are not going to defeat the enemy.'

'Even so, you can't exactly blame them for making enquiries through the International Red Cross,' the soldier insisted.

He began to move towards the door.

'But I do blame them,' said Tompsitt. 'I blame them a great deal. Their people did not act at all circumspectly. The Russians were bound to behave as they did under the circumstances.'

'Certainly hard to see what explanation they could give, if they did do it,' said the airman. '"Look here, old boy, we've shot these fellows of yours by accident" . . . Of course, it may turn out the Germans did it after all. They're perfectly capable of it.'

Everyone agreed that fact was undeniable.

'There's quite a chance the Germans did,' said the curate-schoolmaster hopefully.

'In any case,' said Widmerpool, 'whatever materializes, even if it does transpire—which I sincerely trust it will not—that the Russians behaved in such a very regrettable manner, how can this country possibly raise official objection, in the interests of a few thousand Polish exiles, who, however worthy their cause, cannot properly handle their diplomatic relations, even with fellow Slavs. It must be confessed also that the Poles themselves are in a position to offer only a very modest contribution, when it comes to the question of manpower. How, as I say, can we approach our second most powerful Ally about something which, if a fact, cannot be put right, and is almost certainly, from what one knows of them, the consequence of administrative inadequacy, rather than wilful indifference to human life and the dictates of compassion? What we have to do is not to waste time and energy in considering the relative injustices war brings in its train, but to make sure we are going to win it.'

By this time the Belgian file had been found and handed over to me. The others, having settled to their own satisfaction the issues of the Russo-Polish difference, were now talking of luncheon. Tompsitt had begun telling the curate-schoolmaster about some scandal in diplomatic circles when he had been *en poste* in Caracas.

'Going through the park, Michael?' Widmerpool asked the sailor. 'We might set off together if you can be seen walking with a Pongo.'

The sailor had an appointment in the other direction. I wondered whether in the access of self-abasement that seemed to have overcome him, Widmerpool would make a similar suggestion to the airman, referring to himself as a 'brown job'. However, he required instead my own company. Tompsitt came to the climax of the anecdote which made his colleague suck in his thin lips appreciatively.

'Of course he's a Vichy man now,' said Tompsitt.

'Do French diplomats have mistresses?'

'The Italians are worse,' said Tompsitt pontifically.

'Now then, you two, keep off the girls,' said Widmerpool gaily. 'Come on, Nicholas.'

'I've got to take these papers back.'

'You can cut through the Horse Guards.'

We ascended to ground level and set off through St James's Park. The water had been drained from the lake to decrease identification from the air, leaving large dejected basins of clay-like soil. There were no ducks.

'Rather ridiculous the way those two were talking about women,' said Widmerpool. 'You'd hardly believe how unsophisticated some of these Civil Servants are on such subjects, even senior ones, the Foreign Office as much as any, in spite of thinking so much of themselves. They like to behave as if they are a lot of duke's nephews who've got there by aristocratic influence, whereas they're simply a collection of perfectly ordinary middle-class examinees with rather less manners than most. "The Italians are worse"! Did you ever hear such a remark? I've known Tompy for a very long time, and he's not a bad fellow, but lives in a very constricted social sphere.'

'Who was the other?'

'Some fellow from MEW,' said Widmerpool. 'No real experience of the world.'

There was something to be said for Widmerpool's views, though there had been a time when he had argued the other way. This contempt for those uninstructed in moral licence was new too. It was the sort of subject he was inclined to avoid. His own sex life had always been rather a mystery. There was nothing so very unusual about that. Most people's sex life is a mystery, especially that of individuals who seem to make most parade of it. Such is the conclusion one finally arrives at. All the same, Widmerpool's had more than once shown himself an exceptional mixture of vehemence and ineptitude; the business of Gypsy Jones, for example, in his early days; then the disastrous engagement to Mrs Haycock or his romantic love for Barbara Goring. Few subjects are more fascinating than other people's sexual habits from the outside; the tangled strands of appetite, tenderness, convenience or some hope of gain. In the light of what he had been saying, a direct question could sound not unreasonably inquisitive.

'How do you organize that side of your own life these days?'

I did not feel absolutely at ease making this unconcealed attempt to satisfy curiosity, but, in supposing Widmerpool might be embarrassed, evasive or annoyed, I was wholly wrong. The enquiry delighted him. He clapped me on the back.

'Plenty of pretty little bits in the black-out.'

'Tarts?'

'Of course.'

The solution was the same as Borrit's. I remembered now that Widmerpool had commented favourably, years before, when I told him my own rooms in Shepherd Market were flanked by a large block of flats housing prostitutes. At the time, I had supposed that remark bombast on his part. Now, such a diagnosis seemed less positive. Perhaps, anyway in the course of the years, his remark, 'How convenient', had acquired a certain authenticity. One wondered what cumbersome burden of desire, satisfied or unsatisfied, possibly charged in its fulfilment with some elaborate order of ritual, Widmerpool carried round with him.

'I suppose you have to be rather careful.'

It was a lame comment, which Widmerpool treated with the contempt it deserved.

'I am careful,' he said. 'Is there anything about my life that would lead you to suppose I should not be careful? I believe in thinking things out. Arranging my life, but arranging it in such a way that I do not fall into a groove. By the way, there is a probability I shall go red in the near future.'

'Go red?'

I had not the least idea what he meant. It seemed possible he might have returned to the subject of sexual habits, planning something in that line embarrassing even to himself.

'Become a full colonel.'

He snapped the words out. Failure to recognize a colloquialism had irritated him. The phrase was peculiar to himself. Usually people spoke of a 'red hat' or 'taking flannel'.

'Only a tanner a day more in pay,' he said, recovering his good humour, 'but it's the real jump in rank.'

It was no doubt specifically to inform me of this imminent promotion that he must have come out of the way across the Horse Guards Parade, I thought. By now we had nearly reached the arch leading into Whitehall. He suddenly lost his high spirits, sinking all at once to the depths of gloom, as I had known him do before, one of those changes of mood that would overcome him without warning.

'You never know about promotion till it's in the bag,' he said. 'There are occupational risks where I work. There are anywhere where you may find yourself in the CIGS's entourage.'

'Why him specially?'

'He's quite ruthless, if he doesn't like the look of you. The other day he said, "I don't want to see that officer again. I don't like his face". Perfectly good man, but they had to get rid of him.'

Widmerpool spoke with infinite dejection. I saw what he meant. Given the CIGS was easily irritated by the faces of staff-officers, Widmerpool's, where survival was in question, was a bad bet, rather than a good one.

'No use worrying,' he said. 'After all, I was not affected by all the trouble Liddament made.'

'His Corps seem to have done well in the desert.'

'No doubt Liddament has his points as a commander in the field. Unfortunately, I was blind to them when serving on the staff of his Division. Tell me—talking of those days made me think of Farebrother—had you left the Poles at the time of the Szymanski scandal?'

'Yes.'

'You heard Farebrother was largely responsible?'

'That was being said.'

'He's been unstuck in consequence. Not without some action on my part.'

'I didn't know you were involved.'

'I made it my business to be involved. Strictly between ourselves, the whole disgraceful affair was not unconnected with Prince Theodoric whom we saw at that musical performance the other night.'

'Where does Theodoric come in?'

'That is naturally secret, but I don't mind telling you that the Prince is bringing a lot of pressure to bear one way and another.'

'You mean from the Resistance point of view.'

'I hold my own views on that subject,' said Widmerpool. 'I hear that young woman in red, whose name I asked, is said to be Theodoric's mistress.'

'That's the gossip.'

'I have little or no time for social life, but one keeps an eye on these things.'

A full colonel, wearing the red tabs with which Widmerpool himself hoped soon to be equipped, came out of a door under the arch and turned into Whitehall. Widmerpool pointed after him and laughed.

'Did you see who that was?' he asked. 'I really strolled with you across here, out of my way, in case we might catch sight of him.'

'Was it Hogbourne-Johnson?'

'Relegated to the Training branch, where, if he's not kicked out from there too, he will remain until the end of the war. The man who thought he was going to get a Division. Do you remember when he was so abominably rude to me?'

'That balls-up about traffic circuits?'

'It won't be long now before I'm his equal in rank. I may find an opportunity to tell him some home truths, should our paths cross, though that's unlikely enough. It's only on the rarest occasions like today that I'm out of my office—and, after all, Hogbourne-Johnson's a very unimportant cog in the machine.'

He nodded and began to move off. I saluted—the uniform, as one was always told, rather than the man—and took the Belgian documents back to our room.

3

ONE DAY, SEVERAL WEEKS AFTER the Allied Forces had landed in Normandy, I was returning over Westminster Bridge on foot from transacting some minor item of Czechoslovak army business with a ministry housed on the south bank of the river in the former Donners-Brebner Building. It was lovely weather. Even the most pessimistic had begun to concede that the war, on the whole, had taken a turn for the better. Some supposed this might mean the end of raids. Others believed the Germans had a trick or two up their sleeve. Although it was London Bridge to which the poem referred, rather than Westminster, the place from which I had just come, the dark waters of the Thames below, the beauty of the day, brought to mind the lines about Stetson and the ships at Mylae, how death had undone so many. Donners-Brebner—where Howard Craggs, recently knighted, now reigned over one of the branches—had been badly knocked about in the early days of the blitz. The full extent of the damage was not visible, because the main entrance, where Barnby's frescoes had once been, was heaped with sandbags, access by a side door. Barnby was no longer available to repaint his frescoes. Death had undone him. It looked as if death might have undone Stringham too. At Donners-Brebner he had put me off for dinner because he was going to Peggy Stepney's parents. Peggy's second husband had been undone too. She was married to Jimmy Klein now, said to have always loved her. These musings were interrupted by a tall officer falling into step with me. It was Sunny Farebrother.

'Hullo, Nicholas. I hope my dear old Finn is not still cross with me about Szymanski?'

'There may still be some disgruntlement, sir.'

'Disgruntlement', one was told, was a word that could be used of all ranks without loss of discipline. As I heard myself utter it, I became immediately aware of the manner in which Farebrother, by some effort of the will, made those with whom he dealt as devious as himself. It was not the first time I had noticed that characteristic in him. The reply, the term, was in truth hopelessly inadequate to express Finn's rage about the whole Szymanski affair.

'Finn's a hard man,' said Farebrother. 'Nobody I admire more. There is not an officer in the entire British army I admire more than Lieutenant-Colonel Lysander Finn, VC.'

'Lysander?'

'Certainly.'

'We never knew.'

'He keeps it quiet.'

Farebrother smiled, not displeased at finding this piece of information so unexpected.

'Who shall blame him?' he said. 'It's modesty, not shame. He thinks the name might sound pretentious in the winner of a VC. Finn's as brave as a lion, as straight as a die, but as hard as nails—especially where he thinks his own honour is concerned.'

Farebrother said the last words in what Pennistone called his religious voice.

'You weren't yourself affected by the Szymanski matter, Nicholas?'

'I'd left the Poles by then.'

'You're no longer in Finn's Section?'

Farebrother made no attempt to conceal his own interest in any change that might take place in employment or status of those known to him, in case these might in some manner, even if unforeseen, react advantageously to himself.

'Ah,' he said. 'The Belgians and Czechs. I should like to have a talk with you one of these days about those two Allies, but not now. You don't know how sorry I am that poor old Finn was inconvenienced in that way. I hate it when friends think you've let them down. I remember a Frenchman in the last war whom I'd promised to put in for a British decoration that never came through. No use regretting these things, I suppose, but I'm made that way. We all have to do our duty as we see it, Nicholas. Each one of us has to learn that and it's sometimes a hard lesson. In the case of Szymanski, I was made to suffer for being too keen. Disciplined, demoted in rank, shunted off to a bloody awful job. Tell Finn that. Perhaps he will forgive me when he hears I was made to pay for my action. You know who went out of his way to bring this trouble about—our old friend Kenneth Widmerpool.'

'But you've left that job now?'

'In Civil Affairs, with my old rank and a good chance of promotion.'

The Civil Affairs branch, formed to deal with administration of areas occupied by our enemies, had sprung into being about a year before. In it were already collected together a rich variety of specimens of army life. Farebrother would ornament the collection. Pennistone compared Civil Affairs with 'the head to which all the ends of the world are come, and the eyelids are a little weary.'

'That just describes it,' Pennistone said. '"No crude symbolism disturbs the effect of Civil Affairs' subdued and graceful mystery".'

Among others to find his way into this branch was Dicky Umfraville, who had thereby managed to disengage himself from the transit camp he had been commanding. I asked if Farebrother had any dealings with Umfraville, whom I had not seen for some little time. Farebrother nodded. He looked over his shoulder, as if he feared agents were tracking us at that very moment and might over-hear his words.

'You know Kenneth pretty well?'

'Yes.'

'Umfraville was talking to one of our people who'd been in Cairo when Kenneth flew out there for a day or two, as member of a high-level conference secretariat. Do you know what happened? Something you'd never guess. He managed to make a fool of himself about some girl employed in a secret outfit there.'

'In what way?'

'Took her out or something. She was absolutely notorious, it seems.'

'What happened?'

'Don't let's talk about it,' said Farebrother. 'If there's one thing I hate, it's a woman who lowers herself in that sort of way. I'm afraid there are quite a few of them about in wartime.'

We had by now turned into Whitehall. Farebrother suddenly raised his arm in a stiff salute. I did the same, taking my time from him, though not immediately conscious of whom we were both saluting. Then I quickly apprehended that Farebrother was paying tribute to the Cenotaph, which we were at that moment passing. The preoccupations of wartime often resulted in this formality—always rather an uncomfortable and precarious one—being allowed to pass unobserved. It was a typical mark of Farebrother's innate regard for ceremoniousness in all its aspects that he brought out his salute as if on a parade ground march-past. However, at that moment, another—and certainly discordant—circumstance clouded the scene. Just as Farebrother had been the first to see and pay homage to the Cenotaph, he was undoubtedly the first of us also to appreciate the necessity of taking another decision, a quick one, in a similar field. This resolve also had important implications, though of a very different sort. The situation was posed by a couple walking briskly towards us from the direction of Trafalgar Square: a middle-aged civilian—almost certainly a Civil Servant of high standing—wearing a very old hat on the back of his head, beside him an officer in a full colonel's red capband and tabs. Even at this distance the tabs could be seen to be imposed on one of the new 'utility' uniforms, service-dress tunics skimped at the pockets and elsewhere to save cloth. These innovations always gave the wearer, even if a thin man, the air of being too large for his clothes, and this officer, stoutish with spectacles, was bursting from them. I noticed the uniform before appreciating that here was Widmerpool 'gone red'.

'In life—'

Farebrother had just begun to speak. He broke off suddenly. The way in which he did this, obviously abandoning giving expression to some basic rule of human conduct, made me sure, reflecting on the incident afterwards, that he had seen Widmerpool first. There can also be no doubt that he was as ignorant as myself of his old enemy's promotion. That must have been gazetted subsequent to the Cairo tour of duty. For a split second I had time to wonder whether Farebrother would accord Widmerpool as smart an acknowledgment of rank—after all, it was 'the uniform', even if only a 'utility' one—as he had rendered the Cenotaph. It should be explained perhaps that, although in theory majors and upwards had some claim to a salute from those of junior rank, in practice the only officers saluted by other officers in the street were those who wore red. I was therefore once more preparing to take my time from Farebrother, when he suddenly seized my arm. We were just passing 'the Fortress', Combined Operations Headquarters, then more or less underground, after the war covered by a building of many storeys. At first I thought he wanted to draw my attention to something happening on the other side of the road.

'Nicholas?'

'Sir?'

'A moment ago I was telling you I don't like to see a woman making herself cheap. Women's lives should be beautiful, an inspiration. I thought of that the other night. I was taken to a film called *The Song of Bernadette*. Have you seen it?'

'No, sir.'

He looked at me fixedly. He had put on his holy face, as was to be expected from the subject of the movie, and spoke the words in an equally appropriate tone.

'It's about Lourdes.'

I repeated that I had not seen the film.

'You should, Nicholas. I don't often get out in the evenings, much too much to do, but I think that night did me good. Made me a better man.'

I could not imagine what all this was leading up to.

'You really think I ought to make an effort to go, sir?'

Farebrother did not answer. Instead, he gave another of his quick glances over the shoulder. For a moment I remained at a loss to know why *The Song of Bernadette* had so much impressed him that he felt a sudden need to speak of the film so dramatically. Then all at once I grasped that the menace of saluting Widmerpool no longer hung over us. Farebrother, with all his self-control in such matters, all the years he had schooled himself to accept the ways of those set in authority over him, had for one reason or another been unable to face that bitterness in my presence. Inner disciplines, respect for tradition, taste for formality, had none of them been sufficient. The incident showed

Farebrother, too, had human weaknesses. Now, he seemed totally to have forgotten about Bernadette. We walked along in silence. Perhaps he was pondering the saintly life. We reached the gates of the Horse Guards. Farebrother paused. His gay blue eyes became a little sad. 'Do your best to make your Colonel forgive me, Nicholas. You can tell him—without serious breach of security— that Szymanski's already done a first-rate job in one quarter and likely to do as good a one in another. Do you ever see Prince Theodoric in these days? In my present job I no longer have grand contacts like that.'

I told him I had not seen Theodoric since *The Bartered Bride*. We went our separate ways.

That night in bed, reading *Remembrance of Things Past*, I thought again of Theodoric, on account of a passage describing the Princesse de Guermantes' party:

'The Ottoman Ambassadress, now bent on demonstrating to me not only her familiarity with the Royalties present, some of whom I knew our hostess had invited out of sheer kindness of heart and would never have been at home to them if the Prince of Wales or the Queen of Spain were in her drawing-room the afternoon they called, but also her mastery of current appointments under consideration at the Quai d'Orsay or Rue Dominique, disregarding my wish to cut short our conversation—additionally so because I saw Professer E—— once more bearing down on us and feared the Ambassadress, whose complexion conveyed unmistakable signs of a recent bout of varicella, might be one of his patients—drew my attention to a young man wearing a cypripedin (the flower Bloch liked to call 'sandal of foam-borne Aphrodite') in the buttonhole of his dress coat, whose swarthy appearance required only an astrakhan cap and silver-hilted yataghan to complete evident affinities with the Balkan peninsula. This Apollo of the hospodars was talking vigorously to the Grand Duke Vladimir, who had moved away from the propinquity of the fountain and whose features now showed traces of uneasiness because he thought this distant relative, Prince Odoacer, for that was who I knew the young man of the orchid to be, sought his backing in connexion with a certain secret alliance predicted in Eastern Europe, material to the interests of Prince Odoacer's country no less than the Muscovite Empire; support which the Grand Duke might be unwilling to afford, either on account of his kinsman having compromised himself financially, through a childish ignorance of the Bourse, in connexion with a speculation involving Panama Canal shares (making things no better by offering to dispose 'on the quiet' of a hunting scene by Wouwerman destined as a birthday present for his mistress), from which he had to be extracted by the good offices of that same Baron Manasch with whom Swann had once fought a duel; or, even more unjustly, because the Grand Duke had heard a rumour of the unfortunate reputation the young Prince had incurred for himself by the innocent employment as valet of a notorious youth whom I had more than once seen visiting Jupien's shop, and, as I learnt much later, was known among his fellow inverts as La Gioconda. "I'm told Gogo —Prince Odoacer—has Dreyfusard leanings!" said the Ambassadress, assuming my ignorance of the Prince's nickname as well as his openly expressed political sympathies, the momentary cruelty of her smile hinting at Janissary blood flowing in her veins. "Albeit a matter that does not concern a foreigner like myself," she went on, "yet, if true that the name of Colonel de Froberville, whom I see standing over there, has been put forward as military attaché designate to the French Legation of Prince Odoacer's country, the fact of such inclinations in one of its Royal House should be made known as soon as possible to any French officer likely to fill the post.'"

This description of Prince Odoacer was of special interest

because he was a relation—possibly great-uncle—of Theodoric's. I thought about the party for a time, whether there had really been a Turkish Ambassadress, whom Proust found a great bore; then, like the Narrator himself in his childhood days, fell asleep early. This state, left undisturbed by the Warning, was brought to an end by rising hubbub outside. A very noisy attack had started up. Some residents, especially those inhabiting the upper storeys, preferred to descend to the ground floor or basement on these occasions. Rather from lethargy than any indifference to danger, I used in general to remain in my flat during raids, feeling that one's nerve, certainly less steady than at an earlier stage of the war, was unlikely to be improved by exchanging conversational banalities with neighbours equally on edge.

From first beginnings, this particular raid made an unusually obnoxious din and continued to do so. While bombs and flak exploded at the present rate there was little hope of dropping off to sleep again. I lay in the dark, trying to will them to go home, one way, not often an effective one, of passing the time during raids. My interior counter-attack was not successful. An hour went by; then another; and another. So far from decreasing, the noise grew greater in volume. There was a suggestion of more or less regular bursts of detonation launched from the skies, orchestrated against the familiar rise and fall of gunfire. It must have been about two or three in the morning, when, rather illogically, I decided to go downstairs. A move in that direction at least offered something to do. Besides, I could feel myself growing increasingly jumpy. The ground floor at this hour was at worst likely to provide, if nothing else, a certain anthropological interest. The occasion was one for the merest essentials of uniform, pockets filled with stuff from which one did not want to be separated, should damage occur in the room while away. I took a helmet as a matter of principle.

On one of the walls of the lift, incised with a sharp instrument (similar to that used years before to outline the caricature of Widmerpool in the *cabinet* at La Grenadière), someone quite recently—perhaps that very night—had etched at eye-level, in lower case letters suggesting an E. E. Cummings poem, a brief cogent observation about the manageress, one likely to prove ineradicable as long as the lift itself remained in existence, for no paint could have obscured it:

old bitch wartstone

Quite a few people were below, strolling about talking, or sitting on the benches of the hall. No doubt others were in the basement, a region into which I had never penetrated, where there was said to be some sort of 'shelter'. This crowd was in a perpetual state of change: some, like myself, deciding they needed a spell out of bed; others, too tired or bored to stay longer chatting in the hall, retiring to the basement or simply returning to their own flats. Clanwaert, smoking a cigarette, his hands in the pockets of a rather smart green silk dressing-gown, was present. Living on the ground floor anyway, he had not bothered to dress.

'This raid seems to be going on a long time.'

'Of course it is, my friend. We are getting the famous Secret Weapon we have heard so much about.'

'You think so?'

'Not a doubt of it. We knew it was coming in Eaton Square. Had you not been informed in Whitehall? The interesting thing will be to see how this fine Secret Weapon really turns out.'

It looked as if Clanwaert were right. He began to talk of the Congo army and the difficulties they had encountered in the Sudanese desert. After a while the subject exhausted itself.

'Is there any point in not going back to bed?'

'Hard to say. It may quiet down. I am in any case a bad sleeper. One becomes accustomed to doing without sleep, if one lives a long time in the tropics.'

He put out his cigarette and went to the front door to see how things were looking in the street. A girl with a helmet set sideways on her head, this headdress assumed for decorative effect rather than as a safety measure, came past. She wore an overcoat over trousers in the manner of Gypsy Jones and Audrey Maclintick. It was Pamela Flitton.

'Hullo.'

She looked angry, as if suspecting an attempted pick-up, then recognized me.

'Hullo.'

She did not smile.

'What a row.'

'Isn't it.'

'Seen anything of Norah?'

'Norah and I haven't been speaking for ages. She's too touchy. That's one of the things wrong with Norah.'

'Still doing your secret job?'

'I've just come back from Cairo.'

'By boat?'

'I got flown back.'

'You were lucky to get an air passage.'

'I travelled on a general's luggage.'

A youngish officer, in uniform but with unbuttoned tunic, came into the hall from the passage leading to the ground floor flats. He was small, powerfully built, with hair growing in regular waves of curls, like Jeavons's, though fair in colour.

'We seem to be out of fags,' he said to Pamela.

'Oh, Christ.'

He turned to me. I registered a crown on his shoulder, MC and bar above the pocket.

'Haven't got a cigarette by any chance, pal?' he said. 'We've smoked our last—why, Nicholas? I'll be buggered. Caught you trying to pick up Pam. What cheek. How are you, old boy. Marvellous to meet again.'

'Pamela and I know each other already. She used to drive me in her ATS days, not to mention my practically attending her christening.'

'So you live in this dump, too, and suffer from old Wartstone? If I wasn't leaving the place at any moment, I'd carve up that woman with a Commando knife in a way that would make Jack the Ripper look like the vicar cutting sandwiches for a school treat.'

I was not specially pleased to see Odo Stevens, whose conduct, personal and official, could not be approved for a variety of reasons, whatever distinction he might have earned in the field. At the same time, there was small point in attempting to take a high moral line, either about his affair with Priscilla or the part he had played over Szymanski. Priscilla and Chips Lovell were dead: Szymanski too, for all one knew by this time. Besides, to be pompous about such matters was even in a sense to play into the hands of Stevens, to give opportunity for him to justify himself in one of those emotional displays that are always part of the stock-in-trade of persons of his particular sort. With characteristic perspicuity, he guessed at once what was going through my mind. His look changed. It was immediately clear he was going to bring up the subject of Priscilla.

'It was simply awful,' he said. 'What happened after we last met. That bomb on the Madrid killing her husband—then the other where she was staying. I even thought of writing to you. Then I got mixed up with a lot of special duties.'

He had quite changed his tone of voice from the moment before, at the same time assuming an expression reminiscent of Farebrother's 'religious face', the same serious pained

124

contraction of the features. I was determined to endure for as short a time as possible only what was absolutely unavoidable in the exhibition of self-confessed remorse Stevens was obviously proposing to mount for my benefit. He had been, I recalled, unnecessarily public in his carryings-on with Priscilla, had corroded what turned out to be Chips's last year alive. That might be no very particular business of mine, but I had liked Chips, therefore preferred the circumstances should remain unresurrected. That was the long and the short of it.

'Don't let's talk about it. What's the good?'

Stevens was not to be silenced so easily.

'She meant so much to me,' he said.

'Who did?' asked Pamela.

'Someone who was killed in an air-raid.'

He put considerable emotion into his voice when he said that. Perhaps Priscilla had, indeed, 'meant a lot' to him. I did not care. I saw no reason to be dragged in as a kind of prop to his self-esteem, or masochistic pleasure in lacking it. Besides, I wanted to get on to the Szymanski story.

'You're always telling me I mean more to you than any other girl has,' said Pamela. 'At least you do after a couple of drinks. You've the weakest head of any man I've ever met.'

She spoke in that low almost inaudible mutter employed by her most of the time. There was certainly a touch of Audrey Maclintick about her, at least enough to explain why Stevens and Mrs Maclintick had got on so comparatively well together that night in the Café Royal. On the other hand, this girl was not only much better looking, but also much tougher even than Mrs Maclintick. Pamela Flitton gave the impression of being thoroughly vicious, using the word not so much in the moral sense, but as one might speak of a horse—more specifically, a mare.

125

'I don't claim the capacity for liquor of some of your Slav friends,' said Stevens laughing.

He sounded fairly well able to stand up to her. This seemed a suitable moment to change the subject.

'You were in the news locally not so long ago—where I work, I mean—about one Szymanski.'

'Don't tell me you're with the Poles, Nicholas?'

'I'd left them by the time you got up to your tricks.'

Pamela showed interest at the name Szymanski.

'I sent you a message,' she said. 'Did you get it?'

When she smiled and spoke directly like that, it was possible to guess at some of her powers should she decide to make a victim of a man.

'I got it.'

'Then you were in on the party?' asked Stevens.

'I saw some of the repercussions.'

'God,' he said. 'That was a lark.'

'Not for those engaged in normal liaison duties.'

One's loyalties vary. At that moment I felt wholly on the side of law and order, if only to get some of my own back for his line of talk about the Lovells.

'Oh, bugger normal liaison duties. Even you must admit the operation was beautifully executed. Look here . . .'

He took my arm, and, leaving Pamela sitting sullenly by herself on a bench, walked me away to a deserted corner of the hall. When we reached there, he lowered his voice.

'I'm due for a job in the near future not entirely unconnected with Szymanski himself.'

'Housebreaking?'

Stevens yelled with laughter.

'That'll be the least of our crimes, I'd imagine,' he said. 'That is, the least of his—which might easily not stop at manslaughter, I should guess. Actually, we're doing quite different jobs, but more or less in the same place.'

126

'Presumably it's a secret where you're conducting these activities.'

'My present situation is being on twenty-four hour call to Cairo. I'll release something to you, as an old pal, in addition to that. The plot's not unconnected with one of Pam's conquests. Rather a grand one.'

'You remind me of the man who used to introduce his wife as *ancienne maîtresse de Lord Byron*.'

'This is classier than a lord—besides Pam and I aren't married yet.'

'You don't have to spell the name out.'

I was not impressed by Stevens's regard for 'security', always a risk in the hands of the vain. All the same, not much damage would be done by my knowing that at last some sort of assistance was to be given to the Resistance in Prince Theodoric's country; and that Stevens and Szymanski were involved. That was certainly interesting.

'I'll be playing for the village boys,' he said. 'Rather than the team the squire is fielding.'

'A tricky situation, I should imagine.'

'You bet.'

'I saw Sunny Farebrother yesterday, who took the rap in the Szymanski business.'

'Cunning old bugger. They pushed him off to a training centre for a bit, but I bet he's back on something good.'

'He thinks so. Was Szymanski a boy-friend of Pamela's?'

I thought I had a right to ask that question after the way Stevens had talked. For once he seemed a shade put out.

'Who can tell?' he said. 'Even if there's still a Szymanski. They may have infiltrated him already and he may have been picked up. I hope not. The great thing is he knows the country like the back of his hand. What are you doing yourself, old boy?'

The change of mood, sudden fear for Szymanski—and by

implication for himself—was characteristic. I told him about my job, also explaining how I knew Pamela.

'Won't she be cross if we leave her much longer?'

'She's cross all the time. Bloody cross. Chronic state. Thrives on it. Her chief charm. Makes her wonderful in bed. That is, if you like temper.'

Emphasis expressed as to the high degree of sexual pleasure to be derived from a given person is, for one reason or another, always to be accepted with a certain amount of suspicion, so far as the speaker is concerned, especially if referring to a current situation. Stevens sounded as if he might be bolstering himself up in making the last statement.

'She's the hell of a girl,' he said.

I wondered whether he had run across Pamela with Szymanski in the first instance. In any case, people like that gravitate towards each other at all times, almost more in war than in peace, since war—though perhaps in a more limited sense than might be supposed—offers obvious opportunities for certain sorts of adventure. Stevens, whose self-satisfaction had if anything increased, seemed to have no illusions about Pamela's temperament. He accepted that she was a woman whose sexual disposition was vested in rage and perversity. In fact, if he were to be believed, those were the very qualities he had set out to find. We returned to where she was sitting.

'Where the hell have you two been?'

She spoke through her teeth. There was still a lot of noise going on outside. We all three sat on the bench together. Clanwaert strolled past. He glanced in our direction, slightly inclining his head towards Pamela, who took no perceptible notice of him. He had evidently decided to return to bed and said goodnight to me.

'That was the Belgian officer who gave me your message about Szymanski.'

'Ask him if he's got a cigarette.'

I called after Clanwaert. He turned back and came towards us. I enquired if he had a cigarette for Pamela, saying I believed they had met. He took a case from his dressing-gown pocket and handed it round. Pamela took one, looking away as she did so. Clanwaert showed himself perfectly at ease under this chilly treatment.

'We could have met at the Belgian Institute,' he said. 'Was it with one of our artillery officers—Wauthier or perhaps Ruys?'

'Perhaps it was,' she said. 'Thanks for the smoke.'

Clanwaert smiled and retired.

'One of your *braves Belges*?' asked Stevens. 'Since you've lived here some time, you've probably come across the old girl standing by the door. She's called Mrs Erdleigh. The other evening, I saw her burning something on the roof. I thought she was sending up smoke signals to the enemy—it wasn't yet dark—but it turned out to be just incense, which seems to play some part in her daily life, as she's a witch. We got on rather well. In the end she told my fortune and said I was going to have all sorts of adventures and get a lot of nice presents from women.'

'Not me,' said Pamela. 'You'll have to go elsewhere if you want to be kept.'

Mrs Erdleigh was, indeed, looking out into the street through the glass doors at the other end of the hall. Her age as indeterminate as ever from her outward appearance, she was smiling slightly to herself. This was the first time I had seen her since living in the flats. A helmet was set very squarely on her head and she wore a long coat or robe, a pushteen or similar garment, woolly inside, skin without, the exterior ornamented with scrolls and patterns of oriental design in bright colours. She was carrying a small black box under one arm. Now she set this on the ground and removed the helmet, revealing a coiffure of grey-blue curls that had been pressed down by the weight of the tin hat. These she ruffled with her fingers. Then she took the helmet between her hands, and, as if in deep thought, raised it like a basin or sacrificial vessel, a piece of temple equipment for sacred rites. Her quiet smile suggested she was rather enjoying the raid than otherwise. Nothing much seemed to be happening outside, though the row continued unabated.

'She was mixed up with an uncle of mine—in fact he left her his money, such as it was.'

The bequest had caused great annoyance in the family, almost as much on account of Uncle Giles turning out to own a few thousands, as because of the alienation of the capital sum.

'Must have made it quite lately as the result of some very risky speculation,' my father had said at the time. 'Never thought Giles had a penny to bless himself with.'

'Let's go over and talk to her,' said Stevens. 'She's good value.'

He had that taste, peculiar to certain egotists, to collect together close round him everyone he might happen to know in any given area.

'Oh, God,' said Pamela. 'Need we? I suppose she flattered you.'

'Go on, Nicholas,' he said. 'Ask Mrs Erdleigh to join us, if you know her as well.'

I agreed to do this, more from liking the idea of meeting Mrs Erdleigh again than to please Stevens. As I approached, she herself turned towards me.

'I wondered when you would speak,' she said gently.

'You'd already seen me in the hall?'

'Often in this building. But we must not anticipate our destinies. The meeting had to wait until tonight.'

From the way she spoke, it was to be assumed that she was so far above material contacts that the impetus of our reunion must necessarily come from myself. The magical course of events would no doubt have been damaged had she taken the initiative and addressed me first.

'What a night.'

'I could not sleep,' she said, as if that were a matter for surprise. 'The omens have not been good for some days past, though in general better than for many months. I can see at once from your face that you are well situated. The Centaur is friend to strangers and exiles. His arrow defends them.'

'Come and talk to us. There's a young man called Odo Stevens, who has done rather well as a soldier—been very brave, I mean—and a girl called Pamela Flitton. He says he knows you already.'

'I met your young army friend on the roof when I was engaged in certain required exsufflations. He is under Aries, like your poor uncle, but this young man has the Ram in far, far better aspect, the powerful rays of Mars favouring him rather than the reverse, as they might some— your uncle, for example.'

I told her I had seen the Ufford—where we had first met —now in such changed circumstances. She was not at all interested, continuing to speak of Stevens, who had evidently made an impression on her.

'It is the planet Mars that connects him with that very beautiful young woman,' she said. 'The girl herself is under Scorpio—like that unhappy Miss Wartstone, so persecuted by Saturn—and possesses many of the scorpion's cruellest traits. He told me much about her when we talked on the roof. I fear she loves disaster and death—but he will escape her, although not without an appetite for death himself.'

Mrs Erdleigh smiled again, as if she appreciated, even to some extent approved, this taste for death in both of them.

'Lead me to your friends,' she said. 'I am particularly interested in the girl, whom I have not yet met.'

She picked up the black box, which presumably contained spells and jewellery, carrying the helmet in her other hand. We returned to Stevens and Pamela. They were having words about a bar of chocolate, produced from somewhere and alleged to have been unfairly divided. Stevens jumped up and seized Mrs Erdleigh by the hand. It looked as if he were going to kiss her, but he stopped short of that. Pamela put on the helmet that had been lying beside her on the seat. This was evidently a conscious gesture of hostility.

'This is Miss Flitton,' said Stevens.

Pamela made one of her characteristically discouraging acknowledgments of this introduction. I was curious to see whether Mrs Erdleigh would exercise over her the same calming influence she had once exerted on Mona, Peter Templer's first wife, when they had met. Mona, certainly a far less formidable personality than Pamela, had been in a thoroughly bad mood that day—without the excuse of an air-raid being in progress—yet she had been almost immediately tranquillized by Mrs Erdleigh's restorative mixture of flattery, firmness and occultism. For all one knew, air-raids might positively increase Mrs Erdleigh's powers. She took Pamela's hand. Pamela withdrew it at once.

'I'm going to have a walk outside,' she said. 'See what's happening.'

'Don't be a fool,' said Stevens. 'You're not allowed to wander about during raids, especially one like this.'

'My dear,' said Mrs Erdleigh, 'I well discern in your heart that need for bitter things that knows no assuagement, those yearnings for secrecy and tears that pursue without end, wherever you seek to fly them. No harm will come to you, even on this demonic night, that I can tell you. Nevertheless stay for a minute and talk with me. Death, it is true, surrounds your nativity, even though you yourself are not personally threatened—none of us is tonight.

There are things I would like to ask you. The dark un-
fathomable lake over which you glide—you are under a
watery sign and yet a fixed one—is sometimes dull and
stagnant, sometimes, as now, angry and disturbed.'

Pamela was certainly taken aback by this confident
approach, so practised, so self-assured, the tone at once
sinister and adulatory, but she did not immediately capitu-
late, as Mona had done. Instead, she temporized.

'How do you know about me?' she asked. 'Know when
I was born, I mean.'

She spoke in a voice of great discontent and truculence.
Mrs Erdleigh indicated that Stevens had been her informant. Pamela looked more furious than ever.

'What does he know about me?'

'What do most people know about any of their fellows?'
said Mrs Erdleigh quietly. 'Little enough. Only those
know, who are aware what is to be revealed. He may have
betrayed the day of your birth. I do not remember. The rest
I can tell from your beautiful face, my dear. You will not
mind if I say that your eyes have something in them of the
divine serpent that tempted Eve herself.'

It was impossible not to admire the method of attack.
Stevens spoiled its delicacy by blundering in.

'Tell Pam's fortune,' he said. 'She'd love it—and you
were wonderful with me.'

'Why should I want my fortune told? Haven't I just
said I'm going to have a look round outside?'

'Wiser not, my dear,' said Mrs Erdleigh. 'As I said before, my calculations tell me that we are perfectly safe if we
remain here, but one cannot always foresee what may happen to those who ride in the face of destiny. Why not let
me look at your hand? It will pass the time.'

'If you really want to. I don't expect it's very interesting.'

I think Mrs Erdleigh was not used to being treated in
such an ungracious manner. She did not show this in the

smallest degree, but what she went on to say later could be attributed to a well controlled sense of pique. Perhaps that was why she insisted that Pamela's hand should be read by her.

'No human life is uninteresting.'

'Have a look then—but there's not much light here.'

'I have my torch.'

Pamela held out her palm. She was perhaps, in fact, more satisfied than the reverse at finding opposition to her objections overruled. It was likely she would derive at least some gratification in the anodyne process. However farouche, she could scarcely be so entirely different from the rest of the world. On the other hand, some instinct may have warned her against Mrs Erdleigh, capable of operating at as disturbing a level as herself. Mrs Erdleigh examined the lines.

'I would prefer the cards,' she said. 'I have them with me in my box, of course, but this place is really too inconvenient ... As I guessed, the Mount of Venus highly developed ... and her Girdle ... You must be careful, my dear ... There are things here that surprise even me ... *les tentations lubriques sont bien prononcées* ... You have found plenty of people to love you ... but no marriage at present ... no ... but perhaps in about a year ...'

'Who's it going to be?' asked Stevens. 'What sort of chap?'

'Mind your own business,' said Pamela.

'Perhaps it is my business.'

'Why should it be?'

'A man a little older than yourself,' said Mrs Erdleigh. 'A man in a good position.'

'Pamela's mad about the aged,' said Stevens. 'The balder the better.'

'I see this man as a jealous husband,' said Mrs Erdleigh. 'This older man I spoke of ... but ... as I said before, my dear, you must take good care ... You are not always well governed in yourself ... your palm makes me think of that passage in Desbarrolles, the terrible words of which always haunt my mind when I see their marks in a hand shown to me ... *la débauche, l'effronterie, la licence, le dévergondage, la coquetterie, la vanité, l'esprit léger, l'inconstance, la paresse* ... those are some of the things in your nature you must guard against, my dear.'

Whether or not this catalogue of human frailties was produced mainly in revenge for Pamela's earlier petulance was hard to know. Perhaps not at all. Mrs Erdleigh was probably speaking no more than the truth, voicing an analysis that did not require much occult skill to arrive at. In any case, she never minded what she said to anyone. Whatever her intention, the words had an immediate effect on Pamela herself, who snatched her hand away with a burst of furious laughter. It was the first time I had heard her laugh.

'That's enough to get on with,' she said. 'Now I'm going for my walk.'

She made a move towards the door. Stevens caught her arm.

'I say you're not going.'

She pulled herself away. There was an instant's pause while they faced each other. Then she brought up her arm and gave him a backhand slap in the face, quite a hard one, using the knuckles.

'You don't think I'm going to take orders from a heel like you, do you?' she said. 'You're pathetic as a lover. No good at all. You ought to see a doctor.'

She walked quickly through the glass door of the entrance hall, and, making the concession of putting on her helmet once more, disappeared into the street. Stevens, knocked out for a second or two by the strength of the blow, made no effort to follow. He rubbed his face, but did not seem particularly surprised nor put out by this violence of treatment. Probably he was used to assaults from Pamela. Possibly such incidents were even fairly normal in his relationships with women. There was, indeed, some slight parallel to the moment when Priscilla had suddenly left him in the Café Royal, though events of that night, in some manner telepathically connecting those concerned, had been enough to upset the nerves of everyone present. We might be in the middle of a raid that never seemed to end, but at least personal contacts were less uncomfortable than on the earlier occasion. Mrs Erdleigh, too, accepted with remarkable composure the scene that had just taken place.

'Little bitch,' said Stevens. 'Not the first time she has done that. Nothing I like less than being socked on the jaw. I thought she'd like to have her fortune told.'

He rubbed his face. Mrs Erdleigh smiled one of her slow, sweet, mysterious smiles.

'You do not understand enough her type's love of secrecy, her own unwillingness to give herself.'

'I understand her unwillingness to give herself,' said Stevens. 'I've got hold of that one OK. In fact I'm quite an expert on the subject.'

'To allow me to look longer at her palm would have been to betray too much,' said Mrs Erdleigh. 'I offered to make a reading only because you pressed me. I was not surprised by this result. All the same, you are right not to be unduly disturbed by her behaviour. In that way you show your own candour and courage. She will come to no harm. In any case, I do not see the two of you much longer together.'

'Neither do I, if there are many more of these straight lefts.'

'Besides, you are going overseas.'

'Soon?'

'Very soon.'

136

'Shall I see things through?'

'There will be danger, but you will survive.'

'What about her. Will she start up with any more Royalties? Perhaps a king this time.'

He said this so seriously that I laughed. Mrs Erdleigh, on the other hand, accepted the question gravely.

'I saw a crown not far away,' she said. 'Her fate lies along a strange road but not a royal one—whatever incident the crown revealed was very brief—but still it is the road of power.'

She picked up her black box again.

'You're going back to your room?'

'As I said before, no danger threatens tonight, but I thoughtlessly allowed myself to run out of a little remedy I have long used against sleeplessness.'

She held out her hand. I took it. Mention of 'little remedies' called to mind Dr Trelawney. I asked if she ever saw him. She made a mysterious sign with her hand.

'He passed over not long after your uncle. Being well instructed in such enlightenments, he knew his own time was appointed—in war conditions some of his innermost needs had become hard to satisfy—so he was ready. Quite ready.'

'Where did he die?'

'There is no death in Nature'—she looked at me with her great misty eyes and I remembered Dr Trelawney himself using much the same words—'only transition, blending, synthesis, mutation. He has re-entered the Vortex of Becoming.'

'I see.'

'But to answer your question in merely terrestrial terms, he re-embarked on his new journey from the little hotel where we last met.'

'And Albert—does he still manage the Bellevue?'

'He too has gone forth in his cerements. His wife, so I

137

hear, married again—a Pole invalided from the army. They keep a boarding-house together in Weston-super-Mare.'

'Any last words of advice, Mrs Erdleigh?' asked Stevens.

He treated her as if he were consulting the Oracle at Delphi.

'Let the palimpsest of your mind absorb the words of Eliphas Lévi—to know, to will, to dare, to be silent.'

'Me, too?' I asked.

'Everyone.'

'The last most of all?'

'Some think so.'

She glided away towards the lift, which seemed hardly needed, with its earthly and mechanical paraphernalia, to bear her up to the higher levels.

'I'm going to kip too,' said Stevens. 'No good wandering all over London on a night like this looking for Pam. She might be anywhere. She usually comes back all right after a tiff like this. Cheers her up. Well, I may or may not see you again, Nicholas. Never know when one may croak at this game.'

'Good luck—and to Szymanski too, if you see him.'

The raid went on, but I managed to get some sleep before morning. When I woke up, it still continued, though in a more desultory manner. This was, indeed, the advent of the Secret Weapon, the inauguration of the V.1's—the so-called 'flying bombs'. They came over at intervals of about twenty minutes or half an hour, all that day and the following night. This attack continued until Monday, a weekend that happened to be my fortnightly leave; spent, as it turned out, on their direct line of route across the Channel on the way to London.

'You see, my friend, I was right,' said Clanwaert.

One of the consequences of the Normandy landings was that the Free French forces became, in due course, merged into their nation's regular army. The British mission formerly in liaison with them was disbanded, a French military attaché in direct contact with Finn's Section coming into being. Accordingly, an additional major was allotted to our establishment, a rank to which I was now promoted, sustaining (with a couple of captains to help) French, Belgians, Czechs and Grand Duchy of Luxembourg. As the course of the war improved, work on the whole increased rather than diminished, so much so that I was unwillingly forced to refuse the offer of two Italian officers, sent over to make certain arrangements, whose problems, among others, included one set of regulations that forbade them in Great Britain to wear uniform; another that forbade them to wear civilian clothes. All routine work with the French was transacted with Kernével, first seen laughing with Masham about *les voies hiérarchiques*, just before my first interview with Finn.

'They're sending a *général de brigade* from North Africa to take charge,' said Finn. 'A cavalryman called Philidor.'

Since time immemorial, Kernével, a Breton, like so many of the Free French, had worked at the military attaché's office in London as chief clerk. By now he was a captain. At the moment of the fall of France, faced with the alternative of returning to his country or joining the Free French, he had at once decided to remain, his serial number in that organization—if not, like Abou Ben Adhem's, leading all the rest—being very respectably high in order of acceptance. It was tempting to look for characteristics of my old Regiment in these specimens of Romano-Celtic stock emigrated to Gaul under pressure from Teutons, Scandinavians and non-Roman Celts.

'I don't think my mother could speak a word of French,' said Kernével. 'My father could—he spoke very good French—but I myself learnt the language as I learnt English.'

Under a severe, even priestly exterior, Kernével concealed a persuasive taste for conviviality—on the rare occasions when anything of the sort was to be enjoyed. From their earliest beginnings, the Free French possessed an advantage over the other Allies—and ourselves—of an issue of Algerian wine retailed at their canteens at a shilling a bottle. Everyone else, if lucky enough to find a bottle of Algerian, or any other wine, in a shop, had to pay nearly ten times that amount. So rare was wine, they were glad to give that, when available. This benefaction to the Free French, most acceptable to those in liaison with them, who sometimes lunched or dined at their messes, was no doubt owed to some figure in the higher echelons of our own army administration—almost certainly learned in an adventure story about the Foreign Legion—that French troops could only function on wine. In point of fact, so far as alcohol went, the Free French did not at all mind functioning on spirits, or drinks like *Cap Corse*, relatively exotic in England, of which they consumed a good deal. Their Headquarter mess in Pimlico was decorated with an enormous fresco, the subject of which I always forgot to enquire. Perhaps it was a Free French version of Géricault's *Raft of the Medusa*, brought up to date and depicting themselves as survivors from the wreck of German invasion.

They did not reject, as we sometimes did ourselves, Marshal Lyautey's doctrine, quoted by Dicky Umfraville, that gaiety was the first essential in an officer, that some sort of light relief was required to get an army through a war. Perhaps, indeed, they too liberally interpreted that doctrine. If so, the red-tape they had to endure must have driven them to it; those terrible *bordereaux*—the very name recalling the Dreyfus case whenever they arrived—labyrinthine and ambiguous enough to extort admiration from a Diplock or even a Blackhead.

'All is fixed for General Philidor's interview?' asked Kernével.

'I shall be on duty myself.'

General Philidor, soon after his arrival in London, had to see a personage of very considerable importance, only a degree or so below the CIGS himself. It had taken a lot of arranging. Philidor was a lively little man with a permanently extinguished cigarette-end attached to his lower lip, which, under the peak of his general's khaki képi, gave his face the fierce intensity of a Paris taxi-driver. His rank was that, in practice, held by the commander of a Division. As a former Giraud officer, he was not necessarily an enthusiastic 'Gaullist'. At our first meeting he had asked me how I liked being in liaison with the French, and, after speaking of the purely military aspects of the work, I had mentioned Algerian wine.

'Believe me, mon commandant, before the '14–'18 war many Frenchmen had never tasted wine.'

'You surprise me, sir.'

'It was conscription, serving in the army, that gave them the habit.'

'It is a good one, sir.'

'My father was a *vigneron*.'

'Burgundy or Bordeaux, sir?'

'At Chinon. You have heard of Rabelais, mon commandant?'

'And drunk Chinon, sir—a faint taste of raspberries and to be served cold.'

'The vineyard was not far from our cavalry school at Saumur, convenient when I was on, as you say, a course there.'

I told him about staying at La Grenadière, how the Leroys had a son instructing at Saumur in those days, but General Philidor did not remember him. It would have been a long shot had he done so. All the same, contacts had been satisfactory, so that by the time he turned up for his interview with the important officer already mentioned, there was no sense of undue formality.

Philidor started in Finn's room, from where I conducted him to a general of highish status—to be regarded, for example, as distinctly pre-eminent to the one in charge of our own Directorate—who was to act as it were as mediator between Philidor and the all but supreme figure. This mediating general was a brusque officer, quickly mounting the rungs of a successful military career and rather given to snapping at his subordinates. After he and Philidor had exchanged conventional army courtesies, all three of us set off down the passage to the great man's room. In the antechamber, the Personal Assistant indicated that his master was momentarily engaged. The British general, lacking small talk, drummed his heels awaiting the summons. I myself should remain in the ante-chamber during the interview. There was a few seconds delay. Then a most unfortunate thing happened. The general acting as midwife to the birth of the parley, misinterpreting a too welcoming gesture or change of facial expression on the part of the PA, guardian of the door, who had up to now been holding us in check, motioned General Philidor to follow him, and advanced boldly into the sanctuary. This reckless incursion produced a really alarming result. Somebody—if it were, indeed, a human being—let out a frightful roar. Whoever it was seemed to have lost all control of himself.

'*I thought I told you to wait outside—get out . . .*'

From where our little group stood, it was not possible to peep within, but the volume of sound almost made one doubt human agency. Even the CIGS saying good-morning was nothing to it. This was the howl of an angry animal, consumed with rage or pain, probably a mixture of both. Considered merely as a rebuke, it would have struck an exceptionally peremptory note addressed to a lance-corporal.

'Sorry, sir . . .'

Diminished greatness is always a painful spectacle. The humility expressed in those muttered words, uttered by so relatively exalted an officer, was disturbing to me. General Philidor, on the other hand, seemed to feel more detachment. Appreciative, like most Frenchmen, of situations to be associated with light comedy—not to say farce—he fixed me with his sharp little eyes, allowing them to glint slightly, though neither of us prejudiced the frontiers of discipline and rank by the smallest modification of expression. However, entirely to avoid all danger of doing any such thing, I was forced to look away.

This incident provoked reflections later on the whole question of senior officers, their relations with each other and with those of subordinate rank. There could be no doubt, so I was finally forced to decide, that the longer one dealt with them, the more one developed the habit of treating generals like members of the opposite sex; specifically, like ladies no longer young, who therefore deserve extra courtesy and attention; indeed, whose every whim must be given thought. This was particularly applicable if one were out in the open with a general.

'Come on, sir, *you* have the last sandwich,' one would say, or 'Sit on my mackintosh, sir, the grass is quite wet.'

Perhaps the cumulative effect of such treatment helped to account for the highly strung temperament so many generals developed. They needed constant looking after. I remembered despising Cocksidge, a horrible little captain at the Divisional Headquarters on which I had served, for behaving so obsequiously to his superiors in rank. In the end, it had to be admitted one was almost equally deferential, though one hoped less slavish.

'They're like a lot of ballerinas,' agreed Pennistone. 'Ballerinas in Borneo, because their behaviour, even as ballerinas, is quite remote from everyday life.'

Meanwhile the V.1's continued to arrive sporadically, their launchers making a habit of sending three of them across Chelsea between seven and eight in the morning, usually a few minutes before one had decided to get up. They would roar towards the flats—so it always sounded—then switch off a second or two before you expected them to pass the window. One would roll over in bed and face the wall, in case the window came in at the explosion. In point of fact it never did. This would happen perhaps two or three times a week. Kucherman described himself as taking cover in just the same way.

'Nevertheless,' he said, 'I must insist that things are taking a very interesting turn from the news in this morning's papers.'

'Insist' was a favourite word of Kucherman's. He used it without the absolute imperative the verb usually implied in English. He was referring to what afterwards became known as the Officers' Plot, the action of the group of German generals and others who had unsuccessfully attempted to assassinate Hitler. They had failed, but even the fact that they had tried was encouraging.

'Colonel von Stauffenberg sounds a brave man.'

'I have met him several times,' said Kucherman.

'The right ideas?'

'I should insist, certainly. We last talked at a shooting party in the Pripet marshes. Prince Theodoric was also staying in the house, as it happened. Our Polish host is now buried in a communal grave not so many miles north of our sport. The Prince is an exile whose chance of getting back to his own country looks very remote. I sit in Eaton Square wondering what is happening to my business affairs.'

'You think Prince Theodoric's situation is hopeless?'

'Your people will have to make a decision soon between his Resistance elements and the Partisans.'

'And we'll come down on the side of the Partisans?'

'That's what it looks increasingly like.'

'Not too pleasant an affair.'

'There's going to be a lot of unpleasantness before we've finished,' said Kucherman. 'Perhaps in my own country too.'

When we had done our business Kucherman came to the top of the stairs. The news had made him restless. Although quiet in manner, he gave the impression at the same time of having bottled up inside him immense reserves of nervous energy. It was, in any case, impossible not to feel excitement about the way events were moving.

'This caving in of the German military caste—that is the significant thing. An attempt to assassinate the Head of the State on the part of a military group is a serious matter in any country—but in Germany how unthinkable. After all, the German army, its officer corps, is almost a family affair.'

Kucherman listened to this conventional enough summary of the situation, then suddenly became very serious.

'That's something you always exaggerate over here,' he said.

'What, Germans and the army? Surely there must be four or five hundred families, the members of which, whatever their individual potentialities, can only adopt the army as a career? Anyway that was true before the Treaty of Versailles. Where they might be successful, say at the Law or in business, they became soldiers. There was no question of the German army not getting the pick. At least that is what one was always told.'

Kucherman remained grave.

'I don't mean what you say isn't true of the Germans,' he said. 'Of course it is—anyway up to a point, even in the last twenty years. What you underestimate is the same element in your own country.'

'Not to any comparable degree.'

Kucherman remained obdurate.

'I speak of something I have thought about and noticed,' he said. 'Your fathers were in the War Office too.'

For the moment—such are the pitfalls of an alien language and alien typifications, however familiar, for Kucherman spoke English and knew England well—it seemed he could only be facetious. I laughed, assuming he was teasing. He had not done so before, but so much optimism in the air may have made him feel a joke was required. He could scarcely be ignorant that nowhere—least of all within the professional army—was the phrase 'War Office' one for anything but raillery. Perhaps he had indeed known that and disregarded the fact, because a joke was certainly not intended. Kucherman was a man to make up his own mind. He did not take his ideas second-hand. Possibly, thinking it over that night on Fire Duty, there was even something to be said for his theory; only our incurable national levity making the remark at that moment sound satirical. A grain of truth, not necessarily derogatory, was to be traced in the opinion.

Fire Duty was something that came round at regular intervals. It meant hanging about the building all night, fully dressed, prepared to go on the roof, if the Warning sounded, with the object of extinguishing incendiary bombs that might fall there. These were said to be easily dealt with by use of sand and an instrument like a garden hoe, both of which were provided as equipment. On previous occasions, up to now, no raid had occurred, the hours passing not too unpleasantly with a book. Feeling I needed a change from the seventeenth century and Proust, I had brought Saltykov-Schredin's *The Golovlyov Family* to read. A more trivial choice would have been humiliating, because Corporal Curtis turned out to be the accompanying NCO that night, and had *Adam Bede* under his arm. We made whatever mutual arrangements were required, then retired to our respective off-duty locations.

146

Towards midnight I was examining a collection of photographs taken on D-Day, which had not long before this replaced the two Isbister-like oil paintings. Why the pictures had been removed after being allowed to hang throughout the earlier years of the blitz was not apparent. Mime, now a captain, had just hurried past with his telegrams, when the Warning sounded. I found my way to the roof at the same moment as Corporal Curtis.

'I understand, sir, that we ascend into one of the cupolas as an action station.'

'We do.'

'I thought I had better await your arrival and instructions, sir.'

'Tell me the plot of *Adam Bede* as far as you've got. I've never read it.'

Like the muezzin going on duty, we climbed up a steep gangway of iron leading into one of the pepperpot domes constructed at each corner of the building. The particular dome allotted to us, the one nearest the river, was on the far side from that above our own room. The inside was on two floors, rather like an eccentric writer's den for undisturbed work. Curtis and I proceeded to the upper level. These Edwardian belvederes, elaborately pillared and corniced like Temples of Love in a rococo garden, were not in themselves of exceptional beauty, and, when first erected, must have seemed obscure in functional purpose. Now, however, the architect's design showed prophetic aptitude. The exigencies of war had transformed them into true gazebos, not, as it turned out, frequented to observe the 'pleasing prospects' with which such rotundas and follies were commonly associated, but at least to view their antithesis, 'horridly gothick' aspects of the heavens, lit up by fire and rent with thunder.

This extension of purpose was given effect a minute or two later. The moonlit night, now the melancholy strain of the sirens had died away, was surprisingly quiet. All Ack-Ack guns had been sent to the coast, for there was no point in shooting down V.1's over built-up areas. They would come down anyway. Around lay the darkened city, a few solid masses, like the Donners-Brebner Building, recognisable on the far side of the twisting strip of water. Then three rapidly moving lights appeared in the southern sky, two more or less side by side, the third following a short way behind, as if lacking acceleration or will power to keep up. They travelled with that curious shuddering jerky movement characteristic of such bodies, a style of locomotion that seemed to suggest the engine was not working properly, might break down at any moment, which indeed it would. This impression that something was badly wrong with the internal machinery was increased by a shower of sparks emitted from the tail. A more exciting possibility was that dragons were flying through the air in a fabulous tale, and climbing into the turret with Curtis had been done in a dream. The raucous buzz could now be plainly heard. In imagination one smelt brimstone.

'They appear to be heading a few degrees to our right, sir,' said Curtis.

The first two cut-out. It was almost simultaneous. The noisy ticking of the third continued briefly, then also stopped abruptly. This interval between cutting-out and exploding always seemed interminable. At last it came; again two almost at once, the third a few seconds later. All three swooped to the ground, their flaming tails pointing upwards, certainly dragons now, darting earthward to consume their prey of maidens chained to rocks.

'Southwark, do you think?'

'Lambeth, sir—having regard to the incurvations of the river.'

'Sweet Thames run softly . . .'

'I was thinking the same, sir.'

148

'I'm afraid they've caught it, whichever it was.'

'I'm afraid so, sir.'

The All Clear sounded. We climbed down the iron gangway.

'Do you think that will be all for tonight?'

'I hope so, sir. Just to carry the story on from where we were when we were interrupted: Hetty is then convicted of the murder of her child and transported.'

The rest of the tour of duty was quiet. I read *The Golovlyov Family* and thought what a pity Judushka had not lived at a later period to become a commissar. A month later the Allies entered Paris. George Tolland remained too ill to be moved from Cairo.

4

In DUE COURSE V.1's WENT out of fashion, and V.2's, a form of rocket, became the mode. They were apt to come over in the middle of the morning. Finn was talking to me one day about the transference of Luxembourg personnel from the Belgian artillery (where they manned a battery) to the newly raised army of the Grand Duchy (envisaged with a ceiling of three battalions), when his voice was completely drowned. The dull roar blotting out his comments had been preceded by an agonized trembling of the surrounding atmosphere, the window seeming about to cave in, but recovering itself. I just managed not to jump. Finn appeared totally un-impressed by the sound, whether from strength of nerves or deafness was uncertain. He repeated what he had to say without the smallest modification of tone, signed the minute and put down his pen.

'We've been ordered to take the Allied military attachés overseas,' he said. 'Show 'em a few things. Bound to cause trouble, but there it is. Dempster will be in charge while I'm away. David will probably take the Neutrals when their turn comes, so I shall want you to act as an additional Conducting Officer, Nicholas. Just cast your eye over these papers. It's going to be rather a scramble at such short notice.'

He talked about arrangements. I picked up the instructions

and was about to go. Finn drummed on the table with his pen.

'By the way,' he said, 'I've made it up with Farebrother. He's in Civil Affairs now and he came in yesterday about some matter he thought might concern us. Of course, he's a fellow of great charm, whatever else one thinks. Told me he was going to get married—a general's widow in MI 5. "Won't be able to conceal anything from her!" he said.'

Finn laughed, as if he thought retribution would now claim Farebrother for any sins committed against law and order in connexion with the Szymanski affair.

'Not a Mrs Conyers?'

'That's her name. Very capable lady, I understand. Don't know whether marriage is a good idea at the age Farebrother's reached, but that's his business. Get to work right away on the details of the tour.'

When the day came, the military attachés assembled outside the staff entrance. We did not move off precisely on time, because General Lebedev was a minute or two late. While we waited, another of those quaverings of the air round about took place, that series of intensely rapid atmospheric tremors, followed by a dull boom. This one seemed to have landed somewhere in the direction of the Strand. The military attachés exchanged polite smiles. Van der Voort made a popping sound with finger and mouth. At that very moment Lebedev appeared at the end of the short street, giving the impression that he had just been physically ejected from a rocket-base on to a pin-pointed target just round the corner from where we stood, a method of arrival deliberately chosen by his superiors to emphasize Soviet technical achievement. He was, in truth, less than a couple of minutes behind time, most of the rest having arrived much too early. Possibly the high-collared blue uniform, with breeches, black top-boots and spurs, had taken longer to adjust than the battledress adopted for the occasion by most of the others. Major Prasad, representative of an independent state in the Indian sub-continent, also wore boots, brown ones without spurs. They were better cut than Lebedev's, as were also his breeches, but that was only noticeable later, as Lebedev wore an overcoat. He was greeted with a shower of salutes, the formality of Bobrowski's courteously ironical.

Finn was suffering that morning from one of his visitations of administrative anxiety. He counted the party three times before we entered the cars. I opened one of the doors for General Philidor.

'You accompany us to France, Jenkins—*pour les vacances?*'

'I do, sir.'

'You will find a charming country. I lived there some years ago and was very satisfied.'

He was right about *les vacances*. Undoubtedly the buoyancy of a holiday outing was in the air. Only the V.2 had implied a call to order, a reminder that war was not yet done with. We took the Great West Road, passing the illuminated sign of the diving lady, where I had first kissed Jean Duport years before. I idly wondered what had happened to her, if she were involved in the war; what had happened to Duport, too, whether he had managed to 'sweat it out', the words he had used, in South America.

Although there might be a sense of exhilaration in our party, a crowd of officers unconnected by unit, brought together for some exceptional purpose, always tends to evoke a certain tension. The military attachés were no exception, even if on the whole more at ease than the average collection of British officers might prove in similar circumstances. This comparative serenity was, of course, largely due to the nature of the appointment, the fact that they were individuals handpicked for a job that required flexibility of manner. This was no doubt assisted by a tradition of Continental military etiquette in many respects at variance with our own. Officers of most other armies—so one got the impression—though they might be more formal with each other, were taught to be less verbally crisp, less surly, according to how you chose to assess the social bearing of our own officer corps. I had myself been more than once present at inter-Allied military conferences when the manners of our own people left much to be desired—been, in short, abominable by continental standards—probably more on account of inexperience in dealing with foreign elements than from deliberate rudeness; still less any desire to appear unfriendly—as was apt to be supposed by the foreign officer concerned—for 'political' or 'diplomatic' reasons. However, if individual British officers could at times show themselves unpolished or ill-at-ease with their Allies, other sides of the picture were to be borne in mind. We put up with quite a lot from the Allies too, though usually in the official rather than the personal field.

By the time we entered the Dakota that was to ferry us across the Channel, heavy banter, some of it capable of giving offence among a lot of mixed nationalities, began to take the place of that earlier formality. This change from normal was probably due to nerves being on edge. There was reason for that. It was, indeed, an occasion to stir the least imaginative among those whose country had been involved in the war since the beginning, while he himself, all or most of the time, had been confined in an island awaiting invasion. Such badinage, in fluent but foreign English, was at that moment chiefly on the subject of the imaginary hazards of the flight, some of the party—especially those like Colonel Hlava, with years of flying experience and rows of decorations for bravery in the air—behaving as if they had never entered a plane before. Possibly a hulk like this was indeed a cause for disquiet, if you were used to piloting yourself through the clouds in an equipage of the first order of excellence and modernity. We went up the gangway. Colonel Ramos, the newly appointed Brazilian, swallowed a handful of pills as soon as he reached the top. This precaution was noticed by Van der Voort, whose round florid clean-shaven face looked more than ever as if it peered out of a Jan Steen canvas. Van der Voort was in his most boisterous form, seeming to belong to some anachronistic genre picture, *Boors at an Airport* or *The Airfield Kermesse*, executed by one of the lesser Netherlands masters. He clapped Ramos on the back.

'Been having a night out, Colonel?' he asked.

Ramos, in spectacles with a woollen scarf round his neck, looked a mild academic figure in spite of his military cap. He was obviously not at all well. The sudden impact of London wartime food—as well it might—had radically disordered his stomach. He had explained his case to me as soon as he arrived that morning, indicating this by gesture rather than words, his English being limited. I promised the aid of such medicaments as I carried, when we could get to them.

'I believe you've been having a party with the girls, Colonel Ramos,' said Van der Voort. 'Staying up too late. Isn't that true, old man?'

Ramos having, as already stated, no great command of the language, understood only that some enquiry, more or less kind, had been made about his health. He delighted Van der Voort by nodding his head vigorously in affirmation.

'You're new to London, but, my God, you haven't taken long to make your way about,' Van der Voort went on. 'How do you find it? Do you like the place?'

'Very good, very good,' said Colonel Ramos.

'Where have you been so far? Burlington Gardens? Have you seen the ladies there? Smeets and I always take a look on the way back from lunch. You ought to recce Burlington Gardens, Colonel.'

'Yes, yes.'

Colonel Ramos nodded and smiled, laughing almost as much as Van der Voort himself. By this time we were all sitting on the floor of the plane, which was without any sort of interior furnishing. Finn and I had placed ourselves a little way from the rest, because he wanted to run through the programme again. Colonel Chu, who greatly enjoyed all forms of teasing, edged himself across to Ramos and Van der Voort, evidently wanting to join in. He was not in general very popular with his colleagues.

'Like all his race, he's dreadfully conceited,' Kucherman had said. '*Vaniteux*—you never saw anything like them. I have been there more than once and insist they are the vainest people on earth.'

Chu was certainly pleased with himself. He began to finger the scarf Ramos was wearing. The Brazilian, for a man who looked as if he might vomit at any moment, took the broad witticisms of the other two in very good part. He probably understood very little of what was said. Watching the three of them, one saw what Chu had meant by saying he could 'make himself young'. Probably he would have fitted in very tolerably as a boy at Eton, had we been able to persuade the school authorities to accept him for a while. He left his London appointment before the end of the War and returned to China, where he was promoted major-general. About three years later, so I was told, he was killed commanding one of Chiang Kai-Shek's Divisions at Mukden. Chu must have been in his early forties then, no doubt still prepared to pass as a schoolboy. We floated out over a brilliant shining sea.

'They're not to be shown Pluto,' said Finn. 'I bet one and all of them make a bee-line for it. They're as artful as a cartload of monkeys when it comes to breaking the rules.'

Pluto—Pipe Line Under The Ocean, appropriately re-calling the Lord of the Underworld—was the system, an ingenious one, by which troops in a state of mobility were supplied with oil.

'Not a hope they won't see Pluto,' repeated Finn gloomily.

That sort of thing sometimes got on his mind. He was still worrying about Pluto when we landed at the army airfield. Once more the military attachés were packed into cars. I was in the last one with Prasad, Al Sharqui and Gauthier de Graef. Kucherman, in his capacity as great industrial magnate, had been recalled to Brussels to confer with the new Government, so Gauthier had come on the tour in his place. The Belgians were heavily burdened with economic problems. They had had no Quisling figure to be taken seriously during the occupation, but their various Resistance movements were, some of them, inclined to be fractious. Gauthier was for taking a firm line with them. Prasad, next door to him, had only come with us owing to his own personal desire to do so. His creed and status at home made it doubtful whether it were permissible for him to take part in an expedition that would inevitably lead to eating in public. I had special instructions to see his require-ments in the way of food and accommodation were strictly observed. Al Sharqui, rather shy in this hurly-burly of nationalities and generals, came from one of the Arab states. Like Prasad, he was a major.

'This is like arriving on another planet,' said Gauthier de Graef.

He was right. It was all very strange, incomparably strange. The company one was with certainly did not decrease this sense of fantasy. More personal sensations were harder to define, took time to resolve. I cannot re-member whether it was the day we arrived or later that things crystallized. We were bowling along through Normandy and a region of fortified farms. Afterwards, in memory, the apple orchards were all in blossom, like isolated plantations on which snow for some unaccountable reason had fallen, light glinting between the tree trunks. But it was already November. There can have been no blossom. Blossom was a mirage. Autumnal sunshine, thin, hard, penetrating, must have created that scenic illusion, kindling white and silver sparkles in branches and foliage. What you see conditions feeling, not what is. For me the country was in blossom. At any season the dark ancientness of those massive granges, their stone walls loop-holed with arrow-slits, would have been mesmeric enough. Now, their mysterious aspect was rendered even more enigmatic by a surrounding wrack of armoured vehicles in multiform stages of dissolution. This residue was almost always concentrated within a comparatively small area, in fact whereever, a month or two before, an engagement had been fought out. Then would come stretches of quite different country, fields, woodland, streams, to all intents untouched by war.

In one of these secluded pastoral tracts, a Corot landscape of tall poplars and water meadows executed in light greys, greens and blues, an overturned staff-car, wheels in the air, lay sunk in long grass. The camouflaged bodywork was already eaten away by rust, giving an impression of abandonment by that brook decades before. High up in the branches of one of the poplars, positioned like a cunningly contrived scarecrow, the tatters of a field-grey tunic, black-and-white collar patches just discernible, fluttered in the faint breeze and hard cold sunlight. The isolation of the two entities, car and uniform, was complete. There seemed no explanation of why either had come to rest where it was.

At that moment, an old and bearded Frenchman appeared plodding along the road. He was wearing a beret, and, like many of the local population, cloaked in the olive green rubber of a British army anti-gas cape. As our convoy passed, he stopped and waved a greeting. He looked absolutely delighted, like a peasant in a fairy story who has found the treasure. For some reason it was all too much. A gigantic release seemed to have taken place. The surroundings had suddenly become overwhelming. I was briefly in tears. The others were sunk in unguessable reflections of their own; Prasad perhaps among Himalayan peaks; Al Sharqui, the sands of the desert; Gauthier, in Clanwaert's magic realm, the Porte de Louise. We sped on down the empty roads.

'This car is like travelling in a coffee-grinding machine,' said Gauthier.

'Or a cement-mixer.'

The convoy halted at last to allow the military attachés to relieve themselves. Out of the corner of my eye, I saw the worst had happened. We had blundered on a kind of junction of Plutonic equipment. Finn must have instantaneously seen that too. He rushed towards the installation, as if unable to contain himself—perhaps no simulation—taking up his stand in such a place that it would have been doubtful manners to pass in front of him. On the way back to the cars he caught me up.

'I don't think they noticed Pluto,' he whispered.

It was late that night when, after inspecting a mass of things, we reached billets. A clock struck twelve as the cars entered the seaside town where these had been arranged. By the time we arrived I had forgotten the name of the place, evidently a resort in peacetime, because we drew up before the doors of a largish hotel. It was moonlight. We got out. Finn conferred with the Conducting Officer from Army Group, who was still with us. Then he turned to me.

'They can't get us all into the Grand.'

'No room at the inn, sir?'

'Not enough mattresses or something, though it looks big enough. So, Nicholas, you'll attend General Asbjørnsen,

General Bobrowski, General Philidor and Major Prasad to La Petite Auberge. Everything's been laid on there for the five of you.'

I never knew, then or later, why that particular quartet was chosen to represent the overflow from the Grand. One would have expected four generals—Lebedev, for example, or Cobb, recently promoted brigadier-general—alternatively, four more junior in rank, Gauthier de Graef, Al Sharqui, a couple of lieutenant-colonels. However, that was how it was. One of the cars took the five of us to La Petite Auberge, which turned out to be a little black-and-white half-timbered building, hotel or pension, in Tudor, or, I suppose, François Premier or Henri Quatre style. Only one of the rooms had a bathroom attached, which was captured by General Asbjørnsen, possibly by being the most senior in rank, more probably because he climbed the stairs first. Obviously I was not in competition for the bath myself, so I did not greatly care who took it, nor by what methods. Prasad, like Asbjørnsen, went straight up to his room, but the other two generals and I had a drink in the bar, presided over by the *patronne*, who seemed prepared to serve Allies all night. Bobrowski and Philidor were talking about shooting wild duck. Then Asbjørnsen came down and had a drink too. He started an argument with Bobrowski about the best sort of skiing boots. Philidor and I left them to it. I had already begun to undress, when there was a knock on the door. It was Prasad.

'Major Jenkins...'

'Major Prasad?'

He seemed a little embarrassed about something. I hoped it was nothing like damp sheets, a problem that might spread to the rest of us. Prasad was still wearing breeches and boots and his Sam Browne.

'There's a room with a bath,' he said.

'Yes—General Asbjørnsen's.'

Prasad seemed unhappy. There was a long pause.

'I want it,' he said at last.

That blunt statement surprised me.

'I'm afraid General Asbjørnsen got there first.'

I thought it unnecessary to add that baths were not for mere majors like ourselves, especially when there was only one. Majors were lucky enough to be allowed a basin. I saw how easy it might become to describe the hardness of conditions when one had first joined the army. The declaration was also quite unlike Prasad's apparent appreciation of such things.

'But I need it.'

'I agree it would be nice to have one, but he is a general —a lieutenant-general, at that.'

Prasad was again silent for a few seconds. He was certainly embarrassed, though by no means prepared to give up the struggle.

'Can you ask General Asbjørnsen to let me have it, Major Jenkins?'

He spoke rather firmly. This was totally unlike Prasad, so quiet, easy going, outwardly impregnated with British Army 'good form'. I was staggered. Apart from anything else, the request was not a reasonable one. For a major to eject a general from his room in the small hours of the morning was a grotesque conception. It looked as if it might be necessary to embark on an *a priori* disquisition regarding the Rules and Disciplines of War, which certainly laid down that generals had first option where baths were concerned. It was probably Rule One. I indicated that a major—even a military attaché, in a sense representing his own country—could not have a bathroom to himself, if three generals, themselves equally representative, were all of them at least theoretically, in the running. I now saw how lucky I was that neither Bobrowski nor Philidor had shown any sign of considering himself slighted by being allotted a bathless room. In fact Prasad's claim did not merit serious discussion. I tried to put that as tactfully as possible. Prasad listened respectfully. He was not satisfied. I could not understand what had come over him. I changed the ground of argument, abandoning seniority of rank as a reason, pointing out that General Asbjørnsen had won the bath by right of conquest. He had led the way up the stairs, the first man—indeed, the first general—to capture the position. Prasad would not be convinced. There was another long pause. I wondered whether we should stay up all night. Prasad gave the impression of having a secret weapon, a battery he preferred not to unmask unless absolutely necessary. However, it had to come into action at last.

'It's my religion,' he said.

He spoke now apologetically. This was an entirely unexpected aspect.

'Oh, I see.'

I tried to play for time, while I thought up some answer.

'So I must have it,' Prasad said.

He spoke with absolute finality.

'Of course, I appreciate, Major Prasad, that what you have said makes a difference.'

He did not reply. He saw his projectile had landed clean on the target. I was defeated. The case was unanswerable, especially in the light of my instructions. Prasad looked sorry at having been forced to bring matters to this point. He looked more than sorry; terribly upset.

'So can I have the bathroom?'

I buttoned up my battledress blouse again.

'I'll make certain enquiries.'

'I'm sorry to be so much trouble.'

'Wait a moment, Major Prasad.'

By a great piece of good fortune, General Asbjørnsen was still in the bar. He and Bobrowski had not stopped arguing, though the subject had shifted from skiing boots to tactics.

Asbjørnsen was perhaps getting the worst of it, because his expression recalled more than ever the craggy features of Monsieur Ørn, the Norwegian at La Grenadière, who had such a row with Monsieur Lundquist, the Swede, for sending 'sneaks' over the net at tennis. I hoped no similar display of short temper was in the offing.

'Sir?'

General Asbjørnsen gave his attention.

'Major Prasad has asked me if you would possibly consider surrendering to him the room with the bath?'

General Asbjørnsen looked absolutely dumbfounded. He did not show the smallest degree of annoyance, merely stark disbelief that he had rightly grasped the meaning of the question.

'But—I have the bath.'

'I know, sir. That was why I was asking.'

'I am there.'

'That's just it, sir. Major Prasad wants it.'

'He wants it?'

'Yes, sir.'

'The bathroom?'

'Yes, sir.'

'But—the bathroom—it is for me.'

'It's a very special request, sir.'

General Asbjørnsen's face by now showed at least that he accepted the request as a special one. It was only too easy to understand his surprise, the fact that the idea took some time to penetrate. This was not at all on account of any language difficulty. General Asbjørnsen spoke English with the greatest fluency. As the conception began to take shape in his mind that Prasad's designs on the bath were perfectly serious, the earlier look of wonder had changed to one of displeasure. His face hardened. Bobrowski, who loved action, especially if it offered conflict, grasping that a superbly comic tussle was promised, now joined in.

'You are trying to take General Asbjørnsen's bath away from him, Major Jenkins?'

'It's for Major Prasad, sir, he—'

'I don't believe it, Major Jenkins, I believe you want it for yourself.'

Bobrowski had begun to laugh a lot.

'It is the particular wish of Major Prasad, sir—'

'Look here,' said Asbjørnsen, 'I have the bath. I keep it.'

That was the crux of the matter. There was no arguing. I had hoped, without much conviction, to achieve General Asbjørnsen's dislodgment without playing Prasad's trump card. Now this would have to be thrown on the table. It had become clear that much more discussion of this sort, to the accompaniment of Bobrowski's determination to treat the matter as a huge joke, would make Asbjørnsen more intractable than ever.

'It's a question of religion, sir.'

'What?'

'Major Prasad requires the room for religious reasons.'

That silenced them both. The statement, at least for the moment, made even more impression than I had hoped.

'Religion?' repeated Bobrowski.

I wished he would keep out of it. The bathroom was no business of his. By now I was entirely on Prasad's side, dedicated to obtaining the bathroom for whatever purpose he needed it.

'But this is a new idea,' said Bobrowski. 'I had not thought that was how baths are allotted on this tour. I am Catholic, what chance have I?'

'Sir—'

'Now I see why General Philidor went off to bed without even asking for the bathroom. Like many Frenchmen, he is perhaps free-thinker. He would have no chance for the bath. You would not let him, Major Jenkins. No religion—no bath. That is what you say. It is not fair.'

Bobrowski thought it all the funniest thing he had ever heard in his life. He laughed and laughed. Perhaps, in the long run, the conclusion of the matter owed something to this laughter of Bobrowski's, because General Asbjørnsen may have suspected that, if much more argument were carried on in this frivolous atmosphere, there was danger of his being made to look silly himself. Grasp of that fact after so comparatively short an interlude of Bobrowski's intervention did Asbjørnsen credit.

'You can really assure me then, Major Jenkins, that this is, as you have reported, a question of religion.'

'I can assure you of that, sir.'

'You are in no doubt?'

'Absolutely none, sir.'

'In that case, I agree to the proposal.'

General Asbjørnsen almost came to attention.

'Thank you, sir. Thank you very much indeed. Major Prasad will be most grateful. I will inform Colonel Finn when I see him.'

'Come upstairs and help me with my valise.'

The gruffness of General Asbjørnsen's tone was fully justified. I followed him to the disputed room, and was relieved to see the valise on the floor still unpacked. The bathroom door was open. It seemed an apartment designed for the ablutions of a very thin dwarf, one of Mime's kind. However, spatial content was neither here nor there. The point was, Prasad must have it. I took one end of the valise, Asbjørnsen the other. Prasad was peeping through the crack of his door. When informed of the way the battle had gone, he came out into the passage. Asbjørnsen was not ungracious about his renunciation. Prasad expressed a lot of thanks, but was unaware, I think, that the victory, like Waterloo, had been 'a damned close run thing'. General Asbjørnsen and I carried his valise into Prasad's former room. I helped Prasad with his valise too, on his taking over of the bathroom. As soon as Prasad and I were out in the passage, General Asbjørnsen shut his bedroom door rather loudly. He could not be blamed. My own relations with him, even when we returned to England, never fully recovered from that night. For the rest of the tour I speculated on what arcane rites Prasad conducted in that minute bathroom.

Next morning I rose early to check transport for the day's journey. The cars were to assemble at the entrance of the Grand Hotel, then pick up baggage of the party at La Petite Auberge on the route out of town. The Grand's main entrance was on the far side from the sea-front. It faced a fairly large, more or less oval open space, ornamented with plots of grass and flower beds long untended. From here the ground sloped away towards a little redbrick seaside town, flanked by green downs along which villas were spreading. The cars, on parade early, were all 'correct'. Finn was not due to appear for some minutes. Wondering what the place was like in peacetime at the height of the season, I strolled to the side of the hotel facing the 'front'. On this façade, a section of the building—evidently the hotel's dining-room, with half-a-dozen or more high arched windows—had been constructed so that it jutted out on to the esplanade. This promenade, running some feet above the beach, was no doubt closed to wheeled traffic in normal times. Now, it was completely deserted. The hotel, in café-au-lait stucco, with turrets and balconies, was about fifty or sixty years old, built at a time when the seaside was coming seriously into fashion. This small resort had a pleasantly out-of-date air. One pictured the visitors as well-to-do, though not at all smart, only insistent on good food and bourgeois comforts; the whole effect rather smug, though at the same time possessing for some reason or other an indefinable, even haunting attraction. Perhaps that was just because one was abroad again; and, for once, away from people. In the early morning light, the paint on the side walls of the hotel had taken on a pinkish tone, very subtle and delicate, blending gently with that marine vaporousness of atmosphere so enthusiastically endorsed by the Impressionists when they painted this luminous northern shore. It was time to find Finn. I returned to the steps of the main entrance. The large hall within was in semidarkness, because all the windows had been boarded up. Some of the military attachés were already about, polishing their boots in a kind of cloakroom, where the greatcoats had been left the night before. They seemed to be doing no harm, so I went back to the hall. Finn, carrying his valise on his shoulder, was descending the stairs.

'Good morning, sir.'

'Good morning, Nicholas. Couldn't use the lift over there. No lift boys in wartime. Didn't sleep too well. Kept awake by the noise of the sea. Not used to it.'

I reported the matter of the bath. Finn looked grave. 'Awkward situation, damned awkward. I've always tried to keep out of religious controversy. You handled it well, Nicholas. I'll have a word with Asbjørnsen and thank him. Any of them down yet?'

'Some are cleaning their boots in the lobby through there.'

'Cleaning their boots? My God, I believe they must have found my polish. Which way? I must stop this at once. It will be all used up.'

He rushed off. The fleet of cars got under way soon after this. That day I found myself with Cobb, Lebedev and Marinko, the Jugoslav. The seating was altered as a matter of principle from time to time. I was beside the driver. Lebedev—the name always reminded one of the character in *The Idiot* who was good at explaining the Apocalypse, though otherwise unreliable—rarely spoke; nor did he usually attend more than very briefly—so our Mission working with the Russians reported—the occasional parties given by their Soviet opposite numbers, where drinking bouts attained classical proportions, it was alleged. He was, indeed, commonly held to derive his appointment from civil, rather than military, eminence at home, his bearing and methods—despite the top boots and spurs—lacking, in the last resort, the essential stigmata of the *officier de carrière.*

'I tried to talk to Lebedev the other day about Dostoievski's Grand Inquisitor,' Pennistone said. 'He changed the subject at once to Nekrassov, of whom I've never read a line.'

Cobb was making notes in a little book. Marinko gazed out of the window, overcome with Slav melancholy, or, more specifically—being of the party that supported the Resistance groups of Mihailoviç—dejection at the course British policy appeared to be taking in that connexion.

'Just spell out the name of that place we stopped over last night, Major Jenkins,' said Cobb.

'C-A-B-O-U-R-G, sir.'

As I uttered the last letter, scales fell from my eyes. Everything was transformed. It all came back—like the tea-soaked madeleine itself—in a torrent of memory... Cabourg... We had just driven out of Cabourg... out of Proust's Balbec. Only a few minutes before, I had been standing on the esplanade along which, wearing her polo cap and accompanied by the little band of girls he had supposed the mistresses of professional bicyclists, Albertine had strolled into Marcel's life. Through the high windows of the Grand Hotel's dining-room—conveying to those without the sensation of staring into an aquarium—was to be seen Saint-Loup, at the same table Bloch, mendaciously claiming acquaintance with the Swanns. A little further along the promenade was the Casino, its walls still displaying tattered playbills, just like the one Charlus, wearing his black straw hat, had pretended to examine, after an attempt at long range to assess the Narrator's physical attractions and possibilities. Here Elstir had painted; Prince Odoacer played golf. Where was the little railway line that had carried them all to the Verdurins' villa? Perhaps it ran in another direction to that we were taking; more probably it was no more.

'And the name of the brigadier at the Battle Clearance Group?' asked Cobb. 'The tall one who took us round those captured guns?'

He wrote down the name and closed the notebook.

'You told me, Major Jenkins, that at the beginning of the war you yourself saw a Royal Engineer colonel wearing a double-breasted service-dress tunic. You can assure me of that?'

'I can, sir—and, on making enquiries, was told that cut was permitted by regulations, provided no objection was taken by regimental or higher authority.'

Proustian musings still hung in the air when we came down to the edge of the water. It had been a notable adventure. True, an actual night passed in one of the bedrooms of the Grand Hotel itself—especially, like Finn's, an appropriately sleepless one—might have crowned the magic of the happening. At the same time, a faint sense of disappointment superimposed on an otherwise absorbing inner experience was in its way suitably Proustian too: a reminder of the eternal failure of human life to respond a hundred per cent; to rise to the greatest heights without allowing at the same time some suggestion, however slight, to take shape in indication that things could have been even better.

Now, looking north into the light mist that hung over the waves, it was at first difficult to know what we were regarding. In the foreground lay a kind of inland sea, or rather two huge lagoons, the further enclosed by moles and piers that seemed exterior and afloat; the inner and nearer, with fixed breakwaters formed of concrete blocks, from which, here and there, rose tall chimneys, rows of cranes, drawbridges. The faraway floating docks delimited smaller pools and basins. Within the two large and separate surfaces, islands were dotted about supporting similar structures, the outlines of which extended into the misty distances as far as the horizon. What, one wondered, could this great maritime undertaking be? Was it planned to build a new Venice here on the waters? Perhaps these were docks constructed on an unusually generous scale to serve some great port—yet no large area of warehouses was at hand to suggest commerce, nor other signs of a big town anywhere along the shore. On the contrary, such houses as were to be seen, near or further inland, were in ruins, their extent in any case not at all resembling the outskirts of a city. The roadstead itself was now all but abandoned, at least the small extent of shipping riding at anchor there altogether disproportionate to the potential accommodation of the harbour—for harbour it must certainly be. There was something unreal, ghostly, even a little horrifying, about these grey marine shapes that seemed to have no present purpose, yet, like battlements of a now ruined castle, implied a violent, bloody history.

'*Tiens*,' said General Philidor. '*C'est bien le Mulberry.*'

The Mulberry it was, vast floating harbour designed for invasion, soon to be dismantled and forgotten, like the Colossus of Rhodes or Hanging Gardens of Babylon. We tramped its causeways out over the sea.

'We'll soon be in Brussels,' said Marinko. 'I hope to get some eau-de-cologne. In London it is unobtainable. Not a drop to be had.'

When we drove into the city's main boulevards, their sedate nineteenth-century self-satisfaction, British troops everywhere, made our cortège somewhat resemble Ensor's *Entry of Christ into Brussels*, with soldiers, bands and workers' delegation. One looked about for the Colman's

'Mustart' advertisement spelt wrong, but it was nowhere to be seen. Our billet was a VIP one, a requisitioned hotel presided over by a brisk little cock-sparrow of a captain, who evidently knew his job.

'We had the hell of a party here the other night,' he said. 'A crowd of senior officers as drunk as monkeys, brigadiers rooting the palms out of the pots.'

His words conjured up the scene in *Antony and Cleopatra*, when arm-in-arm the generals dance on Pompey's galley, a sequence of the play that makes it scarcely possible to disbelieve that Shakespeare himself served for at least a period of his life in the army.

'With thy grapes our hairs be crowned?'

'Took some cleaning up after, I can tell you.'

'Talking of cleanliness, would a cake of soap be any use to yourself?'

'Most acceptable.'

'In return, perhaps you could recommend the best place to buy a bottle of brandy?'

'Leave it to me—a couple, if you feel like spending that amount. I understand your people go to Army Group Main HQ tomorrow.'

'That's it—and we've been promised a visit to the Field-Marshal himself the following day.'

At Army Group Main the atmosphere was taut, the swagger—there was a good deal of swagger—a trifle forced; the court, as it were, of a military Trimalchio. Trimalchio, after all, had been an unusually successful business man; for all that is known, might have proved an unusually successful general. A force of junior staff officers with the demeanour of aggressive schoolboys had to be penetrated.

'You can't park those cars there,' one of them shouted at Finn. 'Get 'em out of the way at once and look sharp about it.'

Finn did as he was told. Indoors, the place was even more

like a school, one dominated by specialized, possibly rather cranky theories; efficient, all the same, and encouraging the boys to be independently minded, even self-applauding. Perhaps the last epithet was unfair. This, after all, was a staff that had delivered the goods pretty well so far. They had a right to be pleased with themselves. There was an odd incident while the Chief of Staff, a major-general, addressed the assembled military attachés. In the background a telephone rang. It was answered by a curly haired captain, who looked about fifteen. He began to carry on a long conversation at the top of his voice, accompanied by a lot of laughter. It was on the subject of some more or less official matter, though apparently nothing very weighty. I wondered how long this would be allowed to continue. The Chief of Staff looked up once or twice, but stood it for several minutes.

'Shut down that telephone.'

The captain's chatter was brought to an end. The general had spoken curtly, but most senior officers would have shown far less forbearance, especially in the presence of a relatively distinguished visiting party of Allied officers. Clearly things were run in their own particular way at Army Group Headquarters. I looked forward to seeing whether the same atmosphere would prevail at the Field-Marshal's Tactical HQ.

By this time, the Allied advance into Germany had penetrated about a couple of miles across the frontier at its furthest point. Accordingly, we left Belgium and entered that narrow strip of the Netherlands that runs between the two other countries, travelling towards the town of Roermond, still held by the enemy, against which our artillery was now in action. The long straight roads, leading through minefields, advertised at intervals as 'swept to verges', were lined on either side with wooden crates of ammunition stacked high under the poplars. Armour was moving in a leisurely manner across this dull flat country, designed by Nature for a battlefield, over which armies had immemorially campaigned. The identification flash of my old Division had appeared more than once on the shoulder of infantrymen passed on the route. When we stopped to inspect the organization of a bridgehead, I asked the local Conducting Officer from Lines of Communication if he knew whether any of my former Regiment were to be found in the neighbourhood.

'Which brigade?'

I told him.

'We should be in the middle of them here. Of course we may not be near your particular battalion. Like to see if we can find some of them? Your funny-wunnies will be happy for a few minutes, won't they?'

The military attachés would be occupied for half an hour or more with what they were inspecting. In any case, Finn as usual well ahead with time schedule, it would be undesirable to arrive unduly early for the Field-Marshal.

'I'd like to see if any of them are about.'

'Come along then.'

The L. of C. captain led the way down a road lined with small houses. Before we had gone far, sure enough, three or four soldiers wearing the Regimental flash were found engaged on some fatigue, piling stuff on to a truck. They were all very young.

'These look like your chaps—right regiment anyway, if not your actual battalion. You'd better have a word with them.'

I made some enquiries. Opportunity to knock off work was, as usual, welcome. They turned out to be my own Battalion, rather than the other one of the same Regiment within the brigade.

'Is an officer named Kedward still with you.'

'Captain Kedward, sir?'

'That's the one.'

'Oh, yes, the Company Commander, sir?'

'He actually commands your Company?'

'Why, yes, he does, sir. That's him.'

'You're all in Captain Kedward's Company?'

'We are, sir.'

It seemed astonishing to them that I did not know that already. I could not understand this surprise at first, then remembered that I too was wearing the regimental crest and flash, so that they certainly thought that I belonged to the same brigade as themselves, possibly even newly posted to their own unit. Soldiers often do not know all the officers of their battalion by sight. Indeed, it is not uncommon for the Adjutant to be thought of as the Commanding Officer, because he is the one most often heard giving orders.

'Is Captain Kedward likely to be about?'

'He's in the Company Office just now, sir.'

'Near here?'

'Over there, sir, where the swill tubs are.'

'You stay here, sir,' said one of them. 'I'll get Captain Kedward for you.'

Work was now more or less at a standstill. Cigarettes were handed out. It seemed they had arrived fairly recently in this sector. Earlier, the Battalion had been in action in the Caen area, where casualties had been fairly heavy. I asked about some of the individuals I had known, but they were too young to remember any of them. The L. of C. captain became understandably bored listening to all this.

'Now you're back with your long lost unit, I'll leave you to have a natter,' he said. 'Want to check up on some of my own business round the corner. Be with you again in five minutes.'

He went off. At the same moment Kedward, with the young soldier who had offered to fetch him, appeared from the door of a small farmhouse. It was more than four years since I had set eyes on him. He looked a shade older, though not much; that is to say he had lost that earlier appearance of being merely a schoolboy who had dressed up in uniform for fun, burnt-corking his upper lip to simulate a moustache. The moustache now had a perfectly genuine existence. He saluted, seeming to be rather flustered.

'Idwal.'

'Sir?'

He had not recognized me.

'Don't you remember? I'm Nick Jenkins. We were together in Rowland Gwatkin's Company.'

Even that information did not appear to make any immediate impression on Kedward.

'We last saw each other at Castlemallock.'

'The Castlemallock school of Chemical Warfare, sir?'

On the whole, where duty took one, few captains called a major 'sir', unless they were being very regimental. Everyone below the rank of lieutenant-colonel within the official world in which one moved was regarded as doing much the same sort of job, officers below the rank of captain being in any case rare. Responsibilities might vary, sometimes the lower rank carrying the higher responsibility; for example, the CIGS's ADC, a captain no longer young, being in his way a considerable figure. All the same, this unwonted reminder of having a crown on one's shoulder did not surprise me so much as Kedward's total failure to recall me as a human being. The fragile condition of separate identity, perpetually brought home to one, at the same time remains perpetually incredible.

'Don't you remember the moment when you took over the Company from Rowland—how upset he was at getting the push.'

Kedward's face lighted up at that.

'Why, yes,' he said. 'You were with us then, weren't

you, sir? I'm beginning to remember now. Didn't you come from London?... Was it Lyn Craddock took over the platoon from you?... or Phillpots?'

'Are they still with you?'

'Lyn got it at Caen commanding B Company.'

'Killed?'

'Yes, Lyn caught it. Phillpots? What happened to Phillpots? I believe he went to one of the Regular battalions and was wounded in Crete.'

'What became of Rowland Gwatkin?'

'Fancy your knowing Rowland.'

'But I tell you, we were all in the same Company.'

'So we were, but what a long time ago all that was. Rowland living in my home town makes it seem funny you know him.'

'Is he out here?'

'Rowland?'

Kedward laughed aloud at such an idea. It was apparently unthinkable.

'When I last saw him it looked as if he were due for the Infantry Training Centre.'

'Rowland's been out of the army for years.'

'Out of the army?'

'You never heard?'

Having once established the fact that I knew Gwatkin at all, in itself extraordinary enough, Kedward obviously found it equally extraordinary that I had not kept myself up-to-date about Gwatkin's life history.

'Rowland got invalided,' he said. 'That can't have been long after Castlemallock. I know it was all about the time I married.'

'You got married all right?'

'Father of two kids.'

'What sex?'

'Girls—that's what I wanted. Wouldn't mind a boy next.'

'So Rowland never reached the ITC?'

'I believe he got there, now you mention it, sir, then he went sick.'

'Do, for God's sake, stop calling me "sir", Idwal.'

'Sorry—anyway Rowland was ill about that time. Kidneys, was it? Or something to do with his back? Flat feet, it might have been. Whatever it was, they downgraded his medical category, and then he didn't get any better, and got boarded, and had to leave the army altogether.'

'Rowland must have taken that pretty hard.'

'Oh, he did,' said Kedward cheerfully.

'So what's he doing?'

'Back at the Bank. They're terribly shorthanded. Glad to have him there, you may be sure. I believe somebody here said they had a letter that mentioned Rowland was acting manager at one of the smaller branches. That's quite something for Rowland, who wasn't a great banking brain, I can tell you. Just what a lot of trouble he'll be making for everybody, you bet.'

'And his mother-in-law? Is she still living with them? He told me that was going to happen when we said goodbye to each other. Then, on top of his mother-in-law coming to live with them, having to leave the army himself. Rowland's had the hell of a pasting.'

The thought of Gwatkin and his mother-in-law had sometimes haunted me; the memory of his combined horror and resignation in face of this threatened affliction. To have his dreams of military glory totally shattered as well seemed, as so often in what happens to human beings, out of all proportion to what he had deserved, even if these dreams had, in truth, been impracticable for one of his capacity.

'My God, bloody marvellous what you know about Rowland and his troubles,' said Kedward. 'Mother-in-law and all. Have you come to live in the neighbourhood? I thought you worked in London. Did you hear that Elystan-Edwards got a VC here the other day? That was great, wasn't it?'

'I read about it. He came to the Battalion after I left.'

'It was great for the Regiment, wasn't it?' Kedward repeated.

'Great.'

There was a pause.

'Look here, sir—Nick—I'm afraid I won't be able to talk any more now. Got a lot to do. I thought first when they said a major wanted me, I was going to get a rocket from Brigade. I must make those buggers get a move on with their loading too. They been staging a go-slow since we've been here. Look at them.'

We said goodbye. Kedward saluted and crossed to the truck, where the loading operation had certainly become fairly leisurely. The L. of C. captain reappeared. I waved to Kedward. He saluted again.

'Jaw over?'

'Yes.'

Perhaps as a result of Kedward's exhortations, the fatigue party began to sing. The L. of C. captain and I walked up the road in the direction of the cars, leaving them to move eastward towards the urnfields of their Bronze Age home.

'Open now the crystal fountain,
Whence the healing stream doth flow:
Let the fire and cloudy pillar
Lead me all my journey through:
            Strong Deliverer,
            Strong Deliverer
Be thou still my strength and shield.'

'What a mournful row,' said the L. of C. captain, 'I've heard them chant that one before. It's a hymn.'

Finn was already rounding up the military attachés when we reached the place where the convoy was parked. In preparation for the visit to the Field-Marshal's Tactical Headquarters, some of our party were already wearing their pullovers in a manner popularized by the Field-Marshal himself—though not generally accepted as correct army turn-out—that is to say showing several inches below the battledress blouse. Among those thus seeking to be in the height of military fashion were Bobrowski and Van der Voort.

'I think I keep mine inside,' said Chu.

There was remarkably little fuss about the approach—no hint of Trimalchio here—security merely kept at its essential minimum. The accommodation for the Headquarters was a medium-sized house, built within the last ten or twelve years, one would guess, dark red brick, set amongst a few trees. The place had little or no character of its own. It might have been a farm, but had none of the farm's picturesque aspects. Possibly the manager of some local industry lived there. The fact was, it seemed prophetically built to house a Tactical Headquarters. By an inner wall stood the Field-Marshal's two long motor-caravans, sleeping apartment and office respectively. Here everything seemed quieter, far less exhibitionistic than at Main.

'Will you line up, please, gentlemen,' said Finn, 'in order of seniority of your appointment.'

The prelude to almost all happenings in the army, small and great, is an inspection. This visit was to be no exception. The military attachés were drawn up in a single row facing the caravans. Colonel Hlava, their doyen, was at one end: Gauthier de Graef, the most junior, at the other; with myself rounding off the party. There was a moment's pause, while we stood at ease. Then the Field-Marshal appeared from one of the caravans. He had his hands in his pockets, but removed them as he approached. It was instantaneously clear that he no longer chose to wear his pull-over showing under his battledress blouse. Indeed, he had by now, it was revealed, invented a form of battledress peculiar to himself, neatly tailored and of service-dress material. There was a moment when we were at attention; then at ease again. The last movement was followed by some rapid fidgeting and tucking up of clothes on the part of Bobrowski, Van der Voort and others with too keen a wish to be in the mode. Finn, out in front, was beaming with excitement. This was the sort of occasion he loved. There was a moment's conference. Then the Field-Marshal proceeded down the line, Finn at his side, presenting the military attachés, one by one. The Field-Marshal said a few words to each. It was quite a long time before he reached Gauthier.

'Captain Gauthier de Graef,' said Finn. 'The Belgian assistant military attaché. Major Kucherman himself was prevented from taking part in the tour. He had to attend a meeting of the new Belgian Government, which he may be joining.'

At the word 'Belgian' the Field-Marshal had begun to look very stern.

'You're the Belgians' man, are you?'

'Yes, sir.'

'Some of your people are showing signs of giving trouble in Brussels.'

'Yes, sir,' said Gauthier.

He and Kucherman had often talked of difficulties with the Resistance elements. Gauthier knew the problem all right.

'If they do give trouble,' said the Field-Marshal. 'I'll shoot 'em up. Is that clear? Shoot 'em up.'

'Yes, sir,' said Gauthier.

'It is?'

'Quite clear, sir.'

Gauthier de Graef replied with the deep agreement he certainly felt in taking firm measures. He had already complained of his own irritation with those of his countrymen whom he judged inadequately to appreciate their luck in having got rid of the Germans. The Field-Marshal moved on. He fixed his eyes on my cap badge.

'Prince of Wales's Volunteers?'

The slip was a very permissible one. The two crests possessed a distinct similarity in design. I named the Regiment. He showed no animus, as some generals might, at such a disavowal, however unavoidable.

'Any of 'em here?'

'Yes, sir—one of them got a VC a few weeks ago.'

The Field-Marshal considered the point, but made no move to develop it. Finn smiled very briefly to himself, almost invisibly to those who did not know him, either contemplating the eternal satisfaction his own bronze Maltese cross gave him; more probably, in the same connexion, appreciating this opportunity of recalling a rumour that the Field-Marshal was said to be not in the least impressed by the mystique of that particular award; indeed, alleged to declare its possession hinted at an undesirable foolhardiness on the part of the wearer. Finn, from his personal viewpoint, may even have seen my statement as a disciplined, if deserved, call to order, should that rumour have any basis in truth.

'Speak all these languages?'

'Only a little French, sir.'

'Don't speak any of 'em.'

'No, sir.'

He laughed, seeming pleased by that.

'Now I thought we'd all be photographed,' he said. 'Good thing on an occasion like this. I'll sign 'em for you.'

Smiling like the Cheshire Cat, a sergeant holding a small camera, suddenly came into being. There had been no sign of him a moment before. He seemed risen from the ground or dropped from a tree. We broke ranks and formed up again, this time on either side of the Field-Marshal, who took up a convenient position for this in front of one of the caravans. There was rather a scramble to get next to him, in which Chu and Bobrowski achieved flanking places. Van der Voort, elbowed out of the way by Chu, caught my eye and winked. Photography at an end, we were taken over the caravans, a visit personally conducted by the Field-Marshal, whose manner perfectly fused the feelings of a tenant justly proud of a perfectly equipped luxury flat with those of the lord of an ancient though still inhabited historical monument. Two dogs, not unlike General Liddament's, were making themselves very free of the place, charging about and disregarding the Field-Marshal's shouts. When this was over, the military attachés were led to a spot where a large map hung on a kind of easel.

'You'll want me to put you in the picture.'

With unexpectedly delicate movements of the hands, the Field-Marshal began to explain what had been happening. We were in an area, as I have said, immemorially campaigned over. In fact the map was no less than a great slice of history. As the eye travelled northward, it fell on Zutphen, where Sir Philip Sidney had stopped a bullet in that charge against the Albanian cavalry. One wondered why Albanians should be involved in this part of the world at such a time. Presumably they were some auxiliary unit of the Spanish Command, similar to those exotic corps of which one heard rumours in the current war, anti-Soviet Caucasians enrolled in a German formation, American-Japanese fighting with the Allies. The thought of Sidney, a sympathetic figure, distracted attention from the Field-Marshal's talk. One felt him essentially the kind of soldier Vigny had in mind when writing of the man who, like a monk, submitted himself to the military way of life, because he thought it right, rather than because it appealed to him. Available evidence, where Sidney was concerned, pointed to quite other than military preoccupations:

'Within those woods of Arcadie
He chief delight and pleasure took,
And on the mountain Parthenie,
Upon the crystal liquid brook
The Muses met him every day
That taught him sing, to write and say.'

The Field-Marshal continued his exposition with the greatest clarity, but the place-names of the map continued to stimulate daydreams of forgotten conflicts. Maastricht, for example. It took a moment or two to recall the connexion. Then, oddly enough, another *beau monde* poet was in question, though one of a very different sort to Sidney. Was it Rochester? Certainly a Restoration figure. Something about the moulding of a drinking-cup—boy's limbs entwined, a pederast, and making rather a point of it— with deliberations as to what scenes were to be represented on the vessel? The poet, certainly Rochester, expressed in the strongest terms his disapprobation of army life even in art:

'Engrave not battle on his cheek:
With war I've naught to do.
I'm none of those that took Maestrich,
Nor Yarmouth leaguer knew.'

This feeling that war was something to be avoided at all costs for personal reasons was very understandable; more acceptable, indeed, than many of the sometimes rather suspect moral objections put forward. The references, the engagement at Maastricht and 'Yarmouth leaguer' were obscure to me. The latter was presumably a sort of transit camp, the kind of establishment Dicky Umfraville had formerly been in charge of. Then some memory swam to the surface that d'Artagnan's historical prototype had fallen at Maastricht, though details of the particular campaign remained latent. D'Artagnan was, on the whole, rather a non-Vigny figure, anyway on the surface, insomuch as there seemed little or no reason to suppose he was particularly to the fore when it came to disagreeable and unglamorous army jobs. Musing of this sort had reached Marlborough, his taste for being kept by women, remarks made on that subject to Odo Stevens by Pamela Flitton, the connexion between sex and war in this particular aspect, when the Field-Marshal's discourse terminated. By that time the photographs had been developed. They were signed and handed round. Colonel Hlava, as doyen, made a little speech of thanks on behalf of all the military attachés. The Field-Marshal listened gravely. Then he gave a nod of dismissal. Finn and I packed them once more into the cars.

On the way to Brussels we passed a small cart pulled by a muscular-looking dog.

'Once you would have seen that in my country,' said Hlava. 'Now our standards have risen. Dogs no longer work.'

'That one seems positively to like it.'

This particular dog was making a great parade of how well he was accomplishing his task.

'Dogs are so ambitious,' agreed Hlava.

'The Field-Marshal's dogs seemed so. Do you suppose they were pressing for promotion?'

'A great man, I think,' said Hlava.

I tried to reduce to viable terms impressions of this slight, very exterior contact. On the one hand, there had been hardly a trace of the almost overpowering physical impact of the CIGS, that curious electric awareness felt down to the tips of one's fingers of a given presence imparting a sense of stimulation, also the consoling thought that someone of the sort was at the top. On the other hand, the Field-

Marshal's outward personality offered what was perhaps even less usual, will-power, not so much natural, as developed to altogether exceptional lengths. No doubt there had been a generous basic endowment, but of not the essentially magnetic quality. In short, the will here might even be more effective from being less dramatic. It was an immense, wiry, calculated, insistent hardness, rather than a force like champagne bursting from the bottle. Observed in tranquillity, the former combination of qualities was not, within the terms of reference, particularly uplifting or agreeable, except again in the manner their synthesis seemed to offer dependability in utter self-reliance and resilience. One felt that a great deal of time and trouble, even intellectual effort of its own sort, had gone into producing this final result.

The eyes were deepset and icy cold. You thought at once of an animal, though a creature not at all in the stylized manner of the two colonels at my Divisional Headquarters, reminiscent respectively of the dog-faced and bird-faced Egyptian deities. No such artifical formality shaped these features, and to say, for example, they resembled those of a fox or ferret would be to imply a disparagement not at all sought. Did the features, in fact, suggest some mythical beast, say one of those encountered in *Alice in Wonderland*, full of awkward questions and downright statements? This sense, that here was perhaps a personage from an imaginary world, was oddly sustained by the voice. It was essentially an army voice, but precise, controlled, almost mincing, when not uttering some awful warning, as to Gauthier de Graef. There was a faint and faraway reminder of the clergy, too; parsonic, yet not in the least numinous, the tone of the incumbent ruthlessly dedicated to his parish, rather than the hierophant celebrating divine mysteries. At the same time, one guessed this parish priest regarded himself as in a high class of hierophancy too, whatever others might think.

From the very beginnings of his fame, the Field-Marshal had never ignored Chips Lovell's often repeated reminder that it was a tailor's war. The new spruceness that had now taken the place of the conscious informality of ready-to-hand garments appropriate to desert warfare—to the confusion of those military attachés obliged hurriedly to tuck up their pullovers—was clearly conceived at the same time to avoid any resemblance to the buttoned-up army officer of caricature. It lacked too, probably also deliberately, the lounging smartness of which, for example, Dicky Umfraville, or even in his own fashion, Sunny Farebrother, knew the secret. The Field-Marshal's turn-out had to be admitted to fall short of any such elegance. Correct: neat: practical: unpompous: all that to perfection. Elegant, he was not. Why should he be? It was wholly unnecessary, probably a positive handicap in terms of personal propaganda. Besides, will-power exercised unrelentingly over a lifetime—as opposed to its display in brilliant flashes—is apt on the whole to be the enemy of elegance. One only had to think of the Dictators to see that. Few of the Great Captains of history, with the possible exception of Wellington, had shown themselves particularly elegant in victory; though there, of course, one moved into the world of moral elegance, and, in any case, victory was not yet finally attained.

The cock-sparrow captain, major-domo to VIPs, handed over the brandy bottles in a neat parcel when we arrived back at billets.

'A chap from Civil Affairs was asking for you. I told him when your party was expected back. He said he'd look in again.'

'What name?'

'Duport—a captain. He talked about getting you out for a drink.'

I was off duty that night. Although I had never much

liked Duport, an evening together, if he were free, would be better than one spent alone. If he were in Civil Affairs, it was possible that his branch had received an official notification of our being in Brussels and he wanted to discuss some Belgian matter. It could hardly be mere friendliness, as we scarcely knew each other. I asked where was a good place to go.

'The big brasserie on the corner's not too bad. You'll find all ranks there, but not many senior officers. If you're like me, and see a lot of them, that's a bit of a holiday. What's the food like in England now? Custard on everything when I was last on leave.'

Duport turned up later. I had not seen him since the Bellevue. His reddish hair receded from the forehead, getting grey by the ears. He looked tired, perceptibly older. Like Pennistone, he carried a General Service lion-and-unicorn in his cap, and had changed into service-dress. Uniform did not suit him. Instead of building him up, it diminished the aggressive energy his civilian appearance had always indicated. This lessening of aggression was also signified by a more subdued manner. The war had undoubtedly quieted Duport down.

'I saw your name as Belgian Liaison Officer in London on some document passed to us,' he said. 'Then found you were personally conducting this flight of swans. We run here parallel in a curious way with Army Group, and there are one or two things that could be straightened out if we had a talk. The usual stuff, Leopold's marriage, the Resistance lads. When do you go back?'

'Tomorrow.'

'Then if we had a talk tonight we could straighten out some points about policy. We're very full of work at the moment, as I expect you are too.'

This was a rather different tone from the Duport of former days. We went to the recommended brasserie, as he had no better suggestion. He seemed to have lost some of his old interest in material things. For a time we talked Belgian affairs. Dupont knew all about Kucherman, but had not met him.

'He's one of the ablest blokes they've got,' he said. 'However let's give the subject a rest now. You were cremating your uncle when we last met.'

'How did you come to join the army? At the Bellevue you were talking of sweating it out in South America, if war came.'

'South America wasn't on. As you know I was on my uppers at that moment. Then I got a chance of going to Egypt for a firm that wanted to wind up one of their branches there. Donners had an interest and managed to get me out. Getting back was another matter. The chance of a commission turned up. I took it. Wanted to get into one of the secret shows, but didn't bring it off. I was in the Censorship for a time. Not much to be recommended. Then I had a bad go of Gyppy tummy—with complications. That was what ultimately brought me back to Europe and the mob I now belong to.'

'You haven't seen anything of Peter Templer, have you? Donners was helping to fix him up too—something in the cloak-and-dagger line—but I haven't heard what came of it.'

Duport finished his glass.

'Peter's had it,' he said.

'Do you mean he's been killed?'

'Gone for a Burton.'

'On a secret operation?'

'Yes.'

'I suppose nobody knows more than that?'

Duport hesitated.

'It never struck me you wouldn't have heard about Peter,' he said. 'There was a lot of talk about it all in Cairo

—not the best security imaginable, but then Cairo is not a place for the best security. There was certainly a lot of talk.'

'What happened?'

'I daresay Peter's still officially described as missing, but everyone in the know is aware he's dead, even though the details vary. One story was he was murdered by his wireless operator for the money he had on him, but I happen to know that isn't true. We'll go to another place for the next round.'

We left the brasserie and found a café. It was less crowded.

'Does Prince Theodoric mean anything to you?' asked Duport.

'He's done business with our Section once or twice, but not recently—and of course not on the secret operations level.'

'You knew Peter was involved in that quarter?'

'More or less.'

'I always have a fellow feeling for the Prince, though we've never met,' said Duport. 'He and I always seem to be screwing the same ladies. Bijou Ardglass, for example, now, poor girl, in the arms of Jesus. Have you heard of a young woman called Pamela Flitton?'

'Volumes.'

'You know she was the main cause of Peter's trouble?'

'I was told that—but people don't go and get killed because a piece like that won't sleep with them.'

'Well, not exactly, I agree,' said Duport. 'It was more Peter felt he was slowing up, as I see it. The point is that it all builds up round Theodoric. As you know the good Prince's realm is internally divided as to how best repel the invader. One lot wants one thing, the other, another. Peter went in with the Prince's gang.'

'Was someone called Odo Stevens mixed up in all this?'

'I thought you said you didn't deal with the cloak-and-dagger boys?'

'Something Stevens said off the record.'

'You know him? Young Stevens was a bit too fond of making statements off the record.'

'I was on a course with him earlier in the war. Then he was mixed up with a girl I knew, now deceased.'

'Odo the Stoat we used to call him. These boys make me feel my age. That's what got Peter down.'

'Is Stevens missing too?'

'Not he. I met him in Cairo after they'd got him out.'

'Why didn't they get Peter out too?'

Duport gave one of his hard unfriendly laughs.

'There are those in Cairo who allege proper arrangements were never made to get Peter out. At least they were planned, but never put into operation. That's what's said. These things happen sometimes, you know. Little interdepartmental differences. Change of policy at the top. There was a man with an unpronounceable name mixed up with it all too. I don't know which side he was on.'

'Szymanski?'

'Why do you ask about things when you know the whole story already? Are you from MI 5? An agent provocateur, just trying to see what you can get out of me, then shop me for bad security? That's what it sounds like.'

'Was Szymanski with Templer or Stevens?'

'So far as I know, on his own. Not sure it was even ourselves who sent him in. Might have been his own people, whoever they were. He went there in the first instance to knock off someone—the head of the Gestapo or a local traitor. I don't know. It was all lined up, then a signal came down from the top—from the Old Man himself, they say—that war wasn't waged in that manner in his opinion. All that trouble for nothing—but I understand they got Szymanski out. A chap in the Cairo racket told me all this.

He was fed up with the way that particular party was run. It came out I'd been Peter's brother-in-law in days gone by, so I suppose he thought, as a former relation, I'd a right to know why he'd kicked the bucket.'

'And you really think Pamela Flitton caused this?'

'I only stuffed her once,' said Duport. 'Against a shed in the back parts of Cairo airport, but even then I could see she might drive you round the bend, if she really decided to. I'll tell you something amusing. You remember that bugger Widmerpool, who'd got me into such a jam about chromite when we last met?'

'He's a full colonel now.'

'He was in Cairo at one moment and took Miss Pamela to a nightclub.'

'Rumours of that even reached England.'

'That girl gets a hold on people,' said Duport. 'Sad about Peter, but there it is. The great thing is he didn't fall into the hands of the Gestapo, as another friend of mine did. Pity you're going back tomorrow. We might have gone to the Opera together.'

'Didn't know music was one of your things.'

'Always liked it. One of the reasons my former wife and I never really hit it off was because Jean only knew *God Save the King* because everyone stood up. I was always sneaking off to concerts. They put on *La Muette de Portici* here to celebrate the liberation. Not very polite to the Dutch, as when it was first performed, the Belgians were so excited by it, they kicked the Hollanders out. I'm not all that keen on Auber myself, as it happens, but I've met a lot of dumb girls, so I've been to hear it several times to remind myself of them.'

This revelation of Duport's musical leanings showed how, as ever, people can always produce something unexpected about themselves. In the opposite direction, Kernével was equally unforeseen, on my return, in the lack of interest he showed in Cabourg and its associations with Proust. He knew the name of the novelist, but it aroused no curiosity whatever.

'Doesn't he always write about society people?' was Kernével's chilly comment.

I told Pennistone about Prasad, Asbjørnsen and the bath.

'Prasad merely turned the taps on at the hour of prayer. It was perfectly right that he should have the bathroom. Finn should have arranged that through you in the first instance.'

'I see.'

'Thank God Finn's back, and I shall no longer have to deal directly with that spotty Brigadier who always wants to alter what is brought to him to sign. I have had to point out on three occasions that his emendations contradict himself in a higher unity.'

A day or two after our return, Kucherman telephoned early. It was a Friday.

'Can you come round here at once?'

'Of course. I thought you were still in Brussels.'

'I flew in last night.'

When I reached Eaton Square, Kucherman, unusual for him, was looking a little worried.

'This question I am going to put is rather important,' he said.

'Yes?'

'My Government has come to a decision about the army of the Resistance. As you know, the problem has posed itself since the expulsion of the Germans.'

'So I understand.'

'Were you told what the Field-Marshal threatened to Gauthier de Graef?'

'I was standing beside him when the words were said.'

'They are good young men, but they require something to do.'

'Naturally.'

'The proposal is that they should be brought to this country.'

That was an unexpected proposition.

'You mean to train?'

'Otherwise we shall have trouble. It is certain. These excellent young men have most of them grown up under German occupation, with no means of expressing their hatred for it—the feeling that for years they have not been able to breathe. They must have an outlet of some sort. They want action. A change of scene will to some extent accomplish that.'

'What sort of numbers?'

'Say thirty thousand.'

'A couple of Divisions?'

'But without the equivalent in weapons and services.'

'When do you want them to come?'

'At once.'

'So we've got to move quickly.'

'That is the point.'

I thought about the interminable procedures required to get a project of this sort under way. Blackhead, like a huge bat, seemed already flapping his wings about Eaton Square, bumping blindly against the windows of the room.

'Arrangements for two Divisions will take some time. Are they already cadred?'

'Sufficiently to bring them across.'

'I'll go straight back to Colonel Finn. We'll get a minute out to be signed by the General and go at once to the highest level. There will be all sorts of problems in addition to the actual physical accommodation of two extra Divisions in this country. The Finance people, for one thing. It will take a week or two to get that side fixed.'

'You think so.'

'I know them.'

'Speed is essential.'

'It's no good pretending we're going to get an answer by Monday.'

'You mean it may take quite a long time?'

'You are familiar with ministerial machinery.'

Kucherman got up from his chair.

'What are we going to do?'

'I thought I'd better say all this.'

'I know it already.'

'It's a fact, I'm afraid.'

'But we must do something. What you say is true, I know. How are we going to get round it? I want to speak frankly. This could be a question of avoiding civil war.'

There was a pause. I knew there was only one way out—to cut the Gordian Knot—but could not immediately see how to attain that. Then, perhaps hypnotized by Kucherman's intense need for an answer, I thought of something.

'You said you knew Sir Magnus Donners.'

'Of course.'

'But you have not seen much of him since you've been over here?'

'I have spoken to him a couple of times at official parties. He was very friendly.'

'Ring him up and say you want to see him at once—this very morning.'

'You think so?'

'Tell him what you've just told me.'

'And then—'

'Sir Magnus can tell the Head Man.'

Kucherman thought for a moment.

'I insist you are right,' he said.

'It's worth trying.'

'This is between ourselves.'

'Of course.'

'Not even Colonel Finn.'

'Least of all.'

'Meanwhile you will start things off in the normal manner through *les voies hiérarchiques*.'

'As soon as I get back.'

'So I will get to work,' said Kucherman. 'I am grateful for the suggestion. The next time we meet, I hope I shall have had a word with Sir Magnus.'

I returned to Finn. He listened to the proposal to bring the Belgian Resistance Army to this country.

'It's pretty urgent?'

'Vital, sir.'

'We'll try and move quickly, but I foresee difficulties. Good notion to train those boys over here. Get out a draft rightaway. Meanwhile I'll consult the Brigadier about the best way of handling the matter. You'd better have a word with Staff Duties. It's not going to be as easy to settle as Kucherman hopes.'

I got out the draft. Finally a tremendous minute was launched on its way that very afternoon. Bureaucratically speaking, grass had not grown under our feet; but this was only a beginning. That weekend was my free one. I told Isobel what I had suggested to Kucherman.

'If the worst comes to the worst we can invoke Matilda.'

Neither of us had seen Matilda since she had married Sir Magnus Donners.

'It's just a long shot.'

On Monday morning a summons came from Finn as soon as he arrived in his room. I went up there.

'This Belgian affair.'

'Yes, sir?'

Finn passed his hand over the smooth ivory surfaces of his skull.

'The most extraordinary thing has happened.'

'Yes, sir?'

'An order has come down from the Highest Level of All to say it is to be treated as top priority. The chaps are to come over the moment their accommodation is decided upon. Things like financial details can be worked out later. All other minor matters too. Tell Blackhead he can talk to the PM about it, if he isn't satisfied.'

'This is splendid, sir.'

Finn put on the face he usually assumed when about to go deaf, but did not do so.

'Providential,' he said. 'Can't understand it. It just shows how the Old Man's got his finger on every pulse. I don't know whether Kucherman did—well, a bit of intriguing. He's a very able fellow, and in the circumstances it would have been almost justified. You will attend a conference on the subject under the DSD at eleven o'clock this morning, all branches concerned being represented.'

The Director of Staff Duties was the general responsible for planning matters. When I next saw Kucherman, we agreed things had gone through with remarkable smoothness. The name of Sir Magnus Donners was not mentioned when we discussed certain administrative details. Thinking over the incident after, it was easy to see how a taste for intrigue, as Finn called it, could develop in people.

5

DURING THE PERIOD BETWEEN THE Potsdam Conference and the dropping of the first atomic bomb, I read in the paper one morning that Widmerpool was engaged to Pamela Flitton. This piece of news was undramatically announced in the column dedicated to such items. It was not even top of the list. Pamela was described as daughter of Captain Cosmo Flitton and Mrs Flavia Wisebite; an address in Montana (suggesting a ranch) showed her father as still alive and living in America. Her mother, whose style indicated divorce from Harrison Wisebite (sunk, so far as I knew, without a trace), had come to rest in the country round Glimber, possibly a cottage on the estate. Widmerpool—'Colonel K. G. Widmerpool, OBE'—was based on a block of flats in Victoria Street. Apart from stories already vaguely propagated by Farebrother and Duport, there was no clue to how this engagement had come about. Surprising as it was, the immediate implications seemed no more than that a piece of colossal folly on both their parts would soon be readjusted by another announcement saying the marriage was 'off'. The world was in such a state of flux that such inanities were only to be expected in one quarter or another. Only later, considered in cold blood, did the arrangement appear credible; even then for less than obvious reasons.

'Drove for the Section, did she?' said Pennistone. 'I never remember those girls' faces. I haven't heard anything of Widmerpool for some time. I suppose he's now passed into a world beyond good and evil.'

I had not set eyes on Widmerpool myself since the day Farebrother had recoiled from saluting him in Whitehall. Although, as an archetypal figure, one of those fabulous monsters that haunt the recesses of the individual imagination, he held an immutable place in my own private mythology, with the passing of Stringham and Templer I no longer knew anyone to whom he might present quite the same absorbing spectacle, accordingly with whom the present conjuncture could be at all adequately discussed. By this time, in any case, changes both inside and outside the Section were so many it was hard to keep pace with them. Allied relationships had become more complex with the defeat of the enemy, especially in the comportment of new political régimes that had emerged in formerly occupied countries—Poland's, for example—some of which were making difficulties about such matters as the 'Victory march'; in general the manner in which Peace was to be celebrated in London. In other merely administrative respects the Section's position was becoming less pivotal than formerly, some of the Allies—France, the Netherlands, Czechoslovakia—sending over special military missions. These were naturally less familiar with the routines of liaison than colleagues long worked with, while the new entities, unlike the old ones, were sometimes authorized to deal directly with whatever branch of the Services specially concerned them.

'Not all the fruits of Victory are appetising to the palate,' said Pennistone. 'An issue of gall and wormwood has been laid on.'

By that time he was himself on the point of demobilization. He had dealt with the Poles up to the end. Dempster and others had gone already. The Old Guard, like the soldiers in the song, were fading away, leaving me as final residue, Finn's second-in-command. In a month or two I should also enter that intermediate state of grace, technically 'on leave', through which in due course civilian life was once more attained. Finn, for reasons best known to himself—he could certainly have claimed early release had he so wished—remained on in his old appointment, where there was still plenty of work to do. Other branches round about were, of course, dwindling in the same manner. All sorts of unexpected individuals, barely remembered, or at best remembered only for acrimonious interchanges in the course of doing business with them, would from time to time turn up in our room to say goodbye, hearty or sheepish, according to temperament. Quite often they behaved as if these farewells were addressed to the only friends they had ever known.

'My Dad's taking me away from this school,' said Borrit, when he shook my hand. 'I'm going into his office. He's got some jolly pretty typists.'

'Wish mine would buck up and remove me too.'

'He says the boys don't learn anything here, just get up to nasty tricks,' said Borrit. 'I'm going to have a room to myself, he says. What do you think of that? Hope my secretary looks like that AT with black hair and a white face who once drove us for a week or two, can't remember her name.'

'Going back to the same job?'

'You bet—the old oranges and lemons/bells of St Clement's.'

As always, after making a joke, Borrit began to look sad again.

'We'll have to meet.'

'Course we will.'

'When I want to buy a banana.'

'Anything up to twenty-thousand bunches, say the word and I'll fix a discount.'

'Will Sydney Stebbings be one of your customers now?'

About eighteen months before, Stebbings, suffering another nervous breakdown, had been invalided out of the army. He was presumed to have returned to the retail side of the fruit business. Borrit shook his head.

'Didn't you hear about poor old Syd? Gassed himself. Felt as browned off out of the army as in it. I used to think it was those Latin-Americans got him down, but it was just Syd's moody nature.'

Borrit and I never did manage to meet again. Some years after the war I ran into Slade in Jermyn Street, by the hat shop with the stuffed cat in the window smoking a cigarette. He had a brown paper bag in his hand and said he had been buying cheese. We had a word together. He was teaching languages at a school in the Midlands and by then a headmastership in the offing. I asked if he had any news, among others, of Borrit.

'Borrit died a few months ago,' said Slade. 'Sad. Bad luck too, because he was going to marry a widow with a little money. She'd been the wife of a man in his business.'

I wondered whether on this final confrontation Borrit had brought off the never realized 'free poke', before the grave claimed him. The war drawing to a close must have something to do with this readiness for marriage on the part of those like Borrit, Widmerpool, Farebrother, no longer in their first youth. These were only a few of them among the dozens who had never tried it before, or tried it without much success. Norah Tolland spoke with great disapproval of Pamela Flitton's engagement.

'Pam must need a Father-Figure,' she said. 'I think it's a tragic mistake. Like Titania and Bottom.'

Not long before the Victory Service, announced to take place at St Paul's, Prasad's Embassy gave a party on their

National Day. It was a bigger affair than usual on account of the advent of Peace, primarily a civilian gathering, though a strong military element was included among the guests. The huge saloons, built at the turn of the century, were done up in sage green, the style of decoration displaying a nostalgic leaning towards Art Nouveau, a period always sympathetic to Asian taste. Gauthier de Graef, ethnically confused, had been anxious to know whether there were eunuchs in the ladies' apartments above the rooms where we were being entertained. Accordingly, to settle the point, on which he was very insistent, Madame Philidor and Isobel arranged to be conducted to their hostess in purdah, promising to report on this matter, though without much hope of returning with an affirmative answer. They had just set out on this visit of exploration, when I saw Farebrother moving purposefully through the crowd. I went over to congratulate him on his marriage. He was immensely cordial.

'I hear Geraldine's an old friend of yours, Nicholas. You knew her in her "Tuffy" days.'

I said I did not think I had ever quite had the courage to address her by that nickname when she had still been Miss Weedon.

'I mean when she was Mrs Foxe's secretary,' said Farebrother. 'Then you knew the old General too. Splendid old fellow, he must have been. Wish I'd met him. Both he and Mrs Foxe opened up a lot of very useful contacts for Geraldine, which she's never lost sight of. They're going to stand me in good stead too. A wonderful woman. Couldn't believe my ears when she said she'd be mine.'

He seemed very pleased about it all.

'She's not here tonight.'

'Too busy.'

'Catching spies?'

'Ah, so you know where she's working? We try to keep

that a secret. No, Geraldine's getting our new flat straight. We've actually found somewhere to live. Not too easy these days. Quite a reasonable rent for the neighbourhood, which is a good one. Now I must go and have a word with old Lord Perkins over there. He married poor Peter Templer's elder sister, Babs, as I expect you know.'

'I didn't know.'

'One of the creations of the first Labour Government. Of course he's getting on now—but, with Labour in again, we all need friends at court.'

'Did anything more ever come out as to what happened to Peter?'

'Nothing, so far as I know. He was absolutely set on doing that job. As soon as he heard I was going to work with those people he got on to me to try and get him something of the sort. You ought to meet Lord Perkins. I think Babs found him a change for the better after that rather dreadful fellow Stripling. I ran into Stripling in Aldershot about eighteen months ago. He was lecturing to the troops. Just come from the Glasshouse, where he'd given a talk on the early days of motor-racing. Someone told me Babs had been a great help to her present husband when he was writing his last book on industrial relations.'

He smiled and moved off. Widmerpool arrived in the room at that moment. He stood looking round, evidently deciding where best to launch an attack. Farebrother must have seen him, because he suddenly swerved into a new direction to avoid contact. This seemed a good opportunity to congratulate Widmerpool too. I went over to him. He seemed very pleased with himself.

'Thank you very much, Nicholas. Some people have expressed the opinion, without much delicacy, that Pamela is too young for me. That is not my own view at all. A man is as young as he feels. I had quite a scene with my mother, I'm afraid. My mother is getting an old lady now, of course, and does not always know what she is talking about. As a matter of fact I am making arrangements for her to live, anyway temporarily, with some distant relations of ours in the Lowlands. It's not too far from Glasgow. I think she will be happier with them than on her own, after I am married. She is in touch with one or two nice families on the Borders.'

This was a very different tone from that Widmerpool was in the habit of using about his mother in the old days. It seemed likely the engagement represented one of his conscious decisions to put life on a new footing. He embarked on these from time to time, with consequent rearrangements all round. It looked as if sending Mrs Widmerpool into exile was going to be one such. It was hard to feel wholly condemnatory. I enquired about the circumstances in which he had met Pamela, a matter about which I was curious.

'In Cairo. An extraordinary chance. As you know, my work throughout the war has never given me a second for social life. Even tonight I am here only because Pamela herself wanted to come—she is arriving at any moment—and I shall leave as soon as I have introduced her. I requested the Ambassador as a personal favour that I might bring my fiancée. He was charming about it. To tell the truth, I have to dine with the Minister tonight. A lot to talk about. Questions of policy. Adjustment to new régimes. But I was telling you how Pamela and I met. In Cairo there was trouble about my returning plane. One had been shot down, resulting in my having to kick my heels in the place for twenty-four hours. You know how vexatious that sort of situation is to me. I was taken to a place called Groppi's. Someone introduced us. Before I knew where I was, we were dining together and on our way to a nightclub. I had not been to a place of that sort for years. Had, indeed, quite forgotten what they were like. The fact was we had a most enjoyable evening.'

He laughed quite hysterically.

'Then, as luck would have it, Pam was posted back to England. I should have added that she was working as secretary in one of the secret organizations there. I was glad about her return, because I don't think she moved in a very good set in Cairo. When she arrived in London, she sent me a postcard—and what a postcard.'

Widmerpool giggled violently, then recovered himself.

'It arrived one morning in that basement where I work night and day,' he said. 'You can imagine how pleased I was. It seems extraordinary that we hardly knew each other then, and now I've got a great big photograph of her on my desk.'

He was almost gasping. The words vividly conjured up his subterranean life. Photographs on a desk were never without interest. People who placed them there belonged to a special category in their human relationships. There was, for example, that peculiarly tortured-looking midshipman in a leather-and-talc frame in the room of a Section with which ours was often in contact. Some lines of John Davidson suddenly came into my head:

> 'And so they wait, while empires sprung
> Of hatred thunder past above,
> Deep in the earth for ever young
> Tannhäuser and the Queen of Love.'

On reflection, the situation was not a very close parallel, because it was most unlikely Pamela had ever visited Widmerpool's underground office. On the other hand, she herself could easily be envisaged as one of the myriad incarnations of Venus, even if Widmerpool were not much of a Tannhäuser. At least he seemed in a similar way to have stumbled on the secret entrance to the court of the Paphian goddess in the Hollow Hill where his own duties were diurnally enacted. That was some qualification.

'You know she's Charles Stringham's niece?'

'Naturally I am aware of that.'

The question had not pleased him.

'No news of Stringham, I suppose?'

'There has been, as a matter of fact.'

Widmerpool seemed half angry, half desirous of making some statement about this.

'He was captured,' he said. 'He didn't survive.'

Scarcely anything was known still about individual prisoners in Japanese POW camps, except that the lives of many of them had certainly been saved by the Bomb. News came through slowly from the Far East. I asked how Widmerpool could speak so definitely.

'At the end of last year the Americans sank a Jap transport on the way from Singapore. They rescued some British prisoners on board. They had been in the same camp. One of them got in touch with Stringham's mother when repatriated. It was only just in time, because Mrs Foxe herself died soon after that, as you probably saw.'

'I hadn't.'

He seemed to want to make some further confession.

'As I expect you know, Mrs Foxe was a very extravagant woman. At the end, she found it not only impossible to live in anything like the way she used, but was even quite short of money.'

'Stringham himself said something about that when I last saw him.'

'The irony of the situation is that his mother's South African money was tied up on Stringham,' said Widmerpool. 'Owing to bad management, she never got much out of those securities herself, but a lot of South African stock has recently made a very good recovery.'

'I suppose Flavia will benefit.'

'No, she doesn't, as it turns out,' said Widmerpool. 'Rather an odd thing happened. Stringham left a will bequeathing all he had to Pam. He'd always been fond of her as a child. He obviously thought it would be just a few personal odds and ends. As it turns out, there could be a good deal more than that. With the right attention, Stringham's estate in due course might be nursed into something quite respectable.'

He looked rather guilty, not without reason. We abandoned the subject of Stringham.

'I don't pretend Pamela's an easy girl,' he said. 'We fairly often have rows—in fact are not on speaking terms for twenty-four hours or more. Never mind. Rows often clear the air. We shall see it through, whatever my position when I leave the army.'

'You'll go back to the City, I suppose?'

'I'm not so sure.'

'Other plans?'

'I have come to the conclusion that I enjoy power,' said Widmerpool. 'That is something the war has taught me. In this connexion, it has more than once occurred to me that I might like governing . . .'

He brought his lips together, then parted them. This contortion formed a phrase, but, the words inaudible, its sense escaped me.

'Governing whom?'

Leaning forward and smiling, Widmerpool repeated the movement of his lips. This time, although he spoke only in a whisper, the two words were intelligible.

'*Black men* . . .'

'Abroad?'

'Naturally.'

'That's feasible?'

'My reputation among those who matter could scarcely be higher.'

'You mean you could easily get an appointment of that sort?'

'Nothing in life is ever easy, my boy. Not in the sense you use the term. It is one of the mistakes you always make. The point is, we are going to see great changes. As you know, my leanings have always been leftwards. From what I see round me, I have no reason to suppose such sympathies were mistaken. Men like myself will be needed.'

'If they are to be found.'

He clapped me on the back.

'No flattery,' he said. 'No flattery, but I sometimes wonder whether you're not right.'

He looked at his watch and sighed.

'Being engaged accustoms one to unpunctuality,' he went on in rather another tone, a less exuberant one. 'I think I'll have a word with that old stalwart, Lord Perkins, whom I see over there.'

'I didn't know till a moment ago that Perkins was married to Peter Templer's sister.'

'Oh, yes. So I believe. I don't see them as having much in common as brothers-in-law, but one never knows. Unfortunate Templer getting killed like that. He was too old for that sort of business, of course. Stringham, too. I fear the war has taken a sad toll of our friends. I notice Donners over there talking to the Portuguese Ambassador. I must say a word to him too.'

In the seven years or so that had passed since I had last seen him, Sir Magnus Donners had grown not so much older in appearance, as less like a human being. He now resembled an animated tailor's dummy, one designed to recommend second-hand, though immensely discreet, clothes (if the suit he was wearing could be regarded as a sample) adapted to the taste of distinguished men no longer young. Jerky movements, like those of a marionette—perhaps indicating all was not absolutely well with his physical system—added to the impression of an outsize puppet that had somehow escaped from its box and begun to mix with

real people, who were momentarily taken in by the
extraordinary conviction of its mechanism. The set of
Sir Magnus's mouth, always a trifle uncomfortable to contemplate, had become very slightly less under control, increasing the vaguely warning note the rest of his appearance implied. On the whole he had lost that former air of
desperately seeking to seem more ordinary than everyone
else round him; or, if he still hoped for that, its consolations
had certainly escaped him. A lifetime of weighty negotiation in the worlds of politics and business had left their
mark. One would now guess at once he was an unusual
person, who, even within his own terms of reference, had
lived an unusual life. He looked less parsonic than in the
days when he had suggested a clerical headmaster. Perhaps
that was because he had not, so to speak, inwardly progressed to the archiepiscopal level in that calling; at least his
face had not developed the fleshy, theatrical accentuations
so often attendant on the features of the higher grades of
the clergy. At some moment, consciously or not, he had
probably branched off from this interior priestly strain in
his make-up. That would be the logical explanation.
Matilda, looking decidedly smart in a dress of blue and
black stripes, was standing beside her husband, talking with
the Portuguese Ambassador. I had not seen her since their
marriage. She caught sight of me and waved, then separated herself from the others and made her way through the
ever thickening crowd.

'Nick.'

'How are you, Matty?'

'Don't you admire my frock. An unsolicited gift from
New York.'

'Too smart for words. I couldn't imagine where it had
come from.'

To be rather older suited her; that or being married to a
member of the Cabinet. She had dyed her hair a reddish

tint that suited her, too, set off the large green eyes, which were always her most striking feature.

'Do you ever see anything of Hugh the Drover?'

She used sometimes to call Moreland that while they had been married, usually when not best pleased with him. I told her we had not met since the night of the bomb on the Café de Madrid: that, so far as I knew, Moreland was still touring the country, putting on musical performances of one sort or another, under more or less official control; whatever happened in the war to make mounting such entertainments possible.

'What's his health been like?'

'I don't know at all.'

'Extraordinary about Audrey Maclintick. Are they married?'

'I don't know that either.'

'Does she look after him all right?'

'I think she does.'

Obviously Matilda still took quite a keen interest in Moreland and his condition. That was natural enough. All the same, one felt instinctively that she had entirely given up Moreland's world, everything to do with it. She had taken on Sir Magnus, lock, stock and barrel. The metaphor made one think of his alleged sexual oddities. Presumably she had taken them on too, though as a former mistress they would be relatively familiar. Perhaps she guessed the train of thought, because she smiled.

'Donners has to be looked after too,' she said. 'I'm rather worried about him at the moment as a matter of fact.'

'His job must be a great strain.'

Matilda brushed such a banal comment aside.

'Will you come and see me?' she said. 'We're going to Washington next week—but when we're back.'

'My Release Group comes up reasonably soon. We'll probably go away for a bit when I get out of the army.'

'Later then. Is Isobel here?'

'Last seen on her way to the harem upstairs.'

Sir Magnus had now begun to make signs indicating that he wanted Matilda to return to him and be introduced to someone. She left me, repeating that we must meet when they came back from America. I had always liked Matilda and felt glad to see her again and hear that her life seemed endurable. Widmerpool reappeared at my side. He seemed agitated.

'I wish Pamela would turn up,' he said. 'I shall be late if she doesn't arrive soon. I can't very well leave until she comes—ah, thank God, there she is.'

Pamela Flitton came towards us. Unlike the night at *The Bartered Bride*, she had this evening taken no trouble whatever about her clothes. Perhaps that was untrue, and she had gone out of her way to find the oldest, most filthy garments she possessed. She was almost in rags. By this time the party had advanced too far for it to be obvious to a newcomer whom to greet as host. She had in any case obviously not bothered about any such formalities.

'Hullo, my dear,' said Widmerpool. 'I didn't guess you'd be so late.'

He spoke in a conciliatory voice, making as if to kiss her. She allowed the merest peck.

'I'll just introduce you to His Excellency,' he said. 'Then I'll have to fly.'

Pamela, who was looking very pretty in spite of her disarray, was having none of that.

'I don't want to be introduced,' she said. 'I just came to have a look round.'

She gave me a nod. I made some conventional remark about their engagement. She listened to this rather more graciously than usual.

'I think you ought to meet the Ambassador, dearest.'

'Stuff the Ambassador.'

The phrase recalled Duport. Widmerpool laughed nervously.

'You really oughtn't to say things like that, darling,' he said. 'Not when you're at a party like this. Nicholas and I think it very amusing, but someone else might overhear and not understand. If you really don't feel like being introduced at the moment, I shall have to leave you. Nicholas or someone can do the honours, if you decide you want to meet your host later. Personally, I think you should. If you do, make my apologies. I shall have to go now. I am late already.'

'Late for what?'

'I told you—I'm dining with the Minister.'

'You're giving me dinner.'

'I only wish I was. Much as I'd love to, I can't. I did explain all this before. You said you'd like to come to the party, even though we couldn't have dinner together after. Besides, I'm sure you told me you were dining with Lady McReith.'

'I'm going to dine with you.'

I was about to move away and leave them to it, feeling an engaged couple should settle such matters so far as possible in private, but Widmerpool, either believing himself safer with a witness, or because he foresaw some method of disposing of Pamela in which I might play a part, took me by the arm, while he continued to speak persuasively to her.

'Be reasonable, darling,' he said. 'I can't cut a dinner I've gone out of my way to arrange—least of all with the Minister.'

'Stand him up. I couldn't care less. That's what you'd do if you really wanted to dine with me.'

She was in a sudden rage. Her usually dead white face now had some colour in it. Widmerpool must have thought that a change of subject would cool her down, also give him a chance of escape.

'I'm going to leave you with Nicholas,' he said. 'Let me tell you first, what you probably don't know, that Nicholas used to be a friend of your uncle, Charles Stringham, whom you were so fond of.'

If he hoped that information would calm her, Widmerpool made a big mistake. She went absolutely rigid.

'Yes,' she said, 'and Charles isn't the only one he knew. He knew Peter Templer too—the man you murdered.'

Widmerpool, not surprisingly, was apparently stupefied by this onslaught; myself scarcely less so. She spoke the words in a quiet voice. We were in a corner of the room behind some pillars, a little away from the rest of the party. Even so, plenty of people were close enough. It was no place to allow a scene to develop. Pamela turned to me.

'Do you know what happened?'

'About what?'

'About Peter Templer. This man persuaded them to leave Peter to die. The nicest man I ever knew. He just had him killed.'

Tears appeared in her eyes. She was in a state of near hysteria. It was clearly an occasion when rational argument was going to do no good. The only thing would be to get her away quietly on any terms. Widmerpool did not grasp that. He could perhaps not be blamed for being unable to consider matters coolly. He had now recovered sufficiently from his earlier astonishment to rebut the charges made against him and was even showing signs of himself losing his temper.

'How could you utter such rubbish?' he said. 'I see now that I ought never to have mentioned to you I had any hand at all in that affair, even at long range. It was a breach of security for which I deserve to be punished. Please stop talking in such an absurd way.'

Pamela was not in the least calmed by this remonstrance.

211

Quite the contrary. She did not raise her voice, but spoke if possible with more intensity. Now it was me she addressed. 'He put up a paper. That was the word he used—put up a paper. He wanted them to stop supporting the people Peter was with. We didn't send them any more arms. We didn't even bother to get Peter out. Why should we? We didn't want his side to win any more.'

Widmerpool was himself pretty angry by now.

'Because my duties happen to include the promulgation of matters appropriate for general consideration by our committees—perhaps ultimately by the Chiefs of Staff, perhaps even the Cabinet—because, as I say, this happens to be my function, that does not mean the decisions are mine, nor, for that matter, even the recommendations. Matters are discussed as fully as possible at every level. The paper is finalized. The decision is made. I may tell you this particular decision was taken at the highest level. As for not getting Templer out, as you call it, how could I possibly have anything to do with the action, right or wrong, for which the Operational people on the spot are responsible? These are just the sort of disgraceful stories that get disseminated, probably at the direct instance of the enemy.'

'You were in favour of withdrawing support. You said so. You told me.'

'Perhaps I was. Anyway, I was a fool to say so to you.'

His own rage made him able to stand up to her.

'Therefore you represented Peter's people in as bad a light as possible. No doubt you carried the meeting.'

She had absorbed the jargon of Widmerpool's employment in a remarkable manner. I remembered noticing, on occasions when Matilda differed with Moreland about some musical matter, how dexterously women can take in the ideas of a man with whom they are connected, then outmanoeuvre him with his own arguments. Widmerpool made a despairing gesture, but spoke now with less violence.

'I am only a member of the Secretariat, darling. I am the servant, very humble servant, of whatever committees it is my duty to attend.'

'You said yourself it was a rare meeting when you didn't get what you wanted into the finalized version.'

This roused Widmerpool again.

'So it is,' he said. 'So it is. And, as it happens, what I thought went into the paper you're talking about. I admit it. That doesn't mean I was in the smallest degree responsible for Templer's death. We don't know for certain even if he is dead.'

'Yes, we do.'

'All right. I concede that.'

'You're a murderer,' she said.

There was a pause. They glared at each other. Then Widmerpool looked down at his watch.

'Good God,' he said. 'What will the Minister think?'

Without another word, he pushed his way through the crowd towards the door. He disappeared hurriedly through it. I was wondering what on earth to say to Pamela, when she too turned away, and began to stroll through the party in the opposite direction. I saw her smile at the Swiss military attaché, who had rather a reputation as a lady-killer, then she too was lost to sight. Isobel and Madame Philidor reappeared from their visit to our hostess in purdah.

'The first wife looked kind, did you not think?' said Madame Philidor. 'The other perhaps not so kind.'

After this extraordinary incident, it seemed more certain than ever that an announcement would be made stating the engagement had been broken off. However, there were other things to think about, chiefly one's own demobilization; more immediately, arrangements regarding the Victory Day Service, which took place some weeks later at

St Paul's. I was to be on duty there with Finn, superintending the foreign military attachés invited. Among these were many gaps in the ranks of those known earlier. The several new Allied missions were not accommodated in the Cathedral under the Section's arrangements, nor were the dispossessed—Bobrowski and Kielkiewicz, for example—individuals amongst our Allies who had played a relatively prominent part in the war, but now found themselves deprived of their birthright for no reason except an unlucky turn of the wheel of international politics manipulated by the inexorable hand of Fate.

This day of General Thanksgiving had been fixed on a Sunday in the second half of August. Its weather seemed designed to emphasize complexities and low temperatures of Allied relationships. Summer, like one of the new régimes abroad, offered no warmth, but chilly, draughty, unwelcoming perspectives, under a grey and threatening sky. The London streets by this time were, in any case, far from cheerful: windows broken: paint peeling: jagged, ruined brickwork enclosing the shells of roofless houses. Acres of desolated buildings, the burnt and battered City, lay about St Paul's on all sides. Finn and I arrived early, entering by the south door. Within the vast cool interior, traces of war were as evident as outside, though on a less wholesale, less utterly ruthless scale. The Allied military attachés, as such, were to be segregated in the south transept, in a recess lined with huge marble monuments in pseudo-classical style. I had been put in charge of the Allied group, because Finn decided the Neutrals, some of whom could be unreliable in matters of discipline and procedure, required his undivided attention. The Neutrals were to occupy a block of seats nearer the choir, the wooden carving of its stalls still showing signs of bomb damage.

'I'm glad to say no difficulties have been made about Theodoric,' said Finn. 'He's been asked to the Service in a perfectly correct manner. It's not a large return for a lifetime of being pro-British—and accepting exile—but that's all they can do, I suppose. He'd be even worse off if he'd plumped for the other side. By the way, an ambulance party has been provided in the crypt, should any of your boys come over faint. I shall probably need medical attention myself before the day is over.'

I checked the Allied military attachés as they arrived. They were punctual, on the whole well behaved, whispering together with the air of children at a village Sunday school, a little overawed at the promised visit of the bishop of the diocese, glancing uneasily at the enigmatic sculptural scenes looming above them on the tombs. Among them, as I have said, were many absences and new faces. One regretted Van der Voort. A churchly background would have enhanced his pristine Netherlandish countenance. Colonel Hlava had returned to Prague. 'Russia is our Big Brother' (the phrase had not yet developed Orwellian overtones), he had remarked to me some weeks before he left; even so, when the moment came to shake hands for the last time, he said: 'We can only hope'. Hlava was promoted major-general when he got home. Then, a year or two later, he was put under house arrest. He was still under house arrest when he died of heart failure; a flying ace and man one greatly liked.

Kucherman had gone back to a ministerial portfolio in the Belgian Government, his place taken by Bruylant, a quiet professional soldier, with musical leanings, though less marked than Hlava's and not of the sort to be expressed actively by playing duets with Dempster, had Dempster still been with the Section, not returned to his Norwegian timber. In place of Marinko—out of a job like the rest of his countrymen who had supported Mihailovich's Resistance Movement, rather than Tito's—was a newly arrived, long haired, jack-booted young 'Partisan' colonel, who talked a little French and, although possessing a Polish-sounding name, designated himself as 'Macédoin'. Macedonia was perhaps where Szymanski had come from too. One wondered what had happened to him.

Examining the neighbouring monuments more closely, I was delighted to find among them more than one of those celebrated in *The Ingoldsby Legends*, a favourite book of mine about the time when we lived at Stonehurst. There, for example, only a few feet away from where the military attachés sat, several figures far larger than life were enacting a battle scene in which a general had been struck from the saddle by a cannon ball, as his charger bore him at a furious gallop across the path of a kilted private from some Highland regiment. There could be no doubt whatever this was:

' ... Sir Ralph Abercrombie going to tumble
With a thump that alone were enough to dispatch him
If the Scotchman in front shouldn't happen to catch him.'

Stendhal had seen these monuments when he visited London.

'Style lourd,' he noted. 'Celui d'Abercromby bien ridicule.'

Nevertheless, one felt glad it remained there. It put on record what was then officially felt about death in battle, begging all that large question of why the depiction of action in the graphic arts had fallen in our own day almost entirely into the hands of the Surrealists.

'La jolie figure de Moore rend son tombeau meilleur,' Stendhal thought.

This was against the wall by the side door through which we had entered the Cathedral, at right angles to the Abercrombie memorial. Less enormously vehement, this group too had its own exuberance of style, though in quite another mood. Here a sinister charade was being enacted by several figures not so gigantic in size. What they were doing was not immediately clear, until Barham's lines threw light on them too:

'Where the man and the Angel have got Sir John Moore, And are quietly letting him down through the floor.

I looked about for 'that queer-looking horse that is rolling on Ponsonby', but disappointingly failed to identify either man or beast in the immediate vicinity of the recess. The field of vision was too limited, only a short length of the nave to be viewed, where it joined the more or less circular area under the dome. However, recognition of these other episodes, so often pictured imaginatively in the past when the book had been read aloud by my mother— yet never for some reason appraised by a deliberate visit to St Paul's to verify the facts—mitigated an atmosphere in other respects oddly frigid, even downright depressing. With a fashionably egalitarian ideal in view, those responsible for such things had decided no mere skimming of the cream from the top echelons, civil and military, should be assembled together to give symbolic thanks for Victory. Everyone was to be represented. The congregation—except for those who had a job to do—had been handpicked from the highest official levels to the lowest.

For some reason this principle, fair enough in theory, had in practice resulted in an extension of that atmosphere of restraint, uneasy nervous tension, common enough in a larger or smaller degree to all such ceremonies. The sense of being present at a Great Occasion—for, if this was not a Great Occasion, then what was?—had somehow failed to take adequate shape, to catch on the wing those inner perceptions of a more exalted sort, evasive by their very nature, at best transient enough, but not altogether unknown. They were, in fact, so it seemed to me—unlike that morning in Normandy—entirely absent. Perhaps that was because everyone was by now so tired. The country, there could be no doubt, was absolutely worn out. That was the truth of the matter. One felt it in St Paul's. It was interesting to speculate who, among the less obvious, had been invited to the Service. Vavassor, for example? If so, was he wearing his blue frockcoat and gold-banded top hat? One of the ordinary security guards could look after the front-door for an hour or two. Had Blackhead been torn from his files to attend this Thanksgiving? If so, it was hard to believe he would not bring a file or two with him to mull over during the prayers. Q. (Ops.) Colonel? Mime? Widmerpool?

Meanwhile, the band of the Welsh Guards strummed away at Holst, Elgar, Grieg, finally Handel's 'Water Music'. Bruylant almost imperceptibly beat time with his forefinger, while he listened to these diversions, of which I felt Moreland would have only partially approved. The Jugoslav Colonel, rather a morose young man, did not seem altogether at ease in these surroundings. Possibly to reassure himself, he produced a pocket-comb and began to smooth his hair. General Cobb, contemplating the verdict on life's court-martial, was frowning darkly. I had all my charges in their seats by now, with a place to spare at the end of the row on which the Partisan could leave his cap. Someone might have failed to turn up because he was ill; possibly Colonel Ramos indisposed again. Then I saw Ramos in the back row, anxiously studying the service paper. I checked the list. They all seemed to be there. The Neutrals, in their position further east of the transept, had some of them shown inferior mastery of the drill; at least, not all were in their places in such good time as the Allies. Finn had rightly estimated them a more tricky crowd to manipulate. He appeared to be finding difficulty in fitting his party into the available seats. It was too far to see for certain, but looked as if some flaw had been revealed in the organization. Finn came across the transept.

'Look here, Nicholas. I seem to have a South American too many.'

He clenched his teeth as if some appalling consequence were likely to overtake us as a result of that.

'Which one, sir?'

'Colonel Flores.'

'Can't place his country for the moment, sir.'

'You probably haven't heard of him. His predecessor, Hernandez, was recalled in a hurry for political reasons. It was thought Flores would not be in London in time for this show. There was a misunderstanding. The fact is things have never been the same with Latin America since we lost Borrit. You haven't a spare place?'

'As a matter of fact, I have, sir. I don't know why, because I've checked the list and no one seems ill or late.'

'They may have allowed for the Grand Duchy, whose military representative is in the Diplomatic block. The situation's saved. I'll bring Flores across.'

He returned a moment later with an officer wearing a heavy gold aiguillette, though without the sword that had survived the war in some South American ceremonial turn-outs. Finn, evidently suffering stress at this last minute re-arrangement, had taken Colonel Flores firmly by the arm—rather in the manner of General Conyers, with whom perhaps he had, after all, something in common—as if he were making an arrest and a dangerous customer at that. Flores, obviously appreciating the humour of this manhandling, was smiling. Dark, blue-chinned, with regular features, rather a handsome Mediterranean type, his age was hard to assess. He gave a quick heel-click and handshake on introduction.

'Major Jenkins will look after you, Colonel,' said Finn. 'Must leave you now or your colleagues will get out of hand.'

Flores laughed, and turned to me.

'I'm really frightfully sorry to be the cause of all this

muddle,' he said. 'Especially as a bloody Neutral. Can you indeed accommodate me with your boys over here?'

This speech showed a rather surprising mastery of the English language, not to say unexpected psychological grasp of the British approach in such matters. One never knew what to expect from the South Americans. Sometimes they would speak perfect English like Colonel Flores, were sophisticated to a degree; alternatively, they would know not a word of any language but their own, seemed to find any ways but their own incomprehensible. Neutral military attachés were required to give notification of journeys made further than a given distance from London. The Latin Americans did not always observe this regulation. We would receive official reports from MI5 chronicling jaunts with tarts to Maidenhead and elsewhere. Colonel Flores, one saw in a moment, was much too spry to be caught out in anything like that. He had only the smallest trace of an accent, that hard Spanish drawl that can be so attractive on the lips of a woman. The Flores manner was not unlike Theodoric's, shorn of Theodoric's ever present sense of his own royalty. In fact, anglicization was if anything almost too perfect, suggesting a smoothness comparable almost with Farebrother's. All the same, I immediately liked him. I caused the Jugoslav to take his cap from the spare seat and put it under his own chair, fitting in Flores next to him. If the Jugoslav came from Macedonia, he must be used to rubbing shoulders with all sorts of merging races, ought to have learnt early in life to be a good mixer. Perhaps in Macedonia things did not work that way. If he had not learnt the art, he would have to do so pretty soon, or give up hope of getting the best out of his London appointment. Flores, smiling and apologizing, edged his way along the row, like a member of the audience arriving late for his stall at the opera. He safely reached the place at the end only a minute or two before the fanfare from Household Cavalry trumpets announced the arrival of the Royal Party on the steps of the Cathedral.

There was an impression of copes and mitres, vestments of cream and gold, streaks of ruby-coloured velvet, the Lord Mayor bearing the City Sword point upward, khaki uniforms and blue, a train of royal personages—the phrase always recalled Mr Deacon speaking of Mrs Andriadis's past—the King and Queen, the Princesses, King of the Hellenes, Regent of Iraq, King and Queen of Jugoslavia, Prince Theodoric. Colonel Budd, as it happened, was in attendance. The years seemed to have made no impression on him. White-moustached, spruce, very upright, he glanced about him with an air of total informality, as if prepared for any eventuality from assassination to imperfect acoustics. When the Royal Party reached their seats, all knelt. Prayers followed. We rose for a hymn.

> 'Angels in the height, adore him;
> Ye behold him face to face;
> Saints triumphant, bow before him,
> Gather'd in from every race.'

Under the great dome, saints or not, they were undoubtedly gathered in from every race. Colonel Flores and the Partisan Colonel were sharing a service paper. General Asbjørnsen, legitimately proud of his powerful baritone, sang out with full lungs. Hymns always made me think of Stringham, addicted to quoting their imagery within the context of his own life.

'Hymns describe people and places so well,' he used to say. 'Nothing else quite like them. What could be better, for example, on the subject of one's friends and relations than:

> Some are sick and some are sad,
> And some have never loved one well,
> And some have lost the love they had.

221

The explicitness of the categories is marvellous. Then that wonderful statement: "fading is the world's best pleasure". One sees very clearly which particular pleasure its writer considered the best.'

Thoughts about Singapore: the conditions of a Japanese POW camp. Cheesman must have been there too, the middle-aged subaltern in charge of the Mobile Laundry Unit, that bespectacled accountant who had a waistcoat made to fit under his army tunic, and renounced the Pay Corps because he wanted to 'command men'. Had he survived? In any case there were no limits to the sheer improbability of individual fate. Templer, for instance, even as a boy innately opposed to the romantic approach, dying in the service of what he himself would certainly regard as a Musical Comedy country, on account of a Musical Comedy love affair. On the subject of death, it looked as if George Tolland was not going to pull through. An ecclesiastic began to read from Isaiah.

'The wilderness and the solitary place shall be glad for them; and the desert shall rejoice, and blossom as the rose ... Strengthen ye the weak hands, and confirm the feeble knees ... And the parched ground shall become a pool, and the thirsty land springs of water: in the habitation of dragons, where each lay, shall be grass with reeds and rushes. And an highway shall be there, and a way, and it shall be called The way of holiness; the unclean shall not pass over it; but it shall be for those: the wayfaring men, though fools, shall not err therein ...'

The habitation of dragons. Looking back on the V.1's flying through the night, one thought of dragons as, physically speaking, less remote than formerly. Probably they lived in caves and came down from time to time to the banks of a river or lake to drink. The ground 'where each lay' would, of course, be scorched by fiery breath, their tails too, no doubt, giving out fire that made the water hiss and steam, the sedge become charred. Not all the later promises of the prophecy were easily comprehensible. An intense, mysterious beauty pervaded the obscurity of the text, its assurances all the more magical for being enigmatic. Who, for example, were the wayfaring men? Were they themselves all fools, or only some of them? Perhaps, on the contrary, the wayfaring men were contrasted with the fools, as persons of entirely different sort. One thing was fairly clear, the fools, whoever they were, must keep off the highway; 'absolutely *verboten*', as Biggs, Staff Officer Physical Training, used to say. Brief thoughts of Biggs, hanging by the neck until he was dead in that poky little cricket pavilion; another war casualty, so far as it went. The problem of biblical exegesis remained. Perhaps it was merely a warning: wayfaring men should not make fools of themselves. Taking the war period, limiting the field to the army, one had met quite a few wayfaring men. Biggs himself was essentially not of that category: Bithel, perhaps: Odo Stevens, certainly. Borrit? It was fascinating that Borrit should have remembered Pamela Flitton's face after three years or more.

'I've been in Spain on business sometimes,' Borrit said. 'A honeymoon couple would arrive at the hotel. Be shown up to their bedroom. Last you'd see of them. They wouldn't leave that room for a fortnight—not for three weeks. You'd just get an occasional sight of a brassed-off chambermaid once in a way lugging off a slop-pail. They've got their own ways, the Spaniards. "With a beard, St Joseph; without, the Virgin Mary." That's a Spanish proverb. Never quite know what it means, but it makes you see what the Spaniards are like somehow.'

There were more prayers. A psalm. The Archbishop unenthrallingly preached. We rose to sing *Jerusalem*.

> 'Bring me my Bow of burning gold;
> Bring me my Arrows of desire;

Bring me my spear; O Clouds unfold!
Bring me my chariot of fire!'

Was all that about sex too? If so, why were we singing it
at the Victory Service? Blake was as impenetrable as Isaiah;
in his way, more so. It was not quite such wonderful stuff as
the Prophet rendered into Elizabethan English, yet wonderful enough. At the same time, so I always felt, never quite
for me. Blake was a genius, but not one for the classical
taste. He was too cranky. No doubt that was being ungrateful for undoubted marvels offered and accepted. One
often felt ungrateful in literary matters, as in so many
others. It would be interesting to know what the military
attachés made of the poem. General Asbjørnsen certainly
enjoyed singing the words. He was quite flushed in the face,
like a suddenly converted Viking, joining in with the
monks instead of massacring them.

Reflections about poetry, its changes in form and fashion,
persisted throughout further prayers. 'Arrows of desire', for
example, made one think of Cowley. Cowley had been an
outstanding success in his own time. He had been buried
in Westminster Abbey. That was something which would
never have happened to Blake. However, it was Blake who
had come out on top in the end. Pope was characteristically
direct on the subject.

'Who now reads Cowley? If he pleases yet,
His moral pleases, not his pointed wit;
Forgot his epic, nay Pindaric art,
But still I love the language of his heart.'

But, admitting nobody read the *Pindarique Odes*, surely
the pointed wit was just what did survive? In Cowley's
quite peculiar grasp of the contrasted tenderness and brutality of love, wit was just the quality he brought to bear with
such remarkable effect:

'Thou with strange adultery
Doest in each breast a brothel keep;
Awake, all men do lust for thee,
And some enjoy thee when they sleep.'

No poet deserved to be forgotten who could face facts like that, the blending of conscious and unconscious, Love's free-for-all in dreams. You only had to compare the dream situation with that adumbrated by poor old Edgar Allan Poe—for whom, for some reason, I always had a weakness—when he trafficked in a similar vein:

'Now all my days are trances
And all my nightly dreams
Are where thy grey eye glances,
And where thy footstep gleams—
In what ethereal dances
By what eternal streams.'

Ethereal dances would have been no good to Cowley, by eternal streams or anywhere else. He wanted substance. That verse used to run in my head when in love with Jean Duport—her grey eyes—though she laid no claims to being a dancer, and Poe's open-air interpretive choreography sounded unimpressive. However, there were no limits when one was in that state. We rose once more for another hymn, 'Now thank we all our God', which was, I felt pretty sure, of German origin. Whoever was responsible for choosing had either forgotten that, or judged it peculiarly apposite for this reason. We had just prayed for the 'United Nations' and 'our enemies in defeat'. In the same mood, deliberate selection of a German hymn might be intended to indicate public forgiveness and reconciliation. Quite soon, of course, people would, in any case, begin to say the war was point-less, particularly those, and their associates, moral and actual, who had chalked on walls, 'Strike now in the West' or 'Bomb Rome'. Political activities of that kind might

225

by now have brought together Mrs Andriadis and Gypsy Jones. The Te Deum. Then the National Anthem, all three verses:

> 'God save our gracious King!
> Long live our noble King!
> God save the King!
> Send him victorious,
> Happy and glorious
> Long to reign over us;
> God save the King!
>
> O Lord our God arise
> Scatter his enemies,
> And make them fall.
> Confound their politics,
> Frustrate their knavish tricks,
> On thee our hopes we fix;
> God save us all.
>
> Thy choicest gift in store
> On him be pleased to pour;
> Long may he reign!
> May he defend our laws,
> And ever give us cause
> To sing with heart and voice,
> God save the King!'

Repetitive, jerky, subjective in feeling, not much ornamented by imagination nor subtlety of thought and phraseology, the words possessed at the same time a kind of depth, an unpretentious expression of sentiments suited somehow to the moment. It would be interesting to know whether, at the period they were written, 'reign' had been considered an adequate rhyme to 'king'; or whether the poet had simply not bothered to achieve identity of sound in the termination of the last verse. Language, pronunciation, sentiment, were always changing. There must have been advantages, moral and otherwise, in living at an outwardly less squeamish period, when the verbiage of high-thinking had not yet cloaked such petitions as those put forward in the second verse, incidentally much the best; when, in certain respects at least, hypocrisy had established less of a stranglehold on the public mind. Such a mental picture of the past was no doubt largely unhistorical, indeed totally illusory, freedom from one sort of humbug merely implying, with human beings of any epoch, thraldom to another. The past, just as the present, had to be accepted for what it thought and what it was.

The Royal Party withdrew. There was a long pause while photographs were taken outside on the steps. The Welsh Guards turned their attention to something in Moreland's line, Walton's 'Grand March'. Orders had been issued that the congregation was to leave by the south portico, the door just behind us. It was now thrown open. Finn and I drove the military attachés like sheep before us in that direction. Once in the street, they would have to find their own cars. The last of them disappeared into the crowd. Finn drew a deep breath.

'That appeared to go off all right.'

'I think so, sir.'

'Might have been trouble when we couldn't fit that fellow in.'

'He was quite happy with my lot.'

'Nice chap.'

'He seemed to be.'

'Going back now?'

'I was, sir. Shall I get the car?'

Something was troubling Finn.

'Look here, Nicholas, will you operate under your own steam—leave me the car?'

'Of course, sir.'

Finn paused again. He lowered his voice.

'I'll make a confession to you, Nicholas.'

'Yes, sir?'

'A friend of mine has sent me a salmon from Scotland.'

That was certainly a matter for envy in the current food situation, though hardly basis for the sense of guilt that seemed to be troubling Finn. There was no obvious reason why he should make such a to-do about the gift. His voice became a whisper.

'I've got to collect the fish.'

'Yes, sir?'

'At Euston Station.'

'Yes?'

'I'm going to take the Section's car,' said Finn. 'Risk court-martial if I'm caught. Be stripped of my VC. It's the only way to get the salmon.'

'I won't betray you, sir.'

'Good boy.'

Finn nodded his head several times, laughing to himself, looking even more than usual like a Punchinello.

'After all, we've won the war,' he said. 'We've just celebrated the fact.'

He thought for a moment.

'Another thing about Flores,' he said. 'Just while I think of it. The Foreign Office are very anxious to keep in with his country. They want us to give him a decoration. He's going to get a CBE.'

'But he's only just arrived.'

'I know, I know. It's just to improve relations between the two countries.'

'But we were frightfully stingy in what we handed out to the Allies in the way of decorations after six years. Hlava told me he didn't know how he was going to face his people when he reported what we offered. Foreigners expect something after they've worked with you for ages.'

'The argument is that we like to make our decorations rare.'

'And then we hand one out to a chap who's just got off the plane.'

'It's all a shambles,' said Finn. 'You get somebody like myself who does something and gets a VC. Then my son-in-law's dropped in France and killed, and no one ever hears about him at all, or what he's done. It's just a toss-up.'

'I didn't know about your son-in-law.'

'Long time ago now,' said Finn. 'Anyway, Flores is going to get a CBE. Don't breathe a word about the car.'

He turned away and stumped off towards the car park. It had evidently been a heavy decision for him to transgress in this manner; use a War Department vehicle for a private purpose, even over so short a distance. This was an un-expected piece of luck so far as I was concerned. Just what I wanted. There had seemed no avoiding going back with Finn to duty, when in fact some sort of a break was badly required. Now it would be possible to walk, achieve adjust-ment, after the loaded atmosphere of the Cathedral. One was more aware of this need outside in the open air than within, when the ceremony was just at an end. After all, one did not every day of the week attend a Thanksgiving Service in St Paul's for Victory after six years of war. It was not unreasonable to experience a need to mull things over for half an hour or so. The ritual itself might not have been exactly moving, too impersonal for that, too well thought out, too forward-looking in the fashionable sense (except for the invocation to confound their politics and frustrate their knavish tricks), but I was aware of some sort of inner dis-turbance, though its form was hard to define. There were still large crowds round the Cathedral. I hung about for a while by the west door, waiting for them to disperse.

'So you were lucky enough to be invited to the Service?'
It was Widmerpool.
'I've been superintending the military attachés.'
'Ah, I wondered how you got here—though of course I knew they selected at all levels.'
'Including yours.'
'I did not have much trouble in arranging matters. What a splendid ceremony. I was carried away. I should like to be buried in St Paul's—would prefer it really to the Abbey.'
'Make that clear in your will.'
Widmerpool laughed heartily.
'Look, Nicholas,' he said. 'I'm glad we met. You were present at a rather silly incident when Pam and I had a tiff. At that embassy. I hope you did not attribute too much seriousness to the words that passed.'
'It was no business of mine.'
'Of course not—but people do not always understand her moods. I flatter myself I do. Pamela is undoubtedly *difficile* at times. I did not wish you to form a wrong impression.'
'All's made up?'
'Perfectly. I am glad to have this opportunity of putting you right, if you ever supposed the contrary. The very reckless way she was talking about official matters was, of course, the sheerest nonsense. Perhaps you hardly took in how absurd she was being. One can forgive a lot to a little person who looks so decorative, however. Now I must hurry off.'
'The Minister again?'
'The Minister showed the utmost good humour about my lateness on that occasion. I knew he would, but I thought it was right for Pam to be apprised that official life must take precedence.'
He went off, infinitely pleased with himself, bringing back forcibly the opinion once expressed by General Conyers:

230

'I can see that fellow has a touch of exaggerated narcissism.'

The scene with Pamela had been altogether dismissed from Widmerpool's mind, as he had risen above failure with Mrs Haycock. Just then I had other things to ponder: Isaiah: Blake: Cowley: the wayfaring men: matters of that sort that seemed to claim attention.

A lot of people were still about the streets, making progress slow, so at the foot of Ludgate Hill I turned into New Bridge Street in the direction of the river. There was no need to hurry. A stroll along the Embankment might be what was required. Then my mind was suddenly recalled to duty. Colonel Flores was walking in front of me. Seeing a foreign military attaché, even a Neutral one, was at once to experience the conditioned reflex, by now secondnature, that is to say instant awareness that he must be looked after to the best of my ability, although not one of my own particular charges. I caught him up and saluted.

'I think you're going the wrong way for the official car park, Colonel, it's—'

Flores seized my hand and smiled.

'None of my arrangements have been official today,' he said. 'In fact none of them have been properly conducted at all. My car had another job to do after dropping me at the Cathedral, so I arranged to meet it, when all was over, in one of the turnings off the Embankment. I thought there would be no parking difficulties there, whatever happened elsewhere. Was not that a brilliant idea? You must admire my knowledge of London topography.'

'I do, sir.'

'Come with me. I'll give you a lift to wherever you want to go.'

It was no use explaining that I only wanted to walk by the river for a while, to be left alone briefly, to think of other things for a time, before returning to our room to complete whatever remained to be done. There was a fair amount of that too.

'You know London well, Colonel?'

'Not really. It was all done with a map, this great plan for the car. Am I not a credit to our Staff College?'

'It's your first visit?'

'I was here—what—fifteen years ago, it must be. With all my family, an absolute tribe of us. We stayed at the Ritz, I remember. Now we will cross the road and advance west along the line of the Thames.'

He led the way to a side turning.

'The car should be somewhere near this spot. Ah, here they are. It had to go and pick up my wife and step-daughter.'

An oldish Rolls, displaying a CD number plate, was drawn up by the pavement in one of the streets running north and south. It was a little way ahead. As we approached, two ladies stepped out and walked towards us. They both looked incredibly elegant. In fact their elegance appalled one. Nobody in England had been able to get hold of any smart clothes for a long time now—except for the occasional 'unsolicited gift' like Matilda's—and the sight of these two gave the impression that they had walked off the stage, or from some display of exotic fashions, into the street. Colonel Flores shouted something in Spanish. We came up with them.

'This is Major—'

'Jenkins.'

'Major Jenkins was incredibly kind to me in St. Paul's.'

Madame Flores took my hand. In spite of the sunlessness of the day, she was wearing spectacles with dark lenses. When I turned to the younger one, her charming figure immediately renewed those thoughts of Jean Duport the atmosphere of the Cathedral had somehow generated. This girl had the same leggy, coltish look, untaught, yet hinting at the same time of captivating sophistications and artifices. She was much tidier than Jean had been when I first set eyes on her, tennis racquet against her hip.

'But why was it necessary to be so kind to Carlos?' asked her mother.

She spoke English as well as her husband, the accent even less perceptible.

'Major Jenkins allowed me to sit in his own special seats.'

'How very grand of him to have special seats.'

'Otherwise there would have been nowhere but the steps of the altar.'

'A most unsuitable place for you, Carlos.'

'We are going to take Major Jenkins as far as Whitehall.'

The tone of Colonel Flores with his wife was that of a man in complete control. She seemed to accept this. All the same, she began to laugh a lot.

'Nick,' she said. 'You look so different in uniform.'

'You know each other already?' asked Flores.

'Of course we do,' said Jean.

'But we haven't met for a long time.'

'This is perfectly splendid,' said Colonel Flores. 'Come along. Let's jump into the car.'

It was not only the dark lenses and changed hair-do. Jean had altered her whole style. Even the first impression, that she had contracted the faint suggestion of a foreign accent, was not wholly imaginary. The accent was there, though whether result of years in foreign parts, or adopted as a small affectation on return to her own country as wife of a foreigner, was uncertain. Oddly enough, the fact of having noticed at once that Polly Duport looked so like her mother when younger, made the presence of Jean herself less, rather than more, to be expected. It was if the mother was someone different; the daughter, the remembered Jean. About seventeen or eighteen, Polly Duport was certainly a very pretty girl; prettier, so far as that went, than her mother at the same age. Jean's attraction in those days had been something other than mere prettiness. Polly had a certain look of her father, said to be very devoted to her. She seemed quite at ease, obviously brought up in a rather old-fashioned tradition, Spanish or exported English, that made her seem older than her age. Relations with her step-father appeared cordial. The whole story began to come back. Duport himself had spoken of the South American army officer his wife had married after her affair with Brent.

'He looks like Rudolph Valentino on an off day,' Duport had said.

Colonel Flores did not fall short of that description; if anything, he rose above it. He seemed not at all surprised that his wife and I knew each other. I wondered what sort of a picture, if any, Jean had given him of her life before their marriage. Probably reminiscence played no part whatever in their relationship. It does with few people. For that matter, one did not know what the former life of Flores himself had been. We exchanged conversational banalities. Formal and smiling, Jean too was perfectly at ease. More so than myself. I suddenly remembered about Peter. She had always been fond of her brother, without anything at all obsessive about that affection. His death must have upset her.

'Poor Peter, yes. I suppose you heard over here before we did. He didn't write often. We were rather out of touch in a way. Babs was sent the official thing, being rather in with that sort of world, and as . . .'

She meant that, in the circumstances, her elder sister had been informed of Templer's death, rather than his wife.

'Used you to see anything of him?' she asked.

'Once or twice at the beginning of the war. Not after he went into that secret show.'

'I don't even know where it was.'

234

'Nor me—for certain.'

One suddenly remembered that she was the wife of a Neutral military attaché, with whom secret matters must even now not be discussed.

'It's all too sad. Why did he do it?'

This was not really a question. In any case, to speak of Pamela Flitton would be too complicated. Bob Duport was better unmentioned too. The car was not an ideal place for conversations of that sort, especially with her husband present.

'You must come and see us,' she said. 'We're really not properly moved in yet. I expect you know we've only just arrived. The appointment was quite a surprise—due to a change of Government.'

She mentioned an address in Knightsbridge, as it happened not far from the flat at the back of Rutland Gate, where once, quite naked, she had opened the door when we were lovers. Like so many things that have actually taken place, the incident was now wholly unbelievable. How could this chic South American lady have shared with me embraces, passionate and polymorphous as those depicted on the tapestry of Luxuria that we had discussed together when we had met at Stourwater? Had she really used those words, those very unexpected expressions, she was accustomed to cry out aloud at the moment of achievement? Once I had thought life unthinkable without her. How could that have been, when she was now only just short of a perfect stranger? An absurd incident suddenly came into my head to put things in proportion. Representatives of the Section had to attend an official party the Greeks were giving at the Ritz. In the hall, a page-boy had said to another: 'General de Gaulle's in that room over there'. The second boy had been withering. He had simply replied: 'Give me news, not history.' Jean, I remembered, had become history. Perhaps not so much history as legend, the

235

story true only in a symbolical sense; because, although its outlines might have general application to ourselves, or even to other people, Jean and I were no longer the persons we then had been.

'Where would you like the chauffeur to drop you?' asked Colonel Flores.

'Just on this corner would be perfect.'

There were a lot more assurances, endless ones, that we must meet again, in spite of difficulties about getting the flat straight in the midst of such shortage of labour, and the imminence of demobilization, which would be followed by absence from London. I got out. The car drove off. Jean turned and waved, making that particular gesture of the hand, the palm inwards, the movement rather hesitating, that I well remembered. Vavassor had not been at the Service. He was on duty in the hall when I came through the door. We had a word together.

'Big crowd?'

'Pretty big.'

'Dull day for an affair like that.'

'Very dull.'

'How did the King look.'

'I was too far away to see.'

'All your foreigners?'

'Yes.'

Later in the afternoon I took some letters up to Finn for signature. He was sitting in his chair looking straight ahead of him.

'I got that fish.'

'You did, sir?'

'Home and dry.'

'A great relief?'

Finn nodded.

'Did I tell you David Pennistone is going to join our Paris firm?' he said.

Pennistone, though he would not reveal before he left what his post-war plans were, had said they would make me laugh when I heard them.

'I think the work will appeal to him,' said Finn. 'He wants a change. Tired of all that . . .'

He paused, searching for the right word.

'Liaison?'

'No, no,' said Finn. 'I don't mean his work here. All that . . . philosophy.'

He smiled at the absurdity of the concept.

'Any idea what you're going to do yourself when you get out of uniform, Nicholas?'

I outlined a few possibilities. Even on my own ears, they sounded grotesque figments of a fevered imagination. Finn accepted them apparently; anyway for what they were worth. I excused myself by adding that the whole idea of starting up all that sort of thing again after six years seemed strange enough.

'Remember Borrit?' asked Finn.

It already seemed a hundred years since Borrit had been with the Section, but I admitted his image faintly lingered on. Finn pushed back his chair. He spoke slowly.

'Borrit told me when he was serving on the Gold Coast, one of the Africans said to him: "What is it white men write at their desks all day?"'

Finn nodded his head several times.

'It's a question I've often asked myself,' he said. 'Ah, well. Let's see those files, Nicholas.'

Just before my own release was due, I went to take formal leave of General Philidor, whose staff by this time lived in one of the streets off Grosvenor Square. I looked in on Kernével's room on the way out, but he was not at home. Then, when I reached the pavement outside, someone shouted from a top storey window. It was Kernével himself.

237

'Wait a moment—I'm coming down.'

I returned to the hall. Kernével came clattering down the stairs. Travelling at high speed, he was red in the face.

'Some wine's arrived from France. Come and have a glass. We're in one of the upper rooms.'

We climbed the stairs. I told him this was probably the last time we should meet officially.

'You know that French writer you spoke about? Something to do with a *plage*—in *Normandie?*'

'Proust?'

'That's the one. I've been into it about him. He's not taught in the schools.'

Kernével looked severe. He implied that the standards of literature must be kept high. We reached a room on the top floor with which I was not familiar. Borda, Kernével's assistant—who came from Roussillon and afterwards married an English girl—was there, with a French captain called Montsaldy, who seemed responsible for the wine. There were several bottles. It was a red Bordeaux, soft and fruity after the Algerian years. We talked about demobilization.

'It is true your army gives you a suit of clothes when you retire?' asked Borda.

'More than just a suit—shirt, tie, vest, pants, socks, shoes, hat, mackintosh.'

'Some of the uniform I wore in North Africa will do for civilian life, I think,' said Borda. 'In the hot weather.'

'I carried tropical uniform in the other war,' said Montsaldy, who looked a grizzled fifty. 'It wears out quickly.'

'Me, too,' said Kernével. 'Tropical uniform always makes me think of Leprince. He was a big fellow in our platoon. Ah, Leprince, *c'était un lapin*. What a fellow. We used to call him *le prince des cons*. That man was what you call well provided. I remember we were being inspected one day by a new officer. As I say, we were in tropical uniform. The major came to the end of the line where Leprince stood. He pointed to Leprince. "A quoi, cet homme?"'

Kernével jumped to attention and saluted, as if he were the platoon sergeant.

"'C'est son sexe, mon commandant."

"C'est dégoûtant!"'

Kernével made as if to march on, now acting the outraged major.

'He was an old fellow,' he said, 'white haired and very religious.'

We all laughed.

'Borda's blushing,' said Kernével. 'He's going to be married quite soon.'

That was the last time Kernével and I met in uniform, but we used to see each other occasionally afterwards, because he continued to work in London. Indeed, we shared a rather absurd incident together a few years after the war was over. Kernével had been awarded an MBE for his work with us, but for some reason, the delay probably due to French rather than British red tape, this decoration did not 'come through' for a long time. Kernével, at last told by his own authorities he could accept the order, was informed by ours that it would be presented by the CIGS; not, of course, the same one who had held the post during the war. Kernével, also notified that he might bring a friend to witness the ceremony, invited me to attend. We were taken to the Army Council Room—Vavassor, too, seemed by now to have faded away—where it turned out the investiture consisted of only half-a-dozen recipients, of whom Kernével was the only Frenchman. When the citations were read out, it appeared the rest had performed prodigies of bravery. There were two Poles, an American, an Australian and New Zealander, perhaps one or two more, all equally distinguished operationally, but whose awards had for one reason or another been deferred. The Field-Marshal now CIGS—again not the one whose Tactical HQ we had visited—was a very distinguished officer, but without much small talk. Huge, impressive, *sérieux* to a degree, he was not, so it appeared, greatly at ease in making the appropriate individual remark when the actual medal was handed out. Before this was done, an officer from the Military Secretary's branch read aloud each individual citation:

'In the face of heavy enemy fire ... total disregard for danger ... although already twice wounded ... managed to reach the objective ... got through with the message ... brought up the relief in spite of ... silenced the machine-gun nest ...'

Kernével came last.

'Captain Kernével,' announced the MS officer.

He paused for a second, then slightly changed his tone of voice.

'Citation withheld for security reasons.'

For a moment I was taken by surprise, almost immediately grasping that a technicality of procedure was involved. Liaison duties came under 'Intelligence', which included all sorts of secret activities; accordingly, 'I' awards were automatically conferred without citation. It was one of those characteristic regulations to which the routine of official life accustoms one. However, the CIGS heard the words with quite other reactions to these. Hitherto, as I have said, although perfectly correct and dignified in his demeanour, his cordiality had been essentially formal, erring if anything on emphasis of the doctrine that nothing short of unconditional courage is to be expected of a soldier. These chronicles of the brave had not galvanized him into being in the least garrulous. Now, at last, his face changed and softened. He was deeply moved. He took a step forward. A giant of a man, towering above Kernével, he put his hand round his shoulder.

'You people were the real heroes of that war,' he said.

Afterwards, when we walked back across the Horse Guards, Kernével insisted I had arranged the whole incident on purpose to rag him.

'It was a good leg-pull,' he said. 'How did you manage it?'

'I promise you.'

'That's just what you pretend.'

'I suppose it would be true to say that there were moments when the Vichy people might have taken disagreeable measures if they had been able to lay their hands on you.'

'You never know,' said Kernével.

The final rites were performed the day after I took wine with the Frenchmen in Upper Grosvenor Street. Forms were signed, equipment handed in, the arcane processes of entering the army enacted, like one of Dr Trelawney's Black Masses, in reverse continuity with an unbelievable symmetry of rhythm. I almost expected the greatcoat, six years before seeming to symbolize induction into this world through the Looking Glass, would be ceremonially lifted from my shoulders. That did not take place. Nevertheless, observances similarly sartorial in character were to close the chapter. This time the *mise-en-scène* was Olympia, rather than the theatrical costumier's, a shop once more, yet at the same time not a shop.

Olympia, London's equivalent of colosseum or bull-ring, had been metamorphosed into a vast emporium for men's wear. Here, how often as a child had one watched the Royal Tournament, horse and rider deftly clearing the posts-and-rails, sweating ratings dragging screw-guns over dummy fortifications, marines and airmen executing inconceivably elaborate configurations of drill. Here, in the tan, these shows had ended in a grand finale of historical conflict, Ancient Britons and Romans, Saxons and Normans, the Spanish Armada, Malplaquet, Minden, Waterloo, the Light Brigade. Now all memory of such stirring moments had been swept away. Rank on rank, as far as the eye could scan, hung flannel trousers and tweed coats, drab macintoshes and grey suits with a white line running through the material. If this were not a shop, what was it? Perhaps the last scene of the play in which one had been performing, set in an outfitter's, where you 'acted' buying the clothes, put them on, then left the theatre to give up the Stage and find something else to do. Or were those weird unnerving shapes on the coat-hangers anonymous cohorts of that 'exceedingly great army', who would need no demob suits, but had come to watch the lucky ones?

'Ropey togs,' said a quartermaster-captain.

'The hats are a bit *outré*,' agreed a Coldstreamer with a limp. 'But one of those sports jackets, as I believe they're called, will come in useful in the country.'

Assistants round about were urbane and attentive. They too seemed to be acting the part with almost passionate dedication, recommending the garments available with the greatest enthusiasm. Was this promise of a better world? Perhaps one had reached that already and this was a celestial haberdasher's. The place was not even at all crowded. Most of the customers, if that was what they ought to be called, looked about forty, demobilization groups taking precedence on points gained by age, length of service, period overseas and so on. We wandered round like men in a dream. As one moved from suits to shoes, shoes to socks, socks back again to suits, the face of a Gunner captain seemed familiar. In due course we found ourselves side by side examining ties.

'This pink one with a criss-cross pattern might not look too bad for occasions,' he said thoughtfully. 'We used to meet sometimes, didn't we?'

'Aren't you called Gilbert?'

'At dances years ago.'

Archie Gilbert had been the 'spare man' *par excellence* for every hostess in need, perfectly dressed, invariably punctual, prepared to deal with mothers or daughters without prejudice regarding looks or age, quietly conversational, unthinkable as taking a glass too much or making unwelcome advances in a taxi. His work had been believed to be in a firm concerned with non-ferrous metals, whatever they might be, though it had never been easy to imagine him in day clothes doing an ordinary job. However, in spite of that outward appearance, he had somehow or other taken on a world war. His fair moustache was a shade thicker, he himself had filled out, indeed become almost portly. Otherwise, more closely examined, he had not greatly changed. His appearance, always discreetly military, had, as it were, camouflaged him from instant recognition at first sight. His uniform—he wore very neat battledress, of normal material, otherwise cut rather like the Field-Marshal's— was as spick and span as his evening clothes had always been. We talked of our respective war careers. He had been in an anti-aircraft battery stationed in one of the northern suburbs of London. One pictured a lot of hard, rather dreary work, sometimes fairly dangerous, sometimes demanding endurance in unexciting circumstances. Perhaps experience in the London ballrooms had stood him in good stead in the latter respect. It was impossible to remain incurious about the question of marriage; which of the scores of girls with whom he used to dance he had finally chosen. Perhaps his bachelor gifts were still too overwhelming to be extinguished in matrimony. I crudely asked the question. Archie Gilbert nodded, smiling gently.

'Used I to meet your wife in those days?'

He shook his head, smiling again.

'We ran across each other when I was with the battery,' he said. 'Her family lived just over the road.'

There the matter rested. He divulged no more. We talked of some of the girls we had known in the past.

'Haven't seen any of them for ages,' he said. 'One hears their names occasionally. Usen't you to know Barbara Goring, who married Johnny Pardoe? He was rather odd for a time—melancholia or something—then he went back to the army and did well in Burma, I believe. Rosie Manasch had a lot of ups-and-downs, they say, with Jock Udall. Of course, he was shot by the Germans after that mass attempt to escape from a POW camp. Rosie was a great character. I used to like her a lot.'

He unfolded an evening paper.

'If you were doing liaison work with the Poles, you may know the one who's just married Margaret Budd. Do you remember her? What a beauty. I don't know what happened to her husband, whether he was killed or whether it didn't work. He was quite a bit older than her and distilled whisky.'

He held out the paper. Margaret Budd's bridegroom was Horaczko; the marriage celebrated at a registry office. The paragraph below recorded another wedding at the same place. It was that of Widmerpool and Pamela Flitton. Archie Gilbert pointed a finger towards this additional item.

'That name always sticks in my mind,' he said. 'Barbara Goring once poured sugar over his head at a ball of the Huntercombes'. It was really too bad. Made an awful mess too. Have you decided what you're going to take from the stuff here? It might be much worse. I think everything myself.'

'Except the underclothes.'